'Since its original publication in 2012, *Six Four* has been the sensation of Japanese Crime Literature. It is a joy and a privilege to have the book in English now, and with such a wonderful translation. Not only is it an addictive read, it is an education about Japan, its police and its society, and simply one of the best crime novels I have ever read' David Peace

'A huge hit in Japan and it's easy to see why . . . steadily gathers menace and power until it becomes addictive' *The Times*

'It's very different, in tone, narrative and style, from almost anything out there. Over its 600-odd pages, *Six Four* is the slowest of slow-burn crime novels. It takes the classic elements of the genre but steers decisively away from putting them together in the usual way . . . the twist and the pay-off are worth the wait' Alison Flood, *Observer*, Thriller of the Month

'This is gripping stuff, fast-paced and involving endless conflicts of loyalties, but Yokoyama has something unexpected up his sleeve. A classic plot about a decent cop painstakingly uncovering corruption suddenly turns into one of the most remarkable revenge dramas in modern detective fiction. All the clues are there, in retrospect, but in a kind of shadow plot that will leave even the most observant reader gasping' Joan Smith, *Sunday Times*

'Epic in ambition, it unfurls like a flower in the spring sunlight, steadily increasing its grip as it does so' Geoffrey Wansell, *Daily Mail*

'*Six Four* gives back in abundance everything that the reader is prepared to give . . . this is an idiosyncratic and richly worked narrative, demonstrating that crime fiction can be freighted with the weight and authority of serious literature. The patient reader will find themselves handsomely rewarded' Barry Forshaw, *Independent*

'The plot would grip in any language but, for readers in the west, there is extra fascination in *Six Four* being not just a police procedural but a guide book to Japan . . . Jonathan Lloyd-Davies' English reads speedily and cleanly . . . TV screenwriters have often cited the long-form novel, with its chapter divisions and slow-show narrative, as a model for their work. *Six Four*, though, seems to me a prime example of a complementary phenomenon that began with Larsson's Millennium trilogy – the box set novel. Rejecting the pace and economy of a movie, these stories build incrementally with lingering closeups on people and places. Yokoyama's novel matches the immersive, unnerving, anthropological momentum of Jane Campion's great New Zealand television crime drama, *Top of the Lake*. There's much talk these days of binge viewing; here is a binge read' Mark Lawson, *Guardian*

'In many ways *Six Four* is the literary equivalent of a good TV box set such as Danish TV series *The Killing*. It is totally fascinating, revealing as much about Japan and its people as about the mystery at its heart. Unable to put the book down, I read until 3am every night for a week, the shadows under my eyes growing darker with every hour. But I was rewarded with a shocking conclusion. *Six Four* is unique, remarkable and deserves to sell at least as well over here as it did in Japan' Jon Coates, *Express*

'Slow building, meticulous in its insistence on unfolding all the procedural elements of a Japanese crime investigation and its political ramifications, this is a novel that insidiously grows on you until you are fully captive of its narrative flow and can't put it down' Maxim Jakubowski

'Jonathan Lloyd-Davies's translation is zippy and buoyant . . . like the works of that fine Japanese novelist Haruki Murakami, there is an otherworldly, dream-like quality to the writing that is totally addictive and I ended up hooked. With his insights into both the heroism and corruption of the Japanese police and his sense of poetry, Yokoyama looks set to become the James Ellroy of Tokyo' Jake Kerridge, *Sunday Express*

'In Mikami he has created a most unusual protagonist: we're used to detectives following clues, but a media relations officer? It gives the book a unique feel . . . Yes, there's a brilliant twist near the end, but the novel goes beyond such games, intriguing as they are . . . the real answers are hidden below the bloodstains and fingerprints, and lie further away than simple justice or revenge. Compelling, complex, insightful: a book to be savoured' *Spectator*

'Hideo's portrayal of Mikami owes nothing to the one-dimensional gumshoes of Western detective fiction. He develops his central character with the simplicity of a haiku and complexity of a Kyoto feast . . . [A] well-written epic tale, which reads beautifully in Jonathan Lloyd-Davies's translation. *Six Four* is far more a monument to the idiosyncrasies of Japanese bureaucratic life than it is a simple detective story' Justin Warshaw, *TLS*

'A fascinating insight into Japan's political and legal systems' *Grazia*

'This is an astonishing book, poetically translated, containing one of the most complex central characters in crime fiction. Sometimes publishing sensations exceed expectations; *Six Four* deserves its success – past, present and future' Crime Scene

'The detective novel: investigate, solve, celebrate. If that is the traditional mode of the genre, Hideo Yokoyama's novels stand out for their focus on conflict within the police force itself. We read and we hurt. We hurt and we read. And the climax of the novel stands as *Six Four*'s greatest achievement' *J-Novel Magazine* (Japan)

'The opening reads as corporate fiction, while the latter half of the novel develops into a detective thriller, all but demanding a one-session read as the pieces of the puzzle begin to fall into place. *Six Four* is substantial and a masterpiece, one only Hideo Yokoyama could have written, moving deftly beyond the limitations of the police thriller to successfully fuse the world of the detective novel with that of human drama' *Mystery Magazine* (Japan)

'At first, it might seem as though Hideo Yokoyama is deliberately shunning the juiciest aspects of the genre, yet a characteristic of his novels is the breadth of their coverage, and the author's strong commitment to profoundly moving the reader. *Six Four* is undoubtedly a detective novel of the finest vintage' *Sunday Mainichi* (Japan)

'*Six Four*, Hideo Yokoyama's first novel in seven years, is a tour-de-force that doesn't disappoint. Since his debut, Hideo Yokoyama has brought a unique style to the detective novel and its traditional focus on case investigation. *Six Four* is no different, making a meticulous and striking portrayal of conflict between the media and the police. The author's unrelenting drive to leave nothing untouched has ensured *Six Four* is worth the seven years of quiet' *Mainichi* (Japan)

'The author's overriding objective appears to be in presenting a cross-section of modern society through the ambiguities of the relationships and structures inherent in the police organization . . . The interweaving of the side narrative of Futawatari (a contemporary of Mikami's high-school Kendo club) and his promotion to Inspector into the central conceit of the mystery serves as a further example of the author's remarkable prowess' *Tokyo Jin* (Japan)

'I read *Six Four* more as a treatise on the "internal" and "external" aspects of society than as a detective novel. The characters are forced to stand up against those around them. We see conflict between individuals, in families, with co-workers, the press, the bereaved, retirees from the force, and with civilians. Each highlight the idea of the "in-group" and the "out-group". The relationships may seem commonplace, but such perceptions are regularly overturned, reaping unexpected dividends each time, compelling the reader into reconsidering their view of the world – both in and out of the novel' *The Yomiuri* (Japan)

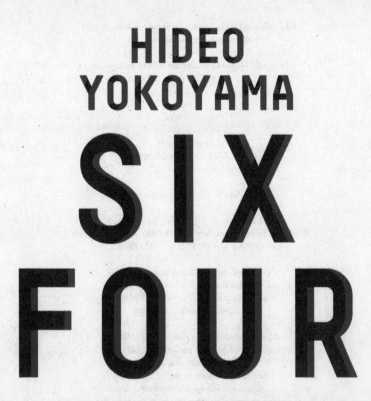

HIDEO YOKOYAMA

SIX FOUR

Translated from the Japanese by Jonathan Lloyd-Davies

riverrun

First published in the Japanese language as *Rokuyon (64)*
by Bungeishunju in Tokyo in 2012

First published in Great Britain in 2016 by Quercus
This paperback edition published in 2017 by

riverrun
an imprint of
Quercus Publishing Ltd
Carmelite House
50 Victoria Embankment
London EC4Y 0DZ

An Hachette UK company

A CIP catalogue record for this book is available
from the British Library

ISBN 978 1 84866 528 6
EBOOK ISBN 978 1 78429 984 2

15

Typeset by Jouve (UK), Milton Keynes

Printed and bound in Great Britain by Clays Ltd, Elcograf S.p.A.

SIX
FOUR

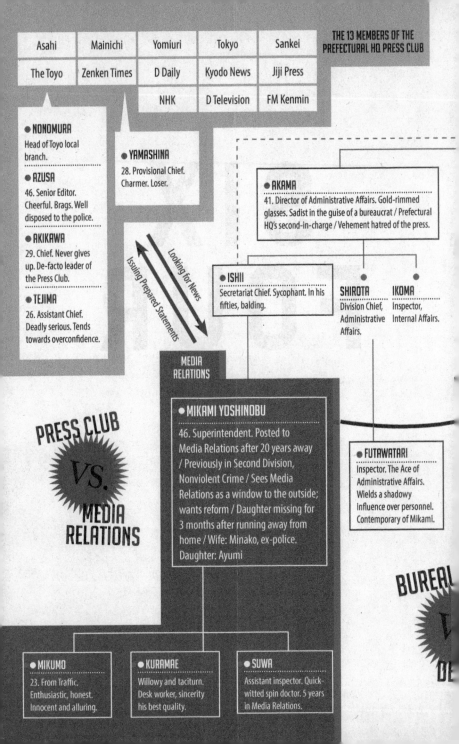

THE 13 MEMBERS OF THE PREFECTURAL HQ PRESS CLUB

Asahi	Mainichi	Yomiuri	Tokyo	Sankei
The Toyo	Zenken Times	D Daily	Kyodo News	Jiji Press
		NHK	D Television	FM Kenmin

● **NONOMURA**
Head of Toyo local branch.

● **AZUSA**
46. Senior Editor. Cheerful. Brags. Well disposed to the police.

● **AKIKAWA**
29. Chief. Never gives up. De-facto leader of the Press Club.

● **TEJIMA**
26. Assistant Chief. Deadly serious. Tends towards overconfidence.

● **YAMASHINA**
28. Provisional Chief. Charmer. Loser.

● **AKAMA**
41. Director of Administrative Affairs. Gold-rimmed glasses. Sadist in the guise of a bureaucrat / Prefectural HQ's second-in-charge / Vehement hatred of the press.

● **ISHII**
Secretariat Chief. Sycophant. In his fifties, balding.

SHIROTA
Division Chief, Administrative Affairs.

IKOMA
Inspector, Internal Affairs.

Looking for News

Issuing Prepared Statements

MEDIA RELATIONS

PRESS CLUB

VS.

MEDIA RELATIONS

● **MIKAMI YOSHINOBU**
46. Superintendent. Posted to Media Relations after 20 years away / Previously in Second Division, Nonviolent Crime / Sees Media Relations as a window to the outside; wants reform / Daughter missing for 3 months after running away from home / Wife: Minako, ex-police. Daughter: Ayumi

● **FUTAWATARI**
Inspector. The Ace of Administrative Affairs. Wields a shadowy influence over personnel. Contemporary of Mikami.

BUREAU

DE

● **MIKUMO**
23. From Traffic. Enthusiastic, honest. Innocent and alluring.

● **KURAMAE**
Willowy and taciturn. Desk worker, sincerity his best quality.

● **SUWA**
Assistant inspector. Quick-witted spin doctor. 5 years in Media Relations.

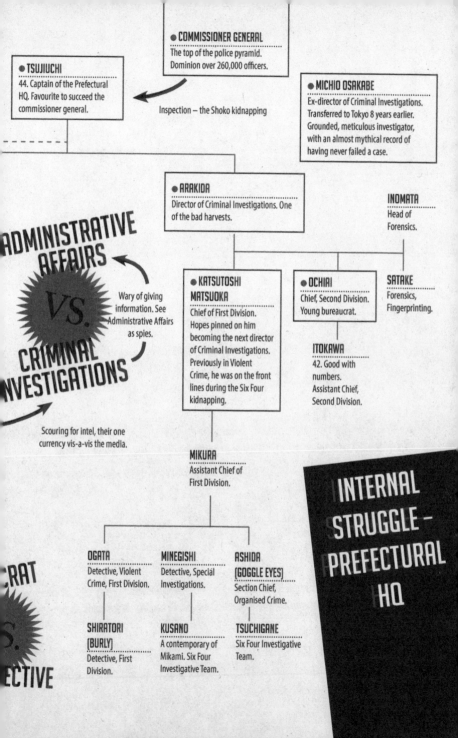

COMMISSIONER GENERAL
The top of the police pyramid. Dominion over 260,000 officers.

TSUJIUCHI
44. Captain of the Prefectural HQ. Favourite to succeed the commissioner general.

Inspection – the Shoko kidnapping

MICHIO OSAKABE
Ex-director of Criminal Investigations. Transferred to Tokyo 8 years earlier. Grounded, meticulous investigator, with an almost mythical record of having never failed a case.

ARAKIDA
Director of Criminal Investigations. One of the bad harvests.

INOMATA
Head of Forensics.

ADMINISTRATIVE AFFAIRS
VS.
CRIMINAL INVESTIGATIONS

Wary of giving information. See Administrative Affairs as spies.

Scouring for intel, their one currency vis-a-vis the media.

KATSUTOSHI MATSUOKA
Chief of First Division. Hopes pinned on him becoming the next director of Criminal Investigations. Previously in Violent Crime, he was on the front lines during the Six Four kidnapping.

OCHIAI
Chief, Second Division. Young bureaucrat.

SATAKE
Forensics, Fingerprinting.

ITOKAWA
42. Good with numbers. Assistant Chief, Second Division.

MIKURA
Assistant Chief of First Division.

INTERNAL STRUGGLE – PREFECTURAL HQ

OGATA
Detective, Violent Crime, First Division.

MINEGISHI
Detective, Special Investigations.

ASHIDA (GOGGLE EYES)
Section Chief, Organised Crime.

SHIRATORI (BURLY)
Detective, First Division.

KUSANO
A contemporary of Mikami. Six Four Investigative Team.

TSUCHIGANE
Six Four Investigative Team.

CRAT
S.
ECTIVE

Snowflakes danced through the evening light.

The man's legs were stiff as he stepped from the taxi. A forensics official in a police-issue overcoat was waiting outside the entrance to the station. He ushered the man inside. They passed a work area for duty officers and continued along a gloomy corridor before taking a side door out to the officers' parking area.

The mortuary stood by itself at the far end of the grounds, a windowless structure with a tin roof. The low rumbling of the extractor fan told him there was a body inside. The official unlocked the door and stepped back. He gave the man a deferential look, indicating he would wait outside.

I forgot to pray.

Yoshinobu Mikami pushed open the door. The hinges groaned. His eyes and nose registered Cresol. He could feel the tips of Minako's fingers digging through the fabric of his coat, into his elbow. Light glared down from the ceiling. The waist-high examination table was covered in blue vinyl sheeting; above it, a human shape was visible under a white sheet. Mikami recoiled at the indeterminate size, too small for an adult but clearly not a child.

Ayumi . . .

He swallowed the word, afraid that voicing his daughter's name might make the body hers.

He began to peel back the white cloth.

Hair. Forehead. Closed eyes. Nose, lips . . . chin.

The pale face of a dead girl came into view. In the same moment the frozen air began to circulate again; Minako's forehead pushed against his shoulder. The pressure receded from the fingers at his elbow.

Mikami was staring at the ceiling, breathing out from deep in his gut. There was no need to inspect the body further. The journey from Prefecture D – by bullet train then taxi – had taken four hours, but the process of identifying the corpse had been over in seconds. A young girl; drowned, suicide. They had wasted no time after receiving the call. The girl, they were told, had been found in a lake a little after midday.

Her chestnut hair was still damp. She looked fifteen or sixteen, perhaps a little older. She hadn't been in the water for long. There were no signs of bloating, and the slender outline running from her forehead to her cheeks was, along with her childlike lips, unbroken, preserved as though she were still alive.

It seemed a bitter irony. The girl's delicate features were, he supposed, the kind Ayumi had always longed for. Even now, three months later, Mikami was still unable to think back on what had happened with a cool head.

There had been a noise from Ayumi's room upstairs. A frenzied sound, like somebody trying to kick through the floor. Her mirror was in pieces. She'd been sitting with the lights off in the corner of her room. Punching, scratching her face, trying to tear it apart: *I hate this face. I want to die.*

Mikami faced the dead girl and pressed his hands together. She would have parents, too. They would have to come to this place, maybe tonight, maybe tomorrow, and face up to the awful reality.

'Let's get out of here.'

His voice was hoarse. Something dry was caught in his throat.

Minako seemed vacant; she made no attempt to nod. Her swollen pupils were like glass beads, empty of thought or emotion. This wasn't their first time – in the last three months they had already identified two bodies of Ayumi's age.

2

Outside, the snow had turned to sleet. Three figures stood breathing chalky clouds in the dark of the parking area.

'A great relief.'

The pale, clearly good-natured station captain proffered his card with a hesitant smile. He was in full uniform, even though it was outside working hours. The same was true of the director, and of the section chief of Criminal Investigations flanking his sides. Mikami recognized it as a sign of respect, in case he'd identified the girl as his daughter.

He gave them a low bow. 'Thank you for getting in touch so quickly.'

'Not at all.' *We're all police.* Skipping any further formalities, the captain turned to gesture at the building and said, 'Come in, you should warm up a little.'

There was a nudge in the back of Mikami's coat. He turned and caught Minako's imploring gaze. She wanted to leave as soon as possible. He felt the same way.

'That's very kind, but we should get going. We have a train to catch.'

'No, no, you should stay. We've arranged a hotel.'

'We appreciate your consideration, but we really do need to go. I have to work tomorrow.'

When he said this, the captain's gaze dropped to the card in his hands.

Superintendent Yoshinobu Mikami. Press Director. Inspector, Administrative Affairs Department, Personnel Division. Prefecture D Police Headquarters.

He sighed as he looked back up.

'It must be tough, having to deal with the press.'

'It can be,' Mikami said evasively. He could picture the mutinous faces of the reporters he'd left back in Media Relations. They had been in the middle of a heated argument over the format of press releases when the call had come in to notify him of the drowned girl. He had got to his feet and walked out without

3

a word, earning the wrath of the reporters, who were unaware of his family situation: *We're not finished here. Are you running away, Mikami?*

'Have you been in Media Relations long?' The captain looked sympathetic. In district stations, relations with the press were handled by the station's vice-captain or vice-director; in smaller, regional stations, it was the captain himself who stood in the firing line.

'Just since the spring. Although I had a brief stint there a long time ago.'

'Have you always worked in Administrative Affairs?'

'No. I spent a long time as a detective in Second Division.' Even now, this engendered a certain amount of pride.

The captain nodded uncertainly. It was unlikely, even in the regional headquarters, that he had seen any examples of detectives switching into the role of press director.

'I would imagine, with your insights into Criminal Investigations, that the press might actually listen to you.'

'I certainly hope so.'

'You know, it's a bit of a problem here. There are . . . certain reporters who like to write what they please, true or not.'

The captain scowled and, without changing his expression, waved towards the garage. Mikami was troubled to see the front lights of the captain's black car flick on. The taxi he'd kept waiting was nowhere to be seen. There was another nudge in his back, but he was hesitant at this point to call another taxi and upset the well-meaning captain.

It was already dark when they drove to the station.

'Here, this is the lake,' the captain said from the passenger seat, sounding a little awestruck as a deeper stretch of darkness appeared beyond the window to the right. 'The internet really is appalling. There is a horrible website, the "Top Ten Suicide Spots" – this lake is listed there. They've given it an eerie name, something like the "Lake of Promise".'

'The "Lake of Promise"?'

'It looks like a heart, depending on the angle. The website makes the claim that it grants you true love in the next life; the girl today, she was the fourth. We had one come all the way from Tokyo not too long ago. The press decided to run an article, and now we've got the TV to deal with.'

'That's terrible.'

'Absolutely. It's a disgrace, peddling articles about a suicide. If we had had time, Mikami, I would have liked to ask you for some pointers in dealing with them.'

As if he were uncomfortable with silence, the captain continued to talk. For his part, Mikami lacked the will to carry out any animated conversation. While he was thankful for the captain's tact, his responses became increasingly terse.

It was a mistake. It wasn't Ayumi. His thoughts were joyless all the same; no different to those on the journey out. To pray she wasn't *their* daughter. He knew all too well that this was the same as wishing she was someone else's.

Minako was perfectly still at his side. Their shoulders pressed together. Hers felt abnormally frail.

The car turned at a junction. The bright light of the train station came into view directly ahead of them. The square in front of the building was wide and spacious, strewn with a few commemorative monuments. It was almost empty of people. Mikami had heard that the building of the station was the result of political manoeuvring; no one had thought to consider actual passenger numbers.

'There's no need to get out, you'll only get wet,' Mikami said quickly. He had the rear passenger door halfway open, but the captain beat him out of the car regardless. The man's face was flushed red.

'Please accept my apologies for the unreliable information and the trouble you've taken to come here. We thought, well, from her height and the position of the mole that she might be . . . I just hope we haven't caused you too much distress.'

5

'Of course not.'

Mikami waved a hand to dismiss the idea, but the captain took hold of it.

'This will work out. Your daughter is alive and well. We will find her. You have 260,000 friends looking for her, around the clock.'

Mikami remained in a low bow, watching the tail lights as the captain's car pulled away. Minako's neck was getting wet in the cold rain. He pulled her slight form close and started towards the station. The light from a police box – one of the *koban* – caught his eye. An old man, possibly a drunk, was sitting on the road, fending off the restraining arms of a young policeman.

260,000 friends.

There was no exaggeration in the captain's words. District stations. *Koban*. Substations. Ayumi's picture had been sent to police departments across the nation. Officers he would neither know nor recognize were keeping watch day and night for news of his daughter, as if she were their own. The police force . . . family. It inspired confidence, and he was indebted – not a single day went by in which he wasn't thankful for being part of such a powerful and far-reaching organization. And yet . . .

Mikami bit down on the cold air. He had never imagined it. That his need for help could have become such a critical weakness.

Submission.

Now and then, his blood felt ready to boil. He could never tell Minako.

To find your missing daughter. To hold her alive in your arms. Mikami doubted there was anything a parent wouldn't put themselves through in order to achieve such a goal.

An announcement rang out along the train platform.

Inside, the train was marked by empty seats. Mikami ushered Minako to a window seat, then whispered, 'The captain's right. She's safe. She's doing okay.'

Minako said nothing.

'They'll find her soon. You don't need to worry.'

'. . . yes.'

'We had the calls, remember? She wants to come back. It's just pride. You'll see, one day soon, she'll just turn up.'

Minako was as hollow-looking as before. Her elegant features shone in the dark window of the train. She looked worn. She had given up on make-up and hairdressers. How would she feel, though, if she realized this only served to draw attention to the natural, effortless beauty of her features?

Mikami's face was also in the window. He saw a phantom image of Ayumi.

She had cursed the way she'd taken after him.

She had made her mother's beauty the focus of her anger.

He slowly pulled his eyes away from the window. It was temporary. Like the measles. Sooner or later, she would come to her senses. Then she would come home with her tongue stuck out, like she had done when she made mistakes as a small girl. She couldn't genuinely hate them, want to cause them pain, not Ayumi.

The train rocked a little. Minako was resting against his shoulder. Her irregular breathing made it hard to know if she was groaning or just asleep.

Mikami closed his eyes.

The window was still there, under his eyelids, reflecting the ill-matched husband and wife.

Since the morning a strong northern wind had been blowing over the plains of Prefecture D.

The lights were green up ahead, but the traffic was backed up and Mikami could do nothing but edge forwards. He took his hands off the steering wheel and lit a cigarette. Work had already begun on another cluster of high-rise apartments, gradually stealing away the outline of the mountains framed through the car window.

580,000 households. 1,820,000 citizens. Mikami remembered the numbers from a demographic survey he'd seen in the morning paper. Close to a third of that population lived or worked within the limits of City D. After a laboured and drawn-out process the city had successfully merged with the neighbouring cities, towns and villages, giving momentum to the process of centralization. Despite this, work on a universal public transport system – the very first item on the agenda – had yet to begin. With only a few trains or buses in service, most of the routes hugely impractical, the roads were overflowing with cars.

Get a bloody move on, Mikami muttered to himself. It was five days into December, and the morning congestion was particularly bad. The radio seemed poised to announce eight o'clock at any moment. He could make out the five-storey structure of the Prefectural Police HQ up ahead. The sight brought an unexpected sense of nostalgia for its cold but familiar outer walls, despite the fact that he'd only been away in the north for half a day.

He hadn't needed to go all that way. He'd known from the start that it would be a waste of time. It was obvious now, a day later. Ayumi hated the cold more than most; it was ludicrous to think she would venture north. Even more that she would decide to throw herself into a frozen lake.

Mikami stubbed out his cigarette and pushed down on the accelerator. Space enough for a few cars had opened up ahead.

Somehow, he managed not to arrive late. Having stopped in the station parking area, he hurried towards the main building. As he did this, force of habit pulled his eyes towards the spaces set aside for the press.

He stopped dead. The area, usually empty at this time of day, was packed full of cars. Correspondents representing each of the news outlets would be gathered inside. For a brief moment Mikami wondered if something had happened. But no – they were here to continue yesterday's discussions, that was all. They would be inside, waiting for him to show.

Gunning for an early start.

Mikami entered the building through the front entrance. It was less than ten steps along the corridor to Media Relations. Three nervous-looking faces looked up as he pushed open the door. Section Chief Suwa and Sub-chief Kuramae, both sitting at their desks facing the wall. Mikumo, at her desk nearest the door.

The cramped space made for subdued greetings.

The room was a little bigger than it had been before the spring, as they'd had the wall to the archive room torn down, but there was hardly room to breathe when the reporters decided all to barge in at once. Mikami had imagined such a situation before he came in, but the press were nowhere to be seen. Feeling as though he'd made a narrow escape, he took his seat by the windows. Suwa approached before he had the chance to call him over. He was unusually reticent when he spoke.

'Sir. Umm . . . about yesterday's . . .'

Mikami hadn't expected this; he'd been getting ready to ask

about the press situation. Late last night Mikami had called his reporting officer, Division Chief Ishii of the Secretariat, and given a full account of what had happened during the ID. He had naturally assumed Ishii would pass the news on to his staff in Media Relations.

'It wasn't her. Thanks for asking.'

The atmosphere seemed to brighten immediately. Suwa and Kuramae exchanged relieved glances and Mikumo seemed to reanimate; she jumped up and took Mikami's mug off its place on the shelf.

'More to the point, Suwa – the press are here?'

Mikami jerked his chin towards one of the walls. The Press Room was on the other side, housing the Press Club, an informal grouping of thirteen news groups.

Suwa's expression darkened again.

'Yes, they're all in there. They were talking about stringing you up. They'll be barging in soon enough.'

Stringing him up? Mikami felt a sudden irritation.

'Oh, and if you could also bear in mind – they think you left because you had a relative in a critical condition.'

Mikami paused briefly before he nodded.

The quick-witted spin doctor. That was Suwa to a tee. He was ranked Assistant Inspector, having come up through Administrative Affairs. With three years of experience in Media Relations and another two in the field as a police sergeant, he had already achieved a deep understanding of the modern-day ecology of the press. While his precociousness could be annoying from time to time, his ability to win the reporters over, transitioning seamlessly between the twin roles of diplomat and spin doctor, was genuinely astonishing. Now that he had further polished his skills during his second posting, the department held him in increasingly high regard.

Mikami's second posting to the office had been less fortuitous. He was forty-six, and the transfer had come after twenty years away. Until the spring, he had worked as the assistant chief of Second Division; prior to that, he had managed a team in the field, investigating corruption and election fraud as a section chief in Non-violent Crime.

Mikami stood and turned towards the whiteboard next to his desk.

Prefecture D, Police Headquarters. Press Release: Thursday, 5 December 2002.

As press director, his first job of the morning was to run through all announcements to be made to the press.

The office received a non-stop deluge of calls and faxes reporting accidents and crimes from within the jurisdiction of the prefecture's nineteen district stations. The recent and widespread adoption of computers meant the same now applied to emails. Mikami's staff would summarize the reports using a template, then attach copies to whiteboards in the office and the Press Room. At the same time, they would get in touch with the prefecture's TV news. It was through activities like these that the force helped facilitate press coverage. Despite this, press releases often ended up becoming sources of friction.

Mikami checked the clock on the wall. It was after eight thirty.

What were they doing in there?

'Sir, do you have a moment?' Kuramae had come over to stand in front of Mikami's desk. His willowy form contrasted with his hefty-sounding name, part of which translated as 'storehouse'. His tone, as usual, was understated. 'It's . . . about the bid-rigging charges.'

'Sure. Did you manage to find out anything?'

'Ah . . .' Kuramae faltered.

'What is it? The CEO's refusing to come clean?'

'To be honest, I wasn't able to—'

'You weren't able to . . . what?'

Mikami's eyes sharpened unconsciously. It was five days since Second Division had made a series of arrests for bid-rigging charges surrounding a project to build a prefectural art museum. They had raided six mid-tier construction companies and brought eight executives into custody, but the investigation was far from over. Their target was Hakkaku Construction, a regional contractor which they suspected had been behind the process. Mikami had heard whispers that the CEO had been quietly summoned to one of the district stations and that, for the last few days, he had submitted to voluntary questioning. If the police successfully brought in the ringleader, it would be big news for the regional papers.

It was common in Second Division for statements – and the formal issuing of arrest warrants – to be delayed until late at night. Mikami had sent Kuramae to get an overview of the current situation, with the hope of avoiding any confusion that might arise should the timing clash with the cut-off point for the next day's news.

'Did you at least find out if the CEO has been brought in?'

Kuramae looked downcast. 'I asked the assistant chief. But he . . .'

It wasn't hard to work out what had happened. They had decided to treat Kuramae as a spy.

'That's fine. I'll go and see them later.'

Mikami watched Kuramae move away with slumped shoulders, then let out a bitter sigh. Kuramae had previously worked in an office job at Second Division in one of the district stations. Mikami had asked him to go in the hope that he would be able to use the contacts he'd made there to extract some new information, but he'd been over-optimistic. Anything you gave Media Relations went straight to the press, who would then use it as a bargaining tool. Many detectives still swore by this belief.

Mikami had been no exception.

Back when he was a rookie detective, Media Relations had been nothing but a department to distrust. *A pawn of the press. A guard dog for Administrative Affairs. A place to brush up for exams.* He had no doubt said as much himself, mimicking the behaviour of his fault-finding superiors. Even from a distance he had found their intimacy with the press distasteful. They would spend night after night drinking, plying the reporters with compliments. At crime scenes they stood aloof, bystanders as they chatted to the press.

Mikami had never considered them to be fellow officers.

Because of this, he had become despondent when, in his third year as a detective, he had received his first transfer to Media Relations. He thought he'd been branded a failure. He took to the work in despair, fully aware of his inability to live up to the task. Then, after only a year, and before he'd even had a chance to learn the ropes, he had received a transfer back to Criminal Investigations.

He had been thrilled by the reinstatement, but had also found himself unable to write off the year-long gap in his detective's career as simply a whim of Personnel. He began to develop a festering mistrust of the system and, with it, an even more potent sense of fear. He buried himself in his work with newfound urgency, all the time wary of the next round of transfers. Even five or ten years later, he still felt on edge. It was true to say that his fear had served to heighten his fierce commitment to the job. He refused to let himself grow lazy, to submit to any form of temptation, to relax in any way – and this brought results. During his time in First Division he was decorated with commendation after commendation, regardless of whether he'd been working in Theft, Violent Crime or Special Investigations.

Even then, it wasn't until his transfer to Second Division that Mikami truly came into his own as a detective. Specializing in non-violent crime, he forged himself an indisputable niche within Criminal Investigations, in both district and the Prefectural HQ.

He still hesitated to call himself a genuine, dyed-in-the-wool detective. And those around him wouldn't let him forget what had happened, even if he'd wanted to. Whenever sensitive case information leaked to the papers, his colleagues and superiors would resist making eye contact. There was a limit to how much he could dismiss as paranoia. The chill horror as the invisible feelers of the witch hunt drew closer was something only those who had experienced it first-hand could understand. Mikami had never been asked to join the hunt for the source of the leaks, no matter how much he'd impressed his superiors with his work, and regardless of his promotion from assistant inspector to inspector. In this respect, the time he had served in Media Relations had been akin to having a 'criminal record'.

You're going to be our new press director.

Mikami's mind had gone blank when Akama, the director of Administrative Affairs, had given him unofficial notification of his transfer earlier in the spring. The only words to enter his mind had been 'criminal record'.

Akama had gone on to lay out the rationale behind the appointment:

'I will not stand back and do nothing while the press continues to chastise us for every mistake we make; they lack integrity, along with any understanding of social justice. It's as though their only goal is to undermine our authority. We've been soft, and now they seek to abuse our trust. That's why we need someone like you, Mikami. A tough press director, someone fierce, someone ready and able to stare them down.'

Mikami had found it hard to accept these words. The police had a tough-guy culture and placed a premium on strength, meaning there was no scarcity of fierce-looking men either in Criminal Investigations or outside it. How did Personnel benefit from taking an inspector at the top of his game, one whose head was filled with the strict application of the criminal code, and assigning him to be protective gatekeeper in a role divorced from the force's original mission?

Akama had spoken of the transfer as though it were an opportunity. It was true that the post was director grade, usually beyond officers of Mikami's rank, and that it guaranteed his promotion to superintendent. Yet, even if he'd stayed in Criminal

Investigations, Mikami had expected to be promoted in two or three years, and he disliked having the carrot dangled before him when the promotion was in some other area of expertise.

He had been certain that his 'criminal record' had influenced the selection. When multiple candidates were considered for a single position, it was Personnel's standard policy, as a kind of insurance, to go with the person who had the most experience in the chosen field. So Mikami's issue hadn't been with the fact that he'd been chosen, but rather with Criminal Investigations having put him forward in the first place.

Mikami had steeled himself and visited Arakida, the director of Criminal Investigations, at his home that same evening. 'The decision's been made' was all the director had said. Exactly as he had twenty years earlier. It had felt to Mikami as if the man had simply dismissed his talent for the job. His disappointment and feelings of dejection were made all the worse for the long years he'd devoted to being a detective.

He was to return to Criminal Investigations in a couple of years. In the meantime, Mikami had taken on the role of press director with a single pledge: to keep his various emotions in check and prevent the rot from setting in. He would *not* repeat his previous mistakes, nor would he let himself become negligent, or squander the time. More than anything else, his long years of hard work had resulted in a physical and mental routine that ensured he couldn't bear to leave any problem unattended.

Reforming Media Relations. He knew he had to make this his first task.

His first move had been to launch an offensive on Criminal Investigations. He needed case information, something he could use as a bargaining chip. In dealing with the press, he understood that raw intel was the only real weapon he had at his disposal. He would confront them armed. He would build a mature relationship where each side kept the other in check. Administrative Affairs would come to interfere less and less, and they could finally break free from that three-sided impasse. In this way, Mikami had outlined his schedule for reform.

The wall which Criminal Investigations – the self-acknowledged bull of the field divisions – had erected to protect itself had been substantial. The same was true of Second Division, Mikami's home for many years, but it was First Division's unwillingness to talk that had, he had to admit, been the most formidable. He had taken to making a daily pilgrimage to each of the divisions during lunch, circling the axis of First Division, striking up conversations with managers to get a feel for any investigations in progress. Outside work he leveraged his personal network to make contact with mid-level detectives. He waited for public holidays and days off, then showed up outside their apartments bearing small gifts. He bypassed politics and gave it to them straight. As he made the rounds, he told them he needed intel so he could stand up to the press.

He had kept his second motivation hidden. He'd been looking towards the future. If he was to return to Criminal Investigations in two years' time, it would be with a 'second offensive'. He had to make sure, during his time as press director, that no one in the department came to view him as an outsider. For better or for worse, he needed to keep them informed of what he was doing in Media Relations; it was a necessary preparation for his return.

His 'pilgrimages' continued for two, three months. While he gained little of actual substance, a second and secretly hoped-for reaction began to surface. What he was doing was unusual for a press director and had caught the attention of the media; the effect was far from insignificant. They had started to pay attention. There were noticeable changes in the way they saw him. He was unique, working for now in Media Relations, but a man whose true home was in Second Division. In a few years he could be in a position of importance in Criminal Investigations, and for this reason the press had treated him with a certain deference from the outset, opting to wait and see. It was as true then as ever that Criminal Investigations was the most crucial source of information for the press. And Mikami's pilgrimages emphasized the 'proximity' between Criminal Investigations and Media Relations. Reporters approached him in increasing numbers. It was the first time the press had voluntarily shown up without an explicit invitation.

Mikami had seized the opportunity, and begun his plan of building up their expectations. He put to use what little information he had, plying it to maximum effect. Speaking to the papers individually, he used indirect phrasing and subtle changes in expression to lay down the scent of cases in progress. He made his presence known by keeping the press close, constructing a solid basis for their interaction, transforming the image of a weak press director. At the same time, he'd been careful not to let them get too comfortable around him. Whenever someone came in to kill time, he remained impassive and played up his stern image. He stood firm, and was quick to shut down superficial criticisms levelled against the police. At the same time, he displayed a willingness to listen to considered arguments. When they wanted to negotiate he gave them all the time they needed. He never sought to ingratiate himself with them, yet allowed for certain concessions when necessary. It had been going well. Mikami had eliminated the imbalance of power that had been to their absolute advantage, and yet they showed no signs of annoyance. They were always hungry for more information. The police were hungry only for good publicity. It was a relationship of convenience, with each side in a different corner, but it was possible nonetheless to find a common ground; all that was necessary was to bring a little trust to those face-to-face moments. The framework for Mikami's vision for Media Relations had continued to come together until Mikami had become convinced his plan was working.

His bête noire turned out to be the director of Administrative Affairs. Mikami had expected an improved relationship with the press to result in less interference, but his prediction had been far from the mark. Akama had become annoyed with Mikami's management of the office, and started to express his reservations at every opportunity. He began to criticize Mikami for his 'defeatist' compromises, bemoaning his liaisons with Criminal Investigations as a stubborn unwillingness to move on. Mikami couldn't understand it. Akama had wanted a strong press director; Mikami had been sure Akama had taken into account his former connection to Criminal Investigations. He had used this leverage to the best of his ability. And it was bringing results. What problem could Akama have? His decision made, Mikami approached Akama directly. He argued the importance of using his access to case information as a tool for more diplomatic dealings with the press. He hadn't been able to believe Akama's response.

'Just let it go, Mikami. If we allow you access to that kind of information there's always a chance you could leak it to the press. You can hardly say anything if you don't know anything. Right?'

Mikami had been stunned. Akama had wanted a stone-faced scarecrow. *Don't act, don't think. Just stare with that fierce look of yours.* Akama might as well have told him that. Media Control, not Media Relations. A genuine hatred for the press. He'd been warped beyond anything Mikami had feared.

Mikami had been unwilling just to give up. Blind obedience to Akama would set Media Relations back twenty years. His reforms were finally in motion – he just needed to push them forward. It was too late to let them come to nothing. The ferocity of his own reaction had amazed him. No doubt it was because he'd felt the breeze of the outside world on his skin. He had learned to see things he'd never even thought of as a detective. It was as if there were a towering wall separating the police from the general public and Media Relations was the only window even close to opening outwards. It didn't matter how narrow-minded or self-important the press were: if that window was shut from the inside, the police would be completely disconnected from the other side.

Something had lit up in the part of Mikami that was still a detective. To submit and play scarecrow for Administrative Affairs would mean severing the few links he had left to his true self. And yet no one was foolish enough to go up against anyone with influence in personnel decisions. If he was posted to some district station in the mountains, then, far from being reinstated to Criminal Investigations, he would, in terms of the organization, become at once someone only vaguely remembered. Viewed differently, however, it had also been a rare opportunity. If the time came when the situation changed and a return to his home department seemed likely, the story of his standing up to the director of Administrative Affairs – the second-most influential man in the Prefectural HQ – would be enough to purge his 'second offensive' and more besides.

With the greatest care, Mikami began to resist Akama. He worked harder to present himself as a loyal subordinate, keeping his emotions at bay while he focused on being true to the cause. He listened quietly but objectively, offering tactful disagreement only when he found himself unable to stomach a particular instruction or order. He also spoke up on certain media strategies he supported, all the while quietly continuing with his plan to reform Media Relations.

He had known he was treading on thin ice. He could feel Akama's irritability in his pulse. And yet he had persisted in making his opinion known. It was clear now that he'd been energized by the risk. For half a year he'd refused to shy away from Akama's piercing glares. He'd felt the rush of combat. He might not have been winning, but he hadn't been losing either.

But . . .

Ayumi's disappearance had changed everything.

Ash tumbled from his cigarette and hit the table. He'd smoked two already. He checked the clock on the wall. Kuramae was visible, his profile a dim shadow at the edge of Mikami's vision. Second Division had refused to share their intelligence. Did that mean their goodwill for him was spent? Kuramae was there as a representative of Mikami. The field divisions would have been well aware of that.

It had to be because he'd stopped visiting the divisions, the detectives. Because his press strategy had regressed to being whatever Akama dictated.

A sudden commotion broke out in the corridor.

Here they come. Suwa and Kuramae had enough time to exchange looks before the door swung open, without so much as a knock.

3

In an instant the room filled with press. The *Asahi, Mainichi, Yomi-uri, Tokyo, Sankei* and the *Toyo*. Then the local press: the *D Daily*, the *Zenken Times, D Television* and the *FM Kenmin*. Their overlapping faces were all hard set. Some were openly glaring, their shoulders tense and angry in a way that suggested their more recent cooperation with Mikami was weakening, too. The majority were reporters in their twenties. It was during times like this that Mikami felt an aversion for their youth, for the way it allowed for such brash behaviour. The reporters from *Kyodo News* and Jiji Press filed into the room a little behind the others. The reporter from the *NHK* was there, too, at the back of the crowd and sticking halfway into the corridor, craning his neck to see in.

All thirteen member agencies of the Press Club were in attendance.

'Let's get on with it.' A surge of disgruntled voices rose from the crowd and the two men at the front, both with the *Toyo*, took a step closer. As the Press Club's representative for the month, it was the *Toyo*'s place to lead proceedings.

'Director Mikami. First, we'd like to hear a proper explanation for your sudden departure yesterday.' Tejima, who had donned a suit jacket, launched the first question.

Toyo. Assistant Chief. University H. Twenty-six. No ideological background. Deadly serious. Tends to overconfidence. Tejima's entry in Mikami's notebook.

'Suwa told us you had a relative in a critical condition. Perhaps so – but does that really justify you getting up and leaving without a single word? And as we've heard nothing from you since, I can't help thinking that your treatment of us is—'

'Sorry,' Mikami interrupted. He hated recalling the reason he had left and to have the press asking about it.

Tejima glanced at Akikawa, who was to his side.

Toyo. Chief. University K. Twenty-nine. Left-leaning. Never gives up. De facto leader of the Press Club.

Akikawa looked nonchalant, his arms folded. He preferred to act big, let the others get on with the heavy lifting.

'Am I correct in assuming that you're offering an apology?'

'That's right.'

Tejima studied Akikawa's expression for a second time, then turned to face the others. Ready to ask their opinion, he began, 'Are you all—'

That'll do, let's get on with it. He nodded at their silent gestures to carry on, then proceeded to open a photocopied sheet he'd been holding over Mikami's desk.

Details of a Serious Car Accident in Oito City.

Mikami had no need to check the document. It was a copy of the press report the office had put up a day earlier. A housewife had been distracted while driving her car and hit an elderly man, resulting in severe, full-body injuries to the victim. While road accidents were common enough in themselves, the details of this particular case had become a cause of conflict with the press.

'Let me ask again – why have you kept the identity of the female driver hidden? You must know you have an obligation to disclose her full details?'

Mikami locked his fingers and met Tejima's icy stare. 'As I explained yesterday, the woman is eight months pregnant. She has been in a state of extreme distress since causing the accident. We can't know how she might react to the shock of seeing her name in the papers, on top of everything else. That is why we haven't revealed her name.'

'That is not a valid reason. You've even kept her address secret – all we have is "Oito City". Mrs A, housewife, thirty-two years old. That's all you've given us . . . how can we be sure she even exists?'

'Of course she's real, and that's exactly why we must consider the effect this might have on her unborn baby. Tell me what's wrong with that.'

They seemed to take Mikami's counter-argument as arrogance. Tejima's expression darkened and the room bustled angrily. 'Since when has that been something the police have to think about? It's an unnecessary consideration.'

'The woman is not under arrest. The man had stepped on to the road in a place with no pedestrian crossing. And he'd been drinking.'

'The fact remains that the driver wasn't watching the road. And here, you describe the man's condition as "serious", where it should say "critical". The old man, Meikawa, he's in a coma, after all.'

Mikami glanced at Akikawa from the corner of his eye. How long was he planning to let Tejima rant for?

'Director Mikami, you need to level with us. This isn't something we can just turn a blind eye to; the potential consequences are too big. We have a duty to question the driver's responsibility in this instance.'

Mikami returned his gaze to Tejima, who was still doggedly persevering. 'So, you want to pass sentence on her by bandying her name around in the papers?'

'Come on, there's no need to put it like that. That's not what we're saying. What we're saying is that it's wrong for the police to make a unilateral decision to withhold a person's name and address. Whether we print the driver's name or not should be up to us, after we've had the chance to weigh it against the public good.'

'Why exactly can't we make that decision for you?'

'Because the facts of the case become obscured. Without the details of the people involved – their names, addresses – we have no means of verifying that the information you provide is correct, or if the cases are properly closed. Also, if the Prefectural HQ gets into a routine of issuing anonymous reports, who's to say the district stations won't start cutting corners in their own statements? Thinking of the worst-case scenario, withholding information like this could be used to bend the truth, even as part of a police cover-up.'

'A police cover-up . . .'

'Listen, all we're saying . . .' Yamashina's lanky frame shouldered in from the side. *Zenken Times. Provisional Chief. University F. Twenty-eight. Third son of a secretary to a member of the Diet. Charmer. Loser.* '. . . is that when someone seems desperate to hide something, well, you start to wonder. Maybe she's the daughter of someone important. Maybe they're going easy because the old man was a drunk.'

'You're being ridiculous,' Mikami said, his voice unwittingly loud.

Yamashina just shrugged, while other voices boiled over. *You're the ridiculous one! Of course we're suspicious when you insist on hiding everything! Were the names of pregnant women withheld before? No. We demand a proper explanation!* Mikami ignored the jeering. If he opened his mouth he would end up shouting, too.

'Let's see, Mikami,' Akikawa said finally. He took his time, unfolding his arms. It stank of drama, as though to suggest that their star performer was about to take the stage. 'What you're afraid of is . . . the police coming under public censure if something were to happen to the woman or her unborn child because her name had come out in the press.'

'That's not it. There are simply some circumstances in which a person involved has the right to privacy.'

'The right to privacy?' Akikawa scoffed. 'Let me get this

right . . . you think we should be discussing the rights of the guilty party?'

'Yes.'

Again the room descended into commotion.

Come on! As if you understand that! Isn't disregarding human rights a particular forte of the police? Who are you to lecture us on that?

'I don't understand why you're so worked up. You know the trend in reporting is increasingly heading towards anonymity. You employ it all the time – on TV, in the papers. Why are you so against us making the decision?'

That's just arrogance. The police don't have the right. Don't you understand anything about press freedom? Anonymous police reports infringe on the public's right to know.

'Come on, Mikami, just give us her name. We're not going to print it if she really is in bad shape.' Yamashina spoke over them again. This time his tone was conciliatory. 'It's not as if it makes any difference in the end. We'd still do our research, get her name and address, even if you were to withhold her details. I imagine it would be harder on her, too – as we know she's pregnant – if we had to find out from her directly.'

'Director Mikami, let's just get this clear,' Tejima implored, speaking up the moment Akikawa refolded his arms. His forehead was oiled with sweat. 'Are you willing to consider giving us the woman's identity?'

'No.' Mikami's answer was immediate. Tejima's eyes grew wide.

'Why not?'

'You know, she was in tears when she pleaded with the officer in charge, asking him not to talk to the press.'

'Hey! Don't make us out to be the bad guys.'

'That's how scary it is. To face having your name in the papers.'

'That's unwarranted. You're just trying to shift the blame.'

'You can say what you want. We're not giving you her name. The decision has already been made.'

The room fell silent. Mikami stood ready for an angry back-lash. But . . .

'You've changed, Mikami.' Akikawa had switched tack. He placed his hands on Mikami's desk and leaned forwards, his expression grave. 'We expected things from you. You weren't like your predecessor, Funaki. You never tried to ingratiate yourself with us, nor did you ever suck up to your superiors. Honestly . . . we were impressed with you after your transfer in. But then you seemed to give up, become indifferent. Now you tow the party line. What happened?'

Mikami was silent. He stared into empty space, loath for them to notice his hesitation. Akikawa continued.

'You were the one to call Media Relations a "window". It's a hard pill to swallow when the same press director chooses to fol-low official policy blindly, like all the other officers. Without someone willing to listen to us in the outside world, someone who has the nerve to be objective and make a stand, the police will never be anything more than a closed-off black box. Are you happy with that?'

'The window's still there. It's just not as big as you thought.'

Disappointment flashed over Akikawa's face. Mikami realized that, rather than seeking to attack or condemn, Akikawa had been making a genuine appeal. His eyes were dispassionate when he returned his gaze to Mikami.

'Okay. I want to know one more thing.'

'What?'

'Your *personal* opinion on anonymous reporting.'

'Personal, official – the distinction's irrelevant. The answer's the same.'

'You really believe that?'

Mikami was silent again. Akikawa said nothing. Each probed the other's eyes. Five, ten seconds. Time seemed to slow down. Finally, Akikawa gave a deep nod.

'Your position is clear enough.' He looked around the

reporters behind him for a while before turning back to face Mikami. 'Then I formally request, representing the consensus of the Press Club, that you reveal the identity of the woman. We ask this not of you but of the Prefectural HQ.'

Mikami's eyes provided his answer: *you know the decision.*

Akikawa nodded again.

'"Give them the woman's name and they'll run it in the papers." Meaning you, the police, have no trust in us whatsoever. Yes?'

The words came out sounding like an ultimatum. Akikawa turned his back on Mikami. The reporters began to file out of the room, their heels loud.

Don't think we're going to stand for this.

A brooding disquiet was all that remained in the cramped room.

4

Had they meant to threaten him?

Mikami let out a heavy sigh; he took the copy of the press report from the desk, scrunched it up and tossed it into the bin. The confrontation had been unlike anything that had come before. Their attacks had been personal. It was the first time he'd seen them seem so thirsty for blood, and he felt all the more irritated for it. Nobody had died; it was just a car accident. News they would hardly have paid attention to if it hadn't become embroiled in the question of anonymous reporting. It was small fry, the kind of news even local papers might not even cover these days.

The office went back to having enough room for its occupants. Suwa's eyes were scouring the paper. He looked as if he wanted to say something but made no attempt at eye contact. Kuramae and Mikumo were both busy finishing work on the bulletin, their deadline looming. They seemed to be waiting for Mikami's mood to settle. Or perhaps they simply felt sorry for him. All three had heard Akikawa's words.

You've changed, Mikami.

Mikami lit a cigarette, crushing it after a couple of drags then drinking down the rest of his cold tea. They'd finally put it in words. For a while now, he'd had the strong suspicion that the press would eventually give up on him. *Back to square one.* He felt indignant as the realization took hold. But perhaps that was nothing more than the result of having overestimated their relationship from the beginning. It was as though he'd hallucinated an oasis in the desert. He hadn't forged enough of a relationship to claim it was broken. The trust between them had been frail enough for a gust of wind to sweep it away. And he would still struggle to answer if someone asked whether his built-in animosity for the press had faded during his time reforming Media Relations.

He had been unlucky, too. Anonymous reporting was tricky. It had become an issue for the police on a national basis. That his turn had come now, when the faith the press had in him had begun to erode, was particularly unfortunate. The woman's name was in a drawer in his desk: Hanako Kikunishi. District had included it when faxing in their report, but a call had come in from the station's second-captain within half an hour of it arriving. *Sorry to bother you. The woman's pregnant, could you keep her anonymous this time?*

Mikami called for Suwa to come over. 'How do you think that went?'

Suwa knotted his eyebrows. 'They did get a little worked up.'

'Because of me?'

'Not at all. I think you did all you could. Win or lose, nothing goes to plan when anonymity is on the agenda.'

His view of the job was similar to Director Akama's. The only difference, Mikami supposed, was that Suwa employed the carrot as well as the stick. A ball of candy, wrapped in the expertise, skill and pride of a natural spin doctor.

Mikami relaxed back into his chair. He watched Suwa move briskly off to answer a call. *Reinvigorated*, Mikami found himself thinking, uncharitably. Perhaps Mikami's arrival had transformed the office into a place difficult for Suwa to do his job. His *raison d'être* had been threatened by a press director with a background as a detective, inexperienced in Media Relations. Mikami wondered if that was how Suwa felt.

Okay, let's see what you can do.

Mikami changed tack. He couldn't allow himself to dwell on

the failure of trust and do nothing about the current situation. Whatever action they ended up taking, if they discontinued their relations with the press, it would be equivalent to a detective refusing to investigate a case.

'Everyone, listen up.'

Having just finished his call, Suwa got to his feet at the same time as Kuramae. Mikumo was on the edge of her chair, looking unsure whether she was included. Gesturing that she didn't need to join them, Mikami waved Suwa and Kuramae over.

'See if you can soften the blow next door. And see if you can't work out who is really pushing this.'

'No problem.'

Suwa had definitely perked up. He grabbed his jacket and, without waiting for further instructions, strode confidently from the room. Kuramae followed, his steps lacking the same self-assuredness. Mikami rolled his neck in a circle. His optimism was keeping his unease at bay.

The Press Room was a unique environment. As rivals in the same industry, the reporters sought to keep tabs on each other; at the same time, they had the solidarity of co-workers in a single workplace. When they came up against the police, this solidarity could grow into a sense of joint struggle. Sometimes – as they had just now – they were able to put up a monolithic front that could put even the police to shame. Even so, when it came down to it, they were all subject to different paymasters. Their companies all had their own unique policies and traditions, and this meant appearances were not always in sync with reality.

Yamashina came back into the room just as Mikami was considering this. His eyes darted around nervously, completely different to fifteen minutes earlier when they'd tried to measure Mikami's mood.

'Got something you want to say?'

He seemed to relax at Mikami's tone, breaking into a grin as he walked across the room.

'You'd benefit from being a little softer on us, you know. Just now? That was crazy.'

'Crazy?'

'They're all furious.'

'You were the one who set them all off.'

'Now why would you go and say that? I was only trying to hold out an olive branch.'

He was scared of the police pulling away. Mikami realized his power had quietly persisted over the more ineffectual reporters like Yamashina.

'How are things in there?' Mikami probed.

Yamashina made a show of lowering his voice. 'Like I said, they're going crazy. The *Toyo*'s angry. Then there's Utsuki from the *Mainichi*. And the *Asahi*'s –'

The phone in front of Mikami started to ring. He picked up the receiver, annoyed at the interruption.

'The director wants you in his office.'

It was Secretariat Chief Ishii. He sounded pleased about something. Mikami could already imagine the look on Akama's face. He felt a sudden foreboding. News that was positive for Ishii was often not so for him.

'You're needed somewhere?'

'That's right.' As Mikami got to his feet he noticed a Post-it note on the floor, hidden in the shadow of the desk's leg. Mikumo's handwriting. He read it, taking care that Yamashina didn't notice.

Call from Inspector Futawatari. 07.45.

Shinji Futawatari. They'd joined the force in the same year. Mikami felt the corners of his mouth tighten. He glanced at Mikumo but said nothing, squeezing the note in his hand. What could Futawatari be calling about? He'd know Mikami was avoiding him. Maybe it was just office business. Or maybe he'd heard about the previous day's ID and felt he should say something as a colleague.

Mikami remembered Yamashina was there.

'We can continue this later.'

Perhaps imagining he'd made progress, Yamashina gave a satisfied nod, sticking close to Mikami as he headed for the door. Just as Mikami reached the corridor, he said, 'Oh, Mikami.'

'What is it?'

'Yesterday – was it true? That one of your relatives is in a critical condition?'

Mikami turned slowly around to face Yamashina. The latter was looking up intently.

'Of course. Why are you asking?'

'Oh, it's nothing,' Yamashina said hesitantly. 'Only, I heard it might be something else.'

Bastard.

Mikami pretended he hadn't heard and started off down the corridor. Yamashina gave him an overly familiar tap on the shoulder before disappearing into the adjacent Press Room. Through the half-open door Mikami caught a glimpse of the reporters, looking stern as they huddled together.

5

Outside of the lunch hour it was rare to pass anyone on the first-floor corridor. *Accounting. Training. Internal Affairs.* The doors to each division were shut tight, keeping prying eyes out. It was quiet. Mikami's footsteps provided the only sound as they echoed on the corridor's waxed floor. *Administrative Affairs.* The words on the faded doorplate seemed to demand a certain feeling of apprehension. Mikami pushed open the door. Division Chief Shirota was sitting up ahead, at the far end of the room; Mikami bowed in silence before walking over, checking the inspector's window desk out of the corner of his eye. Futawatari wasn't there. His light was off, and the desk was clear of papers. If he wasn't having a day off, he was probably in Personnel, on the first floor of the north building. Rumour had it that planning was already under way for the following spring's personnel transfers. Futawatari was in charge of putting together a proposal for changes in executive positions. This fact had been a source of discomfort ever since Mikami had learned about it from Chief Ishii. What did it mean for his own transfer? Had his unplanned return to Media Relations really been the sole decision of Director Akama?

Mikami cut through the room and knocked on the door to Akama's office.

'Enter.' The response came from Ishii. As it had been on the phone, his voice was pitched an octave higher than usual.

'You wanted to see me?'

Mikami made his way over the thick carpet. Akama was

sitting back on a couch, his fingers scratching at his chin. The gold-rimmed glasses. The tailored pinstripe suit. The distant, angled gaze. His appearance was no different than usual – the image of executive management, the kind new recruits were so apt to dream of emulating. At forty-one, he was five years Mikami's junior. The balding man in his fifties, typically sycophantic as he sat bolt upright next to Akama, was Ishii. He gestured for Mikami to come over. Akama didn't wait for Mikami to sit before he opened his mouth.

'It must have been . . . unpleasant.' His tone was casual, as though to suggest Mikami had been caught in an evening shower.

'No, it's . . . I'm sorry to let personal issues get in the way of my work.'

'Nothing to worry about. Please, take a seat. How were the locals? I assume they treated you well?'

'They did. They took good care of me, the station captain in particular.'

'That's good to hear. I'll make sure to send my personal thanks.'

His custodial tone grated.

It had happened three months earlier. Seeing no possible alternative, Mikami had approached Akama for help. He had confided that his daughter had run away from home just one day earlier, and appealed for the search to be expanded from his local district station to include the other stations throughout the prefecture. Akama's reaction had been completely unexpected. He had scrawled a note on the search request Mikami had brought with him, then called Ishii in and instructed him to fax the document to headquarters in Tokyo. Perhaps that meant the Community Security Bureau. Or the Criminal Investigations Bureau. Maybe even the Commissioner General's Secretariat. Akama had then put down his pen and said, 'You don't need to worry. I'll have special arrangements in place before the day is out, from Hokkaido to Okinawa.'

Mikami couldn't forget the look of triumph on Akama's face.

He had known immediately that it contained more than a simple look of superiority at having demonstrated his authority as a Tokyo bureaucrat. Akama's eyes had lit up with the expectation of change. They had become fixated on him, peering from behind those gold-rimmed glasses, desperate not to miss the moment this upstart regional superintendent who had resisted for so long finally capitulated. Mikami had shivered to the core, realizing he'd given Akama a weakness to exploit. How else could he have responded, though, as a father concerned for the safety of his daughter?

Thank you. I am in your debt.

Mikami had bowed. He'd held his head under the table, lower than his knees . . .

'And this, the second time now. I can't imagine how difficult it must be to make those trips.' Not for the first time, Akama was dwelling on the subject of Ayumi. 'I know I've suggested this before, but perhaps you might consider releasing more of your daughter's details? More than just her photo and physical characteristics. There are all sorts of other things – fingerprints, dental records, for example?'

Mikami had of course considered all of these before Akama suggested it. It was close to torture each time he was called out, each time he had to peel the white cloth from the face of a corpse. And Minako's nerves were stretched to breaking. Yet he remained hesitant. Fingerprints. Hand prints. Dental impressions. Records of dental treatment. All were types of data most effectively used in the identification of dead bodies. *I want you to look for my daughter's corpse.* It was tantamount to saying exactly that, and Mikami couldn't bear the idea.

'I'll need some more time to think about it.'

'Well, be quick. We want to keep any losses to a minimum.'

Losses?

Mikami called on his sense of reason, forcing down the surge of anger. Akama was trying to provoke him. Testing the extent of his submission. Pulling himself together, Mikami said, 'What was it you wanted to see me for?'

All the curiosity drained from Akama's eyes.

'The truth is,' Ishii said, leaning forwards in his stead – it was clear he'd been itching to speak the whole time – 'the commissioner general is going to pay us an official visit.'

It took a moment for Mikami to respond. This was not what he'd expected.

'The commissioner general?'

'We've just been notified ourselves. It's scheduled for this time next week, so as you can imagine, we're in a bit of a flap. I can't think how many years it's been since the last commissioner's visit . . .'

Perhaps it was the presence in the room of Akama – a career officer from Tokyo – that worsened the effect. It was embarrassing to bear witness to Ishii's obvious excitement. The commissioner general, the National Police Agency. The commissioner was a man who sat at the very top of the pyramid, above the 260,000 officers in the police force. To the regional police, he was like an emperor. And yet, was an official visit really something to get so worked up about? It was at times like this that Ishii showed his limitations. He held the National Police Agency in awe, looking on with an artless longing, just as a youth raised in the country might dream of the city.

'What's the purpose of the visit?' Mikami asked, his mind already on the job. He had been summoned as press director, which meant there was probably a strong PR element to the visit.

'Six Four.'

This time, it was Akama who replied. Mikami looked at him, taken aback. There was an expectant smirk in Akama's eyes.

Six Four. The term for a fourteen-year-old case, the kidnapping and murder of a young girl named Shoko.

It had been the first full-scale kidnapping to take place within the jurisdiction of Prefecture D. After the kidnapper had successfully made away with the ransom of 20 million yen, the police had tragically discovered the corpse of the kidnapped seven-year-old. The identity of the kidnapper remained unknown. The case was unsolved even after all these years. At the time, Mikami had been working for Special Investigations in First Division and, as a member of the Close Pursuit Unit, had followed Shoko's father as he drove to the ransom exchange point. It was enough to have the painful memory revived, but the greatest shock was to hear Akama – a career bureaucrat and an outsider who'd had nothing to do with the investigation – use the term Criminal Investigations had privately adopted to describe the kidnapping. Behind his back, people referred to him as a data freak, a compulsive researcher. Was Mikami to take it that Akama's network of informers had, after only a year and a half of him being in the post, already infiltrated the inner workings of Criminal Investigations?

Even so . . .

The question was replaced by another. It went without saying that Six Four was the Prefectural HQ's greatest failure. Even in Tokyo, at the level of the National Police Agency, it still ranked as one of the most significant cases that had yet to be closed. At the same time, no one would dispute the fact that, as fourteen years had slipped by since the kidnapping, the memory of the case had begun to fade. What had once been a two-hundred-strong Investigative HQ had, over the course of time, undergone a process of downsizing so that now only twenty-five detectives remained on the case. While the Investigative HQ hadn't been shut down, it had been downgraded internally to Investigative Team. Just over a year remained until the statute of limitations came into effect. Mikami no longer overheard the case being discussed in public. And he'd heard that information from the general public had dried up a long time ago. It was the same for the press, who seemed only to remember the case in one article a year, a token gesture to mark the date of the kidnapping. It was gathering moss; why, now, had it become the focus of a commissioner's visit? *We intend to do everything we can before the statute comes into effect.* Was that what it was, a show of fireworks for the public?

'What is the visit for?' Mikami asked, and Akama's smile deepened in response.

'To make an appeal, inside and outside the force, and to give a boost to the officers still investigating the case. To reinforce our intention never to let violent crime go unpunished.'

'The kidnapping took place fourteen years ago. May I assume the visit is related to the statute of limitations?'

'What could have more impact than the commissioner's message relating to this old case? I am told it was the commissioner's own idea. Although, I do believe his appeal is intended more to reach an internal audience than the general public.'

An internal audience. With those words, everything seemed to fall into place.

Tokyo. Politics.

'Anyway, here's the detailed schedule for the day.'

Ishii picked up a sheet of paper. Mikami quickly pulled out his notebook.

'Note that this isn't official as yet. Right – so the commissioner is due to arrive by car at noon. After lunch with the station captain, he will go directly to Sada-cho and visit the site where the girl's body was discovered. While there, he will make an offering of flowers and incense. Following that, he will go to the Investigative HQ in Central Station and give praise and encouragement to the team. From there he would like to pay a visit to the bereaved family's home in order to pay his respects. There, another offering of incense. After that he wants to take a walking interview between the house and his car. That's the overall picture, as it is now.'

Mikami had stopped scribbling his notes. 'He wants a walking interview?' A walking interview meant the press gathering around him to ask their questions as he stood – or continued walking – outside the house.

'Exactly. That's what the Secretariat has requested. No doubt they feel it will have a more dynamic feel than a formal session, say, in a conference room.'

Mikami felt his mood darken. The unforgiving faces of the reporters flashed through his mind. 'Where does he want the photographs? At the site where the body was found?'

'No. Those would be at the family home.'

'He wants the reporters to come inside?'

'Would it be too small for that?'

'No, not really, but . . .'

'The commissioner paying his respects at the altar, the bereaved parents in the background. That's the picture he wants for the TV and papers.'

The chief executive of the police giving the bereaved his assurances that the kidnapper would be caught. It certainly had impact.

'There isn't much time; make sure you get the family's permission in the next day or two,' Akama said from one side. He had reverted to his normal way of issuing orders.

Mikami made an ambivalent nod.

'Hmm? Is there something you wish to raise?'

'No . . .' He doubted the family would decline to accept the commissioner's visit. At the same time, he felt uncomfortable with the idea of visiting them to make the request. They had hardly exchanged words at the time of the kidnapping. Only the members of the Home Unit had spoken with them in any real detail. And then he'd been transferred. His posting to Second Division had come only three months after the kidnapping had taken place; he had completely lost touch with the progress of the case.

'Okay. I'll check in with the Six Four team first, to see if they can provide me with an update on the family,' Mikami said, choosing his words carefully.

Akama frowned in disapproval. 'I shouldn't think that is necessary. My understanding is that you are already acquainted with the family. No, your request is to be made directly. There's no need to involve Criminal Investigations.'

'But that's . . .'

'This is the remit of Administrative Affairs. Surely it would only complicate matters to bring Criminal Investigations into the fray? Once you have the groundwork in place, I will contact the director personally. Until then, you are to treat this matter as confidential.'

Confidential? Mikami couldn't gauge Akama's true intent. Organizing the visit without Criminal Investigations knowing? It was painfully clear that doing so would only complicate matters even more, and the case in question was nothing less than Six Four.

'Also, with regard to the press . . .' Akama continued, paying no heed. 'As I believe this is the first time you've handled something like this, let me explain a couple of things. The walking interview will give all the appearance of being casual, but it won't do for us to grant the press access to the commissioner without first applying restrictions. Our preparations must be on a par with those for a member of the Diet. It would be untenable if the commissioner were to stumble over any capricious or otherwise irresponsible questions. The first thing you must do is get the Press Club to compose and submit a list of questions in advance. They will have around ten minutes to ask questions on the day. Also, only the paper representing the club this month will be permitted to conduct the interview. And you must impress on them the importance of not asking any awkward questions. Is this clear?'

Mikami looked down at his notes. He accepted that it was necessary to consult with the press beforehand. The question was whether rational discussion was possible, given the current situation.

'I assume the press were . . . vocal again this morning?'

Had Akama noticed his unease? No, someone had probably already told him about the situation in Media Relations.

'What's it really like?'

'Worse than before. I refused to give way on the anonymous reporting.'

'Very good. We mustn't let down our guard. They will only get cocky, try to take advantage, the moment we show any signs of weakness. Force them into submission. We provide the information, and they accept it. You need to drum that into them.'

His talk apparently over, he had started riffling through his jacket pockets, as though having remembered that he had been looking for something. Mikami peered at Ishii out of the corner of his eye. He was scribbling something in red, as exuberant-looking as earlier. Mikami's foreboding had been right on the mark. He felt more weighed down than when he had entered the office.

'Right – if that's everything . . .'

Mikami snapped his notebook shut and got to his feet. Perhaps there was something in his bearing that suggested to Akama a false obedience – he called out just as Mikami was leaving the room.

'You are the spitting image, you know. You must really cherish her.'

Mikami stopped. He turned around cautiously. In his hand, Akama was brandishing the photo of Ayumi the police were using for the search. *The spitting image*. Mikami hadn't told Akama the reason why Ayumi had run away. His face burned regardless. In that instant, his façade of calm crumbled. Akama looked smug.

'The fingerprints, dental records – why don't you discuss it some more with your wife? I just want to do all we can for you.'

Mikami's struggle lasted only seconds.

'Thank you.'

He bowed deeply from the waist. As he did so, he felt the blood coursing through his body.

6

'I don't think I can make it back for lunch.'

'That's fine, there's no need to worry.'

'What will you do for food?'

'I'll manage. I can make do with leftovers, from this morning.'

'Why don't you go and get something from Shinozaki?'

Minako was silent.

'Take the car. It's only fifteen minutes there and back.'

'I think I should finish the leftovers . . .'

'At least order in some soba, from Sogetsuan.'

Again, silence.

'It'll be nice.'

'. . . Okay.'

'Great, do that for today. But it'll really help if you get out a little more.'

'Darling . . .'

She was dying to end the call. The determination expressed itself, as always, through her silence. She was terrified that Ayumi would call, only to find the line busy. They had switched their old phone for a new model, adding call waiting to their contract, alongside the new caller-display functionality that had been rolled out locally in the previous year. Yet Minako refused to be placated, continuing instead to obsess over 'what ifs'.

'Okay, I'll hang up. Just make sure to order something healthy with the soba, okay?'

'I will.'

Mikami ended the call, stepping out from under the wooden pavilion in Joshi Park. The call wasn't the kind he could make from the office, and he didn't like to creep around the station building; instead, he had walked the few minutes it took to reach the park. The north wind was getting stronger still. In lieu of a coat, he turned up his jacket collar and hurried back along the path to the station. The weight of Minako's voice lingered in his ears. He couldn't let them drag each other down. When Ayumi had first gone missing, Minako had almost never been at home. Desperate for news of Ayumi's whereabouts, she had combed the local area with a photo in hand, asking questions and chasing what few leads there were; she had even gone to Tokyo and Kanagawa. Now, she hardly stepped out of the house. The shift had taken place a month ago, after the silent phone call. The call had been followed by another. A total of three in one day. *Ayumi, still hesitant.* The idea had spread and taken root in her mind. She had shut herself inside ever since, waiting all day, every day, for another call. She wouldn't listen when Mikami told her it was bad for her. Buying a new phone had had no effect – her life had changed completely. She started to buy the things she wanted by mail order. She would use food from the delivery companies to make dinner, make do with what was left for breakfast and lunch the following day. Mikami doubted she even ate the latter, when he wasn't there to check.

It had become his daily routine to buy two bento boxes at the supermarket near the station and take them home for lunch. This, at least, made him glad he was no longer a detective. In Media Relations, he could leave relatively early to go home. When something major happened, he still needed to visit the scene of the crime ahead of the press, but, in contrast to his time in Criminal Investigations, he was no longer required to camp night after night in the *dojo* of whichever station had jurisdiction. Most of the time he was free to go home. To be at Minako's side.

The truth, however, was that, even then, he couldn't be sure that his presence was actually providing her with any reassurance. When he was back early or home during lunch he would encourage her to go out, maybe do some shopping, telling her he would keep watch over the phone. She would nod in response but fail to show any signs of leaving. He saw Ayumi reflected in her stubbornness, the way their daughter had locked herself in her room in the days that led up to her running away.

And yet . . . he understood all too well the emotions that drove her to cling to the phone. After two months of silence following their daughter's running away, the moment of the call coming in had, for two parents on the edge of despair, represented confirmation that their daughter was alive. That evening, torrential rain had swept the northern area of the prefecture. The office had been inundated with reports of landslides and Mikami had been late home, so Minako had answered two of the three calls. The first had come in a little after eight. As soon as Minako had given her name, the caller had hung up. The second had come in at exactly half past nine. Minako had later explained to Mikami that she'd known it was Ayumi the instant it had started to ring. The second time she had kept quiet and just pressed the receiver to her ear. Ayumi tended to shrink away from pressure. It was best to give her space. She would talk, she just needed time. Minako had waited and prayed. Five . . . ten seconds. But the caller had remained silent. When Minako finally broke and called out Ayumi's name, the line had been immediately disconnected.

Minako had been beside herself when she called Mikami on his mobile. He had rushed home. *Call, just one more time.* He had waited, hoping against hope. The phone had rung a little before midnight. Mikami grabbed the receiver. A moment of silence. His pulse was racing. He called out to her. *Ayumi? I know it's you, Ayumi.* There was no reply. Mikami let his emotions take over. *Ayumi! Where are you? Come home. Everything will be fine, just come home right away!* The rest, he couldn't remember. He suspected

44

he'd continued to call her name, over and over. At some point, the line had gone dead. He'd fallen into a stupor. For a while, he'd just stood there, rooted to the spot. It was only later that he realized he'd neglected to remember his training as a police officer, as a detective – he'd changed into a father, nothing else; lost sight of the fundamentals; forgotten even to pay attention to noises in the background. They hadn't bought Ayumi a mobile. The call seemed to have been made from a pay phone. He thought he could remember a faint sound, present throughout the call. Had it been breathing, or the murmur of the city, or something else? He'd tried desperately to remember, but nothing came. All that was left was a vague sensation, nothing he could call memory; a continuous sound, one that varied in intensity. His imagination had run wild. A non-stop stream of traffic, a city at night. A phone box on a pavement. An image of Ayumi inside, curled into a ball.

It had to be her, Mikami muttered to himself. His steps were becoming irregular. Without realizing it, his hands had clenched into fists. Who else apart from Ayumi would call three times without saying anything? There was also the fact that they weren't listed in the telephone directory. They didn't live in official police accommodation. After their marriage Mikami and Minako had moved into Mikami's family home in order to take care of his ailing parents. The number had, at the time, still been in the directory, under his dad's name. Illness had eventually claimed his mother, and it wasn't long after Six Four that his father passed away from pneumonia. Mikami had become the new head of the family and, in line with police tradition, applied to remove their personal number from the register. Ever since, it hadn't been included in the annually updated directory. Mikami knew from his experience as a detective that the directory was used for the majority of prank (and obscene) calls. Compared to households with listed numbers, this meant the likelihood of their number being targeted for such calls was minute.

Someone pressing random numbers had got through on a fluke. Emboldened after hearing a woman's voice, they had dialled a second, then a third time. That was, of course, possible. And there were a number of officers in the force who knew his number – after twenty-eight years of service, it was easy enough to imagine two or three who might bear him a grudge. Still . . . what was the point in lining up possibilities? *Ayumi had made the call.* He believed it. Insisted on it. They had no other palpable means, as parents, of clinging to the hope that their daughter was alive. Ayumi had called. She had survived for two months. She was alive now, after three. It was all they could hope for.

Mikami entered the station grounds through the back gate. It had been on his mind the whole month: her hesitation, the three calls. Had Ayumi been trying to tell them something? Or, perhaps, instead of wanting to say something, had she simply wanted to hear her parents' voices? She had called twice, but Minako had answered both times. So she'd tried a third time. Because she'd wanted to hear her father's voice, too.

Occasionally, the thought would come. That Ayumi had wanted to talk to him and not Minako. He'd finally answered on her third attempt. She had tried to speak, but the words hadn't come. She'd wanted him to know. So she'd uttered the phrase in her heart. *I'm sorry. I accept my face as it is.*

Mikami felt a sudden attack of dizziness. It hit him the moment he was through the staff entrance leading to the main building. *Shit, not again.* His vision blackened even as he cursed, his sense of balance deserting him. *Crouch!* His brain issued the command but his hands stubbornly reached for support. He felt the cold surface of a wall. This being his only guide, he waited. Eventually his vision began to creep back. Brightness. Strip lighting. Grey walls. He recoiled from a full-length mirror fitted into one of the walls. He saw the image of himself, his shoulders heaving with each breath. His slanted eyes. His thick nose. His harsh cheekbones. His look was that of an exposed rock face.

Shrill laughter piped up from behind. Someone was mocking him – that was his first thought.

He held his breath and glared into the mirror: a couple of beaming faces passed by. The image was of two women officers from Transport, playing with a training dummy as they walked by.

7

Mikami washed his face in the bathroom. The sweat on his hands was oily enough to repel the water. He dried himself without looking in the mirror then returned to Media Relations. Suwa and Kuramae were sitting on a couch, heads together in conversation. He had expected them to be ensconced in the Press Room, checking on the state of the reporters – why were they back in the office together?

'Something happen?' The words sounded sharper than he had intended.

Suwa stood. He looked crushed, as though his earlier enthusiasm had been a figment of the imagination. Kuramae drifted back to his desk with hunched shoulders.

Suwa's voice was a whisper. 'Sir, I'm sorry. They booted us out.'

'They kicked you out?'

'Yes . . . I don't know what to say.'

It felt like a significant blow. Mikami accepted that the Press Room granted its occupants a certain amount of independence. It was also true, however, that the room was on loan from the police, to assist the press in their reporting. It was disquieting to see that they were willing to shut the police – their landlords – out.

'That bad?'

'There's definitely something happening in there.'

'You think the *Toyo*'s behind it?'

'I do. They're stirring things up, trying to get the others worked up.'

A picture of Akikawa's expression came into Mikami's mind. *Meaning you, the police, have no trust in us whatsoever. Yes?* The words had been cutting.

'Is there anything you can do?'

'Oh definitely . . . I'm sure I can defuse the situation. It's just that I'm not sure we'll be able to do it straight away.'

Suwa's answer lacked confidence. And he didn't seem to be playing it down for effect. Perhaps the issue was serious enough to make even someone as experienced as Suwa feel out of their depth. Mikami sat at his desk. He lit a cigarette and pulled his notebook from his pocket.

'The commissioner's going to pay us a visit.'

'Sir?'

Suwa's eyes widened. Kuramae and Mikumo stopped what they were doing and looked up, too.

'It's an inspection. He's going to visit the crime scene of Shoko's kidnapping, also the family home.'

'When?'

'This time next week.'

'Next week?' Suwa yelped. After a moment he let out a breath and spoke again. 'Well, the timing's particularly bad.'

'For now, if you could just let the press know,' Mikami said, leafing through his notebook. He got Suwa to take a copy of the commissioner's schedule.

'We have ten minutes for the walking interview. That's time for three, maybe four questions?'

'Sounds about right.'

'How do the press decide on their questions?'

'They usually each come up with one, then that month's representative compiles the final list. Most of the time they all ask the same sorts of thing.'

Mikami nodded. 'If you tell them now, when do you think you can get them to submit their questions?'

'That would be . . .' Suwa's words trailed off. Mikami couldn't blame him. It was only moments earlier that the press had unceremoniously booted him out of their room.

'Just tell them I'll need them first thing next week. The executives want a chance to vet them.'

'Sure. I'll give it a go.' He said it with a look of being imposed upon, but followed this with a few quick nods for Mikami's sake.

It'll be fine. Mikami forced himself to feel optimistic. The commissioner general inspecting an unsolved kidnapping: he was sure it would be news enough for them all. They would fall into line. All they needed to do was agree a ceasefire on the issue of anonymous reporting. That would be easy enough. Suwa was partway back to his desk when he did an about turn. He cocked his head to one side.

'I wonder, though . . . why would he be looking into Six Four at this point?'

Six Four. It disturbed Mikami to hear the phrase uttered again, although less so than when it had come from Akama's mouth.

'It's PR, for Criminal Investigations,' Mikami said dismissively, getting to his feet.

Fourteen years since the kidnapping. The term no longer seemed to be the sole possession of the detectives who had worked on the case. Even so, it had made him wary to hear two people, both outsiders to the investigation, deploy the prestigious code name so soon after each other. He'd had the same thought in Akama's office: that information from Media Relations was leaking to Akama. That it had been doing so consistently, since the first day of his appointment.

He spoke without looking at Suwa. 'Right, I'll need you to sort things with the press. I'm going out for a while.'

'Where will you be?'

'Shoko's parents' house. I need to arrange things for the visit.' Mikami glanced at Kuramae. 'Can you come?'

He didn't make a habit of asking his staff to drive him around, but his attacks of dizziness were worrying him. Today wasn't the first time it had happened. He'd been suffering them for close to two weeks.

'Ah, actually, I have to go out to interview the railway division; the police brought in a group causing trouble on the trains.'

While he excused himself Mikumo craned her head upwards from behind, as though to advertise her presence. *Not you* – Mikami swallowed the words rising in his throat. In terms of enthusiasm for her work, Mikumo was many times Kuramae's superior. She had also come up through Transport, meaning she could drive a minibus in her sleep.

Clouds of dust blew through the air outside. As soon as he and Mikumo stepped out of the main building, she raised a hand to her forehead and dashed off into the wind, aiming for the parking area. Within a minute, the press director's car appeared, pulling confidently around to stop alongside the entrance.

'Do you know the address?' Mikami asked, getting into the passenger-side seat.

'Of course, sir,' she said without pause, already navigating forwards.

Mikami supposed he'd been thoughtless to ask. Anyone who worked at the Prefectural HQ but didn't know the address was, it felt fair to say, a fraud. It was Mikumo's youth that had caught him off guard. She had just turned twenty-three; she would have been nine at the time of the kidnapping, only a couple of years older than the murdered girl. Now she was driving him to that girl's home. There was no escaping the fact that an unimaginable span of time had passed.

They stopped not long after leaving the station to buy a gift of rice crackers. The national highway was quiet. The rows of buildings disappeared after they turned right at the junction to the prefectural road, where even the road-side stores began to taper off. Now they were approaching what had, before the city's expansion, been the old Morikawa district.

'Um, sir . . .' Mikumo said, keeping her eyes ahead.

'Yes? What is it?'

'It was a great relief . . . that it wasn't your daughter.' She was talking about the day before. 'I know they'll find her. I'm sure of it.'

Her voice sounded nasal. She looked ready to cry. It was at times like this that Mikami always struggled to find a way to respond. *Just . . . leave it be.* That was as close as he could get to what he really felt. Strict rules were in place to guard the privacy of police officers and their families. Yet this was only the case with regard to those outside the force; within it, stories spread in the blink of an eye. Colleagues would approach with no warning and ask after Ayumi. They did it out of kindness. It was because they were concerned. But no matter how often Mikami reminded himself of this, he was still unable to feel genuine gratitude. Akama's motivations were clearly different, and there were many more who shared his philosophy. Despite the fact that they hardly knew Mikami, these people would assume a concerned expression and worm their way over as soon as they caught sight of him. Some actually seemed pleased, as if Mikami's distress gave them an opportunity to either mend fences, or angle for something in return. These were the ones who were the most likely to voice what seemed like genuine, heartfelt compassion. They would look on, smug, as Mikami bowed and offered thanks. He felt a growing aversion to other people. It scared him. He'd had enough of it.

Still . . .

'Thank you,' he said.

It went without saying that the young female officer sitting next to him was one of the few who did actually merit his trust.

'Oh, you needn't . . .'

She blushed and straightened her back. She was almost

worryingly good-natured. Given that she had chosen to become a police officer, she was already likely to be more straight-laced and diligent than the average person; even with that, Mikami knew she was special. She had grown up in a world where morality, sex and even the values of basic human kindness were in chaos; despite this, nothing about her suggested even the slightest pollution. She was beautiful and innocent. In a way, she reminded him of Minako when she was younger. It was only natural that the majority of single officers were infatuated with her; even in the Press Room, more than a few of the reporters had designs on taking her back to Tokyo with them. Suwa had already mentioned that Akikawa was one of them. It was the main reason Mikami still refused to let her be directly involved with them.

The landscape rolling ahead was rural with a smattering of private houses: the western limits of City D. After a while, the giant pickle factory – almost the size of a leisure centre – came into view, looming over the riverbank marking the boundary of the next village. The house appeared next, still on the factory grounds, a traditional Japanese structure with a tiled roof. *Amamiya Pickles*. The idea of pickling aubergines and cucumbers in small tubs and selling them had been a success, and the business had grown rapidly. The factory had regularly featured in the news; in hindsight, it was likely that it was this success which had caught the attention of the kidnapper.

Mikami gestured for Mikumo to pull over, getting her to park in an empty plot of land a short distance from the family home.

'Wait here.'

It felt insensitive to leave her to sit with the girl's parents. If none of this had ever happened, Shoko Amamiya would now be a young woman of roughly Mikumo's age.

Mikami got out of the car and walked resolutely down the narrow road – back then, an unsurfaced path – leading to the building.

We'll bring the bastard in . . .

Mikami recalled the day he had first entered the house, the burning heat in his chest. Fourteen years had gone by. He had certainly never imagined that his next visit would be to arrange a PR exercise. Whatever the purpose, the visit brought very mixed feelings. Each time he blinked he saw Ayumi. It was going to be difficult to stay businesslike, meeting parents who had already lost their daughter. He straightened the front of his jacket and gazed, without pressing it straight away, at the buzzer marked 'Amamiya'.

8

The heater, having just been turned on, started to click as a warm stream of air flowed into the room.

'It's been a long time.'

Mikami declined the offer of a floor cushion and placed both hands on the tatami before him. Keeping his head low, he slid the box of rice crackers over. Yoshio Amamiya only nodded faintly.

While the walls had darkened a little, the layout and furniture of the living room he'd been shown into seemed unchanged. Amamiya's transformation, on the other hand, had been dramatic and far surpassed that of fourteen years. Fifty-four. It didn't seem possible. His hair had turned white and been left to grow. His skin was pale, leaden. His cheeks were morbidly thin and a mass of wrinkles clustered like knife cuts around his eyes and forehead. It was the face of a man whose daughter had been murdered. A face ravaged by grief and suffering – that was the only way Mikami could describe it.

The next room contained the Buddhist altar. The sliding doors had been left open, making it impossible to ignore the imposing object next to the far wall. There were two photos on display. Their daughter Shoko. Next to her, Amamiya's wife . . .

He hadn't known.

Toshiko Amamiya. When had she passed away?

He had to pay his respects. But it was difficult to find a chance to broach the subject. Amamiya was sitting at the other side of the low table, the very essence of an empty shell. His gaze was hovering around Mikami's torso, but there was a lack of certainty in the sunken eyes, as if he were seeing something else entirely.

Breaking under the weight of the silence, Mikami took out his card.

Amamiya saying his name first. Seeming happy to see him again. Somewhere in his head, Mikami had built up a picture of how he'd expected the reunion to work. So he'd hesitated. *Press Director, not Detective.* He'd felt a growing feeling of shame about the admission, and as a result had missed the opportunity to present his card.

'I'm sorry for not telling you earlier. This is my new position.'

Amamiya's eyes showed no reaction. His right hand was resting on the table. The fingers, together with the skin on the back of them, were wrinkled and dry. The nail on his index finger was cracked at the tip, blackened along with the skin like a blood blister. Every now and then the finger would twitch. But it didn't reach for Mikami's card on the table. *Loss of social function. Reclusive behaviour.* It was as if Amamiya had crossed into that kind of category. Perhaps it was because he wasn't working any more. Mikami had heard that, ever since the kidnapping, Amamiya had left the management of Amamiya Pickles in the hands of his cousin.

'Excuse me, but . . .' He had to ask the question. 'When did your wife . . .?'

Amamiya looked dimly towards the altar. For a while he stayed like that. Eventually, his head came back around. Mikami thought he saw a dark glow in the man's pupils.

'She collapsed from a stroke six years ago. It was last year that she—'

'I'm sorry.' The man's frozen emotions were beginning to thaw. Even realizing this, Mikami didn't think to return the conversation to business. 'She was too young to go.'

'She was. To leave us like that. And without knowing the . . .'

She had died without ever seeing the kidnapper brought to justice. As he perhaps recalled his wife's bitter disappointment, Amamiya's unfocused eyes flickered shut for a moment. Mikami felt his heart ache. Each time he heard the case mentioned, he felt a sense of shame burning in his chest.

One fateful day.

The fifth of January, in the sixty-fourth year of the Showa period. *I'm going to get my New Year presents.* Shoko Amamiya had headed out saying these words a little after midday, only to disappear on her way to the house of a nearby relative. Two hours later, her kidnapper had called the Amamiyas, demanding ransom. The voice of a man in his thirties or forties, slightly hoarse, with no trace of an accent. The content of the call had been textbook. *I've got your daughter. Get 20 million yen ready by midday tomorrow, then wait. She dies if you talk to the police.* Her father had answered the call. He had begged to hear his daughter's voice, but the kidnapper had simply put the phone down.

After a lot of agonizing, Amamiya had notified the police. That was after six in the evening. Within forty-five minutes, the four officers of a Home Unit dispatched from Criminal Investigations First Division in the Prefectural HQ had covertly entered the Amamiyas' residence. At the same time, the local NTT office had called to notify the police that people were in place to trace any more calls. They'd been just a step too late. The kidnapper's second call had come in just moments earlier. *I want used bills. Put the money in the largest suitcase you can buy at Marukoshi. Bring it to the location I'll give you tomorrow, and come alone.*

If we'd only recorded the bastard's voice. If only that damned trace had been ready. These were phrases uttered by every detective who ever came to work on the case, always mingled with a sigh.

At eight the same evening a Special Investigative Headquarters was established in the Prefecture D central police station. Another thirty minutes later Mikami was on his way towards the Amamiya family home, appointed sub-leader of the Close Pursuit Unit, with orders to go through the details of the following day's handover. The officers of the Home Unit were already interviewing the parents. *Did you recognize his voice? Has anything suspicious happened recently? Do you know anyone who might bear a grudge? Are any of your old employees having money trouble?* The parents just frowned, the blood drained from their faces, shaking their heads the whole time.

It was a long night. Nobody slept a wink, just glared at the phone. Not once did Amamiya break his formal *seiza* sitting position. But the third call didn't come in, even after it had started to grow light outside. Toshiko had been making rice balls in the kitchen. She'd made more than everyone could eat then made more rice and started over, mechanically repeating the task. The posture had made it seem like she was praying. But . . .

Her prayers had been ignored.

The sixty-fourth year of the Showa period had lasted for only a week. The fanfare welcoming Heisei had swept it away, as though it had been an apparition. It had most certainly existed. It was during that final year of Showa that a man kidnapped and murdered a seven-year-old girl, before disappearing into Heisei. The code name 'Six Four' was a pledge that the case didn't belong to the first year of Heisei, that they would drag the kidnapper right back into the sixty-fourth year of Showa . . .

Mikami gave the altar a hesitant glance. Toshiko was smiling in her photo. Her youth caught him by surprise. The shot was probably one from a time when she'd still been carefree, from before she could even have imagined that her daughter might be kidnapped. The relaxed smile wasn't that of a mother who had lost her daughter.

Amamiya had fallen silent again. He still hadn't asked Mikami why he was visiting. The emotion was draining from his eyes.

Somewhere else . . .

Mikami cleared his throat. He had no choice but to take the

initiative. He couldn't let Amamiya retreat back into his shell, not before he'd outlined the reason for his visit.

'There's something I have to tell you – that's the reason I'm visiting today.'

Ask, not tell. He should have phrased it like that. He carried on, hurrying as he sensed a shift in Amamiya's mood.

'The truth is, our top executive has expressed a wish to visit you next week. Commissioner General Kozuka, from the National Police Agency in Tokyo. We know a long time has passed since the kidnapping, but it still goes without saying that we want to bring the perpetrator to justice by whatever means we can. The commissioner wishes to encourage the officers working on the case by attending the scene of the crime; he also wishes to visit you here and pay his respects to your daughter.'

It was hard to breathe. The more he spoke, the more his chest seemed to fill with a pungent gas. Amamiya's eyes were on the floor. That he was disappointed was obvious. It was hardly surprising. Mikami wondered if anyone in his position would take what he had said at face value – to be told only now, fourteen years later, that the commissioner general wanted to inject new life into the investigation. *Police politics. PR.* Had he perhaps seen through to the man's true motivation?

Having no other choice, Mikami continued.

'I won't deny that the case has been in limbo. But that's exactly why the commissioner wants to visit. With enough press coverage, there's a chance it might help new leads come to light.'

There was a pause before Amamiya dropped his head in a bow.

'You have my gratitude.'

His voice was relaxed. Mikami breathed out silently, but his relief was tempered by his discomfort at having prevailed on the man. In the end, they always did as the police said. With no other means of exacting revenge, victims were dependent on the force to bring the perpetrator to justice. Mikami understood it now. His hands were tied because his daughter had run away from home, and now he was here, stringing empty words together for the sake of a PR exercise.

Mikami took out his notebook. He flipped to the page with his notes from Akama's office.

'The commissioner's visit is scheduled for Thursday, 12—'

Before he could finish his sentence, he heard the muffled sound of Amamiya's voice. Mikami tilted his head to one side.

But it won't be necessary.

It had sounded like that.

'Amamiya-san?'

'I appreciate the offer, but it won't be necessary. There's no need for someone as important as that to come all this way.'

No need?

Mikami pulled back a little. Amamiya had turned them down. His look was as distant as before, but there had been an unmistakable force to his words.

'But . . . can I ask why?'

'I don't have any specific reason.'

Mikami swallowed spit. Something had happened. He knew it intuitively.

'Have we been amiss, in our—'

'No, that's not it.'

'Then, why . . .?'

Amamiya had stopped talking. He made no attempt to look Mikami in the face.

'What I said just now – there is a real chance of this bringing in new leads.'

Silence.

'The commissioner general is our highest-ranked official. I'm confident the media coverage will be significant. It will be broadcast on TV. The news will reach a great number of people.'

'I do appreciate the opportunity—'

'Please, Amamiya-san. To let a chance for new information like this just slip by . . .'

Mikami realized he was raising his voice and broke off. This wasn't something he could force. The victim was refusing. Wasn't it his obligation to back down? The family home could be struck from the commissioner's schedule without necessarily diluting the importance of his visit. It would reduce the overall impact, yes, but it would still work – internally and externally – if the commissioner visited both the scene of the crime and the members of the Six Four Investigative Team.

But . . .

Akama's profile flashed before his eyes. How would he react if Mikami's report told him the commissioner's offer had been refused? Mikami's pulse throbbed in his temples, punctuating the silence like the ticking of a clock.

'I have a feeling I'll be back.'

Amamiya offered no words in response. He put his hands on the tatami and got to his feet, giving only a cursory nod before he disappeared further into the house.

Why turn them down . . .?

Mikami glanced at the business card and rice crackers, untouched and left behind; he massaged his numb legs before raising himself from the floor.

9

The situation had moved on in Mikami's brief absence.

Members Only: Meeting in Progress.

The cardboard notice had been posted on the door to the Press Room. Suwa was back in the office.

'What's that for?' Mikami motioned his chin towards the corridor. An embarrassed-looking Suwa got to his feet.

'They're discussing anonymous reporting again. It sounds like they're considering a formal written protest.'

Mikami clicked his tongue in irritation. *A written protest.* It would be the first time during his term as press director.

'And the commissioner's visit? Were you able to notify them about that?'

'Mmm . . . I managed to tell them, but they just said they'd discuss it in the meeting. I suspect they're planning to throw a spanner in the works.'

Mikami thumped into his chair and tore the seal off a fresh pack of cigarettes. It was worse than he'd feared. The outlook regarding the press was clouding over, especially now Yoshio Amamiya had said no to the commissioner's wish to go and pay his respects to his daughter.

The commissioner general himself. Six Four. He had been certain the press would bite. His head had been sluggish after the conversation with Amamiya, but now he felt a sudden clarity. He focused on a single point on his calendar.

Thursday the 12th.

He had until then to win over Amamiya and make peace with the press.

'Anyway, I'm planning to take them out for drinks tonight,' Suwa remarked. His breezy tone jarred somehow, amplifying the pressure in the air. Mikami had expected Suwa to gain a new lease of life now he was free from the constraints of Mikami's reforms, but he seemed to be already at an impasse. It didn't bode well, if that was the case.

Suwa had grown as a Media Relations officer, but he remained a man who thrived best on the front line. He hadn't abandoned the traditional methods and would spend his time in the Press Room chatting with the reporters to get a feel for their activities and what they expected. He would advertise his easy-going nature by joining them in games of Shogi, Go and Mahjong. He regularly joined them for drinks, sounding off about a few arrogant executives to gain their trust. To these crude but time-honoured tactics he would add his conversational nous and skills as a negotiator, guiding the reporters until – converted to him – they were converted to the police. He had been to university in Tokyo and could talk about the city, reminisce on classes they'd attended. With the younger reporters, he was able to act as a kind of elder brother. He used these advantages as tools to position himself inside the Press Room, where he could gauge first hand any changes in the atmosphere, and adapt accordingly.

But . . .

There were no guarantees that Suwa's image as a 'young reporter' was still held by the reporters who were holding a meeting in the next room. They were more than just young, they were different. That was Mikami's impression, dealing with them now after a twenty-year hiatus. They were, perhaps in part due to an increase in women reporters, unlike any he had seen before. They were upstanding and straight-laced, almost eerily so. They preferred not to drink and, when they did, they never lost their composure. They were hesitant to spend time on Shogi and Go. He couldn't imagine them sitting around a table in the Press Room, enjoying a game of Mahjong with the police. Some went so far as to speak out against the Press Club, denouncing it as a breeding ground for collusion with the police; this they did with a straight face, even as they reaped the benefits of their membership.

This had caused Suwa – who had always been able to gauge the Press Room's halfway line – to lose confidence. A contradiction had appeared between the image and the reality of the 'young reporter'. The trap had been sprung just as he was coming to believe in himself as a successful Media Relations officer. *We need to bargain with them if we can't negotiate.* This was something Suwa had recently told Mikami, perhaps revealing an encroaching anxiety, despite having occupied his position for so long.

'Sir, I found them.'

Mikumo walked over with a large book in her hands. It took Mikami a second, then he nodded. He had asked her in the car, on the way back, to find the press cuttings from Shoko's kidnapping.

He stubbed out his cigarette. Press policy could wait until the reporters made their move; what Mikami needed to do more urgently was to work on Amamiya. Partly, this came from his sense of duty, but he also wanted to know what the man was feeling inside. However, he needed to find answers to some questions he had first. His hunch was that, in doing so, he would come up with something that would help win Amamiya around.

Why had he turned down the commissioner's offer?

Because the memory of the kidnapping had begun to fade.

Ridiculous. No parent who had lost a daughter could ever rest without seeing the face of her killer.

Because he was disillusioned with the police.

Mikami supposed that was part of it. The police had dedicated vast amounts of time and resources to finding the kidnapper, yet they had been unable to bring Amamiya any results.

Because he held a grudge?

It was possible. The Prefectural HQ had investigated close to seven thousand people, including relatives of Amamiya. His younger brother in particular – Kenji Amamiya – had become a prime suspect and suffered days of rigorous interrogation.

Mikami paged through the archive.

Shoko Amamiya. A first-year student at Morikawa Nishi Primary School. In the photo, she looked young enough to be in nursery. She was wearing the traditional New Year's dress. Her hair had been braided and held together with a pink hair clip; her mouth was pursed, with bright-red lipstick. The picture had been taken at a local photographer's one and a half months before the kidnapping, and in celebration of the Shichigosan festival. Kenji Amamiya had not attended the festivities. Following the death of their father, he had been arguing with his elder brother, Yoshio, over their inheritance. He'd been having problems with money. His business, a motorbike dealership, had been suffering cash-flow difficulties, and he had run up debts of close to 10 million yen with a local loan shark.

It was only natural that the Investigative HQ had made him a focus of their investigation. January the 5th, the day of the kidnapping. Shoko finished her lunch and left the house by herself. She had been planning to visit Kenji at his place, just a half-kilometre to the west. She had no way of knowing about his and her father's battle over their inheritance. She had only wanted a children's make-up kit. Uncle Kenji had always given her money as a New Year's present, but that year he had failed to put in an appearance. Her mother, Toshiko, had warned her against going to see him, but Shoko had won her over with her smile. They lived in an area surrounded by rice paddies, but Shoko's route had traced a path along woodland – a windbreak – which was largely obscured from view. One of the boys from her year had apparently seen her at a point halfway between her house and Kenji's. It was the last sighting. No one saw her alive again.

Later, during the official autopsy, they found the stew she'd had for lunch that day almost entirely undigested in her stomach. That meant she had been killed not long after leaving the house. Kenji had been alone, as his wife and daughter had been out visiting her parents. In his testimony he claimed that Shoko had never turned up and that he hadn't seen her. Despite this, the police – mostly due to a lack of any other reports of suspicious people or cars in the area – continued to treat him as the prime suspect for a long time afterwards. *That wasn't Kenji, on the phone.* They had continued to treat him that way even after Amamiya had assured them otherwise. The Investigative HQ had been leaning towards a theory of multiple kidnappers. As far as Mikami knew, Kenji still wasn't in the clear. He suspected that a number of the detectives on the case still considered him the man behind the kidnapping.

But all Mikami could do was speculate.

The investigation had been ongoing for fourteen years; his knowledge of it barely scratched the surface. He had no access to the specific details of who the police had investigated, or how those people had been cleared; he didn't even know the degree to which Kenji remained a suspect. And when it came to guessing Amamiya's opinion of the police for treating his brother as a potential suspect, Mikami might as well have been grasping at straws.

He leafed further through the archive.

There wouldn't be any articles about Kenji.

Kenji's interrogation, and the investigation surrounding him, had been limited to a select team from the Violent Crime Section. They had maintained strict confidentiality and the information had never made it into the press. What articles there had been covered only the general details of the kidnapping; no information about potential suspects – or anything key to the investigation – had ever made it into the papers. The police had, in line with the gravity of the case, imposed a gag order of the highest level. The kidnapping had also coincided with the flood of articles and

66

reports covering the death of Emperor Showa; the result was an extreme paucity of articles, considering the seriousness of the case.

Anyway, the probability was pretty low that any of the articles held the key to bringing Amamiya out of his shell.

Mikami got up from his chair. The face of an old colleague had been hovering in his head for a while.

'I'm going out for a bit.'

Suwa looked up from his paper. 'Where will you be?'

'Private business. Call me if anything changes in there.'

Suwa nodded deeply. *Something to do with his daughter.* His look conveyed this apparent understanding.

Surely it would only complicate matters to bring Criminal Investigations into the fray?

You are to treat this matter as confidential.

It would be close to a violation of Akama's orders. Mikami knew things would become difficult if Akama got wind of where he was going.

Mikumo, perhaps also thinking of Ayumi, seemed unsure whether she should volunteer her services as a driver. Mikami waved to say it wasn't necessary, then left the room with the press cuttings under his arm. Suwa ran into the corridor almost immediately afterwards. There was something awkward in it.

'Sir, there was one other thing.'

'Yes?'

'I'm planning to invite Akikawa out for drinks tonight, and . . .' His already quiet voice fell another notch. 'Would you mind if Mikumo joined us?'

His eyes were serious. There was even a glint of desperation there. If it hadn't been for that, Mikami would probably have raised his hand to the man's dumpy cheeks.

'You can take Kuramae.'

Suwa's gaze dropped to the floor. Mikami wasn't sure if the curled grin at the side of the man's mouth was a symbol of resistance or a mark of self-derision.

10

Mikami drove his car out of the station.

He was on his way to visit Mochizuki, an old contemporary of his. Mochizuki had been part of the Close Pursuit Unit, as had Mikami himself, and had driven the second car during Six Four's initial investigation. Afterwards, he had remained part of the Investigative HQ, working on the case as part of the team looking into suspects who had debts. When his father collapsed, three years ago, he had retired from the force and returned home to take over the family horticultural business. As was common with the regional police, his official record cited 'personal reasons'. While his retirement did not free him of his oath to confidentiality, he was likely to talk more freely than someone still in the force.

Mikami felt vaguely anxious. Perhaps it was Shoko's name; it had cropped up so many times when he was reading through the press cuttings in the office. And even without that, there were too many things that acted as reminders of Six Four in the area. He was approaching the Aoi-machi junction. His eyes drifted naturally to the blue billboard next to the bookstore. *The Aoi Café*. It looked the same as it had fourteen years earlier. It had been the first stop in the pursuit of Amamiya's car during the ransom handover.

January the 5th. The Amamiya household.

Mikami had spent the night unable to sleep. It was after 4 p.m. on the following day that the kidnapper's third call had finally come in. The police had been caught off guard: instead of Amamiya's home, the call had come in to the office next to the pickle factory. Having slipped through the net, bypassing the tracking and recording apparatus, the kidnapper had introduced himself as 'Sato' and asked to speak to the company president. Knowing he was at home all day, the female receptionist had simply told him he was out for the day. The kidnapper had asked her to give him a message. That he would collect the ransom at the Aoi Café in Aoi-machi. He would be there at four thirty.

The caller's voice had matched the description of the voice Amamiya had heard the previous day. A man in his thirties or forties, slightly hoarse, with no trace of an accent. Because she had happened to answer the call that day, Motoko Yoshida, Amamiya's thirty-two-year-old receptionist, had later ended up having to listen to the voices of hundreds of suspects.

Having no idea what was happening, Motoko had called the company president at home to relay the kidnapper's message. Shoko's parents, and the investigators with them, fell into a state of panic. They had less than twenty minutes until the designated time. They had already prepared a large suitcase and 20 million in cash. To track it, they had concealed a micro-transmitter inside. They had also fitted a pin-size microphone under the collar of Amamiya's jacket, and had finished briefing him to repeat whatever the kidnapper said on the phone. But they didn't have enough time. Even going as fast as they could, they knew it would take at least thirty minutes by car from Amamiya's house to the café.

Amamiya had staggered out of the house, rammed the suitcase into his Cedric and left for the city at a breakneck speed. Katsu-toshi Matsuoka, the chief of the Pursuit Unit, had hidden in the back of the vehicle under a blanket between the front and back seats, prepared for whatever might happen.

The four remaining members of the Pursuit Unit split up into two cars and tailed the Cedric, each keeping a distance of around ten metres. Mikami had been in the passenger seat of Pursuit 1. The signal from the pin-sized microphone in Amamiya's jacket had been weak, transmission limited to a few dozen metres in a built-up area. Mikami's job had been to stay close and listen in to the kidnapper's instructions, as repeated by Amamiya, and relay the details to the Investigative HQ through the wireless set installed in his car.

They had arrived at the Aoi Café just six minutes late, at 4.36. Amamiya had charged inside. The owner had been scanning the customers, holding a pink phone in his hand and calling Amamiya's name. *It's for me!* His voice was tight as he snatched the receiver. Minako had been there, too, seated at the window just metres away, paired with a detective. A few of the female officers, who had left work to marry within the force, had been summoned to assist with the investigation as part of the Undercover Unit, each masquerading as one half of a couple. Minako had been in a conference room inside the Prefectural HQ since first light that morning. When word had come in detailing the location of the exchange, she had rushed out of the station with the detective posing as her husband. They had installed themselves there just minutes before Amamiya's arrival. In the end, he'd been in the corner of her eye for under ten seconds. The moment he'd hung up, Amamiya had sped back out of the café.

As expected, the kidnapper had led Amamiya from one place to another. He told Amamiya a succession of times and places designed to keep him on the road. At first the kidnapper instructed him to take the state road north. Four Seasons Fruits. Atari Mahjong. With the next destination – the Cherry Café – Amamiya crossed into the municipal district of Yasugi. From there he took a right one kilometre on at a set of lights and followed the city road to the Ai'ai Hair Salon. After this, he'd taken a left to join the prefectural highway and continue north.

After leaving Yasugi, he'd entered the rural district of Ozatomura, only to stop soon afterwards at the vegetable wholesaler Furusato Foods. Then, after another five kilometres, the Ozato Grill. Miyasaka Folding Crafts.

By that point, they were already deep in the mountains. Amamiya kept driving, tracing the Futago river as it wound up a steep road, almost too narrow for cars to overtake. It was getting close to dusk. It was already after six. That was when the instruction came in for Pursuit 2, the second car in the Close Pursuit Unit, to break off its chase. The same instruction was relayed to a further five cars from the Intercept Unit, which had joined at various points along the state road and the prefectural highway.

At that point, nobody had known if Shoko was still alive, or if the kidnapper was working alone or as part of a group. They couldn't risk the kidnapper seeing a chain of seven or eight cars on a mountain road usually empty of traffic. Pursuit 1, with Mikami on the wireless, was the sole vehicle left to follow Amamiya's Cedric. It hung back, opening up the space between them; Mikami pushed his seat all the way down to conceal himself from the outside.

They followed the uneven road for a long time. The last place the kidnapper named was the Ikkyu, a fishing lodge close to the Neyuki mountain, which lay on the border of the prefecture. Amamiya had been at the end of his tether. His feet were unsteady as he approached the phone in the lodge. The kidnapper issued more instructions into the man's ear.

You crossed a bridge half a kilometre back. One of the lights there has a plastic cord on it. Throw the suitcase into the river from there. Do it in five minutes if you value your daughter's life.

That was when the kidnapper's reason for asking for an oversized suitcase became clear. He was planning to use it as a raft. For that to work, the suitcase had to be reliably buoyant.

As instructed, Amamiya had turned his car around in the car park and returned to the Kotohira bridge. As was common in depopulated areas, the bridge seemed too grand for its location. A plastic cord had been fastened to one of the mercury lamps, facing downstream on the right-hand side. Amamiya didn't hesitate, and hurled the suitcase over the bridge towards the river, which lay some seven metres below. The momentum carried it under before it shot back to the surface and began to drift with the current. Within a few seconds, it had disappeared from sight. It was now after seven o'clock. Beyond the threshold of the lights, the uniform darkness made it impossible to distinguish between the river, the rocks or even the sky.

The handover point was no longer fixed; now, it was anywhere along the line of the river. The line stretched across ten kilometres, through the pitch black, all the way to the dam at the river's end. The Investigative HQ wasted no time in dispatching a large number of investigators to comb the riverbanks. They knew the kidnapper had to be in hiding nearby, but where and how Shoko was remained unclear, so they couldn't use floodlights or torches. And they had to avoid the noise that bringing vehicles and investigators to the road along the river would make.

The search parties decided they would gather at the bottom of the river, near the southern flanks of Ozatomura, and work their way quietly north up the riverbank. In the darkness, and with only instinct to guide them, the search was erratic.

The Investigative HQ had also been guilty of optimism. They had assumed that the kidnapper – like the search party – wouldn't use a torch. That he wouldn't be able to find or recover the suitcase as it floated downstream in the dark.

They had also trusted in their technology. The micro-transmitter fitted to the suitcase was still functioning. The receiver in the mobile command vehicle displayed a constant green pulse that trailed gradually south.

At that point, they had yet to realize their error.

Just three hundred metres down from where the suitcase had entered the river, near the right bank, was a collection of rocks known locally as Dragon's Hollow. They formed a three-metre cave under the water. *You can get sucked under here, near the right bank*. The locals knew it well as a danger spot, as did canoeists and rafting enthusiasts.

The presence of Dragon's Hollow was the reason the kidnapper had instructed Amamiya to throw the suitcase from the lamp on the right-hand side of the river. When the Investigative HQ later tested their theory in the same conditions, nine out of ten times, the suitcase had been sucked into the hollow.

The kidnapper had waited near the hollow in order to recover the suitcase. He pulled out the money, then returned the suitcase into the river a little further on. The micro-transmitters at the time weren't accurate enough to register the brief pause as anything other than a blip.

Having secured the ransom, the kidnapper would have moved away from the river and retreated into the mountains before climbing down to a nearby village. Alternatively, it was possible he had scaled the mountain and escaped into the next prefecture. The empty suitcase, still floating down the river, had bought him all the time he needed to get away. The suitcase had continued past Ozatomura and Yasugi before finally getting caught in a fishing weir in the northern limits of City D, coming to a stop just before daybreak, at seven o'clock the next morning.

Even then, the police had been unable to act. For as long as there remained a greater than zero chance of the kidnapper showing up to retrieve the case, they couldn't do anything more than maintain a safe distance and keep watch with binoculars; this had lasted until the weir's owner, who had turned up a little after midday, retrieved the case himself. The sleepless game of cat and mouse had lasted twenty hours. *Emperor Showa is dead.* Many of the detectives, including Mikami, didn't hear the news until late that afternoon.

The investigation ended with the worst possible result.

On 10 January, three days after the police had retrieved the suitcase, Shoko Amamiya's dead body was found at a car dump in the city's Satamachi district. A scrap merchant had opened the trunk of a rusty sedan after noticing some stray dogs making a noise nearby. The body was in a pitiful state. The girl's hands had been forced behind her back, tied up with washing line; her mouth and eyes had been covered over with tape. Her throat was swollen and marked with dark purple lines, presumably from a rope.

The early days of Heisei were branded with humiliation. Alongside the rage the police felt against the kidnapper, there was for a long time the sense that Showa had been cheated of its closing days. They'd been unable to look Heisei straight on. The endless TV repeats of Emperor Showa's funeral march seemed to symbolize the dejection of the officers involved in the Six Four kidnapping.

Mikami took a right.

A little further down the city road and the billboard for the Ai'ai Hair Salon would roll into view. An image flashed into Mikami's mind – Amamiya's face. The Kotohira bridge, pale, nebulous in the glare of the mercury lamps. The expression on Amamiya's face hadn't been one of despair. There was hope, bubbling to the surface. *He'd handed over the ransom. His daughter would come home.* He had looked like a man trying to convince himself this was true.

Earlier this afternoon, he had looked different.

His expression had been completely devoid of hope, no longer believing in anything. Amamiya hadn't been robbed of a feeling or an idea. He had suffered the physical loss of the thing he treasured most. Distinctions such as Showa or Heisei meant nothing to him. His only fate was to drift through a world in which his daughter didn't exist.

Mikami pressed down on the accelerator.

Ayumi is alive.

Amamiya faded a little into the distance.

Beyond a new-build housing area and an old farming village, Mikami saw the collection of plastic greenhouses glistening in the sun.

Mikami pulled up alongside the gravel road. The office was a shed-like building that doubled up as a flower shop. Four plastic greenhouses formed a line behind it. This was Mikami's third visit. The last two times, he'd brought some flowers as a gift. He'd been in Second Division at the time, so they couldn't have seen each other for close to a year.

Mikami caught sight of Mochizuki. He was just about to enter one of the greenhouses, pushing a wheelbarrow stacked high with fertilizer bags. He was still wearing the foreign-made, olive-brown jumper that had been his trademark as a detective, but with it he had on baggy trousers and wellington boots. It was a good look.

'Mochizuki!' Mikami called out to his back.

Having no doubt recognized his voice, Mochizuki was already grinning when his portly face turned towards him.

'Well, well. Stranger things have happened.'

'Right, sure. Work does keep me busy, you know.'

The wind was cold outside, but it might as well have been spring inside the greenhouse. Mikami was taken aback by the length of the structure. It was imposing; great ranks of seedlings stretched out like a diagram illustrating the effects of perspective. They were all beginning to bud, but without the flowers Mikami had no idea what they were.

'The reunion was today?' Mochizuki chided. He put a wooden box at Mikami's feet, for him to use in place of a chair.

'I wish. Seriously, things are busy.'

'Sure, in Media Relations?'

He was exactly the same as when he'd been a detective. He made no attempt to hide his aversion to and contempt for Administrative Affairs.

'How's Mina-chan keeping?'

'The same, mostly.'

'Damn – bet she's as good-looking as ever.' He was genuinely peeved. Never the exception, he was one of the many officers who still had a crush on Minako. 'How about Ayumi? She'd be, let's see, in high school now?'

'That's right.' So he hadn't heard yet. Mikami considered telling him what had happened, but he had come out to ask his own questions. He sat up and slid the box forwards. 'Actually, I went to see Amamiya earlier today. Something to do with Six Four.'

Mochizuki looked him straight in the eye. 'I guessed as much.'

Guessed as much? But Mochizuki continued before Mikami had a chance to respond.

'Why did you go to see him?'

'Work.'

'What kind of work?'

'Press-related. An executive from Tokyo wants to come and pay his respects, offer incense. I went to ask Amamiya for his blessing.'

Mochizuki gave Mikami a dubious look. 'That's what you do these days? Light incense?'

'Pretty much. I serve the top brass; I do all sorts of things.'

'So, you went to see him. What happened?'

'He turned me down right there, on the spot. Said a visit by a high-up wasn't necessary.'

Mikami made a quick summary of the events at Amamiya's house. Mochizuki listened, his expression flat.

'He refused to budge. It looked as though he'd given up on the police. It was almost as though he was angry about something,' Mikami said, probing.

Mochizuki only nodded.

'How long has he been like that for?'

'I can't say really. I know he became increasingly withdrawn over the years.'

'Did something happen – between us and him?'

Mochizuki chuckled, reacting to Mikami's use of the word 'us'. 'Come on, Mikami,' he said. 'I left the force a long time ago.'

'That's exactly why I came to see you. You've got more freedom to talk.'

It was still rare for information on the continuing investigation into Six Four to get out, even after the Investigative HQ's downgrade to Investigative Team.

'Do you think he might hold a grudge because of the investigation into Kenji?'

'Absolutely not. He isn't fond of his brother.'

'Right, the inheritance. What actually happened there?'

'That bastard Kenji started pressuring Amamiya – said he'd give up his right to inherit if Amamiya made him managing director of his business. The man's bike dealership was already dead in the water.'

'But Amamiya refused . . .'

'Yeah. I reckon he knew a good-for-nothing like that would drive the company into the ground.'

Mikami nodded, satisfied.

'Okay, so you're sure Amamiya isn't angry because of the business with Kenji?'

'Yeah. I guarantee it.'

'Is he still a suspect?'

'I think, at this point, we have to assume he's innocent. We pushed him pretty hard . . . especially because he was mixed up with some low-level Yakuza.' Mochizuki had started talking as if he were still on the case.

Mikami sighed briefly. 'Hard to believe it's been fourteen years. How's the investigation going, anyway?'

Mochizuki snorted through his nose. 'How should I know? Still, I'll bet it's the same old quagmire. That case was cursed from the outset.'

Quagmire. Mikami had occasionally heard the desolate-sounding word being used in Second Division. It referred to the fact that the Investigative Team was still dealing with a vast number of 'grey' suspects, that it had become stuck. Unnerved in the beginning by the seriousness of the case, Investigative HQ had cast its net too wide. A list had been drafted of seven thousand people. One hundred officers had been assigned to work through it. The detectives didn't have the time they needed to investigate any single individual properly and, as a result, had needed to move on before they could come to any decision. In addition, the detectives had different levels of expertise. Some of those from district had been below par; others, back-up from more remote areas, had been sent from Transport and had no prior investigative experience at all.

Each day saw the investigation becoming more and more slipshod, reports more hastily thrown together. By the time the management realized the problem, it was already too late.

They had a huge number of potential suspects whose status was undecided, accumulated like a mountain of sludge behind them. With the passage of time, the investigations were becoming harder to reopen. And, with each year, cutbacks were made to the number of detectives working the case.

'If Osakabe had been there when the kidnapping happened . . .' Mochizuki said with a sigh.

Mikami felt himself nod. 'Yeah.'

Michio Osakabe had been their greatest general, and Mikami had held him in the highest regard. As a leader, he had been grounded and meticulous, displaying a virtually telepathic ability to communicate his instructions to the rank and file. While he had only retired from his post as director of Criminal Investigations eight years ago, he had, to the misfortune of the Prefectural HQ, been in Tokyo on secondment to the Criminal Investigations Bureau during the year of the kidnapping.

The detectives had mourned their loss. *We would have had the kidnapper if Osakabe had still been directing Criminal Investigations, even First Division.*

Backing them up was his almost legendary record of never having failed to close a case.

And Six Four was only the beginning.

After Fujimura's appointment from Administrative Affairs, people immediately began to complain of a sharp drop in results. It hadn't been until five years ago that Criminal Investigations finally managed to regain some of its vigour, when the post was taken over by Shozo Odate, one of Osakabe's favourites, but he retired after only a year. From that point on it was fair to say that the post had suffered a run of bad harvests, right up to Arakida, the current director. The next reshuffle wouldn't happen for four or five years; it was essentially a waiting game until Katsutoshi Matsuoka was promoted from his current roles as chief adviser and chief of First Division. The man who had hidden himself behind the passenger seat in Amamiya's car during the Six Four kidnapping. At the time, he had been heading up Violent Crime in First Division.

Matsuoka would use me if he were director.

Mikami felt uncomfortable that the idea had popped so readily into his mind. There were issues he needed to address now; it wasn't the time to be looking four or five years ahead.

'If it's nothing to do with Kenji, what else could have turned him against us?'

Mochizuki was slow to respond. His eyes seemed to size Mikami up before he spoke again. 'You've got a good idea already, haven't you?'

The question caught Mikami off guard.

'A good idea? Of what?'

Instead of answering, Mochizuki returned to the last question. 'You remember he had a receptionist called Yoshida? If he's upset about anything, it'll be her, not Kenji.'

Motoko Yoshida. She had taken the kidnapper's third call in Amamiya's office. Mochizuki had ignored Mikami's question, but his curiosity had been piqued nonetheless.

'Why?'

'She was seeing Kenji. How would we put it – double adultery? We had to consider the possibility she was an accomplice, so we were pretty hard on her.'

Mikami hadn't known that.

Still . . .

'Why would that get to Amamiya, though? He didn't like Kenji; if she was with him . . .'

'Thing is, he didn't know about their relationship. Motoko lost her parents when she was young, had been through a lot. Amamiya had been a good neighbour, taken her under his wing and given her a job at his company. She was interrogated for days on end, ended up having a nervous breakdown. She quit her job. If Amamiya has a reason to despise us, that would be it.'

'When did this happen?'

'It wasn't long after you left Second Division.'

'Wait. You're saying Amamiya turned against us that long ago?'

Mochizuki focused on empty space, taking in Mikami's surprise. 'Well, I wouldn't say it happened overnight, because of that one thing. His withdrawal was more gradual. You know how it is when someone's anger or bitterness continues to grow over time.'

'You're right, I suppose.'

'And the fact that we haven't arrested the perp, that's got to factor pretty big in it.'

Was that what it was, after all? Had Amamiya simply become disillusioned with the force for being ineffective – had he run out of patience? If that was the case, Mikami feared he might not be able to make the commissioner's visit happen. Amamiya's scepticism had been building for years; regardless of their sincerity, the police would need to demonstrate a similar investment in time and manpower to remedy the situation. The commissioner was scheduled to arrive in a week. That left little time to win Amamiya over, especially if you took into consideration the time he would need to spend in negotiations with the Press Club. Mikami fixed his eyes back on Mochizuki. The question he'd put on hold was on the verge of coming out.

'What did you mean just now?'

'Hmm?'

'Don't pretend you don't know. You suggested I had *a good idea* of why Amamiya turned against us.'

'Same applies to you. Isn't it time you showed your hand, Mikami?' Mochizuki responded, his tone sharpening. Until that point, Mikami hadn't noticed that Mochizuki was getting angry.

'Showed what hand?'

'Come on – tell me the real reason you came to see me. You're not the type to get worked up about a big shot coming down to light some incense.'

He won't understand.

Mikami grimaced. A visit from the commissioner general. Explaining why it was important in a way that an ex-detective like Mochizuki would understand would be tantamount to admitting he'd become Akama's guard dog.

Mochizuki leaned forwards. 'You're here because you *also* want to ask me about the Koda memo.'

Mikami didn't know how to respond. *The Koda memo? Also?*

Mochizuki was quick to provide the answer. 'I sent Futawatari packing, and now you're here to sweet-talk me. No?'

Mikami just stared. He had assumed Mochizuki had been

poking fun earlier; the words took on a different meaning now. *Stranger things have happened. The reunion was today? I guessed as much.*

Shinji Futawatari had been here too. What for? And what was the Koda memo?

There was only one Koda that came to mind. Kazuki Koda, a member of the Home Unit during Six Four.

'Well? Out with it. What are you up to? The two of you, nosing around, into Six Four. Didn't you two hate each other. Or . . . what? . . . are you all happy families now you're camped in Admin?'

'Just wait a moment,' Mikami finally managed. 'What the hell is the Koda memo?'

'How should I know?'

'Koda – the Koda that left?' Mikami was remembering. Kazuki Koda had resigned. Just six months after Six Four. His brain was finally catching up. 'Why did he leave the force?'

'Officially, the same reason as me. I don't know what really happened.'

Personal reasons. The term was a catch-all; Mikami was starting to get a bad feeling.

'What's he doing these days?'

'He went missing.'

'Missing?'

'Yeah. No one knows where he is.'

'And Futawatari didn't either?'

'Looked that way. He was asking if I knew Koda's address.'

'So, the Koda memo, are we sure it was something Kazuki Koda wrote?'

'Like I just said, I'd never heard of it.'

'But Futawatari seemed to know about it?'

Mochizuki seemed to have come to a realization during the exchange; he stared at Mikami with eyes that had lost their sharpness.

82

'You *are* here for something else . . .'

'That's what I've been trying to tell you,' Mikami half yelled. His head was racing. Had Akama opted for a double-sided approach? Perhaps he was using Futawatari in tandem with Mikami to gather intel to persuade Amamiya to ensure that preparations for the commissioner's visit went smoothly.

No, that wasn't it.

He wouldn't have thought to prepare for that. If he had, that would suggest he'd somehow known in advance that Amamiya would turn the commissioner's offer down.

'What time was Futawatari here?'

Mochizuki scratched his head, looking a little embarrassed. 'A little before midday. He called on the phone, came straight over after that.'

Before midday. Around the time Mikami had been at Amamiya's. Definitely too fast. It ruled out some kind of double-pronged strategy on Akama's part.

In which case . . .

Mikami considered it for a moment, but his thoughts halted when another question popped into his head.

'And he asked you about something called the Koda memo?'

'Yeah. He wanted to know who had it, so I told him I had no idea – told him I'd never heard of the damn thing, let alone knowing who had it now.'

'And that's the truth? You really don't know?'

'Come on, Mikami . . .'

'Okay. He seemed happy with that?'

'Sure, left without a fuss. Even gave me a look to apologize for intruding on my work.'

'And you just let him go, without asking anything back?'

'Hmm?'

'You must have pushed a little, tried to suss out what he was talking about?'

'Naturally. He said nothing, of course. Administrative Affairs,

Internal Affairs; they ask the questions. You don't know what they're up to, and they certainly won't tell you.'

Mikami nodded sharply. He could feel his sympathies shifting to side with the detective's. He felt something close to anger, even jealousy. That this was related to Six Four was certain. Futawatari had trampled barefoot over the holy ground of the investigation. He had emerged from his natural domain, the depths of Administrative Affairs, only to offer a glimpse of a mysterious document neither Mikami nor Mochizuki had known existed: the Koda memo.

Mikami's phone started to vibrate in his jacket pocket. He cursed, checking the display. *Media Relations.*

'Sir. I think you might need to come back.'

Suwa's whispering tone told Mikami something had happened. 'What is it?'

'We've just been told the press intend to issue a formal protest, in writing, to the station captain.'

Mikami hurried back to the Prefectural HQ.

He came to a sudden stop after opening the door to the office. Akikawa from the *Toyo* was perched on one of the room's couches. He'd been calling out to Mikumo, but when he looked at Mikami it was with the same detached expression he'd had earlier in the morning. Mikami took a seat, then levelled his gaze at the man opposite him.

He already knew his opening line.

'You seem determined to make trouble.'

'You've left us no choice, Mikami.'

He was utterly composed. Akikawa had never been the type to curry favour, even one to one. And he was even less likely to do so with Mikumo in the room. She was working on the layout of the bulletin, her expression impassive and doll-like. She'd clearly erected a barrier, deciding to completely ignore Akikawa so he wouldn't get the wrong idea. Suwa adopted a different approach. Like Mikumo, he'd assumed a look of nonchalant disinterest, only his aim was to conceal the agitation in the room. He was acting as though Akikawa's presence were perfectly normal.

Mikami's approach was similar to Suwa's. When he spoke, his voice was measured and calm.

'You don't think you're being a little unreasonable? Threatening to submit a written protest to the station captain out of the blue like this?'

'I've arranged to hold it back for now. If you give us the woman's name by tomorrow evening, we'll withdraw the protest.'

'Sounds like a threat to me.'

'Such a negative word. It's like I said – you left us no choice, flatly refusing to listen in that arbitrary way.'

'We can't compromise on everything.'

'Nor can we. I'm sorry, but I can't let this one go. It's the consensus.'

'Okay – who will it be?'

'Sorry?'

'Who do you intend to submit the protest to?'

'The station captain, of course.'

Mikami felt a chill on his forehead. They really were planning to breach the inner temple of the Prefectural HQ. He pulled out a cigarette and lit the tip.

Time to negotiate.

'Could you lower your sights a little?'

'What do you propose?'

'Address the document to me, or the chief of the Secretariat.'

Suwa had told Mikami during their earlier call. Never, in the history of the station, had the Press Club submitted a written protest to anyone ranked higher than division chief. *I don't think it's ever happened anywhere – for a written protest to be submitted to the captain of any headquarters.* His voice had been stretched to breaking point.

Akikawa was grinning faintly.

'Mikami, are you asking for a favour?'

'I am.'

'You know, it didn't really sound that way.'

'Will you do it if I apologize?'

'Unfortunately not. Consensus, like I said.'

Mikami clenched his fists under the table. 'Okay. At least leave the document with me.'

'Leave it with you? You're asking me to hand you a document addressed to the station captain?'

Mikami nodded; Akikawa suppressed a laugh.

'Why would I do that? You'd only hold on to it . . . the captain would never see it.'

'It's enough to prove you did it.'

Whoever they gave the document to, the fact would remain that they had submitted a written protest to the station captain. Yet Akikawa rejected the idea without hesitation.

'Let's not engage in politics, Mikami. All you have to do is give us the woman's name. It shouldn't be that hard.'

From the corner of his eye, Mikami saw Suwa scratch his chin. The middle ground was to keep the document in Media Relations. Suwa's expression made it clear he'd decided on that as the target.

'We'd like your response by 4 p.m. tomorrow. We'll hold another meeting once we have your answer.'

Seeing that Akikawa was getting ready to stand, Mikami raised a hand. 'There's also the commissioner's visit. Can I assume everything is on track with the questions?'

'That is something to discuss once this is resolved.'

'We need them soon.'

Akikawa flashed a smile, the expression declaring he'd found another weakness.

'More importantly, you're really not going to tell us what this morning was all about?'

'What do you mean?'

'The reason behind the change in you, Mikami. We've had no luck working it out ourselves.'

'Don't you have more important things you should be doing?' The words slipped out, a reflex.

Akikawa looked puzzled. 'More important things . . .?'

'You're representing the club this month, so you need to focus on the anonymity argument: fine, just make sure you don't neglect your actual job. There's also the investigation into bid-rigging charges concerning the art museum. That isn't over yet.'

Akikawa's expression hardened. Second Division's investigation was reaching a climax, and the race for coverage was intensifying. The *Asahi* and the *Yomiuri* had each run pieces covering the story. The *Toyo* had lost its initiative and would, if things continued as they were, have to face a miserable defeat.

'We're working on that, too, don't you worry,' Akikawa said, annoyed but unbeaten. 'I take it it's not illness, something like that?'

'What are you talking about?'

'You know . . . maybe you haven't been feeling well, had to change the way you do your job. That sort of thing.'

Mikami felt a sudden, powerful urge to strike the man.

'I'm just fine, as you can see.'

'Okay. Well, don't think we're going to pull any punches, then.'

Akikawa strode out of the room, sparing a glance for Mikumo. Suwa gave Mikami a quick look then jumped to his feet, following him out. He invited Akikawa to Amigos, the karaoke bar of choice in Administrative Affairs.

It was a while before Mikami felt able to stand. It wasn't just his anger at Akikawa. There was a bitterness in his throat, too.

You could just give them her name, if they want it so badly.

Mikami frowned, concentrating on the cowardly idea that had risen, scum-like, to the surface. If things did come to a head, he could always force a reset by giving them Hanako Kikunishi's name. Doing so might flip the situation to his advantage. There wouldn't be any damage. The press only wanted the police to reveal her identity. He'd already made sure to labour the point that she was pregnant and suffering from high levels of stress. As they tended to be oversensitive when it came to the weak, they wouldn't run an article exposing her true identity. Even supposing they *were* considering it, the story would be three days old if they ran it in the next day's news. No: it was highly unlikely any of them would actually put it in print.

There was, of course, the issue of saving face. If he overturned their policy of not revealing the woman's identity, he would be admitting that the Prefectural HQ had made a mistake. They would also have to ready themselves for this about-turn becoming a precedent, fuelling the press to escalate their demands.

But the loss of face would be nothing compared to what might happen if he failed to act and let the press barge into the captain's office. And worries of losing face would be the last thing on his mind if the trouble disrupted the commissioner's visit.

'I'm going upstairs for a bit.'

Mikumo approached as he got to his feet, looking a little anxious. 'Sir.' Her face was flushed. Her eyes sharp, even angry. 'Please let me go to Amigos with the others.'

Mikami felt his head spin. Suwa had put her up to this. Either that, or she was trying to help, unwilling to stand back and watch him suffer.

'I don't think that's a good idea,' he snapped, hurrying out of the room. He stopped himself after a few steps then turned to face the door again. *Not a good idea?* He turned back into the room. 'Forget about it, for good,' he commanded. Mikumo looked crestfallen. Even Mikami had been surprised by the harshness in his voice.

But the poison was already coursing through his blood. He had for a moment considered taking advantage of the fact that Mikumo was a woman, and he knew he would come to regret it.

It was dark beyond the windows.

Mikami was making his way to the first floor, this time via a different set of stairs from those that led to Administrative Affairs. The red carpet ran all the way up these stairs, starting at the entrance to the station, turning right at the landing to the first floor, and stretching as far as the Secretariat and the Public Safety Committee's office. Mikami pushed open the door to the Secretariat. His gaze met that of Aiko Toda, who was sitting closest to the door. He couldn't see Ishii at his desk.

'Is the chief in?'

'Yes, he's in the visitor's room.'

Mikami glanced at the door set in the right-hand wall. The visitor's room was a kind of annexe within the Secretariat, its main function to host confidential discussions.

'I'll wait.'

He walked over the carpeted floor and settled into one of the couches in the middle of the room, its quality and comfort far superior to the ones in Media Relations. A selection of indoor plants had been arranged at even intervals, doubling up as a screen that could shield you from the office's view if you sat in the right place.

The room was soundless. Even though Mikami had grown used to it, it still managed to put him on edge. His eyes drifted off to the corner furthest to the left. A set of double doors fashioned out of finely grained wood announced the entrance to the captain's office. The lamp was on, indicating that the room was occupied.

The office staff were all hard at work. Even with the chief out of the office, it was rare for them to relax their sense of professional formality. They were polished and always on the ball – all the way down from the vice-chief through the section managers to the rank and file – impressive, even if compared to their colleagues in the Prefectural Government.

The difference was incredible. Although his office was located separately, Mikami was also a member of the Secretariat. Welcoming the station captain from Tokyo. Protecting him. Returning him unscathed back to the NPA. There was no exaggeration in saying that these were the Secretariat's principal duties.

Toda came over with a mug of tea.

'Will he be long?' Mikami asked, keeping his voice low.

Toda inclined her head a little. 'He's been in there for a while, so I wouldn't—'

'Who's he with?'

'Inspector Futawatari.'

Mikami held his breath until Toda left. It was warm when he slowly exhaled. *A second brush with Futawatari in a single day.* It was becoming harder to dismiss it as coincidence. Futawatari would be meeting Ishii to discuss the commissioner's visit, or something else to do with Six Four. Mikami had to assume this much.

His eyes bored into the door. For a moment it was as though he could see Futawatari's scrawny back through it. The sharp, clearly defined lines of his face. The razor-sharp intelligence of those cutting eyes.

But . . .

The look that had been burned in Mikami's retina was altogether different.

A summer day, long ago. It came vividly back: the unfathomable expression, fixed on Mikami as he held out a wet towel in both hands. They'd been in the same class in high school. Both members of the kendo club. It was their last prefectural tournament as third-year students; Mikami had been *taisho* – captain of his team – while Futawatari had reconciled himself to being in reserve. He'd lacked the necessary flair. He'd also been unlucky to find himself in a group of elites many of whom, in their year and the year below, had come up through the local *dojo*. Round one. Mikami had landed a *nukido* – a sharp strike to the abdomen – on the *taisho* of one of their main rivals. He had returned triumphant to the corridor that served as the rest area. Drenched in sweat, he'd looked for one of the wet towels the first years had to get ready but been unable to find any. The bus carrying the team's supporters had been late to arrive, and the junior members had been sent to help unload luggage. Mikami had snapped around, annoyed, his eyes landing on Futawatari.

However much he tried, Mikami couldn't recall what had happened next. He suspected his eyes had barked the order.

Get me a fucking towel.

Futawatari had jumped into action. He'd disappeared behind the stands and reappeared moments later with a cooler box slung over his shoulder. He'd taken out a towel and proffered it in silence. Following the tradition of the club, he'd presented it with both hands. But he hadn't shown any sign of deference. His eyes had remained fixed on Mikami. But their expression had been abnormal. They'd lacked any kind of light. Empty of consciousness or feeling, they'd appeared as black pits. He'd suppressed everything. Taken control. At seventeen years of age, Futawatari had been able fully to conceal all the humiliation, anger and bitterness that would have been seething inside him.

A few months later, on the recommendation of a graduate of the kendo club, Mikami had sat the entrance exams to join the police. When he'd spotted Futawatari in the same examination hall, he'd stared, wide-eyed. *I thought the civil service might be a good fit.* That was all Mikami had managed to get out of him. Even now, Mikami wasn't sure what had motivated Futawatari to chose a career in the force. The kendo club was a sizable organization. A harsh environment where you earned a place to fight by defeating your companions. Mikami had never considered a man like Futawatari, who had never handled a *bokuto* before entering the club, as an equal. He'd worked hard at it; that much was true. Never missed a practice session. Mikami had never heard him whine or complain. And he hadn't been the kind of man who schemed behind people's backs to bring them down. Although maybe that was just the impression he gave. The memories were hazy. *Sure. Of course. I agree.* Mikami couldn't remember much beyond the man's emotionless responses. For Mikami, whose high-school years had been physically and emotionally wild and unrestrained, the reticent and boring Futawatari, forever on reserve, had never been of interest, and nothing dramatic had ever happened to impart the feeling that they'd spent a part of their youth together. Considering they'd been in the same club in the same school for three years, he knew far too little about the man.

Mikami had graduated third in his year in police school. He would never forget his surprise when he learned that Futawatari had graduated first. The greater surprise had been yet to come. Futawatari began to race through his promotion exams, swiftly ascending through the ranks. He focused on administration, specializing in Personnel, and was made superintendent at forty – the youngest in the history of the Prefectural HQ. His record still stood.

He spent the following seven years as an inspector in Administrative Affairs, the key position in managing personnel, enjoying a reputation as the department's 'ace'. He was highly regarded among the career officers, and Mikami had heard he'd been put in charge of drawing up the plans for executive transfers. A succession of directors had taken him in as their right-hand man; he had become the implicit authority behind decisions concerning personnel, and was on his way to becoming truly untouchable.

You're just their pet, nothing more. Mikami had muttered his contempt each time Futawatari crossed his thoughts. It wasn't that he was a bad loser. His position as a detective had furnished him with a sense of pride and exclusivity. He belonged to a no-nonsense world, a family, where influence depended on the number of perps you brought in, a world divorced from the departments that competed to have stars on their collars. His 'record' hadn't disappeared, but he'd beaten it with results. They'd needed him, and he'd always delivered. He'd been far removed from Futawatari's reach in Personnel. He'd never doubted that was the truth.

But . . .

What if Futawatari *had* got to him?

Mikami had always avoided thinking about it. He knew he would become a hostage to the suspicion if he did. He would lose sight of the reason for being in Media Relations; he would lose control. The fear of that happening had compelled him, until now, to look away.

But there it was.

Had his appointment really been down to Akama, and Akama alone?

It had been this time last year. Word had begun to spread that Mikami might receive a transfer to be part of the Criminal Investigations Bureau in Tokyo. *It's looking likely. The decision's all but made.* Mikami had himself heard the whispers. Yet, when the announcement was made, it had been a different story. The promotion to superintendent – and the concurrent transfer to Tokyo – had been awarded to Yasuo Maejima, one of Mikami's contemporaries. Postings to Tokyo were traditionally provided to groom candidates for the post of director. Mikami had been left stranded, as if the passport to his future career had been seized at the moment he boarded the flight. He could have perhaps shaken it off if that had been as far as it went. Told himself he'd never wanted to serve in Tokyo. And, at first, he'd been proud of how well he'd taken the blow. The real shock had come later, when he'd received the informal confirmation of his own upcoming transfer. His 'criminal record' hadn't been the only thing that had crossed his mind. He'd recalled again the eyes like black pits, devoid of light and feeling, from that summer day long ago.

He had suspected something underhand. Futawatari and Maejima had been good friends. They had shared a dorm room in police school and – as far as Mikami was aware – were still close, their friendship extending beyond the professional divide that stretched between Criminal Investigations and Administrative Affairs.

There was a sudden bustle. Mikami glanced at the door to the visitor's room. No sooner had he done so than the door opened and Ishii and Futawatari emerged side by side.

'Mikami,' Futawatari greeted him, the first to speak.

Even more than before, he gave the impression of someone belonging to the elite. Gone was the feeble reserve at the kendo club, the man Mikami could have taken his *bokuto* to and beaten a hundred per cent of the time. Mikami worried he might be unable to keep his voice level.

'Futawatari. Seems you called, this morning?'

Futawatari nodded. 'Ishii just brought me up to speed.'

Which meant the call had been to ask after Ayumi. Concern for a fellow officer? Or had he wanted to confirm something as an Administrative Affairs inspector?

It was a relief. Futawatari's eyes conveyed the message as he strode from the room, not putting it into words. The effect was that of having caught sight of a businessman jumping from one country to the next.

Why are you digging into Six Four? What the hell is the Koda memo? Mikami felt an urge to chase and interrogate him, but he remained where he was. It had thrown him to learn that Futawatari's call had been about Ayumi. But that wasn't all. He'd been unnerved at seeing the virtual display of Futawatari's status. This was his arena. Mikami couldn't expect to win with a half-hearted attack.

'Right then, Mikami.' Ishii waved him over and went back into the visitor's room.

'What did Futawatari want?' Mikami asked, having seated himself on a couch inside.

'Ah yes, that was about the renovation of the headquarters. The work's coming up next summer, so we're getting to the point when we need to start thinking about temporary offices. We're probably not going to be able to avoid having two different sites, so the first thing to decide is where we're going to locate the captain. As you know, the captain's office determines the official address of the police headquarters . . .'

Ishii lacked the ability to lie coherently. Mikami doubted he could have answered so fluently if the two had really been in covert discussions concerning Six Four. Which probably meant it was taking place over Ishii's head. Futawatari was acting on direct orders from Akama. That seemed the more likely scenario, especially when you factored in his status as Akama's right-hand man.

'Anyway, I was planning to call you. How did it go with Amamiya? Were you able to sort everything out?'

The question brought Mikami's thoughts back to the present. He had bad news to report. He straightened himself and lowered his voice a little.

'I'm planning to concentrate on that tomorrow. We have a bigger problem though – there's been a complication with the press.'

'What kind of complication?' Mikami saw a hint of fear cross Ishii's eyes.

'It's the issue of anonymity. They've threatened to submit a written protest to the station captain.'

'To the captain?' The colour seemed to drain from Ishii's face. 'That's . . . you're joking?'

'I'm afraid not, sir.'

'No. Absolutely not – you absolutely cannot let that happen.'

'It was the consensus after a full meeting.'

'No, we can't have that. We can't have that at all. You have to talk them out of it.'

He reminded Mikami of a child having a tantrum. He seemed on the verge of tears. 'They did say they would be willing to reconsider, on the condition that we give them the woman's identity.'

'That . . . no, that's out of the question. The director would never stand for that.'

'But it's better than them barging into the captain's office in protest. There could be consequences for the commissioner's visit.'

'Yes, well, of course. But it was Akama's decision to keep her identity from the press.'

Akama's decision? The accident had taken place in the jurisdiction of Station Y. The decision to conceal her identity had come from them. Mikami had never suspected otherwise.

'Sakaniwa called to discuss it, but it was Akama's decision.'

Right, that made sense.

Sakaniwa was Ishii's predecessor, now the captain of Station Y. He'd been here in the Secretariat until the spring. There wasn't an officer in the headquarters who didn't know the story. He had devoted himself utterly to serving Akama; as a reward, Akama had promoted him to captain, in command of a hundred and thirty officers at Station Y, letting him bypass a number of steps on the career ladder.

Sakaniwa had delegated his decision. No doubt having concluded that the best way to protect himself was to report the incident upwards, he had turned to Akama for advice. Mikami had to admit, that did make it more difficult. Akama wasn't the type to let an underling's opinion sway a personal decision. Even suggesting he reconsider was likely to send him into a rage. *In which case.* Mikami decided to push his next idea. The one that had come to him on his way to the office.

'What if we give them her identity, but unofficially? Without committing it to writing.'

This is just me talking to myself here, but . . .

A while ago, this had been the stock phrase for when a detective slipped the press a tidbit to feed on. Mikami could claim he was talking to himself as he gave them verbal confirmation of Hanako Kikunishi's name. It was a stop-gap, there was no doubt about that, but it still qualified more as *accommodation* than *capitulation*. The force would get by without losing face. Nothing would remain in writing, there would be nothing that could establish a precedent – it would end at one man having muttered something to himself.

'I suppose it's an idea . . . I wonder what Akama would say.' Ishii sighed weakly.

'Can you put it forward, suggest it?'

'Okay. But he's already left for today, a visitor from Tokyo. When would you need an answer by?'

'Before four o'clock tomorrow.'

'Fine. I'll bring it up tonight or first thing tomorrow morning. I can't say which side he'll fall on, so either way you need to work on bringing the press into line. If the worst comes to the worst and they still insist on the written protest, you need to make sure the buck stops with you or me.' Large beads of sweat had gathered on his forehead. 'I'm counting on you for this, Mikami. Keep it in mind that the captain isn't just any old person.'

The sentence caused an image of the captain's face to pop into Mikami's mind, vague and indistinct. He had already known their captain was special. Kinji Tsujiuchi. Forty-four, two years younger than Mikami. He had come to the Prefectural HQ after having worked as chief in the NPA's Accounts Division. His next step would be to return to Tokyo in the spring, taking over as chief of the Personnel Division. All organizations were the same, the police included. You climbed to the top by gaining control over the money, then the people. As such, Kinji Tsujiuchi was currently regarded as the NPA's next in line when it came to taking over the seat of commissioner general.

The next candidate for commissioner general, surrounded by reporters fresh out of university forcing a written protest into his hands. It would be a disaster. It simply couldn't be allowed to happen.

'Is something funny?'

Mikami's head came up in surprise. Ishii's mouth was a tight line.

'What?'

'You were grinning, just then.'

Mikami didn't think he'd been grinning.

'Look, you need to take this seriously. I'm trusting you to keep this from getting out of hand.'

Mikami replied with a perfunctory nod before excusing himself from the room. The lamp was still on, signaling that the captain was there.

He realized what it was the moment he stepped outside into the corridor. *A disaster, one that can't be allowed to happen.* He had laughed at himself for having considered it that way. At his core, Ishii was no different to Captain Sakaniwa. He had offered up his soul to Akama and Tsujiuchi; now he spent his days playing it safe, lost in dreams of the promotional transfer he would probably receive in the next year or two. He wasn't afraid of failure, only that his superior officers might deem him as one. That was why Mikami had been grinning – at having sat with a man like that, for having tried to think up a solution from his perspective.

He paced through the stagnant chill of the poorly lit corridor.

He was an officer in Administrative Affairs. Part of the Secretariat. He had to admit a part of him existed that thought that way. He'd been breathing the air of the force's administrative side for over half a year. It felt as though, through a process of osmosis, an invisible something had risen and insinuated itself through his pores. Things weren't going the way he'd hoped. He had been sincere in his desire to reform Media Relations. He'd made the heartfelt pledge that he would spend his two years here battling for it. Where had this sense of hopelessness come from? The world he inhabited now was one devoid of murder or corrupt politicians, and yet he wasted more energy than he had when they'd been a part of his job; he was exhausting himself, and his confidence was waning.

Not for the first time, Mikami shivered. Futawatari had been in this place for twenty-eight years. He had made this inward-looking world his home, breathing in silence, never resting, the whole time Mikami had laboured as a detective in the outside world. What would that have created? What had it laid to rest? What had it magnified? Mikami felt a creeping unease. What twisted philosophies had made their way into that puny chest, into the mind of the man who, in their high-school years, had never once been given the chance to wield his *bokuto* in a tournament?

A monster in the family.

But gone was the time when Mikami was on the other side. Almost without his knowing it, he'd come to wear the uniform of Administrative Affairs. *It's just temporary.* He would tell himself he could take it off, yet all the while he continued to add layers. He would carry on doing so regardless of his determination not to. There was no guarantee that it wouldn't happen. Over time, the uniform would become his skin – then, his way of thinking fixed, he would never be able to take it off again.

Mikami fought an urge to cry out.

He saw a face appear before him – Ayumi. She turned up every time he got like this. She beamed at him. Like a safety mechanism of the heart, her soft smile remained in his thoughts until his agitation was gone.

14

The night had grown noticeably colder.

It had been just after eight o'clock when Mikami pulled up at home. He'd scanned the entranceway and seen that Minako hadn't left out any bowls from Sogetsuan. *They don't deliver for one.* If he reproached her about it, she'd only give him an excuse like that.

Dinner had been boiled tofu, with a beef-and-potato stew.

Delicious. Maybe delivered groceries aren't so bad, after all. Although I'm sure it's your cooking that does it.

Recently, the words flowed with comparative ease. Mikami had never imagined himself the kind to make small talk, to adopt a loving tone. When he reflected on how he had invested his time and energy, his life at home had always taken second place to his life in the force. This had been true when he was a detective, and it had remained the case after his transfer to Media Relations.

'The bath's ready.'

'Thanks.'

Mikami sneaked a look at Minako's profile as she cleared away the dishes. She was calm. She seemed fine. But it was still the day after their trip, and Mikami doubted the memory of the dead girl's face had faded away. Like him, she was putting on a show of normality so he wouldn't worry unnecessarily.

'I went to see the father from the Shoko kidnapping today.' Mikami said this to Minako's back as she washed the dishes.

'You did . . .?' She turned the tap off and looked around, startled. 'You went to see Mr Amamiya? What for?'

'One of the top men in Tokyo has decided he wants to visit, pay his respects. I was there to ask Amamiya for his blessing.'

Mikami never discussed work at home, but he was happy to do so now if it helped fill the silence. And when it came to Six Four, the kidnapping was, for Minako, too, more than just printed word and hearsay. She had been part of Undercover B, had acted as someone's wife as her unit marked the Aoi Café; she had seen Yoshio Amamiya in the flesh as he'd charged in.

The kitchen fell quiet. Minako took off her apron and walked back to the living room; she folded her legs under the *kotatsu*.

'How were they, her parents?'

'Mrs Amamiya had passed away, last year.'

'Oh . . . that's awful.'

'I know. Without ever finding out who the kidnapper was . . .'

I guess we don't have it so bad. The thought bubbled up like a spring.

'That must have been hard for him,' Minako muttered; her eyes were distant, as though picturing his face from that day.

'He'd aged a lot.'

'Yes . . . not surprising, really.'

'Right.'

'Do you think . . . is the kidnapper going to get away with it?' Minako asked, her face grave.

Mikami grunted. Mochizuki's words from earlier were still ringing in his ears.

'I heard the investigation's stalled.' Minako bit gently on her lip. 'Didn't they think the kidnapper was someone from the prefecture?'

'Yeah, most likely.' Mikami nodded.

The kidnapping itself, the nine businesses the kidnapper had named, the location of the ransom exchange, even the site where the girl's body had been dumped: they had all been in Prefecture

D. The kidnapper had demonstrated an easy familiarity with the roads, along with the names and locations of local businesses. *Extensive local knowledge.* This fact had made the theory that the kidnapper was a citizen of the prefecture difficult to shake off.

'And he had to have accomplices, too?'

'That was the assumption.'

At the time, mobile phones had yet to spread to the general public. The final business the kidnapper had directed Amamiya to – the fishing lodge Ikkyu – had been deep in the mountains. He had then called the resort and instructed Amamiya to throw the suitcase down from the Kotohira bridge, before collecting the ransom at Dragon's Hollow, further down the river. No more than 300 metres separated the bridge and the hollow. After calling the lodge, the kidnapper would have had to have been lying in wait at the hollow only minutes later. And yet there had been no private houses or public phones in the surrounding area. Someone other than the man relaying instructions on the phone, an accomplice, would have been needed to collect the ransom. Everyone in the Investigative HQ had agreed on this.

Although Mikami had agreed, he had found it hard to accept the idea that the kidnappers had been equal partners. He was used to cases of adults kidnapping and locking up other adults, but the thought of a group conspiring to kidnap and murder a seven-year-old girl was, even for a detective with Mikami's long experience, enough to make him shudder. If there had been more than one kidnapper, one would have been the main offender and the other an accomplice. Even then, the leader would have to have wielded absolute power over the latter.

'It might be best to work on the premise of a single kidnapper.'

'How so?'

'It's how a detective's brain works. A solitary offender. We're no good at imagining offenders in groups.'

Minako looked thoughtful

Whether or not the kidnapping had been perpetrated by a

single offender, it was clear it had been planned in great detail, and with extreme care. And brutal cold-bloodedness.

Worse than a monster . . .

Minako opened her mouth to speak. 'He even knew about those rocks, in the river, the hollow. What happened to the investigation into canoeists, the rafting enthusiasts?'

'They're still pursuing it, as far as I know. But . . . well, remember it turned out that people from a surprisingly wide area knew about the hollows.'

This had been discovered some way into the investigation. The *D Daily* had, only a couple of weeks before the kidnapping, printed a large feature article on 'The Enigma of Dragon's Hollow' in its lifestyle section.

'But . . .' Minako seemed a little agitated. 'Even if he *had* got the idea from reading the paper, doesn't that just confirm the fact that he was local? They've been chasing this for so long. Why haven't they found him? I wonder.'

'Yes, well . . .'

580,000 households. 1,820,000 citizens. Mikami hadn't forgotten the demographics in the morning's paper. The prefecture's total population had changed little in the last fourteen years, the flow into local cities more or less equalling the flow out from the countryside. The police had narrowed the range of potential suspects to men in their thirties or forties but that had still left more than 300,000 to investigate.

At the same time, they had had few leads. If Kenji was genuinely innocent, that meant Shoko had been abducted on the single road between her house and Kenji's. The Neighbourhood Unit had swept the area repeatedly but had still come away without a single witness able to confirm the presence of any suspicious people or vehicles. And there hadn't been many people around to start with. As Mikami had reaffirmed earlier in the day, the area was agricultural, with very few private residences. The date of 5 January had also helped form the vacuum. The men who worked part-time on the farms had been in their offices or at the local agricultural cooperative, while the women had been cooped up indoors, busy clearing up after the New Year.

The kidnapper had left only three items. The plastic cord wrapped around the mercury lamps on the Kotohira bridge. The tape over the girl's face. The washing line around her wrists. Each were standard items, sold nationwide, making it effectively impossible to pin down the location of purchase. They had expected to find footprints, but even these had proved evasive. The area around Dragon's Hollow had been composed entirely of exposed rock, while the woods next to it had been carpeted with dry leaves from the beech trees.

All they had left was the kidnapper's voice. Since no recordings of the calls existed, the police had had to depend on the ears of the few people who had spoken with the kidnapper. Yoshio Amamiya, his receptionist Motoko Yoshida and the nine business owners and staff members who had answered the calls for Amamiya at each of the businesses en route to the ransom exchange. None of the officers on the case had heard the kidnapper's voice. And this held true of the members of the Home Unit. The second call had come in before their arrival at the house, while the following day's call had come into Amamiya's office and been answered by Motoko, with no police there to witness it.

They'd been unable to listen to the calls at the various businesses. The Aoi Café had been the only venue they'd been able to reach in advance of Amamiya, and even then they hadn't had the time to modify the phones; they'd also been wary of there being an accomplice in the café, and felt unable to do anything more than keep watch. Mikami had heard that, for the two years that followed the kidnapping, the police had called Amamiya and the others in on a regular basis to take part in 'voice' line-ups. *People with a record of disorderly behaviour. People in heavy debt. Known criminals. Canoeists. Locals of Ozatomura. Ex-employees of Amamiya Pickles. People from Morikawa Nishi, Shoko's primary school. Contractors for and regulars of the nine businesses. Anyone reported to be acting suspi-ciously.* The teams investigating the case picked up anyone on the list who they deemed to have even a minuscule possibility of being a suspect and recorded their voices over the phone. They then asked Amamiya and the ten others who had heard the kid-napper's voice to listen to the recordings several times. The majority of the recordings had been made with the relevant per-son's permission, and Mikami knew that methods not dissimilar to phone tapping had been resorted to for some.

The voice of a man in his thirties or forties, slightly hoarse, with no trace of an accent. *I'll recognize it if I hear it.* Amamiya had been certain. Motoko and the others had sounded confident in their ability to do the same. Despite this, Mikami had not once in fourteen years heard word that the Investigative Team had come up with a hit.

'It'll be difficult if the voice on the phone doesn't lead anywhere.'

As soon as he'd said it, Mikami cursed himself. It was taboo to mention the phone. The atmosphere in the room shifted. Minako said, 'I hope they catch him, somehow . . .' A short while later her eyes drifted to the phone on the low stand.

Another night without the phone ringing.

The room fell silent once Minako had left to go to bed. Mikami slid under the *kotatsu* until the duvet reached his chest. He let out a long breath then switched on the TV. He couldn't handle watching it when Minako was there. Runaways. Disappearances. Silent calls. Suicides. There were so many words that could just come out of nowhere, and each time he worried they might break Minako's heart.

Maybe it was the TV that had got to Ayumi. The idea would come to him now and again. All those variety and entertainment shows, all those commercials. All united in stressing the impor-tance of appearances. Nothing else mattered: if you looked good, you got ahead in life. Men would adore you. Doors would slide open. Your life would be one big party, they said, luring you in, sounding plausible as they claimed it was simply how everybody lived.

Mikami would find himself trying to assign the blame to those behind the screen. Ayumi had been taken into a make-believe world. But she'd been crushed under the empty promises of the tabloids, lost sight of herself.

She'd been full of life in primary school. She'd excelled in swimming and running, and her grades had always been good. She and Mikami had been close. She had always looked up to her dad, the detective, her eyes filled with loving respect – no doubt the result of the stories Minako told her every day.

The change had come after she started secondary school. No, the first signs had been there in her sixth year of primary school. She started to shy away from photos. She threw a leaflet for the school's Parents' Day into the bin at a convenience store. She started refusing to leave the house with Mikami and avoided sitting next to Minako. She had perhaps sensed it, worked out what the other kids were thinking but not saying. Or perhaps someone had actually told her.

You look just like your dad.

It's a shame you didn't take after your mum.

She hadn't attended school on the day of her graduation photo. Her photo had been lodged next to the one containing the smiling faces of her classmates, taken on her own the next day. Her mouth had been clenched tight, her eyes on the floor. *I tried . . . but I couldn't get her to look up*, her form teacher had later called to explain.

A recommendation had meant that her high school had already been decided. *Things will change once she's there. She'll grow up.* A part of him had still been optimistic. At the same time, he had to admit his situation had made it difficult for him to keep a close eye on his daughter; the period had clashed with the shocking news of his first transfer to Media Relations.

Ayumi had attended the school for a little over two weeks. When she stopped going she started refusing to leave the house at all, eventually withdrawing into her first-floor bedroom. She wouldn't tell them why when they asked. When they'd resorted to forcing her to go, she'd bawled like an infant. She spent the daytime in bed, hiding under her sheets. Her day and night cycle reversed as she began to stay up all night and go to sleep when it grew light outside. She began to take meals alone in her room.

Her behaviour had become increasingly eccentric. She'd started to hide her face whenever she did make the occasional trip downstairs. She would twist her head all the way to the right, facing the wall as she edged along the corridor or the side of the living room, because she thought the right side of her face the uglier – although it wasn't until later that Mikami learned that this had been the reason behind her actions.

Minako had been beside herself with worry. She had tried to hide it in the beginning, treating Ayumi as though nothing was out of the ordinary, but it had become too much for her to bear as Ayumi's withdrawal became more and more serious. She had coaxed a reluctant Ayumi into coming with her in the car to visit the town's education consultation centre. There, they were introduced to a therapist who they began to see, driving the hour-long trip each way. Minako bought a doctor's mask for Ayumi, who was still afraid to leave the house, and allowed her to lie across the back seat for the duration of the journey.

The change had come during their sixth session. Ayumi burst into tears, howling her heart out as she finally broke her silence. *Everyone laughs because I'm so ugly. I'm too embarrassed to go to school. I can't even walk outside. I'd rather die than see my relatives. I want to get rid of this face. I want to break it to pieces.* As she continued, she had become increasingly distressed, stamping her feet and balling her fists, hitting the desk over and over again.

Dysmorphophobia. Body Dysmorphic Disorder.

Mikami had found it impossible to accept the therapist's

grim-sounding diagnosis. While it had been horrifying to witness the video of their sessions, he had resisted the idea that his daughter was suffering from a psychological condition. Everyone worried about their looks during adolescence. Wasn't it just that it was hitting Ayumi harder than most? He realized she wasn't pretty in the way that made people fuss over her. She'd inherited a good amount of his genes. But there was nothing about her that was 'ugly'. Anyone would attest to it. Ayumi's looks were no different to those of any other normal girl, the kind you saw everywhere.

The therapist had used the same point to argue that she had a psychological condition. He had stressed the importance of acceptance and recognition; that, as parents, they had a duty to accept their daughter as she was and to respect her as an individual. To Mikami it had sounded trite, and he had struggled to lend a genuine ear to the advice. He'd been angry, too. His daughter had opened her heart to a therapist – a stranger – telling him exactly how much she hated the way her dad looked. Mikami had felt uncomfortable and depressed, and the feeling had grown with each passing day, sapping away his will to talk things over with Ayumi.

Opening up to the therapist had also encouraged Ayumi to lay bare her jealousy of and animosity towards Minako. Perhaps she'd simply concluded that there was no longer any need to keep her emotions bottled up. *Stop staring at me with that face of yours.* After this cruel statement, Ayumi had stopped talking to her mother completely. When she did occasionally look her way, her eyes harboured traces of hatred.

Minako had started to panic; confused, she began to withdraw into herself. It had been hard to watch the way she would knock on Ayumi's door, timid as she held a tray of food in her hand. She had taken to sitting quietly in front of her dresser; instead of putting on her make-up, it seemed as though she was cursing the way she looked. Mikami felt his blood boil. He doubted he would have put up with Ayumi acting this way for so long, not if he hadn't been told she had a 'condition'.

The day had finally come. It was the last week of August.

Ayumi, who was still locking herself in her room, had suddenly appeared in the living room. Her head had been twisted out of view; she addressed the wall when she spoke.

I'm going to have plastic surgery. I'm going to use the money I saved from my New Year's gifts. I need permission, so I need your signatures.

Mikami had asked what she was going to have changed. He could hear the trembling in his own voice. Ayumi had been impassive when she'd answered.

Everything. All of it. I want double eyelids. A smaller nose. Cheekbone and jawline reduction.

She wanted to give up being his daughter. That was how it had sounded. He had pushed Minako, who had taken her daughter by the arms, aside and slapped Ayumi across the face. Ayumi had howled at the wall. He'd never heard a woman scream like that before.

It's all right for you! It's okay for you to look like that, you're a man!

Mikami had lost control. All consideration for her condition disappeared. This time, he hit her with his fist. Ayumi had scrambled up the stairs and taken refuge in her room, locking the door from the inside. *Leave her be!* He'd bellowed the words from the bottom of the staircase as Minako chased up after her. Some minutes later a sound like someone putting their foot through the floor had rung out from above. Then something smashing. An extraordinary noise. Mikami had bolted up the stairs and kicked open the door to her room, then gone in. He'd felt a sharp pain in his foot. The mirror lay in pieces, the glass scattered all over the floor. Ayumi had been balled up in the corner, sitting in darkness. Punching herself in the face. Using her nails to tear at it. *I hate it! I hate it! I hate it! I hate this face. I want to die! I want to die! I want to die!* Mikami had found himself frozen to the spot, unable to speak, scared to do anything in case Ayumi shattered like the mirror.

Mikami had spent the whole night discussing the situation with Minako. For Ayumi in her current state, they were nothing more than the enemy. They had seriously considered checking her into hospital. In the end, seeing no other viable option, they'd called Ayumi's therapist. *I can come tomorrow. You should probably leave her by herself until then . . .*

It happened the evening after the therapist's visit. Ayumi left the house without a word, without even leaving a note.

She's a lot calmer now. Just keep an eye on her, don't make too much fuss.

The words of a professional no doubt providing her with a glimmer of hope, Minako, who hadn't slept at all the previous night, had dozed off in the living room. Ayumi had used the opportunity to run away. They had found an empty bag of doctor's masks in the bin in her room. She'd taken a single shoulder bag. All she had to her name were the few coins and single ten-thousand-yen note she'd taken from the small music box. The bike she'd used to run away with was reported found four days later, discarded on the pavement next to the train station.

While it was true that the work on City D's public transport system had suffered delays, the train station was still the largest in the prefecture. Two private railways used it, alongside Japan Rail, and the bus terminus next to it had services that ran in all directions.

Even so, a young girl in a doctor's mask would stand out. It wasn't as if there'd been a spate of summer colds. Somebody must have seen her. If nothing else, she would have caught the attention of the station staff.

Such hopes led to nothing. Visiting the station during rush-hour, the people had flowed through the automated gates with alarming speed, and the majority waiting for buses or trains had had their eyes trained on mobile phones or magazines. The police officer who manned the *koban* outside the station also claimed not to have seen her. Ayumi had slipped through, completely unnoticed. Either that, or she'd headed away from the station after leaving her bike there.

What evidence did you have to tell us she'd calmed down? Mikami had interrogated the therapist. He'd been unable not to. It was only because of the therapist's advice to try going back to work that Mikami had seen fit to leave Minako and Ayumi alone that afternoon. *You need to avoid provoking her, act as though everything is normal.* Mikami had swallowed the advice and left the house; yet this had been the result. The therapist hadn't shown any signs of remorse. *'I won't cause them any trouble, not any more.' I decided she would be fine when she said that.* He went on to tell Mikami that, in retrospect, the words might of course have signalled an intention to run away.

In Mikami's mind, the sentence had intimated more than a plan to leave home. A number of interpretations had entered his thoughts. She'd said it so they would lower their guard. To say goodbye. Had she perhaps hinted that she would commit suicide? No. Ayumi would never kill herself. She'd definitely said it to get them to lower their guard. She'd known they'd relax their watch if she told them she wouldn't cause any more trouble. There'd been that element of calculation: she hadn't run out of the house in the heat of the moment. Didn't the fact that she hadn't forgotten to take her wallet and a change of clothes prove that?

I want to die! I want to die! I want to die!

High-risk missing person. That was what the 'special arrangements' Akama had spoken of actually boiled down to. Someone vulnerable, with a high chance of becoming involved in an incident or an accident of some kind. Someone likely to attempt self-harm or suicide. Mikami had no argument with Ayumi being classified in this way. He understood that the investigation would become cursory in nature if the threat of suicide was removed completely, whether Ayumi was the child of a police officer or not. As it was, the regional stations had spared no effort in conducting the search. As well as officers on the beat, personnel from Criminal Investigations and Community Safety had also been assigned to the search. Even then, they had yet to pick up any significant leads. He had politely refused when, a month ago, they had suggested that he let them take the search public, which would mean exposing her face to every passerby in the street. Mikami had refused because he'd known that, for Ayumi, there could be no greater hell.

His eyes stung from the glare of the TV set. Five or six girls not too far from Ayumi's age were singing and dancing, looking half naked in their outfits. Each vying to stand out. Staring right into the camera, as if to say, *Look at me, just me.*

If she had only meant to run away . . .

If he'd been one hundred per cent certain that Ayumi wouldn't try to take her own life, that she'd only wanted plastic surgery so that boys would notice her, only shouted abuse at them and charged out of the house because they'd turned down her request, then, even though she was in the middle of adolescence, he felt confident that his anger would have outweighed his concern. At sixteen, she was not yet fully mature, but neither was she a child. There was no reason to let her trample over her parents' dignity. *All daughters leave home eventually. Society's full of families that don't get on. I've seen too many cases of parents killing their children, children killing their parents.* Lining up angry sentence after angry sentence, it was possible he'd convinced himself and Minako into thinking her behaviour was acceptable.

What did Minako think . . .

Of him, for having refused to deal with their daughter's condition?

Of her husband, for having raised his hand to their suffering child?

Minako hadn't tried to blame the therapist. Nor had she tried to blame herself for having fallen asleep. She had searched for

Ayumi with the energy of someone possessed. She'd separated herself, then, from the Minako who had always consulted him before making a decision. He would try talking to her, but she hardly reacted. Her eyes wouldn't meet his, even when he was standing in front of her. It was as though she'd been searching for Ayumi by herself. Once she'd exhausted the possibility of the train station or Ayumi's friends helping, she started buying women's magazines and making calls to the plastic surgeons and beauty clinics that had put out advertisements. *Have you had a young girl come in, wearing a mask? She has a red sports bag. Please call me back if you see her.* She then said, 'I can't get my message across on the phone, I need to ask them in person,' and began to head out every day. To Tokyo. Saitama. Kanagawa. Chiba. If the silent calls hadn't come in, she would have probably extended her investigations to the black-market surgeons.

Mikami could have approached Akama for his help. You couldn't do much with one ten-thousand-yen note. And Ayumi couldn't even approach a plastic surgeon's office without signed parental consent. Yet the fact remained that it was one of the very few leads they had to pursue. And if fingerprints and dental records were means of identifying the dead, then perhaps Mikami should have requested that the focus of the search be shifted to businesses dealing in cosmetic surgery – if nothing else, as a way of searching for an Ayumi who still lived. But he hadn't. Ayumi despised the face she'd inherited. It was the one thing he didn't want anyone else to know. The family's suffering would be too great if the knowledge got out. And he'd wanted to preserve his daughter's dignity. He had pledged to himself that no word of Ayumi's condition, or the things it had made her say, would ever leave the walls of their home.

But . . .

What did Minako think?

A tension like a faint electric current had grown between them. They were aware of each other, but their eyes were firmly shut. Ayumi's absence had brought into relief the parts of their relationship that lacked solidity; at the same time, it formed an unbreakable bond that held them together. She had provided them with a single goal, compelled them to take care of each other, forced them into praying that their relationship would hold out.

Mikami wondered how long that would last.

Midnight. Mikami used the remote control to turn off the TV before he crawled out from under the *kotatsu*. He took the phone from its stand and switched off the room's lights.

He walked down the dark corridor.

Yoshio Amamiya, old and wrinkled. Shoko Amamiya, innocent and sweet, a decorative band in her hair. It was just one of the cases he'd had to work on as a detective. It wasn't until Ayumi ran away from home that he'd really known how the parents must feel, losing their only child like that.

Mikami tiptoed quietly into the bedroom. He put the phone next to his pillow and climbed on his futon. He found the electric foot warmer with his feet and pulled it up until it rested next to his calves.

He thought he heard Minako turn in her sleep.

He glanced across to her futon. Lying inside was a mystery he couldn't solve. Whenever he thought of Ayumi, the way she hated her parents' looks, he couldn't help but recall the question everyone had no doubt asked themselves so long ago.

Why had Minako chosen him?

He was no longer sure about what he thought he'd come to understand. Listening to the ticking of the clock, he fumbled, as though he were squinting in darkness, to trace the genesis of their relationship.

15

Mikami had left the house prepared for a busy day.

The first thing he did on entering the office was check on Mikumo. She was all but allergic to alcohol. Her face became bloated if she'd been drinking the night before. He knew immediately that she hadn't joined the others. This observation also meant he could anticipate the content of Suwa's report as he approached Mikami's desk.

'We don't stand a chance,' Suwa said, his voice croaky.

From the sound of things, he'd spent a good portion of the night singing and having to raise his voice. Next to him, Kuramae looked to be suffering, too. His eyes were bloodshot, half hidden under puffy lids.

'So it's a lost cause?'

Suwa let out an exasperated, alcohol-tinged breath.

'They're still insisting on submitting it to the captain. They're definitely not going to settle for leaving it with us. It seems his editor, Azusa, an old-fashioned reporter with a background in police reporting, is really pressuring Akikawa on this.'

The last part sounded more like intelligence than it did a simple report. Akikawa was getting caught in the middle.

Revealing the woman's identity by thinking out loud. Mikami was leaning more and more towards the idea, but he had yet to hear from Ishii, who was supposed to be confirming Akama's position on the matter.

'Okay, we can forget about the *Toyo*. I want you two to split up – see if you can work on some of the others before the evening. Sound them out about leaving the protest with us; if they're not receptive, make the suggestion that they leave it with Chief Ishii.'

As long as they remained in the dark as to Akama's response, they needed to continue with their attempts to arbitrate peace. If a few of the papers relaxed their positions, that could be used as fodder to bring the *Toyo* around.

The Press Club was a fluid entity. Allegiances shifted in line with the complex interactions of its members, who reacted to each reporter's strategies as well as to the overall balance of power.

When issues like the one they were facing arose, it became even harder to predict the outcome of this type of chemical reaction. The *FM Kenmin*, one of the Press Club's associate members, was perhaps the only one whose stance they could predict. The station received its budget in full from the prefectural government; as such, it had no ability to speak out against anywhere deemed a public office. That left twelve of them. How many would Suwa be able to convert?

Mikami pulled his notebook from his jacket pocket and flipped through the pages.

Toyo. Branch D. Senior Editor. Azusa Mikio. University T. Forty-six. Cheerful. Brags. Well disposed to the police.

Mikami remembered the man's dark face, his narrow forehead. The executive, round-table meeting held once a month between the media executives and the Prefectural HQ. Azusa had shown up once in lieu of his branch head, who had gone down with a cold.

It was worth trying him.

Mikami made a mental note as he reached for the phone. He dialled the number for Ishii's desk. The situation was too pressing to sit back and wait for him to get in touch. The deadline for their official response to the Press Club was four o'clock. He also needed to fix matters with Yoshio Amamiya urgently.

Aiko Toda answered the phone. She told him Ishii was in Akama's office. Mikami asked her to get Ishii to call when he was back, then hung up. Restless, he got to his feet and paced over to the whiteboard near the wall. He ran his eyes over the press reports. Three road accidents between the previous night and the morning. A fire in someone's kitchen. The arrest of a man who had tried to skip out on paying his food bill. All things considered, a quiet night for the prefecture. His phone started to ring just as he turned around. He hurried over and took the receiver in his hand.

'Mikami, could you go and see Akama in his office?'

Ishii hung up without offering an explanation. His voice had sounded heavy. Akama's office, not Ishii's desk. Perhaps it meant Akama wanted to give his response in person.

Three minutes later, Mikami knocked on Akama's door. The director was in there by himself. He moved from his desk to one of the couches without offering Mikami a seat.

'You seem to be particularly bad at managing the press, Mikami. Why did you leave this until it got out of hand?'

He started harshly. A written protest was going to be submitted to the station captain. Mikami understood his urge to get angry, knowing Akama had been told only at the last minute. Even so . . .

'I refused their request to give them the woman's identity, as per your request; unfortunately, this only strengthened their resolve, even more than we could have expected. We are doing our best to remedy the situation, but negotiations are proving difficult. They have a lot of aggravation left to blow off.' He had given his answer standing. Akama still hadn't offered him a seat. It wasn't that it had slipped his mind. He was doling out a reprimand.

'I'm not interested in excuses. They're a waste of my time.'

Mikami felt himself bristle. *You think I have the time to stand here and listen to your sarcasm?*

'They did say they would be willing to withdraw their protest, if we were to give them the woman's identity.'

'I heard from Ishii, you know. About your little expediency, that nonsense about "thinking out loud".'

Expediency?

Mikami looked Akama squarely in the eye. 'There's no risk to us. The exchange would leave no traces in the press, and there wouldn't be any official documents.'

'Rejected,' Akama said coldly. He raised an eyebrow. 'Under no circumstances are we to release her name to the public.'

There was something odd about his tone. It brought to mind a con artist Mikami had investigated some years earlier. The con artist had refused to divulge information regarding a number of his crimes despite clearly wanting to brag, considering it below him to confess to a rookie detective.

Mikami decided he would need to dig a little.

'I understand it was your decision, to withhold her identity.'

'That's right. Sakaniwa phoned to discuss the matter from District Y. I made the call.'

'Could I ask you to reconsider? The press aren't going to relent unless something changes. In light of the fact that the commissioner's visit is so close, could I ask you this one time . . . as an emergency measure—'

'You're pushing it now, Mikami. It's time you stopped clinging to that ridiculous idea and came up with a new strategy.'

His tone had been less cutting than the words themselves. Akama was still caught in the con man's dilemma. Something else was going on. Mikami's unease was only aggravated by the fact that Sakaniwa, a man very much in Akama's favour, was involved.

'Sir, is there something else that is stopping us from revealing her identity, something other than the fact she's pregnant?'

'Of course there is,' Akama answered with surprising openness. It felt as though he'd been waiting for Mikami to ask. 'The issue of anonymity is on the agenda.'

The agenda?

'I assume you are aware that central government is currently in talks on two bills, one on privacy, the other on the protection of individual rights?'

'I am.'

The subject was one that often emerged from the mouths of the press. The legislation was unforgivable, no different to laying open restrictions on the press. They wouldn't stand for it.

'The bills are being subjected to intense criticism from the press, but this is simply their own actions turning full circle – they must reap what they have sown. Whenever there's a big case they swarm in and create more damage for the casualties, all the time underplaying any cases that would reflect badly on their institution. What is it but impudence when such people attempt to lay blame on us and dress themselves up as watchdogs of the peace?'

Akama paused to rub some balm over his lips.

'The two bills will eventually be passed. That is when we'll tackle the question of anonymous reporting. We plan to lobby the government and establish a review committee to discuss official policy on crime victims. We will incorporate a paragraph that gives us the final decision over whether or not to release their identity to the public. While this will initially limit us to crime victims, once the Cabinet decision has been made and we are given the green light, we will be able to stretch the interpretation to fit our needs. We will be in the driving seat from the beginning to the end. We will seize control of every aspect of our press reporting.'

Mikami finally understood . . . why it was that Akama had so relentlessly pushed for such a hard-line approach.

The issue of anonymity had become one of the NPA's projects. Or, perhaps, one of Akama's. From the hints of pride evident in the way he'd talked about 'Cabinet decisions' and 'review committees', it was possible this was something Akama was hoping to push through once he'd returned to Tokyo.

Mikami had already guessed that Akama was unlikely to reverse his decision, but he couldn't help a growing sense of disgruntlement. He knew his idea of 'thinking out loud' didn't run counter to Tokyo's goals. It was standard in the force to treat unofficial or covert actions as though they had never happened.

'If I have your understanding, you may go.'

'Is that the only reason?' Mikami asked, not thinking.

This seemed to throw Akama a little. But only a moment later a spark of curiosity registered under his glasses. 'What are you getting at, Mikami?'

'Is that all – the only reason you have for withholding her identity?' Mikami asked, having switched completely to the role of detective. The con man's dilemma was still there. He could see it. Akama was still hiding something.

'Since you asked . . . perhaps I'll let you into it.' Akama broke into a smile. 'The truth is, the woman in question is the daughter of Takuzo Kato.'

Mikami felt his whole frame tense.

Takuzo Kato. Acting chairman of *King Cement*, and now in his second year as a member of the Prefecture D Public Safety Committee.

'He pushed the decision through?' The words came out like gunfire.

'No, this is just us trying to help,' Akama answered, his expression equable.

In the regions, being a member of the Public Safety Committee was decoration and nothing more. It was an honorary role where the only obligation was to meet once a month with the station captain to hold a casual discussion over some food; it had no particular authority over Administrative Affairs. But the organizational chart painted a different picture. The Prefectural HQ was officially subject to the guidance of the three members forming the committee. Was that why they were helping? No – they would issue an anonymous report as an ostensible act of goodwill, while creating an obligation in the mind of one of the prefecture's most powerful financial authorities, effectively branding him 'pro-police' until the day of his death.

'His daughter really is pregnant. Sakaniwa had initially asked me to suppress the entire report, but, well, the accident was a serious one, and I knew it would be a real pain if the man's family began to kick up a fuss, so I decided to opt for making the report anonymous. Now, I hope I have your understanding on this matter.'

Mikami didn't know how to respond. His initial shock had dissipated, leaving him smouldering with anger and distrust. Hanako Kikunishi, the daughter of a member of the safety committee. He was press director, why hadn't he been told?

'I told you before, Mikami.' Akama looked astonished. 'Your work involves negotiating directly with the press. If you knew the truth, what guarantee would I have had that you wouldn't give something away with a stray look, or something in the way you acted? It's surely easier to be assertive if you don't know anything?'

Mikami felt as if he'd tumbled into a gaping hole, and it took a moment for his emotions to respond. *Be assertive . . . if you don't know anything . . .* The fact of the matter was that he *had* been assertive with the press. He'd been aggressive, even, and all because Akama had kept him out of the loop.

I don't understand why you're so worked up. You know the trend in reporting is increasingly heading towards anonymity.

That's how scary it is. To face having your name in the papers.

Maybe she's the daughter of someone important. He had actually shouted Yamashina down after the man's snide accusation.

He'd been made to act the fool.

Mikami dropped his head to the floor. He felt his face and body flush as a burning shame, furnace-like in its force, began to well up inside him. He'd put on a serious face and made a stand against the reporters, but he'd been ignorant. He could argue that the words hadn't been his own. That he'd simply been carrying out his duty. Yet, he also knew he hadn't stood there simply as a mouthpiece relaying Akama's directions. Was it truly acceptable to give the press full responsibility over dealing with a pregnant woman? Mikami had seen the sense in the position the Prefectural HQ had taken. It was why he'd spoken out, why he'd thought hard about how to put an end to the endless struggle.

But . . .

The HQ's position had been a sham. An utter sham.

Mikami pressed his eyes shut. Akama was right. He *had* told Mikami before. *You can hardly say anything if you don't know anything. Right?* He was a fool for having forgotten. It wasn't the first time something like this had happened. Hadn't Akama always, from the very beginning, sought to treat him as a puppet?

'Anyway, that's by the by. Do you have an update on the arrangements for visiting Amamiya's house?'

Mikami didn't reply. He had reopened his eyes but was still unable to meet the other man's gaze.

'Is something the matter? Speak up.'

Mikami maintained a resolute silence.

Akama's upper body jerked forwards from the couch. His hands came together in a sharp clap, like a sumo wrestler gearing up to attack.

'Look. At. Me.'

Mikami's eyes grew large. His panic reflex kicked in, but the signal was weak. Ayumi's features wavered like a mirage, buckling under the force of his indignation.

Akama slowly looked him up and down, measuring his reaction. His lips came together in a tapered smile. 'It wouldn't do for you to misunderstand, so let me make one thing clear. It would be unwise for you to assume, if you were to be dismissed from your position as press director, that you would ever be returned to Criminal Investigations.'

The image of a resignation letter flashed into Mikami's mind.

In that instant he felt himself lose control of his emotions. *That's it. I'm done for. This is the last time. Why the hell should I have to lick the boots of this sadist masquerading as an officer?* The image of Ayumi disappeared.

Another jumped into its place.

This time it was Minako, her eyes despairing and dark, entreating. Mikami's head seemed to lurch violently. He saw the dance of snowflakes. A white cloth, the ashen face of a district captain, the pallid, lifeless features of a young girl . . . the images tore across his retina in quick succession. Minako's hopes were pinned on each of his 260,000 colleagues. She was counting on their eyes and ears.

Someone was speaking in the distance.

'What is happening with Amamiya?'

No reply.

'Mikami, I am asking you a question. Please respond.'

Akama's voice was close. Too close.

Mikami looked up. He realized his mouth was trembling. 'I . . . we're still in discussions.' The words seemed to sap at his strength.

'Well, look sharp. I need to report to the commissioner's office early next week. Now, there's one more thing you should probably know. The pensioner Committee Member Kato's daughter ran into – he passed away just an hour ago. I have already relayed instructions to Sakaniwa that he not mention this unless the press specifically ask. I expect you to show the same discretion.'

Akama got to his feet. He was a good ten centimetres shorter than Mikami, but it felt as though his eyes were bearing down on him from a great height.

16

The windows in Media Relations had no view. The field of vision was blocked by the archive building, built close enough almost to graze the HQ's main building. Mikami was sitting back in his chair, half turned so he was staring vacantly out at the rusted, red-brown wall of the archive. It wasn't that he was daydreaming. He doubted he would ever have the time to indulge in such an activity, not until the day he died.

A serious accident had become a fatal accident.

It had once been the case that accidents listed as 'fatal' only included those in which the victim died within twenty-four hours of it taking place. It was a trick the police had used to bring down the number of cases involving fatalities. The press had launched an offensive, and now the force integrated deaths outside the twenty-four-hour period into the statistic.

Hiding the fact that the driver was a daughter of a committee member; concealing the fact that the pensioner had died. It was a perfect example of the police seizing control of the process, 'from the beginning to the end'. A noise prompted Mikami to look around; Mikumo had just placed a fresh mug of tea on his desk. He glimpsed the thin frame of someone about to leave the room behind her, an SLR camera in hand.

'And where are you off to?'

Kuramae flinched and came to a stop, backtracking a little before he replied. 'Just Fureai park. The police band is putting on a mini concert, so I thought I could go take a few shots . . .'

The response already in Mikami's throat came straight out. 'Get Mikumo to do it. Didn't I give you instructions to go next door? Hurry up and get over there. I want you to get at least a couple of them on our side.'

Kuramae was standing bolt upright, utterly pale. Mikami averted his gaze. He'd seen an image of himself, superimposed neatly over the man. Kuramae excused himself. Mikumo followed from behind, the camera he'd given her over her shoulder. Mikami made a call, took a quick sip of the tea, then walked sharply out of the office.

The outside world appeared somehow different.

Perhaps it was because he'd become resigned to being Akama's guard dog. He would fully commit to his role as a puppet of Administrative Affairs. He'd made his decision. Now he knew he'd lost even the option of handing in his notice, he no longer cared about the content of his work.

He would keep his mouth shut and do as he was told. He would get results and see it through. That was all there was to it.

There was no reason to let it get to him. Wasn't it what he'd always done? He'd delivered a psychotic killer who had disembowelled three women to the execution chamber. He'd reduced a mayor who had resorted to taking bribes to support his lovers to a grovelling mess in the interrogation room. He'd waged a psychological battle with a con man with an IQ of 160, emerging victorious after staring into his eyes for twenty-two days in a row. He had no reason to consider himself any less capable – having come through the bloodbath of Criminal Investigations, following orders, getting the results – than the office executives who spent their days in a more mundane, nine-to-five existence.

He could play the ferocious watchdog. All he had to do was fight his way through the current situation, through the department itself, then finally gouge out Akama's throat.

As he walked down the corridor Mikami checked his watch. It

was just after 10 a.m. They had less than six hours until the deadline the Press Club had set for their response.

He reflected on the situation with a cool head.

He couldn't reveal the woman's identity. And he couldn't 'think out loud'. Which meant that, at 4 p.m., he would have to enter the Press Club and refuse their terms. The reporters would go on the rampage and descend on the captain's office; they would force him to accept their written protest. If he failed to act, the unthinkable would become reality.

There was only one way he could ensure a soft landing without compromising the department's position. He had to get the press to agree to leave the written protest with either himself or Ishii, then consign it to sleep for ever in the depths of an Administrative Affairs safe.

Akikawa had intimated that the Press Club would hold another meeting after the announcement was made. That was where the outcome would be decided. *I propose, this time, that we leave the protest with Mikami.* He would have to make sure somebody raised the motion. Even given the uncertainty of the club's 'chemical reaction', he suspected Suwa would be able to narrow down a list of reporters who might be receptive to the idea. If they were thorough enough in laying the groundwork, they would be able to convince at least a few of those already on the fence.

The main obstacle would be the hard-liners, those who insisted on protesting directly to the captain. It was no doubt correct to assume that they had overwhelmed the moderates. The issue came down to numbers. They stood no chance of victory, even if the issue was taken to a majority vote, without first converting a few of the more vocal agitators.

I need some kind of hook.

Mikami climbed the stairs to the fourth floor. The entire floor belonged to Criminal Investigations. It had the smell of his old stomping ground. The air was clearly different to that on the first floor. *Criminal Investigations, Second Division*. Mikami pushed open the dark, blackened door.

Kazuo Itokawa's head rose to greet him. His desk, that of assistant chief, had been Mikami's until the spring. Mikami had called ahead from Media Relations in order to confirm that Division Chief Ochiai was out of the office. In the regions, the post of Second Division Chief was essentially a spot reserved for young career officers. Their network meant Akama would immediately learn of Mikami's visit if he showed up in front of Ochiai. Mikami gestured to Itokawa to follow him, crossing into the detectives' office in the next room. He stepped into the 'soft' interrogation room at the far back of the office, then closed the door behind them.

'I owe you one for yesterday,' Mikami said, opening up a folding chair.

'Oh, remind me what for?'

'The kind welcome you gave a member of my staff: Kuramae.'

'Ah, that. I hadn't meant to—'

'No scraps for us dogs, right?'

Itokawa's eyes betrayed a flash of panic.

He was four years younger than Mikami and had worked under him for three years when Mikami had led a team in Nonviolent Crime, First Division. He was good. Especially when it came to numbers. The skill had stayed with him after he'd completed a bookkeeping course he'd enrolled on in vocational high school.

Itokawa settled into the seat across from him; Mikami put both elbows on the metal table and clasped his hands together. Between two detectives, there was no need for preamble.

'Where are you with the bidding over the museum?'

'It's in order, I guess.'

'You've made eight arrests so far?'

'That's right.'

'Is the CEO in today?'

'Well, I couldn't say . . .' Itokawa said, clearly not telling the truth.

Mikami tipped his head to one side, exaggerating the gesture. *We've got the CEO of Hakkaku Construction – the biggest company in the prefecture – in for questioning.* Mikami had received the leaked information just two days earlier, from none other than Itokawa himself.

Mikami let his tone develop an edge.

'The CEO of Hakkaku Construction. He's been called in. Correct?'

'Right, yes. I believe so.'

Believe so?

He was refusing to say for definite. As the division's second-ranking officer, it was highly unlikely he hadn't been informed of whether or not the CEO was being questioned. Mikami decided to switch tack.

'What about the papers? Have any of them started to suspect that he's been brought in?'

'No. Not at the moment.'

In which case, he could use it as bait. Mikami went on without altering his expression. 'Just thank your lucky stars they're a bunch of morons.'

'Yeah, well. Far as I know, they still have their sights on Sogawa.'

'So it seems.'

Sogawa Construction was a mid-size company run by the younger brother of a minister in the prefectural assembly that was plagued by constant rumours of administrative corruption and even involvement with local crime syndicates. Growing tired of this, Hakkaku Construction had severed all ties to the company, meaning that Sogawa was in the clear when it came to the current case. Despite this, however, Second Division had still investigated the company when it had first come to light. The press, unable to declare Sogawa's innocence, due to Chief

Ochiai's continuing insistence that the Hakkaku proceedings remain confidential, continued to trail behind.

'So when do you think you'll make the arrest?' Mikami asked, switching neatly back to the matter at hand.

'I can't really say.'

'Just give me a ballpark figure. Today, tomorrow? Sometime next week?'

'Look, I really shouldn't be . . .'

Itokawa looked distraught. That wasn't like him at all. When Mikami had still been making his pilgrimages to Criminal Investigations, all he'd had to do was sit down with the man to convince him to part, albeit reluctantly, with even sensitive information.

'You've been banned from talking to Media Relations.'

'It's not just you guy—'

Itokawa stopped mid-sentence. He looked ready to kick himself.

Mikami watched as the man's face turned red, imagining how the conversation might have gone if it had been between two detectives. *Not just Media Relations. We need to make sure nobody in Admin gets wind of this.* Admin . . . Administrative Affairs. The Secretariat: under the direct control of the captain. Internal Affairs: in charge of investigating misconduct. Administration: responsible for all personnel decisions.

Something had happened that they wanted to keep hidden from these, the core divisions of the administration. The logical conclusion was that there had been some kind of slip-up in the investigation, that Criminal Investigations had seen fit to impose a gag order.

'Someone hang themselves?'

'No, no, nothing like that. Everything's fine with the investigation,' Itokawa said, flustered.

'All right. So why the gag order?'

'Don't look at me. Though I'm pretty sure it's nothing to do with the investigation.'

'What else could it be?'

'Look, I don't know, but we've been warned to keep our mouths shut in front of you Admin guys. Whatever questions you're asking.'

Keep our mouths shut? Mikami could hardly believe what he was hearing. 'What the hell is going on here?'

'I'm telling you, I genuinely don't know.'

'And you can't talk even to me?' Mikami leaned in some more, but he'd seen that there was no deception or trickery in Itokawa's eyes.

'Try asking the director. I want to know what this is all about as much as you do.'

So the gag order had come directly from the director of Criminal Investigations. Arakida had ordered every officer in his department to clam up in front of Administrative Affairs, without telling them why. It was as though he were trying to imitate Akama's own dictatorial style of management.

'That's why you gave Kuramae the cold shoulder . . .'

'Don't take it personally. What are you after, anyway, Mikami, barging in like this just because I turned him away? Okay, so you don't have much intel over there, but I wonder if you really need to be asking so many questions about the case . . .'

Mikami was suddenly on the defensive.

'I'm just getting things ready, for the press conference.'

'And that's all?'

'What other reason would I have?'

He hadn't meant to hide the truth, but learning about the department's disturbing orders had left him a little wary of revealing his hand.

'Well, if that's all, I've got a meeting that's about to start.' Itokawa took Mikami's response as a chance to wind up the conversation before excusing himself from the room to take a call.

Mikami headed downstairs deep in thought.

The talk had been useful.

While he hadn't been able to extract a date for the CEO's arrest, he had learned that the press had yet to find out about his involvement. Mikami could use the fact that he had been questioned as bait in his negotiations.

The token sense of achievement this gave him was short-lived. His thoughts kept returning to Itokawa's inexplicable pronouncement. *Look . . . we've been warned to keep our mouths shut in front of you Admin guys. Whatever questions you're asking.*

That was unlike any previous gag order Mikami had known. A blanket prohibition on all communications with Administrative Affairs. That was what it sounded like. Akama's words from the previous day forced their way back into his head.

No, your request is to be made directly. There's no need to involve Criminal Investigations.

This is the remit of Administrative Affairs. Surely it would only complicate matters to bring Criminal Investigations into the fray? Once you have the groundwork in place, I will contact the Director personally. Until then, you are to treat this matter as confidential.

Had something happened between Criminal Investigations and Administrative Affairs? The two departments shared a relationship that was the same wherever you went.

It was the same in Prefecture D. As far as Mikami was aware, there were no issues they faced now that could have sparked an open conflict between the two departments.

And yet . . .

Akama and Itokawa's comments. Could he assign the mysterious alignment – like two sides of the same coin – to mere chance? Mikami felt a sudden chill. His mind had brought up an image, of the one man able to engineer coincidence into destiny: Futawatari.

The ace of Administrative Affairs had been acting strangely. Digging into Six Four. Seeking to unearth Criminal Investigation's greatest and most shameful failure. Something must have happened. The conflict hadn't started with Second

Division's bid-rigging; it had started with First Division, with Six Four . . .

Mikami came to a stop on one of the landings. Above him was Criminal Investigations; below, Administrative Affairs. He couldn't help thinking of the landing as a mirror, a perfect reflection of the position he'd found himself in.

17

The deadline was getting close.

'The *Toyo*, the *Asahi*, the *Mainichi* and *Kyodo News* are all lost causes. They're determined to submit the protest to the captain, and they're not going to budge.'

The three of them – Mikami, Suwa and Kuramae – were in close discussion on the couches in Media Relations.

'Who would be willing to consider leaving the document here?'

Mikami's question prompted Suwa to look up from his notes. 'The *Times*, *D Television*, also the *FM Kenmin*. They'll be okay. I haven't had the chance to talk with Tomino from the *D Daily*, but I'm ninety-nine per cent sure they'll be open to it, too.'

The four local outlets. An easy win for Suwa, Mikami supposed. They would have to ask one of them to raise the motion of submitting the protest to Media Relations. Better still, they could ask them all to make the suggestion together.

'How about the *Yomiuri* and the *Sankei*?'

'The *Yomiuri* could go either way. They're supporting the protest on paper, but they're also showing signs of jumping if they think the *Toyo* pushes things too far. The *Sankei* told me they're happy to compromise if it means submitting to the Director of Administrative Affairs.'

'What about the other three?'

'Right, yes.' This time it was Kuramae who responded. He was hesitating, Mikami's earlier outburst having apparently taken its toll. 'So . . . *NHK*, the *JiJi Press* and the *Tokyo Shimbun* are all opting to wait and see. They are against anonymous reports in principle, but don't seem particularly concerned about the written protest. They'll probably side with the majority whatever happens.'

Mikami lit himself a cigarette. He counted the votes in his head. Four for taking the protest to the captain. Four for leaving it with Mikami. Three who were on the fence. One for leaving it with Akama, and one 'unknown'.

The numbers didn't look good.

'Could we get the *Sankei* to agree to leaving it with Chief Ishii in the Secretariat?'

'Not easily. They'd end up losing face in front of the others.'

Mikami nodded once before turning to Kuramae.

'Try the *NHK*, the *Jiji Press* and the *Tokyo Shimbun* one more time. Try to get them on our side by confirming that we suspect the bid-rigging goes all the way to the top.'

'No problems.'

Mikami turned back to Suwa. 'I want you to work on the *Mainichi*. You're free to tell them that we know Second Division has set its sights on Hakkaku Construction.'

'Okay. Although, perhaps, with things as they are, it might be easier to try our luck with the *Yomiuri*.'

'They've run a scoop already.'

Suwa nodded as if to say he'd just remembered. The *Yomiuri* and the *Asahi* had both run feature articles concerning the bid-rigging charges. The papers most starved for a story were, respectively, the *Mainichi* and the *Toyo*.

'So you want me to leave the *Asahi* alone, too?'

'Exactly. I think pushing them might backfire.'

'That's true,' Suwa conceded, then frowned. 'I suppose that leaves the *Toyo*. Are we going to leave them alone, too?'

'No, I'm going to try and get a meeting with one of their editors.'

The *Toyo* relaxing its stance was still the ideal scenario. There was Akikawa's personal influence to consider, along with the fact that the paper was the club's monthly representative. If the *Toyo* agreed to leave the protest with Media Relations, it was likely that many of the others – including *NHK* and the *Jiji Press* – would follow suit. But Mikami knew the relationship was strained, that Akikawa wasn't the type to bite the moment a story was dangled before him. No – if they were aiming to get a quick reversal in what little time remained, their only chance was to go straight to Akikawa's boss and hope for an executive decision.

'There's one more thing.' Mikami lowered his voice to a whisper. He didn't want Mikumo to overhear. 'The old man from the accident passed away. I want you to look into the facts. Make sure the Press Club don't realize what you're doing until the meeting's over.'

After a moment to take it in, they nodded quietly. Mikami checked the clock on the wall. It was just gone eleven.

'Okay, get to it.'

The two men dipped their heads and got to their feet. Mikami also stood. He gave Kuramae's back a light jab as the man made to walk away.

'It's appreciated.'

Sorry I shouted at you. The meaning carried through his words. When Kuramae turned around he was slightly red, and clearly relieved. Mikumo seemed to brighten, too. She stood up from her corner desk, where she'd been hunched at her computer, typing by herself, and walked briskly over to the windows; she flung one open to let in some air. The four of them had to share an office that was cramped and in which they sat at close quarters, and it was easy to feel hemmed in. The slightest altercation or misunderstanding was enough to make it feel suffocating.

Mikami returned to his seat and put in a call to the *Toyo*'s branch office. By a stroke of luck, Mikio Azusa – the man he'd been hoping to speak to – picked up the phone straight away. They had exchanged business cards at the last round-table meeting, but this was the first time they had really spoken. *I've got something I want to discuss with you. Could we meet for lunch?* Azusa seemed happy to agree. *Well disposed to the police* – Mikami was pleased that the man's answer fitted with the impression he had got from the meeting. Hanging up, he saw that Mikumo had joined the others in going out, leaving him alone in the office.

His head suddenly felt clear.

He would meet the editor and buy his allegiance with information on the bid-rigging charges, make sure the protest never reached the captain. He picked up the receiver for a second time. *I won't be back for lunch today.* He'd said this on the way to work but decided to check in regardless.

'Order something from Sogetsuan. You only need to order a couple of portions. If you make one a large, we can heat it up later. I can have it for dinner tonight. All right? Good.' Mikami directed the conversation, ending the call before his wife had a chance to get anxious.

Mikumo returned holding a kettle.

'Sir, is everything okay?'

The question had come out of nowhere. 'What do you mean?'

'It's just that you look pale. Really pale . . .'

'I'm fine.'

Perhaps in response to the curtness of his reply, Mikumo fell silent; she studied him for a while.

'Sir, is there . . .'

'Sorry?'

'Is there anything else I can help with?' Her voice was strained.

'You're already doing all you can.'

'But I want to help . . . with the press.'

Mikami kicked the floor so his chair spun a half-circle around. He couldn't look her straight in the eye. He spoke with his back to her.

'That won't be necessary. Please, don't make this more difficult than it has to be.'

18

Mikami left the station at eleven thirty, despite feeling it was still a little early. Azusa had suggested a Western-style diner not far from the *Toyo*'s office for their meeting.

'Hey, over here.'

Azusa was already there, seated near the windows with a paper open in front of him. Forty-six, the same age as Mikami. His dark features, which had given Mikami an impression of hardiness the last time they'd met, now seemed to suggest – perhaps because it was midwinter – a hard-to-shake bout of ill-health.

'Sorry I'm late.' Mikami dipped his head and seated himself across the table.

'Not at all, I got here too early. So many odd jobs to do in the office. Your call gave me a good chance to sneak out for a bit.'

Face to face, the effect changed and Azusa seemed the very image of good health; he was more easy-going than Mikami remembered.

'Your reputation precedes you, Mikami. When you led a team in Second Division, is it true that you arrested no less than *three* heads of local government on charges of corruption?'

'That was a long time ago.'

'And you spent time in First Division, too?'

'I did. About half my time in each.'

'How about when Shoko was kidnapped?'

'Special Investigations, First Division. As chance would have it.'

'Right in the middle of it, then. What's a kidnapping if not

special? You know, I covered all sorts back when I was in Tokyo.'
Azusa used this to transition smoothly into a run of stories from
when he was chief reporter for the Metropolitan Police, dressing
up his accomplishments to sound like failures. Mikami struggled
to find an opening, and it wasn't until they'd both cleared away
their curries and been given their coffees that Azusa broached the
subject himself.

'I assume you're here to request that I put a stop to the protest?'
Mikami put his mug, which he was already sipping from, back
down on the table. Azusa's sudden change of subject had almost
caused him to spill its contents.

He carefully rearranged the front of his jacket.

'Yes, that's the gist of it. Is there anything you can do to make
them give it to me?'

'I see. Well, I do agree that it's a tad excessive to go straight to
the captain. But I do have to consider the sentiments of my men
in the field . . . and it does seem that your office bears some of the
responsibility for getting them so worked up.'

'I'll admit to that. But the fact remains that the main party
here is a pregnant woman.'

'I understand your point of view on this. But I must also say . . .'
Azusa began to discuss anonymous reporting. While he threw
some of his own theories into the mix, the general thrust was no
different to the argument of the younger reporters. Mikami stole
a glance at his watch as he nodded. It was after one o'clock. The
deadline was less than three hours away.

'Azusa-san,' Mikami said, trying to wrest back the conversation. 'I'm sure, with your knowledge of the police, that you
understand the gravity of a protest landing with the captain of a
prefectural headquarters. I'm not saying you shouldn't protest at
all. However, looking at the precedents, wouldn't you agree it is
perhaps more suitable – at least at first – to lodge the protest with
either the Secretariat or with General Affairs?'

'Hmm. Well, that does seem to be the case.'

He could push it through.

Akikawa is under pressure from this editor with a background in police reporting. Mikami was beginning to suspect that Suwa's information was something Akikawa had made up, maybe to justify himself after Media Relations had footed the bill for his drinks. There was nothing stubborn or radical about the man sitting before him now. Unless the impression was something Azusa was putting on for his benefit, using the techniques he'd perfected in Tokyo.

Mikami pressed again for an answer.

'I don't mean to suggest this isn't an important issue, but it would be unfortunate if we were to let it harm the relationship between the club and the headquarters. If you would be willing to offer your assistance this time . . .'

Mikami had stressed the last sentence.

Azusa looked thoughtful as he answered. 'Very well. Seeing as you went to all this trouble, I'll see if I can talk with Akikawa. As I mentioned earlier, however, my men have an emotional investment in these things, and I'm afraid I won't be able to guarantee his reaction. You are trying to take this over his head, after all.'

Mikami nodded, suppressing any other reaction. A thought had taken shape. He wanted Akikawa to feel the humiliation of having someone bypass your authority. Even so, Azusa appeared to be steering the conversation to an inconclusive end.

'I can't make you any promises. Don't hold it against me.'

Having finished his escape clauses, Azusa reached for the bill on the table. Mikami got to it first. Azusa chuckled.

'There's no need to worry, Superintendent, I'm not going to pay the whole bill. I just wanted to pay my due, that's all.'

'Azusa-san. Please, sit down.'

'Mmm?'

Mikami gave him a look that said: *Just listen.* He lowered his voice to a whisper. 'Tell Akikawa he'd benefit from focusing on the bid-rigging charges.'

Azusa tilted his head a little, focusing his gaze on Mikami. As someone who had ascended the ranks to chief reporter for the Metropolitan Police, he would be well acquainted with the kind of gambit Mikami was about to make.

Mikami was confident it would surpass his expectations.

'For the last few days, we've had the CEO of Hakkaku Construction in for voluntary questioning. If things go to plan, we should be at the stage of making an arrest within the next few days.'

Azusa stopped blinking. A number of his facial muscles tensed and relaxed. Gone was the distinction between rookie and veteran. The expression of a reporter landing a big story was always the same.

The lunchtime crowd had already dispersed. In the comparative stillness of the restaurant, Mikami felt confident he'd closed the deal.

19

It was 4 p.m.

Mikami pushed open the door to the Press Room. Suwa, Kuramae and Mikumo followed from behind. The press were lined up and waiting. Mikami was thrown by their sheer number. Over thirty, at a glance. Close to the club's full roster. Seven or eight were seated on the couches in the middle of the room. Others had positioned themselves around them, on chairs dragged from their respective booths. The rest were on their feet, with no space even to put down chairs. With a pen in her hand, Mikumo did a head count. The previous day's atmosphere of hostility had gone completely. The reporters had all adopted a look that said: *We'll wait and see what you have to say.* Yamashina from the *Zenken Times* was standing directly ahead of Mikami, silent and ingratiating. He'd no doubt only taken the front row so the others wouldn't notice his rather half-hearted demeanour. Akikawa was standing with his sub, Tejima, arms folded, behind one of the couches. On the outside he seemed no less composed than usual. But what about on the inside? What had his boss said to him? What was he feeling as he stood waiting? Utsuki, the *Mainichi*'s chief reporter, seemed in better spirits, suggesting that Suwa had perhaps been successful in his attempt to win him over. At the back of the room, Horoiwa from the *NHK* was standing shoulder to shoulder with Yanase from the *Jiji Press*. Their location perfectly matched Kuramae's report that the two of them remained on the fence.

'Right, is everybody here?' Suwa spoke up. 'Good. In line

with yesterday's request, Press Director Mikami will now read out our official response regarding the identity of instigator of the serious road accident in Station Y's jurisdiction.'

A camera flashed as Mikami took to the floor. It was Madoka Takagi from the *Asahi*.

'Takagi, Takagi. I think we can dispense with that sort of thing. It's not like this is a press conference,' Suwa remonstrated, trying to sound informal.

Takagi's high-pitched voice came back. 'I need a shot for my column. I'm doing a special on anonymous reporting.'

'Okay, well, could you do it from the back? It wouldn't be right to put our faces on this – you know we're not the only ones dealing with this issue . . .'

Having restored the peace, Suwa turned to Mikami and signalled the go-ahead. Mikami cleared his throat and looked down at the sheet in his hands.

'I will now relay our official response. After much deliberation we have reached the decision that, due to the fact of the driver's pregnancy, we will not in this case be able to make her identity known.'

It was no doubt the answer they'd been expecting; there was an almost complete lack of response. Mikami continued to read.

'We do, however, pledge to remain open to any discussions with you, the esteemed members of the Press Club, should a similar issue arise in the future. Thank you.'

The second part had been added as a balance. Mikami had made the suggestion, and Chief Ishii had given his permission to include it just fifteen minutes earlier. Akikawa made an overstated nodding motion before opening his mouth to speak.

'The Prefectural HQ's position on this matter is very clear. We will now hold a meeting to discuss your response. If you'd be so kind as to leave us.'

Following their return to the office, time seemed to stretch out interminably. For the duration, the room was dominated by the clock on the wall. Mikami sat on one of the couches; Ishii across from him. He'd come down from the first floor, clearly nervous about the result. Suwa, Kuramae and Mikumo were restless, too. They were each sitting at their respective desks, keeping busy writing or typing at their computers, but their eyes would drift up the wall to the clock every few minutes.

Four fifteen . . . four twenty . . .

A rubber stopper held the office door open by about five centimetres. They would hear footsteps if any of the reporters started down the corridor.

They'd done everything they could.

Moments before the press had convened their meeting, Suwa had quietly approached the four local outlets in an eleventh-hour attempt to sell them on the 'antidotal' section of the announcement. He'd pleaded their case: *I want you all to raise the motion of leaving the protest with the chief of the Secretariat. Be assured, I'll pay you back for this one.* According to Suwa, Yamashina from the *Times* had agreed, while the others had grudgingly followed suit. If all four of them raised the motion together, even the hard-liners would have to pay attention. They would have no choice but to add it to the agenda.

'They're taking a long time. I wonder if everything's all right,' Ishii said. He looked uncomfortable with the silence.

Mikami nodded without replying.

They were probably arguing. The joint motion wouldn't pass so easily. *The protest has to go direct to the captain.* The hard-liners would persist in their opinion to the end. The talks would come to nothing; it would be down to a vote. There were thirteen outlets in total, meaning they required only seven to vote for leaving the protest with Ishii.

There was a chance they could pull it off.

But they were late out. They should have reached their decision by now.

Mikami was no less concerned than Ishii. Various undesirable outcomes were flashing through his mind. With the progress of time, doubts had begun to surface. Had Suwa actually managed to win Utsuki from the *Mainichi* over to their side? Had he really turned the vote? Had Kuramae managed to spread the bait concerning the bid-rigging charges? Perhaps it was his fault. Had he somehow failed in his attempt to tame Akikawa?

He didn't think so. Azusa had bitten when Mikami had given him the inside information on the bid-rigging.

Happy to do business with you.

Akikawa should be under control. He could strut around, projecting the image of the perfect reporter, but he was still just a cog in a larger machine. He couldn't turn his back on an order from one of the paper's senior editors. While it was unlikely he would actually support leaving the protest somewhere else – not in front of the others – he could no longer advocate lodging the protest with the captain.

It all hinged on the *Asahi* and *Kyodo News*. Perhaps on Ushiyama from the *Yomiuri*, who had a personal grudge against Akikawa. Might he have seen Akikawa's about-turn and, deciding now was the time, changed his mind just to be perverse?

It was now after four thirty.

The stillness rang in their ears.

Four thirty-five . . . four forty . . .

They all turned to look at the door together. *Footsteps.* And not just one or two sets. Mikami was ahead as he flew out of the room. Something like ten reporters were already there, gathered in the corridor. They continued to flood out of the Press Room, the flow pushing the group in the direction of the stairs. Mikami glimpsed Akikawa's face in the crowd. He saw Mikami and walked over. As though on cue, the reporters stopped talking and turned to face Mikami. Mikami searched Akikawa's eyes.

Which is it?

Akikawa answered him flatly.

'We intend to take our protest to the captain, right now.'

Mikami went rigid. He heard someone suck in a breath behind him.

They'd lost.

He sensed all the strength draining from his body. It felt as though they'd hit him, as though they'd decimated a sandcastle he'd toiled over for a whole day so that not a trace remained.

Akikawa's face drew close. He whispered something in Mikami's ear.

'Azusa's going back to Tokyo next week; he's got a bad liver. He seemed grateful for his parting gift. Wanted me to pass on his regards.'

His smirking face pulled away again.

Mikami's eyes were open wide. He'd been played.

Happy to do business with you.

A parting gift. Azusa had never intended to pay his due.

In waves, the reporters began to move towards the stairs. Akikawa disappeared back into the crowd.

Wait!

Mikami had meant to shout, but his voice had deserted him. His vision was failing. His knees buckled, causing him to stumble. He felt something catch him around the waist. One of his hands shot up and caught Mikumo by the shoulder.

'Sir, are you okay?'

'I'm fine.'

'You need to sit down.'

Her voice sounded an age away. His head was swaying back and forth. He rubbed his palm over his eyes, trying to regain his vision.

Hey . . . hey . . . hey!

Shouting, like a broken record. Ishii. He was running after the reporters.

'Stop, you can't . . . not all of you!' Suwa yelled.

Someone screamed right back. 'The vote was unanimous — what else do you expect us to do?'

Mikami brushed Mikumo's hand away. *Unanimous? But that was impossible.* Still hunched in on himself, he began to stagger forwards. He strained his eyes, the light slowly returning, and forced himself to chase after the reporters, on half-numb legs. Mikumo tried to restrain him. Again, he brushed her away.

He was approaching the stairs. He grabbed at the clothes of one of the reporters up ahead and ploughed on through; he grabbed again. He looked up. Kuroyama. Had the ones at the front already reached the first-floor corridor?

I will not let you do this.

He passed the *Mainichi's* Utsuki. Caught up with Yamashina from the *Times*.

'M–Mikami?'

He pawed on past the man's apologetic face. Then past another, and another. *Move, move, move!* He emerged on to the first-floor corridor. At the front, he saw a number of people breach the entrance to the Secretariat. He ran. He could run. He sprinted as fast as he could, breaking through to the front. He crashed into the office. Five, maybe six of the reporters were already inside. Immediately, he saw that the lamp to the captain's office was lit. The captain was still there.

The Secretariat staff were quick to react, a number of them rushing over to blockade the door. It was the moment in which the soft-mannered, suit-wearing, dignified men transformed back into officers of the law. Mikami heard something smash. Aiko Toda was rooted to the spot, having dropped her mug on to her desk.

Mikami pushed his way between the division staff and the press. Akikawa's face was right before his eyes. More than twenty reporters were pushing up from behind.

Everything would be over if they got through.

Mikami stretched his arms out to either side, blocking their path. At first he couldn't speak. He was breathing heavily, his spit dry and sticking to the inside of his throat. He dug his feet in and stared menacingly at the press, and that was when he noticed something odd out of the corner of his eye. Futawatari. He was on one of the couches towards the middle of the room. His eyes were anchored on Mikami. *Those eyes*. Eyes like black pits, all the emotion suppressed. It had lasted only a moment. Futawatari looked suddenly away; he got to his feet and turned away. Threading through the reporters, he walked to the exit and disappeared soundlessly into the corridor.

Bastard's escaping the spray.

'Mikami.'

His head span back to face the press.

'You need to move,' Akikawa said in a low voice. He was holding a sheet of paper, folded in two. The written protest.

'You go in by yourself,' Mikami said, forcing a whisper.

Akikawa levelled Mikami with a challenging stare. 'The decision was unanimous. We're all making the protest together.'

'You've lost our trust, Mikami,' Tejima raised his voice at Akikawa's side. 'How are we to know you won't find a way to punish him if he goes in by himself?'

'Keep your bloody voice down.'

Mikami was beside himself; it felt as though the door might open behind him at any minute.

'The representative goes in – that's final. I won't permit anything else.'

The throng of reporters reacted violently.

'That's absurd. Isn't it true that our taxes paid for that room and its thick carpet? There isn't anywhere that's off limits.'

'Enough! This is a government office; nobody is going in without my permission,' Mikami bellowed over him.

'We don't have to listen to this. Let's get in there!'

At the order, the crowd began to move. Akikawa stumbled as the swell sent him careering into Mikami's chest.

'Don't you dare!'

He used both hands to shove them back. He felt hands pressing against him from behind. Suwa and the rest of the staff were driving him forwards. Akikawa was in the same position. Hardly able to move, the two men struggled as they were pushed together. They touched cheeks. Their faces were flattened.

'Give it up!'

'Get out of the way!'

Akikawa's gums were on show. One arm had come up at an angle, the elbow digging into Mikami's neck. He moved to grab the man's wrist and pull it away. He missed, and his hand sailed through empty air before it caught hold of something else. There was a nasty ripping sound. He had the sheet of white paper in his hand.

It was in Akikawa's, too.

The document had been torn in half.

A stillness descended over the room. Mikami felt the pressure on his back ease then fall away completely. The same was true for Akikawa. Mikami's eyes said the words. *That wasn't on purpose.* He didn't say it out loud. He had no choice but to leave the decision on how to act to Akikawa, and the twenty-plus reporters there with him.

'That was . . .,' someone said weakly. It was Ishii. *That was beyond our control.* Again, Ishii.

Akikawa was staring, half dazed, at the scrap of paper in his hand. His eyes came around to look at Mikami. He made a show of scrunching the paper into a ball and throwing it on the carpet. His voice rang out across the room, dripping with menace.

'As of this moment, the Press Club foreswears all previous association with the Prefectural HQ. I propose we boycott all coverage of the commissioner's visit next week.'

20

The news was showing on the muted TV set, marking the end of another day. Mikami was lying down in the living room at home, vacantly watching the screen. They had hardly spoken. *That sense of failure. Humiliation. The thirst for retribution. Regret.* Unable to process fully the entire array of his emotions during the drive home, Mikami had brought them into the house.

His brain still felt numb.

Akikawa's explosive remark had become the consensus. After the chaos, the press had convened an emergency meeting and formally ratified their boycott of the commissioner's visit.

Ishii had been prostrate on the floor as Akama shouted at Mikami, his anger greater than anything Mikami had seen before. *What on earth do you think you're doing? It's unfortunate that we have such an incompetent press director.* But he'd stopped short of discharging Mikami from his duties. His actions had, at the end of the day, prevented the reporters from protesting directly to the station captain. Akama had interpreted the destruction of the document as a spur-of-the-moment decision, not as an accident. What had been a barbarous act in the eyes of the press had been credited as a lucky break in the eyes of the force, and this had mitigated in part the full weight of Mikami's sins.

Hierarchy . . .

The reflection felt like it had come late. It wasn't just the protest that was on his mind. Why hadn't Captain Tsujiuchi come out of his office? There had only been a door between them. He must have heard the commotion. And Mikami doubted he'd have hidden, scared, behind his desk. He'd probably decided to ignore them. Whatever happened outside his office wasn't his concern. Just another commotion in the provinces. He would have appeared untroubled, happy in his conviction. But how was he able to do that? It was because the captain's office was more than just another room in the Prefectural HQ. It was Tokyo; it was the National Police Agency.

The Prefecture D Police had been diligent in their cultivation of the man's near-divine status. They reported favourable information and insulated him from everything that wasn't good news. They devoted themselves to ensuring that his time in the Prefectural HQ was spent in comfort. He was kept free from germs, sheltered from the troubles and worries of the local police, treated instead like a guest at a spa, and when he returned to Tokyo it would be with pockets full of expensive gifts from local companies. *I enjoyed my time here, surrounded by the warmth of the local community and the officers serving it.* They would feel relief as he recited the formulaic words during his departing speech, then, hardly leaving time for them to gather breath, they would begin to gather information on the personality and interests of the incoming captain.

Mikami lit a cigarette.

They'd made him a part of it. No, he'd made the decision himself. He'd considered every option, used behind-the-scenes tactics with the press, then finally deployed himself as a physical barrier, and all to protect this visitor from above the clouds. It felt as though he'd put himself beyond the point of no return. He'd let himself become a guard dog for Administrative Affairs, both in name and in deed. True to the role, he'd bared his fangs to protect the captain. It was fact; he knew he had to come to terms with it. At the same time, he knew he'd be little more than a failure if he gave up now, with the press mocking him, Akama trampling over him.

Futawatari's expression still hung in his vision.

What had he thought, seeing the young reporters storm around Mikami? Had he laughed at the shame of it? Had he sympathized? Or had he taken a mental note, filing the incident away to use in his performance evaluations?

He had slipped away from the scene. Had he been afraid of getting dragged into the melee? Or had he left having decided it wasn't his concern? Perhaps it simply meant the best way to succeed in Administrative Affairs was to be quick to realize – and expedite yourself away from – any potential danger.

Still . . .

The time would come when they would clash. They were moving on the same board. *Six Four. The Koda memo.* Both were fraught with danger. They would bring the two men into conflict, whether they liked it or not. It was an uneven fight. The game was already in motion and yet Mikami was still in the dark as to its nature. He didn't even know if Futawatari was a partner or an opponent. It was only clear that they would clash. That the fight would be bloody. Mikami could feel it, the certainty there in his gut.

He checked the calendar on the wall. Akama had given him a list of instructions to follow. He was to treat the weekend as a cooling-off period and avoid all contact with the press. He was to work instead on the job he'd been forced to shelve: convincing Yoshio Amamiya to receive the commissioner's visit. Early in the following week, at a round-table meeting scheduled for the ninth, he was personally to outline the process leading up to the ruckus surrounding the protest.

Even Akama, then, had reached the conclusion that it was necessary to try to placate the press. The round-table meetings were attended by the managing editors and branch chiefs from each of the thirteen groups that made up the Press Club. While the meetings were usually convened towards the middle of the month, an emergency session had been set up now, in the middle of the unrest, in order to appeal to the executives before the position of a few aggrieved reporters grew into the stance of the papers themselves.

Would it be enough to defuse the situation? Mikami had only been given permission to 'explain' events, not to offer an apology, or even an excuse.

He stubbed his half-smoked cigarette into his ashtray.

He had resigned himself to having to stand in the firing lane at the meeting, but the burden of having to work on Amamiya was heavy in his mind. The task of convincing him to receive the commissioner general felt untenable, regardless of how many times he might try. He could think of nothing convincing to say to the man. And he was unable to stomach the idea of tricking him into accepting. At the same time, Mikami's desire to understand Amamiya's plight refused to wither away. If anything, it was growing stronger.

What was the real reason behind his refusal? Why was he trying to keep the police at a distance?

If he could only learn the answer, Amamiya's acceptance would come as a natural consequence. Mikami felt sure of it. For now, however, the best he could do – and still call it fair play – was to make an advance visit to the Investigative Team and see what they could offer him. The detectives would have to have some kind of insight into Amamiya's current emotional state, into why it had changed over time.

His main concern was the gag order, imposed by Director Arakida himself. That, and whatever it was Futawatari was up to . . .

But that's all for tomorrow.

Mikami dragged himself out from the *kotatsu* and changed into his pyjamas. Keeping quiet, he walked down the corridor and into the bathroom. He twisted the tap a fraction and used the thin stream of water to wash his face, in silence. His exhaustion clung to the mirror. *This unfortunate face.* The thought had come to him countless times. With no means to switch it for another, or to throw it away, he'd put up with it for forty-six years. The wrinkles had grown noticeably more pronounced under his eyes and on his forehead. The skin was beginning to loosen over his cheeks. He only needed to age a little more, another three or five years, and people would stop commenting on his resemblance to Ayumi.

She's alive, of course she is.

It was because she was alive that she hadn't been found. She was in hiding, that was all. And she had chosen somewhere no one knew; that was why she hadn't turned up. Hide and seek. Tag. She'd loved to pester him to play with her, jumping around like a puppy when he got home from work or was off duty.

Recoiling suddenly, Mikami turned around.

He thought he'd heard something.

He shut off the tap and concentrated on listening.

This time he heard it clearly. The doorbell.

It was almost midnight. He flew out of the bathroom before he'd had time to think. His heart was thumping in his chest. Minako had come out of the bedroom. He took her by the shoulders, gently moving her to one side as he raced the length of the corridor. He switched on the hall light and stepped barefoot down from the tatami, bracing himself as he opened the door.

Cold air. Fallen leaves. A man's shoes.

Yamashina from the *Zenken Times* was standing outside the door.

'Sorry to intrude so late . . .'

Mikami looked back into the corridor. His expression was probably confirmation enough: Minako's white bathrobe disappeared quietly back into the bedroom. He turned back to face the reporter. He levelled the man with a frosty glare, but noted a curious absence of annoyance. Yamashina's nose was bright red. His collars were up and he was rubbing his hands to keep warm.

'Get the hell inside.' Mikami motioned him into the hall before shutting the door on the icy wind.

'I'm sorry about what happened.' Yamashina gave Mikami an apologetic bow, then volunteered an explanation of the events of the club's meeting. He said that Akikawa had been the one behind it all. 'It was the first thing he brought up. That you'd been using dirty tricks to get some of us on your side. That we'd be playing into your hands if we let you split us apart. Then Utsuki . . . from the *Mainichi* . . . he started to join in. After that, we couldn't really suggest leaving the protest with someone else. Fact is, even the local papers started to get angry. Can't blame them, really. I mean, they'd been ready to help out, then they learn you've been dealing with the hard-liners behind their backs . . .'

Mikami said nothing, just listened. For the most part, things fell into place. When he'd first heard that the decision had been unanimous, his reaction had gone beyond mere surprise and anger; he'd simply felt deflated. But he saw now how it might have happened. Their strategy had backfired. And Mikami's own idea of trying to make a deal with the *Toyo* had been the main culprit. By electing to take the matter to Azusa – and over Akikawa's head – Mikami had provoked the latter's anger. Akikawa had taken the story on the bid-rigging as his due, and launched a full-scale retaliation to expose the backhand tactics of Media Relations. The other reporters had started jumping at shadows. Utsuki had started to feel nervous for having been party to the talks with Suwa. *If I'm not careful, I'll end up isolated in the club.* The fear, no doubt, drove his decision to switch sides.

'Still, he's good.'

'Akikawa?'

'Yeah. I'm pretty much universally hated now.'

'Not that I think Akikawa has anything against you personally, or that he's hell-bent on attacking Media Relations,' Yamashina said, assuming the look of someone who knew what he was talking about. 'His target's higher up. You know, the suits . . . the career officers. He's got a bit of an inferiority complex when it comes to people from Tokyo University. That's why

he's being so vocal about protesting directly to your captain . . .
he wants to take a shot at the big cheeses. Basically, he gets off on
acting like he's an equal, wants the attention.'

'There's nothing wrong with the university he went to.'

'Not for most people, sure. But he got a little drunk once when
we were out together, confided in me about it. Both of his parents
graduated from Tokyo University. He'd been on track to go
himself. When he failed his entrance exams, he told me he seriously considered killing himself.'

Knowing who all this was coming from, Mikami was only
half listening. Yamashina's voice dropped to a whisper.

'Anyway, was it true?'

'Was what true?'

'You know, were you really . . . coming to us in secret?'

That was the real reason for his visit – he hadn't come over to
offer an apology. He would know from experience that, if Suwa
had been approaching certain reporters behind the scenes, he
would have used stories or other incentives as bait; that Mikami
would have something Yamashina could use, and that he might
have already leaked it to some of the other papers.

'Take a seat.'

The two men lowered themselves on to the cold step marking
the threshold of the corridor. Mikami felt ready to sympathize
with the mindset of the defeated. Reporters who lacked the flair
to secure leads by themselves would sometimes appear on the
doorsteps of media officials at night. Having failed to pick up a
story, despite repeated trips to see various detectives, they would
knock at the doors of Media Relations staff in the desperate hope
of procuring scraps. It was taboo. Media Relations had been established with the express purpose of equalizing all communications
to the press. There was no doubt that Yamashina was burning
with shame. To visit Mikami was the same as admitting he was a
second- or third-rate reporter, that he lacked the ability to stand
his ground with the detectives. Even then, he'd been compelled to

visit. The mindset of a reporter who couldn't land a story was no different to that of a used-car salesman who couldn't sell a car, or a life-insurance salesperson who couldn't sell a policy.

His discomfort getting the better of him, Yamashina avoided the direct approach.

'Has the beauty queen gone to bed?'

'Yeah.'

'And Ayumi?'

'Yeah, Ayumi, too.'

Yamashina had been coming around every now and then ever since he started working for the *Times*. He had a gift for joking around and often had Minako – and Ayumi, before she fell ill with her anxiety – in stitches. Even when Mikami was preoccupied about his 'criminal record', he had often, until he banned Minako from letting reporters into the house, emerged from his bath at night to find Yamashina standing in his living room.

Mikami was suddenly struck with an odd thought. While his emergence from exile had resulted in him feeling allergic to reporters, he had still, in his following years as a detective, responded to them whenever they turned up outside his door at night. He'd felt something that was neither a sense of camaraderie, nor a feeling of being stuck with them. Their positions were different but they were tracking the same cases. They shared an almost kindred fanaticism.

But did that apply to the man sat next to him? He hadn't changed. He might have been in relatively high spirits, but he was the same old loser, still unable to land a story. And the guy was having a rough time. Two months earlier, Otobe, one of the paper's more competent chiefs, had been headhunted by the *Yomiuri*, leaving Yamashina to fill the position, despite his lack of experience.

The *Toyo* would no doubt run an exposé on the CEO of Hakkaku Construction in the next day's morning edition. It was a big scoop, one they'd only been able to get because of their insistence on protesting to the captain. The exclusive would leave Yamashina with nothing to do but drown his sorrows, despite having agreed to Mikami's conditions and tried to help him save face. Mikami gave a disgusted snort.

He would still make his deadline. The words were already on their way out when Yamashina started to speak.

'Ayumi's shoes . . . I can see they're gone.'

Mikami stared, wide-eyed.

Still looking down, Yamashina continued. 'You know, we can try and help, too. We know the area, we've got feelers all over the place . . .' He spoke in a monotone, the words conveying any number of potential meanings. He looked up and met Mikami's gaze.

On display were the brittle fangs of a stray mongrel, ready to break.

21

The gag order was real.

Earlier that morning Mikami had called Kusano, a contemporary who had been part of the Six Four Investigative Team. While they weren't that close, they knew each other well enough to get a can of coffee each time they met. *I've got something I need to ask you, concerning Yoshio Amamiya.* Kusano had become flustered the moment Mikami had said the words, ending the call and saying he was on his way out.

It was Saturday – a day off for anyone who wasn't working shifts. Mikami connected call after call. The four people he knew relatively well had all told him they were too busy to meet him. The way they'd spoken clearly suggested that they'd been ordered to keep quiet. Akusawa – the fifth person on his list – had broken into apologies the moment Mikami introduced himself. *Sorry, but I can't talk about it. No hard feelings, okay?* Hearing the fear in the man's voice, Mikami had finally been forced to admit that Criminal Investigations had decided, out of enmity or perhaps even hostility, to keep Administrative Affairs out of the loop.

The Iron Curtain.

The outmoded phrase popped into Mikami's thoughts. He had only half believed what Itokawa had suggested in Second Division, just one day earlier, but it had all been true. And the gag order, which had seemingly originated from Director Arakida himself, wasn't even limited to Second Division – it had permeated the entirety of First Division, too.

He shook his head and went outside to collect the post. It was usually his first task of the day to read through the morning papers, but he'd put it off until now. He skimmed through all eight papers. As expected, the headlines in the local section of the *Toyo* and the *Times* jumped out from the page.

Hakkaku Construction CEO Facing Police Questioning.
Possible Arrest Once Charges Confirmed.

Mikami felt the shame fan out inside him. The intentions behind it aside, each of the scoops had come from Media Relations, from his own mouth. He felt a wave of frustration. Akikawa's triumphant grin. The sight of Yamashina charging off to make the morning's deadline. He had no doubt that, for both of them, this was a morning to celebrate.

What did it mean for Media Relations?

The reporters who lost out would be grinding their teeth in frustration. They might overlook the *Toyo*, but they would be suspicious of the *Times* making the story, too, knowing its weakness when it came to Second Division cases, perhaps coming to suspect that Media Relations had played a role in the scoop.

Mikami sighed, closing the paper.

First he needed Suwa to gauge their mood. Akama's cooling-off period applied only to him, and he would need to know how the other papers had taken the news before deciding on a strategy for the coming week.

'Oh, you're going in today?' Minako called from behind him as he was getting dressed.

'Yeah. I'll grab a bite to eat first.'

'Are you sure you can't take the day off? You look exhausted.'

'I'll be fine, I had a good sleep. It'll be busy – bit of a storm until the big cheese gets here.' Mikami offered a smile, hoping not to cause his wife any unnecessary worry. His mind was already on how to breach the wall erected by the gag order. If he was to appeal to Amamiya's good nature, he would need to get information on the man's situation from the Investigative Team.

He already knew, from the five calls he'd made earlier, that procuring the information was going to be no easy task. His connections and friendships wouldn't be much help. There would be nothing he could do if, like Akusawa, they started to fend him off with regretful apologies. Trying to find an opening wouldn't work; to get through the gag order he first needed to track down the real reason Criminal Investigations had seen fit to impose it.

The internal line started to ring in the corridor. When it had been set up, they'd added a long cord so Mikami could carry it into the bedroom or the living room. Mikami took the receiver in his hand, Chief Ishii and Suwa taking up equal space in his mind.

'Sorry to call at the weekend.' It was Assistant Chief Itokawa from Second Division. His voice across the line was muffled. 'The article in the paper this morning, was that you?'

He had to be referring to the scoop in the *Toyo* and the *Times*.

'Nope.' Mikami heard a forced sigh in his ear. 'Have they come looking yet?'

'Four of the papers just came by; I've had another five on the phone.'

'Were they angry?'

'Yeah, frustrated, all of them.'

'What about the boss?'

'Hmm?'

'Arakida, has he called yet?'

'Not yet.'

Nothing from Arakida, who was usually on edge whenever the papers had a scoop. Mikami could assume that meant his mind was on other things.

'Anyway, Mikami . . .' Itokawa began to sound hesitant. 'About our conversation, in the interrogation room. You never heard me say any—'

'Sure,' Mikami cut him off. 'I didn't get anything from you. I don't know anything, therefore, I can't leak anything. Okay?'

22

Mikami made a quick call to Suwa, then left the house by car. He'd decided to pay Takeshi Tsuchigane an unannounced visit. Tsuchigane was one year Mikami's senior, and had been acting sub-leader of the Six Four investigation since spring the previous year. They had never got along, but neither did they dislike each other. And Tsuchigane was living in a home that had belonged to his grandparents; as long as the ban on communicating with Administrative Affairs remained in effect it was a risk to visit any of the detectives who lived in police dormitories, surrounded as they were by colleagues.

The roads were quiet. It didn't take long for Mikami to reach his destination, the residential district of Midoriyama. Keeping an eye on the house numbers, he navigated through a couple of corners before catching sight of his target washing his car outside the front of his house, his back to Mikami. He turned around, looking like a man enjoying his day off, but his expression reverted to the familiar downcast one the moment he realized it was Mikami in the driver's seat.

'Long time no see,' Mikami called out from the car window.

Tsuchigane's eyes drifted down to the tip of his hose. 'It's just as you see Mikami – I'm out here, washing my car in the freezing cold so I can take my wife to the department store to pick out some year-end holiday gifts.'

He was saying he wanted to be left alone. Quite apart from their intended meaning, the man's words drove home to Mikami just how much the case had faded into the background. A two-day weekend. Even for the team working on Six Four, it was no longer the exception.

Mikami got out of the car and held up the box of udon he'd bought on the way. He knew the tradition between detectives: you couldn't turn someone down once they'd brought you a gift.

Begrudgingly, Tsuchigane showed Mikami through to his Western-style reception room. They sat facing each other on cotton couches. Mikami started to talk, acting like they were both detectives. Despite Mikami's efforts, however, it was clear from the way Tsuchigane continued to avoid eye contact that the Iron Curtain was in place between them.

'I'm sorry to barge in like this, on your day off.' Mikami started by making a respectful bow of his head. Tsuchigane was ranked Police Inspector. This made Mikami the senior officer on paper but, once set, the relationship between two detectives never changed.

'I'm here because I have something to ask you. It's about Six Four.'

'Go on, then.'

'Yoshio Amamiya. Did something happen between him and us?'

The look on Tsuchigane's face changed.

'You went to see him?'

'That's right.'

'When?'

'Two days ago. Caught me off guard, I have to say. He's really turned against us.'

'And . . .?'

'I wanted to ask what caused him to change like that?'

'Couldn't say.'

'I seriously doubt that. You're sub-chief of the Six Four Investigative Team.'

'Look – I can't tell you what I don't know.'

Until this point, Mikami had been trying to test the limits of the gag order. He paused before launching into his first real question.

'What the hell's up with Criminal Investigations?'

'Nothing's up,' Tsuchigane replied, becoming testy.

'Okay, can we be honest here? Just tell me why Criminal Investigations has decided to shut out the whole of Admin?'

'What about you? What were you doing, anyway, going to see Amamiya like that?'

'That came from Tokyo. The commissioner wants to visit Amamiya in person, pay his respects. It's my responsibility to get everything in order.'

'Huh, the commissioner?'

'Don't pretend you don't know. Seems pretty safe to assume the two things are related.'

'Like I said, I don't know anything. Go and ask Arakida if you really want to know.'

'Right. Seems he imposed the gag order?'

Tsuchigane gave a quick nod of his head. 'Exactly, so you've got no reason to hound us underlings. Leave me alone.'

'Sub-chief, are you telling me you're an underling?'

Mikami hadn't meant to provoke him, but Tsuchigane snapped all the same.

'What if I am? Anyway, why bother asking? It's obvious Arakida's blown a fuse because you guys have been poking around in things.'

Poking around in things. Mikami shuddered, again seeing an image of Futawatari.

'Just calm down a second. What do you mean, "you guys"? You're including me in all this?'

'You'd deny it? *It's my responsibility to get everything in order.* Well, that's a fucking joke. Didn't you think you should come through us first, if you wanted to talk to Amamiya? But no, you do it in the bloody dark . . .'

'Why do you think I came to see what you had to say?'

'To make a mess of my weekend, no doubt. Shouldn't you be out buying some holiday gifts yourself? Isn't brown-nosing your seniors the best way to get ahead in Admin?'

Tsuchigane was taking every opportunity to stop this being a conversation between two detectives.

'Stop changing the subject. And look, I seriously doubt the gag order was imposed because I went to see Amamiya.'

'Maybe not, but you're not the only one working for Akama.'

'Futawatari came to see you?'

'Why the hell would he do that? You're here, aren't you?'

'Unrelated. I don't know what he's up to.'

'And you expect me to believe that?'

'So . . . he didn't come to see you?'

'Not to see me. But my staff keep sending things up the chain. He's been asking around the rest of my staff – right down to the new recruits.'

'Down to the new recruits . . .'

'Don't act so fucking surprised. You Admin bastards, are you really so glad Amamiya's severed all connections?'

Severed all connections?

Mikami only just managed to keep his surprise from showing. So it was more than merely a falling-out. Tsuchigane had just told him the relationship had completely broken down.

'So what's the next move? Report in to the boss? Sure. Do it. No skin off my bloody nose.'

'Was that what Arakida told you?'

'What?'

'Akama's minions are sniffing into Six Four. He wants to get the press to cover the break with Amamiya. Keep your mouths shut around Admin. Is that it? Is that what he told you?'

'What else could it be? You tell me if you bloody know.'

Tsuchigane looked genuinely interested. He was speculating, that was all. It had been the same with Itokawa back in Second

Division – he hadn't been let in on the background to Arakida's imposition of the gag order either.

'So all connections were severed?'

'Huh?'

'Us and Amamiya.'

'Still pretending you don't know . . . Wasn't that why you went to see him, to get to the bottom of it?'

'Why did things get so bad?'

'There isn't any bloody reason. It's just time. Atrophy, whatever. Just you wait – if we catch the kidnapper, he'll be here thanking us, all teary-eyed.'

Because they hadn't found the kidnapper. Mikami acknowledged that had to be one of the reasons. But was it the only one?

'You brought Motoko Yoshida in for questioning, in the beginning.'

'Excuse me?'

'I heard she'd had a bad time of it, that Amamiya took her under his wing afterwards.'

Tsuchigane clicked his tongue, his mouth contorting.

'You were a detective, for god's sake. You'd have treated her as a potential accomplice, too, if you'd heard she'd answered a call from the kidnapper in the office.'

'No need to emphasize the past tense, please.

'Oh, really? Yeah, well, maybe if you stopped grilling a fellow fucking detective . . .'

'So there's a chance he came to bear a grudge because of the questioning.'

'See, you're losing your touch over there in Admin.'

'Losing my touch? What are you—'

'Just listen. Amamiya wasn't in love with Motoko Yoshida. He loved Shoko, his one and only daughter. He treasured her. And she was kidnapped, murdered. I can tell you right now – the only person he didn't consider a suspect back then was his own fucking wife.'

Mikami recognized the intensely charged air of fieldwork.

'You know that's probably true even now. They're all suspects in Amamiya's eyes. Everyone – from the workers at his factory to his kid brother.'

Mikami nodded gravely. No detective, present or past, could get away with not doing so.

Nothing had happened other than the kidnapper being still at large. With the passage of time, the relationship between Amamiya and the Investigative Team had simply faded to nothing. It had to be true; this was coming from the sub-chief of the team itself, someone who had stuck with the case from the very beginning. And yet . . .

There was no guarantee that Futawatari shared his opinion.

'I'm sorry I took up your time.' Mikami got to his feet, then acted as if he'd remembered something. 'Reminds me – Koda, from the Home Unit. I heard he left the force?'

Tsuchigane looked instantly wary. 'Right. That was a long time ago.'

'Do you know what happened to his memo?'

'What bloody memo?'

'You know, the Koda memo.'

'That's the one thing I want to ask *you*. What the hell is this Koda memo thing?' Tsuchigane's expression made it clear he genuinely didn't know. One of the officers on his team had reported it to him; that had been the first time he'd heard of it.

'I don't know either.'

'You lying bastard, you set me up.'

'The thing is, nobody seems to know where he is.'

'It's not that rare for someone who's left the force to end up drifting.'

'Are there any leads at all?'

'I don't know any.'

'Okay. Well, see you again.'

Mikami bowed. Tsuchigane frowned and took a step closer. Mikami had suspected he might.

'Go to the source. You find out what this Koda memo thing is, and come and tell me. If you do that, I'll put in a good word with Arakida.'

Their eyes met.

'I'll do what I can.'

'Come on, you can do better than that. I doubt you plan to run errands for the first floor until the day you retire.'

23

I need to go higher.

Mikami would approach First Division Chief Katsutoshi Matsuoka. His hands were digging into the steering wheel. He had learned enough to know that he was on the verge of something big. It fitted perfectly with everything Mochizuki had said back in the plastic greenhouse.

It was Administrative Affairs that had set out on the offensive. On orders from Akama, Futawatari was digging around Criminal Investigation's weak spots. His sights were set on Six Four. In his hands, he held a card called the Koda memo.

But what was it?

Mikami had surmised from Tsuchigane that Amamiya's split with the Six Four Investigative Team was no longer strictly confidential. It was no doubt far from ideal as far as the department was concerned, but Tsuchigane had all but said they'd given up trying to patch the relationship together a long time ago. They had decided there was nothing they could do to stop Administrative Affairs from finding out – if anything, they were showing signs of taking a belligerent 'what of it?' stance.

Keeping one hand on the steering wheel, Mikami lit a cigarette.

The fact that the relationship had failed wasn't the real issue; no, the root problem lay in whatever it was that had *caused* the split. Mikami was increasingly sure of it. The relationship hadn't simply come to an end – Amamiya himself had made the conscious decision to end it. And yet Tsuchigane had flatly denied the existence of any problem. Mikami hadn't sensed that he was lying or trying to throw him off.

Unless . . .

They'd kept Tsuchigane out of the loop. The idea had already taken shape in Mikami's mind. *Something at the highest levels of confidentiality.* If that was what it was, it was possible. If something existed that was so potentially explosive they'd seen fit to block the information from the sub-chief of the Six Four Investigation Team, and if the Koda memo was at the core of that something, then the Iron Curtain policy – which had seemed reckless before – began to assume an air of necessity. One big secret. Something only a handful of high-ranking officials were privy to. That was why Arakida had obscured his reasons for imposing the gag order not only from the lower ranks but even from the Six Four team.

The executive block came into view up ahead.

Matsuoka would talk. *He'll talk to me.* Mikami willed it to be true. A long time ago, he'd worked two years under Matsuoka in the Criminal Investigations Division of one of the district stations. Matsuoka respected his skill on the job and his qualities as an individual. He'd invited Mikami to become part of the Close Pursuit Unit he'd led during the Six Four kidnapping. If it was true for anyone, Mikami was confident Matsuoka wouldn't mistake him for a stooge for Administrative Affairs.

Mikami pulled into the parking area behind the building. The executive block was split into apartments, over three storeys. It contained fifteen households, each representing the individual division chiefs in the Prefectural HQ. Mikami hated the idea of being seen, but he knew he needn't be concerned on Matsuoka's behalf. If Futawatari was the implicit authority when it came to Personnel, Matsuoka was, in turn, the de facto head of Criminal Investigations. Regardless of department, the division chiefs were all aware that he was the *real* head of investigations, and his second role – as Arakida's chief adviser – meant that his official rank was also higher than the others'. His presence in the department was staggering, his determination suggesting he'd made a blood pact with the force. People would turn a blind eye even if he were to receive a personal visit from an officer in Administrative Affairs. And, in Mikami's favour was the fact that the career officers' network of informers did not stretch this far. Chief Ochiai of Second Division lived by himself, and as such was staying in another complex, one with smaller apartments. But Mikami was still tense as he hurried from his car, trying to conceal the sound of his footsteps as he climbed the stairwell.

He already knew Matsuoka's apartment was on the second floor. Number 302. A nameplate bore the family name. Mikami pushed the buzzer before he could even think about changing his mind. A female voice responded almost immediately. The door opened a fraction and a jumper-clad Ikue – Matsuoka's wife – popped her head through the gap. She seemed surprised to see him.

'Mikami?'

'Ikue, it's good to see you.'

'You, too.'

She flicked off the chain and opened the door fully. Her eyes creased in a smile. Ikue had been an officer, too. She and Minako were close. Even so, Mikami was struggling to remember the last time he'd spoken to her.

'Sorry to turn up out of the blue like this. There's something I was hoping to discuss with the chief adviser. Is he around?'

'Oh, he left for work, not too long ago.'

'Did a case come up?'

'No, no, nothing like that.'

Mikami had a bad feeling. Going in at the weekend, even without a case on.

'I see. Good to see you again, Ikue.'

He made to leave but heard Ikue quietly calling from behind. When he turned around he saw she was frowning, looking worried.

'Have you . . . had any word from Ayumi at all?'

The question didn't rattle him at all. If anything, he felt a warm sense of friendship, and the tension subsided from his shoulders. Matsuoka must have brought it up at home. The two of them were concerned about Ayumi.

'We had a call, a while back.'

The words soothed as they came out. Ikue's eyes seemed to double in size.

'When? Where from?'

'About a month ago. We don't know where she called from, though. She didn't say anything.'

'Nothing at all?'

'That's right. She called three times, but was silent the whole time.'

Ikue looked as if she was searching for something to say. Her expression suggested hesitation. No doubt the words 'prank call' were there in her head.

'I'll go and see if I can find Matsuoka in the office.'

The feeling of awkwardness stayed with him all the way back to the car. He drove away with a new carelessness. He'd begun to doubt his own convictions. Hadn't Ikue's embarrassment simply been a reflection of what he himself really believed? *The calls had been someone messing around.* Could he truly say he didn't suspect it, deep down? It felt disloyal even to think it. Something else to add to the list of things he couldn't discuss with Minako.

Fifteen minutes later, Mikami pulled up the handbrake in the parking lot of the Prefectural HQ. He stopped by the duty officer's office next to the building's entrance. The face of a young detective was visible through the small reception window. His eyes remained frosty as he acknowledged Mikami, although perhaps only in reflection of the latter's expression. Mikami muttered a quick greeting as he opened the door and grabbed the key to Media Relations. He stepped back into the corridor, picking up speed the moment he was out of sight again; he began to charge up the stairs.

The fourth floor, together with the offices of Criminal Investigations, were bathed in silence. First Division sat at the end of the corridor. There was no doubt this was his home ground, but gone was the time when he could walk around without feeling self-conscious.

Mikami took a few breaths, edging the door open a fraction. Matsuoka was ahead, at the far end of the room, sitting at his desk with his back to the window. He was going through some papers. He was the only one in.

'Can I come in?'

'Ah, Mikami.'

Matsuoka wouldn't have been expecting Mikami to turn up, but he showed no outward indications of surprise. He gestured for Mikami to sit; Mikami bowed and sat himself on the edge of one of the couches. He was aware it was a weekend. With the Iron Curtain in place, he would never have been able to waltz into First Division and have a one-on-one conversation with a man like Matsuoka on a weekday.

'How did you know I'd be here?'

'Went by your apartment first.'

'Right, of course. Sorry you had to go out of your way.'

And . . .?

Matsuoka's fingers interlocked as his eyes asked the question. From his expression it was clear he had already worked out the reason for Mikami's visit.

Mikami knew he couldn't launch straight into business. He had to contend with the force of Matsuoka's personality. He was the commander-in-chief of all investigations. A legitimate successor to Michio Osakabe. Despite this, there wasn't a hint of arrogance about him. His eyes were enough to convey the breadth of his experience. And it was his unshakable confidence that allowed for his expression of kindly benevolence. Mikami couldn't count the number of times he'd wished he could exhibit such power with nothing more than a look.

'I think it's time I admitted defeat. I'm getting the cold shoulder wherever I go,' Mikami said, smiling. Brothers separated only by age. Memories from his easy-going days in district were surfacing in full force.

'I would hope so,' Matsuoka joked. He hadn't even faltered.

'I tried First Division, Second Division, too; both were a complete disaster.'

'Glad to hear it.'

'Sir, the gag order – does it have your blessing?'

'It does.'

Mikami's smile withered under Matsuoka's casual response. It had been in the back of his head that the gag order had been imposed at Arakida's sole discretion, that Matsuoka had been secretly uncomfortable with it. He now knew that wasn't the case. The Iron Curtain had been granted the full support of the de facto head of Criminal Investigations; it was the department's legitimate policy.

'Can you tell me what happened?' Mikami asked, keeping his voice down.

Matsuoka stared right back, looking intrigued.

'You mean to say you don't know?'

Akama didn't tell you?

It was the moment Mikami's position in Administrative Affairs was made clear.

'I don't know.'

Something formed in Matsuoka's eyes. Pity? Mikami had nothing to be ashamed of. He might have been superintendent in name only, just one of Akama's limbs, but the fact that he didn't know was also proof that he hadn't truly switched to the other side.

'I haven't traded my soul away, not yet.'

It was the best he could muster in response, but Matsuoka did nothing more than blink to show he'd heard. Had it come across as a complaint? Or did he suspect Mikami of only having said it so he'd lower his guard?

Mikami shuffled forwards, reducing the distance between them.

'I know that, whatever started this, it has something to do with Six Four.'

'I see.'

'I went to see Yoshio Amamiya. I know he's severed all ties with us.'

Matsuoka nodded in silence.

The chief of First Division had admitted it. What came next was key. Mikami leaned forwards across the table.

'What led to the breakdown?'

'I can't tell you.' His voice carried weight. Was this the point where the gag order came into effect?

'What's the Koda memo?'

'I can't tell you.'

'Was it what triggered the gag order?'

'I can't tell you.'

'Okay, what about the commissioner's visit? That has to be part of it.'

There was a pause, silence. Meaning: *Yes, the commissioner's visit is part of it.*

'Ask your boss,' Matsuoka said, his voice low as he got to his feet.

'Wait.' Mikami was standing, too. 'I can't be like Futawatari. Nor do I ever intend to be.'

Matsuoka watched him silently. Mikami thought he saw pity in his eyes.

'Sir, I'm asking you. Just tell me what this is.'

No response.

'What happened – between Criminal Investigations and Administrative Affairs?'

'What would you propose to do with the information?'

The response halted Mikami's excitement. His mind raced. *Which side do you intend to be on?* Was that what Matsuoka was asking him? His chest burned. It went without saying. *With Criminal Investigations.* The words forced themselves up from deep in his gut. Yet . . .

All that escaped his throat was a dried-up sigh.

He felt a shiver run through his body. It was as though he'd finally woken up. The whole morning he'd been working to find something he could use to convince Amamiya. That was the reason he was here now: in order to carry out Akama's wishes. Circumstances were forcing his hand, perhaps, but the truth was that he was even now trying to gather intelligence for Administrative Affairs; he was no more than a cog in its wheel.

I'm on your side. He wouldn't say it. He *couldn't* say it. The moment he did he would become a traitor to both sides – a bat, something between bird and beast. A molten thing; he would lose any individual identity.

Mikami's eyes fell to the floor.

He'd been naive. Matsuoka was concerned for Ayumi's well-being. Even now, he considered Mikami one of his own. Yet Mikami had let nostalgia for his time in district get the better of him, let the dam burst on the inner detective he was supposed to be keeping in check. He'd mistaken the proximity of Matsuoka across the table for the proximity of the department itself.

'Try thinking about why the commissioner's coming.'

Mikami looked up at the sound of his voice.

What . . .?

Matsuoka had turned so his back faced Mikami. He'd plunged his hands into his trouser pockets and was slowly stretching his neck from side to side. Mikami was stunned. *Of course.* It was Matsuoka who had taught him the technique of 'thinking out loud'. He'd adopted the same pose in district, without fail, whenever he wanted to suggest something to a reporter who was getting the wrong end of the stick.

What did he mean? Mikami had no idea. Akama had already explained the reason behind the commissioner's visit. It was PR, a message for the public, and at the same time designed to boost confidence that the commissioner wouldn't shun Criminal Investigations.

Yet Matsuoka had—

There was a loud thud. The door to the division opened and Director Arakida strode in, his sizable frame rocking as he did so. He immediately caught sight of Mikami. His slanted eyes narrowed even further.

'What's Media Relations doing here?' He was close to shouting. Mikami straightened his back. He had no idea how to respond. 'That was you, wasn't it?' His eyes drilled into him, now full of accusation. 'This morning – the *Toyo*, the *Times*. Let me guess, you got something from that hotline you have with Itokawa?'

'That wasn't me . . .'

'Well, who the hell leaked the story?'

'I intend to look into that.'

'You *intend* to?'

'That's right.'

'Not that it matters. We'll know soon enough.'

The pitch of his voice had dropped sharply. *Don't think you'll get away with this.* Arakida flicked a glance in Mikami's direction, communicating his message, then he gestured for Matsuoka to follow as he started towards his office.

'If you're not CID, get out.'

The door slammed as he delivered the barbed comment. The number one and number two of Criminal Investigations disappeared into the director's weekend office. They were on full alert. It was as though they were getting ready for war.

24

The north wind stung Mikami's cheeks.

Back in his car he shoved the key into the ignition and started the engine, but instead of pulling out, he took his cigarettes from his jacket pocket. He lit one and savoured the smoke, immobile in the driver's seat as he gazed out of the window, focused on the building he'd just come from. His heart was still thumping hard. He could hear Matsuoka's words, a continuous loop in his ears.

Try thinking about why the commissioner's coming.

What reason would Tokyo have to level its sights on the Criminal Investigations Department in Prefecture D? What was their real motive?

Matsuoka had told him to ask his boss, but Akama wouldn't disclose the secret even if he did. He would kick him out, and say he'd already explained it. He hadn't given any hint of the con man's dilemma when it came to the commissioner's visit. Akama had given orders and left no room for compromise. He didn't trust Mikami, never had. Ayumi's disappearance was holding him back, but Akama also knew Mikami would tear off his Administrative Affairs' suit the moment this leverage became irrelevant.

Mikami checked the car's digital clock. It was already gone 1 p.m. He felt an increasing sense of duty, as well as urgency. How could he get something to use in convincing Amamiya? It had been obvious from the ferociousness of Arakida's expression that, if Mikami simply charged around blind, the gag order wouldn't budge an inch. It hadn't been the look of a man on the defensive. He'd been warlike, determined – and he was intent on keeping Administrative Affairs from interfering. That was it. Criminal Investigations was doing more than simply trying to protect itself. On the far side of the Iron Curtain, it was making preparations for a counter-strike.

You need to start with the Koda memo.

The words formed on Mikami's breath. It wasn't possible, at this stage, to be sure such a document even existed, let alone work out what it contained. Futawatari was operating on the basis that it did exist. Focused on this one point, he was attempting to break into the territory of Criminal Investigations. The Koda memo was the key, it had to be. Criminal Investigations staging a mutiny. Amamiya refusing the visit. The commissioner's real reason for making the visit. Mikami was increasingly convinced the memo was the way to unlock all three puzzles.

It was no stretch of the imagination to suppose that the memo was something Kazuki Koda had written. Koda had been with Violent Crime in First Division when the Six Four kidnapping had occurred, and he'd been one of four officers assigned to the Home Unit stationed in Amamiya's house during the kidnapping. Something had gone wrong while he was there. Something that had resulted in Amamiya losing confidence in the police. The Koda memo contained the details of what had happened.

Mikami felt that he wasn't too far from the mark.

The fact that Koda had resigned only six months after the kidnapping only served to reinforce the theory. The official record of his resignation cited 'personal reasons', but the truth was that he'd been pressured into leaving the force because he'd written about whatever it was that had occurred in Amamiya's home. Either that, or the existence of the memo had come to light after his resignation and the issue was still smouldering away even now.

But . . .

Mikami's thoughts leapt back fourteen years. He'd been there, too. The night of the kidnapping, he'd been in Amamiya's house as part of the Close Pursuit Team. He'd been in the same room as the Amamiyas – and the Home Unit – until after 4 p.m. the following day. As far as he could remember, nothing resembling an argument had taken place during that time. Could something have happened that he hadn't picked up on? Could it have been after he'd left?

Koda had written the memo – all he needed to do was ask him. Yet Mochizuki had told Mikami that Koda had gone missing. Criminal Investigations was also unaware of his current location; unable to track down the source of the fire. It was why they were so terrified of Futawatari digging around.

Whatever the situation, the most direct source of information would be the Home Unit. If he managed to find out what had caused it all from someone on the team, he would be able to infer the subject of the memo. The date of Koda's disappearance, his last known whereabouts – it was likely that the members of the Home Unit knew these details, too.

Mikami looked up at the sky.

The four members of the Home Unit had left directly for Amamiya's house. Urushibara had been in charge; Kakinuma, his sub. Each had been pulled from Special Investigations, First Division, which was where Mikami had been stationed at the time. Koda had been number three. He had been brought in from Violent Crime, his familiarity with the neighbourhood around Amamiya's house having secured him the place. The final member of the unit had been Iwate, an officer from Forensics; he'd been put in charge of recording and tracing calls. His first name refused to surface. He was the eccentric type, a bespectacled analyst with rimless glasses who had transferred in from an R&D job in telecommunications with NTT.

Urushibara had since been promoted and was now the acting captain of District Station Q. At the time, he'd been the section chief of Special Investigations, Mikami had been sub-chief of the same, Urushibara's direct subordinate. Yet it had never felt like he'd worked for him. The section had been organized into two teams which functioned independently of each other; Mikami had managed one, Urushibara the other. The section had little experience when it came to kidnappings. The only real knowledge they'd been given had been the case manual, already drummed into their heads, and the few dusty sets of apparatus they could put to use in such an investigation. They had dealt with a couple of kidnappings before Six Four – one when the owner of a real-estate company was taken hostage by a crime syndicate; another when a violent husband had abducted and locked up his ex-wife – but none that had involved both a child and a ransom. For better or worse, this had biased the nature of the work sent to Special Investigations, and Mikami had spent the majority of his time in district dealing with a surplus of cases concerning serious professional negligence. Just before the kidnapping occurred, Mikami's team had been focusing on dealing with the aftermath of a fire that had resulted in the death or injury of seventeen workers, while Urushibara's had, following a landslide at a gravel stope, been out conducting daily tests in order to build a case for the prosecution.

Even if they had been part of the same team, Mikami doubted he could have ever grown to like Urushibara. More than anyone else, he'd used Mikami's 'exile' as an excuse to treat him coldly, and had also, no doubt to harass him, developed the habit of making coarse remarks about Minako. *How about it, is she a moaner?*

Even so, there had been nothing remiss in his conduct as chief of the Home Unit. He'd helped calm Yoshio Amamiya's frayed nerves and provided encouragement to his despairing wife, Toshiko, speaking in calm and level tones even as he extracted the information necessary to help with the investigation. They had ended up waiting until the next morning for the kidnapper to call. Yet even when the tension in the room had reached the point of becoming unbearable, the occasional conversation between the two men had remained candid and free from accusation.

You should try to rest a little.

No, thank you. I can relax better like this.

It's going to be a long day. You need to sleep a little, for your daughter.

Amamiya had responded by nodding, finally relaxing from his formal posture. At that point at least, a relationship of trust had been growing between the two parties.

What had come next? What had happened to spark Amamiya's emotional withdrawal?

Mikami suspected it would be next to impossible to get Urushibara to talk about it. Whatever his shortcomings, he was a man who had from a young age waded undaunted through the world of criminal investigations. His sense of belonging was adamantine, nothing a promotion to captain could shake.

What about Kakinuma? Mikami hadn't heard anything about him being transferred away from Six Four. If he remembered correctly, the man had joined the Investigative HQ from Special Investigations and continued to work there even after its downgrade to 'team'. It seemed abnormal for someone not to receive even a single transfer in fourteen years, but, Mikami supposed, it could simply be testament to the magnitude of the case. Kakinuma gave the impression of frailty, but he was surprisingly gutsy. He was quick on his feet and could hold his own against a professional architect when it came to his knowledge of buildings and construction. They'd been on different teams and Mikami could count the times they'd shared drinks on a single hand, but there was no reason to suspect he'd be anything but receptive to an approach. The hitch was that he wasn't in a position to think of Six Four as something that had happened in the past. Assuming he was still part of the Investigative Team, the gag order would carry more weight for him than with anyone else.

The image of a man in blue overalls suddenly revealed itself.

That was it. Kakinuma had entered Amamiya's house under the guise of being there to fix a gas leak. Together with Koda, who had been in the same disguise, he had busied himself handling communications with the Investigative HQ: a radio, issuing a continuous flow of orders and directions; a mobile phone – before they'd come into widespread use, larger than the radio itself. With a practised hand, Kakinuma had used them both to relay every scrap of information Urushibara had gleaned from the Amamiyas back to HQ. By night-time the members of the other units had begun to arrive in the house; just as Mikami had, they circled around the back of the pickle factory so as not to be seen. Officers to assist with Kakinuma and his unit. Officers who were only there briefly to collect something of Shoko's – photos, a hairbrush. Matsuoka had been there too. He had formally introduced himself to Amamiya, saying he would hide in the car with him if the kidnapper demanded that a member of the family deliver the ransom. By dawn, a group of female officers had arrived with the specific goal of providing support to Amamiya's wife. They huddled quietly with Toshiko in the kitchen while she continued making rice balls.

A chain of images flashed into Mikami's mind, all of Mizuki Suzumoto. She had come in as a shift officer to help Toshiko. She was Minako's senior by one year, and had also been in Criminal Investigations in Mikami's district station. He had seen her recently, just a couple of weeks ago. Worried about Minako once she'd stopped leaving the house after the silent calls, and knowing that Mizuki had been like an older sister to her, Mikami had approached her to ask for help. The memories of her in Amamiya's house began to take shape. She had first shown up in the afternoon, the day following the kidnapping. She had donned an apron and done the washing-up. She had massaged Toshiko's back. She had made tea and handed it around. And she had still been there even after Mikami had left. Her skills of observation were formidable. What might she have seen? What might she have experienced?

Of course . . . *Hiyoshi*.

The name seemed to come from nowhere. Hiyoshi from Forensics. The fourth member of the Home Unit. He'd been all but invisible, quiet throughout. With no way of knowing when the kidnapper might call, he'd been unable to leave the open-reel tape recorder for even a moment. He'd been as white as a sheet. It was hardly surprising. He was a civilian, an engineer; he worked for the force, but he wasn't an officer. He spent his time at work cooped up in a lab, and, apart from cases when his professional advice was needed as a matter of urgency, he had never been required to visit a crime scene, much less work full-time on the site of a criminal investigation. His inclusion in the team had been notable by its irregularity. Every officer in Special Investigations had passed training in setting up and using the recording and tracing equipment. Even supposing Urushibara and Kakinuma had been unable to perform the task due to their other duties, they could easily have brought in someone else from the section to cover them. Hiyoshi had only become involved because of his background at NTT. Facing its first real case of kidnapping, the Prefectural HQ had grown nervous. Desperate for a strong opening gambit, but showing concern at Special Investigations' lack of experience outside of professional misconduct, the HQ had seen fit to bend the investigative rulebook, pinning its hopes on the expertise of this one man.

Maybe he's the one I need to go after . . .

Mikami felt increasingly sure of it. He had hardly spoken to the man, but he knew Hiyoshi wouldn't be the type to let friendship influence a negotiation. They were both part of Criminal Investigations, but staff in Forensics shared a mindset that was closer to that of an academic, and they were not interested in station-wide power games. He might reveal their secret without even realizing it. It was certainly possible. Staff in Forensics were also, as a rule, not subject to departmental transfers. Hiyoshi would still be there, in the lab.

Mikami tried to contain the anticipation that was rising within him.

First was Mizuki Suzumoto. It was ten years ago that she'd married a banker and resigned from the force; her family name had changed to Murakushi. Although he felt bad going to her with another request for help, it also made for a good opportunity to thank her for the last time. She had rushed over to see Minako the very day Mikami had called. They had sat together and spent a long time talking over things. The network of female officers is small and close. Mizuki had graduated from the same high school as Mikumo.

Mikami took his phone from his jacket pocket. He brought up his list of contacts, but couldn't find anybody under Suzumoto or Murakushi. Cursing himself, and after a moment of indecision, he chose to hit the third speed-dial number instead of calling home.

'Sir, what is it?'

Mikumo answered, already aware of who was calling.

'Sorry to disturb you. Can you give me Murakushi's home number?'

'Mura—?'

'Mizuki, from your school. Mizuki Murakushi. You did say you two sent each other cards at New Year?'

'Right, sorry. Hold on just a second.'

If he'd called home, Minako would have wanted to know what he was doing. Lacking the time to go into the details, he would have only caused her more worry.

'Sorry to keep you. Have you got something you can write this down with?'

'Sure, go ahead.'

Mikami had jotted down the number and was just about to hang up when Mikumo spoke again, sounding rushed. 'Sir, can I do anything to help?'

'You already did. Just get some rest. We're going to be busy next week.'

The cold stares of the reporters darted through his mind. Monday would be another crucial point for the HQ's relationship with the press.

Mikami shook his head and hung up. He called the number he'd noted down. It was a Saturday, so he expected Mizuki's husband would be at home; as he listened to the phone ring, it didn't seem to matter.

'Hello, yes?' It was Mizuki who answered the phone, breathing heavily.

'It's Mikami. Uh, is everything okay?'

'Oh, yes, sorry. I was just on the balcony, had to run to get the phone.'

'Right. Do you have the time to talk?'

'What, has something happened to Minako?' she asked, suddenly apprehensive.

'No, nothing to do with that. Thanks, by the way. You really were a great help.'

'You know she called me, yesterday.'

'Hmm?'

'She didn't say?'

Mikami stumbled over what to say. He hadn't expected that at all. Minako, usually so desperate to stay off the phone, had actually made a call?

'Not yet. I spent the whole night running from one thing to another.'

'So that's not what you're calling about?'

'No. I've got something I need to ask you, about an old case.'

'Something to do with Six Four?'

He was surprised by her reaction, but she was an ex-officer of the Prefectural HQ, and he supposed Six Four would be the first case to come to mind after what he'd said.

'Yeah. You haven't lost your touch. Would you mind?'

'Is it anything difficult . . .'

'Potentially a little.'

'Okay, well, why don't you come over? My husband's out with Yoshiki, playing football. Unless you're not in the area?'

'No, I am, I'm near the office.'

'That settles it – come over. I've got something I wanted to talk to you about, too.'

Her last sentence convinced him that they needed to meet. He wanted to know what Minako had called her about.

'No problem. I'll be there in ten minutes.'

He already knew the way to the Murakushis' apartment. He spun the car around and left the parking area. Over the dashboard he spotted an insubstantial figure crossing the road, causing him to catch his breath.

Futawatari.

With a serious profile, he strode into the main building of the headquarters. Working at the weekend. Was he headed for Administration? Personnel? Surely he wasn't planning to barge in on Arakida and Matsuoka in Criminal Investigations?

The glass of the entrance doors flashed, reflecting light as they closed behind him. Mikami pulled his eyes away, then slowly pressed on the accelerator.

25

The only way to rationalize the size of the living room Mizuki showed him into was to remind himself she was married to a banker.

'You're sure this is okay, with your husband out?'

'It's fine, don't be silly. Find yourself a seat while I put on some tea.'

Perhaps it was the effect of being on home territory, but Mizuki gave the overall appearance of being a little rounder than when he'd seen her a couple of weeks earlier.

'Don't go to any trouble. I don't have much time either,' Mikami said. He heard a laugh from behind the kitchen counter.

'As self-centred as always, then.'

'Probably a bit late for that to change.'

Mikami relaxed. There was something in Mizuki's easy-going and frank manner that compelled him to loosen up. She had a large face with small eyes. Nothing about her fitted the definition of beauty. *And that's what's so good.* The old thought came back to him, vivid and suggestive.

'How has Minako been since I last saw her?' Mizuki asked, setting down a teacup and saucer. She was still working up to what she really wanted to ask.

'You told me she called you. How did she seem?'

'She sounded down.'

'What did you talk about?'

'Nothing important, I don't think.'

Mikami felt as if she'd dodged the question. She was still debating whether or not to confide in him.

'How is she normally?'

'Not too bad most of the time.'

'But not all of the time . . .?'

'She's a lot better than she was.'

'Does she leave the house at all?'

'No, that's still the same.'

'But you haven't had any more calls, since the last ones?'

'No.'

'You know, I can't help wondering—' Mizuki broke off. She seemed to be thinking about something.

'Wondering what . . .?'

Her eyes flicked up to meet his. 'Do you mind?'

'Go on.'

'The silent calls you had. I keep asking myself . . . if they really were from Ayumi.'

It came as a painful blow. First Ikue, now Mizuki, too.

'It was Ayumi. I'm certain of it.'

'There's something I kind of neglected to mention before. We had a silent call. I think it was around three weeks ago. It was a Sunday, so my husband answered; he kept saying hello but whoever was calling just stayed silent, so my husband started to shout, asking who it was, saying we were a police family, that kind of thing, but the phone just went dead after a while. Anyway, what matters is that—'

'Just the one?' Mikami asked, cutting her off.

'Just the one. I don't know, maybe finding out we were police scared them off . . .'

'We had three calls. All on the same day. We're not even in the directory.'

'I know. But we're not either, haven't been for more than ten

189

years. My husband . . . the way he looks, he used to worry no one would marry him. So he rushed to buy this place, even though he couldn't afford it. And guess who fell for that . . .'

Mikami laughed, snorting through his nose. He had never seen her husband, and didn't feel comfortable talking about him.

'Anyway, I mentioned the phone directory and he said he'd only been listed for the first few years, that he'd had the number made private after too many of those annoying sales calls. I checked the new one over there, just to be sure, but our number definitely isn't in there. But we still had the call. I'm sure hardly anyone has their number listed these days . . . it's not like it used to be. It's just hassle, there's no upside to it.'

'True enough.'

Stuffed on to one of the shelves of the gaudy bookcase Mizuki had pointed at was a new-looking phone directory. *Hello Pages. Prefecture D, Central to East. 2002.* You didn't need to check to see it was getting thinner with each passing year. Even so, it was thicker than the North or West sections, which came attached as flimsy little supplements.

'Do you know of anyone who might have a grudge against you?'

'I can't say no for sure. I'm sure some people have it in for my husband. You know, a lot of people were left without work when the bank downsized. They'd have good reason to resent the people who kept their jobs.'

'It's possible.'

'But look at society these days, there are so many weird people out there, there have to be some who enjoy calling up random numbers. That reminds me: Mikumo said her parents had one, too. That was when I called her to organize a get-together for us female officers, not too long ago.'

'Okay. Look, what are you trying to say?' Mikami was becoming conscious of the time.

'What . . . I'm . . . saying . . . is that it might be an idea *not* to fixate on the calls. The way things are going, Minako's not going to last much longer. Mentally or physically.'

'But they're—'

'I know. They're the only evidence you have that indicates that Ayumi's alive and well. She is alive, of course she is. She's a daughter of the police. Officers are looking out for her across the country. They will find her. She will come home – I'm sure of it. And that's why Minako has to take care of herself until that happens. It's your job to support her, right? The fact that no one said anything during the calls, it's really getting to her; she can't handle it. She said it felt like Ayumi was saying goodbye.'

Mikami looked up to meet Mizuki's eyes. 'She . . . said that?'

'Yes, when she called yesterday. It scared me a little. That's why I thought I should tell you. You need to alter your approach a little. I think it would help if you were the one to say it – suggest the calls might not have been from Ayumi. That she would have said something if it had been her.'

Mikami blinked and saw Minako's downcast features.

Usually desperate to hang up, she had actually used the phone to call Mizuki. On the drive over, Mikami had wondered if it was the pain of having to ID the girl's corpse that had pushed her into making the call. Maybe he'd been half right. The silent girl underneath the sheeting had communicated nothing but 'goodbye'.

Mizuki's worries touched on Mikami's greatest concern: that he couldn't trust Minako's outward appearance to convey the truth. *Ayumi had been saying goodbye.* Minako would choke on the despair if she ever decided that that was the truth.

'Okay. I'll think about it.'

'Yes, please do. I'll try calling her again, too.'

'Thank you.'

'Don't be silly. I'm just concerned for Minako's happiness. I'm glad you're letting me help.'

This didn't translate well. *Concerned for Minako's happiness . . . because I know she's had a hard time in the past.* Mikami had previously suspected that Mizuki knew a side to Minako he didn't. Despite the circumstances, he felt his emotions spike, hitting his pride as a man rather than as a father or a husband.

'You went to see Amamiya at home?' Mikami was slow to nod, disorientated by the sudden change in topic. Minako must have told her about it during their call. 'What did you want to ask me about? I was only there for half a day, mind.'

'I need to know when you arrived and when you left.'

'It was the day after the kidnapping, so 6 January. I got there after midday. I think you were there at the time.'

'That's right.'

'I was there until 9 p.m., when Nanao came in to take my shift. How is she these days, anyway?'

For a long time, Nanao had headed up the women officers' section in Administration in the Prefectural HQ – she was the only female officer in the prefecture to have been promoted to police inspector.

'I couldn't say. I never see her at work.'

'But you're both in Administrative Affairs?'

'Different offices. I did hear she doesn't laugh so much now that she's a police inspector.'

'It must be stressful. It's not easy, you know, for a woman to carve out a career in the force. Anyway, sorry, what else did you want to ask?'

Mikami chose the most direct of all the questions in his head. 'Did you notice any arguments or trouble between the Amamiyas and the Home Unit while you were in the house?'

'What kind of trouble . . .?'

'It would take too long to go into it now. I went to see Amamiya a couple of days ago, but he wasn't receptive to what I had to say. I got the impression he was angry with us for something. I'm trying to work out what that something is.'

Mizuki looked at Mikami through narrowed eyes. 'Well, that does sound odd. You saw him about something press-related?'

'Like I said, it's a long story.'

Mizuki chuckled. 'Still a detective on the inside. Tell me this, tell me that, never revealing your own hand. I'd always thought Admin was more about bartering: you scratch my back and all that . . .'

'Nice.' Mikami felt a pang at being called a detective. 'So come on, how did relations with the Home Unit seem to you?'

'The Home Unit. That would be Urushibara, Kakinuma . . .'

'And Koda and Hiyoshi.'

'Mmm.' Mizuki folded her arms in a distinctly masculine gesture. 'I was in a bit of a state myself. You were there, I'm sure you remember. You could hardly breathe it was so tense in there, right up until Amamiya-san had to rush out with the ransom. I doubt anyone could have actually *argued* during that . . .'

That fitted Mikami's own impression. 'What about afterwards? Did you see anything out of the ordinary in the run-up to that night?'

'Cut out that fierce look. This isn't an interrogation.'

Mikami grimaced. If Mizuki ever became a suspect in a crime, she'd give even the best detectives a hard time.

'Sorry. If there is anything you can remember . . .'

'I can't . . . I don't think I saw anything. Did you have anything particular in mind?'

'Someone from the Home Unit arguing with Amamiya's wife? Anything like that?'

'She passed away, you know.'

'Yeah. I found that out when I went to see him.'

'I went to her funeral. Nanao had called to tell me about it. I'd only been there for half a day, but I suppose I was on the team looking after her . . . You know, thinking about it now, I can't remember anyone from the Home Unit being there.'

The shock of this forced Mikami to ask her again. 'No one? You're sure?'

'I think so. But, no, I'm pretty certain there wasn't any kind of trouble. I can't think why anyone in the team would have a reason to fight with Toshiko.'

'Hold on for a second. What about Kakinuma? He wasn't at the funeral either?'

'I didn't see him there, no.'

'And Urushibara, the chief of the Home Unit?'

'Well, I didn't see him. I did have a pretty good look, too. I'd expected he would be there.'

It was hard to digest. Koda had resigned. Hiyoshi was with Forensics. It was feasible enough that they might not have attended. But it was difficult to imagine Kakinuma – a man who had continued to devote himself to the case even after his time in the Home Unit – neglecting to put in an appearance. The same applied to Urushibara. He might have since become a district captain, but it seemed ridiculous that the man who had led the Home Unit would demonstrate such an uncaring attitude. Even putting social graces aside, for an officer of the law it was all but compulsory to attend such ceremonies.

They hadn't forgotten . . . something had prevented them from going. That had to be the case. Meaning it was true – something *was* stopping them from crossing Amamiya's territory.

'Was anyone else there from the force?'

'Yes. Matsuoka was there, and the officers from the Investigative Team. A few others.'

'What was the atmosphere like?'

'One of mourning. What else could it have been? We failed to bring in the kidnapper.'

'What about Amamiya himself?'

'He had his eyes on the ground the whole time. He looked like an empty shell. Like he couldn't hear any of the condolences people offered.'

'And flowers, wreaths?'

'None that I remember. Not from us, at least.'

It was possible Amamiya had refused to accept any. It was

normal for a wreath to be delivered bearing the station captain's name.

'Ah! But yes,' Mizuki said, suddenly louder. 'There was something.'

'Flowers?'

'No, no, something out of the ordinary. But it wasn't anything to do with Toshiko. It was the man with the glasses . . . from Forensics, I think.'

'Hiyoshi.'

'That's him, yes. He was crying.'

'Crying?'

'Off in one of the corners.'

Mikami struggled to keep up. She wasn't talking about the funeral. She was back in Amamiya's house, fourteen years ago.

'Why?'

'I'm not sure. I noticed his head was drooping over the recording equipment, not too long after Amamiya had left. I thought he might have got too tired, maybe fallen asleep, so I went over and looked into his face to check. His eyes were bright red. When I asked what the matter was he just started to cry.'

Mikami felt his neck tense. It was the first solid fact he'd come across. 'What happened next?'

'Well, I didn't know what to say. That was when Koda hurried over; he all but pushed me out of the way. He kept tapping Hiyoshi on the shoulder, saying something into his ear.'

'What did he say?'

'I couldn't hear. It looked like Koda was trying to console him.'

Mikami remembered the scene from the time he'd stepped into Amamiya's house. Hiyoshi, white as a sheet. Utterly overwhelmed. Did this mean it had been more than just stress?

'Thanks. I think I'll go and pay him a visit.' Mikami drank the rest of his cold tea and got to his feet.

'Oh, okay. I'm sorry if I wasn't much—'

'Give me a call if you remember anything else.' Mikami handed her a note with his mobile number.

'About Minako?'

'Either of the two.'

'Okay. I think I've already told you all I know about—'

'Have you ever heard of the Koda memo?'

'The Koda memo? I don't think so. Is that something Koda wrote?'

'Forget I said it,' Mikami said, avoiding her gaze as he made his way to the door.

'Try not to be too . . . distant, okay?' Mizuki's voice chased him from behind. 'Right now you're all Minako's got. She's totally dependent on you.'

For whatever reason, Mikami found it hard to be thankful for the advice.

'Thanks for your time.'

'Call again, okay?'

Mikami thought he saw a hint of pride in the woman's small eyes and wondered if it was because she'd managed to keep her and Minako's secret for another day.

26

Dead leaves swirled around Mikami's feet as he made for the car.

The kind of man who cried in front of others. Sentimental. It wouldn't be hard to get him to talk. Mikami sank into the driver's seat, feeling encouraged. He used his mobile to call Minamikawa. Two years Mikami's junior, Minamikawa worked in the Prefectural HQ's forensics division. He and Mikami shared the same hometown, and they went out for drinks a couple of times each year.

'Hello?'

'Minamikawa, it's Mikami. Sorry for the weekend call.'

'No problem . . . how are things?'

His voice had grown tense. Mikami continued with a sinking feeling.

'I've got something I need to ask you. One of your lab staff – Hiyoshi; glasses. Do you know his address and phone number?'

'No, sorry.'

'Really? You don't know it?'

'I don't work with those guys.'

'Stop messing around. I know you're all like family over there.' Mikami tried to sound confident, but he could already feel his shoulders sagging. Even Forensics had been told to keep away from Administrative Affairs.

'If you've been told not to say, at least admit it.'

'Fine – I'm not allowed to say anything.'

'When did they come around?'

'Yesterday. Out of nowhere.'

'And they didn't tell you why, I suppose?'

'Do you know what this is about, Mikami? I'd like to know if you do.'

'Ask Arakida.'

Mikami snapped his mobile shut and started the car. He didn't have the luxury of waiting until Monday. He would contact the head of Forensics, get Hiyoshi's address, then go and see him in person before the day was out. He could no longer trust the department's neutrality, but he could hope that the head proved to be more amenable – as an academic – than the others.

Mikami was back at HQ in seven minutes. The detective on duty leaned briefly from his window, surprised to see Mikami for a second time in one day. Mikami ignored him and walked into the room; he opened the box containing the keys. The one for Media Relations was missing from its hook. Someone on his staff was in the building. He stole a glance at the hook for Administration. Not there. Futawatari was still in.

Mikami made his way down the corridor, half dark due to the energy-saving policy. He walked into Media Relations. As expected, he saw Mikumo, sitting at the desk closest to the door. She got quickly to her feet. She was wearing full uniform.

'What are you doing here?'

'Sir. The deadline's almost up for the bulletin. I thought I could come in and get a little done now.'

Her desk was littered with proofs and photos, all for the press bulletin. Mikami didn't doubt that her schedule had suffered because of the problems they were having with the press, but it seemed unlikely that that was the only reason behind her deciding to come in on a weekend.

'Sorry I had to call earlier.'

'Not at all, that's fine.'

'Call Kuramae, get him to come in and help.'

Mikami sat at his desk and unlocked the bottom drawer. He

pulled out a list of phone numbers for officers and staff in executive-level accommodation and began to go through it. *Inomata, Head of Forensics.* The sheet contained both his private and work numbers. The internal line would be best. Mikami doubted Inomata would be able to place him from a name if he called his private number. Using the internal line would put Inomata into a state of readiness; Mikami would only need to introduce himself as press director before moving straight on to his questions. He reached for the phone on his desk. As he did, he became aware of Mikumo's profile. *It's nothing she can't overhear.* Reassuring himself, Mikami dialled the number.

After a few rings, Inomata picked up the phone. He seemed perhaps five years Mikami's senior.

'Please accept my apologies for disturbing your weekend. This is Press Director Mikami.'

'Not a problem. What can I do for you?'

He came across as a good-natured old man.

'There's something I need to confirm, if possible. Would you be able to give me the address of someone on your staff? His name is Hiyoshi.'

'Hmm? I don't remember anyone with that name working for me.'

'I'm sorry?' Mikami raised his voice before he could stop himself. He looked up at Mikumo. She was busy moving her pen, her face over her desk. Mikami pulled the mouthpiece closer. 'Are you positive?'

'If the head of Forensics hasn't heard of him, I'm quite sure he doesn't exist. Perhaps there's been some kind of mistake? A mix-up with another department, something like that?'

Mikami was listening for signs of the Iron Curtain, but could pick up nothing out of the ordinary in the way Inomata was speaking.

'And you haven't had any transfers? Anyone who moved on to something else?'

'Not since I started here; not one.'

That was when Mikami realized something. It was only seven or eight years ago that Inomata had moved into his current position. The HQ had headhunted him from the Prefecture D Institute of Technology, having set up the role specially.

'Forgive the question, but could you remind me when you joined us?'

'Eight years ago . . .'

'And you're absolutely sure there wasn't anyone here by that name?'

'I'm not senile quite yet.'

He sounded a little affronted. Ignoring this, Mikami asked his next question.

'In which case, I'm very sorry to have to trouble you, but could I ask you to check with the staff rota from fourteen years ago?'

'Sorry? Staff rota . . . fourteen years ago?'

'Please. I believe, as head of the division, it should be in your possession.'

'Well, I must say it's a bit sudden . . . Don't you have that in the main building?'

'No. We don't maintain a comprehensive list in case of religious cults or the extreme left getting their hands on it.'

'I see . . . of course.'

The confidence had drained from his voice. Seeing his opportunity, Mikami chose to press the matter. 'Speed is of the essence. If you can't find the rota, you'll need to try something else. Maybe you can ask someone on your staff who might know. I would appreciate it if you called me – Mikami in Media Relations – the moment you have an answer.'

'Ah . . . of course. I'll try asking someone.'

'Also, I think you might find that he resigned. If so, I would appreciate it if you could find out the date he left as well as the reasons he gave for his decision.'

He had quit the force, Hiyoshi, just like Koda had.

The magnitude of this discovery left Mikami on edge even after the call was over. Hiyoshi had left the force, too, at the very least eight years earlier. It was possible that, like Koda, he had resigned when the memory of Six Four had still been fresh in everyone's mind. The real question was *why* he'd chosen to leave. Whether the decision had been related to the tears he'd shed in Amamiya's house.

Mikami saw Mikumo get up from her chair. She started towards the cupboard. She'd probably decided it was time to put on some tea. Mikami checked the wall clock: three fifteen. Knowing Inomata wasn't a police officer, it seemed impossible to gauge how long it might take him to call back.

A short while later Mikumo came over with a tray and a mug of tea.

'I heard your parents had a silent call, at their place.' The words came without conscious thought.

Mikumo drew a quiet, surprised breath.

'Mizuki Murakushi told me. When did it happen?'

'Right, yes. They said it was about a month ago.'

'How many calls?'

'They said two.'

'On the same day?'

'Yes, I think that's what they said.'

'I see . . .'

The response hung awkwardly.

One month ago. It was around the same time he and Minako had received the calls. And again, more than just once. Mizuki's call had also come in around the same period, close to three weeks ago. *Look at society these days, there are so many weird people out there.* It was possible Mizuki's comment hadn't actually been too far off the mark. Two coincidences coming together was making Mikami think that maybe someone had been out there, getting off on silent-calling random numbers. He let out a quiet sigh just as his desk phone started to ring. He checked the clock. Only twenty minutes had passed. He glanced at Mikumo as she walked back to her desk, then picked up the receiver.

'Mikami, this is Inomata. I got what you wanted.'

His voice was much brighter. *All right then.* Mikami got himself ready.

'Go ahead.'

'I had a look around and found the staff rota. Let's see . . . yes, here we are, Koichiro Hiyoshi. Is that the man you're after?'

'Is there anyone with the same family name?'

'No, no, just Koichiro Hiyoshi. He was in our physical-evidence lab. Here's the information you needed. First his address: 1256, Osumi-machi, City D. His phone number is—'

Mikami felt he'd had a stroke of luck as he recorded the details. Addresses bearing a four-digit house number were usually in the older residential areas. It was almost certainly the address of his parents' house. And the name Hiyoshi traditionally indicated the eldest son of a family. All of this meant there was a strong possibility he was still living at the address in Osumi-machi.

'I asked some of our older employees, too. Apparently, the reason he left was . . . do you remember that kidnapping that happened fourteen years ago?'

Mikami caught his breath. His hand tightened around the receiver.

'Yes.'

'He took some time off after that, three months or so. When he didn't come back we decided to treat the case as voluntary resignation. They didn't know the exact cause, but it seems Hiyoshi had been posted to work in the house with the victim's family – ah, hello? Are you getting all of this . . .?'

'Yes, keep going.'

'Well, it didn't last long, but it seems he was very withdrawn by the time he'd come back to work. He stopped talking to other people altogether. After a while, he just stopped turning up to the lab. That's the general gist. He was . . . with us for close on two years. Before coming here he'd spent just under a year with NTT. That's all the information I could get.'

'That's perfect. I really appreciate your help,' Mikami said, genuinely meaning it as he slipped the paper he'd written the address on into his jacket pocket.

27

It took Mikami fifteen minutes to reach Osumi-machi by car.

The streets were lined with large old houses, the tall walls surrounding them suggesting concealed, manicured gardens. Mikami parked off to the side of a children's playground. The sun was already low in the sky. He continued his way on foot, using a copy of a local map to guide him. He picked up speed as he moved.

Hiyoshi's family home was situated just around a corner; it had an old, tiled roof and a nameplate set into a stone column that read *Hiyoshi*. It was large even compared to the others. Thick pine branches arched over the road, and there was a white-walled building for storage alongside the main structure. There was a garage, too; the door was closed but, judging from the width, it probably housed a number of cars.

Hiyoshi was from a wealthy family. Mikami felt his enthusiasm wane as a number of emotions, including a good measure of disdain, rose to the surface. Hiyoshi had only been in Forensics for two years; NTT, less than one. Perhaps he was simply the type to throw in the towel each time something bad happened at work. Mikami still didn't know why Hiyoshi had cried at Amamiya's, but the man's tears already seemed to carry less weight. Mikami sighed, then he circled around to the side and rang the bell. It was bowl-shaped, lacking a camera or intercom function, just a single button that reminded him of early Showa, possibly even Taisho.

Mikami waited for a while, allowing for the size of the building. Eventually, he heard the clicking of wooden sandals. The small timber door opened and a woman in her early sixties emerged, dipping a head that was streaked with grey. Her appearance wasn't that of a domestic helper. Mikami decided she had to be Hiyoshi's mother, but there was something about her that suggested a deep melancholy. She eyed Mikami suspiciously, then in a clipped tone asked, 'And you might be . . .?'

He bowed his head, bending formally from the waist. 'Sorry to disturb you, ma'am. My name is Mikami, and I work for Administrative Affairs in the police headquarters. I understand that your son used to work in Forensics. Is he in, perhaps?'

'Oh, I see.' Her eyes seemed to double in width. 'Police. What could you possibly want with my son?'

'I need to talk to him about something that's come up.'

'*Talk* to him? I can't imagine there is anything left to say, not at this stage. Really, we're the ones who need to talk to you. Treating him with such cruelty . . .'

'I understand your anger, ma'am.'

Mikami instinctively switched gear. *Hiyoshi had resigned because someone had mistreated him.* It was possible the resentment was unjustified, that Hiyoshi's mother had simply chosen to ignore her son's frailty; either way, what mattered was that Hiyoshi – and his family – were under the impression that he'd suffered maltreatment.

'Yes, well, it really was unbelievable.' The bitterness twisted her features. 'He was working for NTT Computers, in communications! The police chose him to help with a new case, and, well, when he saw how useless you all were at that sort of thing, he thought he could make himself useful by joining Forensics. Then, of all things, that kidnapping . . .'

Perhaps thinking of the eyes and ears of her neighbours, she suddenly told Mikami to come in, pulling him through the wooden door. It closed behind them. They stood hemmed in between the tall wall and a patch of head-height fatsia, the recess feeling damp and humid despite it being the cold season. Keeping her voice down, Hiyoshi's mother continued.

'It was unforgivable. To throw my son right into a barbaric case like that. Then to call him incompetent . . . after such a tiny little mistake. Don't you people in the police have families? Was that normal behaviour for you? Try putting yourself in the shoes of the parents – we devoted ourselves to raising our son in a loving environment. He was devastated; the whole thing has ruined his life. How on earth do you intend to take responsibility for that?'

Mikami wasn't sure how to respond. The virulence of her anger gave the false impression that she was talking about something that had happened earlier that day or the day before.

'I'm here to offer an apology, and to talk to Hiyoshi if I can. There's still a lot about what happened that we're not clear on.'

'*You're not clear on?*' Her shoulders came up, hostile, as she stuck her chin out in accusation. Her mouth was trembling. 'Are you trying to tell me *you don't even know* what you did to my son?'

'Do you know who told your son he was incompetent?'

'I'm sure you're fully aware of who it was.'

'Please, ma'am, if you could tell me. I am planning to make a thorough investigation into the matter.'

'I don't know – whoever was in charge at the time. I remember Hiyoshi telling me, "I made a mistake, I'm incompetent." Ever since, he's just been . . .'

He hadn't told her what had actually happened.

'You mean to say it was Hiyoshi himself who said he was "incompetent", not somebody else?'

'What are you trying to imply? He would never say such a thing, not unless someone had said it to him first. The poor boy was completely morose, he hardly ate. He looked terrified. It was one of your people. Someone said something to him, and it ripped his heart in two.'

Mikami prickled with each accusation.

'Did Hiyoshi explain to you what his mistake was?'

'He wouldn't say a thing. Can *you* tell *me*? Did he really do something wrong? Or was it someone else trying to make him take responsibility for their mistakes?'

Mikami nodded to show he understood how she felt. He got the impression she'd already told him everything she knew.

'I'll try to ask him directly. Please, if you'd let me see him.'

'Impossible,' she snapped back.

'Five minutes, that's all I need.'

'He won't see anybody. Nobody at all.'

'Nobody at all?'

'Nobody. Not even family . . .'

She brought a hand up to cover her mouth. Tears formed in her eyes and they began to lose focus. Mikami held his breath as he waited for her to continue. In his mind he saw a number of potential scenarios. She looked back at him with reddened eyes.

'Fourteen years. It's been *fourteen* years. He's been shut up in his room since the day he stopped going to the lab. He won't talk to me, to his father. That's how badly you people have hurt my son.'

Mikami looked up at the sky.

A recluse.

The worst-case scenario – suicide – had been in the back of his mind. But this hit him with even greater force.

'May I ask how old he is now?' Mikami asked, forgetting about work.

'Thirty-eight. He'll be thirty-nine next month. I don't know what we can . . . How we can . . .'

Hiyoshi's mother hid her face in her hands. The sound of sobbing leaked through.

The whole thing has ruined his life. Mikami had assumed it was an exaggeration, but not now. It all made sense.

'How do you communicate with him?'

She looked up sharply.

'Just how is talking going to help? It's not as though any of you care. Not after all th—'

'I had a similar situation, with my daughter,' Mikami said, cutting in. A pain ran through his chest, brought on by the knowledge that he'd said this in part to accomplish something for work. 'It's been hard on my wife. She lost the ability to communicate and—'

'Did she come back out?' This time, Hiyoshi's mother interrupted him. 'Your daughter. Did she come back out?'

'. . . yes.'

The ache in his chest grew worse. It was true, she had come out of her room. But . . .

'How did you convince her?'

The hunger in her eyes caused Mikami to flinch. She moved closer, stark desperation on her features. Mikami cursed himself for having brought it up, but it was too late to crush the woman's hopes.

'We argued, just let everything out.'

I hate this face. I want to die!

It's all right for you! It's okay for you to look like that, you're a man!

Mikami felt himself going pale. His head started to feel numb. He prepared himself for the dizziness to come. He stood firm. It passed in a few seconds. He told himself he was fine, and continued.

'We also took her to see a therapist. That helped her let her feelings out.'

Hiyoshi's mother gave a doubtful nod, her eyes flicking to the ground. Her disappointment was plain to see. They'd had fourteen years. They would be long past any discussions of whether or not to take their son to therapy.

'Are you able to discuss your feelings at all?' Mikami said.

She seemed distracted. 'Oh, no . . . Every day I put a letter under his door, but he hasn't answered a single one of them.'

'Have you tried taking a harder line on it?'

'His father did, a few times in the beginning. But it only made things worse.'

Mikami's eyes lingered on the woman's frail-looking shoulders. He was caught somewhere between professional integrity and personal feeling.

'Would you allow me to try, with a letter?'

'Of course . . . thank you,' she answered, hardly listening. Her eyes hovered impassively over one of the windows of the house, a room – no doubt her son's – on the first floor, the curtains closed.

28

The family diner lacked its usual weekend bustle. It was already dark outside.

Perched on a bar seat at the edge of the counter, Mikami glanced down at his watch. Exactly five thirty. The waitress had already brought over the rice pilaff and coffee he'd ordered, but he ignored them and continued to sit, arms folded and staring at the sheet of writing paper. He'd bought a pad from a convenience store on the way and had already smoked five cigarettes from the pack he'd picked up at the same time. *I'll drop it in your letterbox this evening. I'd appreciate it if you could pass it on to your son.* Those were the words he'd left with Hiyoshi's mother, but he couldn't think of a single thing to write.

He exhaled and leaned back into the chair.

He wanted to help. Driven by that one idea, Hiyoshi had leapt into the world of the police. *He wanted to do good.* Mikami wanted to take Hiyoshi's mother's words at face value, but it seemed too nice a fit. Something else must have happened, to make Hiyoshi consider switching jobs after only one year. While not a godsend, it was possible he had seen in the police force's ignorance of computer systems the perfect excuse to escape – painlessly – from his job at NTT.

But in Amamiya's house, his confidence had suffered a terrible blow.

I made a mistake, I'm incompetent.

What kind of error could Hiyoshi have made?

Taking into account his role at Amamiya's, it had to be something to do with the recording equipment. The first thing that came to mind was that he'd made a recording error. That he'd somehow failed to record the kidnapper's voice during a call. Without doubt, that would have been a disaster. It would also mean that the unorthodox move of adding someone like Hiyoshi to the team had ended up backfiring. But it couldn't have been that. Hiyoshi simply hadn't had the opportunity to make that kind of error. The Home Unit had yet to arrive at the house when the kidnapper's call came in. And there hadn't been any more calls after they'd arrived – there hadn't been a chance to make a recording.

Even so . . .

Mikami's thoughts shifted abruptly.

What was Koda's involvement in all of this? It was one of the key factors, but it remained completely opaque. What might have motivated Koda to draft the memo, supposing it contained details of Hiyoshi's mistake?

Mikami knew nothing about Koda as a person. What kind of relationship had he had with Hiyoshi? Hiyoshi's mother had suspected someone of trying to make her son take responsibility for their mistake. An unwelcome thought came into Mikami's head. Hiyoshi's failure had been due to doing something Koda had asked of him. Koda had made a show of consoling the man while actually intimidating him into silence. The possibility was there. There was just one thing keeping in check the idea that Koda had been the source of the outburst, and that was the impression Mizuki had of the man in her memory.

Hiyoshi was the key to finding out. All Mikami had to do was convince him to open up, and he would learn everything he needed to know about the background to the Koda memo.

Mikami put a light to his sixth cigarette. He took a drink of his coffee and, pen in hand, focused on the sheet of paper.

The pen didn't move. Mikami's heart and brain refused to

engage. Ten, twenty minutes ticked by as he sat there doing nothing. His forehead was slick with sweat. The more his impatience grew, the more he felt an emptiness spread through his mind.

To hell with this . . .

He had to admit defeat. Having failed to commit to a single word, he felt an overwhelming sense of powerlessness. He'd been convinced that getting someone to open up would be an easy task. He'd lost count of the number of criminals he'd broken in the interrogation room. He'd got them to expose their every thought, to confess all the lies, all the truths, to discard all appearances and reveal hidden layers. He'd used force: the unrivalled, overwhelming force of the badge.

Mikami focused again on the paper.

What he needed now was words, not force. Something genuine. Something that could reach out to a man's heart.

I don't have them.

If he'd had even a fraction of that type of ability, Ayumi would never have grown so distant. Words were weapons; the razor-sharp tools of psychological warfare instruments that could lacerate a man's heart. Mikami had never changed, even outside work. He wondered if he had ever made a genuine attempt to say something with the aim of actually connecting to another person.

'Would you like a fresh coffee?'

Startled, Mikami looked up. He turned around to see a waitress, probably a student, standing with her head cocked to one side. There was something about the gesture and her smile that looked a little off for this kind of place – she was probably new.

'That would be great, thanks.'

Mikami prodded the cold rice with his spoon. The waitress had looked a bit peeved to see the untouched plate. There was a phrase Mikami recalled whenever he couldn't drum up an appetite. It was something one of his father's old wartime buddies had muttered during one of his visits, a long time ago. *Every time I had a meal, it was like a fresh start.* Mikami started eating, realizing only then that he'd forgotten lunch. *Right.* He decided to blame that for his sudden dizziness at Hiyoshi's house. He ate about half of the rice then put down the spoon, leaving space for dinner when he got home.

He lit a cigarette. It wasn't the fresh start he'd hoped for, but his agitation had subsided somewhat. He breathed out smoke. His objective side was staring at the truth. He wouldn't be able to reach Hiyoshi. He had to forget about him, go after Urushibara and Kakinuma instead, keep an eye out for any news of Koda's whereabouts. The white sheet glared at him from the side of the counter where he'd pushed it, but he knew he was out of time. If there was even a slight chance he would succeed, then maybe, but he couldn't allow himself the luxury of clinging to a task he considered impossible. He couldn't call that work.

He stowed the paper and pen in his bag and reached for the bill.

'Would you like a refill?'

The textbook question chimed in his ears.

'I'm good, thanks.' Mikami said this without looking around; he heard a faint laugh. He froze, thinking for a moment she'd laughed at his appearance. He looked around. The waitress from earlier came into view next to him.

'No problem. Just let me know if you change your mind, okay?'

This time, her tone was chatty. Mikami turned his head and looked her in the face. She wasn't what he would call pretty. She had narrow eyes and a nose that pointed up at the end.

'Oh, sorry, was that annoying? I was just happy. You know, that's the first time anyone here's ever said thanks for something.'

She gave another soft giggle. Mikami was still unable to respond. His eyes followed her even as she walked away. A strange idea had taken hold of him. The girl had been some kind of omen. He could think of no other explanation for what had just happened.

Mikami stayed in his seat for the next hour.

He sat facing the sheet of paper. The pen stayed on the counter. He spent periods of time with his eyes closed. His brain felt useless, like something borrowed. Drowsiness enfolded him. A single image flickered at the back of his retina: Hiyoshi, wandering through a vast, twilight forest. Now and then he caught glimpses of Ayumi threading her way between the trees. She was lost in there. They both were. Although . . . maybe he was the one who was lost.

The letter of persuasion ended up being a short message.

I want to know where you are. I'll come by if it's somewhere I can visit.

Mikami had wasted too much time indulging himself. He added the numbers for his mobile and home phones, grabbed the bill and hurried across to the register.

His eyes tracked around to find the waitress. Perhaps she'd gone through to the back or maybe finished her shift. She was nowhere to be seen.

29

The 7 o'clock news came on the radio.

The lights seemed stuck on red. A powerful glow emanated from the window of a building, apparently a crammer school. Waves of people started to emerge. Navy duffel coats. Tartan scarves. Pink, woolly gloves. A couple of high-school girls cycled by, one then another, both dressed in winter garb no different to what Ayumi would wear.

She said it felt like Ayumi was saying goodbye.

Mikami was on his way home. He had delivered his message to Hiyoshi's mother; by then, he had started telling himself he could get the rest of his work done using the phone at home.

Minako had set out boiled fish with some pickles. *That was quick. Yeah, faster than I'd expected. Let me heat something up for you.*

She sounded energetic, and spoke more than usual. She seemed to be making a visible effort. Mikami didn't really have much of an appetite. The fried rice wasn't the only thing lying undigested in his gut. But he still found himself enthusiastically commenting on how good the food smelled. Seeing Minako in good spirits was like seeing the sun through a cloudy sky. He learned the reason soon afterwards.

'Mizuki said you paid her a visit?' She introduced the subject not long after he'd started eating.

'You called her?'

'She called me, just this evening.'

Mikami came close to cursing out loud. *Bloody gossip.* 'I just popped over, had something I wanted to ask her about.'

'She said you looked overwrought.'

Mikami laughed. 'She's always over-reacting. I'm still getting used to it in Media Relations, that's all.'

'You think it would have been better if you'd stayed a detective?'

'It's hard to say. This is less of a strain, physically.'

'Psychologically, though . . .'

'Exactly, that part's difficult. Still, it'll never be fun and games, not so long as I stay in the force.' Mikami continued to smile as he said this, but Minako sighed a little.

'But they've got you dealing with Shoko's kidnapping, even though you're in Admin.'

'Mizuki told you that?'

'Don't be silly, darling. You told me. You said someone important was visiting from Tokyo, that was why you had to go to Amamiya's house.'

Mikami flicked at his chopsticks. He'd been talking for talking's sake for so long it was easy to forget the things he'd said.

'It isn't going well?'

'It's definitely not going to plan. It's proving difficult to get Amamiya's permission for the commissioner's visit.'

'The visitor is . . . the commissioner?' Minako stared in blank amazement, causing Mikami to panic a little.

'Only on a whim. It's like sightseeing for him.'

'But, why wouldn't . . .?'

'Hmm?'

'Amamiya, why wouldn't he give his permission?'

'Probably because we haven't found the kidnapper. That's enough to turn anyone against us.'

'And you have to bring him around?'

Minako's expression had hardened. The commissioner general

of the National Police Agency. Having been an officer herself, she understood the weight of the title.

'I'm going to try to talk him round, that's all. If I can't, then I can't. The commissioner can still go to the site of the kidnapping, it's no big deal.'

'But—'

'I'll be fine. You don't need to worry.'

'Mizuki said it, you know.' She spoke as if she were confessing something.

'Said what?'

'That she could tell you were exhausted. But that I was the only one who could tell if things were really bad or not.'

'Nosy cow . . . thinks she knows it all.'

Mikami used the coarse language to hide his annoyance. He thought he understood Mizuki's intentions, though. Minako had been in a dark place, focused on one single thing, so Mizuki had grabbed her by the shoulder and tried to shake her up. She had no doubt decided it would help Minako to worry about her husband. It was unpleasant to feel that someone was poking through their marriage, but Mikami also recognized gratitude; it came naturally as he watched Minako that night, her eyes staying focused, not drifting to the floor.

It was the main reason for his decision to broach the subject.

'I only found this out today. Seems they had a call at Mizuki's, too.'

'What kind of call?'

'You know, a silent call.'

Minako's cheeks twitched a little. 'They did . . .?'

'Yeah. Around the same time we had ours.'

Mikami tried to speak evenly, but his monotone seemed only to exacerbate the tension in the room.

'How many?'

'Just the one.'

'Right.'

Minako fell quiet. It was hard to read her reaction. Had she dismissed it as something unrelated? Or had she started to worry about some kind of possible connection? Depending on her reaction, Mikami had been ready to tell her about the two calls that had come in to Mikumo's family home, but now it seemed too cruel.

'The calls we had were Ayumi. It has to be: she called three times.'

Unable to stop himself, Mikami tried comforting her. He immediately cursed himself for doing so. Couldn't he just leave it at that? What was the point in having tried to talk if he let the conversation slip back to square one?

'Still . . .'

You never know, it could have just been someone fooling around.

The words reached the tip of his tongue. But he couldn't bring himself to say them out loud. It became impossible the moment he imagined Minako's reaction, the look on her face. Besides, he found them hard to accept himself. Some other people had received silent calls. That was all there was to it. There was nothing to ponder over. It was nothing more than speculation to question whether the calls had been from Ayumi or from some prankster. If so, they needed to believe in the better scenario. They would start to lose clarity the moment they stopped believing.

Even so . . .

In order to stop Minako's imagination from getting the better of her, he still needed to address Ayumi's silence during the calls. He had to think up a reason that wasn't 'saying goodbye'. *A silent farewell.* He needed a story of some kind, something to help Minako realize her fear was imagined.

'She must have been afraid I'd shout at her. You know, the way she hung up without saying what she'd wanted to.'

The words came out sounding forced. Minako gave him a hard look. She was no doubt considering the reason for Ayumi's silence, as well as why Mikami had decided to bring the subject up.

'Although she got half of what she wanted. She'd wanted to hear our voices. Yours, then mine. I think that was why she called.'

'Maybe in your case,' Minako said plaintively.

'Why would you think that?'

'I answered the first two calls, but she called a third time. It was your voice she wanted to hear.'

'Nonsense. I bet she was happy she got to hear you twice.'

'No, you're wrong.' Her mouth had started to tremble. 'She didn't care about hearing my voice, nor did she have anything to say. I mean, if she had—'

'That's enough.' Mikami raised his voice, then hurried to continue. 'Look . . . don't. It'll be no use if we let ourselves lose hope. Right?'

Minako dipped her head. For a moment it looked as though she would stay there, looking at the floor.

'It *was* Ayumi – she made the calls. I doubt it, too, sometimes, but it's okay to feel like that. She's out there, and she's fine. And if she's fine, if she's doing well, the truth is that the calls don't really matter at all.' He tried his best to sound confident.

'I suppose so.' Minako looked up. She was trying to smile.

'It'll be fine.'

The moment he'd said this to reassure her, the phone started to ring. Minako seemed to float in the air, halfway up. If it had been work, the internal line would have rung in the corridor.

'Don't get up. I'll answer it,' Mikami said softly.

He leaned over the low stand and peered into the display. It was a local number, but one he didn't recognize. He picked up the receiver, not rushing, so as to conceal his anxiousness from Minako. Putting it to his ear, he heard a familiar voice greet him.

'Hello. Is that Mikami?'

It was Division Chief Ishii. Mikami fought an urge to yell at the man. Why the hell hadn't he used Mikami's work number?

'What is it?' Mikami said, discarding formality.

'Ah, I was just wondering how it was going. With Amamiya.'

'I was just working on it.'

'What, at home?'

The snide tone went beyond sarcastic. After having prostrated himself before Akama the previous day, Ishii had jumped down Mikami's throat before leaving. *Don't think I'm going to go down with you, Mikami.*

'Hang on a moment.'

He whispered to Minako that it was Ishii, then carried the phone out to the corridor. It took all the effort he could muster. What would be going through Minako's head? Had his words managed to comfort her even a little?

The bedroom was ice-cold.

'Sorry about that. I've come across something I think I can use as leverage in bringing Amamiya around. I'm going to go and see him again, probably tomorrow.'

'Meaning you haven't managed it yet.'

Isn't that what I just said?

'This is far from acceptable, Mikami.'

'I'll do my best.'

Mikami flicked on the room's electric heater. He decided it better to wait a while before going back into the living room, and settled himself down. Either way, he'd been planning to put in a call to Urushibara's home before the night was out. He was impatient to end Ishii's call, but it seemed he hadn't called only to taunt.

'The round-table meeting, on Monday. You're planning to make an apology for the trouble surrounding this anonymity issue, yes?'

'I was told to go through what happened, not to offer an apology.'

'It's the same thing.' There was an uncharacteristic brashness in the way Ishii said this. 'Anyway, I'm getting ready to call around, make the necessary invitations, but I can't help thinking an apology might not do the trick by itself . . . that we probably need to sweeten the pot a little. However this goes, it's absolutely necessary that we convince the press to withdraw their intention of boycotting the commissioner's visit.'

'Okay. What do you mean when you say "sweeten the pot"?'

'In a nutshell, some additions to the services you provide in Media Relations. Sending the press information on breaking cases, even if it comes in late at night or on a holiday. Emailing reporters individually, if they opt in. That sort of thing.'

Mikami snorted loudly. He'd known that a few of the headquarters in other prefectures had rolled out an emergency-bulletin service, but only in cases where Media Relations was well staffed; such a system went far beyond the resources of an office of four.

Besides . . .

'And this is your idea?'

Akama would never submit a proposal like this. To offer these kinds of extra services was no different to offering the Press Club an apology.

'Shirota's, actually.'

'Shirota, from Administration?'

The name came as quite a surprise. Shirota was officially ranked highest among the division chiefs in Administrative Affairs, but his authority did not extend to matters involving the Secretariat.

'He's going to be at the meeting, and he's expressed his concerns. He's aware of the trouble we're having with this.'

'Still, I doubt the press would back off, even if we were to offer such blatant concessions.'

'Maybe not the reporters, granted, but the executives aren't as worked up as the front line. This kind of bargaining works. It plays up to their egos.'

'How about scheduling the meeting for an earlier date? Wouldn't that be enough to let them know we're treating the issue seriously?'

'You don't get it, do you? If we bring the meeting forwards that will only raise their expectations. They'll want an apology – at the very least, some kind of compromise. Basically, we're going to give them a gift to take home, in place of those things.'

Mikami had to stop himself from sighing.

'What you're suggesting is too much. The reporters will only get lazy, more than they are now, if we start sending them individual emails. They won't need to phone us for stories, let alone drag their sorry asses into the station.'

'Perhaps, but what do we care if they get lazy?'

'I would need more staff, if you expect us to cover holiday and night shifts. There is no way I can do it with the resources I have now.'

Mikami had hoped this would end the conversation, but it only prompted more taunting from Ishii.

'Now that doesn't sound like something a hardened detective would say. I thought you guys liked to fight to the bitter end, even when you know something is impossible?'

Like you have a fucking clue.

'Do you have Akama's approval on this?' Ishii went silent on the other end of the line. He hadn't mentioned anything to his boss. 'No, I don't suppose you do. He wouldn't tolerate such a weak stance,' Mikami said, using Akama to deliver the final blow. It felt underhand, like mentioning family in the interrogation room.

Still . . .

'It'll be fine. That's the reason I'm going to call around the papers first. I'll tell them about the new services on the phone, and you can remain ambiguous about it during the meeting. Just say something like, "We will continue to improve on the work we do." Akama should forgive that much. If by some chance he does flare up, just tell him it was an empty promise.'

'An empty promise?'

Was he suggesting they make the statement but do nothing to follow it up?

'Shirota told me he thought Akama would let it pass.'

He'd been smart enough to get Shirota on his side. Having to prostrate himself before Akama had taken its toll. Fearing he'd lost Akama's confidence, he had taken out insurance. Either that, or he was simply planning ahead. Akama would sooner or later return to Tokyo, but Shirota was a born-and-bred local and would remain a key figure in Prefecture D until the day he retired.

'All we need to do is survive the meeting. Even if we can't get away with doing nothing, we'll only be committing to a verbal promise and, as for the new services, well, we can just add them slowly, bit by bit.'

Mikami didn't see the point in responding. For yet another night, he was sitting at the same table as Ishii. He experienced a tide of self-derision, weaving its way up through layers of anger.

'So that's what we're doing. I'm counting on you, Mikami.'

There was no response.

'Mikami, are you still there?'

Again, silence.

'Look, I'm sure you realize this, but we're close to being pushed out of the ring with regards to this anonymity issue. If we don't straighten it out by the time of the commissioner's visit, we're both going to be—'

'I need to ask you something,' Mikami said, having made up his mind. The core problem he needed to crack was nothing to do with the round-table meeting.

'Huh, well, that came from nowhere.'

'Futawatari, from Administration; he's been acting strangely. Do you know anything about what he's doing?'

'Acting strangely? I can't say I've noticed anything . . . How so?'

'He's poking around the Shoko kidnapping.'

'He's what? I don't see what that has to do with him.'

That's why I'm asking you.

'You don't know if he's working under our orders?'

'Our orders?'

'I'm asking whether or not he's operating on instructions from Akama?'

'I can't imagine he's doing anything. He's got his hands full with the project to build a new headquarters.'

'He's up to something, that's for sure. Why do you think Criminal Investigations has gone into lockdown? Because our ace is digging into Six Four.'

'That's the first I've heard of it. Nobody's mentioned anything to me.'

He was getting ready to flee.

'What about Shirota? Have you seen him doing anything that seemed odd?'

'Nothing I've noticed . . . You think he might have Futawatari working for him?'

'That depends on whether you can draw a line to link him with Akama and Futawatari.'

'If he thought it was dangerous, I imagine Shirota would simply turn a blind eye. He does have a particular aversion to taking responsibility for things.'

Look who's talking, Mikami thought.

'If it's bothering you, why don't you try asking Futawatari directly? You joined the force together, and didn't you both do kendo in high school? I suppose you haven't seen much of each other since, being in Criminal Investigations and Administrative Affairs, but, well, you're here now, you should just go see him, ask him in person.'

'That's exactly what I plan to do.'

Mikami hung up. It took a while for the irritation to subside. The outpouring of Ishii's empty and insincere words had left him on edge. *I was just happy. You know, that's the first time anyone here's ever said thanks for something.* The girl's voice echoed like something from another age. *Words reach people.* Mikami decided he was a fool for having believed it, even for a moment. For having left a message for Hiyoshi. What words were there to reach someone who had lived the last fourteen years locked away in isolation, someone who had switched off every last channel to the outside?

Mikami jumped to his feet and walked back through to the hall. He grabbed the internal line and went into the bedroom again, using his free hand to pull the cord with him. Station Q, Urushibara's home. He already knew the number. Rather than just finishing his work over the phone, Mikami's plan had been to get on with some work that he could only do on the phone. He was going to launch a surprise attack. He would agitate; trick Urushibara into revealing the truth. The man might have grown used to sitting in the captain's chair, but he'd been a skilled detective with an extraordinary talent for intuition. If Mikami chose a head-on approach, Urushibara would almost certainly cotton on to the fact that Mikami's hand was empty.

But maybe, over the phone . . .

Mikami checked the time on the alarm clock: 8.15 p.m. The perfect time. Urushibara would be winding down for the night, having finished dinner and his bath. Mikami picked up the handset and dialled Urushibara's home number. He swallowed a mouthful of spit.

Someone picked up after the third ring: Urushibara. His voice shot up an octave once Mikami had introduced himself.

'Mikami. It's been a long time.'

'Yeah, it has.'

'How's life been treating you? Still having a good time with Minako, I assume?'

An opening jab. He was putting on a show of being the same old Urushibara, while his thoughts raced to pin down the reason for Mikami's call.

'How are you?'

'Not bad, not bad. It's pretty laid-back down here. Got everyone else doing my work for me.'

'Sounds great. You should give me a call. I'd be happy with a job like lead detective.'

'Haha. I'd probably consider it if I thought you were being serious. Anyway, to what do I owe the sudden call? Someone screw up a press report or something?'

'Nothing like that. Actually, there's something I wanted to ask you.'

'Huh. Come on, then . . . out with it.'

'I met with Hiyoshi today,' he said, keeping it simple and listening for Urushibara's response.

'Hiyoshi . . .?'

'Koichiro Hiyoshi, the one who used to work in Forensics. The one who screwed up during Six Four, ended up leaving the force.'

The line went quiet for a moment, but when he spoke again Urushibara seemed completely unfazed. 'Right, I do remember there being someone by that name. Remind me what he did that was so bad?'

It was Mikami's turn to fall quiet for a moment. His lie about having met Hiyoshi hadn't shaken Urushibara at all. He'd even countered by asking about Hiyoshi's mistake in return. Obviously, Urushibara hadn't let his armour rust in the slightest.

Mikami carried on regardless.

'It was after your unit entered Amamiya's house. He'd been in charge of recording the calls.'

'And?'

'He made a fatal error.'

'Uhuh . . . and?'

'You shouted at him, called him incompetent. Then he left the force.'

'And?'

Urushibara was trying to dictate the pace of the conversation. Show no reaction, keep the story going . . . it was a technique detectives liked to use.

'It hit him hard. After leaving Forensics, he spent the next fourteen years locked up in his room at home. But I'm guessing you know all this?'

'Uhuh . . . and?'

'I told him I'd listen to whatever he wanted to say, whether he wanted to complain or confess.'

'Right . . . and?'

He was probing to find out the extent of what Mikami knew. It was getting difficult. If Mikami went too far, if he failed to temper the falsehoods with enough truth, he'd end up with Urushibara's high-pitched cackle in his ear.

'He'd been in tears, clutching the recording equipment. Even though the Amamiyas were there, too.'

It was too late to alter course now. He heard a quiet intake of breath, and Urushibara's voice seemed suddenly closer.

'And? Did Hiyoshi confess to anything?'

Mikami clasped his mouth shut. *Could he let himself say it?* He let the silence make his bluff for him, but Urushibara saw through it.

'Look, Mikami, I've got no idea where you're going with this. What the hell was this screw-up you keep alluding to? And me calling him incompetent? I certainly don't remember having done that.' His tone suggested he knew he had the upper hand. 'Where did you dig up all these false accusations? And what's with the Internal Affairs act? Isn't Media Relations there to give the press a pure and just picture of us?'

'I don't believe the accusations are false.'

'Of course they are. I guarantee it. Who was it that fed you all this nonsense?'

'It was in the Koda memo,' Mikami said, going all out.

'The what—?'

His voice seemed to have clouded over. Mikami guessed he'd elicited the man's first genuine response.

But . . .

'I see. You and Futawatari, you're a team in this.'

It felt like a punch to the nose.

'He turned up at the station yesterday, hadn't even made an appointment. Said he wanted everything I knew about this thing called the Koda memo.'

Futawatari had beaten him to it again.

Mikami felt his whole body flush. He had intended to mount a surprise attack, to land the decisive blow, but his failure had been decided before he'd even picked up the phone. Futawatari's direct approach had given Urushibara the time he'd needed to prepare. Urushibara had raised his guard the moment he'd answered Mikami's call. He'd been able to sidestep Mikami's questions while dictating the course of the conversation. He'd even had his own final counter-attack ready.

You and Futawatari . . .

'They've managed to tame you, too, is that it? Really, for you and that dog to get together . . .'

'We have nothing to do with each other.'

'You share the same master in Akama. So you're Fido and he's Benji: that's about the only difference between you.'

He seemed to be enjoying the goading. But Mikami wondered if it was genuine. Could he really be so laid-back after having had Futawatari march in on his territory?

'Here's what I know. The Koda memo contains details of an error made by the Home Unit, one grievous enough to cost you your job.'

'And you read it?'

The response came so fast Mikami ended up stalling.

Laughter resonated in his ears.

'No, I don't suppose you did. You can't read something that doesn't exist.'

His voice was triumphant. Mikami wondered if it could be true. The Koda memo didn't exist. It had, once, but now it was gone. Could that be the source of Urushibara's confidence?

'It was an entertaining story, I'll give you that. Call again when you have another.'

Mikami couldn't just give up.

'I got the intel from someone who *has* read the memo.'

'Who . . . Futawatari?'

'I'm not at liberty to say.'

'Right, right. At least come out with it. What was this fatal error you say would have cost me my job?'

Mikami sank his teeth into his lip. He should never have let Urushibara ask the question.

'Well? Come on.'

'At this point, I'm not at liberty to say.'

Urushibara cackled again.

'How about we call it a day on the Internal Affairs act? I'm going to hang up. I heard you out because you're an old friend, but I'm under Arakida's direct orders not to discuss anything with Admin.'

Mikami seized on the words. 'So you're just another Fido.'

'I'm sorry?'

'You're sticking to the gag order, even though you don't know what it's all about . . .'

After a short pause, Mikami heard Urushibara cursing under his breath. 'Mikami, are you trying to test my patience?'

'No, I want to ask you, do you know what's behind the gag order? Tell me if you do.'

'You tell me. What do I need to say to make you happy?'

It sounded like Urushibara was trying to duck the question.

He'd been there when it had happened, so he'd known Criminal Investigation's secret from the start. But even with that knowledge, he hadn't been made aware of what the reason was behind the current, station-wide secret that had come into being so suddenly. They had shut him out.

If that was the case . . .

'What would happen if the memo found its way to the commissioner?'

'The commissioner . . .? What are you trying to say?'

He'd taken the bait.

'You know about the commissioner's visit next week?'

'Yes. What of it?'

'It's the only reason the gag order is in place. Criminal Investigations wants to hide all traces of the memo's existence.'

'Look, I don't know about any of this. What are you getting at?'

'I'm sure you do know. This is Tokyo we're talking about here. Arakida won't protect you, not when push comes to shove.'

'You're pushing—'

'He'll assign all the blame to the Home Unit. That's just how he operates. Trust me, I learned the hard way.'

There was no response.

The silence gave Mikami hope.

But . . .

'You're still pissed off with the Director, is that it?'

What . . .?

'Not everybody gets the transfer they wanted; the system doesn't work that way. You need to let it go. Spend two or three years towing the line and you'll get what you deserve, eventually.'

Urushibara was goading him back. It was obvious enough, but Mikami refused to ignore it.

'That's not what this is.'

'Despise Arakida, despise the whole department. That it? And now you're bringing me into the fray with this fucking interrogation. Pain in the ass.'

'No, that's not—'

'No? Then why the barbed phone call?'

'This is just . . .'

'. . . you doing your job, right. I'm asking you if that's all this is. Are you sure this isn't just some pretext for exacting revenge on Arakida, on your whole department? Are you certain that's not what this is?'

'I'm certain.'

The determination in his voice resonated through his skull.

'Okay. Well, at least act that way. Sure, Arakida is just some bullshitter with no talent apart from giving out orders. But the brass is the brass. If you really do want to work with us again, you'll need to pay him – and the department – a little more respect. We can talk after that.'

Urushibara had missed the mark. He'd shot short of any vital areas. It was a chance to open up a new line of questioning.

'Were you ordered to stay away from the funeral?'

'Funeral? What funeral?'

'Toshiko Amamiya's. I take it you know she passed away?'

'Ah, sure, I'd heard.'

'Why didn't you attend? You were in charge of the Home Unit.'

'That day, I was—'

'A detective would have made sure to be there.'

Urushibara started to say something but stopped midway, perhaps experiencing a wave of bitter nausea. The man had done his best at Amamiya's. No one would have seen anything else.

'You were ordered not to go. So as not to provoke Amamiya. Tell me if I'm wrong.' Urushibara's breath was a forbidding rumble over the line. 'Where is the Koda memo?'

'Enough.'

'Are you prepared to lose your job for a talentless bullshitter?'

'You're deluded. Stop obsessing over this crap – and make sure to enjoy yourself tonight.'

The line clicked off.

Mikami's hand jumped immediately to redial, but he stopped himself from calling back. The build-up wasn't something he could reproduce. Urushibara's presence had begun to recede with the silence, and now he seemed as remote as the dead.

Mikami was hit by a sudden exhaustion. This was gradually painted over by a sense of futility. Mikami had tried to throw Urushibara off balance, but the man had been steady on his feet. It was only to be expected. The result would have been much the same, whether he'd had time to prepare or not. Even so, Futawatari's lack of subtlety was maddening. Mikami wouldn't have expected to outsmart a seasoned detective like Urushibara, not one to one like that. He'd been testing for a reaction. Out to get a sense of things. But he was reaching above his station. His empty success in Administrative Affairs had given him the confidence to try his hand at cross-examining a detective. But to what end? Urushibara had seen through him. And it wasn't the first time it had happened. He'd been going from place to place, hawking the Koda memo, only ever managing to aggravate and irritate Criminal Investigations. Like a poor shot, he was shooting wildly to make up for an inability to aim. Mikami couldn't help but feel discouraged. Mikami was sure Ushibara had been unnerved when he'd brought up the commissioner's involvement, but he knew that wouldn't be enough in itself to make a man like him give in.

That left Kakinuma. Mikami's thoughts were already moving on. He didn't expect him to shed any light on the matter. Kakinuma was still part of the Investigative Team. He was younger than Mikami and lower in rank, and as such it would be easy for him to put the phone down, saying that he wished to remain uninvolved. Mikami's only hope was to appeal to Kakinuma's sense of justice. To get the approach right, he would have to go and see him in person.

Tomorrow.

Mikami felt weighed down as he got to his feet. He put the

handset back on the cradle in the hall, trying to look normal as he walked back into the living room. Minako was watching TV. The sight reminded him of how things used to be. Had she changed for the better? Or was she just trying to make an effort to do so?

'Anything wrong?'

'No, everything's fine.'

'I ran the bath.'

'You go first.'

'Well, I think I might be catching a cold . . .'

'Maybe you should go to bed then. Don't worry, I won't use the phone again tonight.'

Mikami imagined them in five or ten years, having the same conversation as today. It had become routine for them to worry about each other while pretending everything was normal.

He took a long bath. After this he sat in the living room having a drink, then went into the bedroom. Minako was already lying on her futon, the cordless phone in its usual place next to her pillow. The slender nape of her neck appeared orange under the glow of the lamp.

Still awake. That was the impression Mikami got.

Make sure to enjoy yourself tonight . . .

Urushibara's heartless jab had haunted him during his bath and while he'd been having his drink in the living room. He hadn't made love to Minako for a long time. Together, they had brought Ayumi into the world. Together, they had watched her tear herself apart. They hadn't been able to make love since, either from desire or from a will to create new life.

Mikami breathed silently as he slipped into his futon.

They would have two children. Although they'd never discussed it officially, they had shared the same unspoken understanding. But the desire for a second child had fizzled out after Ayumi, while she was still growing up. It had become clear, even though she had never said anything, that Minako no longer wanted another child. Ayumi had taken after her father. Had Minako been secretly afraid that their next child might be another girl, but take after her?

Mikami closed his eyes.

He'd been young. Working theft in Special Investigations, First Division. Minako had been based in the annexe, doing an office job for Transport Regulation. A number of cars had been broken into at the station's riverside car park and, with the reputation of the force on the line, Special Investigations had been deployed to look into the matter. One of the cars had been Minako's, and Mikami had been tasked with interviewing her. He only remembered her voice. He hadn't been able to look her properly in the face. The next year, they ended up working in the same district station. They would swap greetings whenever they saw each other. That was the extent of their relationship. She dazzled him, and he'd already decided he was unworthy of a woman like her. One day, without any forewarning, she presented him with a road-safety charm. *It's a bit silly, but here you go.* She'd looked embarrassed. He had been so amazed he hadn't been able even to thank her.

He could make out her gentle breathing. She was so close.

Do you regret all this?

Again he found himself silently voicing the question, unable to bring himself to say it.

30

Mikami drove his car from the house before nine o'clock the next morning. It was Sunday.

Kakinuma had just got married around the time of the Six Four kidnapping and had been living in a police dorm in Chuo-machi which had family-sized apartments. He'd entered Amamiya's home as part of the Home Unit and had afterwards remained on the case as a member of the Investigative HQ. He'd been there ever since, so it seemed safe to assume he would still be in the same apartment.

From the outside, the dorm was easily mistaken for a medium-sized municipal apartment building. Generally referred to as the Chuo Standby Hall, the complex consisted of six individual blocks, and Mikami's memory from the one time he'd visited before told him Kakinuma lived somewhere on the ground floor of the right-hand-side building. Mikami eased on a baseball cap and a pair of glasses before stepping out of his car. The communal letterboxes were gone, no doubt a precaution against the nefarious activities of the various cult religions.

His memory had been shaky at best. After wandering, lost, for a while, Mikami finally found the nameplate with 'Kakinuma' on it on the first floor of the building second from the right. It also displayed the name of Kakinuma's wife, Meiko, together with those of their three children.

Mikami presumed that Urushibara would have called the night before to make sure Kakinuma kept quiet. It was with this in mind that he pushed the buzzer. Almost immediately afterwards, a high-pitched female voice shouted, 'Coming!' and the door slipped open on the chain.

'Yes, how can I help?'

Meiko peered out from inside. Mikami could hardly believe his eyes. She looked as young as the day he'd first met her, all those years ago.

'My name is Mikami. I was with Special Investigations, back when—'

Meiko piped up before he could finish his sentence. 'Oh, of course! I remember. You were working with my husband.'

She kicked on a pair of sandals and stepped out.

Something about her reminded him of Mizuki Murakushi. She wasn't particularly good-looking, but had an easy-going smile that could disarm anyone. Her wedding to Kakinuma had coincided with Mikami's mother's passing away, so he'd been unable to attend their reception; because of this, he had only met Meiko twice, the first time at a party First Division threw in Kakinuma's honour, the second when he visited the married couple's new home with a few colleagues from work. Almost fifteen years had passed since then. And yet Meiko was so full of energy it was no exaggeration to say she looked like a woman in her twenties; she certainly didn't look like a mother of three.

'My husband always talks about you. I wouldn't be surprised if you found your ears burning every now and then?'

Mikami answered with an awkward smile. The stories were probably of the *Beauty and the Beast* variety.

'He says it every time he's had a couple of drinks. "That Mikami, he's the real thing. Guy's a real detective."'

Mikami tried to dismiss her words as flattery, but Meiko was adamant.

'No, he really means it. He says you're the only detective he knows who made a name for himself in both First *and* Second

Division. He sounds really proud when he talks about what you've achieved.'

'He's exaggerating.'

Conscious of eyes and ears around them, Mikami stepped into the entranceway. He heard the pattering of footsteps and a young girl of early primary-school age appeared with a younger child, possibly already in nursery, whose features made it hard to tell what gender he or she was. Another boy was at the end of the hallway, probably secondary-school age, leaning slightly to one side as he looked on.

'Is Kakinuma in?' Mikami asked, already sensing that he wasn't.

Meiko pursed her lips as she scooped up the youngest of her children. 'You've just missed him. He left about ten minutes ago.'

'For Central?'

While it had suffered a downgrade in both size and status, the Six Four Investigative HQ was still based in Central Station.

'I don't think so. It was definitely work, though.'

'I hear he gets his weekends off these days?'

'He does. Although I'm not so sure that's a good thing. Oh, I really hope the kidnapper's caught. He did such horrible things to that poor little girl.'

Meiko peered into the face of the kid in her arms. The child shrieked with laughter, finally revealing to Mikami that she was a girl.

'It's been non-stop since the marriage. Sometimes I wonder if I actually married the case. I know Kakinuma will suffer if the kidnapper isn't caught. I doubt he'll ever get over it, you know, if the statute of limitations kicks in and he's transferred out.'

Mikami made a deep nod.

'He says he wishes you were back on the case. That he's sure you'd be able to crack it.'

Mikami felt a sharpness in his chest. A part of him seemed to be watching the scene from above.

'Your husband will apprehend the kidnapper, I'm sure of it. Nobody knows the case better.'

'I do hope you're right. Then, if he gets three straight promotions, I'll have nothing else to say on the matter.'

She broke into laughter, giving Mikami an opportunity to move in.

'Am I right to assume you had a call from Urushibara last night?'

'Oh! Yes, that's right. And another, from someone called Futawatari.'

This time Mikami managed to keep his expression from changing. He'd been wondering if Futawatari might ring, too.

'Was that the first time he's called?'

'Oh no, he calls every now and then. Although it's sometimes Kakinuma who phones him.'

'Sorry, I meant Futawatari.'

'Ah. Yes, first time. And it wasn't just the call; he came over, late last night.'

Mikami couldn't help but feel impressed by the man's legwork. Yet again, Futawatari had beaten him to it.

Meiko's smile clouded a little. 'All Kakinuma said was that he was someone important from Admin. What's he like?'

'What do you mean?'

'I didn't get to see him. We pretended I was out when he came over.'

'Ah, right.'

'Is he Internal Affairs, that kind of thing?'

Mikami smiled instinctively. 'No, nothing like that. He's in Personnel, joined the force the same year as me. I'm sure it was something to do with that. Kakinuma hasn't changed jobs for fourteen years now; it's possible Futawatari was checking in to see if he wanted to try something else.'

Meiko seemed to accept this. 'I see. How silly of me, I should have introduced myself.'

'Is your husband . . . looking to move somewhere else?'

'Yes, I think so. But whenever he's had a few drinks he always complains that his hands are tied until the statute kicks in.'

His hands . . . tied. It sounded as though someone was holding him back.

The girl in Meiko's arms began to tug at her hair. Mikami took advantage of the distraction.

'Kakinuma has a mobile number?'

'Oh, I'm sorry.' She looked up and clasped her hands in apology. 'I'm under strict orders not to give the number to anyone.'

'I understand.'

Don't tell anyone, even if they're police. It was something all detectives told their families. Mikami resolved to try again later. He was just about to bow and leave when Meiko spoke again.

'Although, I wonder if he might have gone there?'

'I'm sorry?'

'There's a supermarket, in Matsukawa-machi. Tokumatsu. Do you know it?'

'I think so. Next to the pachinko parlour?'

'That's the one. You know, there's a chance he might be there, parked near the entrance to the car park. I go there to shop every couple of days; I've seen his car a few times now.'

Surveillance?

'Parked on the street?'

'That's right. He's using one of the side streets, off the main road. Wide enough so his car's not in the way, of course,' Meiko said, defending her husband, having misunderstood the question.

'And he's in the car, alone?'

'Yes. I wonder if he's found someone he's staking out? I tried calling out to him one time, but he got really angry. Even told me I had to stay away.'

He'd be angry with her again. She'd refused to give out her husband's mobile number, but that meant nothing now she'd told

Mikami where he might be. Although she had volunteered the information herself, Mikami felt awkward, as though he'd taken advantage of her good nature.

'I'll try him there, thanks.'

'Yes, please do. Sorry you had to come all this way.'

'It's no problem. I should be the one apologizing, for barging in on you like this. When I see your husband, I'll tell him I just happened to be passing by.'

Meiko let out a happy shriek. 'If you wouldn't mind. He'd probably be angry with me otherwise.'

She didn't seem overly concerned, even as she said this. *A good family*. He turned to leave but looked back almost immediately.

'His car . . .'

'It's a dark-green Skyline. A real old banger.'

'Thanks. Next time I'll make sure I'm not in such a rush.'

Mikami looked back a final time as he heard a little voice.

'Bye-bye.'

The little girl shyly hid her face in her mother's chest, her features an attractive mix of both parents'.

31

Mikami turned right when the lights at the intersection turned amber.

He hadn't taken everything Meiko had said as fact. If Kakinuma *was* by himself, he wouldn't be on official surveillance duty. What was he up to? Mikami mulled over the question as he sped down the bypass.

He crossed into Matsukawa-machi. The area was full of large, out-of-town superstores. As it was December, the streets were bustling. Cars and consumers zipped back and forth with concentrated purpose. Mikami couldn't miss the gigantic sign announcing the Tokumatsu supermarket. He took a left and made his way down the side of the store before taking a right at the next junction to circle around the back.

His foot came down hard on the brakes.

I'll be damned . . .

On the left side of the road, parked ahead of five or six cars lined up against one wall of a consumer electronics store, was Kakinuma's dark-green Skyline. Mikami pressed on the accelerator to approach from behind. He made a quick check of the exhaust. There was a faint trail of white smoke. He edged a little closer. The inside of the vehicle came into view through the rear window. A head, the hair short, sat in the tipped-back driver's seat. Mikami drove straight on, glancing to the side as he passed by. The profile of a man. Kakinuma. He was looking directly ahead. Less than ten metres away in that direction was the entrance leading into the Tokumatsu car park. A couple of uniformed guards were busy directing the heavy traffic, guiding customers in and out with red batons. *Kakinuma's watching the cars, or the customers.* But Mikami dismissed the idea almost as soon as it came. The Skyline was parked too close to the entrance. He was also at the front of the row of other cars, meaning he was in plain sight of anyone driving out. The rules of surveillance suggested his target would be fifteen metres further on – the back entrance to the pachinko parlour. Either that, or the main entrance to the multipurpose building across the road.

Mikami made a left, then another, navigating his way through the side streets until he was behind the line of parked cars. He pulled up behind the last vehicle and cut the engine; he got out of his car and into the street. *Guy's a real detective.* The words Meiko had told him sat heavily in the pit of his stomach. He approached the Skyline as though it were an interrogation room. When he reached it, he lightly rapped his knuckles against the driver-side window. He sensed Kakinuma jump. His eyes opened wide when he turned to see Mikami standing there. *Open up.* Mikami formed the words with his mouth. Kakinuma stumbled over himself, unlocking the door. The car was parked flat against the wall, so the passenger side was off limits. Mikami pulled open the rear door and climbed into the back of the car. He grabbed the fabric of the passenger seat and pulled himself forwards so he could see Kakinuma from the side. The man had gone completely pale.

'What are you doing here?'

Mikami didn't give him any time to think up an excuse. Kakinuma managed little more than a grunt in response.

'Are you waiting for someone? Or keeping your eye on someone?'

Surveillance. Routine mapping. Mikami was sure Kakinuma was engaged in one or the other, but the view through the windscreen didn't seem to fit now he was inside the car. The car park was, as he'd thought, too close. The interior of the car was in plain sight, almost inviting people to look in. At the same time, the two entrances – those of the pachinko parlour and the multi purpose building – seemed too far away, making it a stretch to keep tabs on someone with the naked eye.

'We're moving,' Kakinuma blurted, letting off the handbrake. He put the car into drive and started to press down on the accelerator. Mikami reached out, pulling the handbrake back up in almost perfect unison, making the car jerking forwards before coming again to an abrupt stop, sending the two of them pitching forwards. One of the men directing the traffic turned around in surprise, having no doubt registered the screech of the tyres.

Mikami sat back in the seat and said, 'I'm not here to get in the way. Just carry on like I'm not here.'

'I'm done for the day.'

Done for the day? What did he mean, *done for the day*?

'It's fine, just carry on as you were. I want the kidnapper to see justice, too; no less than you do.' Mikami heard Kakinuma swallow. 'I'm here for something else. You can keep looking ahead, that's fine. Just hear me out.'

'What do you want?'

Mikami looked into the rear-view mirror. He could see Kakinuma's eyes. They shied away from meeting his.

'I went to see Hiyoshi yesterday, the one who used to be in Forensics.' Mikami held back from saying he'd met him, intimating only that he'd been to his house. Kakinuma was blinking more rapidly now. He would have had warning of Mikami's attempted ambush from Urushibara's call, but physical reactions weren't something you could fully suppress. 'His mother told me all about what happened. That her son had made a fatal error at Amamiya's. That the captain – that Urushibara – had yelled at him for being incompetent. This is all correct, I take it?'

'I don't . . . I don't know.'

His voice broke into a falsetto as he replied.

'That Hiyoshi left the force, that he spent the next fourteen years refusing to leave the house. Did you know about that?'

'No . . .'

'He'd been crying, hadn't he? The second day you were with the Amamiyas.'

Kakinuma's eyes were restless, moving in the rear-view mirror. 'I didn't know.'

'Somebody saw it. Koda was trying to comfort him. What were you doing?'

'I can't remember. I . . . was probably busy talking with HQ.'

Mikami leaned forwards again, bringing his face right up to Kakinuma's. The man's ears had gone bright red.

'Do you know about the Koda memo?'

'No.'

The answer had come too quickly. Kakinuma's half-open mouth was trembling slightly.

'Koda wrote about Hiyoshi's mistake. Yes?'

'I just told you—'

'But Urushibara covered up both the mistake and the memo. Because he was afraid he'd lose his job.'

'Mikami, I don't know an—'

'Are you the kind of person who abandons his team mates just to protect his boss?'

Mikami put everything into the words. Kakinuma's neck stiffened. His arteries were pumping visibly.

Mikami waited for Kakinuma's reaction.

Kakinuma eventually opened his mouth to speak. 'I don't know what you're talking about.'

Mikami let out a heavy sigh. All Kakinuma's physical reactions had registered positive. But not his words. Mikami had guessed it might go this way. Kakinuma was on the far side of a dark river; appealing to his morals alone wouldn't get him across.

'Do you mind if I move off now?' There was a firmness to his voice. His hand was already on the handbrake.

'Keep doing what it is you're doing.'

'I already told you, I'm done.'

'*What's* done?'

'My job. What I'm doing here.'

They were talking at odds to each other. The mood in the car became increasingly one of irritation.

'I'm pulling out.'

'Don't you dare,' Mikami threatened. His brain felt like it was on the verge of some kind of realization.

'Anyone can see us here. If you want to talk, can we please do it somewhere else?'

'You're the one who parked here . . . where anyone can see us.'

Something clicked when he put it into words. Kakinuma had done this on purpose: there was no other explanation. Kakinuma had wilfully ignored the rules of a stake-out: he'd *meant* to park somewhere where he stood out. The man's shrunken pupils flicked a glance at Mikami in the mirror.

'I can drive you back to your car.'

'I'm just back there. I'll get out once we've finished talking.'

'We haven't finished yet?'

'Not yet.'

Mikami had run out of moves. And it pained him to pressure Kakinuma any more. The image of Meiko was there in his mind. He'd seen their three children. Kakinuma was no different to him. He was unable to do the right thing, even if he wanted to. He was protecting his family.

Mikami sensed his will to fight wither away. He felt a wave of resignation washing over him. Yet he found himself increasingly curious about the strange disconnect in their conversation. Kakinuma had maintained his position without breaking, but, instead of letting his guard down, with each passing second he seemed to be growing more agitated. He looked like he was choking. He was holding the handbrake halfway down, desperate to get away.

No, that wasn't it.

He wasn't trying to get away. He was trying to get *Mikami* out of the way.

Why?

Mikami lifted his eyes and studied the view out of the windscreen.

'If you've got something else to say could you hurry up and say it?' Kakinuma pleaded. It was the voice of someone facing a very specific crisis. 'Mikami, please!'

Mikami said nothing.

'If not, I'll have to ask you to leave.'

Kakinuma swung around in his seat, blocking the view from the window. Mikami shoved him out of the way and stared ahead.

'Mikami, you've got what you came for!'

Kakinuma was all but screaming, but Mikami's focus was unshakable. His eyes were being drawn towards a single point. He had the feeling you had when a face you'd been waiting for suddenly appeared in the middle of a vast crowd.

Kazuki Koda.

The car-park entrance. One of the two guards on traffic duty was Koda. His eyes were half hidden under his cap and, from the looks of it, he'd changed significantly in the last fourteen years; still, Mikami was sure it was him. The narrow eyes, the tall nose, the compact mouth. Each was a match for Mikami's memory.

Kakinuma's head had slumped on to his shoulders. Witnessing the depth of the man's despair was all Mikami needed to solidify his astonishment. As though a cloth had been whisked away, everything came into view. Kakinuma hadn't been on surveillance. Nor had he been trying to map someone's routine. He was here as a demonstration of intent. His closeness to the object of his surveillance was deliberate: he was to show his face, intimidate Koda. *Don't talk to anyone about Amamiya's. We can make things difficult, whenever we want.*

Kakinuma probably made sure Koda was aware of him on a

regular basis. He was there to drum it into Koda that they intended to keep him under long-term surveillance. That was the role Kakinuma had been assigned.

Mikami shuddered as he fixed his gaze on Kakinuma's stooped back.

'All this time?'

No answer.

'Really? You've been doing this . . . for fourteen years?'

Kakinuma let out a groan, and cradled his head in his hands. He'd been following orders. Urushibara's confidence, Mikami now realized, had stemmed from this framework of intimidation.

'I'm sorry I got in your way. I'll get the rest from Koda.'

Mikami put his hand on the handle to open the door. Kakinuma let out a subdued cry, then twisted all the way around. There were tears in his bloodshot eyes.

'No . . . just let him be.'

'You're in no position to say that.'

'No, you're right. You're absolutely right. But it's not what you think. This isn't about intimidation or surveillance – not any more. It's just habit now. For me. For Koda, too.'

'Habit?'

'It's what happens after fourteen years of doing this. *Ah, he's here today* – that's really all it is now. We don't see each other outside of that. It's become an unspoken agreement. It's how I've made it this far – Koda, too.' Kakinuma threw his head into a deep bow. 'I'm begging you, Mikami. Don't make any trouble. If you go after him, with your charisma . . . he might well say something. If he does, I'll have no choice but to report it.'

Mikami refrained from nodding.

'I've been watching him since the beginning. He's had nothing but pain since he left. Can't land himself a decent job. He might have left by his own volition, but everyone's prejudiced against someone who's resigned from the force. And he left so suddenly he wasn't even able to get a letter of recommendation. He's had to go from one job to the next. All physically hard. Now, he's finally married, got himself a family. He's started to settle into a new life. That's why—'

'Tell me what happened.'

'Hmm?'

'Amamiya's house. If you don't want me to get it from Koda, tell me.'

'But, I—' Kakinuma broke off, a hopeless look spreading across his face.

'I'm the same as you. I'm here to get my job done, too.'

Again, no answer.

'I didn't see you. We never spoke. Okay? Now talk.'

Kakinuma closed his eyes. Finally, he gave a weak shake of his head.

Mikami started to open the door. Something took hold of his wrist. The grip was strong. 'This isn't just about Koda. I have a family, too.'

'So do I.' Mikami grabbed Kakinuma. 'Listen. No one will ever hear your name from my mouth. You, me, Koda – we will all get through this. Nothing will happen to our families. Tell me if there's a better way of doing this.'

There was a long silence.

Kakinuma raised his head. He stared regretfully at Koda in the car park, then, eventually, turned slowly back around. The mouth he'd been holding shut dropped part-way open. He brought up a hand to massage his throat. There was another long pause before he was able to muster any words.

'We missed our one chance to get the kidnapper's voice on tape.'

Mikami caught his breath. *Huh?*

'The recording equipment . . . it didn't work.'

His head was racing.

Missed our chance to get the kidnapper's voice . . . Recording equipment . . .

He didn't understand what Kakinuma was trying to say.

'What do you mean? That call came in before any of you were even—'

'There was another call.'

Mikami swallowed a breath.

Impossible . . .

'It's true. There was another call, one apart from the two that went on public record. And we screwed up our chances of getting it on tape.'

The words rang in his ears.

'It was just before your unit arrived. We had a third call from the kidnapper. We'd been ready. Everyone was in place to record and trace the call. Then . . .' Kakinuma swallowed, visibly pained. 'The moment the phone started to ring, Amamiya almost lost it . . . he tried to pick it up, forgetting everything we'd told him. We managed to stop him, and contacted NTT. Hiyoshi was switching on the recording equipment at the same time. But the machine wouldn't come on. The tapes didn't move. He started to panic, tried flipping the switch off and on again, but the tapes just wouldn't move. The phone continued to ring the whole time. Amamiya must have been terrified it would go dead – he picked up in the middle of the chaos.'

He picked up? The detective in Mikami reacted immediately.

'Did the kidnapper talk to him?'

'Yes.'

'What did he have to say?'

'He warned Amamiya to steer clear of the police. Said he was watching him. Amamiya swore he hadn't contacted us and begged to hear his daughter's voice, but the line went dead. The call was too short to finish the trace.'

'Was it the same voice as the previous times?'

'According to Amamiya, yes.'

'Did you get to hear it?'

Kakinuma shook his head regretfully. 'No one heard it but Amamiya.'

'What about headsets?'

'I had mine on before. Koda, too. But we'd taken them off to help Hiyoshi, he was in such a panic. We were in the middle of checking the power, the slack on the tapes, when Amamiya . . . Anyway, that's what happened.'

The car fell silent. The press officer in Mikami was late to catch up. The police had covered up their error. They'd deceived the public, consigned to the dark a call from the man behind a kidnapping and a murder.

It was unimaginable. It should never have been allowed to happen. It was at that point that Mikami finally felt a shiver go through him.

'Who made the decision for the cover-up?'

Silence.

'You're wasting my time. Spit it out.'

'The chief.'

'Urushibara? What did he actually say?'

'That we didn't need to report it. That Amamiya understood. That we were never to speak of it to anyone, whatever happened.'

'Did he try to sweet-talk Amamiya into playing along?'

'I don't think so. Amamiya was actually apologizing to us, at least immediately after the call. He kept saying he was sorry he'd answered without checking first.'

At least immediately after the call . . .

'But that changed over time. Amamiya decided he couldn't forgive us for the error. That was the reason the relationship broke down?'

'I can't really say; I've got orders to stay away from him. All I know is that the papers covered the case in exhaustive detail after the embargo was lifted. I'm certain he would have noticed that we hid the third call.'

Was that what it was? Had Amamiya turned his back on the police because of the cover-up, not because of the error itself?

'What time did the call come in?'

'Seven thirty, on the dot.'

That was only an hour before Mikami had arrived. He hadn't sensed anything out of the ordinary. Although . . . whatever he'd seen, he would probably have considered it a product of the situation, of being in the house of a family whose daughter had been kidnapped, just as he'd written Hiyoshi's paleness off to stress.

'What did you say to NTT?'

It was one thing to commit an error, but they'd requested a trace and would have needed to follow that up.

'We told them the call had been a wrong number.'

'That's what Urushibara told you to say?'

'Yes.'

'Was anyone giving him orders during all this?'

'No. The way things were, he needed to make split-second decisions, there and then.'

Meaning responsibility stopped with the Home Unit. But, if that was the case . . .

'What's the Koda memo?'

Mikami had expected Kakinuma to put up a last-ditch fight, but he didn't even pause.

'I don't know what it is, not exactly, but I do know that Koda was sick with anger. He turned on Urushibara when he learned the kidnapper had got away with the ransom. *The whole team's responsible for this. We need to report it to HQ. All four of us should stand in the firing line.* Urushibara just shouted back: *Why would you want to alienate the public? Spare me the amateur politics until we've caught the damn kidnapper.* I said the same things to him, begged him. I said he needed to put up with it, keep it quiet.

'Believe me, I knew exactly how he felt, but I really didn't think it would benefit the investigation to kick up a fuss over a single mistake. And a part of me thought Urushibara had a point. Koda kept quiet after that. Then, later, he seemed to be in agony, after everything started to go wrong, after Shoko was found dead. In the end, Urushibara couldn't stop him. It was after we'd pulled out of Amamiya's house. Koda wrote up a report detailing the error and posted it through the director's letterbox.'

Mikami's head lurched.

The error had been reported, fourteen years earlier. The director of Criminal Investigations had been made aware of the cover-up. This wasn't the first time a secret the Home Unit had sought to bury for ever had come to light. The man in the top position in Criminal Investigations had known about it, too, and as far back as the kidnapping itself. Yet the facts had never been made public. The Koda memo had been stamped out of existence. They had decided to endorse Urushibara's conduct. Koda had tipped them off and resigned from the force, yet no one had tried to stop him. On the flip-side was Urushibara, the man behind the whole cover-up – promoted to captain.

A systematic cover-up. Orchestrated by the Prefectural HQ. That was the truth behind the Koda memo.

'Koda's got a strong moral core. He's also a good man, and he honours his obligations. Every year, on the anniversary of Shoko's death, he goes to offer incense at her grave. He even made a quiet visit to Toshiko's grave after she passed away last year, to pay his respects.

'That's why your hands are tied.'

'Sorry . . .?'

'You know what I'm talking about. You're the only one who can watch Koda. That's what this is.'

'Yeah . . . I suppose so. The director's secret was passed down the lines.'

'Of course,' Mikami said, feeling disgusted.

He could see a man in a guard's uniform, his trousers, flapping in the biting wind. Fourteen whole years. All because he'd been true to his conscience.

'He must really hate us.' What was supposed to be a sigh came out as words.

'Not really,' Kakinuma muttered. 'You know, I think he feels grateful now.'

'Grateful?'

'This is the first time he's been able to hold down a proper job. Urushibara put in a good word.'

Mikami grunted when he heard this. It was probably true; the security agencies were essentially an old-boy network for the police. Under normal circumstances, an allegedly unstable element like Koda would never be able to find work with them.

'Koda came begging, asked the chief to forgive him.' Kakinuma dabbed a finger over his eyes. 'He asked Urushibara to let it go, help him out, said he just wanted a normal life with his wife and child.'

Submission. Mikami felt it in his chest. A deep sympathy. *An officer. A security guard.* The only difference was the uniform. Off in the distance, Koda was laughing. He was in gloves, holding a red baton. Chatting with the shoppers through their car windows. Nodding happily away. He'd had his fangs removed. He was no longer a threat to the force. Yet he was still subject to Kakinuma's regular surveillance. By the same measure, Kakinuma was being made to recall what had happened. They were two sides of the same mirror, the strategy functioning also to keep Kakinuma, who understood the truth of the cover-up, in check. *This is you, if you go shooting your mouth off.* Even though he'd been the one keeping watch for fourteen years, Kakinuma would have been instilled with a fear that was much the same as Koda's.

Mikami felt the sudden urge to set them free, both of them.

'Okay, I'm going to leave now. Just let me know one more thing. Why did Hiyoshi start crying in Amamiya's house?'

'That was because . . . he felt responsible.'

'That's all?' Kakinuma grimaced. 'Urushibara said something to him. Yes?'

'. . . yes.'

'What did he say?'

'It was about Shoko.'

'Tell me exactly what he said.'

'He told Hiyoshi that if the worst came to the worst . . . that it was his fault.'

32

Mikami's foot eased down on the accelerator.

He was heading east on the prefectural highway, having taken his leave of Kakinuma. He was going to visit Amamiya. He didn't know if the new information was enough to talk him around, but he felt it was enough to warrant a second attempt. The truth was that he wanted to go directly to Urushibara's in City Q and beat the truth out of the man. He could feel the bile rising in his throat. This wasn't something he could just build a wall around or keep apart from his emotions. There was anger, but that wasn't all. He felt dismay, too. They'd had a chance to get the kidnapper's voice on tape. If they'd succeeded, they could have broadcast it to the nation. They could have used voice fingerprinting to pare down the list of suspects.

He rammed his palm into the steering wheel. One after another, the negative emotions boiled up from within.

The police had messed up their one chance to record the kidnapper's voice. What would have happened if this had got out to the public at the time? The case had ended in the worst possible way, with the kidnapper making off with the ransom, then with the discovery of Shoko Amamiya's dead body. The police had, in the course of their investigation, failed to procure evidence that could have led them directly to the perpetrator. *The tapes hadn't moved.* There would have been an outcry. Management's heads would have rolled. Mikami doubted even that would have been enough to quell the fire. For as long as the case remained unsolved, the press would have seized every opportunity to bring up the mistake, continued, regardless of the passage of time, to rub salt on old wounds. The police would face endless condemnation: *if only you'd recorded the kidnapper's voice that time.*

And yet . . .

The crime they'd committed was the greater one.

This wasn't an old injury. The truth that needed to be faced was that the wound was still festering, just hidden under bandages. The police had made an inexcusable mistake during a full-blown kidnapping case then they had systematically covered it up and lied to the public for fourteen years. If something like that was to reach the press, be broadcast all over the news . . .

That thought alone was horrific. However fatal, their failure to make the recording was still nothing more than an error. Covering it up had been a deliberate act. And they had gone so far as to hide a call from the kidnapper, crushing in their hands information that could have been fundamental to the case. It was a criminal act, unworthy of any investigative body. The Prefectural HQ would have no means of defence if the truth came out. It would suffer attacks that were of a different magnitude to the censure it would have received if it had first confessed to its mistake.

That wasn't all. Kidnappings were different to other cases. Mikami knew, having read up on the documentation concerning national press policy since his appointment as press director, how dangerous they could be.

Kidnappings brought with them the extremely delicate issue of the Press Coverage Agreement. The agreement had first come into being as an apology for a history of unregulated and irresponsible reporting of kidnappings. There is no way for the police to protect a victim once a kidnapper who has warned his target not to call the police learns, either from the papers or the TV, that the police have become involved. Because of this the press are required to sign an agreement whenever a kidnapping takes place, stating that they will refrain from reporting anything about the case until either the kidnapper's arrest or the safe return of the victim. It falls to the police to bridge the resultant vacuum of information. They are obligated to offer updates and real-time reports on the progress of the investigation. This is where the difficulty begins.

In reality, the Press Coverage Agreement is a slip of paper signed by various agencies of the press, but *not* between the media and the police. Despite this, the police take a leading role in the administrative task of setting it up; this is because they are usually the first to learn about a kidnapping, and also first to make a judgement whether the victim's life is at risk. They present the general details of the case to the members of the Press Club, then request them to sign a coverage agreement. In most cases, the press accept the terms, giving the agreement the impression, from the outside, of having been made between the police and the press.

The end result is the press signing the document, while entering into a 'gentleman's agreement' with the police.

On the surface, this resembles a promise made with the goal of protecting innocent life, but the reality is that it's more like a negotiated contract. On the one hand, the police want the press to agree; if this happens, they can focus on the investigation without having to keep an eye on reporters' movements. On the other hand, the press find themselves having to put aside their freedoms and the public's right to know, but they are able at the same time to gain leverage from this to argue for greater checks and balances; also, being the side having made a concession, they are in a strong position to pressure the police into full and complete disclosure of all case information. Considered objectively, the contract means the press can sit back and watch as a vast amount of case-specific intelligence – more than they could obtain by themselves – comes tumbling into their hands. But nobody sees it this way. Each time a kidnapping occurs, one to two hundred reporters and cameramen push their way into the police station dealing with the case. While they might turn up in high spirits, the inability to conduct any real interviews, combined with being packed into a claustrophobic press area, leads to a gradual build-up of frustration; finally, they begin to suspect the police of trying to control them. *We curbed our freedoms to help with your investigation.* The sense of having done the police a favour spreads through the room, and if the police try to hold anything back while the agreement is still in effect, the press tend to become a hysterical crowd and launch a full-on attack.

What about during Six Four? It went without saying that there would have been a coverage agreement in place. But the Prefectural HQ had concealed the kidnapper's third call, forsaking their obligation to provide case information. They'd gone back on the promise they'd made to the press, and in the worst way possible. The bond of trust between the police and the media had been severed fourteen years ago; it had nothing to do with the present issue of anonymity.

The press would have lashed out, torn any confidence in the authority of the police to shreds. And that would have been only a small sign of the storm yet to come. How many reporters would there have been, jammed together in the Six Four press room? Even the new recruits would be veteran reporters by now. Many would be editors, branch heads; many more would hold key positions in their respective head offices. They had all been there. They would have all felt shock, then outrage, at the deception; they would be vocal in their censure of the force. Their voices would become the voices of their companies, then the voice of the mass media, as it rallied against the NPA. The opposition party would have gained political traction. The media's impassioned lobbying might have even influenced debates over bills on privacy and individual rights.

Damn fool . . .

Mikami let out a harsh grunt.

Urushibara's crime deserved the harshest punishment. One

district police inspector's attempt to shirk responsibility could have brought the entire organization to its knees. But . . . no, the real war criminal was Director Seitaro Kyuma, who had been in charge of Criminal Investigations at the time. He had turned a blind eye to one individual's deception, and in the process had made it a crime committed by the organization itself. The letter Koda had delivered to him had been a cry from the heart. But Kyuma had crushed it underfoot. The man had thought himself an intellectual, always dressed sharply, but he'd lacked any real skill when it came to actual case work: he'd chosen to reward Urushibara for the decision he'd made in the field.

Fair enough, he'd done it to protect the force. Both the magnitude of the case and the scope of the error itself made the information too dangerous to be made public. The timing had been off, too. It had been days since the error had taken place, Shoko had been found dead and the force had already been facing mounting criticism. Mikami understood how difficult it would have been to stand before the lines of cameras and admit there had been another phone call.

Even so . . .

It would have come down to self-protection. Kyuma had been close to retirement and had already been promised a golden handshake and an executive role in the private sector. Whatever his circumstances, he was an executive who had looked after his own interests; in doing so, he had chosen to leave his successors with the parting gift of a live grenade. *We can defuse it if we deal with it internally.* Perhaps Kyuma had concluded as much, but that only proved he was as narrow-minded as the rumours had said. The reality was that there had already been a whistle-blower, in the form of Koda, and that the girl's father also knew the truth. It was a barely sleeping giant, one that might be chanced on or woken up at any moment.

It truly was a cursed legacy. *The director's secret was passed down the lines.* Kakinuma's words. When he was about to retire, Kyuma had confided the truth to his successor, Tadahiko Muroi. The failed recording. The cover-up. The Koda memo. Muroi had no doubt been stunned, but he would have realized he'd become complicit the moment he heard the words. If he had let the facts come to light, the press conference to mark his promotion might have ended up marking his resignation. So Muroi had done as instructed, he'd taken the poison. It was probably during his reign that the framework for maintaining the secret – the surveillance and intimidation of Koda, after he'd left the force – was put in place. Muroi had primed Kakinuma for the role and appointed Urushibara to head up the operation. Keeping the Home Unit under lock and key was integral to preventing any leaks, so the blanket ban on Kakinuma's transfer was added to the legacy. Criminal Investigations' greatest secret. Carried down the line by eight successive leaders, all the way to the present day – to Arakida.

Mikami's mood darkened.

Michio Osakabe was among the eight. As was the celebrated commander Shozo Odate. He had acted as a go-between for Mikami and Minako, and he'd been a father figure to the entire department. Still, they couldn't have done anything. The potential danger of revealing the cover-up would have grown with time. They'd been handed a live grenade, and it had harboured more destructive energy than ever before. It wouldn't have been about self-protection; it was all they could do to bury it as deep as possible.

Mikami nudged open the driver-side window. Cool air brushed his cheek. The north wind rustled the remaining leaves on the winter trees dotted along the pavement.

He needed to reset his line of thought.

He thought he could see through to Arakida's way of thinking. Perhaps he had grown worried, sensing some kind of hidden motive behind the commissioner's visit. Soon afterwards, word had reached him that Futawatari was digging around to find information on the Koda memo. It would have felt as though someone was sniffing around the hole in which he'd buried the grenade. Like a cornered animal, he'd panicked, sensing the danger, and had imposed the gag order before the night was out. *Was there a real chance he would lash out, if he was pushed?* Whatever Arakida did, Mikami felt certain Matsuoka wouldn't take it quietly. He would be prepared to fight Tokyo directly if he perceived a threat to the department.

Mikami sensed he was beginning to understand the reason behind Futawatari's actions, together with the aim of Administrative Affairs. They were working to remove any and all obstacles to Tokyo's agenda. Did it forward this agenda to condemn the Six Four investigation? They would expose the department's shortcomings, its weaknesses, then hold them up to its throat, hoping to breach the castle without spilling blood.

Was that the plan?

Even so, the knowledge that the bomb concealed within Six Four was related to a cover-up, that it had the potential to bring down not only the department but also the entire Prefectural HQ, clouded Mikami's understanding of what Futawatari was trying to achieve. There was no guarantee it wouldn't turn into a hornets' nest. Yet he had gone from one place to the next, openly enquiring about the Koda memo. That was no different to advertising the bomb's existence. It was a hallmark of inspections made in Administrative Affairs – whether to do with Personnel or Internal Affairs – that they were carried out in silence, in the shadows. More to the point, its inspectors were experts at measuring risk, always conscious of the public mood and wary of any possible legal action. They would expose the force to danger despite their duty to protect it. Were they capable of such a thing? If the truth came out, the Prefectural HQ would face the censure of every one of the 260,000 officers across the nation, together with the condemnation of the NPA. It would be a disastrous loss of face. The HQ would be stripped of its autonomy and forced into performing ablutions, into spending a long winter under the roof of Tokyo's scrutiny. It would become a lame duck. Wouldn't that be the outcome Futawatari feared the most?

Although . . .

Was there anything to suggest Futawatari had made any progress? Mikami had been in Criminal Investigations until the spring, but it was only fifteen minutes earlier that he had finally learned the truth about the Koda memo. Futawatari had failed in his attempt to get to Kakinuma. Urushibara definitely wouldn't talk. And the field officers were all subject to the gag order, banned from talking to Administrative Affairs. They wouldn't let their guard down in front of the enemy's star player. The rank-and-file officers weren't even aware of the facts. The odds were stacked against Futawatari. It was safe to assume he had still to get to the truth. He'd overheard someone talking about something called the Koda memo; that was the extent of what he knew. He had no idea what it said. He wasn't aware of the danger, and that was why he was going after even the newly recruited detectives asking after it.

Mikami's line of thought stopped there.

Futawatari must have overheard the memo being mentioned. But where?

His theory, only half thought through, took a sudden hit. This was Criminal Investigations' dark secret, handed down from director to director. It wasn't anything you could simply overhear. Where the hell could Futawatari have got wind of it? Had somebody told him? Was it Akama, whose orders he was working under? He'd known the detective's code name for the case. Mikami had to admit that anyone overseeing an entire department had access to streams of information that were entirely off limits to anyone of a lower rank. Mikami refused to buy it. His authority meant that any number of people would seek to curry his favour, but it still didn't make sense that he would have heard a code name that had never made its way around the headquarters as a whole.

Mikami felt at sea again. The mystery of Futawatari expanded to take over his thoughts. Futawatari knew something he wasn't supposed to have heard about. He was discussing something it was taboo to speak of. The man's dark eyes flickered in and out of Mikami's mind, devoid of emotion.

Futawatari was doing something without realizing the risk. No. It was unthinkable. Mikami was more and more sure of it. Futawatari had always weighed the risks against his actions – it was how he'd made his name as the department's ace.

Why was he doing it, even though he knew it was wrong?

Futawatari fully understood the dangers posed by the Koda memo. He might not know the contents, but he had already worked out that it was potentially explosive. No doubt he had immediately set out to learn what had happened. Two of the officers from the Home Unit had resigned from the force. Koda's whereabouts were unknown. Hiyoshi had become a recluse. And relations with Amamiya had broken down. These facts alone would have suggested that the memo – itself classified, and bearing Koda's name – was more than just a sheet of paper. He'd caught a whiff of gunpowder. But it was Six Four, and he'd known he would have to proceed carefully in case it brought down headquarters. Yet he had continued to accelerate his investigation.

Why?

Because his position had left him no choice. As far as Futawatari was concerned, 'the police' had become more than just the Prefectural HQ. More than just a department to uphold public safety, Administrative Affairs was in many ways a regional branch of the NPA. Futawatari was an inspector for the Prefectural HQ, but he was also a loyal servant to Tokyo. He had been quick to climb the ranks and be singled out, earn the trust and attention of many career executives, but, having done this, he was no longer able to move independently of their various machinations. The commissioner's visit was in four days. Futawatari would have been instructed to bring Criminal Investigations into line, to make sure of its compliance. He was running out of time. And the Koda memo was the only weapon he had. He had decided to use it as his opening gambit, all the while averting his eyes to the danger it constituted to the station.

This time, the theory spread like water, saturating his thoughts. Futawatari was in the same boat as he was. They were both under pressure, backed into a corner. Beneath his poker face Futawatari's eyes were bloodshot, fixated on the clock and the calendar. The commissioner's visit was the watershed moment, in four days' time. The deadline.

Of course.

Everything became clear. The commissioner's visit would intensify the feud between the Tokyo faction and Criminal Investigations. The idea had been there, subliminal. But that wasn't what would happen. The battle would be short, and decisive. And the countdown had already begun. The matter would be settled before the visit was even completed. The visit was more than just a formality, more than just ceremony or symbolism – it was going to be the sentence. Commissioner Kozuka would deliver the reality of Tokyo's goal in person. He would make some kind of important announcement. It was probably safe to assume that much.

His heart skipped a beat. He didn't know *what* the commissioner would say. But he knew *where* and *when* he intended to say it. *Outside Amamiya's house.* During the walking interview scheduled there.

Mikami caught his breath. His subconscious suddenly became aware of a red light up ahead, which forced him to slam on the brakes. He was a good way past the stop line when the car finally came to a halt. He looked around, but there were no cars or pedestrians to be seen. He was at a small intersection in the middle of a farming area, already in what had been the district of Morikawa, before its absorption into the city. Just minutes from Amamiya's house.

He felt a strong urge to turn back. His role was painfully clear. *Bring Amamiya around. Change his mind.* But this was much more than just groundwork for the visit. The commissioner intended to use the walking interview to issue a public message to Criminal Investigations. And the power of the media – in print and over the airwaves – would set the outcome in stone. If that was the true goal of the Tokyo faction, it meant that Mikami would be helping to set up the gallows on which to hang Criminal Investigations. He would act as producer, ensuring the final scene had as much impact as possible. It would be his job, as press director, to oversee the entire proceedings.

The lights changed and Mikami drove on, but he made a sharp turn as soon as the pickle factory came into view. There was a small park he remembered, down the road and along the river. Rows of poplar and camphor. Outdoor gym machines. An old, dilapidated phone box. The trees had grown impressively, but otherwise it was as he remembered from fourteen years earlier. Even the phone box was still there. The spread of mobile phones was forcing most of them out of commission; perhaps, in the wake of Six Four, the families having stopped coming here with their children, the park and its surroundings had been lost from memory.

Mikami pulled up alongside the phone box.

He would lose any chance of returning to Criminal Investigations. He was staring his greatest fear right in the face. He'd been repressing the love he felt for being a detective but it came rushing to the surface now that he realized he might never be one again.

Having had no other choice, he'd submitted to Akama's will. He'd taken everything on board and donned the uniform of obedience. That didn't mean he'd stopped hoping. That Ayumi would come home. That Akama would be transferred back to Tokyo. That, given time, everything would change for the better. That he would be able to shrug off his fake persona, continue his reform of Media Relations and return to Criminal Investigations with his head held high. How many times had he wished that?

But they wouldn't forgive him. Plotting. Conspiracy. Betrayal. Removing his disguise would only make him stand out as a traitor. Tsuchigane's words came forcefully to mind: *I doubt you plan to run errands for the first floor until the day you retire.*

Just take the gallows apart.

He nodded slowly, the voice in his mind a whispered invitation. If he abandoned his task of persuading Amamiya, talk of the commissioner visiting him would go away. With the situation as it was, the chance he would change his mind was minimal even if Mikami *did* try to talk him around.

Mikami decided he would see Amamiya again; he needed the alibi for when he saw Akama. But he wouldn't make any real effort to twist the man's arm. That way, the visit to his house – and, with it, the interview – was sure to be cancelled. Mikami didn't doubt that the commissioner would still make his announcement. Perhaps at the scene of the kidnapping. Perhaps in front of the Six Four Investigative Team. But it would be weak. The impact would pale into insignificance compared to it being made at the victim's home. *We only got by because Mikami's the press director.* It was a little petty, but there would still be hope if people inside Criminal Investigations commented on his actions. Akama would be furious, but his anger would be directed at Mikami's incompetence in failing to convince Amamiya; he wouldn't suspect Mikami of having encouraged Amamiya not to take part. Even if he did somehow realize Mikami's sabotage, there was a limit to the punishment he could issue, a line he couldn't cross. He might have used Ayumi as leverage in controlling Mikami, but he wouldn't be able to completely disregard a girl who was – as far as the police were concerned – family. He had authorized the search himself, and he couldn't change that, whatever happened between him and Mikami.

Everything changes with this decision.

Even though Akama had clearly demonstrated that he had done it only to make him into his puppet, the gratitude and obligation Mikami had felt when Akama sent the fax ordering the search to Tokyo had, until now, tempered his will to fight. If he were able to dispel those emotions, particularly now his reforms had ground to a halt, there would be no more reason to bend to Akama's will. There was, of course, the fear of being transferred somewhere else. If Akama decided he had sabotaged the commissioner's visit, he would be tossed off to some post in the mountains. But if his career as a detective was to end in demotion, it was still better than being on the receiving end of a dishonourable discharge. If the alternative was remaining in Administrative Affairs as the man who took a shot at Criminal Investigations, he would rather start from scratch in the middle of nowhere. The smallest paths are still paths. As long as he didn't resign, Ayumi's status as family wouldn't change. The 260,000 officers that made up the force would be sure to . . .

His phone started to vibrate in his jacket pocket.

He checked the display. His home phone. *Minako?* He pushed the answer button, hardly daring to hope.

'What is it?'

'Sorry, I know you're at work.' She was speaking quickly. Excited.

'Did something happen?'

'It's just something I've been wanting to say. Ayumi called us on 4 November, right?'

Mikami couldn't remember the date offhand. But if that was the date Minako gave him, it wouldn't be wrong. 'Yeah, that was it.'

'Mizuki told me the silent call they had was on Sunday, the seventeenth.'

'You called her?'

'Yes. I couldn't stop thinking about it so I just called to check. Anyway, that means you were wrong.'

'Wrong? How do you mean?'

'Ayumi called us thirty-four days ago. Mizuki's call came in three weeks ago.'

'That's not what I said?'

'You said they both called around the same time.'

She was sounding critical now.

'Okay, well, one was a month ago and the other three weeks. They're not too—'

'It's completely different. They were almost *two weeks* apart. They're completely unrelated, I'm positive.'

Mikami found himself at a loss as for what to say, realizing now that this was the only reason for her call. It meant she'd been dwelling on it since the previous night.

'You're right. They can't be related.'

He'd finally said it. Something like a sigh came over the line. Minako told him she needed to free the line.

Silence returned to his ears.

Mikami wound the driver-side window all the way down. Fresh air filtered into the car. He could hear the sound of the river. Even then, it felt hard to breathe, the sense lingering that his windpipe was constricted. He opened his mouth a little and tried to take in a deep breath, but only ended up coughing violently. His emotions followed soon after, as he came to realize the scale of his omission.

How could he expect Minako to come with him to some station in the mountains? She would choose to stay, to wait for the call. To wait and hope for Ayumi just to turn up one day. Would he go by himself? Would he leave her alone as he tried to reforge his career in such a remote location?

An optimist to the last, Mikami jeered inwardly. He was still looking for his place in the force. Dreaming of somewhere to lay his bones to rest, as a hero detective, using Ayumi's suffering as his excuse. Why hadn't he noticed? If he was sent away, if he and

Minako were separated, their family would never be whole again. He slammed a fist into his kneecap.

Had he forgotten? He would be a guard dog for Administrative Affairs. Hadn't he already decided that?

'Talk Amamiya into it.' Mikami issued the order to himself.

33

Amamiya was out.

Having seen the man as the embodiment of grief only three days earlier, Mikami hadn't even considered the possibility that he might not be in. He was living alone now his wife, Toshiko, had passed away. It was likely he was doing his own shopping and cooking. Mikami circled around to the side of the building to check for his car. There was only a bike. He was out in the car, although that didn't necessarily mean he had gone far. There were no real shops in the area, and the Prefecture D public-transport system was bad wherever you went, so you needed a car for errands even if you lived in town.

Mikami drove for about fifteen minutes before settling himself down in a family diner next to the prefectural highway. It was the same as the one he'd visited the previous day. The inside was a little bigger, and this one had benefited from what looked like a recent redesign; even so, over half the tables were empty, despite it being midday on a Sunday.

'Are you ready?'

A middle-aged waitress arrived to take his order, probably a housewife working part-time; her vaguely belligerent tone suggested she was having a bad day. Mikami considered the contrast to the waitress from the previous day. It seemed a rare coincidence in this kind of family diner to run into two waitresses who let their personal feelings show through at work.

What had Amamiya eaten?

Mikami decided that was where he should start. He needed to get closer to the man's feelings, to try to put himself in the suspect's shoes, as detectives were apt to say. Work out his emotional narrative. Then he would take careful aim and deliver the line that would bring him around.

He lit a cigarette.

Amamiya had seen the error take place in front of him. Yet, instead of losing his temper, he had actually apologized for taking the call without having been given permission.

His response wasn't particularly unusual. He had been completely dependent on the police. When they had asked him to cooperate with the Home Unit, he had agreed out of a desperate wish to recover Shoko, his only daughter. Their single-minded focus would have been plain to see. He would have sat with them, their hearts as one as they waited for the kidnapper's call. The phone had started to ring. Amamiya had panicked, seeing the tapes hadn't started, but he hadn't had time to get angry. He'd been scared it would annoy the kidnapper to be kept waiting. He'd wanted to hear his daughter's voice. Above all else, he'd been terrified that the phone would stop ringing. Feeling he had to do something, he had answered it.

They would have tested the recording equipment beforehand. It would have been working when they set it up. It was possible that the failure had been down to a faulty connection, not an actual problem with the machine. Maybe they could have got the kidnapper on tape, if only Amamiya had let the phone ring just a few more times. He might have come to the same conclusion after the call ended. He had broken his promise and cost the police a valuable lead. He saw himself as having disrupted the solidarity of the team. He found himself apologizing. No doubt it had been a true representation of his feelings.

Even so . . .

At the time, he had still believed his daughter would be coming home.

Some ash fell on to his knee. He flicked it away, pulled an ashtray towards him and stubbed out his cigarette. He mulled over an idea as he did so. It had been fourteen whole years. Amamiya wouldn't have spent the whole time wallowing in grief. He'd had a lifetime of opportunity to revisit, deliberate, ask questions, to examine the case in exhaustive detail.

What conclusion would he have come to, in his heart, about the error? Nothing about the call had ever come to light, even after the press had set out the case in minute detail – in the papers and on TV – once the embargo had been lifted. Kakinuma had probably been right to say that Amamiya would have realized the cover-up was motivated by fear of public criticism.

After Shoko's body was found, the Home Unit had been left with nothing more to do. They had worked with Amamiya, all together as one entity, but then they had moved on. *Running away.* It was possible Amamiya might have interpreted it this way. Nobody had shown up after that. Not even last year, after Toshiko's death.

Mikami had been part of the Six Four investigation, albeit only in the beginning. He was qualified enough to express his regrets on behalf of the Prefectural HQ. He would make a formal apology, to Amamiya, then to his wife and daughter at the Buddhist altar. He wouldn't need to be explicit – Amamiya would know what he was apologizing for.

Would his apology be enough to get Amamiya to open up? It was possible. He'd trusted the police in the past; maybe he'd been waiting all this time for a tiny shred of decency in the form of an apology. The question was whether or not Mikami could do it properly. He had to. He needed to get Amamiya on their side. For Ayumi's sake. So his family could be complete again.

But he would be apologizing to a man who had lost his family for good.

It'll be fine . . .

Mikami reached for the bill just as his phone started to vibrate.

Again? He saw a brief image of Minako, but it was someone else – although he hadn't been wrong to be wary.

'I need an update on Amamiya.' It was Ishii, sounding even more agitated than he had the night before.

Mikami scanned his surroundings before answering in a low voice, 'I'm working on it.'

'Haven't you been to see him yet?'

'He wasn't in.'

'Where are you now?'

'Somewhere nearby.'

'I just had a call from Akama. Asking the same thing.'

Akama was conscious of the deadline. He'd planned to make quick work of setting up the gallows, to stay ahead of Criminal Investigations. He hadn't foreseen that Amamiya would put up a fight.

'You know what that means, right? He's chasing us to get it done.'

'Yes, of course.'

'Well? Go and keep a watch on the place. We can't go back to Akama saying he was out, now can we?' Mikami said nothing; Ishii heaved a sigh. 'It's okay for you, you don't have to deal with this directly.'

The line went dead, the signal apparently failing. Ishii didn't try calling back. Amamiya didn't figure into his idea of 'directly'; nor did anyone else who had been involved in the case. He didn't know anything about it, and he didn't *want* to know anything about it. But even then, he was getting caught up in the waves Six Four was making. Mikami saw the image of Koda waving a red baton. He saw the tortured look on Kakinuma's face; Hiyoshi's mother, her face buried in her hands.

If the worst comes to the worst, it's your fault.

Mikami pulled his bag over and opened it; he took out the writing pad he'd bought the day before.

It's not your fault.

That was all he wrote. He'd never genuinely tried to save Hiyoshi.

Do a good deed, and it'll find its way back to you. It was something his dad used to say. *One good turn deserves another.* That was what he'd meant, but he'd lacked a proper education and always had his own way of saying things.

Mikami downed the rest of his tepid coffee, then got to his feet. He wasn't even sure what it meant to be *good* any more, not really. Thinking she might be good luck, he looked around, hoping to catch a glimpse of the waitress, but she was nowhere to be seen.

34

It was just after 2 p.m., but the clouds that had gathered made it seem already dark outside.

Amamiya's car was back in its parking space. Mikami touched the bonnet as he walked by. Already cold. He couldn't have gone far, unless it was the wind that had cooled the engine.

Mikami pressed the buzzer and used his hands to press the creases out of his suit. There was a long pause, enough to suggest nobody was in. Finally, the door opened and Amamiya appeared from inside. He looked empty. The chalky, white skin. The gaunt cheeks. Although he did seem very slightly healthier than three days earlier; Mikami realized that this was because he'd trimmed his overgrown white hair.

'Please excuse me for disturbing you a second time.' Mikami came forwards in a deep bow. Amamiya didn't respond. His eyes, obscured under his creased skin, silently asked him the reason for his visit. 'Can I ask you to hear me out one more time? I promise this will be the last time.'

Amamiya was silent.

'Please. It won't take long.'

There was another pause before Amamiya let out a faint sigh. 'Come in, then.'

'Thank you.'

Mikami followed the man's thin form inside. Amamiya showed him into the living room, as before. This time, Mikami asked before sitting down.

'Do you mind if I pay my respects?'

He was ready to be turned down, but Amamiya nodded quietly and walked off into the altar room. It happened just as Mikami let the relief sink in – his eyes landed on a name he hadn't expected to see. *Koda*. It was written on an envelope, as the sender, and was poking out of a letter rack mounted on the living-room wall. *The Koda memo*. Mikami knew it instantly. Koda must have sent Amamiya a copy of the memo he'd left in the director's letterbox, no doubt setting down everything that had happened leading up to the cover-up.

That was the reason for Amamiya's . . . .

But it didn't matter, not any more. Amamiya would have learned about the deception even if Koda hadn't told him. Mikami had to apologize. He'd been lucky to get this opportunity to offer incense. Amamiya had turned to face him, holding the lit candle.

Mikami gave a deep bow then stepped into the room. The tatami was cold under his feet. He moved the purple floor cushion to one side, then knelt before the altar. The apology was on the tip of his tongue. He clasped his hands together. He gazed up at the altar. On the shelf were two photos, one of Shoko, the other Toshiko, each placed in front of the memorial tablets. Both were smiling openly.

Their expressions seemed to blur.

Mikami was confused and his sudden emotions caught him off guard. By the time he noticed the heat in his eyes, the tears were already flowing. He didn't know what to think, or what it was that had made him burst into tears.

He took out a pocket tissue and dabbed it over his face. His fingers were trembling as he reached for the incense. It took him two, three attempts to lock them around one of the sticks. He was aware of Amamiya standing there, behind and off to one side. He reflected that no act could have been so convincing.

He held the stick of incense over the lit candle. His hands were still shaking, making it difficult to catch the flame. Amamiya's wife and daughter continued to smile. New tears came. They tumbled past his cheeks to hit the tatami. All he wanted to do was get away. It felt like an insult to their spirits, to be crying in front of them without even knowing the reason why.

He managed to place the incense so it stood up. He brought his hands together, but then held them up to his forehead. He did it to stop himself crying out loud.

He couldn't manage a prayer. Not even the simplest of blessings.

He turned on his knees to face Amamiya. Keeping his head down, he placed both hands on the tatami. Through misted vision he caught sight of Amamiya's hands and knees. His focus fell on the tip of the man's index finger. The nail was black with clotted blood; it felt, for a moment, like a manifestation of Amamiya's disgust.

The tears continued to flow. He'd forgotten everything he'd intended to say. He pushed his forehead on to the matted floor.

'Forgive me. I'll come back some other time.'

His voice was thick and clogged. He pushed himself back to his feet and gave Amamiya a quick bow before heading along the hallway to the door. He was already in his shoes when he heard the voice coming from behind.

'There was something . . . you wanted to talk to me about?'

'It's fine. I can come back.' Without turning around, he started towards the door.

'Was it the visit you'd mentioned? The man coming from Tokyo?'

Mikami stopped where he was.

'It's . . . it's fine. I'd be happy for him to visit.'

Mikami turned slowly. Amamiya was standing in the middle of the hallway, eyes still half down, but looking straight at him.

'Are you sure?'

'You said it would be Thursday? I'll make sure I'm in.'

35

Mikami's eyes felt dry.

He was heading for the city. For Akama's home. His mind was trained on his destination; his emotions, still shaken. His tears had persuaded Amamiya to change his mind. They had been unexpected. *This is for Ayumi. For Minako. Do whatever it takes.* Had some part of him thought that way? Amamiya had been touched. He'd seen the tears as an apology and reconsidered his position. It was terrifying. Mikami had managed to pull it off without consciously doing anything. He'd persuaded Amamiya to come around . . .

His mood gradually eased as he drove away from the man's house. Means aside, he had achieved what he'd set out to do. He'd clawed back the victory he'd all but given up on, and by the time the area of town containing the directors' housing came into view he thought he could glimpse a little light poking through the clouds. A part of him felt relieved at his own shamelessness. Something had got into him. To burst suddenly into tears before another man. He'd never done it before; he certainly never wanted to do it again.

Calculation also drove his rush to report in to Akama. *An incompetent press director.* Time seemed to have ground to a halt between them since Akama's explosion of two days earlier. And there was no guarantee he could reconcile things with the Press Club before the day of the commissioner's visit. He was glad to have Amamiya's blessing, but it meant nothing if the press were to boycott the interview. That was why he needed to make sure of Akama's reaction while his success with Amamiya was still fresh. If he failed to do that, his obligation to Criminal Investigations would rear its head once again. Now he'd set up the gallows, he wouldn't let Akama keep him in the dark about the reason behind the commissioner's visit – not any more. Criminal Investigations' crime, and its punishment. Meeting Akama was the only means he had of getting to the truth.

The area containing the houses of all the directors was bathed in weekend quiet. Mikami parked on the road and walked the ten metres to the intercom to Akama's house. He pressed the button.

'Mikami? What on earth do you think you're doing?' Akama answered, obviously annoyed. He had no doubt given up on Mikami producing a positive result. Career officers disliked visits during their downtime, but Mikami knew Akama had called Ishii to check on their progress with Amamiya.

'I've got some news, it's about Amamiya.'

'Hmm? What?'

Maybe the connection was bad; Akama didn't seem to hear. There was a short pause before the front door swung open. Mikami didn't recognize him for a moment. He was in a casual jumper with loose-fitting trousers, and he wasn't wearing his glasses. Mikami's eyes were naturally drawn to the man's curved shoulders, his scraggy chest, which drove home the effect the man's expensive, tailored suits and gold-rimmed glasses had on his projection of authority. When he spoke, however, there was no doubt who it was.

'What's wrong with you, coming here directly? You report through Division Chief Ishii.'

'Amamiya has granted us his permission,' Mikami said quickly.

Akama looked at him, surprised. He gestured for Mikami to step into the doorway but remained on the step above, donning a pair of slippers but showing no sign of inviting him further into the house.

'The commissioner can enter his house. Offer incense at the altar. Yes?'

'He gave me his word.'

A woman laughed from somewhere inside. Akama had probably invited his family from Tokyo for the weekend. He still looked irritated. Mikami was sure it was a reaction to having an underling intrude on his private space.

'Okay. Will we have enough space for all the cars?'

'There should be plenty of room in front of the house.'

'That's too close. Can you arrange it so the commissioner can leave the house then walk a little before the reporters come in?'

'If they park on the road, that should leave enough space.'

'Will the house be visible in the background, if we do it that way?'

Akama's attention to detail served to bolster Mikami's confidence. Tokyo was fixed on securing Amamiya's house as the venue for their announcement.

'What's important is the picture for the cameras. Once the commissioner has paid his respects at the altar, he will emerge – looking dignified – from the house, then take the reporters' questions outside. Can you set it up to work like that?'

'It shouldn't be a problem. If we make sure the cameras are on the road, the house should show up in the background.

'*Should* isn't good enough, Mikami. Make sure you rehearse it the day before. We need to be absolutely certain before we go ahead.'

Akama had yet to say a word of thanks. All the same, his frown had eased and it was clear he'd relaxed somewhat. It also didn't seem like he was going to raise the issue of the proposed boycott. He was perhaps confident the issue would be rectified during the following day's round-table meeting, when they would have a chance to discuss it *properly* with the branch heads. Unless . . . he had something else up his sleeve.

More laughter piped up from inside the house.

'You're dismissed, if that's all you have to report. I'm supposed to be—'

'Sir,' Mikami cut in. He couldn't let his chance to ask pass by. 'Sorry, but there was one other thing I wanted to ask about.'

'What is it?' Akama shot a glance into the house. He was getting restless.

'What is the commissioner aiming for with this announcement?'

Akama's eyes betrayed a momentary indecision. But that was all. 'What are you trying to say? You know, you'd do well to think before you speak, Mikami. The commissioner is there to answer the questions from the press.'

'Yes, of course.' Mikami knew he'd get nowhere making Akama angry. And yet . . . 'Criminal Investigations is on edge.'

'Oh, is it now?'

'The situation might get out of control. If we continue to hold the Koda memo at their throats—'

'The what?' Surprisingly, Akama gave him a puzzled look. Was he pretending not to know? Or had he really never heard of it? 'I don't know what you're talking about. It would help, Mikami, if you made sense.'

'But—'

Mikami stopped himself there. If he really didn't know, it would only complicate the matter. What Mikami wanted to find out was the reason for the commissioner's visit.

'I just want to understand the whole picture, as press director. If you could tell me Tokyo's aim in this, that would help a lot.'

'That's enough. Don't you think it's time you learned, Mikami?' Akama said, looking as if he'd had enough. 'What would be the point of your knowing, hmm? Media Relations is just a speaker on a wall. The broadcasting room is somewhere else entirely. Only a select few get to take the microphone.'

A speaker on a wall. A select few. Not knowing how to respond,

Mikami dropped his eyes to his feet. As he did, a pair of white socks came sliding into the hallway.

'Papa, are you still busy?' came a voice.

The socks were attached to a little wide-eyed girl in her first or second year of secondary school. Her eyes caught Mikami's and she darted behind a bannister, hiding playfully in the shadow. Akama's stern façade collapsed.

'I'm sorry, darling. Papa won't be much longer now.'

'We'll miss the start if we don't go now.'

'It'll be okay, it won't start right on time.'

'Mum's worried the roads'll be busy.'

'Okay, Achan, you go ahead and get in the car with Yoshi.'

Mikami had overstayed his welcome. He'd done enough. With this in mind, he bowed to take his leave.

'Sorry to have intruded.'

When he turned around, he heard a stifled giggle. Turning, he saw the young girl, still half concealed, and watching him out of one eye. She had one hand over her mouth, trying to hold back laughter. An unspeakable emotion washed over him. He felt himself shiver. It was as though he'd caught a glimpse of himself through the girl's eyes. The way he looked to other people, not the way he looked to himself in the mirror or in a photograph.

Ayumi felt suddenly close by. He felt a need to cover himself with something. The girl's crescent-moon eyes, which were no doubt full of charm, seemed at that moment to resemble those of a felon or a demon.

36

Back outside, the heavens threatened to open at any moment. Mikami couldn't tell if it would be rain or snow; the thick clouds could go either way.

As he walked back to his car, his phone started to vibrate in his jacket pocket. Something told him it had also been doing this while he'd been standing outside Akama's house. He checked the caller display. Mizuki Murakushi.

He heard a noise and looked up. Akama's garage door was sliding open. A metallic-silver sedan slowly emerged from inside. Akama was at the wheel. His wife was in the passenger seat, dressed to go out. Two heads bobbed in the back. The car drew closer. Passed by. Mikami kept his head down.

He glanced up at the side and back mirrors. The car continued to pull away. The brake lights came on. It turned a corner. Even then, Mikami found it hard to shake the sensation of those eyes, laughing as they watched him.

Something in his pocket was vibrating again. Shaking himself out of his reflections, he pushed the answer button.

'I know, you're at work. Should I call later?'

Despite the suggestion, it was clear she had no intention of hanging up.

'No, it's fine. I'm on a break. What is it?'

'I had another call from Minako, about an hour ago.'

'Okay.'

Hearing what he had expected to hear, Mikami felt a mixture of relief and annoyance.

'She kept asking about the silent call we had. I think she wanted to convince herself it was nothing to do with the ones you had, that yours were from Ayumi, after all.'

'Uh-huh.'

'Well? Did you have a proper talk to her about it?'

'Yeah. Can't say if it went well or not, though.'

'You think it might have backfired? She did sound a little cross with me.'

'Maybe.'

'Hmm?'

Perhaps that had sounded a little cold. 'I'm pretty sure it didn't backfire. Don't worry about it.'

'You think so? Oh, you know how worked up I get when I think of Minako having to deal with this by herself. I had another call, too, from the Matsuokas.'

The name threw him for a moment.

'Oh, not *Chief Matsuoka*. His wife, Ikue. She said you visited their apartment?'

'That's right.'

'Right. Anyway, she didn't seem to think the calls were from Ayumi either. She said she hadn't been sure, about what you'd told her.'

Word had spread around the female officers' network. Mikami began to feel irked. When people started to talk without involving himself or Minako he couldn't help doubting their good intentions, regardless of any apparent sincerity.

'I asked around a bit . . . and it turns out almost everyone's had a call at some point. They had one at the chief's family home, too, only a couple of months back.'

'Huh.'

'Would you try talking to her again?'

'Sure.'

'If she insists the calls were from Ayumi after you've talked it through, well, it's probably best just to go with it. The worst thing would be for her to feel isolated. Just say it was my idea – tell her I'm a meddling gossip, something like that. Whatever happens, she needs to believe you're on her side.'

Mikami reconsidered his frustration, but it was still hard just to say yes. Mizuki was helping more than most sisters would.

'Mikami? Are you still there?'

'Yeah.'

'Are you angry?'

'Why would I be?'

'Are you sure? Maybe I shouldn't have suggested anything in the first place . . .'

'Don't worry about it. Minako makes her own decisions.'

'What do you mean?'

He clicked his tongue, frustrated at having to answer yet another question. 'Just that she's not the type to let herself get swayed by anything you or I say.'

'I don't think that's true for you. She believes in you from the bottom of her heart. You should be more confident in yourself.'

He didn't like the sound of what she was saying. Was she planning to talk about a Minako he didn't know, out here among the directors' housing block?

'Okay, thanks for letting me know. I have to—'

'Wait. Oh, no, this won't do. You sound like you've given up completely. Are you sure the two of you aren't fighting? Is it because of me?'

'It's nothing to do with that, like I said.'

'But . . .'

'We're just not on the same level. The truth is, I can never tell what she's thinking.'

'Since Ayumi ran away, you mean?'

'No. Right from the beginning.'

Mikami wondered if he'd accidentally imparted something he

hadn't meant to. Mizuki fell silent, sighing before she spoke again.

'In that case, I'll tell you how she feels.'

'There's no need.'

'I'm telling you. I couldn't stand it, not for you two to come unstuck when you most need to be there for each other. You can't let that happen, not even a little bit. Especially if you haven't communicated properly in the past.'

'Look, I was a detective. I didn't have the time to—'

'You know that's not what I'm talking about. It's no use throwing up a smokescreen, Mikami, I know what it is you're worried about. We all know everyone was surprised when the two of you got married. They said it was one of the prefecture's seven great wonders. I mean, you *were* in the same station, but not for long, and it wasn't as though you worked together – she was in Traffic, you were in Criminal Investigations. The other men were genuinely amazed. All wondering what you'd done to get a girl like that. But the thing is, *you* don't know what you did either. I'm right about this, aren't I?'

Mikami felt his chest tighten.

'I'm going to tell you what you did. When you were there, in that station together—'

'You needn't bother.'

'Just hear me out, okay? One day, she went through a bad experience, and spent the whole night crying. But she didn't drag the problem to work – you know how seriously she took being a policewoman. She put her feelings to one side, did her make-up and dragged herself, smiling, back into work. She greeted everyone normally, carrying on with her work as though nothing had happened. She took lunch with her workmates, chatting away without showing any signs of being down. So nobody noticed. Then, when she was on her way home, she happened to bump into you outside the side entrance. You gave her a funny look and said, 'Are you okay?' That was all you said. That was when she started to take notice of you. She said she gave you a road-safety charm not too long after that.'

Mikami could only remember fragments. 'That was just . . .' he said without thinking. 'That was just a wild guess. I probably just said it to get her attention, either that or I'm some kind of clairvoyant.'

'This isn't something to joke about. This is where you ask me the reason she spent the whole night crying, right?'

Mikami started coughing. 'That's enough, just stop,' he finally managed.

'No, it's not enough. I can't stop now I've said this much and broken my promise, anyway. What's the point otherwise? And listen, it's not what you're thinking. But it's not something you'd put in a wedding speech either. One of her friends committed suicide. A high-school friend, from the same year; they'd been in the calligraphy club together. The people in the club were close and continued to meet after they all moved on from the school. Anyway, the girl who killed herself did so leaving behind a scribbled note on her desk. "Don't tell Minako." That was all it said.'

'*Don't tell Minako?* That she was dead?'

'Minako wondered if the message had been intended to keep her from going to the funeral. It really frightened the girl's parents. They called Minako on the phone, asking if something had happened between them. But there hadn't been anything, nothing at all. Minako had been busy, so they hadn't even seen each other for a while. Yet the fact remained that she'd been mentioned by name. Her friend had died and left instructions to keep her in the dark – and she didn't find out until the day of the wake. She still went, you know. It must have been torture. She told me she felt like an intruder the whole time. As though she'd been denied permission to grieve, even though she was suffering at having lost a friend. She left to go back to her dorm room without staying for the final rites; that was when she finally started crying.'

Mizuki's rapid-fire voice broke off.

'Did they find out the reason for the suicide? Had she left anything else?'

'Nothing. She'd separated from her husband and was living by herself. They'd been married three years but had no kids. I don't know why they ended up living apart, but it must have had something to do with her suicide. Her husband had been in the calligraphy club of a nearby boys' school. They'd originally met during a summer getaway organized between the two clubs. They'd fallen in love and ended up getting married. From what I know, her husband was good-looking and smart, popular with the girls.

'This next bit is just my own speculation, okay? He'd seen Minako during the same summer trip, and he'd fallen in love with her at first sight, so her friend had had to work hard to win him over. When they were first married she felt like she had all the happiness in the world. But then it started to go wrong, and she ended up by herself, started to think of suicide, and that was when she saw Minako. She wanted to leave something to get her own back. So she decided to leave that note.'

It sounded like more than empty speculation. 'You think Minako . . . had something to do with their separation?'

'Oh, come on, Mikami! What I'm trying to say is that having someone with Minako's looks around all the time would have made the other girls uneasy. Even supposing the girl's husband-to-be *hadn't* fallen for Minako during their summer trip, she would still have been afraid that he would. She'd have been going crazy with the worry. Believe me, the majority of normal women have experienced that sort of thing. So do you see? She was fighting with *herself*. But she never realized it was all in her head. She set herself up against Minako, then she won her man and sealed her victory, ending up on a high that was ten times, a hundred times, greater than normal. Then everything fell apart . . . in just three years. I don't know if it was something to do with him, or something else entirely, but I know she would have had so many regrets; then I suppose she gave in to despair, and started to feel hostile towards a carefree, happy-looking Minako. So maybe she decided she wanted Minako to have a taste of her own suffering.'

Carefree? Happy?

'Why would she assume Minako was—'

'Minako wouldn't have known any of this was going on, not at the start, not at the end. That's why. She wouldn't ever have considered that they were in competition, wouldn't have known she'd lost any lead. She would have been genuinely happy for her friend's marriage, never in a million years considering she'd lost anything. I'm sure her friend had no reason to feel the way she did. But I don't think she could have left such a heartless note if she hadn't got to the point of thinking that Minako had in some way pushed her into the marriage, and been responsible for the mess that followed. She would have wanted her husband to break down in tears at her funeral, feel the guilt, all the regret and the pain. She didn't want Minako to share in their final meeting. She wouldn't have wanted anyone to distract him from her, not even for a moment. I don't know whether any of this is true or not, but it was still a horrible thing to do . . .'

Horrible, but understandable. Mikami understood the implication. After a moment's silence, Mizuki started to laugh.

'Anyway, you shouldn't take the last bit seriously. Just my imagination running wild. Pure fancy. All I'm trying to say is Minako's special enough for that kind of thing to be true. Believe me, I had a hard time, too. It was a nightmare when she got out of police school and got posted to work for me. I thought: *Seriously? Why would someone like you want to be a policewoman? Do you want to test yourself, take pride in your job? Don't you think you're being a little greedy?* Back when she joined, women were still treated like mascots in the force, so we were all fighting for a little more recognition. Along comes Minako, the very definition of a mascot, and we're all crying that we don't need any more women like that.

'Of course, the truth was, we'd enjoyed being fussed over a little. That stopped quickly enough. The younger officers couldn't take their eyes off Minako, and her bosses were clearly smitten, regardless of whether they were telling her off or complimenting her on a job well done. To be honest, we were beyond jealousy; most of the time it just felt like we'd had the wind taken out of our sails.'

Mizuki let out another chuckle. She'd realized she was straying from the point.

'I'm only telling you this because of the circumstances – she was actually bullied at work. I was guilty of it, just a little. But she was strong. Took the nonsense in her stride. She lived for her job. More than most of the men, really. It was so impressive, to see someone so beautiful yet so totally unconscious of it. I realized she was a hard-working and decent person. Even then, it was difficult to feel close to her.

'It was easy to see, watching from the sidelines, that she received special treatment. When I was feeling uncharitable, I would suspect it was all an act, that she was just *pretending* not to notice the effect she had on people. It wasn't until I heard the two of you were getting married that I was able to feel a genuine affection for her. I couldn't believe it when she told me. Actually asked if she was pulling my leg. Ah, don't take it the wrong way, I'm not trying to imply she undersold herself or anything. You were a young detective with a bright future, and don't forget I also knew why she'd given you the charm. That's how it was, anyway. It was a decisive moment. Everyone relaxed around her when they learned she was taken, and by you. Everyone's opinion of *you* – well, that went down the drain. They were all, *Look at him, head over heels in love – he'd never looked at anything but case work*.'

Mikami snorted.

He had relaxed into the story. He'd stopped wondering about the reason for Mizuki's diversion, and had been listening to her discuss Minako's difficult situation, and her own speculation as to what had caused it, as though he were skimming over an unpleasant scene in one of his favourite children's stories. He felt a pleasant fatigue and warmth in his chest. Mizuki's reflections on the past had taken the edge off his mood. If he'd looked up and seen anyone else, anyone other than the man who was approaching, he would have stayed on the phone and continued to listen to his good friend.

'Sorry,' he said. 'We'll have to talk later.'

He snapped the phone shut, pulled the key from the engine and opened the car door, the whole time keeping his eyes fixed on Futawatari.

37

Two pieces on the same board. The coincidence no longer came as a surprise.

The same seemed true for Futawatari. He continued down the house-lined street, drawing closer without a single alteration in his expression or pace. He was dressed in a suit, as usual. Did he have business with Akama? Or had he just emerged from another building? He'd been closest to the houses where Captain Tsuji-uchi and Director Arakida lived when Mikami had first noticed him. It made sense if he'd been here visiting the captain. Akama hadn't heard of the Koda memo. That meant the chances were good that Futawatari was operating under the direct orders of the captain himself.

Mikami stood waiting outside his car. When Futawatari was close enough, he called out to him.

'Akama's out if you're after him.'

Futawatari continued to approach in silence. Now he was closer, Mikami could make out the severe expression on his face. He seemed to be avoiding eye contact, but not by much.

'Working hard, I see,' Mikami said, looking him square in the face.

'You, too,' Futawatari replied, walking straight by and keeping his eyes ahead.

You bastard . . .

Mikami spun around and started after him. He followed Futawatari's wispy frame from behind, moving slightly to the side, and caught up with him at the far end of the wall outside Akama's house. At the intersection, Futawatari turned towards a smaller road. His dark-blue sedan was visible in the distance, parked ahead on a wider section.

'Confidential discussions with the captain?' Futawatari didn't answer. 'Right, the silent treatment. That's cold even for you.'

'I don't have the time.'

Mikami could see he actually meant it.

'I found out what's in the Koda memo.'

He'd said it to freeze Futawatari in his tracks. It didn't work. His steps shortened as he pulled his keys from his pocket and pushed the button, unlocking his car.

'What do you intend to do to Criminal Investigations?'

Still mute, Futawatari reached towards the driver-side door.

'Look, just wait.' Mikami lowered his voice, putting himself between Futawatari and the car.

'Didn't I just tell you I don't have the time?'

Futawatari glared at him. Mikami glowered back.

'Neither do I.'

'Go and do what you need to do, then.'

'What is the commissioner planning to say?'

'It doesn't concern you.'

'I think it does. Don't think I'm going to play a role in taking down Criminal Investigations without knowing the reason first.'

'As if it matters.'

Mikami was dumbstruck. *As if it matters.* Had he heard correctly? He let his voice drop to a whisper.

'Listen to me. The Koda memo is a veritable Pandora's box. That thing's capable of destroying the entire headquarters, not just Criminal Investigations.'

'What if it does?'

'I'm sorry?'

'Get *out* of my way,' Futawatari snarled, reaching again for the door.

Mikami took him by the wrist.

'Is it your plan to sell us out to Tokyo?'

His hand was knocked away with surprising violence.

'Don't be so narrow-minded. There are no distinctions; no headquarters, no Tokyo. The police force is monolithic.'

Futawatari took his opportunity. He shoved Mikami out of the way. His lanky frame slid into the driver's seat; he keyed the ignition. *Wait*. Mikami's cry was lost against the noise of sudden acceleration. Mikami started walking then broke into a run. He got into his car and pulled out. The road Futawatari had headed for was littered with traffic lights. He could still catch him.

He couldn't ignore what Futawatari had just said.

The police force is monolithic.

Mikami made a sharp turn to rejoin the main road. His eyes were focused directly ahead. *There*. Futawatari's dark-blue sedan was stuck at a red, two sets of lights ahead.

Mikami had already guessed that his interests weren't going to be compatible with Futawatari's. But he'd hoped, regardless. He'd hoped that they were both torn between their allegiances, single bodies with two minds, existing in a world where hierarchy was everything; that the man's conflicted state would come to the surface if he challenged him face to face; that Futawatari might finally drop his mask of indifference.

But he'd been wrong.

Mikami hit the accelerator the moment the lights turned green. He pulled ahead of the small yellow car to his side and crossed into the right-hand lane; he accelerated past a truck then slid back to the left. The dark-blue sedan was ten cars ahead. The sky was already growing dark. *Perfect*. Mikami pulled the sun visor close to his eyes, then used one hand to remove his tie. Spying an opportunity, he passed the next car in front. The road was full of Sunday drivers. They were either driving far too slowly or jumping mindlessly around, forcing him to concentrate. He repeated the cycle of accelerating, decelerating. The sedan was only four cars ahead now. He settled into the standard routine for close pursuit.

What kind of police officer lets himself be tailed?

Mikami pulled at the wheel, abruptly switching lanes. The back of Futawatari's head was visible through the sedan's rear window. *Something urgent.* Where was he going? Who was he hoping to see? Mikami would follow him until he stopped, back him into a corner, force him to confess his true intentions.

The sedan took a left at the next junction, entering an older road that followed the river. The road narrowed to a single lane on each side. Mikami maintained his tail, keeping two cars between them. There were no more buildings outside the window, just a flood plain stretching off to the left. The road snaked through a gentle curve as it followed the river. At each bend the two cars ahead would slide momentarily to one side, giving Mikami a clear view of the sedan's rear lights.

The station wagon just ahead started to brake. At the front, Futawatari was slowing down. His indicators flashed to turn right. He taxied to let an oncoming car pass, then left the road at a crossroad intersection.

Mikami followed after him, turning slowly so as not to give himself away. He saw the sedan take a left at the next junction, into a quiet, old-fashioned residential district. Mikami finally realized where Futawatari was going. Instead of a destination, the name of a man Mikami knew lived nearby came into his head.

But that's . . .

Mikami edged forwards, not daring to breathe. He glanced down the street the sedan had entered. His eyes registered the shock first. The car was parked next to a hedgerow of red photinia. Outside the house of Michio Osakabe.

Futawatari's thin profile vanished through the door.

38

The hazy winter sun was getting ready to set.

Having decided to wait, Mikami circled around to park at a sports complex down towards the flood plain. He kept his eyes glued to the road. He intended to keep watch until Futawatari was gone.

He tried to map Futawatari's movements in his head. When he'd seen him near Akama's house, he'd felt sure he'd been there to see Tsujiuchi, but maybe the truth was that he'd emerged from Arakida's house across the road. That would mean he'd been there to launch an attack on the enemy camp. Arakida had then turned him away, and he'd decided he would extend his reach to the department's alumni – unless he'd somehow got wind that Osakabe had been connected to the cover-up, and decided to make an attempt on the summit.

The line seemed to come together. Still, Osakabe was on a level far above even the other directors. Like the highest executives – albeit in a completely different way – he was, for the people of the Prefectural HQ, someone who existed above the clouds. It was unthinkable under any normal circumstances to barge into his home with the aim of extracting information. Futawatari was on a rampage. Only someone who thought himself above the other sections, part of the elite, would be capable of such a thing. Whatever his thinking, it was safe to assume the proximity of the deadline was forcing Futawatari to become more brazen.

It doesn't matter; Osakabe won't listen.

Mikami flicked an eye to the display on the dashboard: 4.40 p.m. Fifteen minutes since Futawatari had entered Osakabe's home. Just as he was thinking this, Mikami saw the sedan pass in front of him. *There.* Mikami didn't miss the face, caught briefly in the streetlights. Futawatari's expression had been grave. He'd have had less than ten minutes to talk. It was no surprise. A man like Osakabe would never play host to Administrative Affairs for long.

Mikami set off towards the director's house. He would find out what was behind Futawatari's covert manoeuvring. Osakabe would tell him the real reason for the commissioner's visit. It seemed likely he would know. He was party to everything that had happened, not just the contents of the Koda memo. Futawatari must have realized this; it was probably why he'd decided to visit him in person.

Mikami was in the middle of the right turn at the intersection when his phone went off in his jacket pocket. He finished the turn, then pulled up to the side of the road. It was Ishii. Mikami swore under his breath, then pressed answer.

'What do you think you're doing, Mikami?' Mikami had never heard him sound so agitated.

'Sorry?'

'Don't pretend you don't know. I just had a call from Director Akama. He said you'd already fixed things with Amamiya?'

Mikami realized he'd forgotten to report in after his encounter with Futawatari.

'Sorry, a lot of things were going on.'

'But you managed to report to Akama? What possessed you to go over my head on this? You should have called me first . . . How do you think this looks for me, having to admit I didn't know?'

'I'll be more careful in the future,' Mikami said, making it clear he was ending the conversation, but the message didn't seem to get through.

'You wanted to take the credit directly, I assume? I don't know how you do things over in Criminal Investigations, but that kind of behaviour just isn't acceptable here.'

The words just washed over him. Ishii wasn't even on the same board.

'There is no Criminal Investigations, no Administrative Affairs.'

'I'm sorry?'

'I'll make sure I'm more careful in the future,' Mikami repeated, and ended the call.

As if it matters, he muttered to himself. He flicked on his headlights and pulled back on to the road. He turned the first corner and the car's beam fell on the vivid red of the photinia. He parked where Futawatari's car had been and walked briskly up to the front door. He felt himself tense when he saw the name on the plate. *Osakabe*. His throat dried up. He hadn't phoned ahead. He hadn't even worked for Osakabe, not directly. On any other day, he wouldn't have been able to push the buzzer. But this wasn't any other day, not for the Prefectural HQ. And Osakabe had admitted a man who had no knowledge outside of Administrative Affairs – he wouldn't turn away someone with years of experience as a detective. Mikami worked up his courage, then pushed the buzzer.

It felt like a long wait. The door finally opened to reveal the face of an elegant old woman, her white hair neatly plaited. It was the first time Mikami had seen Osakabe's wife.

He bent forward from the waist, the form of the gesture letting her know he was from the police.

'Please forgive the sudden intrusion. My name is Mikami. I'm with the police headquarters.'

He held out his card and Osakabe's wife accepted it in both hands. She showed no signs of surprise at his visit, so soon after Futawatari's.

'Press Director Mikami?'

'That's right.'

'May I ask why you're visiting?'

'There's a matter I wanted to discuss with Director Osakabe, if possible.' Director, even after retirement. That would never change.

'Of course. If you could give me a moment while I pass on your message.' She disappeared briefly before emerging again. 'Please, follow me.' She gestured for him to enter, then led him along a cool hallway before showing him into the guest room.

Mikami's legs were as stiff as posts.

'Sir. Thank you for agreeing to see me,' he said, intoning clearly. He felt like a newly recruited officer again.

Osakabe was sitting next to a low table on the floor. Eight years retired. Aged sixty-eight. He'd lost a little weight around his cheeks and neck, giving him a sinewy appearance that was in line with his age, but his eyes were sharp as they regarded Mikami, and commanded no less authority than they had during his time in active duty.

'Sit yourself down.'

Mikami obeyed, folding his knees. He declined Osakabe's offer of a cushion and sat awkwardly in formal *seiza*. Osakabe folded his arms. Face to face, his presence was overwhelming.

'Please excuse me for barging in like this. My name is Mikami, I'm in charge of Media Relations. I was assistant director in Second Division until the spring when—'

'Just tell me why you're here.'

'Of course.' Mikami forced himself to move on. 'Inspector Shinji Futawatari was just here. I wanted to know the reason for his visit,' he said, getting straight to the point.

Osakabe's expression told him to continue.

'I'm sure you know this, but the headquarters is coming apart. Criminal Investigations and Administrative Affairs are at odds with each other over the commissioner's proposed inspection of the Six Four investigation. The commissioner is scheduled to arrive in four days, but relations are strained to breaking.'

Osakabe remained inscrutable. He looked like someone heading up a case meeting, waiting for his subordinates to finish their reports.

'I think Commissioner Kozuka is planning to make an announcement, one that will have severe repercussions for Criminal Investigations. Futawatari is helping set the stage, asking questions of officers in the department.'

Osakabe said nothing.

'I wondered if he might have come here with the same purpose?'

'I told him I had no idea what he was talking about,' Osakabe said flatly.

Mikami's head started to race as he felt a surge of something like kinship. Osakabe had just told him he'd kept Futawatari in the dark. He was addressing Mikami as though he were in Criminal Investigations.

'What did he try asking you about?' Mikami tried pushing a little, but Osakabe said nothing else. 'If I can be honest . . . I still don't know what Tokyo intends to do. If you know what they're planning, it would be a great help.'

The silence seemed to deepen. What would happen if he were to bring up the subject of the Koda memo? Would Osakabe's involvement in the cover-up compel him to walk away? There was no choice. Futawatari would have addressed the subject.

'I believe Futawatari would have mentioned something called the "Koda memo". Am I right to assume that?'

'As press director, what is your interest in this?'

This threw Mikami. Had Osakabe asked this defensively? Or did he want to clarify Mikami's position first, before he moved on to talk about the core issue? *I told him I had no idea what he was talking about.* Stunned by Osakabe's words and swept up by the murky, detective-like atmosphere of the room, Mikami had – despite the question being an obvious one – forgotten to explain his own stance.

'My . . .'

He could feel the sweat on his palms. Whatever Osakabe's reasons for asking, now the question was in the air Mikami knew the conversation was over unless he answered.

'It's true that I am currently based in Administrative Affairs. That I am therefore under an obligation to follow my commanding officer's orders. And while I don't know Tokyo's goal in this, I realize I am a part of the plan. But—'

I haven't sold my soul.

'I only want to know what's necessary in order for me to do my job as press director, as the person in charge of managing the sites during the commissioner's visit. That's why I'm here.'

'How would you use the information?'

'I would keep it to myself and carry out my orders.'

'Meaning you would commit yourself to Administrative Affairs but remain a detective?'

'No, I . . .'

Mikami stopped, reconsidering. It would be foolish to pretend he belonged in Administrative Affairs, not after he'd come here driven by his loathing for Futawatari. Osakabe was right. Mikami couldn't erase the part of him that was still a detective. Even if he *had* sold his soul, he was still a detective in flesh and blood. He needed something that fundamentally differentiated him from Futawatari. Osakabe had turned Futawatari away, but Mikami had been confident he wouldn't do the same to him.

'Yes, I think you're right. That's just a part of me now, I can't do anything about it. I won't forget that I'm a detective, whatever it is I end up doing.'

'You want to go back?'

'I can't deny it. But—'

'So you're saying you'd like to have an easy run of things?'

'An . . . easy run?'

'Sure. The job's an easy one. Easiest in the world.'

Mikami didn't understand what he was hearing. The job was

easy? Was that what he'd meant? Or had he meant *being there* was easy? Being a part of Criminal Investigations, where he could be himself. Where he'd left his desk, his pride, his achievements . . .

Osakabe unfolded his arms.

'Return to your post. There's nothing so foolish as wasting the present for the future.'

What?

'Today is for today. Tomorrow is for tomorrow.'

Mikami was stunned.

Osakabe was already on his feet. Mikami needed to make the decision.

'Please, wait.'

He had to say it: it was the only thing that would keep him there.

'I believe you know the truth about the Koda memo. If the information gets out, it will harm your reputation, too.'

Osakabe peered down at him. His eyes were quiet, philosophical, as though he'd let go of everything years earlier.

'Return to your post. Chance can define a lifetime.'

'It could bring the department down.'

Osakabe ignored the question to the end.

So you're going to run?

Osakabe walked out of the room, leaving nothing but a brush of air wafting across Mikami's cheeks. The sound of his footsteps receded along the hallway. As though it was a custom of the house, his wife came quietly in to take his place, carrying a cup and saucer.

'Some tea before you go?'

There was something reassuring about her voice. Mikami felt the tension slip away from his back and knees. *Ten minutes, on the dot.* He didn't doubt Futawatari had been left with the same bitter aftertaste, drinking tea after Osakabe had left the room.

39

In the cold air outside, Mikami became aware of the heat in his face.

In their fight for information, both he and Futawatari had suffered a painful defeat. While that was true for this particular round, however, the fact remained that Futawatari knew Tokyo's intentions, while he didn't. For his part, Mikami had learned the secret of the Koda memo. Yet, try as he might, he hadn't been able to get Futawatari to talk, and Osakabe had presented an insurmountable rock face.

But that wasn't all . . .

Return to your post.

Chance can define a lifetime.

Fatigue convinced him to go home. He made a detour to Hiyoshi's home and left the letter he'd written with the man's mother: *It's not your fault.* Now that Kakinuma had confessed to the truth, he had less need to reach Hiyoshi, but he knew he'd feel bad if he abandoned him now without having first delivered his words.

At home, Minako had prepared mackerel and a vegetable stir-fry. Although she wasn't smiling, her expression had softened a little. Mikami had expected her to bring up the phone calls again but, dressed in her apron and perhaps satisfied after their conversation earlier in the day, she showed no signs of wanting to raise the subject.

When they'd started to eat she said, 'Did something good happen at work?'

Mikami blinked at the sudden question. 'Why, do I look different?'

'A bit.'

It was probably his relief showing through at finding Minako in a good mood. Although it was possible it was the other way around. He'd arrived home in good spirits, and she'd let his mood raise hers, too. That would explain it. It was the effect of the talk he'd had with Mizuki Murakushi. She'd helped fill one of the many gaps in the jigsaw puzzle of their marriage. It might have remained obscured beneath his self-consciousness, his other worries, but the warmth he'd felt when listening to Mizuki reminisce about Minako had already been integrated into his deep memory, settled into a place where it couldn't be overwritten. It wasn't just fatigue that had urged him to come home. He was sure of it.

'You do look tired, though. Is anything wrong?'

'Got through a major obstacle, actually. Amamiya has agreed to let the commissioner visit him.'

Mikami had expected her to take this as good news; instead, she tilted her head to the side.

'Oh? Hadn't he turned you down already?'

'Yeah, the first time.'

'Huh. I wonder why he would . . .'

Mikami didn't want to tell her that he'd cried at the Buddhist altar.

'I think he probably realized I was being sincere.'

'That must be it,' Minako agreed, encouraging him, but the look of surprise was still there.

Mikami felt sure that Amamiya had been moved by his reaction. He thought the tears had probably fallen because he'd seen Ayumi in the photographs; he was certain of it. Amamiya had lost his daughter; he would have sensed something was wrong in the way Mikami had acted.

Still . . .

Was it that he'd seen Ayumi? Mikami had asked the question

several times during his drive back home, but he hadn't been able to find a satisfactory answer.

'I need to make a short call for work,' he called to Minako, who had just started on the dishes. He picked up the phone and headed into the bedroom.

Amamiya's feelings on the matter aside, the hurdle of the commissioner's visit had been cleared. As of tomorrow, Mikami could go back to working on the press – he would be involved in tough negotiations right up to the visit itself.

He would return to his post.

Mikami switched on the heater and settled heavily on to the floor, crossing his legs. He checked the alarm clock. Exactly half past seven. Ishii was probably still fuming, having not called back since. He would be lying if he said the next day's round-table meeting didn't weigh on his thoughts, but the first call he made was to Suwa at home.

Suwa's home line was busy.

Feeling slightly out of the loop, Mikami lay back on the floor and stretched, the phone still in his hand. He pictured Suwa, busy canvassing the various reporters. Suwa understood his 'post' perfectly. He would complain, but it was clear he loved what he did.

Getting restless, Mikami sat back up and pressed redial. This time the phone rang at the other end. Suwa's wife picked up and told him her husband was out on a job. Mikami decided to call Suwa's mobile directly. As he listened to the ringtone, he could feel a growing anticipation.

'Suwa speaking.'

The background blare of karaoke accompanied his voice.

'It's Mikami. Where are you?'

'Sir. I'm in Amigos, with a few of the reporters.'

Manning his post, of course. Even at the weekend. *Anonymous reporting. The written protest. The boycott.* Mikami felt each of the issues come back into focus.

'Is Kuramae there with you?'

'Yes, he's here, too.' It sounded as though Suwa had already had a fair amount to drink.

'Who's there from the press?'

'Just give me a moment.' Suwa seemed to be making his way out of the bar. The karaoke in the background was replaced with the sound of cars going by. 'Sorry. I forgot to ask, how did it go with Amamiya?'

'Yeah, good. He gave us permission to go ahead.'

'Wow, that's great! Fantastic.'

'How about things on your side?'

'Ah, right, well, I'd put out a call for everyone to come out and celebrate the owner's birthday, although it's actually next month – sorry, beside the point – anyway, the way it's ended up it's more of a "strengthen our defences" thing.'

Strengthen our defences? He meant the only people who had shown up were the moderates, the ones still sitting on the fence.

'Who have you got?'

'Let's see. There's the *Kyodo News*, the *Jiji Press*, *NHK*, *Tokyo*. As far as the local press goes, I've got the *D Daily*, the *Zenken Times*, *D Television* and the *FM Kenmin*.'

'So no one from the *Asahi*, the *Mainichi* or the *Yomiuri* . . .?'

'Sorry to say it, but yeah, that's right.'

'What about the *Sankei* and the *Toyo* . . .?'

'The *Sankei* turned me down flat. Said they couldn't come out drinking until the whole thing was behind us. As for the *Toyo* . . . well, Akikawa did look like he intended to come. He definitely sounded interested when I told him Mikumo would be here.'

Mikami almost shouted. Only barely managing to restrain himself, he asked the question in a whisper.

'Is Mikumo there with you now?'

'Yes, but of her own accord. I only brought her along because she insisted,' he said defiantly.

'We'll talk about that afterwards. What else do you have to report first?'

'Right – so, Akikawa made it sound like he'd be coming, but he hasn't shown up. I just tried his office again but they said he was out covering a story. I get the feeling he's going to run something in the morning edition. I wonder if it's related to the bid-rigging charges?'

It was a regular occurrence for one of the papers to release a story the morning after the others had been out drinking.

'What's the atmosphere like?'

'Hmm? How do you mean?'

'Does it seem like the boycott's going ahead? What are the fence-sitters telling you?'

'Ah, right. Well . . . that's the . . . problem.' Suwa's skill in forming whole sentences seemed to be suffering, along with his ability to think logically. 'Basically, they all think the boycott is going too far. The commissioner's Six Four inspection is big news, so of course they want to cover it. It seems the original idea – in their last GM – was to boycott the entire visit, but now they're saying the boycott only applies to the interview outside Amamiya's house.'

'So they want the best of both worlds . . .'

'Yes. What it boils down to is that they're planning to boycott the walking interview as a kind of sanction, even as they sneak out coverage of the rest of the visit. I think it's just posturing. That interview is clearly the highlight of the inspection – they all want to be there, they all want full coverage. I'm certain they're all agreed on that. It's just . . .' His voice tapered off. 'They're just unwilling to cooperate unless something changes.'

'What would it take to bring them around?'

'Well . . .' Suwa hesitated.

Mikami guessed the mood in Amigos was riding against him.

'It's fine – just say it.'

'First, they want you to make an official apology. Verbally and in writing . . . Then – and they don't mind if this is unofficial – they want a verbal apology from Captain Tsujiuchi or Director Akama. I think if we can meet those demands . . . There's also—'

'There's more?'

'Someone is apparently pushing for your replacement rather than an apology. I don't know who it is, but it's someone aligned with the hard-liners. My guess is that it's the *Toyo*.' He gave his conclusion without hesitation, despite his earlier wavering.

'Someone's after my head?'

'Just a small fraction among the hard-liners.'

'And what do you think?' Mikami wanted Suwa's honest opinion of things.

'If you ask me, they're getting carried away. If we give in to their demands at this stage, who knows where they'll draw the line in the future? But, well, to be honest, I also don't believe they're being totally unreasonable. They might not need your head, but they probably do need an official apology so they don't lose face. And they've got their bosses breathing down their necks. What matters is how it looks. If they at least seem to be getting their way, the moderates will come together to end the boycott.'

Mikami felt like he'd been put on a leash. And by his own staff, not even just the reporters. 'Do you think they'd actually cancel the boycott, though, even if I were to apologize? Don't forget we thought we knew how the votes would fall, for the written protest.'

'Well, I can't offer any guarantees. But we've got to make sure they don't go through with the boycott, whatever happens; we'll have to make do with the hand we've been dealt.'

Mikami gazed into empty space.

'If we were to issue an official apology, how do you think that would affect our influence in the Press Club?'

'There shouldn't be any cause for concern. I've seen a number of similar cases in the past, and I'm pretty sure we've never lost ground after an apology. It usually seems to help . . . if anything, the relationship with the press tends to improve afterwards.'

It came across as a sales pitch. He didn't seem to think the apology came at any great cost.

'Do you think we can keep it to our floor?'

'Hmm?'

'Akama won't authorize the apology. If word of it reaches the first floor, he'll stop us from going ahead.'

He'd lobbed the ball into Suwa's court. *Can you do it?*

Suwa seemed to get the message. 'We should be able to contain it. Yes, not a problem.'

'Good. Let me give it some consideration.' Mikami sighed, then took a deep breath. 'Is Mikumo still there with you?'

'Ah . . .'

'She's not something to put on display. I told you we're not resorting to those kind of tactics. Tell her to go home, right now.'

'But she only came out because she wanted—'

'I won't say it again – send her home, now.' Mikami raised his voice and Suwa went quiet. His disapproval was palpable across the line. 'Look, if you've got something to say, just say it.'

Suwa put on a patient tone. 'There's nothing to worry about. I'll take responsibility for her. She's just here to lighten the mood a little. I'm not going to let anyone take her home.'

Mikami saw red. 'Don't be a fucking idiot. We're police; we don't use women like that. I'll slit my own stomach in front of them, if that's what it takes – but you send her home this instant. Do you understand?'

Suwa refused to stand down.

'You have to think about Mikumo's own view on this. She *wants* to help out. If you keep her from interacting with the press, well, all she's got is admin work. I told her, *You don't have to come.* I told her she had to put up with the status quo because that's what you wanted. Do you know what she said? That you were discriminating. *I want to do the same as the rest of you.* That's what she said.'

Discriminating. It didn't sound like something Mikumo would say.

'Put her on the phone.'

'Okay, but she's had quite a bit to drink.'

'I don't care. Put her on.'

For the few minutes he was kept waiting, Mikami ran dozens of possible angles through his head.

'Sir, it's me.' Mikumo's voice was quiet, but not in a way that made her sound intimidated.

'I thought I'd made myself clear before. Why did you disobey my orders?'

She didn't answer,

'This isn't part of your job.'

'I'm Media Relations, too . . .'

'I had desk workers in First. Do you think they went chasing after killers?'

'I want to make myself useful.'

'You're more than useful already, without doing this.'

'I don't think so. Not at all.'

Mikami let out a sigh. He readied himself for the next line. 'I'll admit I did consider it, that one time. I thought maybe we could use someone to help ease things with the reporters. But I never thought about using you. Just a girl in general.'

Mikumo refused to yield. 'I'm a trained policewoman. I'm here because I think this is part of my job.'

'The reporters won't see it that way.'

'I can't change what I am. And you can think I'm trying to take advantage of that if you want to. But I can't continue to turn a blind eye to the trouble we're having with the press. I know what we're trying to do. We're the window that links the headquarters to the outside world. I've been reading up on the media, too. I can hold my own talking about press issues. And I can be a calming influence when everyone else is getting heated up. Besides, the reporters listen to what I've got to say.'

'You're being naive.'

'Forgive me, sir, but I believe you're the one who's being naive.'

What . . .?

Mikami's grip tightened over the phone.

'What have I said that was naive?'

'Just tell me what you want me to do. I can get you the information. I'm not afraid to dirty my hands a little.'

'You're drunk.'

'I'm not.'

'If you want to really make something of yourself, you should leave the police. Someone with your determination and talent – you could choose anything.'

'I joined the force because I wanted to become an officer. I'm proud of what I do. I'm motivated by it.'

'But you must have realized it by now – the force isn't kind to women. A lot of men can't hack it here either.'

'It's not fair.'

Mikami's eyes stretched wide. 'Not fair . . .?'

'I can see how hard it is for you, in the office. It's clear you're unhappy with the way things are done, with having to put aside your ideals, having to use dirty tricks, that you're trying to tell yourself you've got no other choice. You're making yourself ask Suwa and Kuramae to do whatever they can, even though you obviously hate doing so. You're angry with yourself for doing it. Everyone can see it. But . . .' Her strained voice began to waver. 'It's not fair to use me as a surrogate. It's cruel. You're trying to keep me pure, keep me away from the dirty work, so you can feel better about yourself. I can't take it any more. It's horrible. I want to contribute, to help with what we're here to do.'

Mikami stared up at the ceiling. All the fire seemed to have drained from him.

Even when Mikumo told him the battery was about to die, he had nothing to say in response.

40

It was after 10 p.m. when Mikami finally sank into his bath.

Still so early, he thought to himself.

It had felt like a long day.

Mikami's thoughts were losing their clarity. He felt the distinction between what he knew and what he didn't begin to slip away. His fatigue spread into the warm bathwater. Every time he closed his eyes he felt his drowsiness grow heavier.

The wind was blowing.

The frosted glass rattled in the windowpane. The house had always been old, even in Mikami's earliest memory.

We should do the place up, his dad would say.

One day, his mother would reply.

The afternoon sun, filling the room. The faded tatami. The round dining table. On it, he could see a cake box from a local patisserie, some bottles of beer. His dad's wartime buddy was visiting. Close-cropped hair. Bronzed profile. His whole body shook when he laughed. He turned to look at Mikami. His eyes lit up.

You really take after your old man, kid.

His mom smiled, as if to say, *He really does*. His dad showed yellow teeth, cracking a smile that looked half proud, half pained.

Just hang in there. Do a good deed, and it'll find its way back to you.

Mikami remembered now. The friend had started to cry when Mikami's dad had uttered his favourite phrase. He'd been on the way out, finished doing his laces; he got back to his feet and turned around, his face creased up.

He had no doubt lost lots of good friends.

Taken countless lives.

He didn't show up again after that. He'd messed his hands through Mikami's hair, as though Mikami were his own son. He'd come with gifts of chocolate and ice-cream . . . had the good deed ever found its way back to him?

Dad . . .

His father had existed in the shadows. When Mikami remembered him, he was always standing behind his mother. It wasn't that he'd been intimidating, or that he'd let Mikami's mother take charge of raising him; it was just that he'd been quiet, as though afraid to step out from the safety of her shadow. Mikami had also, for his part, kept his mother between them. He'd never been able to relax when she was out of the room, left alone with his dad. He'd found it difficult to relate to the melancholy in his eyes, the ruggedness of his face, hands and fingers. He had no memory of his dad ever holding him. His DNA had taken precedence, Mikami having taken after him, yet, when he died in the year of the Six Four kidnapping, he did so without having ever opened up to his son.

'Dig in, dig in. It'll melt if you don't get a move on!'

Mikami had finished the cake, but he hadn't smiled. As his dad's friend cried at the door he'd stolen a look, and felt somehow that the man deserved it.

Don't worry, it's just because you're a boy. His mother had always been relaxed like that, easy-going. Despite this, she'd been completely at a loss – far more than his father had been – the first time Mikami had introduced them to Minako. Her eyes had lost focus, swimming before she blinked and looked at him again. He remembered it even now. It was the same look she'd had when she'd suspected him of keeping back change many years before. *Have you been a bad boy?*

Mikami smiled.

She'd definitely over-reacted.

It came back to him now: it was on her recommendation that he'd first gone to kendo at his local club. She'd wanted him to be strong, honourable, more than she'd wanted him to learn the abacus or become proficient at calligraphy. The training had been punishing. If not for the excitement he'd felt each time he donned the mask, he doubted he would have lasted long. Inside the mask's metal enclosure, with his restricted vision and close breath, he'd felt like he was in a hideaway, a top-secret base made from old boxes. He'd never been conscious of wanting a disguise, but that had no doubt been a part of it, too. The thirteen horizontal bars obscured his features. The one vertical bar hid the shape of his nose. Apart from the two eyes peering through the gap of the *monomi*, he was lost in shadow. He stopped being a face. He stopped needing a face. For a short while, he'd been able to transform into something special. And when he'd started to become conscious of girls, grown spots on his face, it was under the sweaty confines of his kendo mask that he had felt most at ease.

A mother's wishes, the way he'd looked, kendo. It had seemed natural to follow that line and become an officer of the law.

Mikami squeezed the hand towel and rubbed it over his face. He could feel his craggy features through the fabric.

The job's an easy one. Easiest in the world.

It can give you the resources to hide from the world – maybe that was what Osakabe had wanted to say. It was widely known that the job wasn't easy. An endless supply of detective novels, documentaries and TV dramas had conditioned the general population into thinking that they understood the difficulty, anguish and misery of the job. They had flicked a switch each time Mikami introduced himself. It meant he hardly needed to say anything himself – it was easy in that sense of the word. It was also easy for a detective to ignore the various difficulties, anguish and miseries of everyday life. There was always new prey to hunt. Matsuoka had summarized it aptly in a speech to motivate the officers in district: *I won't allow any complaints. You're all here to enjoy yourselves. We're being paid to get out there and hunt.*

Detectives understand the concept of justice, but they lack an instinctual hatred of crime. Their only instinct is the chase.

Mikami had been no different. *Identify the perpetrator. Corner him. Take him down.* The daily grind served to polish to a dull glow the mindset of the detective, eroding as it did any vestiges of individuality. Nobody tried to resist the process. If anything, they welcomed it, thirsted for more. For these people, the desire to stay in the hunt went far beyond any monetary considerations. It was their sole hobby, their greatest entertainment.

Mikami only had to ask Koda. A man who'd had his licence stripped, who had instead become one of the hunted. Someone whose only motivation to work was to support his wife and child. *Try asking him if being a detective had been hard.*

Mikami exhaled deeply.

The commissioner would arrive in four days. The most important thing was to keep his cool. He would side with Administrative Affairs, for the sake of his family. The part of him that was still a detective would scream.

He felt a sudden rush of adrenalin.

Wait – this isn't the time for sitting back . . .

What announcement was the commissioner planning to make? What would happen as a result? Mikami had yet to discover what it was.

A face flashed through his mind – the man who had kindly acted as a go-between in helping arrange his marriage. Osakabe was unwilling to help, but he could still try Odate. He had been one of the directors party to the cover-up. He was a greatly respected figure, second in estimation only to Osakabe himself. It was entirely plausible that he might have information on the commissioner's plans. He had collapsed from a stroke at the beginning of the year; when Mikami had taken him a gift in the summer he'd been at home and working on his rehabilitation. He'd been sorry to hear of Mikami's transfer to Media Relations, and promised, with a slightly frozen mouth, to have a sharp word with Arakida.

Odate would talk. If Mikami asked him to . . .

His excitement passed, the enthusiasm suddenly leaving him, as though sucked away.

It would be too cruel. Odate had only been retired four years. The wound would be far from healed. It would be hard on him to have one of his officers – one he'd been fond enough to act as a go-between for – turn up and prise open the partially desiccated sore. Would he consider doing it even knowing that Odate was still in recovery?

Futawatari would do it. He wouldn't even hesitate before pushing the buzzer.

He probably already had.

If the ace of Administrative Affairs had been there already, Odate wouldn't have to ask Mikami the reason for his visit. He would only need to sit there in silence and look into Odate's eyes. Wait for the man to come out with his final testimony.

Mikami shook his head.

He gazed at the steam rolling over the ceiling. For a while he did nothing else.

What was Mikumo doing now? She was probably still *in Amigos*.

Cruel . . .

It's not fair to use me as a surrogate . . .

Mikami tried to imagine her expression when she'd said the words.

You're only able to speak like this because you're a woman, Mikami had thought, irritated during the first half of their conversation. Then Mikumo had broken the taboo. The last person he'd wanted to hear say the words had told him exactly what he'd hoped never to hear. He'd been shocked and saddened, but the feeling went beyond her having landed a blow on him. He'd felt a concurrent surge of self-disgust and astonishment, realizing that the very thing he'd been looking for had been right there in front of him. Mikumo had been there the whole time. She was quiet, but he knew more than anyone that she was a quick thinker, that her eyes and ears were keen.

But . . .

It was because she was a woman. He'd realized it when she'd called him cruel. He'd never intended to use her as some kind of trophy. Nor had he ever thought to keep her untarnished on his behalf. He had wanted to protect her, that was all. Having failed to do the same for his wife and daughter, he'd chosen Mikumo to keep close, thinking he might be able to keep her safe for a year or two, for as long as he remained her boss.

He had been using her as a surrogate after all. Playing an unfair game. Perhaps he *had* been cruel to her.

Amigos. Laughter. The tang of alcohol . . .

He began to wonder if his attempts to maintain her innocence might have had the opposite effect. Was it possible her passion for the job had nothing to do with her decision to shun her womanly virtues? Mikami started to get worried. She'd told him she wasn't afraid to get her hands dirty. How far had she decided she would go?

I want to contribute, to help with what we're here to do.

'Darling?'

Mikami started, thinking he'd dozed off and imagined Minako's voice.

'Are you okay?'

She was calling out from the next room, where the sink was. She was worried he'd been in the bath for too long.

'Yeah, I'm fine. Getting out now,' he replied, but he remained where he was.

He didn't feel like he'd had time to warm up. Had he really

been in the bath long enough to justify her worrying? Their daily rhythms — washing, bathing, using the toilet — had all suffered since their daughter had run away. He would become engrossed in brushing his teeth. Not because his thoughts were on Ayumi, just focused on keeping the toothbrush in motion. So he didn't have to think. *Turning away from reality.* Sometimes he was convinced that was what he was doing.

But he had never pictured her dead. He made sure he didn't focus on the negatives.

She was alive.

And yet . . .

He couldn't see anything beyond that.

If she was alive, it followed that she would be out there somewhere. On her feet . . . moving around . . . eating . . . sleeping. But he couldn't picture her doing any of those things.

In her mind, the whole world was laughing at her. She hated people looking at her. He couldn't imagine in any detail her going about a normal life outside of home, not in that state of mind. What would she do for money? For a place to sleep? Most high-school girls ran away to get a job, a boyfriend, even to the red-light districts — but none of those cases fitted Ayumi. How would she support herself? Was she living on the streets? It seemed unlikely that a young homeless girl would slip through the net cast by 260,000 officers. Could someone have taken her in? If they had, who? It felt as if it would be a criminal act for anyone to take in a sixteen-year-old girl and not notify her parents or the authorities. She was locked up somewhere. Was that the only possible conclusion? Would he have to spend the rest of his life haunted by the thought?

It was better not to think at all, to ensure that Minako had no reason to dwell on it. *Ayumi is safe and well.* He made sure to draw a line under any other thoughts, forcing the subject to a close. For her part, Minako didn't try to talk of anything else. She discussed the calls, but anything more was taboo. Ayumi, holding the receiver in a public phone box. It was the only image they had of her in the outside world, the only one they permitted.

'She'll come back to us.'

Mikami tried saying the words he always said. He listened to the way they sounded. Whatever happened while Ayumi was away was immaterial. She just needed to come home. They would make it work.

'Just come back.'

A drop of condensation trailed down the dark window. Mikami's eyes felt heavy. The drowsiness was relentless this time. He wondered where he'd put Minako's road-safety charm.

Darkness fell.

He saw a hand.

Minako, in her white kimono, smiling gently as she reached down with both hands.

41

As expected, the week failed to start normally. Mikami was woken by a call from Akama, which arrived even before the alarm he'd set for 6 a.m. went off.

'Have you seen the morning edition of the *Toyo*?'

'Not yet.'

'Well, get a move on and read it.' Akama sounded ready to explode. Still in bed, Mikami told Akama he would call back. He hung up the phone, threw a dressing gown over his nightshirt, then hurried outside to the letterbox. The *Toyo* had run some kind of scoop. His mind went first to the bid-rigging charges, but he dismissed the idea, realizing that Akama wouldn't have called so early for that.

No, he thought.

The Public Safety Committee. The pregnant woman. The old man's death.

'Is it something in the papers?'

Minako was already up by the time he came back into the living room, the papers bundled in his hands. She had just finished turning on the heater. She was frowning, looking nervous.

'Seems so. Could you get me a coffee?'

Having coaxed her into the kitchen, he spread open the sheets of the *Toyo*, then leafed through to the local section.

Two headlines in bold jumped out from the page.

GIFT VOUCHERS BUY SILENCE
DETENTION FACILITIES IN QUESTION

A chill ran across his forehead. He noticed as soon as he started to read that the article was a detailed report with a parent write-up in the national pages. He quickly scanned across to the general news. *There.* The article lacked the detail of that in the local section, but the headline stood out nonetheless.

PREFECTURE D POLICE HEADQUARTERS. FEMALE DETAINEE ABUSED.

His eyes recoiled from the page.

The article contained an account of gross misconduct, allegedly having taken place at Station F, in the north of the prefecture, that August.

A police sergeant in his fifties who was in charge of detainees has allegedly abused a woman in her thirties. While she was in custody on charges of suspected theft, the officer forced her to let him touch her breasts and genitalia over consecutive nights.

Mikami snapped back to the local section.

'You'll get out sooner if you do what I say.' The officer had black-mailed the female detainee into permitting his misconduct. The female detainee later received a suspended sentence and, following her release, demanded an apology from the sergeant, protesting that he had taken advantage of her vulnerability, claiming his actions had been 'unforgivable'. When she threatened to lodge an official protest with Station F, the sergeant offered her 100,000 yen in gift vouchers and begged her not to disclose the misconduct to his superiors.

Mikami drove his fist into the paper. They wouldn't have gone this far without having first secured some kind of evidence. He could feel the bile in his throat. He admitted it was sometimes difficult to find evidence of decency within the force, but still – to think someone so twisted had the gall to masquerade as an officer of the law . . .

He flicked through the remaining papers. None contained any mention of the story. The *Toyo* had secured an exclusive. Suwa's gut feeling had been on the money. Akikawa had failed to show up at *Amigos*: it was safe to assume that he'd been hard at work on the article.

Still, it didn't make sense. Why hadn't he known about the story before seeing it in the paper? Reporters always made sure to visit the executive the night before they ran a scoop of this magnitude – it was a necessary rite to request official confirmation of the facts to back up their story. Had they lacked the time, the information coming in too close to the printing deadline? Mikami supposed it was possible they had been confident enough of the truth of the story that they had deemed it unnecessary to seek official confirmation. Even then, however, they would usually call in advance to warn that the article would be in the morning paper; a surprise attack would only make it harder to approach the police for more information down the line.

And there was something else that didn't seem right . . .

Minako had already brought him his coffee. He touched the mug to his mouth but stopped there. Picking up the internal line, he called Akama's home number. The call connected after just one ring.

'Okay, I saw it.'

'It was written by one of our reporters,' Akama said. It was a statement of fact.

The *Toyo* had a correspondent in charge of news in the area around Station F. Akama went on to say that the reporter, a contract worker in his sixties, had just put in an apologetic call to Kobogata, the captain at Station F: *I just read the article in our morning edition. So, this really happened?*

'It was apparently the first Kobogata had heard of it.'

The captain had called the sergeant over. The sergeant had given a full confession. Kobogata had called officers from the Criminal Investigations Division and carried out an emergency arrest, citing indecent assault by a public official. An official from Internal Affairs was en route from the NPA in Tokyo, and a press conference had been scheduled to be held in the station at 9 a.m.

That was as far as things had progressed.

'I can't wrap my head around it. We didn't get a single call – they didn't call me; they didn't call Shirota or Internal Affairs. From what I hear, this is unheard of. What do you make of all this?'

The brain asking its limbs for an opinion: it had never happened before. Akama was genuinely shaken. The scoop had made it to the national press. Mikami wondered if a call from Tokyo had interrupted his sleep.

'I think it's likely the reporter was tipped off; someone close to the source.'

'That's not what I'm asking you. I want to know your opinion as to why an article slamming us has found its way out at this *particular* point in time.'

Of course.

It was an attack on Administrative Affairs. The idea had come to him as he read the article: that Criminal Investigations had leaked the story to the *Toyo*; that they'd done an about-turn on their defensive stance, moved on to the offensive.

The fact that the article had been about the detention facilities had been suspicious from the start. The facilities were officially under the jurisdiction of Administrative Affairs, but the reality was that they were the territory of Criminal Investigations. *The cells are a breeding ground for wrongful convictions. The police use them as prison substitutes*: Criminal Investigations had distanced itself from the facilities, from an organizational standpoint, in a bid to stave off complaints from human-rights groups, but there wasn't a station in the prefecture where the facilities were run exclusively by officers from Administrative Affairs. Many belonged to the department in name only, their background being in detective work; others were serving an apprenticeship with a view to becoming wardens or guards; they would often return to the facilities after a day of investigative work and keep watch over the detainees, filing detailed reports to Criminal Investigations.

What this boiled down to was that, while Criminal Investigations had full access to the facilities, whenever an issue cropped up concerning their management, it was Administrative Affairs, as the official managing department, who ended up shouldering the blame. Criminal Investigations might have lacked the means with which to expose malpractice from the more closed-off divisions at the department's core, but it would have had ready access to a backlog of material in the case of the detention facilities.

Still . . .

Could they really have done it?

It seemed hard to believe; Akama's apparent certainty meant that Mikami had to be careful in how he responded.

'Sir, are you saying you think that this is Criminal Investigations trying to send us a message?'

'A message? This is a blatant and unconditional threat. Seeing as they went after the detention facilities, they probably decided to take a small hit and deal us a serious blow.'

Take a small hit?

The article wouldn't have hurt them in the slightest. Anyone in their fifties who was still a police sergeant was either gullible to a fault or just organizational flotsam. It went without saying that he wouldn't have any experience of active duty, or in any of the department's more high-powered roles. They had procured an 'outsider' for their sacrifice, making sure Administrative Affairs alone bore the brunt of the scandal.

It felt increasingly likely that it was the work of Criminal Investigations.

'Might you be the cause, Mikami?'

The question left him stunned. *The cause? Of what?* 'I'm not sure what you mean.'

'You don't remember fiddling around behind the scenes, per-haps accidentally stirring up more trouble than was necessary?'

Don't be an idiot. He came close to saying it. If anyone fitted that accusation, it was Futawatari.

'I don't remember doing that, no.'

'Well then, did you seek to incite them on purpose?'

'Excuse me?'

'You seem to have been paying visits to various people in Criminal Investigations. I believe I especially banned you from doing that?'

Mikami gritted his teeth. *So that's how it is.* Akama hadn't given him the reason for the commissioner's visit, yet he was still ready to suspect betrayal.

'I have nothing to hide. I've been getting the information I need in order to do my job, nothing more.'

'Yes, well. You need to give this one final push, for your fam-ily's sake, too. I will have Ishii attend the round-table meeting on his own; you can concentrate on finding out how this article came about and deal with the aftermath. Captain Kobogata will need some assistance. I want you to send someone from your team to be at the press conference in Station F. And I want to know how it went – what was asked, what the answers were – as soon as it's done. I hope that's understood.'

The call rang off before Mikami had a chance to respond. Mikami put the phone down, careful to be calm as he sensed Minako behind him.

For your family's sake, too.

Never one to give up an advantage, Akama had tested the slack on Mikami's reins.

Mikami was still glaring at the phone when it started to ring. It was Suwa. He sounded out of breath.

'Sir, have you seen the *Toyo* this morning?'

'Yes.'

'That bastard Akikawa. I knew it.'

'The guy doesn't know when to stop.'

'It's my fault. I should have had him monitored.'

With the apology, Mikami remembered the call the previous night, when he'd given Suwa a dressing-down about Mikumo; fortunately, the new problem helped mask any awkwardness.

'The *Times* called – some of the others, too – they all want to know if the story's true.'

'Okay. You can tell them it's mostly accurate. And that you believe the sergeant is already under emergency arrest.'

'Really? He's been arrested already?'

'Yeah.'

'So it's like it said in the article?'

'It's probably safe to assume that, yeah.'

Suwa heaved a long sigh. Any officer would share the same sentiment. That feeling of being let down. *For God's sake, just stop dragging our name through the mud.*

'What are they doing now, having missed the scoop?'

'Some of them have already started calling for a press conference.'

'There's one scheduled for 9 a.m. in Station F. Do you think you could go?'

'Absolutely. I'll head into the office first, and keep a watch on things for now.'

Sensing he was about to hang up, Mikami held him back.

'Do you have any idea as to Akikawa's source?'

Do you think it was Criminal Investigations? The question was implicit in the words. He wondered if Suwa was somehow connected to Akama, and if the connection went both ways. Was he aware of the trouble surrounding the commissioner's visit?

'Oh . . .' Suwa paused before continuing, a little awkwardly. 'Not really. Not yet, anyway. I'll try asking around.'

'That would be great,' Mikami said, ending the call. He reflected on the cruelty of testing his own staff. Suwa didn't know about the trouble. Mikami had needed to consider his own relationship with the man before worrying about any possible connections he had with Akama. He hadn't brought Suwa in on the big picture, the same way Akama hadn't with him. He hadn't told Kuramae, or Mikumo.

He was struck by a cold realization.

He'd never intended to forge a real connection, not in Administrative Affairs. He would return to Criminal Investigations within two years. The veiled decision, made eight months earlier, seemed now to have been fatally short-sighted.

42

It was seven thirty when Mikami arrived at the Prefectural HQ.

Suwa was already in the office, apparently having just arrived. Mikami was also at her desk, talking on the phone. From the side, her face seemed a little puffy. She looked his way. Nodded a greeting. She had on only a smattering of make-up, almost nothing at all; it was, perhaps, a mark of her new resolve.

Suwa stepped in front of him, as though to block Mikami's line of sight.

'I sent Kuramae next door to check up on the situation. There may be some way to turn this to our advantage.'

Mikami thought he understood the implication. The *Toyo* had enjoyed a run of exclusives. And today's article had detailed a case of gross misconduct – grade-one material. The rest of the papers would be despairing. They had come together to rally against anonymous reporting, yet the *Toyo* – which had assumed a leading role in pushing the agenda – had emerged the sole victor; the others would see the *Toyo* as having taken advantage of the chaos and betrayed them; they would feel compelled to reconsider the validity of their united front.

'Relations must be strained right now. I don't think we'll have any trouble bringing the moderates into our camp. If things go well, we might even be able to convince them to abandon their boycott of the commissioner's interview.'

Mikami gave him a cautious nod.

It was no doubt the case that things had changed in the wake of the *Toyo*'s unexpected article, but Suwa's expression didn't carry the confidence of his words. It was only the previous night that he'd been insisting an apology was the only way to gain ground. Had he lost his nerve overnight? Media Relations acting of its own accord, without Akama's knowledge: Mikami realized the proposition carried a lot of risk for an assistant inspector like Suwa, one of the department's rising stars. It was nothing he could blame him for, but Mikami felt disappointed. Suwa still remained a loyal servant to Akama.

'Good morning, sir.'

Mikumo got to her feet and dipped her head. Mikami had already noticed that she had finished her call. She stood with her chin pulled back, unnaturally formal and stiff. She was going to tell him she was sorry for the way she'd spoken on the phone. But she wasn't going to apologize for going to Amigos. That was clear from the subtle narrowing of her eyes.

'I dug a little into the guard.' Suwa stepped between them for a second time. In his hands were a number of sheets, faxed copies and something that resembled a personnel file. 'His name is Yoshitake Kuriyama. Fifty years old. Have you heard of him before?'

Mikami told him he hadn't. There was a slight recognition – they had both been in the force for a long time – but he was sure at least that there was no one of that name in Criminal Investigations.

'After graduating from college, he spent the majority of his career manning *koban* and small substations. He was transferred to the detention facilities after complaining to his boss that his back pains were getting worse.'

He wasn't Administrative Affairs. That was Suwa's way of stating this fact.

'What about honours, disciplinary actions?'

'Nothing of note. There's a mark against him for having misplaced paperwork relating to lost property, but that was a long time ago.'

'Do you know how he's thought of, in general?'

'Not too well, it seems. I've just asked someone at Station F. He was a bit depressive, guarded. Liked to act important. Bit of a mess, really. They did say he was relatively good-looking, that he'd been somewhat of a hit in the local bars.'

Mikami felt a wave of nausea.

'Okay. Did you get anything on the woman?'

'Also less than salubrious.'

Her name was Natsuko Hayashi. Thirty-seven years old. She'd worked at a massage parlour and was currently romantically involved with a known offender who specialized in breaking and entering. Her husband was serving time on charges of repeated opportunistic theft.

Mikami couldn't hold back a scornful laugh.

'Quite the couple. Don't tell me she was in on charges of theft, too?'

'Yes, for stealing a bag. From a schoolgirl trying to buy a ticket at the train station.'

Mikami stretched his neck in a circle, letting it all sink in.

'Seems odd that he owned up.'

'Hmm?'

'Kuriyama. It's not as though his name was on those vouchers he gave her. Why not tell the captain she'd made it all up?'

'Right. Well, it seems she had made a written statement. He would have realized there'd be trouble if his boss – or his family – ever found out; seems she managed to cajole him into writing out an apology.'

Decisive, physical evidence. Had the *Toyo* known about that? If they had, then that would explain their being confident enough to go ahead with the article without first obtaining confirmation from the executive.

'Meaning it's possible Hayashi was the source?'

Suwa's eyes hung unfocused for a moment; he blinked a few times, then looked back towards Mikami.

'Doesn't seem likely, though, right? I mean, she already had the gift vouchers. They're probably why she thought about blackmailing Kuriyama in the first place. She wouldn't have benefited from taking the story to the press.'

'Okay. Who do you think handed Akikawa the story?'

Unlike on the phone, Suwa's response was immediate. 'I don't have a name, but I'm pretty sure the source was a detective.'

'What makes you think that?' Mikami asked, his expression unchanged.

'It was something my contact in Station F said, someone in Admin. He told me no one had known about Kuriyama's misconduct and that, even if they had, it would have been suicide to leak the story to the press. He said it simply didn't make sense for anyone in Admin to be the source.'

'Doesn't the same logic apply to detectives? After all, they think they're the ones in charge of the facilities.'

'Sure, but the official jurisdiction lies with Admin. And they're pretty damn serious about maintaining confidentiality; it's practically beaten into them.'

Unlike detectives, they keep their mouths shut. Suwa gave the impression that this was what he wanted to say. He phrased it differently, keeping the same expression.

'Hayashi might have mentioned it in passing, to one of the detectives . . . what Kuriyama was doing to her.'

'And the detective just happened to mention it to the press?'

Catching on to Mikami's irritation, Suwa leaned in closer. 'My contact did say that people were acting a bit strangely in the Criminal Investigations Division.'

'Strangely? How so?'

'I mean, it must have been a shock, to see the morning paper. The captain called everyone in, so they're all there in the station, but . . . the thing is, none of the detectives is showing any sign of surprise; he said it's as though they already knew what was going to happen, that they're just pretending they didn't.'

'You won't find a detective who shows his surprise openly.'

Even as he said this, Mikami couldn't help feeling Suwa was probably right. They were talking about a dodgy masseuse and a husband with a penchant for breaking and entering. The couple would be well known among the station's detectives. The atmosphere in the interrogation room would have been comparatively relaxed, more so than if she'd been a first-time offender. The chances were high that she would have opened up to one of the detectives if the guard had been abusing her. Although, judging by the fact that nothing had happened at the time of the offence, her approach had perhaps been more of an implication than a direct accusation. Either way, what mattered was that the story had probably spread through the division, then, as a secret shared between detectives, to the other stations, possibly even to the Prefectural HQ.

The conclusion was that the leak had probably come from Criminal Investigations. The rumour had made its way to Director Arakida's office. He had ordered one of the detectives in Station F to look into the facts. Then he'd used the most effective tool he had to pressurize Administrative Affairs – the *Toyo*, with its circulation of 8 million copies.

Mikami looked back at Suwa.

'You think the leak came from Criminal Investigations in Station F. Is that right?'

'Yes.'

'That Akikawa went all the way to some district station in the middle of nowhere to get the story?'

'I don't think he went anywhere to get the story. Someone leaked it to him. He's pretty well known. Anyone who'd worked here before would know his name.'

'Why leak the story?'

'Going by how big it is, I'd say whoever it was wanted to go straight for the captain. Kobogata has a reputation for being difficult, almost obsessively so. Plenty of people would be happy to see him go.'

So that was the reasoning behind his 'detective' theory. It certainly wasn't implausible. Still, Mikami felt confident Suwa would have come up with a different theory, had he known about the conflict surrounding the commissioner's visit. If he was going to tell him, it had to be now. It felt like the only way he could secure Suwa's loyalty – to bring him directly into the fold, make sure he didn't hear it from Akama first. But it was a difficult subject to broach. He had yet to understand many of the core elements himself. It felt wrong to give Suwa only a general summary, highlighting the disquiet and nothing else; it was like handing him a body bag without revealing what was inside.

'I should probably be heading out.' Suwa flicked a quick glance at his watch. 'There was one more thing I wanted to ask first.'

'Go on.'

'This is the first time Kobogata will be leading a press conference of this kind. We might need to hold his hand a little.' His voice dropped to a conspiratorial whisper. 'I can get him to drop something about Hayashi's . . . background. Either at the end of the conference or later, when everyone's chatting, so it feels like an off-the-record comment. Some of the papers might drop the story if they learn she used to be a "masseuse", that she's involved with a convicted criminal. Even if they go ahead, they'll have to exercise a little more caution in the evening editions.'

Mikami let out a brief sigh.

'You think some of the reporters suspect she was the one who instigated it?'

'If we can get a question like that to come out – that's our best-case scenario. The captain can remain silent, let the reporters draw their own conclusions.'

It was a good idea. But Mikami wasn't without reservations.

'Saying nothing could work. But we shouldn't try to redirect this, whatever happens. Even supposing Hayashi *had* lured Kuri-yama into doing what he did, he's still lowlife scum. We can't have it looking like we're trying to defend him. The coverage will be much worse if the reporters think we're taking his side.'

Mikami had to rush at the end. The phone on his desk had started to ring.

'How's the Press Room?'

It was Ishii. Suwa seemed to be hanging on for instructions; Mikami jerked his chin to tell him he was free to go.

'Quiet, for now.'

'It really is one thing after another. Because of this, I've ended up having to do the apologizing at the round-table meeting.'

Mikami had expected Ishii to be furious, but he came across as surprisingly buoyant. 'You'll do a good job. Just remember: we're not apologizing, only explaining what happened.'

'Yes, yes. It'll be fine.'

'It's possible it might get a little heated, in light of the trouble in Station F.'

'Nothing to worry about. Captain Tsujiuchi has decided not to attend this time.'

Mikami had expected this. If the captain went to the meeting, he would have to field questions concerning Kuriyama's misconduct, indecent as it was. He would have to apologize. To make sure this didn't happen, Shirota or Akama would have to lower their heads in his place. The question was whether the veteran reporters, who were all too familiar with such tricks, would turn a blind eye to the captain's absence.

Mikami waved to Suwa as he left. Mikumo reacted, looking up.

'How do you plan to explain the captain's non-attendance?'

'Well, the meeting's due to start at one o'clock, right? We decided to set the timing of Kuriyama's disciplinary hearing so that the two clash. The press will see that he's busy dealing with the situation, get the impression he's taking it seriously.'

There was a hint of pride in the way Ishii said this. The idea had probably been his own.

'What did Akama have to say?'

'He said the idea was a good one.'

'Not that. About the *Toyo*'s scoop.'

'Nothing in particular. He was in a really bad mood, of course.'

Mikami ended the call without further questions. Ishii was outside the net. He was simply excited about the upcoming visit of a luminary from Tokyo; he wasn't party to the true objective behind it. Mikami reached for the external line at the corner of his desk.

I'd like to come over, tonight if possible. Mikami dialled Shozo Odate's home number, intending only to make the request. He was still hesitant to do anything that might harm his benefactor, but he couldn't sit back and do nothing. The commissioner's visit was now only three days away.

He stole a glance at Mikumo as he listened to the phone ring, trying not to be obvious by studying the wall first. She was at her corner desk, typing on her keyboard with practised hands. But he could tell her attention was on him. She was waiting until he got off the phone. Mikami felt his chest constrict. He looked away. She wanted him to assign her work, ignoring the fact that she was a woman. He was only just realizing exactly how hard that was. She'd been loyal, a good follower, until the previous night. He felt a stabbing sense of loss. It seemed Akama wasn't the only one who wanted full control over how his staff behaved.

No one was picking up. Perhaps Shozo Odate was out enjoying a morning stroll with his wife, as part of his rehabilitation. As he'd waited on the phone, Kuramae had come back into the room. He walked over the moment Mikami hung up. He looked bloated, suggesting he'd consumed a fair amount of alcohol during the night's activities.

'What's it like in there?'

'They've all just left for the press conference in Station F. The atmosphere was tense right up until they left. Apart from the *Toyo*, they were all huddled together, whispering in groups of two or three.'

'Like they were ready to boil over?'

'Yeah, that's kind of how it felt,' Kuramae said, clearly not feeling very confident. He still hadn't been able to get the reporters to open up to him.

'Was Akikawa there?'

'No, I didn't see him. His sub was there until a moment ago – Tejima.'

'Okay. If you see him, tell him I want to have a word.'

'I will.'

Mikami considered the conversation over, but Kuramae continued to hover, looking like he had something to get off his chest.

'Yes?'

'Right . . . I . . . it's just that I finished compiling the information on Ryoji Meikawa.'

'Meikawa?'

'The pensioner, who died in the car accident?'

Mikami remembered. He'd given Kuramae instructions to look into what had happened, but he'd only said it in passing and hadn't expected a report.

'Did you find something?'

'Yes, it turns out he was from Hokkaido.' Kuramae seemed to expect surprise. 'From Tomakomai, actually. He came from a poor family and hardly made it through primary school. He came down here before he turned twenty and spent the next forty years working at a factory making food paste. Let's see here . . . he was seventy-two at the time of the accident, so he'd been retired for twelve years. After losing his wife eight years ago, and with no nearby relatives, he'd been living by himself in a run-down apartment and getting by on his pension. He owned the property but rented the land.'

Mikami didn't know how to react. Was this Kuramae's idea of digging into the facts?

'What did you learn about the accident?'

'Right, yes. The cause of death was blood loss resulting from ruptured organs. There were no witnesses to the accident itself, so I wasn't able to find anything to corroborate or refute the driver's claim that the man had crossed blindly in front of her. The man had been drinking at a bar near the scene of the accident, not far from where he lived. According to the owner of the bar, it was a monthly treat for the old man to visit the bar and have a couple of glasses of *shochu*. He told me he'd been sad to hear of the accident. He said the man had been thoroughly enjoying his drinks, that if he'd left five minutes earlier or later the—'

'Keep looking into it.'

Mikami cut him off, noticing Akikawa had just walked into the room.

'Sorry I wasn't there last night. I was really hoping to come out, just couldn't get away . . .'

His sugary voice was directed to where Mikumo was sitting. Although she usually looked impassive, she smiled in return, as if to say, *maybe next time*, further exacerbating Mikami's sense of unease.

'Akikawa. Just the man I was looking for.'

'I'm touched, Mikami,' Akikawa joked, helping himself to a seat on one of the couches.

Reporters never failed to exhibit a morning-after buzz the day after an exclusive. It was always a mix of fatigue and self-satisfaction, causing Mikami to wonder if lust was the closest approximation to what the press felt when they were chasing a story.

Mikami settled down next to him.

'Week's off to a fine start, thanks to you.'

'Just doing my job. How did the others react?'

'You can get that from Tejima.'

'Fair enough. What was it you wanted to talk about?'

Akikawa was gradually regaining his usual cool. Mikami realized it was the first time they'd seen each other since their clash in the Secretariat.

'Why didn't you call to confirm the story before running it?'

'Just exercising my rights.'

'Who was your source?'

'You expect me to reveal my source? Come now, Mikami, that's not like you.'

'You got a handshake from Station F.'

'Mikami. Why keep asking when you know I'm not going to tell you?'

'No, you got the information directly from Arakida.'

Mikami made his move. A pause, indicating a bullseye. But Akikawa did nothing more than blink slowly.

'It's a big risk.'

'I'm not following.'

'There's nothing more expensive than a free lunch,' Mikami said threateningly.

Akikawa's cheeks twitched. The look on his face resembled dread. Someone like Akikawa would know it all too well. It was dangerous to snap up a story being dangled before you. You ended up with a debt of obligation; if you weren't careful, you could end up becoming a tool for the police to manipulate, an opening for the police to infiltrate.

Akikawa made a show of sighing.

'So, I take it you didn't call me here to discuss the apology?'

'Sorry?'

'Your apology to the Press Club, for what happened in the Secretariat. You know, I could have sworn you'd called me to go through the preparations.'

Akikawa hadn't been at Amigos, but it seemed as though news of Suwa's legwork had reached him anyway.

'Would you call off the boycott, if I did make an apology?'

'That's why I came here, to give you my answer. Which is "no".'

'What about the others?'

Akikawa frowned, clicking his tongue. 'You really don't get it. If the Press Club stopped functioning every time one of us ran an exclusive, it would have come apart long ago.'

It could have been confidence. It could have been a bluff.

Akikawa got to his feet. 'I'll be in the branch office. You can reach me there if anything comes up.'

'You're not going to Station F?'

'I've already sent Tejima. I'm going to attend the one here, in the headquarters.'

'Here?'

Mikami shot a look at Kuramae. He caught Mikumo's eye in the same movement. Both faces told him they didn't know.

'We're not holding a press conference here.'

'Uh-huh, sure.' Akikawa strode calmly from the room, showing no surprise at the answer.

Something was going to happen. He had another play.

Was he planning something? Or was it the *Toyo* – did they intend to unveil something during the round-table meeting? Or could it be . . .

He thought about it for a moment.

The *Toyo* had got its exclusive from Arakida. Mikami was sure of this now, after his talk with Akikawa. Perhaps it was this sudden certainty that made him sense the shadow of Criminal Investigations in Akikawa's bravado.

43

One o'clock. The round-table meeting had commenced on schedule. Kuramae had gone to take notes, Mikumo to help serve tea, leaving Mikami on his own in the office.

The reporters who had gone to Station F were still there. Suwa had reported in to let him know that the details they'd given the captain about the woman Hayashi had already taken effect. The press were already chasing her story, looking for holes in the *Toyo*'s article. Mikami didn't doubt their motivation, but he knew their efforts were futile as long as Hayashi had written evidence. Thanks to Suwa, they had been able to dissuade the reporters from accepting the story at face value, and in time for the evening-edition deadlines. Their follow-up articles would be conservative in comparison to the size of the scoop.

Mikami put the phone down again. He had tried Shozo Odate a few more times but still hadn't managed to get through. It was possible he wasn't out on a walk, that he'd gone to the hospital or the rehabilitation centre for treatment.

Mikami was about to pull out a cigarette when his eyes spotted a clear plastic file lying on his desk. It was Kuramae's. He'd left it there on his way out. It contained a number of sheets, all filled with his neat writing. He'd said it was his report about Meikawa – they'd only got halfway through it. Mikami felt no particular need to finish it, but he had been thrown by the points Kuramae had decided to focus on.

Kuramae was the typical office type, his best feature his

commitment to the job. He'd spent time in Second Division in district, filling in at a desk job for someone who was on long-term sick leave, but he also had experience in Transport and Local Community; in the Prefectural HQ, he'd spent time in Welfare. Having been shunted through so many divisions, he lacked a territory he could call his own. People who failed to specialize tended to get trampled on in the force, and Kuramae was a case in point. It was hard to reconcile the passion he'd poured into compiling and delivering this particular report with his usual dependence on Suwa to help him out.

Perhaps it felt personal somehow, reminding him of his father or someone of his father's generation. Whatever the reason, to let himself get so distracted when the office was riding turbulence like this . . .

'I'm coming in.'

The door cracked open and Mikumo stepped into the room. She usually stayed away until the meetings were over, but Mikami had suspected she might duck out of this one and wasn't surprised to see her.

'How's it going?' he asked.

She stood to attention in front of her desk.

'Chief Ishii is still giving his speech.'

'What is he talking about?'

'Anonymous reporting, and the provision of new services.'

'What is the reaction like?'

'He's only just started, so everyone is still listening. It's pretty quiet.' She went on to explain that the local and major press were all represented by their respective branch heads or editors in chief – not a single one had sent someone to take their place.

'The Press Club likes to call itself the "Four Seasons", did you know that?'

'Just the name.'

'You don't know why?'

'No.'

'It's because there used to be twelve member agencies. They made the comparison with the number of months in a year. They didn't like it when the *FM Kenmin* joined; in the end, they decided to keep the name because its membership was only provisional.'

He'd been hoping to alleviate the tension, but Mikumo's expression only stiffened. Probably because he was on edge. It wasn't anything rational. She'd made a stand. Defied an order. He understood that he'd driven her to do it, at least in his mind, but it was hard to face up to the truth here in the office.

Especially if . . .

As he'd feared, Mikumo wasn't going to let her chance to apologize slip by.

'Sir, about last night—'

There's no need. Mikami cut her off. There was nothing worse than having someone ask forgiveness when they'd done nothing wrong. 'Let's just move on, shall we? How did it go after our call?'

She looked unsure.

'I'm asking seriously. I just want to know what you thought about it, about dealing with the reporters.'

'Okay . . . Well, I think I learned a lot.'

'About?'

'We talked a lot. I think I got a good feel for their side of the story.'

'Their side of the story?'

She gave an awkward nod.

'One of the things that shocked me the most, when I started here, was the hostility of the reporters. It reminded me of when I worked for Transport in district. Whenever we caught someone who was parked illegally or speeding, they always got angry; they would throw insults, treat us with contempt, make cutting remarks. Some would get aggressive and make threats, criticizing us for trying to make a quota, doing the work for its own sake. That was when I started to think that – at least when it

342

came to the general public – what we did was a kind of necessary evil. It seemed the same with the reporters. They were reluctant to show any understanding. Decided we were the bad guys. That's what it felt like to witness their aggression every day. But then—'

'Sorry, just hold on,' Mikami cut in, unable to stop himself. One of the phrases she'd used he repeated in a wave of indignation. 'You thought we were a *necessary evil*?'

Mikumo looked a little anxious but was ready to defend herself. 'I only meant to say there's a part of that, in what we do, as far as the public is concerned.'

'Those people were annoyed at getting a ticket. And they saw a woman so they thought they could get away with shouting. That's all.'

'Maybe. But they were right in that I had a quota to fulfil.'

'And it's also a fact that cars parked illegally block the way for fire engines, ambulances.'

'That's what I kept telling myself, to justify the work. But it wasn't like when I was working in a *koban*. I couldn't take pride in my work. I spent a lot of time debating with myself about whether we *were* a necessary evil.'

She wouldn't last. Even supposing she got through her time in Media Relations, she would be torn to pieces in some other office.

'Listen, we're not here to discuss personal feelings. This isn't your home and I'm not your father. The force is far from being any kind of mother figure.'

Mikumo stared at him, unblinking. There was a pause before she let out an almost imperceptible, shaky breath. She brought a hand up to her chest. She was trying to control her feelings.

'Let's go back to your report on Amigos.'

'Okay.'

'The reporters consider us a necessary evil. Is that what you want to say?'

Mikumo quickly shook her head. 'I used to think so – but I

was wrong. They are definitely sceptical. And they strongly believe they have to work to keep us in line. But they don't doubt for a minute that we're a necessary part of society. Far from it – they deal up close with so much violent crime I think they're actually afraid, for the sake of the public, of what might happen if we start to lose our authority. If I'm right, I think there's hope yet.'

'Hope?'

'For making Media Relations into an open window.'

It felt like a punch to the chest.

'Yes, but you've seen the reality of how things are now. We're no such thing.'

Mikumo started to nod, but reconsidered. She looked as though she was holding herself back.

'You once told me you thought the *koban* performed that function?'

'Yes, sir.'

'Always open to the outside. With a more direct connection to the people. Was that what you meant?'

'Yes. But also that it demonstrates through what it does on a daily basis that we're essentially good. Everyone who expresses an interest in joining the force is the same. They want to help other people, contribute to making the world a little better. Officers new to the force don't try to hide their sense of purpose, their will to do good. And that kind of frank openness has a positive effect on the press.'

Mikami had underestimated her – he'd assumed she was just letting off steam about her time in Transport, but she'd boomeranged back to talking about the press.

'How so?'

'Reporters aren't aggressive or hostile with officers in the *koban*. I think that something about the atmosphere there helps them forget about the conflict; they wake up for a while. There's a single-minded focus to the role of a *koban* that causes them to

344

remember their original motivations – the sense of duty, of what's right – for joining the press.'

The room was briefly quiet.

'You think we lack that quality here?'

Mikumo bit her lip. Her arms and fingers were locked straight.

'If you've got something you want to say, just say it.'

Nothing.

'More personal feelings?'

'No,' she answered immediately, her voice constricted. She took a pained breath then looked up. 'I don't think we can become a window if we continue to focus on *tactics*. The more calculated we are, the more we exacerbate the hostility.'

Mikami made his face impassive and folded his arms.

'Go on.'

'Of course. We shoulder all the responsibility for dealing with the press. As far as they're concerned, we're more than just a portal to the inside; in many cases, they think of us as an embodiment of the organization itself. If we show them nothing but calculated moves designed to keep control over them . . . I worry they'll see that as applying to the whole police force. I wonder if we can't be a little more relaxed in our approach, less structured, more open-minded. I understand that tactics are sometimes necessary, I do, but if we really want to become a two-way conduit, isn't the best tactic *not* to rely on strategy any more than we need to?'

Mikami had closed his eyes.

It felt like someone was telling him it was wrong to kill, even as he stood amidst a bloody crime scene. Applying the fundamentalist grammar of the *koban* to Media Relations wouldn't poke even a pinhole through their thick walls, let alone a window.

The gap in enthusiasm brought on a wave of lethargy.

However impassioned her speech, Mikumo's image of Media Relations was one that was free to think up new approaches;

sadly, that just didn't fit with the reality of the office, entangled as it was in executive politics.

And yet . . .

If anyone was capable of opening a window to the outside, it was Mikumo. While he'd felt discouraged by her missionary zeal, like sun shining through a biting wind, another part of his mind had caught sight of a fleeting but welcome hope. And not just because she was uncontaminated, or a woman. She had grown wings in the course of a single night, and he'd seen in that a limitless potential. The impossible stopped being so. *She* could connect with the reporters. *She* could wade through the scum of one-upmanship and ambition, clear the waters for a younger, more naive earnestness to shine through.

She was right, he knew it. Tactics could never genuinely move a person. He wanted to believe they were both gazing at the same peak, even if they saw different routes, even if a landslide had left them both unable to move. He hadn't forgotten: two sides were needed to shake hands.

They were trying too hard to be smart.

'Sir,' Mikumo started, sounding formal. 'Please, let me work with the reporters.'

Mikami tutted. He made a wincing smile, surprised she'd even ask at this point.

I'm not afraid to dirty my hands a little.

He could still hear the words from the night before aching in his ears, but he felt confident now that she wouldn't do anything rash. She'd just told him the best tactic was to minimize tactics.

'Sign up for once-a-week training – on how to make an arrest.'

'Sir . . .?'

'Did anyone try to touch you, make a pass?'

She looked scandalized. In the next moment, the look dissolved into a smile.

'No, nothing of the sort. I think I actually scared them off.'

'I can see where they're coming from,' Mikami said, breathing out, checking the clock on the wall.

It was five minutes to two.

He'd expected the meeting to have ended by now, but Kuramae had yet to return. Sensing what was on his mind, Mikumo put on a serious face and bowed. She told him she was going to help with clearing up after the meeting and walked out.

Mikami leaned into his chair. He lit a cigarette. He took what felt like his first normal breath in a while. Eventually, he let out a chuckle.

He thought back to the look on Mikumo's face as she'd turned around briefly on her way out. All the formality had gone from her eyes. He'd recognized it as a measure of gratitude, affection in the way one would think of a parent, but he'd also seen traces of the particular familiarity that was shared after a romantic encounter, even the joy of discovery he'd witnessed in Akama's daughter when she'd found herself able to communicate with a single glance. Inside everyone is unlimited potential. People might work for you, but that doesn't mean their emotions are any less valid.

Mikami knew it well enough – he'd spent twenty-eight years working for other people. He understood that no one was unquestioning in their obedience, just as he realized that no leader could ever hope to understand the inner workings of their staff. Yet they still made themselves gods. Whenever someone was newly appointed to them, they would tend to classify them as this or that kind of person, applying brightly coloured tabs to shoehorn them into the role they wanted performed.

Mikami had been the same at home.

Even at home.

A gentle wife who kept to herself. A daughter, spoiled but kind at heart.

He'd been quick to label them for whatever reason, then leave the classification unchecked, unaltered, as five, then ten years had gone by.

Had he known Ayumi at all?

Mikami felt himself tense, recognizing the onset of his dizziness. Everything around him started to go black. His vision blurred and spun. He pushed his elbows out and lay his face flat on the desk.

Ayumi was standing there, inscrutable, as his head lurched.

44

The only sound was the ticking of the office clock.

As before, the attack abated after five minutes. All that remained was a lingering echo, like a fading cramp in the leg, causing Mikami to forget all ideas of check-ups and hospital appointments.

Even after half past two, neither Kuramae nor Mikumo had come back. Nor had anybody called to let him know the meeting was over. Knowing they were due to discuss anonymous reporting, he had expected the press to deliver lengthy, padded-out speeches, but this was taking too long even with that in mind.

He had finally got hold of Odate. His wife had called out with the vitality of a young woman when he'd given her his name.

'Mikami. It's been a long time.'

'Sorry I haven't been better at staying in touch.'

'Not at all, we know things are busy. How are Minako and Ayumi? I trust they're well?'

'Yes, thank you.'

Mikami had decided not to tell the truth, not wanting to add to the strain the director was already under. Even so, it had been three months already. He'd expected the information to have reached him by now. That it hadn't only provided a glimpse into the solitude of retirement, of growing distant from the force, even for a man like Odate, who had worked his way up to becoming director of Criminal Investigations.

'Do you mind if I ask what you're calling about? My husband

is resting at the moment. It's the rehabilitation exercises, they really wear him out. I do sometimes wonder if they're actually doing any good . . .'

Laughter flooded into his ear. While Odate's retirement had meant an increased separation from the force, it had also allowed him a peaceful life at home. Where his wife had previously been reserved, always a few steps behind her husband, she was now bright and open, perhaps relieved of the hidden burden her role had exacted.

'How is the director coping?'

'Really quite well, actually. The mouth is still a problem, of course. Should I get him to call you when he's up again? Although I'm sure he'll be getting me to do the calling.' She laughed again at the little joke.

'Actually, I wanted to ask whether I could come over tonight, depending on the director's condition, of course.'

'Oh! I'm sure he'd be delighted.'

The internal line started to ring on his desk. Odate's wife seemed to pick up on the sound.

'Okay, I'll be sure to pass on the message.'

'That's appreciated. I won't impose myself for long. I'll call to let you know when I'm leaving the office.'

There wasn't anything to suggest that Futawatari had been there ahead of him. Feeling a measure of relief, Mikami ended the call. He reached for the ringing phone, assuming it would be either Suwa or Kuramae.

'Mikami. This is Urushibara.'

Mikami reeled with the sudden change. What the hell could Urushibara want? Two days had passed since Mikami had called him. Urushibara had found it easy to fend him away, but that had been before he'd learned the truth about the Koda memo.

'What is it?'

Mikami was instantly suspicious, but that wasn't all. A blast of animosity had forced his voice into a whisper. He was the man who had buried a call from the Six Four kidnapper to cover up a recording error. The man who had broken Hiyoshi by blaming him for Shoko's death. The man who had been promoted to captain, and remained unscathed even after he'd committed Koda and Kakinuma to a cycle of surveillance that had lasted fourteen years.

'What's the matter? Did I catch you at a bad time?'

'Just tell me what you want. I don't have the luxury of free time a captain has.'

'Let me guess, Minako turned you down last night?'

That was as far as he got with his usual remarks. Mikami had been about to hang up when the man's voice registered in his eardrum, suddenly tense.

'What did you do to Koda?'

Mikami froze. 'Koda . . . Koda as in Koda memo?'

He was stalling for time, but Urushibara kept coming.

'I know you met him.'

Mikami was at a loss as to how to reply. He struggled to understand what was happening. *Impossible.* Could Kakinuma have reported in to his boss?

'There's no point denying it, Mikami. Answer me.'

Mikami knew he had to be careful; he didn't want his reply to backfire. He saw in his mind an image of Kakinuma, of the man's wife, the face of their young child in her arms.

'You bastard . . . you're not planning to play dumb, I hope?'

Mikami didn't know what to say.

'Talk! Tell me what you did to Koda.'

Just stay calm.

Urushibara's the one who's worked up. Not me.

'I didn't do anything.'

'Quit the lies. Kakinuma told me he saw you.'

The picture was coming into focus. *Kakinuma had seen him.* That was the only thing he'd said to Urushibara.

'Seen me? Where?'

'Anywhere, wherever. Just admit to it. You went to see him – you went to see Koda.'

'And what if I had?' Mikami asked, leaving only the suggestion. He had regained his composure.

'What did you go to talk to him about?'

'Nothing I'd need to tell you.'

'Why, you—'

Urushibara broke off, his breathing heavy in Mikami's ear. When he spoke again it was as a detective.

'You sent him into hiding. Right?'

Mikami blinked slowly.

As I'd suspected. He'd lost Koda. Just days before the commissioner's scheduled visit, Koda – the man who knew everything about the cover-up – had dropped out of sight. Mikami thought of the situation this would have put Kakinuma in. He'd lost Koda, the target of his watch; fretted over how to report it in – finally, he'd decided to give Mikami's name. He'd told Urushibara that he'd seen Mikami approach Koda outside the supermarket, at the car park.

'I didn't send him anywhere, and no, I'm not sheltering him either.'

'But you know where he is.'

'No.'

'Tell me what you said to him.'

'I just bumped into him, outside a supermarket car park. I asked him how he was doing, but he looked busy, so I didn't say anything else.'

'It won't help you to lie, Mikami. I know you said *something*. Why else would he have bolted?'

'You say he's gone, but are you sure? He's got a wife, a family.'

'I'm asking the questions.'

'I don't understand this at all. What on earth could I say that would give him cause to run away?'

'That's, well, that's . . .' Urushibara faltered. 'Whatever it was you were asking about on the phone. That nonsense about – what? – the Koda memo?'

'If it was nonsense, why would Koda jump ship?'

'You bastard . . .'

Mikami felt sure it was Futawatari's handiwork. He'd finally tracked Koda down, then pressured him for the truth behind the memo. But was that enough? Koda could have just pretended not to know. What would cause him to disappear in such a hurry? He'd suffered for so many years – was it just fear taking over? He'd hoped to protect the normal life he'd finally managed to obtain. He'd become terrified of Futawatari as the latter pried into his past, sought a temporary hiding place. It was certainly possible, but for him this kind of self-defence actually served to protect Criminal Investigations – Mikami couldn't see how he could have disappeared in a way that threatened Urushibara or Kakinuma.

'Go and see the director.'

'Hmm?'

The door opened as he was replying; Kuramae came into the room. His stiff expression made it clear there had been some kind of unexpected development. Mikami held up a hand to catch his attention, then wrapped it around the mouthpiece.

He spoke under his breath.

'I don't think I heard you properly.'

'I told you to report to the director.'

He had heard correctly: Arakida intended to continue Urushibara's interrogation.

'Hey, Mikami, are you listening to me?'

'Which director?'

Mikami wanted to test the response. When Urushibara answered it was in an unnaturally quiet voice.

'I don't think that's even a question, for people like you and me. Am I wrong?'

'What am I reporting in for?'

'You'll find out when you get there. Just get yourself up to the fourth floor, right now.'

'It's unfortunate, but the directors are all engaged in a meeting with the press.'

Urushibara slammed down the phone. Mikami put his down, feeling as if he were sealing off a demon. He glanced up to the clock before turning to face Kuramae. It was five to three.

'What happened?'

'Yes . . .' Kuramae frowned, apparently in some difficulty. 'The press are demanding we hold a press conference, in light of the morning's news, and that Akama issues an official apology.'

What?

'Who was first to say it?'

'Nonomura. The head of the *Toyo*'s local branch.'

Toshikazu Nonomura. High-handed, he liked to think of himself as a star among the major players.

'What was the reaction?'

'They went along with it . . . but only I think because they lacked any good reason to block it. They want you to attend an emergency meeting in Akama's office to get the preparations started.'

Mikami caught his breath. It was like watching rocks emerge from a receding tide.

Akikawa's words.

I'm going to attend the one here, in the headquarters.

45

Mikami was late to the meeting.

Suwa got back just as he was leaving the office; they'd stood at the door and brought each other up to speed. The reporters had started to file in, back from Station F. Mikami had only spared them a glance as he'd hurried up the stairs, but by the time he reached Akama's office the couches were already lined with frowning faces. Akama. Shirota. Ishii. And Division Chief Ikoma, from Internal Affairs. Mikami had half expected Futawatari to be there, too, but he was nowhere to be seen. That decided it. He *was* acting on Captain Tsujiuchi's direct orders.

Akama's eyes were like arrows, targeted on Shirota.

'What possessed you to agree like that? *We'll have to discuss the matter.* All you had to do was say something along those lines.'

'I'm sorry.' Shirota had gone white. 'I decided the number-one priority was to ensure the commissioner's visit went smoothly; that it wouldn't have been wise to argue in a press conference.'

'And so you decided to offer me as a sacrifice?'

'Sir, I would never . . .'

Mikami had a notebook in his lap. It contained Kuramae's notes from the round-table meeting. He had scanned them briefly before coming in.

> Nonomura: *Without wishing to sound like I'm blowing our trumpet here – could I trouble Director Akama for his opinion on the news from Station F?*

Akama: It is a most unwelcome situation. I can assure you all that we are all treating this with the greatest—'

Nonomura: Sorry, I didn't mean here and now. If we could prevail on you to hold a press conference on the matter ... I believe you had a suicide in another of your detention facilities, just a couple of years ago. At this point, I imagine it is necessary for Director Akama to offer a full and public explanation, detailing the system you have in place for managing detainees.

'What's happening with the press? Do they know about this?' Akama turned to look at Mikami. His gold-rimmed glasses seemed arched, mirroring his questioning eyes and raised eyebrows.

'Most of the reporters just got back from Station F. Their bosses have already appraised them of what happened in the meeting; they're apparently discussing when the conference will take place.'

'I can't believe this is really going to go ahead.'

Graceless defeat. That was what it sounded like.

'I've got Suwa looking into it.'

'Get him on the phone.'

Mikami nodded. He excused himself and flipped open his mobile. Suwa answered immediately.

'How's it looking down there?'

'They want us to hold the conference at 4 p.m.'

'Do they have a venue in mind?'

'The Press Room should be fine.'

'Four o'clock, in the Press Room.' Mikami repeated the details for the benefit of everyone there.

He checked his watch: three twenty-five.

'Are they putting their questions together?'

'I don't think so. The only paper really behind this is the *Toyo*, so I think they'll be happy if they get a picture of Akama lowering his head and apologizing.'

Wary of Suwa's voice being heard, Mikami pressed the phone harder against his ear.

'So it's unlikely the club will put forward any official questions.' Mikami repeated this out loud, summarizing Suwa's meaning.

Akama's head came forwards, looking impatient. 'What about TV?'

'Will the TV have cameras there?'

'Yes. The association just called in the request.'

Mikami nodded in silent confirmation. Probably having pictured himself on the news, Akama put a fist to his forehead and threw his head back.

'This is a joke. We're playing right into *their* hands.'

Criminal Investigations' hands.

Akama let out a heavy sigh, the gesture conveying both resentment and resignation.

'We don't have time for this. We should begin preparing. Ikoma, the suicide took place before I assumed my post. According to my predecessor, we were not at fault. May I assume this understanding is correct?'

'Yes.' Ikoma looked up, his eyes curiously tranquil for an inspector from Internal Affairs. 'In view of the exceptional circumstances, we decided the suicide didn't suggest there was anything at fault in the facilities or with their management. No dismissals were made. The press were mostly happy with the decision, and no articles were printed condemning our treatment of the case.'

Ikoma was right. Mikami had read the article at his desk in Second Division. A middle-aged man detained for trying to skip a restaurant bill had killed himself during the night in one of Station T's cells. The method had been unprecedented – he'd been lying with his back to the guard on duty and choked himself on his vest, having pulled it through the cuff of his shirt and then forced it – and his fist – down his throat. Thinking the man was asleep, it had taken the guard more than three hours to realize something was wrong. Charges of negligence had seemed inevitable, but the focus of the investigation shifted after a number of detainees who had shared the man's cell came forward to give evidence, testifying they hadn't noticed anything wrong or heard a single groan. Internal Affairs had been confident in its press release stating that circumstances had made the man's suicide extremely difficult to detect. It was also discovered that the man had stolen funds from work and spent the money on women in hostess bars. When his transgressions had come to light he'd run away, abandoning his family; his death had been a final, selfish act. Some of the reporters had even come forward, sympathizing with the police for the whole situation.

But . . .

A short while later, Mikami began to hear rumours.

That the guard had failed to keep an eye on the monitors showing the cells. That the guard had been asleep as the man lost consciousness, his legs kicking in agony. Most of what he'd heard had been like that. Had Station T been behind the cover-up, or had Internal Affairs decided to lead the whitewash in the interest of protecting the organization as a whole? It wasn't hard to guess the tricks they might have used to secure the testimonies of the man's fellow detainees. He doubted they would have taken the risk of openly pressuring them into giving false statements, but they could perhaps have suggested it was up to the detainees themselves if they wanted to draw certain conclusions. Making a good impression meant getting out of detention sooner. Rather than calculated strategy, it would have been desperate prayer. The truth, no doubt, was that the detainees had picked up on what was happening and volunteered to play nice, and that Station F and Internal Affairs had opted to accept the 'harmless' deception.

Mikami watched Ikoma from the side.

His eyes hadn't wavered when he'd said it wasn't a problem, but Mikami couldn't know whether the man's faith was as unyielding on the inside. He'd only been transferred from Security Second Division in the spring, so there was the possibility he didn't know. Either that, or he was simply avoiding mention of the rumours so he could argue impunity later on.

Akama glanced around the people gathered there.

'All right, then. The *Toyo* is hoping to build up the theme of negligence and repeated misconduct, to make more of this than there is. I can't imagine much worse than them running that as a headline in the papers tomorrow morning.'

Mikami felt a sudden chill. An even worse possibility had just occurred to him. What if the *Toyo* knew for a fact that the guard had dozed off?

'We will issue a statement committing ourselves to a severe tightening-up of discipline in the captain's name,' Akama announced. 'The statement will be enough for the papers; it will make the headlines and prevent the *Toyo* from achieving its aim. Always assuming there are no other problems regarding the suicide, we still have to address the misconduct at Station F. I will inform the press that we are taking disciplinary action, and that the officer in question has been dismissed. Ishii, I assume this has already been done?'

'Yes, earlier this morning.'

'Good. I will then make a formal apology to the citizens of the prefecture. After this I will move on to my second statement – announcing that the captain has sent notices to all stations in the prefecture that they are to work to the standards laid out in the regulations governing the facilities. After this, I will move to questions. The *Toyo* will no doubt ask about Station T. I will emphasize that the suicide did not result from negligence and dispel any ideas of repeated misconduct.'

Wasn't that just playing into the *Toyo*'s – no, Criminal Investigations' – hands? They'd loaded their third arrow. They would wait for Akama to refute the claims of negligence, then shoot for his heart. They would bring up the talk of the guard having fallen asleep and request another investigation. Akama would hesitate. His panic would be broadcast all over the evening news. It would reach even the commissioner's circles.

Or maybe . . .

A different scenario came to mind.

They wouldn't say anything. As with the cover-up during Six Four, the negligence would never come to light and, because of that, it would become an indispensable tool. Criminal Investigations had no reason to make open threats, even less to bring the public into the fray. What they wanted was a table in the shadows at which to hold their negotiations – and a sharp blade, to press up against the throat of the administrative faction. That was it. They would force Akama into committing himself during the conference. Then they would move in and attack from behind the curtains. Once he'd gone on public record about the lack of any negligence, they would whisper into his ear that, in fact, the guard had fallen asleep. That they could leak that factual tidbit to the press whenever they wanted.

The third arrow was doused in flame.

Would they really release it? Maybe it would end up as a game of chicken. Criminal Investigations was afraid of Administrative Affairs' own arrows – also doused in flame. They were already suspicious that Kazuki Koda was in their hands.

Go and see the director.

You'll find out when you get there.

Urushibara's words replayed themselves in his ear. How much of the truth would Arakida give him?

'We've got fifteen minutes,' Ishii said. Even now, he wanted to make something of the fact that he paid attention to detail.

Akama dismissed everyone, but ordered Mikami to stay. It hadn't come as a surprise.

'Well? Come on, then.'

No sooner had the door closed than Akama waved him closer. Mikami shifted to where Shirota had been sitting, so that he faced Akama directly. Immediately he saw the director's blue veins and bloodshot eyes.

'Did you find out who the source of the article was?'

Mikami nodded, feeling no resistance to telling him. All he needed to do was confirm Akama's suspicions.

'The leak came from Director Arakida. I believe he gave the story to Akikawa directly.'

'That bastard! *I knew it.*'

Mikami felt himself tense. Akama resembled a wild animal, the way he'd bared his gums. After a while he spoke again, his voice back to normal as it filled the room.

'I assume I have Arakida to thank for Nonomura's speech, too?'

'Most likely, yes.'

'Just who the hell do they think they are? Do they have no shame?'

Akama's voice became a bark for the second time. He fell silent, then brought his foot up and kicked the desk. His anger seemed to come in waves, swelling, then pulling away again. He drew himself into a stooped position. Stared at a single point on the floor. His hand tensed into a fist, slowly unfolded again. He was trying to keep his anger in check.

'I have lots of things I need to do, you know, when I go back to Tokyo. I didn't want to waste a single calorie of my energy, not in a backwater station like this. I have things to do for the sake of the nation. Otherwise, what's the point in all this? Why doesn't anyone understand?'

His anger peaked again. His face flashed bright red.

'This is a fucking joke. They think they have me cornered, but this apology is a waste of time. Doesn't mean a bloody thing.'

It didn't seem that way to Mikami. This was the worst-possible scenario for Akama. Tokyo's intention had been to conceal the true purpose behind the commissioner's visit until the day itself, then launch a lightning strike on the Prefectural HQ to relay the 'word from above'. That was why Akama had restricted access to the information. Instead of bringing Shirota or Futawatari into the fold, he had manipulated Mikami, savouring his success at having brought him into line. But the information had somehow got out. The first slip-up had been to let Criminal Investigations discover the NPA's plan. The second had been to let the backlash escalate into an actual counter-attack. Akama had been forced into this predicament. A threatening article had been printed in the lead-up to the commissioner's visit, incurring Tokyo's wrath; Akama had failed in his attempt to fix the situation and now had to offer a public apology. His ability to function as one of the Tokyo elite would be cast into doubt. And his drop in estimation wouldn't end there. The trap set by Criminal Investigations, waiting for him in the Press Room, would see to that.

Should I warn him?

Mikami had been pondering the question ever since the door had closed. It was only speculation. Yet the story of Criminal Investigations' plot came together neatly in his mind, too plausible simply to dismiss. Was he going to do nothing, let his superior officer attend a press conference he was sure was a trap?

Akama's phone started to ring on his desk. It was Ishii.

'Fine,' Akama said. He put the phone down and got to his feet. 'Let's get this over with.'

Still uncertain, Mikami got to his feet. He followed Akama out of the room and down the corridor. He had no reason to feel loyal to the man in front of him. Yet he felt the betrayal nonetheless. The dishonesty seemed to constrict his chest.

He found himself unable to side with Criminal Investigations. He couldn't think of a single reason to protect them. Was it because of the way they'd treated him as an exile? Was it because he'd caught a glimpse of the dark history behind Six Four? No. It was because he didn't yet know what Tokyo was trying to do. He could tell himself he was still a detective at heart, but, as long as he was unable to imagine the danger Criminal Investigations faced, it was impossible to see things from their perspective.

And he had his own perspective. He had the feeling that he was also a victim, of Criminal Investigations having interfered with his current job, of them having violated his territory. Their trap had been laid right at the feet of Media Relations. Arakida was trying to use the press as a weapon and had set the stage for his war right in Mikami's office.

Even so . . .

Mikami didn't feel angry. And that was why, he realized, the skin concealing his true feelings – his guilt because he hadn't warned Akama about the trap; his hostility for Criminal Investigations – had peeled cleanly away. Both were nothing more than footnotes. By the time they reached the stairs, Mikami had become slave to a single idea. Akama's wiry frame stood there before him.

If he were to warn him about the trap . . .

If he were to hold out his hand, rescue this weakened, panic-stricken tourist . . .

Akama would change the way he looked at him.

Someone I can trust.

If that happened, Mikami would never have to worry about being transferred away.

Sir . . .

Mikami was on the verge of speaking up when Akama turned suddenly around. 'You should use this as a chance to make your apology, too.'

He'd said it almost without thinking.

All the tension seemed to dissipate in an instant.

Apology? About what . . . who to?

'To the Press Club. You need to fix the clash you had over anonymous reporting. Get on your hands and knees if you have to – just make sure the press withdraw their intention of boycotting the interview.'

Mikami couldn't think of anything to say. He wouldn't show himself as weak before the press. Akama had just crossed the line Mikami had drawn for himself.

'If that's not enough, assure them that all future announcements will include the full identity of everyone involved. We only need the commissioner's visit to be a success. Once it's over, you can rescind your statement, cause all the trouble you want.'

He had to have misheard.

An empty promise . . . but this was something completely different to Shirota's suggestion of fleshing out their services. Akama was telling him to lie, and about anonymous reporting, the most incendiary issue his office faced.

'You should see yourself.' Akama smiled, without looking amused. 'We'll have to put up with it for three days. But there's nothing to worry about. Criminal Investigations can wriggle all it wants. Come Thursday, it'll be gone.'

46

The press conference had been continuing without issue.

'. . . in light of the aforementioned circumstances, I am able to report that a disciplinary committee was convened in the Prefectural HQ earlier today at which it was decided, after a thorough discussion, that the actions of Sergeant Yoshitake Kuriyama, aged fifty, were in clear violation of the propriety and behaviour that is expected of an officer of the law. As such, Sergeant Kuriyama has been placed under emergency arrest and has today been dismissed from the force . . .'

Twenty-three reporters. Five TV cameras.

Akama was sitting at the centre of the table put out for the conference, talking in a monotone. Not having had the time to put together a full statement, all he had to hand were a few quickly drafted notes. Shirota was at his side, every now and then passing along a sheet with more scribbled notes.

Mikami was watching the reporters from the corner of the room. Apart from the two representing the *Toyo*, they all seemed to be in varying states of despondency. No one had shown displeasure when Mikami had walked into the room. The atmosphere had clearly changed from the previous week. Perhaps it *was* possible to turn the boycott around, if, as Suwa had suggested, they were able to capitalize on the other reporters' resentment for the *Toyo*. And Mikami had been freed from his responsibilities. The format of the apology had been left to Shirota's discretion. Mikami didn't doubt that the lie of full disclosure would prevent the boycott from taking place, but he also suspected that the same might be achieved without breaking any promises – if he directed his apology at the melee surrounding the written protest.

But his mind wasn't focused on such preparations. Those kind of thoughts raced along on the surface of his consciousness but failed to breach the deeper layers of emotion.

Come Thursday, it'll be gone . . .

Alarms were flashing red, deep in his mind. In the end, he'd let Akama take his seat without even hinting at the trap. *Gone.* The impact of that one word had been too much.

Was Mikami reading too much into it? Akama hadn't been in a normal state when he'd made the utterance. His pride had been injured, his standing in Tokyo placed under threat. It might have been a vengeful remark, an exaggeration of the trouble Criminal Investigations would no doubt have to face. It might have been nothing more than a battle cry. And yet the alarms continued to flash, growing brighter still. What could 'gone' mean, supposing it hadn't been an exaggeration? It went beyond concepts like shock, loss and damage. What it seemed to suggest was an 'end', an 'extinction'.

'. . . we are treating this case with the utmost severity. To make sure nothing like this ever happens again, Captain Tsujiuchi has called on all nineteen district stations to reinforce their controls concerning the management of the detention facilities.'

Akama gave Shirota a signal. They both stood; it was part of the ritual. The cameras flashed in waves.

'We offer our most sincere apologies to the citizens of our prefecture and to the nation, to the victim of this heinous crime, and to everyone else affected. I believe I speak for everyone in the Prefectural Headquarters when I say that we intend to do all we can to recover the goodwill and trust lost due to our shortcomings in this case.'

The two men came forward in a bow.

Shutters clicked as countless flashes went off, bathing the front of the room with an otherworldly brightness. Akama raised his head after a few seconds, followed soon after by Shirota. They retook their seats.

'We will take questions now.'

Mikami's eyes were trained on Akikawa. But it was Tejima, next to him, who was the first to raise his hand.

'I seem to remember someone killing themselves in one of your detention cells, a couple of years ago. In light of today, wouldn't you agree there might be a fundamental problem in the management of the prefecture's detention facilities?'

The question.

Akikawa had followed through on his pact with Arakida, with Tejima as his mouthpiece.

'When you say *fundamental problem* . . .?' Shirota asked in response, holding a hand to his ear. Tejima floated a sly grin.

'Oh, you know, that maybe you don't see managing the facilities as important, so you don't post any of your better officers to the job. That sort of thing.'

Akama indicated that Shirota was to respond in person.

'I can assure you this is not the case. We believe the management of the facilities to be of paramount importance. As such, we assign some of our best officers to work there. With respect to the case you bring up from two years ago, the conclusion was that the suicide had taken place in exceptional circumstances – the man having chosen to adopt a highly unorthodox method – and that nothing suggested negligence in the facilities or their management.'

The answer.

Mikami shifted his focus back to the two reporters from the *Toyo*. They showed no signs of having any further questions. Tejima was scribbling in his notepad while Akikawa was an image of composure, arms crossed in front of him.

Mikami breathed out in silence.

Akikawa had decided to keep the detail about the guard's 'cat-nap' on hold. No — it was more likely that Arakida hadn't told him about it yet. It wouldn't benefit him to have given away anything more the previous night; if he was planning to use the story as leverage, it made sense to keep it secret for now. He might have won over a local police reporter, but that didn't mean he would underestimate the reach of one of Tokyo's major papers. If he leaked two stories – both hinting at the same thing – he couldn't guarantee that the *Toyo* wouldn't choose to ignore Akikawa and come down from Tokyo with the intention of exposing the conflict raging in the Prefectural HQ.

'Are there any more questions?' Shirota asked, hinting that he wanted to bring the conference to an end.

No hands came up, and no one spoke. The whole thing had been for the *Toyo*'s benefit. The atmosphere was phlegmatic, the assembled faces bored.

'This concludes the conference.'

Akama and Shirota both stood; they bowed and made their way towards the exit. What they were thinking was clear from the way they walked, in their relaxed shoulders. *We got through it.* They wouldn't realize it had all been a trap until later that night.

Mikami walked out of the Press Room.

Go and see the director.

The press had to come first. He could go and see Arakida afterwards. He would request a meeting with them in his capacity as press director, rather than turning up because he'd been summoned. He wouldn't be able to hold out, not without the armour his work provided.

Criminal Investigations . . . gone. He hoped the meaning behind those words would be apparent on Arakida's face.

47

Mikami called everyone to his desk, this time including Mikumo.

He tasked them to find out what each of the twelve papers – excluding the *Toyo* – wanted, before the day was out. The current mood was hostile towards the *Toyo*. How many would cave in with regard to the boycott if he tried bringing the 'press director's apology' to the table again?

'See if you can get everyone on the fence to come down on our side. Make sure we have the majority, then set them up for a general meeting tomorrow.' Mikami realized he was raising his voice. He caught Suwa's eye and added, 'It's okay, Akama wants me to offer an apology.'

Suwa seemed finally to breathe. He slapped himself on the sides of his cheeks to fire himself up, effectively starting again. He looked ready for business when he addressed Kuramae and Mikumo.

'Right – let's go put an end to this damn boycott.'

They heard footsteps in the corridor.

Suwa twisted sharply around and paced away from Mikami's desk, in his element as he greeted the two reporters who had just entered. Yamashina from the *Times* and Yanase from the *Jiji Press*.

'Suwa, how much do we owe you?'

'Five thousand.'

They'd come in to settle the bill for the previous night's drinks. Yamashina caught Mikami's eye as he fished out his wallet. He wanted to say thanks for the story on the bid-rigging charges.

'You've got a pretty good voice, Yamashina,' Mikumo flattered. She looked slightly flushed, perhaps from working up the courage to speak.

'Me? Haha.' Yamashina smiled shyly, pointing a gratified finger at himself. 'No way, not as good as—'

'Yanase, you got a moment?' Suwa cut in. He gestured towards the couches, businesslike all of a sudden.

Yanase cocked his head to one side while Yamashina's smile faded, the latter clearly wondering why Suwa hadn't extended the request to him, too. Yanase took a seat and gave Suwa a questioning look. Suwa sat so close Yanase had to shunt along the couch.

'Let's start where we left off last night. Everything will work out if we offer a proper apology. That's what you think, yes?'

He was keeping his voice and his expression low-key. Yanase, the de facto head of the moderate faction, put on a pained look.

'Well, I suppose . . .'

'Great. We'll all be looking for new positions if the commissioner's interview goes down the drain. If we're unlucky, we might even get booted from the force.'

Yamashina was peering at the couch, still on his feet. Suwa ignored him and focused on Yanase.

'See if you can't spread the idea among the others. We know everyone wants good coverage. That walking interview – it does make for a good shot.'

'Well . . . yes, but it *was* decided at the GM. It'll be difficult to overturn the decision to boycott that one.'

'And GMs are great for changing decisions, too, right? Set one up for tomorrow.'

'I don't know . . .'

'It's not as though the last one was normal. I imagine it was like a hornets' nest after the tumult outside the captain's office.'

'True. But the vote was unanimous; that does carry a lot of sway.'

'I hope you're not planning to leave me and Kuramae destitute here. What about Mikumo? She'll be sent back to work in the *koban*.'

'Of course that's not what I want. Don't forget that management's weighing in on some of us. And this all started with anonymous reporting – some of the papers have you blacklisted, at least until they get some tangible concessions from you.'

'We've already told you we're planning to improve on our services. And we're going to apologize, too. We're taking this seriously.'

'Well, I can see that. But—'

'Hey,' Yamashina interjected from the side. 'I could suggest it. That we hold another GM.'

Suwa feigned annoyance.

'Yamashina, I'm trying to have a talk with Yanase.'

'I'm saying I'm happy to make the suggestion, Suwa. You want us to convene another meeting? No problem. Although I can't guarantee what the outcome will be.'

Suwa kept his eyes on Yanase and said nothing. There was a pause, then Yanase sighed and the issue was settled.

'Fine. Yamashina, if you're happy to make the suggestion, I'll back you up.'

Mikami felt again as if he were watching a master craftsman at work. With two papers supporting the motion, the GM would be sure to go ahead.

The two reporters disappeared back into the corridor; Suwa began to discuss with the others their plan for approaching the remaining papers. The foundations were already in place for overturning the boycott. Mikami got up from his seat.

'I'm just heading to the first floor.'

It was the truth – there was something he wanted to discuss with Shirota. But he was the only one who seemed to care about what he was doing. The others nodded as though they were on autopilot, and Mikami felt suddenly alone.

48

Mikami spent less than five minutes in Administration, having succeeded in his mission to obtain Futawatari's mobile number from Division Chief Shirota. *You don't know it? Isn't he from your intake?* That was the closest Shirota got to questioning him about his enquiry. He'd shot a glance at the inspector's desk, then tilted his head and paged through his organizer. Mikami was reminded of Shirota's approach to office politics: *don't ask too many questions.*

Mikami exited the corridor via the steel door leading to the emergency staircase. He pulled out his mobile and dialled the number he had just got. He wanted to get more on Koda before his meeting with Director Arakida. Had Futawatari managed to make contact? Did he know where Koda was now? The call went straight to voicemail. He was in a meeting with someone, perhaps. Or maybe it was his policy not to answer calls from unknown numbers. Mikami ended the call without leaving a message. It was, without exception, the caller who had the advantage. He would lose the initiative if he let Futawatari call back at his convenience.

Fine. I'll do this empty-handed.

Mikami walked back into the corridor and started towards Arakida's office. He still couldn't claim to have fully merged into his title of press director. It was proving hard to maintain his cool. He decided to use the stairs and not the lift, climbing to the fourth floor on foot, but far from helping his composure he found himself increasingly conflicted. On the one hand, there was his acute mistrust of Arakida; on the other, the obligation he still felt to Criminal Investigations, tangled like original sin around his heart. Then there was his own muddied position. *Come Thursday, it'll be gone.* Mikami's thoughts spiralled as he paced along the fourth-floor corridor. It was growing dark outside, as thick clouds blotted out the sky beyond the windows – they were a mix of black and grey.

Criminal Investigations, First Division.

Mikami pushed hard on the door.

He willed Matsuoka to be in, but he wasn't at the desk that faced the door at the back of the room. Assistant Chief Mikura craned his neck up from the next desk along. He'd joined the force a couple of years after Mikami. The discomposure that spread across his face was clear to see even from a distance. *I wouldn't say he's got the balls of a flea. But an ant's? Sure.* Mikami recalled the way someone had once described the man.

He pointed a thumb at Arakida's office.

'He wanted to see me.'

Mikura got to his feet without saying anything; he hurried to the door of the director's office and knocked. He put on a show of listening for a response, cautiously opened the door, and popped his head through. When he emerged again he said, 'Go on in,' without making eye contact.

The last time Mikami had entered the director's office had been in the spring. That time, at least, he had been admitted as a detective.

'Sir.'

Mikami bowed from the waist, having stopped a fraction before meeting the carpeted floor.

'Ah, Mikami. Good of you to drop in,' Arakida said breezily.

He took off his reading glasses and circled around, his imposing frame moving from his desk to one of the couches. His expression was no different to his usual one, but Mikami knew it was a thin veneer, that, like Urushibara, underneath, he would be alert and ready for battle.

'Come on, then, no need to be formal. Take a seat.'

Mikami complied. Arakida flipped open a glass-covered box of cigarettes and offered Mikami a smoke.

'No, thanks.'

'What, you quit?'

'No.'

'Tell me, how are things?' he prodded. Mikami cocked his head in lieu of a response. 'The first floor, I mean. In a bit of a fluster?'

'I . . . I don't know.'

'Huh, right. I'm sure we only loaned you out for times like this . . .'

Mikami understood what he was trying to imply.

You're either with us, or you don't come back.

'Urushibara told me you wanted to see me. What was it you wanted to ask?'

'No need to rush. You'll find out soon enough.'

Mikami's discomfort was considerable. Was Arakida trying to work out how much he'd changed in the eight months since his exile from Criminal Investigations?

'I hear things are bad in Media Relations. You been picking fights with the reporters?'

'Actually, the biggest problem is not knowing the source of the *Toyo*'s leak.'

Mikami's attempt at a subtle counter-attack caused Arakida to narrow his eyes.

'Are you implying it was me, Mikami?'

'Do you intend on having a *chat* with Akama?'

'Did he send you to find out?'

'No.'

'No, I have no intention of meeting him. Why would I want to look into the face of that damned mantis? Besides, he's small fry as far as Tokyo's concerned. I could pressure him, and it wouldn't change a thing.'

The third arrow would be fired at Tokyo. That was what it had sounded like. Mikami saw an image of Maejima, already on secondment to the Criminal Investigations Bureau. Would they use him? Or someone in Prefecture D?

'Where's Matsuoka?'

'Hmm? Why do you ask?'

'He wasn't at his desk.'

'Politics isn't his forte, as I'm sure you know. Solving the next case is all he thinks about. He's out visiting the Six Four team, priming the pumps even as we speak.'

Politics.

Was that what he'd said?

'You know Matsuoka was thinking about making you a team leader?'

Mikami cut the switch to his emotions as a reflex. Still he felt flustered to see the smug look on Arakida's face. The man's giant frame came slowly forward, over the table. He intertwined his fingers and began to speak in a whisper.

'Realistically, I think we could probably stretch to director, over in central. The position's due to open up next spring.'

Mikami felt his insides lurch.

When Arakida spoke next his voice echoed throughout the room, suddenly powerful.

'There are two matters of business.' He'd done away with his outer skin. Before Mikami was the avaricious face of a man entrenched in war. 'First – where is Koda?'

'I don't know.'

'Maybe not. But Futawatari does.'

'I don't know.'

'Does Admin have Koda, yes or no?'

'I don't know.'

'Well, get out there and find out!'

Mikami said nothing. It had been more than a threat. Arakida was testing Mikami's allegiance.

'Who gave you orders to look for Koda?'

'I ran into him by chance.'

'What did you say to him?'

'We exchanged greetings, that was all.'

'What did you get from him?'

'Like I said, we exchanged greetings.'

'Why did you come here today?'

What . . .?

'I am asking you why you came to see me today.'

'Because you called me.'

'Just that?'

'Also, because I'm press director. If nothing changes, the trouble will spread to involve the press and—'

'I'll bet you came here with an expectation.'

'An expectation of what?'

Arakida didn't answer. The expression on his face suggested that Mikami should try asking himself.

There was no need.

'Take my advice. Take off that ill-fitting disguise. Even if you end up clashing with Akama, I'll make sure you make it back here.'

Mikami levelled his gaze on Arakida. He let his thoughts charge the silence.

The answer is no.

The silence held until Arakida clicked his tongue in frustration.

'You'd be acting differently if you knew what Tokyo's real motives were . . .'

Mikami recoiled. That would have been his final question, and he'd expected Arakida to refuse to answer.

Was he going to tell him?

'The second matter of business.' As though turning a page, Arakida steered the conversation back to the beginning. 'You seem to have a talent as an *instigator*.'

'An instigator?'

'Yes. Someone whose job is to cause trouble and get the ball rolling. Some are paid professionals, tasked to incite violence during peaceful demonstrations. Ring any bells? That's right – the clash you staged with the press in the Secretariat, after all the talk of the written protest. It's because of your handiwork there that they decided they would boycott the commissioner's interview.'

'I couldn't do anything to stop that. It certainly wasn't my plan.'

'Then make it your plan. Agitate some more. Get them riled up, make sure they go through with the boycott.'

I'm sorry . . .?

Mikami's eyes sharpened.

'I don't see any reason to do that.'

'Because you don't think they'd go through with it anyway?'

'No, because I would be remiss in my duties.'

'I want to know how things look. Is it likely they'll go through with it, or will they call it off?'

'Avoiding the boycott is looking difficult. But that doesn't mean I don't have a hand I can play.'

'Then don't play it. Just stand back and watch. Surely your conscience can forgive that?'

'That won't do.'

'You don't care what happens to your home?'

'This is all just bullets flying over my head. I don't even know what it was that kicked this off in the first place.'

The room was silent once again. This time the quiet was longer, more oppressive. Arakida's giant frame shifted. Then he let out a sigh, seeming to sag as he leaned back into his couch.

'Then let me tell you,' he said gravely. 'Once you know Tokyo's intentions, I hope you will reconsider your position.'

Mikami gave a cautious nod. His hands tensed over his knees.

'This is a sequestration.' Arakida glowered into open air. 'The bureaucrats intend to take over the post of director in Criminal Investigations. The NPA intends to make us into a fiefdom of Tokyo.'

49

Mikami could hardly feel the ground under his feet.

He stood on the emergency stairs, having come through the steel door at the end of the corridor. He couldn't think of anywhere else to go. The sun was long gone. The wind was strong, but it didn't feel cold at all. Mikami's body continued to generate heat regardless of how much was stolen away.

Sequester the director's post.

The decision had come first, after which they'd drafted the scenario of the commissioner's visit into Six Four. Commissioner Kozuka would march right into the headquarters. He would pay his condolences at Amamiya's house and pledge to arrest Shoko's kidnapper and murderer. It would be more than just paying lip service. Directly afterwards he would use the walking interview to reveal the strategy with which he intended to back up his words. His intention was to post one of Tokyo's best career officers as director of Criminal Investigations, thereby strengthening links with Tokyo and helping the Prefectural HQ achieve its full potential as it continued its investigation into the Six Four kidnapping.

It was just a front. The case was frozen solid; it wouldn't budge an inch, even if they did send in someone from Tokyo. It would end with the new director issuing orders for the sake of making his presence known; he would throw the investigation into disarray, squandering both time and resources as he demanded report after report. Tokyo, perfectly aware that they had no chance of solving the case, had decided to use Six Four as a smokescreen to hide their hostile takeover of the director's job. *Just you wait and see.* It didn't matter if they solved Six Four or if the statute of limitations kicked in – whatever happened, the bureaucrats would hold on to the director's chair after it was all over.

Mikami gazed upwards. The pitch-black, starless sky drank up the wind.

Come Thursday, it'll be gone.

They had no doubt set their sights on Prefecture D. The current system of local directors had resulted in a run of poor candidates, and the situation seemed as if it was going to continue for years to come. Six Four had been fourteen years ago. Out of all the cases of kidnapping and murder that had happened since, it was the only one in which the perpetrator was still at large.

Mikami could ask what it was that had prevented Tokyo from extending its feelers until now. They hadn't hesitated to set aside a position for themselves in Second Division, under Arakida's direct authority. With the sole justification of zero tolerance when it came to discrepancies in the unmasking of corruption and election violations, they had dispatched young career officers to head up divisions across the country. They could have taken over the director's position long ago, used their state-invested powers to assume a 'bigger is better' approach, without resorting to such roundabout means. Yet they hadn't.

Why disrupt that balance now?

They would have expected local resistance. Criminal Investigations was certainly putting up a vicious fight. Tokyo may have set its sights on the debacle that was Six Four, but what was the good in seizing the position if it meant unilaterally destroying the tacit understanding that had benefited them so much until now?

It had to be something else. He could try to apply logic, but nothing he came up with would be correct.

It was hegemony. Seizing power was an instinct of the central command. Most likely some large cog had ground into motion somewhere in Tokyo. They would pick away at the autonomy of the regional police. Pull down the curtain, see through to their ambition of a centralized police authority. Was their announcement going to be the opening gambit? A trial run? Whatever the case, it would send shivers down the spines of any medium to small regional headquarters with its own Criminal Investigations Director. Just one failed case could result in them losing the post. The precedent would give rise to a fear that would spread and multiply until it fostered a terror of the NPA.

Was that their real aim? Punishment as example. Putting Arakida's decapitated head on display to drive home the real power of the central authority.

A wind picked up, hitting Mikami from the side.

The NPA intends to make us into a fiefdom of Tokyo.

Mikami squeezed his hands until they hurt. He could feel the blood coursing through his body. The blood of a detective. It was the only way he could parse the intensity of emotion, making his entire body feel like a clenched fist.

50

The lamp indicated that Captain Tsujiuchi was still in his office.

Mikami strode across the Secretariat, heading directly for Chief Ishii's desk. His hands were still balled tight. The temperature in the room should be comfortable, but it felt like a sauna, the heat almost suffocating.

Ishii was sitting with his chair swivelled to one side, fiddling with a remote control. He seemed restless. The evening news was about to start, showing the footage from Akama's earlier press conference.

'Oh, Mikami . . . what is it?'

'I want to talk to the captain. There's an urgent matter I need to discuss,' Mikami said.

Ishii's eyes stretched into circles. 'What could be so urgent?'

'I'd prefer to speak to him personally.'

'Ridiculous. Well, come on? Have you raised it with Akama?'

'He's not here.'

Mikami had already stopped by Administration. *I expect he doesn't want to see the news*. Shirota had said this, also fiddling with a remote in his hands as he did so.

'Okay, well, just tell me what it is you want to say. If it's important, I will relay it to the captain.'

The conversation had already exhausted Mikami's patience. He bowed sharply to Ishii, then started for the captain's office at the back of the room.

'Hey . . . what are . . . *stop*!'

Ishii's voice became a screech. Mikami ignored him and kept walking. He knocked on the distinctive wood-textured door.

'Come in.'

Mikami could only just make out the subdued response.

'Mikami!'

Ishii had jumped out from behind his desk, shrieking now.

'Mikami, stop right there!'

Mikami felt something grab his arm. He brushed it away and pushed the man's feeble chest. Ishii stumbled backwards a couple of steps before careering on to his backside. His eyes were full of shock as they peered up. Mikami looked away and pushed open the door.

'Thank you, sir.'

Everyone in the office got to their feet, but too late. Mikami was already making his way into the captain's office. He closed the door behind him. The heavy sound served to cut off the outside.

Even the air in the room felt alien. Subtle, indirect lighting. Space enough to hold a cocktail party. Leather couches with a dozen or so armchairs. Thick carpet, woven with an intricate pattern. Tokyo's place in the Prefectural HQ. The NPA. That was why Mikami was there.

Kinji Tsujiuchi was sitting at his desk.

His eyes came up to scan Mikami, unpleasant as they traced a line from his head to his feet. Mikami had been here two times in the past, but he'd never exchanged more than simple greetings with the captain.

'Mikami, wasn't it? Press director.'

His voice was soft, showing no signs of reproach for Mikami's disrespect in pushing his way through Ishii.

'That's right,' Mikami said, just as he heard a knocking from behind.

The door opened, shunting him forwards into the room. Ishii's face was as bright red as a monkey's.

'Sir, please forgive the intrusion. I'll get him to leave right this—'

Mikami talked over him. 'I have something urgent to discuss. Would it be possible for us to talk in private?'

'Mikami, you . . .' Ishii said, his voice low, simmering with indignation.

Tsujiuchi glanced at them both in turn, his open curiosity showing through. 'Ishii, you can leave us alone.'

'But, sir . . .'

'It's fine. It's refreshing to hear from people in the field, every now and again.'

'But, sir, you're already due at the—'

'I shouldn't like to repeat myself, Ishii.' Tsujiuchi gave Ishii a reproachful look, causing the man to recoil as though he'd been physically whipped.

'Of course, forgive me. I can give you both five minutes. I'll call in when the time is up.'

'I'll ring the buzzer for you when we're finished.'

There was nothing else Ishii could say. He gave an almost comically deep bow and stepped out of the room, his eyes pleading with Mikami.

'Come over, take a seat.'

'Thank you.'

Mikami was able to move smoothly across the floor. The blood coursing through him made it easy. He sat upright on the couch. Tsujiuchi was right in front of him. A wide forehead giving the impression of a keen intellect. Thick brows. Cool, elongated eyes.

'What did you want to talk about?'

'I have something I want to ask.'

'A question, rather than a discussion?' The curiosity visibly drained from his eyes. He had possibly been looking forward to listening to the bellyaching of a field officer. 'Fair enough. Out with it, then. I'll answer if I can.'

Mikami tipped his head in thanks. He focused his eyes around the bridge of Tsujiuchi's nose. He couldn't be sure that Arakida had been truthful. With Akama gone from the building, he had no choice but to ask the captain himself.

'It concerns the orders you gave Futawatari.'

'Futawatari? I don't remember seeing him recently . . . did he say I asked him to do something?'

Was he pretending not to know?

'The commissioner general is due to visit us, on Thursday.'

'Indeed.'

'He is planning to install an officer from Tokyo as the new director of Criminal Investigations. I've heard this is what he plans to announce.'

'Quite right.'

Mikami felt a stabbing in his chest. The captain had vaulted clean over the hurdle.

'What of it?'

'I wanted to know the reason for the decision.'

'The reason? Why, the kidnapping, of course. It's a public appeal, a gesture to show we don't intend to give up.'

'So it will be a temporary measure?'

'I don't see what you're getting at . . .'

'If the case is solved, for example. Am I correct in understanding that the position will be returned to us?'

'I don't know, although I'd wager that's yet to be decided. You'd do better to ask the commissioner, when he gets here.'

'So it's possible the change could be permanent?'

'As I said, I don't know. I believe some district stations alternate between the two. Mostly, it seems to be case by case.'

'Meaning it rests on the availability of the right people.'

'Quite. Personnel is key. Our Criminal Investigations department has suffered quite a bit, in that respect.'

Mikami was becoming increasingly crestfallen. What had been a dotted line was quickly filling in, becoming fact. He'd finished testing the truth of Arakida's words.

The NPA intends to make us into a fiefdom of Tokyo.

Mikami slid forwards on the couch.

'Criminal Investigations is vehemently against this happening.'

'So it seems,' Tsujiuchi replied equably.

'Some people have begun a call to arms.'

'Which is exactly why Akama has left for Tokyo. We've just had word that someone is posting a dangerous memo around head office.'

Mikami was dumbfounded.

'It details a number of cases of misconduct in Prefecture D, none of which has been made public. It's a veritable letter bomb. I'm sure whoever it is intends to warn off the commissioner.'

They'd released their third arrow. Was it Maejima? Had Arakida ordered him to take on the role of instigator?

'Well, it'll be interesting to see how the Commissioner's Secretariat reacts,' Tsujiuchi added, as though the matter didn't concern him. 'I wonder, have you ever heard the phrase, "Don't send Kennedy to Dallas"?'

'Dallas . . .?'

'It describes an aide's intuition. Their ideal is to keep their charge far from danger. Yet, in many cases, the people they've sworn to protect have a nothing-ventured-nothing-gained philosophy and actually prefer putting themselves in danger. This tests the aide's decision-making powers, forcing them to evaluate the threat posed – in this case, the potential damage to the commissioner in the estimation of the public.'

Tsujiuchi kept his gaze firm, expecting a response.

'Are you suggesting we're Dallas?'

'Let us hope that *isn't* the case. If the danger looks genuine, perhaps the commissioner will reconsider his trip. Although, in that case, his announcement would lack authority if it were made from Tokyo, and there would be zero PR value in doing so.'

The commissioner, stepping bravely into the field only to have his podium taken away. The press, siding with Criminal

Investigations. If they came to such a conclusion, would the Commissioner's Secretariat be forced to regard Prefecture D as another Dallas?

'Are we finished here?' Tsujiuchi said. 'I am due to have dinner with the governor this evening. The old fox needs humouring if we're to secure a decent portion of the budget.'

He seemed tired of the conversation. It was as though he'd closed a book: it was obvious even from a glance that his mind was already elsewhere.

Mikami felt his blood boil. Tsujiuchi didn't care. Not once had he stopped to consider the pain this would cause the regional police.

'Have you talked this through with Criminal Investigations?' Mikami said. 'Positions like this are important in any organization. People will try to protect them if they feel they're under threat. Especially if the change happens suddenly, without warning.'

Tsujiuchi was staring in blank amazement.

'Why get so worked up? I thought Criminal Investigations was a thorn in the side for you people. Too cocksure, always trying to hide away anything vaguely worthy of attention. Believe me, the quickest way to effect change is to replace those at the top. You'll find a vast improvement in the way they communicate with Administrative Affairs. Both sides will find it easier to get their jobs done.'

Mikami genuinely considered that Akama might be the lesser evil. He was at least conscious of the way he tormented others; that, at least, was human.

Why get so worked up?

'I was based in Criminal Investigations until the spring. I worked as a detective for twenty-four years. Based on my experience, I—'

'Ah! I did wonder . . .'

. . . if that was why you jumped into their ring.

Mikami imagined how he would continue, but missed the mark.

'It was the shoes. Your shoes. I have to say, I thought they were a mess when you came in.'

Shoes? A mess?

Mikami was thrown by the sudden change of tack. He looked down and studied his leather shoes; the right one first, then the left. They looked fine. Perfectly clean. What had the captain seen to make a statement like that? They were well worn, true, but Minako made sure to buff them every single day. Any scuff marks were concealed under black polish. There was nothing about them that was *a mess*. The shine had perhaps dulled a little from the day's use, but that was all.

'How long does it take you to get through them?'

Tsujiuchi had switched to making small talk.

'When I find shoes I like I always buy a couple of pairs. But it's so hard to wear them out, and before you know it the second pair's mouldy . . .'

Mikami was still gazing at his own feet. He hadn't even blinked. He was seeing Minako, crouched in the entranceway. Mikami had always had polished black shoes to put on – even when he'd worn the synthetic leather police-issue shoes. Even after that, when he'd started to buy more comfortable shoes. Even after Ayumi had run away. The line of Minako's mouth would always relax once she'd finished polishing and arranging his shoes.

What have I . . .

The shiver spread from his core, propagated down his limbs. He felt like he was coming out of a spell. His actions were indefensible. He'd gone over Akama's head, tried to communicate with Tokyo directly. He'd shoved Ishii to the floor and forced a one-on-one audience with the captain of the Prefectural HQ, bombarded him with question after question. The future commissioner general.

One of the untouchables.

He felt his head go numb. His vision closed in. It wasn't uncomfortable. If anything, the sensation was almost pleasant.

'These days, detectives wear trainers. Even then, they get through a good number of pairs each year.'

The words came flowing out.

'Hoo, is that so?'

'They do it because they have a need to bring criminals to justice. It's nothing rational. Detectives work on instinct alone.'

Tsujiuchi inclined his head.

'Try to understand their perspective. They're itinerant hunters. Always moving from one case to the next. It's the only language they understand.'

'*Itinerant hunters.* Certainly has a nice ring to it.'

'The post of director of Criminal Investigations is the pinnacle of their community. If they're deprived of something to look up to, they will panic.'

Tsujiuchi barked with laughter. 'That scoundrel, the pinnacle of their community? Besides, he came up from Security.'

'I'm referring to the position as a symbol, something that's about more than the individual who holds it. The further you delve into the regions, the more indispensable that kind of symbolism becomes.'

'I see.' Tsujiuchi's tone had changed. 'You wish to interfere in personnel decisions . . .'

Mikami's anxiety was still captive to his numbness, but his respect for the hierarchy of the force was ingrained in his bones. He tensed, the unavoidable result of facing a superior officer's displeasure.

'This has been interesting. Perhaps we can do it again sometime.'

Tsujiuchi craned around, reaching behind him to push the buzzer on his desk.

'Sir, could I ask you to at least suggest it to Tokyo? That they need to reconsider this?'

Ishii flew into the room before Mikami had finished. The division staff followed from behind, stony-faced. Tsujiuchi was beaming.

Mikami got to his feet and made a salute.

'Sir, if you could at least give some though to—'

Get him out! A number of hands took hold of him on Ishii's command, pulling him backwards with astonishing force.

Amidst the chaos, he could hear Tsujiuchi's voice.

Don't let anything like that happen again.

Mikami was escorted through the office and into the adjoining annexe. The TV on the desk was showing pictures of Akama. Perhaps because of this, Ishii became conscious of his surroundings, keeping his voice low as he snarled.

'What do you think you're playing at, Mikami? What on earth did you say to the captain?'

'Let go of me, now!' Mikami threw off the hands still holding him. It felt as if he were on fire.

'You need to tell me, Mikami. What did you say to—'

'As if telling you would change anything.' The TV flashed white. Akama was bowing, luminescent under the wave of camera flashes. 'None of you knows a bloody thing. Craning upwards the whole time . . . you can't even see that the ground's cracking under your feet.'

'I'm afraid you're the blind one, Mikami. What do you think will happen if you make the captain angry? *We're* the ones who are going to suffer for this – the Prefectural HQ. We're all going to feel the blowback for what you've done.'

'Damned fool! That's why they make idiots of us. The Prefectural HQ belongs to us. Don't think I'm going to stand by and let those bastards do what they want.'

Mikami drove his fist into the TV.

Akama's face contorted before being sucked into darkness, scattering into the air as countless fragments of glass.

51

There was someone else who deserved to be hit.

Mikami burst out of the Secretariat and strode down the corridor; he swept open the door to Administration. The noise was loud enough for most of the staff to look up in surprise.

Futawatari . . .

He wasn't there; his desk was still empty. Shirota was also nowhere to be seen. Section Chief Tomoko Nanao, who was in charge of looking after the female officers on the force, turned in her chair before getting to her feet.

'What happened to your hand?'

He hadn't noticed until she'd pointed it out. His right hand was covered in red, the skin torn between the base of his index finger and the back of his hand. Drops of blood hit the floor.

'Is Futawatari in the building?'

'No, he left.'

Before her reply, Nanao had started jogging towards one of the wall lockers.

'Will he be back?'

'Not today. He said he was going to go home straight afterwards.'

In that case. Mikami crossed the floor and walked into Akama's office, not even bothering to knock. The director's cologne was still in the air, suggesting he'd been there only moments earlier. Nanao came rushing in holding a first-aid kit. She set about finding disinfectant and bandages, then held her hands out.

'Let me bandage you up.'

'I can do it.'

'It's fine, let me.'

'I can do it. Just leave it with me.'

He shut her out, then pulled a wad of cotton wool from the box. He applied this to the wound and used his teeth to unroll the bandage, then proceeded to wrap it around his hand. He was still doing this when he walked over to Akama's desk, its master now absent, and perched himself unceremoniously on the edge. He took out his phone and scrolled to Futawatari's number, then used Akama's phone to make the call.

It would show as Akama's direct line. Futawatari would surely have to answer.

The call connected after only a couple of rings.

'How can you say this doesn't matter?' Mikami didn't wait. 'I found out what Tokyo's planning. If this doesn't matter, what the hell does?'

'How did you get this?'

'From Captain Tsujiuchi.'

'No – who gave you my number?'

'You fucking dolt. Don't you understand what this is? This isn't some plot to take over Criminal Investigations. This is a plot to *destroy the whole Prefectural HQ*. Are you aware that that's what you're taking part in here?'

He didn't answer. Footsteps. Noise in the background. A car door shutting.

'Futawatari . . .'

'I thought I'd already told you. There are no distinctions; no headquarters; no Tokyo. The police force is monolithic.'

'That's the kind of delusional crap Tokyo comes out with. How can we call ourselves the regional police if we don't even own the director of Criminal Investigations?'

'Cool down. Nothing bad is going to come of this. If anything, it'll be a boost for efficiency.'

Efficiency? The comment mirrored what Tsujiuchi had said.

The quickest way to effect change is to replace those at the top. You'll find a vast improvement in the way they communicate with Administrative Affairs. Both sides will find it easier to get their jobs done.

He felt like he finally understood. That, for the first time, he'd touched on what it was that Futawatari believed in. He'd been hell-bent on weakening Criminal Investigations, on creating a dominant and unshakable Administrative Affairs. That was what Mikami had always suspected, but he'd been wrong. His Tokyo mindset. His orders from Tsujiuchi. They weren't the only factors motivating Futawatari's behaviour.

'Are you scared by it?'

'Hmm?'

'The director's chair, Criminal Investigations.'

Futawatari said nothing. He made no attempt to ask what Mikami was talking about.

Bullseye.

Futawatari would know more about it than anyone. The hierarchical order couldn't be changed. For someone who had made superintendent at the young age of forty, the only post waiting for them on promotion was director of Criminal Investigations. The hidden force behind all personnel decisions would become the face of Criminal Investigations. The ironic truth awaited him in just over ten years, and he was scared of it. He might have been skilled in Administration, but, as someone who didn't know the first thing about being a detective, all that lay ahead of him was a barren desert, a secret betrayal. The shrine would be carried, but it would be empty. He would be disgraced, become one more addition to the list of failed candidates. For someone who had spent so long effectively in control of the organization itself, it was an unacceptable outcome. In this context, the talk of the 'sequestering' had seemed like good news.

'Is something wrong? Tell me.'

'You should try to make more sense when you talk.'

'You know exactly what I'm talking about. Your plan to forge a utopia for yourself.'

Tokyo's trust in Futawatari was absolute.

Each of the career officers from Tokyo posted to the prefecture had left with the impression that Futawatari could get things done, having recognized him as an indisputable high-flyer with regard to personnel and organizational management. That wouldn't change just because one of those officials bore the title of Criminal Investigations Director. A bureaucrat was a bureaucrat. As someone held in high regard in Tokyo, Futawatari had guessed that his word would trump that of other officers in Criminal Investigations. So he would volunteer himself for a role in the background, settle into the position of Community Safety Director, just one rung down, invoking the power of his counsel to influence Criminal Investigations. Choose profit over fame. That interest, more than anything, was what was guiding the man's actions. In Personnel, he'd defined the careers of so many others, but the whole time he'd been trying to think up a way to round off his own.

'Give me an answer. Are you planning to sell us out, just so you can build your own personal paradise?'

'You're still not making any sense.'

'You want to be a pantomime puppet for Tokyo, to pull the strings in the dark. Is that the long-cherished dream of the regional elite?'

'I'm ending this call.'

'If you really are some kind of top dog, you need to step up to it. I'm trying to tell you I think I'd rather have you in the director's chair, if the alternative was a *suit* from the NPA.'

Futawatari made a surprised sound, then, quieter, he said, 'You sure about that?'

Mikami focused on empty space. The man's dark eyes felt close. The weird sensation of Futawatari passing him the towel felt suddenly real again.

'You shouldn't take it so seriously. It's a symbol. It hardly matters who actually sits there.'

Mikami couldn't follow. A symbol? Was he still talking about the director's job? 'Are you sure you're one of us, Futawatari?'

'The detectives will do their job, regardless of who's at the top. Isn't that right?'

'Family's family, whether the old man's a slave driver or a waster. The position isn't something an outsider on transfer can ever hope to fill.'

'They'll get used to it in a month. In two, they'll have adapted completely. That's how it works with personnel – no exceptions.'

'So self-important. All you ever manage is to shuffle people irresponsibly between rooms.'

'You're a perfect example, Mikami.'

'Excuse me?'

'You stood your own against the press. Right before the captain's office.'

Mikami caught his breath.

'A fine member of the Secretariat, in anyone's eyes.'

Mikami clenched down on his back teeth. Blood seeped visibly into his bandage.

'You say that one more time.'

'Don't take it the wrong way. I meant it as a compliment.'

'Say it to my face. Come here, Akama's office, right now.'

'I guess that part of you never changes, Mikami.'

Had he laughed?

'You need to face up to reality. We're not in the *dojo* of the kendo club any more.'

52

Diluted, the whisky tasted like water. Even on the rocks it tasted like water. Inebriation failed to come.

The Tsukinami, a small bar built into the front of a residential building, managed by a married couple in their sixties. It was one of Mikami's few genuine hideaways, unknown by either Criminal Investigations or Administrative Affairs. He'd come to know it after the owner had delivered a stray dog to Mikami's *koban*. He'd been coming back for twenty-five years. The *mama-san* was as unyielding as a boar, while her husband was the kind to say whatever popped into his head. The result was that they were continually, both then and now, bickering behind the counter. For Mikami, whose habit it was to sit at the far side of the counter, their interaction was a source of both irritation and envy.

He'd forgotten who he was; he'd forgotten his family. He had taken the opportunity of Akama's absence to force his way into the captain's office. That alone was grounds enough for a transfer. He'd knocked Chief Ishii to the floor, broken property belonging to the Secretariat. If he hadn't injured himself, if he hadn't been bleeding, and if Ishii had been any less a coward, he knew he would right now be filling in a long report in some basement part of Internal Affairs. If he'd been thinking of his family at all, he should have warned Akama about Criminal Investigations' trap. He'd even had the option of playing both sides, of pretending to take Arakida's proposal on board. Even given that the chances of it actually happening were slim, he should have taken out the insurance of the job at Central Station, in case Criminal Investigations ended up victorious. There, he could get by without having to move away. He could be with Minako as they waited for their daughter to come back.

The ice clinked, shifting in his glass.

He'd put up with everything so far. And all for his family . . .

No. That wasn't it. He'd used them as a shield. He'd been selfish. He'd made sacrifices each time his place in the force had come under threat, and he'd always blamed his family. The truth was clear enough. He could keep going without a family, but he'd fall apart if he lost his place in the force. Unless he first recognized that, accepted that was who he was, he'd never be able to find his true place in the world.

Mikami's phone was vibrating in his jacket pocket. It might have been doing so the whole time.

A number of faces came forward, but the call was from none of them. It was Assistant Chief Itokawa of Second Division, sounding harried. Forgoing preamble, he launched straight into talking about the bid-rigging charges. He told Mikami that they had substantiated the charges against the CEO of Hakkaku Construction – who had been in for voluntary questioning – and issued a warrant for his arrest, but that the CEO had started coughing up blood before they could process the arrest and had been checked into hospital. At first Mikami wondered why Itokawa was volunteering inside information, but the reason was coming next. The *Yomiuri* and the *Sankei* had somehow managed to get word of the warrant and had called in to notify their intention of covering the story. Itokawa had begged them to wait, but they hadn't listened.

'Anyway, thought I'd give you some advance warning. It's going to be chaos tomorrow morning.'

An image of Arakida flashed before his eyes. Mikami checked his watch, then put a call through to Suwa's mobile. It was eight forty-five. Suwa was in the Wan Wan Tei, a transvestite-run bar he'd recently unearthed. Having failed to get anything from the press in the headquarters, he'd improvised with a 'social studies meeting' led by Mikumo. He sounded tense at first, Mikami having left the office without explaining the reason for his bandage, but his tone reverted to normal when Mikami told him about the warrant.

'That explains it,' he said. 'Ushiyama from the *Yomiuri* and Sudou from the *Sankei*, they're both missing.' He lowered his voice. 'Another scoop. I hope that this isn't going to mess up our chances of stopping the boycott.'

'I want a report, first thing in the morning,' Mikami instructed.

He palmed the phone shut. The clamour on the line was replaced with the racket of karaoke. A group of ten or so men and women of various ages – by the look of things, work colleagues – were gathered around the carpeted *zashiki* area. A slightly premature end-of-year party, according to the barkeeper.

Mikami felt restless. Suwa, Mikumo, even Kuramae – they would all be the same. They were focusing every resource on averting the boycott. And no wonder. The commissioner was due to visit in only three days. It was their job to manage the press. What else would they be doing?

An image of Yoshio Amamiya came unexpectedly into his thoughts. The appearance had been sudden enough to feel like a revelation, the insight he needed to break through the wall of his dilemma. Mikami felt the colour drain from his face.

The commissioner general is our highest-ranked official. I'm confident the media coverage will be significant. It will be broadcast on TV. The news will reach a great number of people.

His own words. He'd tried to build up Amamiya's expectations, with a view to getting him to agree to the commissioner's visit. But it hadn't worked. Amamiya had long ago given up expecting anything from the police. He felt bitter towards them, having learned of the cover-up of the kidnapper's call. He'd seen the visit for what it was, a PR exercise. That was why he hadn't even considered Mikami's entreaty. He hadn't given in to any new expectations. He hadn't changed his mind because of anything Mikami had said. He'd been shocked, moved even, when he'd broken into tears – but that was all.

Even so . . .

He'd said the words.

. . . there is a real chance of this bringing in new leads.

Mikami emptied his glass.

It had been a revelation, after all. Stuck in a local skirmish, he'd looked up at the sky and caught sight of a shooting star. *A promise*. One he'd made in the outside world, away from any consideration of Criminal Investigations or Administrative Affairs.

He felt a shift, a weight tipping the scales. The commissioner would never forgive a boycott. Whatever happened, Mikami had to ensure his voice made the papers and the airwaves. For Amamiya. And in order to take responsibility for what he'd said.

He realized his mind was made up. There had never been any real 'promise'. And if the only way of stopping the boycott was lying to the reporters, that wouldn't even constitute finding a third path as press director. All he'd done was find another extreme, following the polar opposites of Criminal Investigations and Administrative Affairs. *It doesn't matter. It's enough*. He would use the excuse of Amamiya to force a change in direction.

A very Mikami way of settling the dispute.

'Look, he's got a smirk on him,' the *mama-san* teased.

'Leave him be. Probably felt good to land one on his asshole boss,' the barkeeper said next to her. 'He just wants to drink by himself. Can't you see that?'

They were gearing up to start again. Mikami turned his chair so his back was facing the counter. The uproar coming from the *zashiki* was at its peak. The apparent leader of the group, a man in his fifties, was howling out an off-tune ballad. The rest were clapping in time; from the looks on their faces, it was clear they were still half at work. The women were already fidgeting, ready to leave.

Mikami was counting on Suwa. On Mikumo. Even on Kuramae. Everything would turn out fine if the Press Club held a GM to overturn the boycott. His made-up assurances would become real. Media Relations would survive.

Mikami's gaze met with that of a woman in the group. She let out a snigger and whispered something in the ear of the woman next to her.

He looked away and flipped a cigarette into his mouth. Still bickering with her husband, the *mama-san* held out a lighter; a flamethrower-sized lick of fire burst out. The man sitting next to him chose that moment to open a conversation. Mikami had seen him there, probably once before. He thought he remembered the man being a doctor, but it turned out that, after failing to gain entrance to medical school for three straight years, he'd ended up as head of administration in a hospital that had been in his family since his grandfather's generation. Mikami told him the bandage was because he'd fainted, and ended up – despite his mood – having to give the man an outline of his symptoms. The man nodded gravely. 'It could be Ménière's disease,' he said, before asking whether the dizziness came from the left or right ear first. *You're not even a doctor*, Mikami thought ungraciously, even as his hand came unconsciously up to his left ear.

He called a taxi.

When he left, it was to the *mama-san*'s smile, the barkeeper's look of concern, and the glances that rippled through the group of women. Inside the vehicle, he noticed his hand was still on his left ear. He recalled the cold touch of the phone. Ayumi hadn't said a word. In her silence, she'd left nothing more than a suggestion. *Was that what it was?* Mikami wondered. Had she called so he'd ask the questions himself? *What have you ever done as a parent? Did you ever try to understand anything about me?*

Mikami got out of the taxi to see Yamashina standing next to his front door; that was when he realized how drunk he was, and in how bad a mood.

You bastard.

He'd been with the others at the Wan Wan Tei but had become uneasy when he'd noticed that the chief reporters from the *Yomi-uri* and the *Sankei* were missing and decided to call over. He'd probably come hoping to secure a tidbit for himself. *Ayumi's shoes . . . I can see they're gone.* He thought he'd get lucky again – it was clear from his expression. He was walking over with an obsequious smile, making a show of how cold it was. Mikami waited with his feet firmly in the ground, then reached out with his bandaged hand. He grabbed Yamashina by the scarf and pulled him in until he was breathing down the man's bright-red ear.

'Don't get me wrong, Yamashina. I didn't feed you news on the bid-rigging because I like you. I did it out of charity. Because of the way you resemble an abandoned dog in the rain.'

He shoved the man, now frozen and bolt upright, to the side, before striding in through the front door. Minako came straight out. She'd started to say that Yamashina was outside when she noticed his bandaged hand and broke off.

'Just an accident, cut myself a little,' Mikami said, easing off his shoes.

Minako was obviously suspicious but refrained from asking any more questions. She composed herself again then told him that Director Odate's wife had called, at around eight o'clock.

Mikami's heart stopped. He looked at his watch. It was already after ten.

I'll call to let you know when I'm leaving the office.

A shiver ran through him. It was like waking from a dream. Reality flooded in, replacing the squandered time he'd spent immersed in noise and drink. He ran down the hallway and into the living room, his mind an empty space; he took hold of the phone and started to dial the director's number. His fingers stopped. He couldn't remember what came after the area code. He rammed his fist on to his forehead. Still unable to remember, he started to flick through his notebook.

Sitting formally, his knees together on the tatami, he listened to the phone ring. He'd broken a promise he'd made to his benefactor, despite being the one who had instigated contact. The moment he'd learned of Tokyo's intentions from Arakida, he'd written Odate off as no longer useful. The truth was, he'd stopped expecting anything even before that. Odate hadn't known about Ayumi running away from home; he'd been consigned to the past. How would someone like that have access to inside information on the commissioner's visit? Mikami had realized this but asked to meet up regardless. To keep his worry at bay. Because he'd been desperate to do *something*.

The call connected.

'Mikami. It's great to hear from you.' While the good humour in her voice was unchanged from lunchtime, Odate's wife had lost a little of her earlier cheer.

'I'm so sorry. I really don't know how to express my—'

'Oh, don't be silly, we know you're busy. Right, I'll put my husband on then. He's been up waiting for you.'

Her voice petered out; the time that followed seemed to stretch on for ever. What he heard next was more breathing than a voice, almost like interference on the line. Perhaps he'd been half asleep already. Or he'd been feeling bad and forced himself to stay up.

'Director . . .'

'Ah . . . yes, this is Odate.'

Mikami went through every apology he knew. He denied having had any business to discuss. 'I just wanted to see how you were. I'll come over soon . . . I'll make sure of it.' The whole time, Odate's breathing was close in his ear. Every now and then this became a wheeze. Mikami had suggested he get some rest and was just about to hang up when Odate managed some words.

'Thank . . . you for . . . the call.'

He'd sounded genuinely grateful. Mikami pressed his fingers into his brow. Even after he'd ended the call, he didn't leave his formal seated position. *Shozo Odate, Criminal Investigations Director, Prefecture D.* Was he proud of his accomplishments? Or was that all gone now, vanished like a dream? What had a life in the force given him? What had it taken away?

The ferment inside Mikami had settled. The Prefectural HQ would lose its remit over the director of Criminal Investigations.

The idea of keeping his promise to Amamiya scattered like mist. He couldn't base his decision on a make-believe story he'd come up with when he was backed into a corner. What he needed was the truth. A light that would shine right through his dilemma.

He needed something else.

A genuine third path.

53

'Seven out of the thirteen said they were ready to call off the boy-cott. Although . . .'

Mikami had still been at the kitchen table when he'd answered Suwa's call. Unable to sleep the previous night, he'd been camped there until the morning. Much of the time he'd spent asking himself questions. He'd been left with a single answer. But could he really pull it off? He'd been lost in thought when the unexpected call had arrived.

'. . . that was last night. We're probably back at square one, with this morning's commotion. I don't think we're going to be able to convince anyone into holding a GM now.'

He'd sounded like he'd given up.

The storm in the morning papers had been unprecedented. As forewarned, the *Yomiuri* and *Sankei* had both run long articles detailing the arrest of the CEO of Hakkaku Construction. And it hadn't ended there – the pages of the *Asahi* and *Mainichi* had also contained unanticipated scoops. The *Asahi*'s article was about a traffic official in Station S hushing up his niece's speeding ticket. That had been enough of a blow, but the greatest surprise had been the *Mainichi*'s article: 'Guard Asleep for Detainee Suicide of Two Years Ago?'

Mikami had reached the office by 7 a.m. Suwa, Kuramae and Mikumo all arrived soon afterwards. They'd ended up arguing with the reporters when the latter had demanded a press confer-ence. Akama hadn't shown up in his office. Ishii had poked his head into the room at one point but had left without issuing a single order or word of advice, either spooked by the rancour of the reporters, or by seeing the bandage on Mikami's hand. Working at his own discretion, Mikami had set about making the various preparations for a press conference. When he'd finished calling the relevant divisions, debating the content and response to each of the articles, and arranging the schedule itself – thirty minutes each, starting with Second Division, then Transport, then Administration – it was already gone eight thirty.

He could hear Arakida's shrill laughter. He had forced Akama into claiming a lack of negligence, then overturned it by leaking the fact that the guard had actually been dozing off. The *Toyo* might have fired the initial volley, but there was nothing to say they had to deliver the fatal blow themselves. Arakida would have realized that result wouldn't change, whichever paper he used. And it was the safer way to do it. By seeding the information through different papers, he was making it harder to see through to his involvement.

The story on the bid-rigging had most likely been a calculated leak, too. And it was easy to imagine a detective in Station S hearing about the speeding ticket. *Arakida* – he was the principal instigator. And judging from the fact that he'd opted to release the information about the guard having been asleep, rather than keep it in reserve together with the volley of arrows accompanying it, it seemed safe to assume that the misconducts listed in Tokyo's 'letter bomb' would be both numerous and deadly in their destructive potential.

The morning was long. The atmosphere remained feverish throughout, in both the office and the Press Club. Each of the three press conferences had ended in complete chaos. The press had asked a succession of barbed questions, cursing each time they thought the answer evasive; as the deadline for the evening edition drew closer, there were even scenes of reporters shouting each other down. It was impossible to predict what would happen next. The reporters appeared possessed as they busied themselves with calls and writing copy, and this left no room to bring up the proposal of a GM. Mikami hadn't even been able to find out if Yamashina and Yanase had made good on their promise to Suwa.

Mikami took a late lunch at his desk.

The traffic of reporters coming and going had finally petered out, and, with the rest of the staff out on reconnaissance, he was alone in the room. The only sound was him sipping his tea. He realized he hadn't taken lunch at home since the whole commotion broke out over the commissioner's visit; not once. What was Minako eating? Was she eating at all?

'Has it settled down?'

Akama's call came in just after 2 p.m. He told Mikami he was still in Tokyo, that he'd be there until late that night, finally giving a hint as to the gravity of the situation.

'How did you deal with the issue of the guard?'

'Ishii held a press conference; he stuck to his guns, maintaining that we were still looking into the matter.'

Akama's breathing seemed to steady. But only for a moment.

'And the *other* matter?'

'Sorry?'

'The boycott. Did you manage to get it turned around?'

His voice was low enough to be inaudible. Someone else was nearby.

'I haven't had the chance to discuss it yet.'

'Why?'

'The press are still reeling after this morning.'

'What about the apology?'

'No, not yet.'

'Well? Have you told them we won't issue any more reports anonymously?'

'They're still—'

'Then get a move on and tell them, you simpleton!'

Mikami let his eyes close. He pictured himself overlooking the cluster of skyscrapers in the Kasumigaseki part of Tokyo.

'Of course, sir.'

The phone went dead the moment he finished speaking. He lit a cigarette. His mind was calm. The smoke pricked at his eyes. Through it, he saw Suwa come into the room.

'How are things in there?'

'Calmer . . . a little, but no one's speaking to each other.'

'And the GM?'

'. . . is looking difficult. Yamashina told me he'd tried raising the subject; I can't say if he actually did or not.'

'Whatever happens, I doubt they'll be happy with an apology from me.'

Suwa nodded silently.

'Call Kuramae and Mikumo in.'

'Sir?'

'I've got something I want to say to all of you.'

Kuramae walked in as Mikami was saying this. He stopped by his desk, then came over with a sheet of paper in his hands.

'Well?'

'Right. Well, according to Yanase, Yamashina hasn't even—'

'Not that. What's in the paper?'

'Ah, yes, this is . . . some more on Meikawa. Supplementary information.'

Exactly as Mikami had suspected. Suwa looked dumbstruck.

'Is it important?' Mikami asked.

Kuramae lowered his head in puzzled concentration. 'Oh. I'm not sure if it's important in the general sense. It's just that . . .'

'Just that what?'

'I just thought it might be important . . . for *him*.'

This came as a subtle jolt. Mikami had been thinking something similar even that morning, when the sky had still been growing light. *Amamiya's transformation*. He remembered how, Amamiya having had his beard and hair neatly trimmed, Mikami had hardly recognized him on his second visit. Was it possible that he'd been leaning towards accepting the visit even before Mikami had burst into tears? Going out. Getting his hair cut. It was possible these had been important steps for a man like Amamiya.

The promise existed. Mikami had kept the idea in his head, allowed it as speculation.

Still, whatever his promise to Amamiya, Mikami's mind was already set. The third path. He would do whatever was important to him.

'Call Mikumo in.'

54

Mikami put up a notice to indicate that there was a meeting in progress, shutting the door for the first time since he'd become press director because of the office's policy of never turning anyone away. Suwa and Kuramae were on chairs across from the couch. Mikumo had pulled a folding chair up next to them. Having hurried back, she was out of breath.

'It's time we settled the anonymity issue.' Mikami introduced the topic and looked at each of the others in turn. 'The breakdown of relations with the press, the boycott – looking back, it all started with our disagreement over anonymous reporting. It's been a curse ever since. So we're going to take it down.'

Take it down? Suwa gave a questioning frown.

'We will no longer withhold information from our press reports. From this point forwards, our policy is on principle to be full disclosure.'

The look on all three faces changed. Suwa's eyes rolled briefly to the ceiling.

'But Akama won't stand—'

'This is *his* idea.'

'Really? Akama gave his blessing to this?'

'He said we could make an empty promise to the press, if it would stop the boycott.'

Suwa rocked back in his chair before coming to sit upright again. 'So, you're proposing we lie to them?' he said, half coughing.

'No. We're going to work, on principle, with full disclosure. It should be fine.'

'So . . . actually go ahead with it?'

'Exactly. We're going to turn Akama's scheme on its head, use it to pave the way for full disclosure.'

Suwa's mouth twitched. Kuramae looked speechless. Mikumo was staring, rapt.

'You want us to lie to Akama, and not to the press?' Suwa's response made his irritation clear.

'We are going to use him to pave the way for change.'

'Change? A change for the worse, maybe. I don't understand it. Why lie to our superiors and do something so reckless? Full disclosure for everything is just irresponsible. Can we just give out the name of the driver, even though she's pregnant? What about juveniles? Are we to ignore the laws governing juvenile crime? What about cases involving the Yakuza? If the names of people involved crop up in the press, who's to say the Yakuza won't go looking for retribution? Then there are the suicides. And double suicides. What about when people have a record of mental illness? We can't leave these kind of decisions to the press . . .'

'That's where Media Relations comes in. That's our job. We give them everything, but when a case needs discretion we sit down with the reporters and get them to agree to withhold the information. Think about it. Do you think there's a difference between our criteria and theirs for this kind of thing? As long as we're doing our jobs properly, they won't deviate far off course – look at how vocal they are on privacy, on individual rights.'

'But isn't that just wishful thinking? You know personally how much trouble they can cause. They're a mob with a fancy name. There's nothing to guarantee they won't unexpectedly break ranks or get out of control.'

Suwa represented the office's past and its present. Nothing would change unless Mikami managed to bring him on board. He leaned over the table, weaving his fingers together.

'I want to have faith.'

Suwa was wide-eyed. 'Faith? In that lot?'

'That's right. For anonymity at least, we should give up on strategizing, try trusting them. Think of it as a test run to see how far they're willing to cooperate.'

'Come off it. Having faith is fine, but this isn't the place for it. As police, it's our job to manage the press. And we can't do this – whether it's anonymity or something else – unless we maintain the advantage of knowing more than they do.'

'Do you really believe that?'

'I'm not sure what you're trying to suggest,' Suwa said, his head swinging forwards in defiance. 'I've been working with the Press Club for six years. I know how scary things can get when we lose the ability to keep them under control.'

'Scary? Come on. Have you ever suffered any real damage? You say things get scary. Are you sure you're not simply afraid of what might happen to the force?'

Suwa replied with a sharp nod. 'That should be obvious. I am a member of the Prefectural HQ. It's my job to be scared for the organization as a whole, and it's my duty to act in line with whatever policies have been decided.'

'This isn't our policy. This is Tokyo scheming.'

'I realize that much. All the more reason we can't go against it. We're individuals, sure, but we're also a part of something else.'

Mikami sucked in a long breath. Suwa had helped him clarify exactly what he needed to say. 'Managers move on, but our duty to the force is unchanging. We should be deciding in Media Relations on how to manage the press. The four of us should make our own decisions.'

Suwa shook his head. 'No – the entire organization is underpinned by the executive. If we ignore their instructions, what right do we have to call ourselves Media Relations?'

'Individuals make up an organization. I don't see any problem with an organization reflecting the will of the individuals inside it.'

'It sounds like desperation, sir.' Suwa's tone hardened. He shot a contemptuous look at the bandaging on Mikami's hand. 'You need to think of your position. The moment you – as press director – announce our intention to go with full disclosure it becomes our official policy.'

'Of course.'

'Once we give them that right, it becomes next to impossible to take it away again. They would fight, much more than if they'd never had it to begin with.'

'That's why we won't take it away. We'll see it through.'

'That's fine for you. No doubt you'll be happy to have established a policy. But what comes next? Come the spring, we'll still be tied to what you said, left to suffer for it.'

'I'm leaving in the spring, am I?'

'Don't pretend you don't know. You know that's what's going to happen – that's why you're talking about full disclosure. You ignored direct orders, you bulldozed your way into the captain's office and you lost it in front of the entire Secretariat. You'll be transferred come spring. That's why . . .'

Kuramae was frozen to the spot. Mikumo's ears had gone bright red. She looked like she was the one under attack.

'I'm just asking if we can't be a little more realistic?' Suwa switched to a more conciliatory tone. 'We can think of some other way to prevent the boycott, one that doesn't involve lying to anyone. The first thing is to apologize. Apologize, whatever might happen. If they're unwilling to listen, we can push our way in and do it anyway. We can get down on our hands and knees. I'll help. Kuramae and Mikumo will, too. We can stay vague about our stance on anonymity, but we'll show we're willing to try a compromise. "We'll do all we can to include full details in our reports. We assure you we'll do everything in our power to accommodate the opinions of the Press Club." You can give them something like that. They want to interview the commissioner. There's a chance they'll settle for something like that, even if they do realize it's non-committal.'

'Did you join the force to make recommendations like that?'

'Sorry?'

'What about the next time? Do you intend to do the same – put off making any actual decisions, right up until the day you retire?'

Suwa flashed his teeth. 'Choosing to be vague is a fine decision in itself. I'm fully prepared to shoulder responsibility for any suggestion I make.'

'You're just putting the issue on hold. *That's* what causes suffering later on.'

'What I'm saying is that the decision to put things off can be the appropriate one in certain circumstances. Even without that, I can't agree that offering full disclosure is the correct thing to do. What about the woman in this case? Wasn't it you who decided it was the right decision for us to withhold her name from the press?'

'That was my original stance. Then I learned that Hanako Kikunishi is the daughter of the chairman of King Cement.'

They all stared at him, speechless.

'But, doesn't that mean—'

'Exactly. They knew she was the daughter of someone on the Public Safety Committee. That's why they wanted to keep her name out of this.'

There was a long silence.

Suwa's mouth twisted, as he processed the new information.

'It's possible that . . . that even in that case it was still the right decision. If the committee was damaged at all, that would reflect on us, too.'

'You really mean that?' Mikami stared at him.

Suwa pulled a crooked smile. 'I guess you really are a detective.'

'Meaning?'

'You detectives couldn't care less about the organization. We could lose face, be torn apart, but to the detectives it's someone else's business. They look down on all the other jobs. Laugh, sneer. In a way, they're no different to the bureaucrats.'

'You think I'm like that?'

'You don't agree? Look – you're only here on a temporary basis. This is a stop-gap thing until you return to Criminal Investigations. You think it's ridiculous; you're doing it because you've got no other choice. But people forge careers here, too. A huge proportion of officers go about their jobs with no reference to case work. You wouldn't feel a thing if you were driven out from Admin. You were on your way out in any case. And it's that mindset that lets you think you can be reckless, just like the bureaucrats.'

Mikami had stopped feeling angry. Instead, he felt a heavy melancholy. Staff pinned labels on their superiors, too. And in Media Relations, the black mark against him – the 'criminal record' – was reversed: it was his having been a detective. This meant that Suwa hadn't thought to re-evaluate his initial opinion of Mikami, not once in eight months.

Mikami drew a long breath.

'There's one last thing I want you to know. Tokyo is planning to take over the post of director in Criminal Investigations. The commissioner's inspection is camouflage. His real purpose is to make that announcement.'

Suwa's mouth fell open and he slowly tipped his head so he was looking at the ceiling.

'I won't be returning to Criminal Investigations. I went against an order to ensure the boycott went ahead.'

Someone knocked at the door. Nobody got up to answer it. Another knock. No one moved. There was a pause, followed by the sound of footsteps moving away.

'I agree with Suwa's recommendation,' Mikumo said, suddenly volunteering her opinion. 'I think it's the right decision to keep our position vague for now.'

'I do, too,' Kuramae said after her. 'I'm happy to get on my hands and knees. If we do that, whether the boycott goes ahead or not shouldn't—'

There was still a way out. Mikami's resolve was unshaken.

'That's all I want to hear about strategy. Sometimes, when all other avenues are exhausted, a new route makes itself known. We're going to give up on strategy. We're going to try having some faith in the outside world.'

Kuramae didn't nod. Neither did Mikumo; he'd expected her to agree.

'Don't you see? The force can't keep itself going properly, not alone. It's rotting on the inside and no one can even see it. It doesn't matter that the reporters can't be trusted, that the world's corrupted, it's still better to connect than let ourselves remain isolated.'

Mikami felt a surge of pain in his hand. Without realizing, he'd tensed it into a fist. Mikumo's hands were white over her knees. Both were trembling. Kuramae let out a long, insubstantial breath. He gave Suwa, sitting next to him, a helpless look.

Mikami relaxed his hand and flexed his fingers.

'Suwa . . .'

He didn't respond. Only his neck was visible. He'd curled forwards to stare at his feet. Mikami waited a few seconds. Suwa showed no signs of coming back up.

'. . . I want you to pretend we never had this talk.'

Mikami stood.

'You two as well. I'm going next door. All of you are to remain here, on standby, until I get back.'

'You're going to abandon Criminal Investigations?'

A whisper. Suwa's eyes were angled up at Mikami.

'Okay. You've shown us your resolve. But . . . are you sure about what you're doing? You're talking about your home ground. Are you really planning to stand by and let the bureaucrats get away with this?'

Mikami turned to the door.

'This is my home ground now. And no, I don't plan to let the bureaucrats *or* Criminal Investigations get away with a thing.'

55

Mikami had always wanted there to be more of a walk. Stepping out of Media Relations, you reached the Press Room before you'd had any time to think.

This time it didn't matter.

He didn't hesitate as he pushed the door open. The room was full of reporters. A few looked up but chose to ignore him. They were all huddled together in groups, according to their respective papers. Ushiyama, Kasai and Ami Kiso were there from the *Yomiuri*. Sudou and Kamata from the *Sankei*. Horoiwa and Hayashiba from *NHK*. Kakei and Madoka Takagi from the *Asahi*. Akikawa and Tejima were both there from the *Toyo*, the former whispering something to the latter. Utsuki from the *Mainichi* looked sulky, his feet flung over a desk; Kadoike from *Kyodo News* was lying down on one of the couches. The room was oddly quiet, especially considering that the majority of the other news agencies were in there, too. Even those that had made a story had missed two. It was hard to gauge their mood; with no outright victors, the Press Room's usual rapacity was gone. No one tried to speak to Mikami, even though they'd all seen him come in. It was as though they were all saying they had no further need for Media Relations now the three conferences were over.

Mikami spoke up, unwavering.

'I have an announcement to make. If you could make sure everyone is here.'

He had addressed the *Toyo*'s desk. Just as he finished, Ushiyama, who'd been sitting ahead of Mikami, got to his feet with a note in his hand. He sighed and gave Mikami a look that said *whatever you want*. He walked straight by and left the room. Sudou muttered a gruff 'excuse me' and started for the door after him. A number more filed by on either side, their faces impassive and mask-like. 'Just give me a second . . .' Mikami had started to speak when he heard a voice in the corridor behind him.

'Ushi, Ushi. Come on, there's no need to act like that. The press director told you he had an announcement, right?'

It was Suwa. Ushiyama was responding.

He's only going to request we call off the boycott. I don't have the time to do that again.

I know, I know. Equable and calming. *No point jumping the gun, though, it won't take a minute. You, too, Sudou. It's a big thing for you guys.*

A few moments later the two men trudged back into the room, Suwa patting them on the shoulders. The other reporters trailed back in behind them, despondent looks on their faces. Kuramae was next. Mikumo followed him. She closed the door behind her and stood with Suwa and Kuramae so they blocked the exit.

Mikami turned back to the reporters. His state of mind was already different to that of moments earlier. He could feel the support behind him.

'What the hell do you think you're doing?'

Tejima spoke first. Akikawa was still sitting next to him, glaring in Mikami's direction. None of the other reporters tried to hide their aggravation. *Is this detention or what? What right do you have to keep us here?*

'If everyone's here, I'll proceed with the announcement.'

'We don't want an apology if that's what this is. You can leave.'

Tejima was cold. He'd made the statement as though it was already consensus. Backing him up was the fact that no one had raised an objection. Yamashina was there at the far end of the

416

room, as was Yanase from the *Jiji Press*, but it was too much to expect them to say anything now.

'I'm not here to offer an apology.'

'Well, what *are* you here for?'

'I'm here to announce a new policy on anonymous reporting.'

'A new policy?' Tejima shot Akikawa a sideways glance. He scanned the room before coming back to Mikami. 'Okay, everyone's here. Might as well let us have it.'

Mikami nodded. He felt a wave of tension from behind.

'From now on, our policy will be based on the principle of full disclosure.'

Everyone froze around him. A moment later, the room burst into uproar. Akikawa spoke up to calm the noise.

'What's the condition?'

'No condition.'

'You want us to call off our boycott of the commissioner's interview?'

'No condition means no condition. We're hoping you'll consider doing that, of course, but I'm not going to make it a bargaining point.'

Again the room fell into a state of turmoil. Ushiyama's voice carried over the others.

'What brought this on?'

'The decision was made after careful deliberation. We're going to make a leap of faith, and trust in your discretion.'

'This came from your boss?'

'This came from me.'

'Right, so it could be turned around? If your boss decides against it.'

'No.'

There was a pause. Ami Kiso raised a hand, at Ushiyama's side. 'So you don't object to us seeking confirmation from Director Akama?'

'Not at all. He's not in today, though.'

'Mikami,' Akikawa said, reclaiming the floor. 'Why *the principle* of full disclosure?'

Mikami stared right back.

'Because there will be cases in which I'm sure we'll both agree that an anonymous report will be best.'

'Why would we agree to something like that? I don't see it. Tell me – what kind of cases?'

'I wouldn't tell anyone the name of a rape victim. Much less would I ever stick it in a report on a board, detailing a name and address. If you were to insist I do that, I would have no choice but to step down from my position as press director.'

'Well, but . . .' Akikawa stumbled for a moment. 'That's an extreme scenario. What I'm worried about is you extending the interpretation. We'd be right back where we started if you were able to dictate to us the cases *you* deemed important or unique.'

'Does the press need to know the name and address of a victim of rape?'

'That's why I'm—'

'*If* we decide to make full disclosure the norm, you won't have to fight to maintain face any more – you will all be able to make cool, rational decisions. What I'm hoping is that, instead of us having to force our opinion on to you, you will become able to sit down and think these things through: whether or not you really need to know a particular name, whether a given piece of information is important or not.'

'It's presumptuous. Essentially, you're trying to brainwash us. We will not accept the proposal unless you remove the "principle" clause.'

'Then you can consider the proposal withdrawn. It's like I said. I'm only here talking to you like this because I trust your good judgement. If you continue to imply that you can't trust ours, the proposal is null and void.'

'So you're just going to turn on us?'

'Hold on,' somebody said. It was Horoiwa, chief reporter for *NHK*. 'We should at least consider this.'

Yamashina and Yanase joined in.

'Horoiwa's right. It doesn't make sense that we reject this outright.'

'Full disclosure as the guiding principle. That's a big step forward. It at least gives us room for discussion.'

Kadoike from *Kyodo News* provided another voice in favour.

'If he's willing to make this proposal, the least we should do is explore the option.'

You're right. The moderates caved. *We can talk this through. We should hold a GM. Definitely – we can hold a GM to make the decision.*

Akikawa was visibly shaken. His mouth was moving but nothing emerged. The other hard-liners remained silent, but it looked as though the majority were in agreement.

It happened just as Mikami thought the matter had been decided.

'How about some proof?'

All eyes searched for the speaker. It was Madoka Takagi from the *Asahi*.

'Proof . . .?'

'You talk about full disclosure, but that doesn't mean anything. What we need is proof. The road accident in Oito City. The driver was a pregnant woman. Can you give us her name and address now?'

The words came like those of a god – one hell-bent on destruction.

'Hold on there, Takagi!' Suwa let out a shrill cry. 'You really want to drag that up again? We put the lid on that already. And you couldn't run it in an article at this point.'

'We never finished talking about that. It's still relevant. Things only got this bad between us because we wanted her name and you refused to budge. I'm not sure you're entitled to talk about moving forward unless we resolve that matter first.'

'But . . .'

He stopped there. Suwa's eyes darted through empty space. He'd only called attention to the validity of her argument. The tide had already begun to shift. More people were speaking up in support of her request, both moderates and hard-liners. *She's right. We have to get that sorted first. We can hold a GM afterwards.* Akikawa seemed also to be regaining his poise. He made a survey of everyone in the room then sprung to his feet.

'All right. We renew our request for Media Relations to provide us with the name of the driver. Are there any objections?'

No. The answer echoed through the room. Akikawa turned to face Mikami. It looked like he was grinning.

'Then it's decided. Mikami, words are easy enough. We'd appreciate a gesture of goodwill to prove your intent.'

Mikami shut his eyes. His eyelids twitched. Suwa. Kuramae. Mikumo. It felt as though he could hear their hearts beating behind him. He'd expected it would come down to this. He hadn't foreseen the specifics, but it had seemed inevitable that to make a serious go of making Media Relations into a two-way window he'd have no choice but to tear open a few of the veins linking him to the force.

He opened his eyes.

'Fine. We accept the request.'

Sir! He felt someone tug his jacket from behind.

'I'll need to go and fetch the documents,' he said, and left the Press Room.

His staff were huddled together. Suwa cried out the moment they were inside the office.

'Are you really planning to tell them?'

'We have to honour our promise.'

'It's a terrible idea. Really bad. It'll all be over if they realize the connection with King Cement.'

'Her surname's different now. If we're lucky . . .' Kuramae said, inciting Suwa to shout him down.

'They're not that bloody stupid!'

Mikami opened one of the drawers in his desk and pulled out the relevant sheet of paper. He scooped up Kuramae's clear folder with it.

'Sir, don't do this.' Suwa blocked the way. He looked desperate. 'This is equivalent to a case of rape. *I can't tell you her name.* That's what you need to tell them.'

'If I do that this will never end.'

'Sir,' Mikumo said, her hands clasped together, entreating. 'When I talked about being less structured, that we didn't have to rely on strategy, I was being naive. I was being stupid.'

Her head was hanging low when Mikami answered.

'It hit me when Takagi was speaking. You can't open a window from the inside. If we're going to make this work, we need to try stepping outside.'

Mikami walked through them, into the corridor. Suwa grabbed his arm as soon as he was out.

'Sir, this is the last warning I can give you. *Don't go through with this.* You'll lose your job if you do.'

'I'll do what I can to make sure I don't.'

'It won't make a difference. Everything will be over.' Suwa's grip was strong. 'I . . . if possible . . . I'd like to keep on working for you.'

The corridor was completely quiet.

Mikami took hold of Suwa's hand. He moved it slowly away.

'If that's really true, you have to let me do this.'

Suwa dropped his head, resigned. Mikumo's face was in her hands. Kuramae hovered like a ghost. Mikami wrapped one hand around the doorknob of the Press Room. He placed the other on Suwa's chest.

'Stay here.'

'But—'

'This time you stay on standby. If you were in my position, you'd ask me to do the same.'

56

The reporters had arranged themselves formally, looking like an orchestra waiting for the first wave of the conductor's baton.

'I'll make the announcement.'

At this, the reporters opened their notebooks.

'The name of the driver involved in the Oito accident is Hanako Kikunishi. "Hana" using the character for "dazzling". "Ko" as in "child". "Kiku" as in "daily", and "nishi" as in "west". She is thirty-two years old. Her address is 1-15-3, Sayamamachi, Oito.'

His voice was met with the sound of pens scribbling. In a few seconds they had finished and looked back up.

It was the moment of their victory over anonymous reporting. They'd succeeded in learning the driver's identity. Yet they showed no sign of arrogance. The anger was gone. They'd relaxed. This seemed true even for Akikawa.

'I have more information,' Mikami continued. *Stepping outside.* 'Hanako Kikunishi is the daughter of Takuzo Kato, the chairman of King Cement.'

The reporters were silent. One by one, their expressions transformed as the revelation sank in. *Kato, from King Cement . . . Isn't he . . .? He's on the Public Safety Committee!* Their expressions sharpened abruptly.

'Is that why you kept her identity secret?'

'I'll leave that for you to decide.'

'Sorry?'

A few of the reporters jumped to their feet. *You've got to be kidding. How corrupt can you get?* Utsuki, Ushiyama and Sudou each shouted criticism in turn.

'The fact that she is the daughter of a committee member does not factor into the equation,' Mikami continued, standing his ground. 'It remains a fact that Hanako Kikunishi is eight months pregnant. That she is in a state of shock, at having caused the accident. It is with this in mind that I ask you again to refrain from including her details in your coverage.'

Mikami's voice was lost amidst cries of indignation. He caught Akikawa's gaze and held it, unsure if it was anger or serenity that he was seeing.

'I have more.'

The clamour petered out, the reporters' eyes those of people hungry for fresh prey.

'The injured party, Ryoji Meikawa, passed away. It happened in hospital on the sixth, two days after the accident took place.'

'You kept that from us, too?'

'You decide.'

There was no outburst this time. The tension in the room seemed to break. 'This is beyond a joke,' someone said. Within seconds, the reporters had taken on a look of astonished incredulity. Everyone standing sat noisily back down. *So this is it, this is the truth. Fucking police.*

Akikawa got idly back to his feet. He seemed to embody the atmosphere in the room.

'As expected, it's obvious we can't trust you. You're not fit to sit at the same table as us. I'm sorry to have to say it, but it's the only conclusion we can draw.'

'You're like a broken record.' Mikami couldn't stop the words. 'I'm not talking about the force as a whole. And I'm not asking you to put your faith in something as abstract as that. I'm in here, having cast off that role. What I'm asking you to decide is whether or not you can trust *me*.'

'Mikami, we're not . . .'

'You need to put your banners down, too. How can I hope for a proper discussion when I'm talking to organizations, insubstantial bodies – the *Toyo*, the *Yomiuri*, the *Mainichi*, the *Asahi*?'

'We've heard enough for today.'

'I'm here putting my job on the line. You can at least hear me out.'

Akikawa was the only one still defiant. The rest had given in, looking away but listening.

'This isn't like you. You've won, you've had your victory, you've got full disclosure. Why not use it? Why are you so happy to let it go? Maybe you prefer the fight. Is that it? I've taken a leap of faith. I've told you everything there is to tell. Are you saying that's not enough? You condemn the police for being corrupt and untrustworthy. Does that mean you can't even shake my hand? Are you so desperate to go back to the beginning and repeat your futile war? If that's what you want, then go ahead. You make this a fight between organizations. Go and report everything I said to your superiors. Lodge a complaint with mine. You'll get yourselves a new press director in no time. Then you'll be free to start the fight again.'

The room felt empty, it was so quiet. Everyone was still stunned. Some were looking away. Others had their eyes closed. A few had balled hands against their foreheads. Many were staring at something specific. The floor, a notebook, their hands.

'That's all I have to say on the accident in Oito City.' *Although*, he muttered to himself, then decided to continue. 'Actually, there is a little more.' Mikami pulled the document from the clear file in his hands. 'Some more on the man who passed away, Ryoji Meikawa. The cause of death was blood loss from internal damage. He'd been on his way home, after a couple of glasses of *shochu* at a bar nearby.' Mikami scanned the rest of the page. He'd been taken by an overwhelming desire to read it all. 'He was born in

Tomakomai in Hokkaido. He'd had a poor background, and hardly made it through elementary school. He left his hometown to look for work, before turning twenty. He worked for forty years at a factory making food paste, staying there until his retirement. After that he lived on his pension. He lost his wife eight years ago. They had no children. He had no relatives living close by. He'd been living in a small, tenement-style flat . . .' Mikami didn't know if the reporters were even listening. He continued regardless. 'The property was in his name, the land rented. His hobby was growing vegetables in planters. He didn't gamble or play pachinko; his only monthly extravagance was to visit the bar, the Musashi, and enjoy a couple of glasses of *shochu*.'

Mikami flipped to the next page. It was the additional information Kuramae had just brought him.

'According to the bar's owner, it was five years ago that Meikawa had first started showing up. He was generally quiet when he drank, but a failing tolerance for alcohol meant that in recent years he'd come to share a little about his life. His mother had been kind, but she'd died from an illness when he was eight. He never talked about his father. He had an elder sister, but had lost touch. He said he'd gone to Tokyo first, but had never been specific about how he'd ended up in Prefecture D. He never went back to Tomakomai in over fifty years. He was colour blind but had hidden this at work. Because of this, he never made any friends there. He had a lot of trouble with the colour red, but had an above-average sensitivity to blue. His real dream had been to become a photographer, taking photos of the sky and the sea.'

Mikami felt a pressure around his eyes.

'He used to say that meeting his wife was the best thing that ever happened to him. He'd been badly ill a couple of times, always had a low salary, caused her nothing but hardship, but she'd always been devoted and never complained. He'd taken her on a holiday, a tour around some hot springs, but they'd never taken a trip abroad together. He'd bought a magnificent gravestone for her, his second-biggest purchase after his home. After she passed away he spent most of his time watching TV. Mostly variety shows. He hadn't found them particularly interesting, but had enjoyed the fact that everyone seemed so cheerful.'

Mikami's voice became harsher. The notes were driving home the deplorable downside of anonymous reporting. They hadn't simply suppressed the identity of Hanako Kikunishi, they'd been complicit in stamping out the proof of Ryoji Meikawa's existence in this world. He'd met with a sorrowful end, but the clash over anonymous reporting had robbed him of the chance of having his name in the papers, of the opportunity for someone who loved him to read it and mourn his passing.

Mikami continued to read.

'The owner said Meikawa had been in a good mood on the day of the accident. That he'd told him he'd found his answerphone flashing when he got back from some shopping a few days earlier. There hadn't been a message, but he never received sales calls or wrong numbers, and said his phone hardly ever rang. It was old so he had no way of finding out where the call had come from. *Who could it have been? Who could it have been?* he'd said, cocking his head. The owner said he'd never seen him look so happy.'

Important . . . for him.

Everything on the page was significant. The last two lines detailed the results of the official inquiry. It took an effort to read them out.

'After contacting the police in Hokkaido, Meikawa's sister was discovered to have already passed away. Contact was made with distant relatives, but they refused responsibility for the ashes.'

Mikami let his hand fall to his side, the sheet with it. The reporters were still in a state of bewilderment, but they'd all turned to look his way. They were looking directly at him. Mikami felt an urge to say something else – something he hadn't intended to say. Something he couldn't have said if it had felt even the slightest bit underhand.

'I want you to cover the commissioner's visit. I don't know if Amamiya is hoping the coverage will unearth new leads. But he's given his consent for the visit and for you to cover it. Please – help us honour his wishes.'

57

Mikami felt a sudden wave of exhaustion.

He sank back into his chair. Inside Media Relations, the atmosphere was as if they were awaiting sentence. When Suwa got back in, he gave Mikami a heartfelt salute. He'd no doubt had his ear on the door, heard everything. 'Great work' was all he said. Mikumo's eyes were puffy, probably from crying. She said something but Mikami couldn't make it out.

Kuramae was . . .

. . . at his desk in the corner, staring at his computer screen. He had a grave, almost troubled look, the expression in harmony with the general atmosphere of the room. It seemed like camouflage. Nothing conscious, or defensive, simply the natural state of a desk worker who made up the undergrowth of the organization.

It was probably ironic. Only Kuramae, out of all of them the least interested in PR, had managed to distinguish between the inside and the out. The relationship was the same as that between Criminal Investigations and Administrative Affairs, Media Relations and the Press Room. They were all separate entities but, viewed from above, it became clear they inhabited the same well. Suwa, of course, but also Mikami, and even Mikumo – they had all looked deeper into the well to find their answers, forgotten to gaze up at the sky. It hadn't been the press. The real links to the outside had been Meikawa and Amamiya. They'd let themselves become blind to something as obvious as that.

What would the reporters think? Would they realize they were accomplices, occupants of the same well? Both sides had left an elderly man's corpse exposed to the elements. Would they be able to accept the truth? They'd become obsessed with finding the driver's identity and, as a result, let the article fall by the wayside; they'd overlooked the death of a pensioner, someone whose name they could have learned with one call to the hospital or town hall. *If they feel even a little remorse, we can all move forwards.* The only way they could open a window to the outside was to work together.

Suwa came over.

'Nobody's gone to lodge a complaint upstairs.'

Right.

'And they've just started their meeting.'

Good. It worked, then.

Mikami realized he had his eyes closed. *No surprise. I didn't sleep at all last night.* His exhaustion was pushing his thoughts towards sleep.

Papa, not yet!

You can't open your eyes yet.

Not yet. Not yet, not yet, not yet.

Papa, you cheated!

I told you it was too early to open your eyes!

Someone was shaking him. He opened his eyes.

How about now?

'Sir.' He saw Suwa's face in close-up. 'It's the press. They're here.'

When he sat up, a pink blanket slid off his shoulders. A group had assembled before his desk. *A crowd*, his mind interpreted. He glanced at the clock on the wall. He'd been asleep for thirty, maybe forty minutes. He looked at the reporters properly this time. Akikawa, Utsuki, Ushiyama, Sudou, Yanase, Horoiwa, Yamashina, Kadoike, Namie . . . The chief reporters were there from each of the thirteen member agencies of the Press Club. He slapped his cheeks and pulled his chair back so he could see the whole group. Akikawa silently held out a sheet of paper. Mikami took it, also saying nothing.

Questions: Commissioner General Walking Interview. Prefecture D Police Headquarters, Press Club.

They'd called off the boycott.

Mikami sensed Suwa, to his side, breathe a huge sigh of relief. The sheet of paper contained a list of five questions. Mikami scanned through them. Each was generic, concerning things like the commissioner's impressions during his visit, the planned course of the Six Four investigation; there were no hints of malice or hostility.

'We don't need a new press director. That's our consensus,' Yamashina said. The man's usual goofiness was gone; his bearing revealed instead a determination that took Mikami by surprise.

When he looked around he saw the others all wore similarly earnest looks. Even Akikawa seemed to have lost his usual sneering sarcasm; he resembled nothing more than a young man passionate about his job. Mikami thought he felt a breeze on his cheek. He turned to check the windows, but they were closed.

'Oh, and this, too.'

Akikawa placed a two-page document on Mikami's desk. Kuramae's report on Ryoji Meikawa. Mikami had stuck it to the whiteboard in the Press Room on his way out, together with a copy of his other announcements.

'Let's just say we didn't see this. This bit should be our job, after all.'

Right. Mikami gave him a deep nod, maintaining eye contact. He'd meant it as a handshake. Akikawa didn't return the gesture, but a subtle motion of his eye told Mikami he hadn't brushed it off either. He turned around. The other reporters bowed at Mikami, then followed Akikawa out. Mikami made sure to look directly at each of them. No victors. No losers. How long had it been since the last time he'd seen them leave like this?

No sooner had the door closed behind them than Suwa punched his fists into the air, calling out in silent triumph. Mikumo clapped her hands silently, standing up and smiling through tears. Kuramae arched forwards, breathing a sigh of relief before impressively missing a high five Suwa threw his way.

Mikami rolled his chair backwards and picked the blanket up from the floor. He held it out. *Here.* Mikumo hurried over. As he handed it to her, he said, 'You should be proud. This only happened because we chose not to go with strategizing.'

'Sir . . .'

Mikami craned to look past her emotional face; he called out to Kuramae.

'You know, you ought to teach the press a thing or two about good research.'

Mikami caught Suwa's gaze as he laughed. He didn't let the moment pass.

'Suwa, thanks.'

He spun his chair around to face the windows. Suwa could interpret it as an attempt to hide awkwardness; that was fine. He dropped his eyes to the sheet on his knees.

Generic questions.

With just over a year until the statute of limitations kicks in, what do you intend to do to make sure the case is solved?

The preparations were in place for the execution.

The problem of Dallas was solved. How would Criminal Investigations respond? How many people would get dragged into their final struggle?

He'd been true to his duty as press director but had had to make significant sacrifices in order to get this done. It was possible he'd lose more as events unfolded. But his mind felt clear. The feeling of unease and regret was easing off. A clarity that felt like salvation spread through his mind.

Lots of laughter came from behind.

There was one thing he knew for sure. That it was here, in Media Relations and not in Criminal Investigations, that he'd finally secured himself a loyal following.

58

Mikami left the Prefectural HQ just before 5 p.m.

Minako had called him at the office, sounding distraught. They'd had another silent call. Unlike before, this time the display had given them the caller's number. The area code was City D.

Mikami's gut feeling told him it wasn't Ayumi. Less instinct, perhaps, more like habit, an application of the brakes to avoid false hope. He was afraid of what might happen if they both hoped it was true but it fell apart. His body gave more open signals. He could feel his hands sweating against the steering wheel. His foot grew heavier on the accelerator, and he raced through more than one set of amber lights.

Minako was pale, waiting outside the house. The front door was open, so she could hear the phone if it rang.

'She's close, I can tell,' Minako said with unblinking eyes.

'Let's go inside.'

Mikami grabbed the handset in the hallway and carried it into the living room, pulling the cord from behind. Too impatient to take off his coat, he crossed his legs on the tatami and started to dig through the phone menu.

A number came up on the display. The area code was undoubtedly one from the city. The number had ten digits. Mikami frowned at a sudden sense of déjà vu. Something told him he'd seen it recently. Amamiya's home number crossed his mind as a possibility, but he didn't want to disillusion Minako with only a vague memory.

'What was it like?'

'The same as before. They ended the call without saying a word.'

'Did you give your name when you picked up?'

'No. I just picked up . . . I didn't say anything at first.'

Meaning it wasn't a wrong number. Lots of people would hang up without apologizing, but they'd would at least say hello if whoever picked up was silent.

'How long were you on the phone for?'

'Oh, I don't know. Not long. I said hello a few times, then the line went dead.'

'Did you notice any particular sounds in the background?'

'Noises? I don't think so. I couldn't hear anything.'

'Okay, so maybe inside someone's house.'

Caller display services were advertised everywhere; its application was probably widely used and understood. If the call had been a prank, or something malicious in nature, he would have expected the caller to have withheld their number.

Perhaps it was Amamiya after all. Estranged from society, it was possible he didn't know about the new service. He might have called to discuss the commissioner's visit but become flustered and hung up when he heard a female voice.

The same reasoning held for Ayumi, too. She would never imagine them buying a phone with the new function. Had she wanted to talk to him and not Minako? No. It was the same trick as before – she was making the silent calls as a test.

Mikami picked up the phone.

'I think it's best to try calling back.'

'Hmm?' Minako appeared not to have considered this option.

'We can make a call to this number. That way, we'll find out who made the call.'

Mikami felt his cheeks draw tighter even as he spoke. Minako's expression hardened. As though coming back to herself, she gave him a resolute look.

'Yes. Please.'

'Could I get a glass of water?' Mikami asked, loosening his tie. Having managed to get Minako into the kitchen, he slipped out his notebook and deftly flipped through the pages. *Different.* The number didn't match Amamiya's. Was it true, then? Could Ayumi be here in the city?

Minako came jogging back in. Mikami's thirst had been genuine. He gulped down the cup of water, picked up the handset, and pressed redial.

He wondered if it might be one of Ayumi's friends. The phone kept ringing. Minako shuffled her knees and face closer. Somebody picked up. A second later, a female voice sounded in Mikami's ear.

'This is the Hiyoshi household.'

Mikami was dumbstruck. The technician from Forensics. The recluse. It was Koichiro Hiyoshi's home number.

'Hello? Who is this, please?'

'This is Mikami, from the police headquarters. I came to visit a few days ago.'

He assumed she'd made the call. He wondered if something had happened to Hiyoshi that had prompted her to get in touch.

But . . .

'What do you want?'

The jaundiced reply was unexpected. 'We had a missed call; I'm just calling back.'

'Sorry? I don't understand.'

It's work, Mikami whispered to Minako, holding his palm around the mouthpiece. 'We had a call, about half an hour ago. Our phone lets us know . . .'

She started to panic when he explained about the caller-display function.

'But . . . I was out, doing some shopping.'

Hiyoshi had called in his mother's absence. That was what had happened. Mikami had given his mother two short messages to pass on, one three days ago, another the day after that. *I put them under his door.* He nodded now, remembering her words. Hiyoshi had read them. And he'd called the number Mikami had noted on the bottom.

'Is your son still in his room?'

'I . . . I think so.'

'Could you put him on the phone?'

'On the . . .? Oh . . .'

She stumbled to a halt, perhaps hesitant to make waves. Even nightmares became mundane after fourteen years.

Still . . .

'We should consider this an opportunity. Your son made the call.' Mikami couldn't stop the words. 'Has he done that before? Has he ever tried to call someone before?'

'No, not once. Although, I can't say for sure . . . when I've been out.'

'Is the phone cordless?'

'Hmm? Oh, yes, it is.'

'Good. Could you tell him I'm on the phone and leave it outside his door? I'll see if I can't talk to him.'

'Yes, yes, of course.' Her voice shot up a pitch. 'Please. If you could. That would be wonderful.'

Mikami heard a pattering of slippers. She was rushing. Going upstairs. She stopped, started calling out to her son. Her voice was soothing, mixed with fear. There was a scuffing noise, then the sound of slippers moving away.

The silence that followed was painful. It was easy to picture the phone, lying there on the floor. Ten seconds passed. Twenty. Thirty. Mikami waited, resolute, his entire being focused on listening, intent on not missing even the slightest sound.

Minako's head popped unexpectedly into view. *What is it?* He held up a hand to stop her from whispering. The hand tensed and he waved her away.

He thought he'd heard something. A door, opening. That's

what it had sounded like. White noise came down the line. Some-one had picked up the phone. Mikami had the handset pressed so hard over his ear the sound felt like a physical force.

The door closing again . . . A creaking sound, a bed or a chair . . .

Confident Hiyoshi had the phone in his room, Mikami opened his mouth to speak.

'Hiyoshi?'

No answer. Mikami waited a moment. He couldn't even make out the man's breathing.

'This is Mikami. I'm press director at the Prefectural HQ. You called my number a short while ago.'

No response.

'It's okay. Phones these days have—'

Mikami broke off, having realized something. Hiyoshi had been working with new technology during his time at NTT. He would have been fully versed in computer technology, long before he became a recluse. He would have a computer of his own. Which meant it was safe to assume he would know about the growth of the caller-display function. He'd known about it and let his number show on purpose.

The call had been an SOS.

'Did you read my notes?'

No answer.

For Hiyoshi, time had come to a standstill. It had stopped back at Amamiya's, the moment Urushibara had whispered into his ear.

If the worst comes to the worst, it's your fault.

'Everything I wrote is the truth. None of it was your fault.' He heard an intake of breath. 'Hiyoshi . . .'

Silence.

'Hiyoshi. I know you can hear me.'

Again.

Mikami's sense of his presence seemed to slip away. But . . . he was still on the line. Still listening. Holding his breath, waiting for the continuation. *I have to say something.* Mikami needed something that would resonate. Something that would find its way to a heart forced to bear responsibility for the death of a young girl, a heart that had been shut away for fourteen years.

He closed his eyes and drew a quiet breath.

'It was a terrible case . . .' Mikami had started. 'For the girl, and her parents, of course. But also for her friends, for the school, for the area she lived in. For us, too.'

Nothing.

'And for you, Hiyoshi. It must have been terrible, miserable. You ended up having to join us in Amamiya's house, even though you'd never expected to work in the field. The recorder didn't work, even though it had during your testing. And you couldn't have had anyone more repugnant in charge of your unit. The case was cursed with bad luck. Everything that could go wrong did. And the girl ended up losing her life. I understand your pain. I understand the need to blame yourself. But Shoko died because the kidnapper murdered her. It wasn't because of you.'

Still no response.

'Okay, so there was an error with the recording. A costly one. But there's something you need to know – that wasn't the only mistake made during the investigation. They were everywhere; the whole case was littered with them. I'm not just saying that. There isn't much we do that isn't a mistake of some kind, during an investigation. That time the mistakes just happened to come together in a single result – our failure to save the girl. The kidnapper's still at large, even now. Every officer in the prefecture has to shoulder that burden. To say it's any one person's responsibility is ludicrous. It's good that you feel accountable. It's proof you're a decent, caring human being. But it's wrong to assume blame on everyone's behalf. No one can endure that. It's self-indulgent. The blame needs to be shared. All the pain and suffering, it needs to be apportioned equally between every single officer who took part in the investigation. Do you understand?'

437

He felt like he was in an airless vacuum. He'd never contemplated the existence of a silence so perfect. Hiyoshi's hand was probably clamped over the mouthpiece, hard enough to make it numb. He was listening; every part of him concentrated in his ears.

'I don't know if you remember, but I was there, too. I met Amamiya, and his wife. I followed his car when he left to deliver the ransom. I was there, watching, when he threw the suitcase from the bridge into the river. It still hurts me physically, every time I think about it. I get attacks of remorse, of shame, each time I pass by any of the businesses the kidnapper listed — it all comes back to me. It passes, sure. It's not there all the time, like it is with you. It's not constant, but it's stayed with me. I haven't forgotten. I couldn't forget. Nor do I ever want to forget. We all carry a part of it — me, Koda, Kakinuma. We're not allowed to ease each other's pain. Shoko and her parents wouldn't forgive it. That's why we quietly split the blame. We will carry it to our graves, without ever mentioning it or making excuses. You could spend the rest of your life dwelling on it, and it wouldn't be enough. The only way we have of keeping Shoko alive is to keep her in our minds. That's why we have to share the burden.'

Still nothing.

'I don't know if you're listening. I think you are.'

It began to feel like he was shouting into a void. Into a deep forest. Into an ocean the sun couldn't reach. *I want to know where you are. I'll come by if it's somewhere I can visit.* The words in his first letter.

'Why the silence? You called because you wanted to reach out.'

'. . .'

'It's okay to talk. I'll listen, whatever it is.'

'. . .'

'Try and say something.'

The silence exacerbated the sense of darkness. Mikami felt its pull. He felt something close to panic.

438

'Fourteen years. It's been fourteen years.'

'. . .'

'You can't spend fourteen years in one room. That's why I wanted to write you the notes. I want to know where you've been. The places you've visited. Are you in heaven? Hell? The bottom of some ocean? Somewhere in the sky? I want to know how you can stand being alone. Tell me so I can understand. Can no one else join you there? Not even family?'

'. . .'

'I was in a diner when I wrote the notes. I spent a long time trying to come up with something to put down; they're the end result. I wrote exactly what I feel. I really do want to know. Tell me. Where are you now?'

'. . .'

'What can I do so we can meet? Tell me how to reach you. If that's too much for now, let me hear your voice at least. Just a single word will do. Anything.'

The line went dead following a burst of static.

Ayumi . . .

Mikami had fallen into a trance-like state. It felt as though his soul had been sucked through to the other side.

No, not Ayumi . . . Or was it . . .? Was it possible that, in that silence, all worlds were connected?

He realized he was still holding the phone. He let out a long, deep breath. Pulling himself together, he redialled their number. Hiyoshi's mother answered. *He didn't say anything.* Through tears, she still showered him with gratitude.

He felt exhausted. It was a trial even to stand up from the floor. It took him a while to notice Minako. She was sitting at the table in the kitchen area. The chair was turned away. It was a shockingly lonely image. Her thoughts would be on Ayumi. Or maybe on him, for having expended so much effort on someone other than their daughter. He glanced at his hand. He'd used it to wave her away . . . He felt a sudden rush of fear. He moved away from the phone and into the kitchen. It took all the courage he could muster to sit across from her. With a visible effort, she looked up.

'Anything wrong?'

The question was automatic. Mikami made a face, acting as though he'd been put upon. 'It was someone who used to work in Forensics. He quit the force in the aftermath of the kidnapping. Ever since, he's refused to leave his room.'

'Right . . .'

'It's been fourteen years. His mother's having a hard time coping.'

Minako said nothing.

'I thought there might be a chance I could help.'

'You're such a good man,' she snapped, immediately dropping her face into her hands. The gesture made it clear she regretted what she'd said.

'Minako . . .'

Unconsciously, he reached for her fragile shoulder. It pulled away to leave his hand swimming in mid-air.

He felt suddenly helpless. He gazed into her face, the features obscured under the shadow of her hair. He couldn't think of anything to say. Seeing no other option, he drew his hand steadily back. His mobile started to vibrate in his jacket. The muffled sound seemed to echo through the whole room. Agitated, Mikami took it out and flicked it open.

It was Suwa.

'Akama's back. He's asking to see you.'

'Okay.' Mikami stood and turned his back to Minako.

'Can you make it back to the station?'

Mikami walked a little. He stepped around the kitchen counter and got to the sink before turning to face Minako again. She radiated despair.

'No.'

'Okay. I'll go and report what's happened. I'll tell him we've agreed to full disclosure and convinced the press to call off the boycott. I won't go into any more of the details.'

'Appreciated.'

Suwa fell silent, staying on the line even though they'd finished the conversation. Mikami lowered his voice to a whisper.

'It was an unrelated call. You can let Kuramae and Mikumo know, too.'

'Yes, sir.'

Mikami closed up his mobile and walked back to the table. As though switching places, Minako stood to get dinner ready. The sound of the knife was muted. From behind, she gave an impression of being alone, of being an elderly woman preparing her own dinner. They didn't talk during dinner, or after they'd moved into the living room. Mikami turned on the TV. He flipped to a channel showing a run-of-the-mill quiz programme. Minako inhabited the edge of his vision. Her eyes were on the TV but focused on some other place. The caller hadn't been Ayumi. He knew Minako would be suffering after making that barbed comment. He ought to say something, but he was hesitant, the feeling of rejection still lingering in his hand. His head was buzzing with Mizuki Murakushi's story. *Are you okay?* He wondered if he'd really said the words. He was starting to wonder if Mizuki had just made it up. Even after they'd got married he couldn't be sure. They'd been together for over twenty years, but he couldn't remember ever noticing a shift in her mood and saying something to comfort her.

They were in bed by eleven o'clock. Minako had suddenly said goodnight; he'd replied that he was tired and that he'd join her. His every sense told him he had to. More than anything, he understood how important it was to stay at her side. They might both have been praying for their daughter's safety, but that didn't make their relationship anything more than that of a normal marriage. He was certain the insecurity and fragility that was creeping between them was no different to the kind that existed between every husband and wife.

The bedroom was cold. Minako switched off the small lamp next to her futon. The white of the handset she kept by her pillow faded into dark, followed by the after-image. Mikami kept his breath quiet on his own futon. He felt uncomfortable even turning over. He could make out the faint sound of Minako's breathing. His chest felt constricted, as though the oxygen in the room was getting thin. He wasn't the slightest bit drowsy. Five minutes felt like an hour. After a while, probably unable to sleep herself, Minako let out a quiet sigh. It sounded like she'd given in.

'Can't sleep?' Mikami said, using the darkness as an ally. 'The wind's died down outside.'

'It has . . .'

'I suppose it's hard to sleep when it's too quiet.'

'Right.'

'Sorry . . .'

'For what?'

'For being on the phone for so long, on a day like today. For getting so worked up, for the sake of a stranger's son.'

Minako didn't say anything.

'One good turn deserves another . . . do a good deed, and it'll find its way back.'

Still, silence.

'Do you regret this?'

He sensed Minako turning his way.

'Regret what . . .?'

'Getting together, with me.'

A short pause.

'Do *you*?'

'Me? What reason would I ever have to regret marrying you?'

'Well . . . okay, good.'

'And you?'

'No, of course not.'

'Okay.'

'Why would I? Don't be so silly,' Minako said, reprimanding him gently.

To Mikami, it sounded like someone who was trying their best. He'd ruined her life. Out of all the paths her life could have taken, he'd led her down the worst. The thoughts came like tidal waves.

'You could have stayed in the force.'

'Hmm?'

'You gave up being an officer because you married me. Don't you regret that?'

'Why would you ask me that?'

'It's something Mizuki said. She told me you worked harder than anyone else.'

'I was thinking of leaving, even before we got married.'

'You were?'

'I wasn't suited to the job.'

Not suited? It was the first he'd heard of it.

'That doesn't sound right.'

'I was full of energy at the start. I really thought I could do something to help, to make the world a better place, you know?'

'And you did, no doubt about it.'

'No, that wasn't it. It took a while, but I realized it eventually – I'd only joined the force because I wanted to be loved.'

In the dark, Mikami stared, open-eyed.

'I just couldn't warm to people, to society. All those cases, accidents, all those egotists. I started to hate everything. That was when it dawned on me that I was only doing my job so I could feel loved – I wanted people to show me gratitude. When it hit me, I didn't know what to do. I got cold feet about the whole thing. How could someone like that ever hope to protect people? Why had I ever thought about doing something so off the mark as keeping the peace? That was when . . .'

There was a long pause.

'I thought, maybe I could protect a smaller world. Maybe I could build a family. Protect it. That much I thought I . . .'

Her voice clouded over.

Mikami sprung up. He turned around and put his hand under Minako's duvet. He traced the mattress until he found her slender arm and took hold of her hand. She held his back, her grip weak.

'It's not your fault.'

Again, Minako said nothing.

'Ayumi . . . she's not well.'

' . . .'

'Maybe it's because of me that she's like this. I never tried to get to know her, not really. I thought I could just leave her be and she'd grow up all on her own.'

' . . .'

'And she inherited my face. It's been a big obstacle for—'

'That's not the reason,' Minako said, cutting him off. 'Maybe it isn't even about what we did right, what we did wrong. Maybe we just weren't right for her.'

Mikami's head spun. *Not right for her?*

'What do you mean?'

'It's possible we'd never have understood her properly, however much we tried. Just because we're her parents, it doesn't mean we know what she's thinking.'

Mikami felt himself flinch.

'How can you say that? We lived under the same roof for sixteen years. You gave birth to her, you raised her—'

'It's not a case of how long. There are some things you just can't understand. Parents and their children are different people; it's not so strange that this happened.'

'You think it's a mistake she was born to us?'

'That's not what I'm trying to say. I just wonder . . . whether Ayumi just needs somebody else. Someone other than us.'

'Who?'

'Someone has to be out there. Someone ready to accept Ayumi

as she is, who won't try to change her one way or another. Someone who'll tell her she's perfect, who'll stand silently by her side
and protect her. That's where she belongs. She'll be free to be herself, do what she wants. Not here, not with us. That's why she left.'

It was painful to listen. What was she trying to say? Was she
giving up hope? Was she trying to tell him she was ready to let
go? Or was she simply clinging to an idea, some kind of hope?
Whichever the case, it was the dark making her talk. It had taken
a small idea, nothing genuine, and amplified it, until it came to
dominate the infinite space before them.

'It just doesn't make sense.'

Mikami rested his head back on the pillow. Their hands had
come apart without either having consciously let go.

'It does make sense. I know, because I was the same. I never felt
like I belonged at home, even as a child. The feeling was always
there.'

'You?'

'My parents seemed really happy together, right? The truth is
they were really unhappy. There was a girl at my dad's work who
he'd been involved with for a long time. My mum was always
unstable as a result. I remember you said you were glad there was
someone to look after him when he remarried a few years after
she passed away. That was the girl from work.'

Mikami felt dizzy. Something else he was hearing for the first
time. This made sense of the fact that Minako hardly ever got in
touch with her father.

Even so . . .

'We're not like that.'

'Of course not. But their problems weren't the reason I didn't
belong. I didn't find out about the adultery until much later, and
my parents were good to me most of the time. Still, I felt alone.
I never told them how I felt. And I never got the impression
they knew. I'd just assumed they wouldn't understand. I don't
know why.

'I always felt like I was coming back to an empty house, even though Mum would be there when I got back from school. *How was school?* I already knew everything she'd ask, and my answers were all fixed. It all seemed pointless. The feeling of emptiness didn't change even when Dad got back. Even now, thinking back, it's only the empty spaces I can remember. The wind or the sun coming through the window. The worn-out couch. The *kokeshi* doll, gathering dust on one of the shelves.'

Her voice had trailed off. Mikami shut his eyes. The dark became darker still. Had she fallen asleep? Was she staring at nothing? She was quiet. Mikami had begun to lose sense of time, even the feeling of being on his futon, when he heard her speak again.

'The woman's son. I hope he comes back to her.'

'Hmm?'

'The man from Forensics. I hope he's able to come back.'

To come back . . .

'Yeah. I do, too.'

'Because . . . it could be you.'

'What could?'

'You could be that someone, for him.'

You think so . . . ?

Mikami stopped thinking. He couldn't think any more. He breathed out. As though it was a sign, it carried him into the dark.

59

The next morning Mikami found his shoes polished as usual.

The commissioner was due to arrive in one day. He geared himself up and left the house. Anything could happen in the next twenty-four hours. For the moment, the papers had been empty of surprises. With nothing to suggest a repeat bombardment from Criminal Investigations, the pages had been filled with news articles catching up on the previous day's scoop.

The first shock had come a minute after his arrival in Media Relations. Kuramae and Mikumo had already been out, gathering details of a land survey for the new station building; Suwa had been by himself, brooding as he waited for Mikami.

'Did you hear the news?'

'What news?'

'There was a tip-off. It made its way around Criminal Investigations, late last night.'

'A tip-off?'

'About Administrative Affairs being in cahoots with Tokyo, conspiring to take over the director's job – something to that effect. Anyway, word spread around the detectives, and now even the smaller district stations know about it.'

The instigator. Was it Arakida's plan to get every last detective up in arms?

'Where did you get this?'

'A detective, someone I know from my intake. He was all riled up, called me a traitor.'

Mikami hadn't had a single call at home. If Suwa was being targeted due to his background in Administrative Affairs, Mikami, with his history as a detective, knew he'd become an even bigger target. *Bastard got greedy, sold us out.* He wondered if that was what they were saying on the other side.

He picked up the external line, and dialled Amamiya's home number. It felt more like a call to confirm, to double-check, than to run through the following day's schedule. The phone had rung a few times when Kuramae came back into the office; Mikumo followed soon after.

Nobody picked up at Amamiya's end. Mikami waited a while before trying again, but all he saw was the lonely image of the phone ringing by itself in the man's empty living room. Twenty past nine. Maybe he was still in bed.

Mikami put his notebook back in his jacket pocket and got up from his desk. The internal line started to ring, stopping him. It was Akama. He told Mikami to report immediately to the first floor.

The air inside Akama's office was still.

Ishii had been summoned, too. He was perched on the edge of one of the couches, his back hunched. He didn't look around, although he would have heard Mikami come in.

Akama acknowledged him with a quick flick of his eyes. He'd aged in just one day. That was Mikami's immediate impression. Harried, dehydrated. Hair not combed properly after a night's sleep. Fingers that twitched on the couch armrest. The details all spoke of the magnitude of the stress he'd no doubt faced in Tokyo.

'I just finished talking with Ishii.'

As he took his seat, Mikami threw a sideways glance at the man. Head drooping. Eyes staring. Mouth half-open. Whatever he'd been told, it had put him in shock.

'Criminal Investigations apparently called him at home, issuing threats. He came to discuss the matter with me.'

Mikami saw what was coming.

'What kind of threats?'

'Someone's spreading information through the department.'

'What information?'

'That Tokyo is planning to sequester the director's post in the spring. That the commissioner intends to make the announcement tomorrow.'

Mikami watched Akama in silence.

Akama watched him back, clearly hoping to gauge something from his reaction. 'You knew.'

'Yes.'

'You received a threatening call, too?'

'No. No one's been in touch.'

'So, you've been in contact with them?'

Mikami said nothing in response. He felt the muscles pulling together over his forehead. Akama broke eye contact. It looked as though he'd done so to avoid an argument.

'I'm not looking to blame you here. I heard from Suwa that you managed to placate the reporters. A job well done. It certainly raises you in my estimation. Why then . . .' Akama looked back up '. . . would someone like that go crashing into the captain's office? I hear you gave him your opinion? That you even urged him to reconsider the matter of the director's post?'

Mikami's eyes had fallen to Akama's chest. He didn't know how to revisit the emotions he'd felt at the time, even now, as Akama raised the subject. He couldn't think of a single thing to say, not a single excuse.

'Which one is the real Mikami?'

He gave no answer.

'You need to make your allegiances crystal clear. The commissioner is due to be here *tomorrow*.' Akama's tie swayed as he leaned in. 'Mikami, I wonder if you truly understand what this means. We are talking about the commissioner general, in person. He is more than an individual, more than the pinnacle of a government bureaucracy. He embodies the *entire police authority*.'

'If the commissioner is the embodiment of the force, the director of Criminal Investigations is nothing less than the embodiment of the police in Prefecture D.'

Akama removed his glasses. His hand was trembling faintly.

'Is that your answer?'

'I just told you how it is. As press director, I have no intention of lending them my support.'

'If that really is the case, admit to it. You know something. What is Criminal Investigations planning to do?'

'I don't know.'

'I seriously doubt that's true. You must have heard *something*.'

'My position precludes me from knowing anything.'

'I've always held you in good favour, Mikami. Don't disappoint me now.'

'I'm not doing this for your benefit,' he said, before thinking what he was saying.

Akama's eyes widened.

'So you do—'

'Was there anything else?'

'Why, you—'

'I have to go and see Amamiya. I need to make sure everything's in place for tomorrow.'

Akama's eyes drifted for a moment. Then he nodded, put his glasses back on, and crossed his hands over his knees.

'Yes, good. Make sure to consider every eventuality.'

Mikami got to his feet. He gave a deep bow of his head, Akama's expression seeming to leap out at him as he did. His head was dipped low, his eyes upturned and steady, so he looked like a wild animal getting ready to pounce.

'While you're here, have you come to a decision about sending your daughter's photo nationwide to help with the search?'

It didn't come as a surprise. At this stage, the leash he had Mikami on was doubtless his only lifeline. Mikami made another deep bow of his head. It was a salute, marking the conclusion of eight months.

'Thank you, I appreciate the concern. Thank you again for the special consideration you've been kind enough to show us until now.' Mikami brought his head back up. 'I would like you to remember one thing. If – heaven forbid – your daughter were ever to run away from home, *we're* the ones who would search for her. The 260,000 police officers stationed in regions throughout the nation. *Not* the bureaucrats in Kasumigaseki.'

Mikami walked out without waiting for a reaction. His pace picked up as he strode down the corridor. Ishii was coming up from behind. He seemed about to enter the Secretariat, but his footsteps quickened; he jogged up to Mikami.

'Mikami, there's nothing we can do about it.' He didn't know how to vent his anger. It was clear from the look on his face. Down around his belt, his hands were clenched into fists. 'It can't be helped. It's beyond our control. We couldn't change it even if we wanted to.'

Ishii would have had one – *I swear to protect our home* – a day in his youth, when he'd pledged the same.

Mikami held back from nodding.

Instead of heading immediately downstairs, though, he stayed and watched Ishii trudge, exhausted, like a sun setting, through the doors of the Secretariat.

60

Yoshio Amamiya was out.

The front door was locked and his car was gone. Mikami waited half an hour, but he showed no signs of coming back. He wrote a note on one of his business cards and wedged it into the letterbox. *I'll try again this afternoon.*

Mikami felt uneasy. He wasn't worried about Amamiya having second thoughts; instead, the feeling came from his not knowing why Amamiya had decided to accept the commissioner's visit in the first place.

His team were sitting in the guest area when he got back to the office. They were going through some last-minute checks, huddled over photos and a map marked with the route planned for the next day's inspection. *What do we do if someone turns up with a new cameraman? Do we need a signal for when they need to leave the site where the body was found? Do we have enough spaces for the press during the visit to the Investigative HQ in Central Station? Any more notifications of roadworks scheduled along the commissioner's route?* With the ease of a seasoned professional, Suwa was relaying a list of points to confirm. Kuramae was scribbling them down as fast as he could, but failing to keep up. Mikumo seemed like an elder sister, providing the relevant details and more whenever one of the men asked her a question.

Mikami felt his tension subside. What he saw before him now was no different to anything he'd seen before, but it felt new and welcoming. At his desk, he ran through the day's schedule.

12.00: Commissioner arrives. Lunch with Captain
Tsujiuchi.

13.20: Visit site of Shoko's body in Sadacho. Offering of
flowers and incense.

14.15: Commissioner provides encouragement to
Investigative HQ in Central Station.

15.05: Commissioner pays respects at Amamiya home.
Offering of incense.

15.25: Walking interview outside Amamiya home.

It's really happening.

Mikami lit a cigarette and closed his eyes. What were Criminal Investigations doing? He didn't think for a moment they'd get through the day without something happening. Arakida had spread word of what Tokyo intended to do to every detective in the prefecture. He'd put everything in place to transform Prefecture D into another Dallas. What was he planning for his next – *no, his last* – move?

Time moved irritatingly slowly for the rest of the morning. Nobody called, and the reporters were mostly absent. 'Everything's good and ready,' Suwa had said. 'As long as nothing unexpected happens.' He hadn't forgotten to add that final part. Yet the office remained tranquil, and no news came in to suggest anything had happened in Tokyo.

Mikami joined the others when they ordered food for lunch. Gulping down the warm soba noodles, he found himself worrying whether Minako had eaten. What had she been feeling the night before? It was difficult to untangle the threads of the conversation they'd had in bed. It felt as if it might have been a critical juncture; at the same time, it felt as though they'd wandered into some sort of fable-like other world.

I just wonder . . . whether Ayumi just needs somebody else. Someone other than us.

I should have bought a bento and taken it back. He came seriously to

453

regret not having done so, with too much time on his hands even as late as the afternoon. No plays from Arakida. No calls from Akama. The calm before the storm, maybe. Perhaps the storm had already passed, the decisive battle won on a scale he wasn't even aware of.

It was after 2 p.m. *I should go back to Amamiya's.* Mikami was just getting to his feet when Suwa, who had been checking on the next room, came back in. He looked puzzled.

'I'm going to take a quick look at the fourth floor.'

'Why?'

'One of the *Yomiuri* reporters was trying to get hold of First Division for some stats on breaking and entering . . . he was complaining about the lines being busy.'

'Investigative Planning?'

'Right. He thought he'd try out Assistant Chief Mikura's desk, but again no one answered.'

Under normal circumstances, Mikami wouldn't have paid it any more attention.

'Go check it out.'

It didn't feel right. Having sent Suwa on his way, he pulled over the internal line and pushed the number for Investigative Planning. The line was busy. He tried again, this time opting for Mikura's desk. *No answer, the same as the* Yomiuri. He kept trying, but the result was the same.

Something's wrong.

Even if Mikura *was* out of office, a nearby member of staff would surely pick up instead. Mikami took a chance and tried First Division Chief Matsuoka's number. Nothing. No answer. Taking the next step, he called Director Arakida's phone. The line rang uselessly. Matsuoka and Arakida, both out of office. Mikami let the ringing continue, ten, fifteen times, but there was no one running to answer it.

Calm down, he told himself, then tried the number of the assistant chief of Second Division. *I can ask Itokawa.* The two divisions were next to each other, straddling Forensics. If something major was happening in First Division, he'd notice whether he wanted to or not.

He couldn't believe it. Itokawa wasn't answering. *Second Division, too . . .?*

Mikami lifted his head.

'Go check Second Division and Forensics. And the Mobile Investigation Unit.'

Kuramae and Mikumo were on their feet before he finished, forgetting even to salute as they dashed from the room. Mikami's fingers were unsteady as he dialled Forensics. *Here, too?* Nobody picked up. He flicked through his directory and dialled Mobile Investigation's main unit. They were located just across from Second Division. The line was busy.

The external line started to ring in front of him. It was Suwa. He sounded out of breath.

'Something's definitely up. There's only one guy up here manning First Division.'

'One?'

'A desk worker, youngish. He's fielding all the calls.'

'Did you check the detective area?'

'I did. Completely deserted.'

'Ask where everyone went.'

'But . . . he's busy with the calls.'

'Wait for a gap, and ask.'

Mikami ended the call and picked up the internal line again. Mobile Investigation, West Dispatch Unit. *No answer.* He had just clucked his tongue in annoyance when someone picked up.

'Mobile Investigation, West Dispatch.'

Whoever it was was almost shouting. And young.

'This is Mikami, from Media Relations in headquarters. Is your captain there?'

There was a short pause. 'I can't put him on.'

'Why not?'

'He's gone out.'

'Where to?'

'I don't know.'

'You don't know?'

'Sorry, I've got another call—'

The external line was ringing again. Mikami picked up after slamming down the internal line. He heard Mikumo speaking in a subdued voice.

'There's no one here except for Satake, from Fingerprinting. He's on the phone.'

Kuramae was the next to call.

'Sir . . . Chief Ochiai is the only person in the Second Division office . . . he looks panicked. He's shouting to someone on the phone, saying all his staff are gone, asking where they went.'

They had all vanished, leaving their career-officer chief by himself.

Abandoning their posts? No, some kind of insurrection.

Mikami shuddered.

Criminal Investigations had disappeared. First and Second Division. Mobile Investigations. Forensics. They had all vanished without trace.

61

It didn't seem real.

Mikami charged up the stairwell. He ran into Ishii, who was coming down, on one of the landings.

'Mikami! Is it true? That no one's in Second Division?'

Mikami didn't stop. Bringing up an arm, he knocked Ishii to one side and continued up. He was out of breath as he walked along the fourth-floor corridor. The sound of ringing echoed from each of the division offices. Kuramae and Mikumo were both standing in the corridor, looking anxious; most likely, they'd been shut out. They hurried over as soon as they saw him.

'Go and check the department garages. I want to know whose cars are here and whose are missing.'

Mikami gave his instructions as he walked by; picking up speed, he pushed open the doors to First Division. Two heads in the whole office. Suwa's looked around in surprise. He was standing next to the island of desks that made up Investigative Planning but was clearly hesitating, somehow diminished by being in enemy territory. The young desk worker was on the phone. He had another in his right hand; another was off the hook on a desk a little further off.

'Sorry, the phones haven't stopped ringing,' Suwa whispered.

From what he could gather, they were all regular business calls. Mikami nodded, standing in front of the man, where he'd have no choice but to acknowledge his presence. Hashimoto. Mikami knew his surname, but that was all. He failed to conceal his fright. He looked away, then turned his back. *Hey*. He didn't respond. Mikami pressed firmly down on the cradle of the phone Hashimoto was using.

'Huh . . . what the . . .'

Hashimoto wheeled around, eyes wide. Mikami depressed the cradle on the second phone, then brought his head in close.

'Where is Arakida?'

'I don't know.'

'What about Matsuoka?'

'I don't know.'

'And everyone else?'

'Out, work . . .'

Another phone started to ring on a nearby desk. Hashimoto made a move to go over, but Mikami side-stepped to block the way.

'Please move. I can't do my job with you here.'

'I don't think *anyone's* doing their job. Not Arakida, not any of you.'

'That's not true.'

'Where are they?'

'I already told you, I don't know.'

'Someone must have given you a number to call if something important came in.'

'No.'

'You think you can do your job without one?'

'You don't need to worry.'

'Think for a moment. Even minding the office, you're an accessory to this.'

'Accessory?' Hashimoto wailed. 'If anyone's an accessory to anything, it's Admin, and the NPA.'

'Good. You should be taking out your frustration on *us*. What the hell are you doing taking it to the outside? Criminal Investigations, vacant. You're turning a blind eye on crime, on murder. You think you're still officers of the law?'

'You're in no position to lecture us.'

'I need to talk with Arakida. Tell me where he is.'

'Right, sure.'

When hell freezes over. It was written on his face. A phone rang on a desk towards the back of the room. This time, Mikami stood aside, letting Hashimoto dash over. He couldn't afford to waste time wrestling with an underling. He caught Suwa by the shoulder.

'Stay on him. He'll let something slip eventually. And call me the moment anyone higher than inspector turns up.'

His mobile started to buzz. Kuramae.

'I just finished checking the garages. So . . . all the cars from Mobile Investigations are missing, as are most of the enforcement vehicles. The Forensics mini-van is gone, too.'

That much was standard.

'What about management?'

'Right . . . uh, hang on.'

Mikumo replaced him on the line.

'Director Arakida and Chief Adviser Matsuoka's cars are still here, as is the Mobile Command Centre's. The same for the chief of Forensics', and the captain of Mobile Investigations'.'

Which meant they were still inside the headquarters.

'Hold the line.'

Keeping the phone line open, Mikami stepped out of First Division. He walked the length of the corridor and pushed against the wind to open the steel door leading to the emergency staircase. Directly ahead was the north building, beyond a connecting passageway. Off to the right, the three-storey annexe housing Transport and the red-brown roof of the archive warehouse. Mikami leaned over the guardrail and peered straight down. Two small figures stood in the courtyard outside the garages – Kuramae and Mikumo.

'What about people?'

He spoke into his mobile; Mikumo's answer was immediate.

'We didn't see anyone in the area.'

There.

Three heads, closer to the annexe than the garages. Making their way across the courtyard. Carrying something on their shoulders. It looked cylindrical. A carpet? A roll of paper? A large map? They entered a blind spot and disappeared around the back of the building. The route led to a wall. A dead end; there wasn't anything there. Except . . . an emergency staircase, outside the back of the building. Transport only took up the lower couple of floors. The second floor housed the station's assembly hall.

Mikami held his mobile to his ear.

'Mikumo, go back to the office. Act as though nothing's happening. Tell Kuramae he's to report in to First Division.'

He called Suwa after hanging up.

'I've sent Kuramae your way. Get him to take over what you're doing – I want you in the assembly hall.'

'The assembly hall? You think that's where—'

'Yeah, I do.'

62

Under siege . . .

Mikami thundered down the emergency stairs, the metallic noise of each step reverberating through his skull. Each jolt pulsed up his legs, drumming so hard it felt like he might come apart.

He jogged through the courtyard and entered the annexe via the main entrance. He stopped to listen. Footsteps, coming from above. He took the goods lift to bypass the stairs. He didn't even have time to catch his breath. The bell rang as the floor indicator switched to '2'. The doors opened to the double doors of the assembly hall, a large notice reading AUTHORIZED PERSONNEL ONLY, and two men, both of whom turned to glare in his direction. The one with the beard, fierce-looking with goggle eyes, was Section Chief Ashida from Organized Crime. The other, Mikami had never seen before; younger, with a crew-cut and an abnormally large upper body. He was getting ready to salute when Ashida said something, halting him midway.

Bingo.

Certain he'd found the right place, Mikami started to walk, maintaining eye contact with the two guards. Ashida took a lazy step forwards to head him off. His scowl deepened as the distance between them continued to close; finally, he raised both hands in a *stop* gesture.

'That's far enough, I'm afraid.'

The words were courteous enough but the threat was implicit in his tone and in the look on his face. Mikami continued walking until his chest pressed up against the man's hands. Ashida was half a head taller. He'd always had to hunker forwards, each time he'd come to Mikami for his opinion on gang-related fraud. The man had a peculiar talent for forgetting obligations and grudges, switching from one day to the next. Right now, Mikami resented him for it.

'Not even going to ask my business?'

'That won't be necessary.'

'Out of the way.'

'No unauthorized personnel, sorry. Nothing I can do.'

'You're saying I'm *unauthorized* . . .?'

'Perhaps I should clarify?'

'Please do.'

'I'm under orders to send any NPA spies packing. It's a fucking disgrace. I don't know what the hell they gave you. For a detective who devoted so many years to bringing in the dirt, to betray us like this . . .'

Mikami heard the words, but his mind was already beyond the doors. *What was happening in there?* There were no sounds escaping through the door. He was six steps from the threshold. Maybe seven. Crew-cut was fully alert, marking the midpoint between the doors.

'I don't have time for games. Let me talk to whoever's in charge.'

'Not going to happen.'

'They're inside, yes? Arakida. Matsuoka, too.'

'Who knows?'

He shrugged, giving Mikami an opening. His eyes fell to his still-bandaged right hand, which shot straight up towards Ashida's exposed neck. He widened his stance as it connected with the man's throat, sending Ashida's large frame reeling backwards. He clamped his other hand over Ashida's as it came snapping up to grab at his wrist. Crew-cut shifted menacingly forwards. It was the moment Mikami had been waiting for. He wrenched his hand from Ashida's throat and shoved the stumbling man into his partner, dodging to one side as he did. He ducked as a log-sized arm exploded through the air next to him then he broke into a run, directing all his momentum into a kick that landed in the middle of the doors.

The spectacle burst open before him. *Incredible*. The single word travelled directly from his eyes into his brain, devoid of any emotional content.

Shocked at the sudden noise, all the faces inside turned around. There were fifty . . . a hundred. Maybe more. All packed together. Long desks stretched from one side of the large space to the other, proportionate to the vast number of personnel. As though time had ground to a halt, they all stopped what they were doing – carrying boxes, moving whiteboards, setting up communications, spreading outline maps on the floor – and stared. Not all of the faces belonged to detectives. The chief of Forensics was there. Next to him, the assistant chief of Community Safety. Towards the back of the room, the vice-captain of Mobile Investigations. Also the chief of Local Community, the assistant chief of Transport Regulation and the captain of the Vehicular Patrol Unit.

It wasn't just Criminal Investigations. Apart from Administrative Affairs, every function of the Prefectural HQ was taking part in the preparation to stand siege.

Mikami was horrified. What were they doing about the rest of the prefecture? Were the police still functioning? Would they be able to respond if a new case came in? What about the car patrols? Foot patrols? The officers in the *koban*? Accident-response teams? Was it possible? Was this to be the Prefectural HQ's endgame under Arakida's direction? This went beyond mere sabotage. In order to force the commissioner into calling off his trip, the director had decided to take the safety of the entire prefecture hostage, send the tremors all the way to Tokyo.

It was an act of insanity. If Mikami was right, it was nothing less than a *coup d'état*.

He couldn't take a step further. Ashida had him in a full nelson from behind. *Just you try it.* The man whispered angrily into his ears.

'I've seen you all!' Mikami bellowed into the hall.

Seconds later, Crew-cut had the doors shut and was glaring into Mikami's eyes, his own dripping with enmity.

'You're riot squad, right?'

The man looked back with an expression that said: *what else?*

'Then report to your unit *right now*. You're not paid to protect us.' Mikami shook his head violently. Ashida's hold didn't budge. 'Let me go, now.'

'I don't think so, Mikami. Not after a dirty trick like that.'

'Dirty trick? Weren't they *your* speciality?'

'Mikami, not in front of our friend here.'

'Okay, just let me go.'

'No more trouble?'

'Trouble, right . . .'

'No more chances, Mikami. I'm going to have to ask that you leave quietly.'

Mikami hadn't seen any key faces. *Director Arakida. Chief Adviser and First Division Chief Matsuoka.* Had they been in there? Or were they . . .

He heard footsteps. It was Suwa, running up the stairs. Crew-cut overreacted, dropping immediately into a low fighting stance. As Suwa recoiled in fright, Ashida gave him a casual greeting. Mikami suddenly regained his freedom of motion. A pair of hands shoved him on the back, propelling him forwards.

'Suwa, do me a favour and show your boss out.'

It was clear by Ashida's tone that he and Suwa knew each other, either from school or from having joined the force together. Suwa seemed to be at a loss for words. Just as in First Division, he seemed to be intimidated. That was why Mikami had called him. The star player of Media Relations was useless if he lived in fear of Criminal Investigations. Mikami beckoned him over, flexing his neck and shoulders. Now he could move again, he realized just how strong Ashida's grip had been. The atmosphere hadn't relaxed. Crew-cut stood like a rock, utterly silent, even more determined to let nothing pass. Ashida was massaging his neck, but none of the tension had left his frame. He was an ox, someone who'd fought in national-level judo tournaments when he'd been younger. *Even so . . .*

Mikami couldn't just turn tail and run. He couldn't picture himself worrying at his desk. He drew Suwa closer and held up a hand, whispering in his ear.

'Go to the toilets, on the first floor.'

'Sorry?'

'I need a pole. Get a mop, take off the end.'

Suwa seemed to convulse. As he walked away, Mikami gave him a sharp nudge. Ashida snorted as he watched Suwa stumble his way down the stairs.

'Make all the reports you want. Or was that a call for back-up?'

Mikami turned back towards Ashida.

'You think we're the enemy?'

Ashida issued another snort. 'You? You're just small fry. It's the sharks in Tokyo – they're the ones trying to devour everything in their way. I can't excuse them.'

'You get eaten if you're weak. What right do you have to complain?'

The light in Ashida's eyes shifted.

'You mean that?'

'Arrest every murderer we've failed to bring in. String up every corrupt mayor out there. Wipe out organized crime. No one will come looking to take your jobs then.'

'You've let greed get the better of you. Becoming a damned mouthpiece for Tokyo . . .'

'You're all deluded. Getting all teary-eyed over a single posting. Are you really willing to abandon the 1,820,000 citizens of Prefecture D just to protect a single, useless job?'

'What the hell are you talking about? When have we ever given up on the people?'

'Go back to school, start at square one. If we turn our back on keeping the peace, we might as well be inciting violence. If we do that, as representatives of the state, we're worse than the gangs you deal with.'

Mikami looked behind him. Suwa had just got back. He was pale. His unnatural gait told Mikami he had the pole hidden behind him.

'Now!'

Suwa instinctively complied. A moment later, the pole was in Mikami's hands. It felt too long. But it would do. And Mikami knew he could trust his right hand, having already used it on Ashida's throat.

'You shit,' Ashida growled.

He was already retreating. As a former practitioner of judo, he would know to be afraid of the sword. The same wasn't true of Crew-cut. He looked completely unperturbed. His riot-squad training had probably kicked in. His shoulders had come up and he looked about to charge. It wouldn't be a problem to take him down. But could Mikami do it without hurting him?

Mikami faced him, tensing his grip on the pole. In that instant he saw an image of Futawatari. Where was he during all this? Failing to keep Criminal Investigations in check, he'd actually spurred them to rampage. Had he seen no choice but to surrender?

'Crush the bastard,' Ashida ordered.

Crew-cut drew back his chin and crossed his arms to shield his face. He was going to throw himself in, let his body do the work; taking a hit or a jab was irrelevant. His eyes were wide and alert. The solid muscles over his shoulders suddenly tensed. *Come on then*. It happened the moment Mikami sank into deep concentration. A click came from the door behind Crew-cut.

It opened.

The tension took on another form. A man stepped out – Assistant Chief Mikura. *An ant's balls . . .* He stood there with authority, not looking that way at all. It didn't look like he was there to control the noise outside the door. He looked straight past Ashida and Crew-Cut, focusing his gaze on Mikami.

'We need to talk.'

'About what?'

The pole was still raised. Mikura stepped forwards but kept himself just out of range.

'There's a message from the director.'

'Don't make me say it again – about what?'

'You need to get the press to sign a coverage agreement.'

He couldn't make sense of the man's words.

'What are you talking about?'

'We've had a kidnapping.'

'A . . . kidnapping?'

'That's right. We have a name, Sato. He's issued a demand for 20 million in cash.'

Mikami's eyes blinked in disbelief. *Sato. 20 million yen.* All the colour around him seemed to drain to sepia. In his mind, he saw an image of Shoko Amamiya's death mask. *The spectre of Six Four.* He turned to look at Ashida. Crew-cut. Then Mikura. Each of their expressions attested to the truth. It wasn't a siege. The communications equipment. The maps. The sheer number of investigators present. They were getting everything in place. The assembly hall had been established as the base of operations – the Investigative HQ.

The pole rolled on to the floor with an audible *clunk*. With the sound, everything Mikami had believed in until that moment began to fall apart.

63

Six Four. They would drag the kidnapper back into the sixty-fourth year of Showa, put him in cuffs. A pledge, unfulfilled even though they were fourteen years into Heisei – now a voice from Showa had emerged to call them back. *Sato. 20 million yen.* Was it a copycat? Someone out for a kick? Or was it . . .

Mikami pulled Mikura into a small room located to one side of the hall. Suwa was having difficulty unfolding their chairs; his hands were shaking, refusing to obey him.

'Give me the details,' Mikami said, taking a seat.

Mikura remained standing, having turned down the offer. 'The victim is a girl from a high school in Genbu City.'

A girl. High-school student. The resemblance to Six Four began to degrade. The victim wasn't in primary school – she was someone in high school, Ayumi's age. Genbu's population was 140,000. It was located in the middle of the prefecture, fifteen kilometres east of City D. Station G had jurisdiction.

'Here.'

Mikura held out a couple of sheets from inside his jacket pocket. The standardized header jumped from the page in printed font:

Attn: Press Club, Prefecture D Police Headquarters
Regarding: Proposal for Press Coverage Agreement
11 December, Heisei 14. Criminal Investigations Director, Prefectural Headquarters.

Mikami grabbed the sheets.

*As of 11 December, Heisei 14, a kidnapping investigation —
detailed below — is being held under the jurisdiction of Station G.
It is believed that press coverage may present a danger to the victim's safety. As such, the following terms are proposed to establish
a Press Coverage Agreement to regulate reporting activities.
While the agreement remains in effect, Criminal Investigations
agrees to convey all details of the progress of the investigation to the
press.*

Terms:
- *The press agree to refrain from interviews and all other reporting
  activities for the duration of the investigation.*
- *Should the victim be discovered or be brought into safe custody, or
  in the case where it is decided that reporting activities no longer pose
  a danger to the victim, a representative of the Press Club may enter
  discussions with the director of Criminal Investigations regarding
  the termination of the agreement.*
- *Once the details of termination have been agreed upon, the Press
  Club may decide the date of termination.*
- *In cases where the investigation continues (and the agreement
  therefore remains in effect) for an extended period of time, a representative of the Press Club is to hold ongoing discussions with
  Criminal Investigations to discuss possible amendments to the
  agreement.*

Mikami skimmed the page, then turned it over. His interest
lay in the details that followed.

Details:
*Kidnapping and ransom of a female high-school student, Genbu
City.*

Here, the contents were recorded in an untidy scrawl.

Victim C (17). Eldest daughter of A (49, self-employed) and B (42, housewife). Second-year student in private high school.

Their identities were being kept anonymous. Mikami felt his cheek twitch.

Kidnapping reported at 11.27, 11 December. Victim's father, A, called 110 to notify Contact Management in the Prefectural HQ of his daughter's kidnapping.

Mikami checked his watch. Two thirty-five. Already three hours since the kidnapping was reported. Mikami's eyes bored into the page as he continued.

Calls from the kidnapper:

#1 Made to home phone from C's mobile at 11.02, 11 December. B answers. Kidnapper does not give name, speaks in altered voice (helium or similar) and issues ransom demands.
'I've got your daughter. If you want to see her alive again, get 20 million yen ready by midday tomorrow.'
B phoned A's office. A reports kidnapping to 110.

#2 Received 12.05, 11 December. As before, kidnapper speaks in altered voice, call made from C's mobile. A answers, having rushed home.
'This is Sato. I want used bills. Put the money in the largest suitcase you can buy at Marukoshi. Bring it to the location I give you tomorrow, and come alone.'

Urgent investigation is in process.
End.

Mikami was speechless. He was horrified. The similarities to Six Four were unbearable: *midday tomorrow, 20 million yen, Sato, used bills, Marukoshi, the largest suitcase, come alone.* Even the detail of the kidnapper not giving his name during the first call then calling himself Sato was the same. *The voice of a man in his thirties or forties, slightly hoarse, with no trace of an accent.* That was the only difference. No – even that was unclear, because the kidnapper had altered his voice.

The same man . . . a repeat offence. Nothing in the details refuted the possibility. Even so, Mikami had a gut feeling that that wasn't it. During Six Four, nothing had happened to suggest the kidnapper was doing it out of enjoyment. The crime was desperate, urgent, executed to obtain the large sum of money to be paid out for the ransom. It didn't make sense that the same person would show off by staging a repeat performance. Even supposing it was him, he would surely have made every effort to strip away any resemblance to Six Four, made sure that there was nothing to suggest a link between the two cases.

Mikami felt like he was coming back up for air.

This wasn't Showa calling them back. The case belonged to Heisei. It was new, unrelated to Six Four. And the kidnapping had taken place only moments – no, it was already three hours – earlier.

'You need to make sure the agreement is signed, without delay.'

Mikura's voice sounded from above, completely lacking any self-awareness. *Without delay.* Mikami looked at him through upturned eyes.

'How dare you.'

'Hmm?'

'It's been three hours since the kidnapping was reported. After this long, and with a flimsy sheet like this, do you really think they're going to just smile and play along?'

'I don't see why not. Besides, it's my understanding that a

provisional agreement comes into effect automatically, the moment we notify them of a kidnapping.'

'That's right.' It was a safety measure, to stop the press from taking advantage of the time between notification and the signing of the agreement. 'But what do you propose if they decide not to sign? If they refuse after having discussed the terms, the provisional agreement ends and they get a free reign on reporting. What you need to understand is that they only agree to our terms because we promise to give them detailed intel from the investigation, and at the earliest opportunity.'

'And you have it now.'

Mikami struck the papers in his hand. 'This is barely even an outline. I need all the details covering the last three hours – on the progress of the investigation, and everything you know about the kidnapping. The moment the press hear of this you'll have hundreds of reporters and camera units charging in from Tokyo. You won't be able to control them with this kind of attitude.'

'Well, of course not,' Mikura answered, sounding offended. 'If necessary, I am able to supply extra information myself, to the extent of my knowledge.'

'Okay, good. Then give me some more. First, I need full names. Let's start with the victim herself.'

Suwa fumbled for his memo pad. His pen remained still in his hand.

'I can't give you their names.'

'What?' Mikami's anger spilled over. He'd read the files on the press and kidnapping. There were no precedents for any headquarters giving the press anonymous information. 'Why not?'

'It can't be helped.'

'Why?'

'Because . . . there's a chance this is a hoax. That someone's just pretending to copy Six Four.'

'A hoax? You think it's a hoax just because it resembles Six Four?'

'Not just that.'

'Then tell me why. The calls were made from the victim's mobile, right?'

Mikami glanced down at the papers. *Call made from C's mobile.* No ambiguity. Which meant that the parents' home phone had caller-display functionality. And that the investigators had already finished confirming the record with the phone companies.

In which case . . .

'So you've got reason to believe that the kidnapper found, maybe stole, the daughter's phone? You've got something that suggests that?'

Mikura gave a churlish sigh and shook his head.

'No, that's not what I mean. Just that, at the moment, we can't dismiss the possibility that this is the girl's own doing.'

Her own doing? Mikami drew back. The daughter staging her own kidnapping?

'She has issues, you see. She hardly goes home, only when it's to ask for money or pick up a change of clothes. She's *registered* with the high school, but spends all her time – day and night – hanging around with friends. The truth is, her whereabouts have been unknown since she left home a couple of nights ago. It's our view that she's either teamed up with a man she knows, or that someone's putting her up to this. We don't know if she's making a real attempt at getting the 20 million or if she's just done this as a prank. She's capable of either.'

It didn't sound right.

'The girl's seventeen. Are you saying this *boyfriend* looked fourteen years back to research Six Four?'

'With a mobile, she could contact someone in their fifties, even local Yakuza, in just minutes. Even if the guy was younger, it's easy to find out about Six Four. You only need enter "kidnapping" into your computer . . . it's all Six Four. And unsolved means successful, so it's easy to see why they'd choose it as a model.'

Mikami didn't agree. The idea didn't hold together. It sounded made up, a fancy born of hypothesis and conjecture.

'That's why you can't give me the girl's name?'

'It's cause enough. It will be fatal if we were to announce her name to the public – bearing in mind she's a juvenile – and then have the case turn out to be a hoax.'

'Publicly? Don't misunderstand this. We give the press her name in a private capacity. They can't print a word with a coverage agreement in place, not until the ban is lifted. Even if it did end up as a hoax and the agreement was nullified, they *still* couldn't print her name – she would fall under juvenile law. There's no danger of her name getting out.'

'That's not what would happen. The press would crowd around her home the moment the agreement was lifted. We're talking about a high-school student who faked her own kidnapping. There's money, men, family breakdown. It's a goldmine for them. The tabloids will come and join the fray, as will the TV. Whether or not her name gets out, the family will become the victims of a media storm.'

Mikami was tired of hearing this kind of excuse. No – he was tired of reeling it out himself.

'That's why Media Relations exists, to prevent that from happening. Just let us get on with our job.'

'I can't, the case is too big. The girl will end up being the focus of all the excitement that gets generated around a kidnapping and ransom – the anger, too, if it's a hoax.'

'It's because the case is big that I'm telling you this. What if it turns out not to be a hoax? That's when the real bloodbath starts, unless you have a coverage agreement in effect.'

'Hence we're preparing for both eventualities. We keep her identity secret, but we also convey everything we know about the case. Like I just told you.'

'The identity is non-negotiable. Take me to Arakida if you're not prepared to tell me yourself.'

'I'm in charge of this. Nobody else will respond to you,' Mikura said, matter-of-fact.

He'd left Mikami with no room for leverage. When dealing with a big case, it seemed even someone with 'ant's balls' was able to step up their game.

Mikami checked his watch, his restlessness trumping anger and frustration. The situation was worsening with each passing moment. The reporters didn't even know the kidnapping had occurred. Three hours and twenty-four minutes since the report. Already dangerously close to cover-up territory. Mikami pulled off the clip fastening the two sheets and pressed the one containing the details into Suwa's hands.

'Copy that down.'

'Sir?'

'When you're done, notify the Press Club.'

There was sudden fear in his eyes. 'Sir, like this? Without the names?'

'That's right.'

Suwa was staring into empty space, no doubt having glimpsed the maelstrom of anger that would ensue. This was yesterday's today. They were trying to resurrect anonymous reporting despite the promise they had just made – and for a kidnapping and ransom, a case the press would unanimously deem of the utmost importance.

'Suwa.'

'But . . . sir . . .' Suwa's expression was the same as that of yesterday.

It would be close to impossible to repeal the right, once we've given it to them. The resistance would be many, many times that of if they hadn't had it in the first place.

That's why we won't take it away. We'll see it through.

They would be closing the window.

But the situation was too pressing to hold off. And there were other reasons to notify the press as fast as possible. Their tentacles were not to be underestimated. Each of the papers had its own unique web of contacts, covering the entirety of the prefecture. If one was to notice something unusual in Genbu . . . If they started to sniff around, not knowing it was a kidnapping . . . And if the kidnapper was to notice their activity . . .

An image of Ayumi flashed into being under closed eyelids, her face puffy with tears. There was nothing to guarantee the kidnapping was a hoax. No reason to assume it was. The life of a seventeen-year-old girl hung in the balance – every moment counted.

'Copy it down, now! I want the press notified – and the provisional agreement in effect – in the next five minutes.'

'They'll never sign the official agreement, not without names. They'll riot. We won't even be able to hold a discussion.'

'Tell them we're working on a second and a third announcement to follow. Do what you can to get the foundations in place.'

'I can't do that, not in—'

'You will. I'll get the names. All I'm asking you to do is keep the peace until then. You'll be press director one day – you've got to do it.'

Everything went quiet. Suwa's eyes were distracted when he looked at Mikami. Finally, he collapsed into a chair, bit down on his lip and opened his memo pad, holding the report in one hand.

Mikami's eyes came back up.

'I can't give you their names,' Mikura said, anticipating Mikami's question.

But Mikami had something else in mind when he pulled out his notebook and pen. 'Do you know if the kidnapper is male or female?'

'Sorry, what?'

'The helium. What did the girl's mother think?'

'Uh . . .'

'I don't have time to mess around, Mikura.'

The man wanted to object, but nodded. 'She couldn't tell whether the voice was male or female.'

Mikami was still writing when he asked his next question. 'What about an accent?'

'She wasn't sure. I don't think it would stand out either way, not with the helium, not unless the accent was particularly strong.'

'The kidnapper didn't give a name during the first call?'

'According to the girl's mother, no. But she was pretty distraught.'

'*She dies if you talk to the police.* Did they say anything like that?'

The kidnapper had during Six Four, on the first call.

'I don't think so.'

Mikami's eyes travelled to Suwa's hands.

'Yet it still took her parents twenty-five minutes to report it in. What were they doing?'

'Trying to call their daughter on her mobile. And they were worried about reporting it. The kidnapper hadn't made it explicit, but they were still afraid their daughter might be killed if they involved us. They'd had to discuss it first.'

Suwa had flipped his pad shut and was getting to his feet. Mikami finished writing and tore the page from his notebook. He handed this and the first sheet of the proposal over.

'I'm counting on you.'

Suwa made a deep nod, looking determined. 'I'll be waiting for the follow-up,' he said quietly, before jogging out of the room.

Mikami knew he couldn't return without the names. His mind made up, he turned back towards Mikura. Just then, his phone went off in his jacket pocket. It was Ishii.

'Mikami, were you able to—'

'There's been a kidnapping.'

'A kidnapping?'

'I'm getting more details. Suwa is en route to Media Relations.

Get in touch with him,' Mikami dictated. He ended the call. As he did, Ishii's voice had rattled, shrill against his eardrums.

But, that means the commissioner can't—

Mikami folded his phone shut and placed it on the desk. *The commissioner's visit.* He had forgotten all about it. The shock and mystery evoked by the kidnapping had had no effect on Ishii. His position as an office worker, a police officer in title alone, had let him forge an instant connection between the case and what was happening the following day.

Ishii was right. Exactly right. There was no way Commissioner Kozuka could come, not now.

They were in the midst of a brand-new kidnapping. To imagine the commissioner walking into this chaos to inspect a kidnapping from fourteen years earlier . . . Mikami couldn't think of anything more absurd. What would he do, then? Would he force through the inspection, anyway, but reframe it as a visit to the front lines? Or would he use the kidnapping as an excuse to seize control? Would he arrive with a team from the bureau to lead the Investigative HQ, parade NPA leadership as established fact? No, it was too risky. If the kidnapper were to escape, it would be the same as entering into a suicide pact with the Prefectural HQ. They would lose face before the nation and never be able to bring up sequestration again. The visit would be postponed or cancelled outright. As of now – unless the kidnapping was solved straight away – the visit would not be going ahead.

There was no great impact. Mikami's emotional dial registered no disappointment, no sense of comfort; no exhilaration. All he was left to do was contemplate the irony, almost predestined, of the outcome. *The spectre of Six Four ending the Six Four inspection.* The prefecture had become Dallas after all, but because of *Sato*, not because of the Prefectural HQ or Criminal Investigations.

'Is that enough for now?' Mikura sounded impatient.

Mikami examined the man again. He looked into his eyes, trying to see right through them. Still an ant, but a confident ant.

That had been the impression from the start. Mikura's composure made it hard to imagine that he had, only three and a half hours earlier, been appointed as one of the lead investigators in a kidnapping case, even though it might turn out to be a hoax. *They saw it as a lucky break* – the idea was repugnant but it was there, regardless. The kidnapping had saved Criminal Investigations from the commissioner's visit.

'Well, if you don't have any more questions, I'll—'

'Of course I've got more bloody questions. My information is three and a half hours out of date,' Mikami said, abandoning decorum as he opened his notebook again. 'Come on, then . . . the girl's mother tried calling her daughter on her mobile. What happened next?'

'She couldn't get through.'

'That's still the case?'

'Yes. There's no signal from the phone at all; the battery's probably been taken out.'

'Who's the provider?'

'DoCoMo.'

'Have you been able to contact any of her friends?'

'Her parents don't even know their surnames, so . . .'

Mikami flipped a page. 'So they did a bad job of raising her?'

'They smothered her. It seems her delinquency probably resulted from their excessive interference, when she was in primary and secondary school.'

'Whose opinion is that?'

'A city counsellor. One her parents took her to see once.'

Mikami felt a throbbing in his ear.

'Why did she go home two nights ago?'

'To pick up some clothes.'

'How was she acting? Anything out of the ordinary?'

'She didn't say anything, although for her that's apparently normal.'

Mikami turned to a new page.

'What about warnings, of the kidnapping?'

'They had some silent calls.'

The throbbing again.

'How many?'

'Not sure. We're still getting information from the parents.'

'When did they get the calls?'

'Around ten days ago.'

'And the number?'

'Hmm?'

'They've got caller display, right?'

'Ah, yes. They said the call was made from a phone box.'

Mikami felt a door creak open in his mind. He was letting his emotions get in the way.

'Anything else of note?'

'The girl's mother said she saw a black van she didn't recognize parked near the house.'

'When was that?'

'Three, maybe four days ago.'

'Could they think of anyone who might bear them a grudge?'

'They didn't think so.'

'What about the phone? Were there any reports of it being lost?'

'How do you mean?'

'From the girl. Maybe at a *koban*?'

'Oh, we haven't asked that. Still, if she had, this wouldn't be a kidnapping—'

'Have you asked the *koban* to report in?'

'Well, no, we—'

'You need to do that. Not just for phones – there's a chance it came in as a bag.'

Mikura gave him a perfunctory, uninterested nod.

Mikami turned a page and continued.

'When did the Home Unit get there? How many officers?'

'I don't know the exact time. Five officers.'

'Did you get the second call on tape?'

'We didn't get there in time.'

'What area was the kidnapper calling from?'

'Uh . . .?'

'I'm asking which base station picked up the outgoing signal? You have a three-kilometre radius around the station. You have checked with DoCoMo, right?'

'All I know is that the call originated inside the prefecture.'

He'd dodged the answer. Was he hiding something?

'Find out and let me know.'

'Okay, I'll ask.'

'Her father is self-employed; what kind of business is it?'

'Telling you that would give away their identity.'

'Okay, so a business with few competitors. Some kind of store?'

'I suppose, yes, that's right.'

'Based?'

'In Genbu, in the city.'

'Are they well off?'

'They said they could just about put the ransom together.'

'Does the girl have any other siblings?'

'Yes, a younger sister.'

'How old?'

'Eleven. Year six in primary school.'

'Year six . . .'

Mikami stopped writing. The kidnapper had chosen the elder, not the younger of the two.

'Exactly – that's one of the reasons we thought it might be the girl's own doing.' There was something like pride in his voice.

'Maybe the kidnapper was poorly organized. Maybe the crime was sexually motivated at first. Maybe the kidnapper was someone she knew. Surely there are lots of possible interpretations?'

'Well, yes, I suppose.'

Mikura was acting disinterested, just as he had when Mikami had asked about the lost-property reports. Something was wrong.

The kidnapping had only just taken place. In light of that, weren't they putting far too much emphasis on the idea that it was a hoax? Was that why Mikura's statements lacked any sense of urgency?

Maybe there was more. Maybe they had evidence, something decisive enough to convince the Investigative HQ that the case was a hoax. It would make sense then. It was possible Mikura's self-possession stemmed not from the cancellation of the commissioner's visit but from the optimism he had regarding the case.

Mikami closed his notebook.

'Why are you keeping Admin out of this?'

'Excuse me?'

'In the assembly hall I saw management from Security, Community Safety, even Transport. Why were you so quick to bring them in, yet kept us out for three and a half hours?'

'It's just a matter of priority,' Mikura answered, with no hesitation. 'We would need to dispatch the riot squad for the search if any of the girl's things were found. Transport can pretend to be pest control while carrying out number plate checks, collecting fingerprints. Community Safety can—'

'What about Logistics?' Mikami asked, cutting him off. 'I'm pretty sure the first thing you need to establish an Investigative HQ is a budget and equipment.'

'We didn't think of it straight away. But that can be fixed retrospectively, unlike the investigation.'

'What about PR, can that be fixed retrospectively? Didn't you see a problem in delaying things with the press? Did Arakida tell you it was fine?'

'That's . . .'

Mikura hesitated. Mikami'd hit the mark.

'You kept us out deliberately. That's it, isn't it?'

'No, that's not—'

'How long were you planning to keep us out, if I hadn't shown up?'

Mikura fell silent.

'Do you understand what you've done? A high-school girl is missing. Her parents received calls from someone purporting to be her kidnapper. Yet your mind was on something *other* than the case. This is a sham. You let an internal struggle influence the investigation of a kidnapping. No – you *used* the kidnapping . . . as retaliation against Tokyo? As a warning? Insurance? How could you support something so reprehensible?'

'You're the sham.'

Mikami ignored him and carried on. 'You know it's a hoax. That's why you're reacting this way.'

'We know nothing of the sort. It's possible it's a hoax, that's all. Our focus is on bringing the kidnapper to justice. You're being paranoid if you think we're shutting you out. You're only making the accusation because you're feeling slighted.'

'If that's true, why keep her identity secret?'

'I already told you. For as long as the chance exists, however remote, that this is a teenager's hoax—'

'I don't mean from the press! I'm asking you why you're keeping their identities secret from Admin.'

Mikami's phone started to vibrate across the top of the desk. Keeping his gaze locked on Mikura, he reached to pick it up. It was Kuramae.

'Sir, I managed to discover Chief Matsuoka's whereabouts. He went to Station G in one of the enforcement vehicles.'

'You're sure?'

'Ah, yes. Five or six phones started ringing together so I answered one without thinking . . . anyway, it was from Station G.'

'Okay, good work. Go back to the office and chase it up with Suwa.'

Mikami ended the call. Mikura looked as though his response was ready.

'Go on, then.'

'We no longer feel able to share important information with Admin. You sold us out to Tokyo.'

'Yeah, and I'm sick of hearing that. If you insist this isn't all a sham, give me the identity of the girl and the family.'

Mikura let out a shallow sigh, then added coolly, 'This isn't Admin's business. Nobody needs to know, ever.'

Mikami felt his head pitch. *The true essence of the police. Utterly self-contained*. Mikami had shared the same opinion. In his many years working as a detective, he'd taken this kind of exclusion as a matter of course. But . . .

Now a part of him saw things from the outside.

This isn't Admin's business.

Nobody needs to know, ever.

He could already see how a reporter would respond.

A, self-employed. B . . . C . . . How can we be sure they even exist?

64

The dust was swirling, getting into Mikami's eyes.

He got into his car, rubbing them as he checked the digital display. Three fifteen. He took out his mobile and called Media Relations. The moment it connected, his ears were subjected to a barrage of noise. Angry shouts, hurled back and forth. *You think this is some kind of joke? Give us their names! Was everything you said a plain lie?* The reporters were irate, and Suwa was taking the fire. Mikami got a vivid sense of how close they were.

Mikumo had answered the call. He heard a female voice.

'Can you hear this?'

'Hello? Can you hear me?'

'Have all of the papers been notified?'

'Sorry, sir, I can't really hear . . .'

Mikami raised his voice. 'Is the provisional agreement in effect?'

'Ah, yes . . .' There was a rustling; the din quietened a little. It sounded like Mikumo had ducked under her desk. 'Yes, it is. But a lot of the papers are refusing to comply unless we give them the names. They're threatening to send reporters into Genbu.'

'The agreement is still binding, however temporary. Make sure they don't go against it.'

'They're saying after three and a half hours it's too late. One said they already had someone in Station G earlier today, to cover an accident; now they intend to send someone else.'

'You can't let them. Tell them they're not to go anywhere near Station G. If they do, they're in direct violation.'

'Kuramae's trying to talk them down. He's telling them it's a possible hoax, that that's what's delaying the release. They're not listening, though. They're really worked—'

'I've got another report. Can you take this down?'

'Sure, one second.' The level of noise jumped sharply, then became muffled again. 'Okay, go ahead.'

Mikami read out Mikura's additional information. His ears picked up on the jeering between each sentence. *Where's your boss now? Get him here, this instant!* His absence was fuel to their fire.

'That's everything. Hand the notes to Suwa.'

'Sir . . . do you have the girl's name?'

'Not yet.'

Silence.

Her dismay was evident even on the phone. She could probably see that Suwa was close to breaking.

'Tell him to hold on.'

'Are you coming back?'

'I have to go to Station G. Let Suwa know, but be quiet about it.'

'When will you be back?' Her voice sounded desperate, but he knew he couldn't answer, as things were. He had no guarantee he'd even be able to meet with Matsuoka. 'Just an estimate. Can you say roughly when—'

'Tell Kuramae to go to Supplies in the Prefectural Government.'

'Sorry, where?'

'There's a conference room on the fifth floor of the west wing, it's got a capacity of over three hundred people. We need to use it for the press conference. For now, he can tell Supplies it's for an important case. We'll need space in the underground parking area, too, enough for all the press from Tokyo and neighbouring prefectures.'

'Okay, I'll pass on the message. Can I help?'

'Make sure the press understand what they *can't* do. Get them to call their head offices in Tokyo. They can't use vehicles with

486

their names on, or any kind of logo. They have to conceal the radio antennas on their broadcast vans. Tell them they aren't – under any circumstances – to go anywhere near Genbu. Also that there's a strict ban on parking in the Prefectural HQ. They aren't to do anything to give themselves away en route, and they have to use the underground car park at the Prefectural Government. From there, they need to use the goods lift and move quietly to the fifth floor.'

'But . . . that's impossible.' She was almost crying. 'They're not listening to anything we say. They'll never listen to me—'

'Tell them individually, one by one.'

'They're unanimous in saying they won't sign an official agreement. They won't stop shouting. They won't call their head offices.'

'They'll be coming whatever happens. Every paper will send all the reporters they can spare. Most likely, they're already on their way.'

No answer.

'You don't have time to think; do it now. The life of a seventeen-year-old girl is hanging in the balance. We can't arrest the kidnapper. What we *can* do is make sure the press don't get her killed.'

He started the engine without waiting for an answer.

'You're right. I'll do what I can.'

Her voice was obscured by the shouting in the background, but her determination was clear.

Mikami accelerated sharply. He pulled past the swirls of dead leaves and out of the Prefectural HQ. He rode the prefectural highway east. If traffic was light, it would take less than half an hour to reach Station G. *The life of a seventeen-year-old girl is hanging in the balance.* The words had left a bitter taste in his mouth. Not because he'd deployed them to coax Mikumo into action. Not because he felt any less concern for C now the idea of a hoax had been planted in his mind. It felt real. *Ayumi's smile. Shoko's death mask. High-school uniforms. Hair decorations, the* shichigosan festival. *Girls walking in the streets. A bright-red coat in a shop window.* Mikami's vision conjured images, mixing with memory and emotion to give C a tangible reality, furnishing her with warmth and a pulse. And yet . . .

Something was interfering with the picture.

Do they even exist?

Mikami spun the wheel, putting his foot down to overtake two cars ahead of him.

The Investigative HQ were placing too much emphasis on the theory that C had orchestrated the kidnapping herself. *They'd started with the conclusion and worked their way backwards.* Seeing Mikura's calm detachment, suspicion had wormed its way into Mikami's head. Under any normal circumstances, it would suggest he was holding some kind of trump card. If they did have some kind of irrefutable evidence that it was a hoax, then there was no case. No need to set up an Investigative HQ. And yet they had staged a dramatic occupation of the assembly hall. They had demanded that the press sign a coverage agreement, and been careful also to float the possibility that the case was a hoax. *We can stop the commissioner's visit.* Someone had had the idea. They'd decided C could play the role of instigator and were taking advantage of something they knew was a hoax to magnify the disturbance.

Mikami put a cigarette in his mouth. His hand stopped before he lit it.

But was that really it?

Was it really just chance?

It felt too perfect. Why now? The commissioner was due to arrive and claim the director's head. But a kidnapping occurred the day before the visit. A kidnapping and ransom, the kind of case that happens maybe once in every ten years in the regions. And the kidnapper was imitating Six Four, playing off the ostensible reason for the commissioner's visit: *Get 20 million yen ready by midday tomorrow*. Midday was the time scheduled for the commissioner's arrival. The lines might have been a carbon copy of Six Four, but the timing had to be more than simple chance.

They had made it look as if C was the perpetrator of the hoax, when in fact it was on a completely different scale . . .

Mikami stopped at a red light. He lit the cigarette he had in his mouth.

Do the girl and her family exist?

The answer was perhaps yes *and* no. The family existed, but not as victims of a kidnapping. It seemed possible, because Mikami knew what the police were capable of when they put their mind to something. It wouldn't be difficult to procure a victim. The investigation was a sham. Or worse . . . He didn't want to believe it, but the hypothesis stuck because he knew they *could* do it if the decision had been made.

The case was a kidnapping. Their first step would have to be setting up a 'victim's house'. As NTT would maintain records of any calls made, they wouldn't be able to use the phones of police officers or their relatives, or anyone belonging to police-affiliated organizations, for the 'victim's phone'. The quickest way to do it would be to use someone already in deep cover. It didn't have to be someone in the underworld. They would prefer some citizen they had on a leash, someone in their debt who had a weakness they could exploit, someone under their control. That way they would have no reason to fear double-dealing, or the truth slipping out. For this particular role, a married couple who lived outwardly normal lives.

Mikami thought back to one of the guards outside the assembly hall – Ashida from Organized Crime. Goggle Eyes. He had once saved a family who were running a *ryokan* business from going through with a suicide pact. The man had liked to play around and had got himself involved with a girl who was part of a Yakuza scheme; they had started blackmailing him. They raped his wife, took photos, filmed every last detail. The man had approached Ashida in private, and he worked behind the scenes to settle things with the Yakuza. They agreed to leave the man alone, but on the condition that Ashida turn a blind eye to the blackmail and violence. Ashida received a commendation from the station captain when, three months later, a couple of guns were found in one of the Yakuza group's lower-ranking offices. Mikami had later heard that Ashida had his own private room in the *ryokan*, and that the photos and tape of the owner's wife were kept there in a safe.

The case wasn't even unique. There were many couples out there hiding an unsavoury background or running from debt who would suddenly find life difficult if their secrets got out. The longer your service as an officer – particularly in the case of detectives – the greater the number of potential 'collaborators' in your network. Most crimes would never happen without there first being some kind of secret.

Yes, it would be easy enough to get a couple to act as parents. *All they needed then . . .*

Mikami stubbed out his cigarette and started forwards. The road was looking busy; he pulled in front of a truck, then back into the left lane.

All they would need then . . . was a daughter. A son would have worked just as well. If necessary, they could have got by without a kid at all, just used three different phones. One could be designated as C's, and a detective could use it to call in as the kidnapper. If they wanted to avoid the risk of using an active police officer, they only needed to ask their network, or someone already retired.

There was another possible scenario. If there *was* a 'C', some-one who hadn't come home and who didn't know that her parents were collaborating with the police, the whole kidnapping could have been created around her disappearance. She would have had to 'misplace' her phone after leaving home two nights ago. People dropped their guard; it wouldn't have mattered whether she kept it with her or in a bag, and people aren't as sensitive as animals when they're asleep. Getting the phone would have been easy for a detective working theft, someone who knew every trick in the book. If that was the case, she might have gone to a *koban* to report the phone missing. Or stolen. Whatever the case, she would remain 'kidnapped' unless the Investigative HQ decided actively to seek out the information.

Mikami realized he was moving into territory beyond normal speculation. That, if anything, the theories were closer to pure fancy. But, even then, he couldn't laugh them off.

Because the report was anonymous.

Any tale of make-believe, however far-fetched, could come alive when hidden behind a screen of anonymity. It could walk freely. Any and all developments were plausible. When it came to weaving a tale, anonymity was omnipotent, a delusion itself, one that allowed for an infinity of choice.

Through force of habit, Mikami eased off the accelerator. The billboard for the Aoi Café swept into the corner of his view. The starting point of the Six Four pursuit. If the kidnapping was real and not a hoax, if the kidnapper genuinely hoped to re-enact Six Four, then, come tomorrow, the café would be filled for the first time in fourteen years with investigators posed as couples.

If the kidnapper was Criminal Investigations, the café would be empty. The kidnapping wouldn't progress to the stage of the ransom. They only had to maintain the pretence until midday tomorrow, the time of the commissioner's scheduled arrival; at that point, they could be certain the visit would be cancelled. Still, it was likely that everything would be decided before the day was even out. Once word came in of the commissioner's decision to cancel, the case would suddenly begin to resolve itself.

Mikami let the car pick up speed again. Twenty-five to four. It was taking longer than expected.

Their objective achieved, the Investigative HQ would turn to damage limitation. Having used and enraged the press, they would use disappointment to sedate them. First, they would announce that they had taken C into custody, that the kidnapping had been fake, organized by her. That was where the idea of the hoax – already seeded – would come into its own. They would issue statement after statement, until the press were sick and tired of it all. *The girl had been acting alone; no one had forced her. She'd only wanted to hurt her parents. She'd copied an old case she found on the internet. She'd got the helium cans playing bingo at a party. She was sorry; she regretted what she'd done.*

And so on . . .

They would use the girl's age as a shield, maintaining the family's anonymity. The story would never make the mainstream news. *Press and police led on wild-goose chase during alleged kidnapping.* The papers would write sullen, anecdotal articles at most. Their anger would wither away, as would any desire to follow up the story. Even if they did want to chase it up, they would lack any direction to explore it with. *Genbu. A self-employed father. Second-year student at a private high school. Seventeen years old.* The city council and the school would be bound by confidentiality and would function as brick walls. And Criminal Investigations could convince the family to leave the prefecture.

More than anything, they had the power of fiction on their side. There was nothing to guarantee that the girl's age, or the information pertaining to her schooling, matched anything on record. There was no proof she even existed.

This isn't Admin's business. Nobody needs to know, ever.

Mikura's words would become fact. The press would never know the truth, not to mention the public. They'd chosen kidnapping. They'd known they would have to stage a kidnapping. It felt more and more plausible. The public wouldn't hear about it until it was all over. A tornado was raging in the Prefectural HQ, but it was nothing more than a storm in a teacup. No one would die and no one would be hurt. It would be reported as a hoax, so there would be no public outcry. It had impact enough to stop the commissioner in his tracks, but it carried no risk of future recrimination. It was the only viable option.

Criminal Investigations was getting ready for the endgame. Tokyo would find itself in the midst of a hurricane. They would recoil in blind horror when they were told the hoax had been the final play of the Prefecture D Criminal Investigations Department.

That's right . . . they're planning to tell Tokyo the truth.

Keeping the deception hidden was like not telling an enemy state that you'd successfully developed weapons of mass destruction. It meant nothing unless it convinced Tokyo to abandon its plans. Criminal Investigations would find a way to confess, in the process making sure Tokyo never suggested another Six Four inspection. They would send Tokyo a decapitated head, force the conclusion. How would the NPA react? Would it take it in silence, bury it deep in the ground? Or would it seek revenge and take Arakida's head, put it on public display?

Mikami gazed upwards.

The apex of Station G was visible in the distance, the *Hinomaru* flag twitching in the wind. Two minutes past four. The heavy clouds meant it was already half dark.

Matsuoka's the key . . .

Mikami muttered the words. He was sure Matsuoka would help unlock the truth, put Mikami's delusional theories to rest with a single word. It went without saying that he would have nothing to do with the sham investigation. Thinking back, it was from Matsuoka that he'd first heard the phrase. *We've been accorded the hands of god. We wash in dirty water but that doesn't mean we let it taint us. No matter how desperate you are to make an arrest, regardless of if the detention cells are empty, the one thing you must never do is permit a sham investigation.*

It came down to this: if Matsuoka was in Station G, heading up the front line of the investigation, and if his expression was that of a man hard at work, Mikami could dismiss the idea of Criminal Investigations staging a fake kidnapping.

He'll be there. I need him to be.

Matsuoka would refer to his own personal morality when choosing whether or not to divulge the family's details. That was why Mikami thought he had a chance. Regardless of whether or not he had proof that it was the girl's hoax, Matsuoka's core ideal was that a person had to reap what they sowed. He wouldn't treat the girl any differently because she was young. If Mikami confronted him one on one, honestly and rationally, there was a chance he'd cave in. And his position meant he could make the decision alone.

Mikami lit a cigarette.

He had no intention of repeating his earlier mistake. Barging into Criminal Investigations would only result in a repeat performance of the fiasco outside the assembly hall. But how was he to secure a private meeting? He needed somewhere to catch the lead commander of a kidnapping investigation by himself. It was possible that would be more difficult than getting him to talk.

Mikami frowned at the scene ahead. The station was within reach, but the traffic had come to a standstill. Eight minutes past four. He clucked his tongue as this became nine minutes past.

An image of Suwa presented itself. It seemed as if this was the first time he'd been able to picture someone on his team in detail, for one of them to appear as more than just an impression.

Hold on a little longer . . .

He stubbed out the still-long cigarette and flicked on the car's headlights. Putting them on full beam, he spun the wheel and pulled out into the oncoming lane. He put his foot down and accelerated past the unmoving cars.

The importance of full disclosure . . .

This was no longer just for Media Relations. Mikami couldn't allow anonymity to run wild; it was a monster, feeding on doubt to multiply indefinitely.

65

Mikami's hearing seemed amplified.

He could make out the dripping of water. Every few seconds a drop would strike one of the sinks, forming a regular pattern.

Station G, the third-floor toilets. Mikami was holding his breath, lying wait in a cubicle at the far end of the room. The angle was bad, so he couldn't make anybody out through the gap in the door. That left him dependent on sound. Footsteps. A sigh. A cough. Humming. Conversation, if people came in together. When he was a detective in Second Division, a reporter from the *Sankei* had often caught him this way. Mikami would ask how he knew it was him, but the reporter had always smiled and said: *it's a secret.* The reporter had finally revealed his trick when he'd called in to say goodbye, after Mikami's transfer became official. *When you wash your hands, you put the tap on full . . .*

Matsuoka always washed his face. A lot of people did, but Matsuoka had another habit when he did. After turning off the tap, he would always snap the water from his hands, a sharp movement not unlike flicking raindrops from an umbrella. The gesture made an audible *swish*. That was the sound Mikami was listening out for. He'd heard it many times when they'd been together in division.

He checked his watch. Five to five. Already thirty minutes since he'd sneaked his way in. The air in the cubicle was cold, the heating in the building apparently not extending to the corner of the toilets. Mikami propped up his jacket collar to lessen the chill, rubbing the back of his hands in turn.

He opened his mobile. No missed calls. Knowing the vibration would be too loud in silent mode, he'd set it to 'driving'. He'd called his office from the car the moment he'd arrived at the station to let his team know he'd be out of contact for a while. The phone had rung a long time before Suwa had finally picked up. As before, the tempest had been blaring in the background. Mikami had quickly given his message, then asked a question.

'Has anyone been in touch to say the visit has been cancelled?'

'No, they haven't.' Suwa had put on a snappy tone, disguising the caller from the reporters. As he hung up, he said, 'We need those spare parts as soon as possible, okay?'

A sound.

Mikami concentrated hard. Footsteps, in the corridor. Hurrying. Getting closer. At the entrance to the toilets . . . Passing by . . . The steps grew closer together. Whoever it was was going downstairs.

Only five people had entered the room in the last half-hour, and none of those had been in the last fifteen minutes. They had started a meeting, either in Criminal Investigations or the conference room beyond. That had to be it.

Mikami's theories were already losing substance, even though he hadn't seen Matsuoka. His head had begun to clear the moment he'd entered the parking area behind the station. He'd seen row after row of sedans – CID vehicles, to those who recognized them – most likely called in from neighbouring districts. At a glance, Mikami had counted four from Violent Crime in the Prefectural HQ. There wasn't a single small or compact vehicle, meaning the station staff had been made to move their personal cars somewhere else.

What he'd seen was something he'd recognized from his years as a detective – *a case in progress*. The image had also driven home how difficult it would be to bring everyone under the same illusion. If the kidnapping was a hoax, one led by Arakida, the truth would have to remain under wraps until they had the decapitated head ready for Tokyo. A handful of people managing the investigation would have to battle hard to achieve that. And it would mean having to lie to every detective gathered here. Perhaps they'd ordered the investigation without disclosing the identity of the family. Or they had disclosed their identities but not told any of the detectives they knew the investigation was a sham. Both were taboo, and both came with significant hazards. Detectives are expert at detecting lies. There was the possibility that their plan to protect Criminal Investigations could backfire, lead instead to the end of the department, if mistrust and anger started to poison the ranks.

Knowing that, could they have revealed to everyone that the investigation was a sham? No, that was impossible. The plan was maybe feasible if it involved only a handful of people . . . but it would be nothing less than reckless to bring the entire department into it. Arakida would realize that. The key unit for a detective – their bible and their rulebook – was the individual. News of Tokyo's intention to sequester the director's post had spread through the ranks, uniting everyone against the NPA, but that wouldn't be enough for the whole department to taint itself by being party to a sham. One after another, detectives would step down from their jobs. They would break confidentiality. Every generation of detectives had decent men, men like Koda.

The fact that the entire department was mobilized and functioning could only mean . . .

Mikami's eyes flicked to the side.

Footsteps.

This time, there was no need to concentrate. It was a crowd. The meeting was over. They were all heading in his direction. There was a slam as the door opened. Mikami automatically ducked his head back down.

Two. Another coming in behind them.

'Should probably take off our ties.'

'Yeah.'

They were talking casually, but Mikami didn't recognize their voices. Urinating. The footsteps outside began to fade as everyone headed downstairs. Someone was using the tap, at the sinks. Washing his hands. Another tap came on over the sound. What was the third person doing? The sound of water stopped. Two sets of footsteps, heading for the door. 'See you later.' Had that been for the one still there? There was no answer. If he'd responded with a nod, that would suggest he was their superior. Outside, the footsteps moved slowly away. Another tap came on. The sound of someone washing their hands. And . . . their face. Was it Matsuoka? The tap stopped. Mikami focused his entire being on listening. His fingers were already on the lock inside the door.

Another slam. Someone else had come in. 'Hi.' The man who'd just come in spoke. Mikami couldn't move. He hadn't heard the snap of hands. It was possible the sound of the door had masked it. Even if that had been the case, Mikami knew he couldn't risk leaving the cubicle when there were two people in the room. The man's footsteps retreated along the corridor. The second man left shortly afterwards.

A long wait followed.

Six o'clock . . . six thirty . . . seven . . . How many times must he have checked his watch? No one had tried to call his phone. What had happened to Suwa? Had he managed to hold his ground? What about Kuramae and Mikumo – were they making progress? Were the press honouring the provisional agreement? Why hadn't Akama or Ishii tried to get in touch?

Someone else walked out. There had been a constant flow of people, but Mikami still hadn't heard the sound he'd been waiting for. It was possible he'd missed it. Or that Matsuoka wasn't even in the building. The doubt worsened Mikami's anxiety. He was chilled to the bone. Most of the time, he was sitting on the toilet with the lid down, standing only occasionally to stretch his arms and legs. It was nothing compared to the extreme conditions he'd often had to endure for stake-outs in the past, but his pulse would still race each time someone entered the room, never sure when they might knock on the cubicle door.

Eleven minutes past seven. He'd just glanced at the time when the door opened again. He heard the clicking of footsteps on tiles. The man's pace was calm and composed, not slow, not hurried. Mikami's eyes stretched open. He couldn't remember the way Matsuoka walked. He'd never consciously thought about his pace, the sound his feet made. And yet . . .

It's him. He knew it instinctively.

Urinating. More footsteps. The tap came on. He was washing his hands . . . rinsing his face. The tap stopped; with it, the sound of the water. Mikami pressed his ear against the gap in the door.

Snap.

Mikami walked slowly out of the cubicle. He saw the man's shoulders first. His hands were still horizontal, pivoted like knives beneath his arms.

'Sir.'

What would it take to make him register surprise? When Matsuoka turned around it was as though nothing was wrong; he gave Mikami a casual greeting and glanced at the bandage on his right hand. Still . . . he was there. The de facto leader of Criminal Investigations was there, leading the investigation at the front.

Mikami walked closer. His knees felt weak, frozen.

'I don't mean to ambush you. I was just hoping we could talk.'

'Huh. You taking cues from the press these days?'

'I couldn't think of another way to speak to you.'

Matsuoka took a handkerchief from a trouser pocket and dabbed it over his wet face. 'I'm busy, as I'm sure you know. Make it quick.'

Mikami nodded once. 'I need to know the identity of the family.'

'I can't tell you.'

He responded without even pausing. But he hadn't sounded hostile.

'Sir. I can't keep the press under control if the family are kept anonymous – not in the case of a kidnapping. They're refusing point-blank to sign the coverage agreement.'

'Huh . . .'

'Sir?'

'That's it? That's why you're here?'

'Yes, sir.'

'*I haven't traded my soul away, not yet.* I believe that's what you said?'

There was a steely light in his eyes. He was referring to their conversation in First Division. Criminal Investigations or Administrative Affairs – throughout the conversation, Mikami had focused on the two positions and nothing else.

'Did you find out the real motive behind the visit?'

'Yes, from Arakida.'

'And yet you still work for Admin. Go to such lengths.'

'I'm not doing this for Admin *or* for Tokyo. This is simply my duty as press director. If you could think of it that way.'

'Uh-huh.'

'I can see why you don't believe me. All I can ask is that you do. This is what I have to do as press director. It is absolutely imperative that I rein the press in and get them to sign a coverage agreement. I can't go back without the names.'

Matsuoka tilted his head to one side.

'It's that important?'

'Sorry?'

'I'm asking if it's important enough to justify you waiting in ambush for me.'

Mikami took a long breath.

'I have no doubt it seems ridiculous from a detective's point of view. Unrelated to our original vocation as officers of the law. That's how I used to think, too. Keeping the peace was about making arrests. The world, a hunting ground. Now I know better. There are 260,000 officers out there, each with their own role to play.

Detectives are just a minority. The majority of our officers work out of sight, away from the limelight. They haven't been awarded the *hands of god*. But they take pride in what they do, regardless. And without their pride and their hard work – every single day of the year – an organization as huge as ours would never function. Media Relations has its own pride. Detectives mock us for reaching out to the media, but there's no shame in that. Kowtowing to Administrative Affairs, letting them force us to sever all links to the outside world – *that* would be worthy of shame.'

Matsuoka folded his arms. He was thinking about what Mikami had said. Or Mikami himself.

'I haven't sold my soul. But nor am I clinging on to my past as a detective, not any more. The distinction between Criminal Investigations and Administrative Affairs is irrelevant. All I have to do is make sure I carry out my duty to––'

The door swung suddenly open. A man came in, probably another detective. Mikami avoided his gaze. *It's over.* Just as the thought arose, Matsuoka turned around and addressed the man.

'Use downstairs.'

'Ah, of course.'

The man saluted, still looking surprised. He hurried out. Mikami looked up, using the look to convey his gratitude. He readied himself to continue.

'In many ways, Media Relations is semi-private. Sometimes it's important for us to stand our ground against Criminal Investigations. There are rules that must be adhered to for a kidnapping. Rules for the police, rules for the press, too. It's our job, in Media Relations, to ensure that both sides respect and follow these guidelines. Please, I'm asking you again. I need to know the identity of the family.'

Matsuoka relaxed his arms. His eyes were piercing, relentless.

'And so the toilet, right?'

Mikami nodded. Something else had struck him in that moment.

'That's not all, though. I need to help my team. They're battling with this even as we speak, back at HQ.'

Matsuoka's eyes drifted off. He stood like that for a while, clearly running it all through his mind. It happened without warning. Matsuoka turned his back to Mikami. He plunged his hands deep into his pockets.

Thinking out loud . . .

It hit Mikami like an electric shock. *Thank you.* Mikami mouthed the words, pulling out his notebook.

'Ma-sa-to Me-sa-ki,' Matsuoka said, his voice low. '"Masato" using the characters for "truth" and "person". "Me" as in "medicine", and "saki" from Nagasaki. Forty-nine.'

Masato Mesaki.

'He owns a sports store in Genbu. The address is: 2-4-6, 2 Chome, Ota-machi.'

Mikami was concentrating on getting it all down. His writing was a mess. He got ready for the rest.

But . . .

He looked back up, startled. Matsuoka had turned to face him again. His hands were out of his pockets. What was wrong? What about the girl's mother? What about – most importantly – the girl herself? C . . . the victim of the kidnapping.

'That's all I can give you.'

'But . . . this won't be—'

'Did you not hear me?' he threatened.

But it was too late to turn back. 'Please, reconsider. The press won't sign the coverage agreement without the girl's name.'

Matsuoka fell silent.

'If an agreement isn't put in place, the press will stampede. Hundreds of reporters, photographers. They will get in the way of the investigation.'

Still, silence.

'It's a hoax, the girl's own doing. I heard someone mention the possibility, back in HQ. I'll give the names to the press; at the same time, I'll impress on them the importance of not releasing them publicly. Even if I didn't – they understand that much. They would never think to print the name of a young girl.'

'I can't.'

'Why?'

'Some things must never be spoken.'

Never be spoken? Something felt wrong. Matsuoka had sounded as if he was cornered. Flickers of doubt resurfaced in Mikami's mind. He no longer suspected Criminal Investigations of having staged the kidnapping, but he hadn't completely discounted the idea that they were using it to their advantage. That they had realized the kidnapping was a hoax but were keeping the truth hidden, had decided to head up a full-scale investigation in order to force Tokyo into retreat. Mikami had to ask. Matsuoka was the most distinguished detective in the headquarters; he was like an elder brother.

'You have proof it's a hoax. Is that why you can't tell me?'

Matsuoka didn't answer. Maybe he *couldn't* answer.

Mikami's pulse was rising.

'Tokyo taking control of Criminal Investigations. I feel the shame, too. But if what you're doing here is taking advantage of some hoax – whatever the circumstances behind it – this investigation is nothing more than a sham – it's heresy.'

'There's a phrase: "It takes a heretic to catch a heretic."'

Mikami was sure he'd misheard. He couldn't believe someone like Matsuoka had just said that.

Matsuoka chuckled. 'Don't look so grim. There's the possibility the kidnapping's a hoax. But we don't have evidence to back it up. I've got people doing their best to find out, as we speak.'

'Well, if that's the case—'

'Don't push it.' Matsuoka's eyes glinted sharply. 'I'm leaving the rest to you. Mobilize that pride you told me about, show me your office can handle the press.'

Mikami pulled back. Unable to meet the man's commanding

gaze, his eyes fell to Matsuoka's torso. *I'm leaving the rest to you.* The words had struck him hard. It felt like someone pulling him out of a dream. *Of course.* Matsuoka had given him all he needed. Mikami had obtained what he'd come for. A name – Masato Mesaki. And an address. The rest – the names of the wife and daughter – they could find out for themselves. He didn't think Matsuoka had given the order, but the words had made the decision for him.

He checked his watch. Ten minutes past eight. *Get a move on.* Right now, the most important task was to speed back to the Prefectural HQ. Mikami looked Matsuoka square in the face. He kicked his heels together and bowed.

'Thank you, sir. I'll be on my way.'

'Before you go, I also have a request.'

He hadn't expected that. *A request?*

'I'd like to borrow Minako for the day, tomorrow.'

His surprise became astonishment.

'I don't have enough female officers. I need someone with normal-looking hair, in style and length.'

For the Undercover Unit, for tomorrow . . .

Mikami struggled to come up with an answer. It was true that Minako didn't look like an officer, or even that she'd ever been in the force. And she already had experience working undercover. She'd been in the Aoi Café when Amamiya had come charging in. Mikami wanted to say yes. He wanted to help the investigation. But it wasn't his decision. Minako couldn't do it, not in her current state. It would be cruel to ask her to help.

Mikami was searching for a way to turn him down when Matsuoka spoke.

'She's stopped leaving the house, right?'

It felt like a hand had grabbed his heart. *Of course.* Matsuoka's wife would have told him. And she would have found out on the phone, from Mizuki Murakushi.

'It'll help her to get some fresh air. I understand her need to wait by the phone . . . but I have the feeling she'll come around if it means she can help someone.'

Mikami felt his head slump. The words were touching. He saw a vivid picture of Minako in his mind. *Helping someone. Someone other than Ayumi.*

'It's up to you both. Tomorrow at 7 a.m. Officer Nanao will be in the assembly hall in HQ.'

Mikami bit down on his lip. *Nor am I clinging on to my past as a detective.* He had no way of retracting his earlier statement and had no intention of doing so. But he felt the ache nevertheless.

To work for this man, just one more time . . .

66

The tornado had moved on.

But it had left Media Relations scarred. The desks and couches had been pushed against the walls. Chairs were overturned. The floor was littered with paper.

Suwa was alone in the office. He looked transformed. His eyes were abnormally red, his eyebrows arched; even his close-cropped hair seemed to bristle with anger. Yet these were only surface details. He had the look of someone unbreakable, some-one whose true potential had been shaken out of a deep sleep. He looked victorious, not worn.

'Great work, sir.' His voice was ragged, like a politician's after a hard-fought election.

'I think that's my line.'

'Mesaki's name, it did the job. Turned everything around.'

Mikami had called in from the parking area in Station G. That had been fifty minutes ago.

'What about the forecast for the coverage agreement?'

'They're on a conference call discussing it. It'll probably take a while yet, but we should have it signed before the day's out.'

'Really?' Mikami asked, genuinely surprised. 'They'll sign with just Mesaki's name?'

'Oh, they know the girl's name. They did the research them-selves, all of them.'

Right, of course.

'Here are the names.'

Suwa held out a sheet of paper, saying he'd asked Administration to do the research in Station G.

Mutsuko Mesaki (42)

Kasumi Mesaki (17)

Saki Mesaki (11)

Ka . . . su . . . mi. Mikami read out the girl's name. The sound seemed similar to that of Ayumi. *Masato. Mutsuko. Kasumi. Saki.* Lined up together, the names were unmistakably those of a family. Mikami felt a new emotion come into play. *How wonderful – if it did turn out to be only a hoax*. Her parents would be anxious to know their daughter was safe and well.

He shook his head.

'How are Kuramae and Mikumo? Is the conference room ready?'

'Yes – Kuramae managed to get everything together. He's there now. We have ten people helping. Five from the Secretariat, five from Administration. Mikumo is in the underground car park, helping organize the cars from Tokyo. She's got a few people from Welfare and Officer Development.'

Right . . . they'd need help to get everything done. Nanao would be in the assembly hall. Matsuoka had already told him that. Which meant Criminal Investigations must have called her in from Administration, to take charge of the female officers. The practical demands of the case were helping to bring down the wall between the two departments. After a delayed start, the Prefectural HQ had begun real preparations for the investigation into the kidnapping.

'Have you seen Futawatari?'

'The inspector? No.'

'What about the conference room?'

'Kuramae would have probably mentioned it, if he was there.'

'Right . . .'

'Do you want me to look for him?'

'No, it doesn't matter.' Mikami changed the subject. 'The conference room, is it filling up already?'

'We've had more than a hundred reporters arrive from Tokyo. There'll be more, too.'

'What about our lot?'

'Our lot?'

Suwa broke into a smile and chuckled. Unable to keep it down, he let this become a loud, open-mouthed laugh. It looked to Mikami as though he'd let go of a huge burden. He suddenly remembered his father's wartime buddy, his exaggerated laugh.

Huh. Guess I forgot how to laugh.

Mikami gave Suwa a pained grin. 'Yeah, maybe "our lot" was a bit of a stretch.'

'Sorry, it was just . . .' Suwa muttered. He rubbed his hands down his face. 'The ground troops left for the conference room. The more senior reporters are out at the assembly hall. It's locked, so they can't get in. It shouldn't be long before they give up and join the others.'

'What about the timetable for our announcements?'

Suwa looked down at his desk. He leafed through a pile of hand-written memos. 'Okay. When the agreement's in place, once every two hours. We can add paper bulletins in between when necessary. We're also supposed to hold emergency announcements if there's a call from the kidnapper, or some other major development. That's true for the duration of the provisional agreement, too.'

'We can't chair a conference every two hours.'

'It's only for the time being. This is the first day of the case . . . we probably can't avoid it.'

'Is this what the Press Club is asking for?'

'That's right. They're asking for every last detail of the case and investigation, as we're keeping the girl's name anonymous.'

'Two hours won't be enough. If we gave them every detail we'd be in there until the morning. Do they expect us to keep the lead investigator there the whole time, under house arrest?'

'Ah, yes . . . there was that, too.' Suwa's expression clouded over.

'Second Division's Chief Ochiai has been appointed to make the announcements. That's according to Criminal Investigations.'

'They're fucking kidding,' Mikami blurted out.

During a kidnapping, tradition dictated that press announcements were to be made by the director of Criminal Investigations or the chief of First Division. The chief of Second Division was both lower in rank and from an unrelated office: what were they hoping to achieve in standing him before the press? And Ochiai was a young bureaucrat, with no experience of active field duty. He wouldn't stand a chance fielding questions on a kidnapping.

Was that the plan? Were they going to usher him in with only a half-empty sheet of paper? The move was straight out of Akama's playbook. *If you don't know anything, you can't say anything.*

'It won't work.'

The reporters would run riot, hundreds of them. Knowing this, Arakida had still decided to offer up Ochiai. There was something he needed to keep from the press. Something he was afraid would slip out if he was pressed. That was why he'd opted to use a puppet.

But was that true?

Mikami no longer thought the kidnapping was a sham. And the idea that Criminal Investigations was taking advantage of a hoax had also been disproved, now that Matsuoka had told him they didn't have evidence either way. Mikami couldn't see anything that would break under investigation – no chinks in their armour.

His mind still felt clouded. There was something he couldn't pin down, the vague sense that something was out of place . . . It was why he was still asking questions.

But it was just nitpicking without any evidence, without something tangible. Mikami was forced to accept that, apart from their treatment of the press, Criminal Investigations was doing a good job of managing the investigation so far. They were aware the case could be a hoax, perpetrated by Kasumi Mesaki herself, but showed no signs of being negligent, of cutting corners. They'd sent First Division Chief Matsuoka to shore up the front line at Station G; they'd gathered detectives specializing in violent crime and had begun preparations to station undercover officers, all the while remembering to cooperate as necessary with the other divisions. The ransom was going to be delivered tomorrow. The case and the investigation would undergo significant developments. Yet Mikami felt no rush of anticipation. *Something has to be wrong.* He felt unbalanced, as though he'd sat on a chair with only three legs.

He couldn't call it his detective's intuition, not any more. And there was no sense of it being anything new, any insight he'd derived from his experience in Media Relations. Yet the idea persisted. That something was going on in the background.

'Like I said . . .' Suwa was on the phone. From the sound of things, talking to one of the smaller tabloids. '. . . the conference is only open to members of the Press Club.' He was having to repeat himself.

Word of the kidnapping was already out.

Mikami took out his mobile and called Kuramae, who answered immediately.

'Sir, that was great work,' he said, sounding surprisingly upbeat.

'Thanks – you, too. What's the headcount up to?'

'I'd say . . . over two hundred.'

'Have you had any trouble?'

'There were some fights over seating, but nothing major.'

'I need you to make an announcement. Tell them there's been a leak; get them to double up on security. We need tight checks on anyone coming and going. And make sure no one does anything stupid like order food in.'

'Yes, sir. I'll let them know.'

Mikami checked the clock on the wall. Already gone half past nine.

'Thanks, I'll be coming over soon.'

Mikami hung up. He was about to call Mikumo when Suwa got off the phone. He looked as though he'd overheard Mikami's conversation.

'Sir, you just reminded me, when you mentioned food. You should eat before you head across.'

On a shelf in the refreshments area was a plate of what looked like fried rice, wrapped in cling film. The surface was clouded with condensation, making it difficult to discern the contents. Suwa said that Mikumo had ordered them all food. Mikami realized he needn't worry, if she'd remembered that in the middle of everything else. She would be on top of everything that needed to be done.

By the underground passage, the west wing of the government office was five minutes on foot. Two if he ran. Mikami started on the food, deciding to eat half. It was cold and soggy, but it filled his stomach.

'Are you going to check in with the first floor?'

'I'll leave that until later.'

'They took quite a beating. The press had Akama in a corner at one point.'

'Did they say anything about the commissioner?'

'No, not yet. But, realistically, it's not going ahead, not with all this.'

'Right.'

'The timing really is crazy,' Suwa said, reaching towards his desk. The phone was ringing again.

The timing . . . crazy. The comment had doubtless been offhand. He wouldn't have meant anything by it. But it had been enough for Mikami's spoon to pause in mid-air. A kidnapping mimicking Six Four, one day before the commissioner's inspection into the fourteen-year-old case. That had to be the source of the cloudiness he felt.

'Sir . . .' Suwa's hand was over the mouthpiece. 'It's Chief Ishii. The commissioner's office just called. The commissioner's visit has been cancelled.'

Mikami thought back to Futawatari as he climbed the stairs.

It would mark his first failure since coming to the Prefectural HQ. He'd lost because of a kidnapping that was beyond his control. No . . . he'd lost even earlier. His threats concerning the Koda memo had come to nothing. He'd acted boldly and out of character, but he'd only managed to provoke Criminal Investigations unnecessarily; without any tangible results, he'd been forced to stage a quiet retreat. It looked that way at least. Whatever the truth, Mikami knew he no longer had to worry about those eyes. He could concentrate on his job without fearing he was going to be cut down from behind.

Administration was half dark. The fluorescent ceiling lights were off, leaving the curtains, couches and carpet pale orange in the glow of the wall lamps.

'Because we're not here, officially,' Ishii said, before anything else.

The reporters had left him frayed. Partly it was the lighting, but each wrinkle on his face seemed to convey the shadow of exhaustion. Akama was . . . lying on one of the couches, shoes still on. Hands and legs sprawled, eyes were empty. He showed no interest in Mikami. Mikami felt the same.

'Definitely not postponed?' Mikami directed the question at Ishii.

'They just said it was called off. We can assume cancelled, although they didn't say it outright.'

Was he unhappy? Relieved? His voice seemed to contain both emotions. Mikami realized he'd sounded the same when he'd told him about the kidnapping. *But, that means the commissioner can't—*

'Is the coverage agreement going to be okay?'

'Yes, just about.'

'Well, I guess that's something. They gave us a real beating, you know. What can we do? Doesn't matter how much they shout at us to give them the girl's name. I told them to go to Criminal Investigations, but . . . they were so confrontational . . . wouldn't stop yelling.'

'I'll tell the press the visit's cancelled, then.'

He was already on his feet. Mikami bowed silently at Akama still lying on the couch, then started for the exit.

He heard a voice from behind.

'Is this Criminal Investigations' work?'

Mikami turned back around. Akama was still staring at the ceiling, his eyes glazed over.

Mikami felt a chill run through him.

'No, sir,' he replied. 'It's the work of a monster.'

68

Inside was Tokyo.

It was 10 p.m. Mikami entered the conference room on the fifth floor of the regional government's west wing. The first thing he noticed was the difference in temperature compared to the corridor. The room was the largest they had, but it was cramped and airless. Countless rows of desks and chairs. Lines of TV cameras. He almost tripped on a cord running across the floor. It was impossible to navigate the walkway without hitting a shoulder or an elbow or bumping into a bag. The room buzzed with conversation, the voices overlapping to form an oppressive low-level drone.

He caught sight of Kuramae. He had on an armband that said *Media Relations*, and was standing at the stage towards the back. It took a few minutes to reach him. A long desk had been set up for the announcements; towards the centre was a huge jumble of TV and radio microphones.

'Tomorrow's been cancelled.'

Kuramae's eyes lost focus; no doubt, he'd forgotten all about the commissioner. 'Ah, the visit. Cancelled?'

'Yes. Can you tell our lot? Use your phone if you can't get to them in person.'

'Our lot . . .?'

'Our reporters.'

'Ah, yes, of course. No problem.'

He jumped down from the stage and disappeared into the crowd, apparently able to guess their whereabouts.

Mikami made a fresh survey of the room. It was the first time he'd faced this many reporters. It would probably be the last. A horde of cameramen had set up camp directly below the stage. They were roughly dressed and squatting; 'loitering' seemed the best way to describe them. The reporters were gathered behind them. Their heads were packed together, behind long desks that were joined to make a jagged horizon. Not all wore serious expressions. Some looked puzzled; others nonchalant, or anxious; some looked excited. There were defiant eyes. Impatient mouths, desperate to be heard. A veteran-type wearing black-rimmed glasses, sitting, relaxed, with his arms folded. Another in a long coat and scarf, the playboy kind, probably with the TV. People were yawning. Yammering on the phone. Making others crease up with laughter. Some were there for the long haul, with rucksacks and sleeping bags. A few groups had rudimentary tents. There were a good number of women. One was angrily shouting instructions to a younger man. Another was calling out in a high-pitched voice, happy to see someone she knew. A round-faced woman, probably a news reporter, was using a compact to fix her make-up. All of them looked at home. The confidence and arrogance that accumulated from travelling the country, hopping from one big case to the next, showed through in a shamelessness they weren't even aware of.

The local reporters were buried somewhere inside. If Mikami hadn't kept his eyes on Kuramae's back, he would have struggled to find them. He caught sight of Tejima, from the *Toyo*, who was handing his business card to a middle-aged man with slicked-back hair and a down jacket. No doubt a star reporter from head office. Tejima's smile was forced. He saw Utsuki next, from the *Mainichi*. He looked worried. Then he burst into a smile. Kuramae had just called out to him. Takagi was there, too, from the *Asahi*, standing by herself. The group next to her seemed to be co-workers, but she wasn't joining in their conversation. Kasai was there from the *Yomiuri*, Yamashina from the *Times*. Both looked decidedly uncomfortable. They were the locals, but they were acting subdued. That was why they didn't stand out. Whenever Mikami looked away, he all but lost them in the swell of unknown faces.

He'd suffered from being too close to the local reporters, with each side having to be careful about what they said. He felt nostalgic for it now, with the air in the conference room so fully transformed into that of the capital.

Ochiai would have to stand in front of them all. With each announcement, he would be made to declare himself a simple puppet. As press director, Mikami could hardly bear to think of it, about the bloodshed that was to come . . .

He saw Mikumo; she was standing towards the entrance. In uniform, it was easy to make her out, even from a distance. Realizing he was looking her way, she stretched up a hand and waved. She looked like someone who'd spotted a lover's face in a crowd. He'd never seen her look so happy. She'd made sure the press adhered to the rules that came with a kidnapping case. She'd directed every last one of their cars into the underground car park. She had no doubt forgotten to smile, too. She started making her way over but came to a sudden stop, ambushed by a group of reporters who'd seen her armband. A group crowded around her, at least half due to her looks he thought. Mikami called her phone, watching as she hurried to pick up.

'Thanks for all the help.'

Her face lit up before she replied. 'It was nothing.'

'Did you get to eat?'

'Sir?'

'The fried rice.'

'I'm actually in the middle of a diet so—'

'I need you to do something, then you need to eat.'

'Of course. What is it?'

'Lend Kuramae a hand. The commissioner's visit has been cancelled. He's letting the local press know.'

'Okay. Do you know where he is?'

'The middle of the room, towards the passageway on the right. Give him a call on his mobile.'

Mikumo was dialling. Kuramae reacted. Mikami kept watch until Kuramae had the phone next to his ear, then stepped off the stage. The after-image of Mikumo's smile was already fading.

The inspection . . . cancelled.

The reporters weren't the only ones who needed to know.

The commissioner general is our highest-ranked official. I'm confident the media coverage will be significant. It will be broadcast on TV. The news will reach a great number of people.

He walked to a corner of the room, where a small administrative area had been set up behind a partition. *Prefecture D Police Headquarters: Authorized Personnel Only.* There were five folding chairs behind the screen. No one was inside.

. . . there is a real chance of this bringing in new leads.

A promise, he'd thought, at least for a while.

He opened the phone in his hand and called Yoshio Amamiya's home number. He checked his watch. Twenty past ten.

No one was picking up. The phone rang ten times. Was he already in bed? This wasn't something Mikami could leave until the morning. Twelve times. Thirteen. Each ring weighed heavy in his chest.

Someone picked up. But . . . no one spoke. All Mikami could hear was silence. He had to force the words out.

'Sorry to disturb you so late. I'm trying to get hold of Yoshio Amamiya.'

'This is Amamiya.' The voice was indistinct.

'This is Mikami, from the Prefectural HQ. I came by the other day.'

'Yes. What is it?'

'Tomorrow's visit. I'm sorry to say this, but . . . due to unforeseen circumstances . . . we've had to cancel it. Please accept my apologies for not letting you know until now.'

There was a long silence. It seemed to last for ever.

'So . . .' Amamiya's voice. 'No one's coming?'

Mikami could see the man's neatly trimmed grey hair. Was he disappointed? Had he – even if just a little – perhaps hoped that something would come of the commissioner's visit?

A promise. In Amamiya's mind, Mikami's words might have been exactly that.

Mikami's head slumped.

'I don't know how I can make this up to you. You listened to me, even though I'd turned up out of nowhere. You even agreed to let us go ahead. And yet this . . .'

Another long silence.

Why was it cancelled? Mikami wanted to run from Amamiya's unspoken question.

'Thanks for letting me know . . .'

Mikami's head sank lower as he listened to the man's voice. Then . . .

'How are you now?'

What?

'Are you better?'

Mikami was stunned. *Of course.* His shameful display of tears before Shoko's altar. 'My last visit . . . I don't know how to express my . . . having to—'

'Not everything is bad. There's good out there, too.'

The words were soft. It felt like the first time he was hearing the man's real voice. Amamiya had lost his only daughter; the kidnapper was still out there. How could a man who had been through that sound so gentle?

Mikami apologized again then ended the call. He was at breaking point. His fingers were tight over the bridge of his nose. If he'd stayed on the phone any longer, he would have shed tears again.

He took a deep breath and punched himself over the chest; two, three times. There was one more call he needed to make. He cleared his throat, tried out his voice until he felt ready.

'Honey, your voice . . .'

Minako picked up on it straight away.

'It's nothing.'

'Is something wrong?'

The standard question hit him harder than it usually did.

'Sort of. I'm not going to be back tonight. Make sure you lock all the doors, and get some rest. One more thing . . .'

I should ask. Mikami tensed his stomach.

'Matsuoka wanted you to help with something. On an investigation.'

'Help? What investigation?'

'There's been a kidnapping.' Mikami felt his voice tighten. 'Matsuoka wants people for an undercover unit, for tomorrow.' He heard her take a sharp breath. 'He said he'd understand if you couldn't help out. It's up to you.'

'Who . . . who was kidnapped?'

'A seventeen-year-old girl, still in high school.'

Silence.

'It's fine if you want to say no; I don't mind, and Matsuoka said the same. Only . . .'

If it means she can help someone. Mikami wanted to convey Matsuoka's words.

Or maybe Amamiya's . . . *Not everything is bad. There's good out there, too.*

'Minako?'

A pause.

'Minako . . .'

'Yes, I'll do it.'

Mikami's head came up. He could almost picture the determination on her face. It was because of him that she'd said it. But that was okay. It felt like progress, if only a fraction. When the phone rang immediately after he'd ended the call, he answered without even checking the display.

Maybe she'd changed her mind . . .

'This is Futawatari.'

You had to call right now, didn't you? The thought shot right through him.

'What is it?'

'Can I help with anything?'

Mikami was thrown. He waited for Futawatari to continue.

'I heard about the kidnapping. Is there something I can do to help?'

'No,' he said, his thoughts picking up speed. 'Got time on your hands?'

'Not particularly.'

'You sure about that?' Mikami's anger was flaring up. 'Didn't go as planned, huh?'

'What?'

'Admit it. You failed. You didn't achieve anything.'

Mikami had meant the words to be a knockout blow, but Futawatari was unshaken when he replied.

'I'll admit, there was some miscalculation on my part.'

Miscalculation? The commissioner's visit had been crushed by a twist of fate, a kidnapping. Was he saying he'd failed to take the possibility into account?

'You flatter yourself. A miscalculation . . . that's a joke. How the hell do you account for something like this in your plans?'

'At least it ended well.'

What?

A face poked out from behind the partition; Suwa, with an urgent look. Mikami held up a hand to say he was hanging up. He spoke into the phone.

'You're not needed here. Go and clean the office or something.'

Suwa started to speak the moment Mikami ended the call.

'The press – they've signed the agreement. The first announcement is scheduled for 11 p.m.'

69

It marked the beginning of a long night.

They shut the doors and drew blackout curtains over the windows to prevent light from leaking out. Two hundred and sixty-nine – the total number of reporters Administration had admitted to the venue.

Mikami was on the stage with Ochiai.

Testing . . . testing . . . testing. His voice crackled slightly over the wireless microphone. Kuramae, over at the entrance, raised a hand to signal that he could hear. His voice was audible throughout the room.

'My name is Mikami, press director for the police headquarters.'

He was blinded the moment he opened his mouth. The herd of cameramen at the front had, as though conducting testing of their own, all started taking photos at once.

He took a deep breath.

'Eleventh of December. 23:00 hours. We hereby convene our first press conference regarding the case of a kidnapping and ransom in Genbu City, in accordance with the rules and regulations stipulated in the Press Coverage Agreement. Superintendent Ochiai – Second Division Chief – will chair proceedings. We appreciate in advance your cooperation and assistance while the agreement remains in effect.'

Huh? A voice came from directly behind the line of cameramen. *What do you mean, the chief of Second Division? Bring us the director, or the chief of First!*

The man had a goatee, and looked to be in his mid-forties. Mikami didn't recognize him, but Akikawa was there next to him. Slick was there, too, the man who'd been with Tejima. It was the *Toyo*.

Mikami whispered to Ochiai: 'Ignore him and go ahead.' The twenty-seven-year-old superintendent nodded, before taking his place at the centre of the long desk. Side parting. Broad forehead. Intelligent eyes. He looked honest. It was the only positive; probably his only lifeline. Mikami noticed he was trembling. Itokawa, the assistant chief of Second Division, had previously told him that Ochiai tended to crack under pressure, that he was prone to panic.

'Thank you. I hereby begin our first announcement.'

His voice was a little high-pitched. A rustling spread through the room. Even the sound of notebooks opening seemed to carry weight when everyone did it at once. Ochiai looked down at the piece of paper in his hands.

'For a general overview of the case details, please refer to the summaries in your hands. At the current time, there have been no further developments in the case or the surrounding investigation. Six hundred officers are engaged on work pertaining to the preliminary investigation. Five to seven detectives are already in the victim's home, working hard on solving the case.'

Ochiai's head came back up, the look on his face saying he had finished.

The room was silent. *That's it?* They all wore the same expression. Mikami hurried from where he stood at the edge of the stage to stand behind Ochiai.

Flesh it out a little, give them some more detail. He didn't get the chance to voice the words in his head.

'Thank you.'

Ochiai was getting to his feet.

'The next announcement is scheduled for 01:00 hours.'

Is this some kind of joke? It was the only sentence Mikami could make out. The floor started to rumble; the entire room shook as the uproar hit the stage. The cries were sharp, almost physically painful, and unrelenting, no matter how much time passed.

Ochiai was in his seat again, his knees having given way. All the colour had drained from his face. No doubt his mind was blank, too. Mikami tried whispering to him. After getting no response, he tried shouting into the man's ear. *Read the outline!* Ochiai's hands shook as he leafed through what he had. Mikami looked down, then away, in shock. The sheets were empty. All they contained was the blank template Suwa had put together. Arakida really had gone through with it. They'd given him nothing. Ochiai was a puppet.

Mikami took hold of the wireless microphone, but no words came out. He knew he'd just make things worse. Whatever he said, it would be like petrol on a fire. His only job was to stand there and bear the brunt of the shouting and jeering.

A hand shot up. From the *Toyo* camp. It was Akikawa. Not to attack. It looked like an offer of help. Mikami thought he heard something . . . *microphone.* Acting on instinct, Mikami jumped from the stage and made his way through the cameramen. He held the mic out like a baton, his eyes meeting Akikawa's. Their gaze seemed abnormally strong. Akikawa clasped his hand around the mic then turned away to face the gathered reporters.

'My name is Akikawa, I'm with the *Toyo*. We represent the Press Club here in Prefecture D.' He repeated this three times before the noise began to subside. 'I understand your anger. For a long time, the Media Relations division here has left a lot to be desired. We have been forced time and again to demand changes in policy.'

A chill ran down Mikami's back. Did he intend to stir them up even more? *An olive branch.* Was there no room for such things in his current state of mind?

'It goes without saying that them sending us the Second

Division Chief is just another example of this. As representative of the Prefecture D Press Club, I intend to lodge an immediate complaint and force them to send the Criminal Investigations Director or First Division Chief.'

He was drunk on adrenalin. The full extent of the man's ego, only glimpsed on an everyday basis, was coming out.

'At the same time, it would be a waste for us to let the first announcement end like this. It would waste important time. As representative for the Prefecture D Press Club, I would like to propose that we be patient at this time – use it to ask the questions we need answers to. We must find out the details of the kidnapping. Do you agree?'

His voice echoed off the walls. After a pause, Goatee and Slick began to clap at either side, their expressions nominally supportive of their subordinate's effort. This caught and scattered clapping spread through the room.

'Okay.'

Akikawa turned forwards again. He levelled his gaze on the stage and Ochiai. He looked desperate, as though starved of oxygen. It wasn't his ego. Nor was he hoping to offer a way out. He was defending the honour of the local press. But it was too dangerous. Whatever Akikawa's intention, if the announcement were to turn into a Q&A session . . .

'Chief Ochiai. I propose to open with a few questions from the Prefecture D Press Club. I will then pass the mic around for more questions. Is this acceptable?'

Mikami wanted to step in, but he had no plausible grounds for doing so. His hands were tied.

Akikawa took a deep breath. 'If you could start by explaining the headquarters' thoughts regarding the case. What is your stance on the possible connection to the Shoko kidnapping from fourteen years ago?'

'C . . . connection?'

The response was weaker than he'd feared.

'We know the kidnapper copied the wording during the call. Putting aside the possibility of a hoax, do you or do you not believe a connection exists between the two cases?'

'We can't say . . . at this juncture.'

'Meaning you have nothing to actually prove a connection?'

'I believe so . . . although it's not certain as yet.'

'Okay, now we need some specifics.' Akikawa waved the sheet containing the overview. 'This is far too generalized, nowhere near enough. We need to know the details you've learned from the girl's parents; their financial situation, work record . . .'

Ochiai flicked ineffectually through the summary in his hands. 'Uhh . . . we haven't received any reports on that as yet.'

The room broke into a murmur. Goatee and Slick were frowning.

Akikawa was showing signs of distress. *Just give me a proper answer.* His expression was pleading.

'Have you had anything from the kidnapper? Another call, for example?'

'No.'

'Where were the first two calls made?'

Again, Ochiai's eyes fell to his papers. Mikami felt a shudder. *From inside the prefecture.* If Ochiai gave an answer like that, the reporters would riot again. His only chance was to keep saying 'Nothing reported'. Mikami held up a no-go sign. Ochiai was still flicking through the pages. *Look at me. Look at me.*

Akikawa's breathing was heavy in the mic. 'All we have on this is "Prefecture D". Where in the prefecture? You must have finished checking with DoCoMo . . .'

The question could become the olive branch they'd needed. It could become the final blow.

Ochiai looked up. He had the terrified look of a man cornered.

'I . . . don't know.'

Then bring us someone who does! The shout became a signal for the room to bare its teeth. Countless jeers came together, blasting hot air towards the stage. Ochiai's honest appearance was no longer of any use. He looked afraid. *That's enough, surely. Give it up!* Some of the shouts were aimed at Akikawa. Goatee turned to him with a look of disgust. *What have you been teaching them?*

'One more question!'

Akikawa refused to give up the microphone. His neck and ears were bright red; he looked despairing.

'Chief Ochiai, is the kidnapping a hoax?'

For the second time, he repeated himself three times. This time, the shouts didn't die away. *He's wasting our time! Call yourself a representative? Why don't you go and fetch the director!?*

'Chief Ochiai, it's imperative that you answer this. Does the Investigative HQ really suspect the kidnapping is a hoax? Yes or no?'

'I don't know at this—'

'That is not satisfactory. You're here representing them – answer the question. Is this a hoax perpetrated by Kasumi Mesaki?'

The question came out as an inhuman wail. The tumult dropped to a minimum. All ears were trained on Ochiai, awaiting his response.

Ochiai's gaze was hovering in mid-air. The microphone picked up a murmuring.

'Kasumi . . . Mesaki . . .?'

Akikawa froze. His eyes stretched open, incredulous.

Mikami looked up at the ceiling. *Unbelievable.* Ochiai hadn't even recognized the name. 'C' was the only name he'd been given.

They're in violation of the agreement! The noise level shot to maximum in under a second. Everyone was on their feet. Only one man stood out – Akikawa. His shoulders were slumped, as though under heavy rain. The microphone was limp at his side.

70

They had escaped to the Prefectural HQ.

The next announcement is scheduled for 01:00. With that, they had taken flight. Suwa had manned the front while Mikami and Kuramae had supported Ochiai, one on each side of him as they'd guided him through the room. One of Kuramae's jacket pockets had been torn; Suwa had lost an armband. Ochiai had disappeared back into the Investigative HQ, smoothing down his dishevelled hair. Mikami had been refused entrance, the number of guards on the door bumped up to six. Getting Matsuoka was out of the question: he was out on the front line. That left Arakida; getting him to make the announcements was their only hope of salvaging the situation. But he refused to break his golden rule of holding the fort; they couldn't even get a meeting, notwithstanding Mikami's attempts to threaten Mikura, and the local reporters' endeavours to use the sheer force of their number to get through the guards.

Ochiai ended up holding the one o'clock announcement. He was only able to do this because the Investigative HQ had given him a little more information on the girl's family.

Masato Mesaki had 7 million yen in savings. He'd inherited land – thirty square metres in size – and taken out a twenty-year loan to build the house they lived in. He leased out the ground floor of a building in the city, where he ran a store specializing in sports equipment. Until ten years ago, he'd been a salesman for a car dealership that sold luxury imported cars.

Mutsuko Mesaki was the elder sister in a relatively well-off agricultural family; she had no work history. Her family was going to help them with part of the ransom money.

Kasumi Mesaki's school attendance amounted to thirteen days only in the first term of the year, and none at all in the second term. She'd left the house on the night of the 9th, a little after 8 o'clock. She'd been wearing a leopard-skin coat, and hadn't been seen since.

Things held for the opening ten minutes. But once Ochiai had finished reading out the notes, he returned to being an empty vessel. He failed to give an answer to even a single question properly. Making it worse was his stubborn refusal to use names, still referring to the members of the family as A, B and C.

Disorder became convention. The yelling to and fro became incessant. Goatee and Slick from the *Toyo* were gradually asserting their control over the room. They were intent on dragging Arakida into the conference room, but he was proving surprisingly resilient. Having realized this, they had decided to work on Ochiai, hammering away and making him their courier pigeon. One would ask a question. Ochiai would fumble for an answer. Each time, they forced him to go back to the Investigative HQ to get the answer. *Get a move on! Run!* He would be sent out under a hailstorm of shouts. From there he would take the lift to the ground floor and stumble his way down the pitch-black underground passageway before climbing the staircase to reach the Investigative HQ. Once there, he would be given a non-committal answer, then have to run back to the conference room. *How does that answer the question? Get back over there.* He would step back into the lift. Mikami accompanied him on each trip. Having beseeched Mikura to consider Ochiai's position, demanding he get Arakida to take the stage, he finally grabbed him by the collar and rammed his head into one of the walls, losing his only avenue of negotiation.

Three o'clock. As Mikami had feared, the conference had

become endless. Ochiai's two-way trips had become standard drill.

Let us have all your questions, then we can try to get all of your answers together. Mikami had tried to appeal to Goatee, but the man had refused to listen. Their strategy was to drag Arakida out from the shadows. The whole point was to parade Ochiai's suffering before the Investigative HQ, over and over again. And he was thoroughly worn out. His eyes were vacant, legs weak; in the lift, he would occasionally sink to the floor. Mikami couldn't understand Arakida's game plan. All he knew was that the man's hatred of career officers had let him turn Ochiai into a joke. Was he making an example of him? Mikami had begun to suspect even that. And yet . . .

The one o'clock announcement was still in session even after half past four. Hard-liners would pipe up across the room each time Ochiai left, lobbying to declare the agreement null and void. The suggestion had only failed to take hold because many of the reporters remained wary of the potential consequences. What would happen if a group their size all scrambled, unrestrained, to cover the story? A kidnapping was a kidnapping; that didn't change, however the police treated them, and there was nothing to prove it was a hoax dreamt up by the girl. That set off warning lights. If they started to move around blindly, without the police there to guide them, and if that were to lead to the girl losing her life . . . It was a trump card they could use in applying pressure, but it would be difficult to actually break the agreement. Which meant it was maybe better not to shout about it, not to reveal a chink in their armour. It was a dilemma. They were caught in a deadlock which was feeding their anger and volatility; they were unable to retreat, yet unable to advance.

Five o'clock became just another waypoint. Ochiai was reaching his limit. His utter exhaustion had left him sluggish and, it seemed, increasingly confused. Even the hot towel and energy drinks Mikumo had prepared were failing to help. Suwa and

Kuramae were now taking turns helping him back and forth between the Investigative HQ. Most of the time Ochiai would return with next to nothing, cueing another bombardment. Goatee and Slick were merciless as they sent their carrier pigeon on one errand after another. *We're almost there. They'll break soon enough.* Mikami had started to overhear comments like these. He hadn't seen Akikawa for a long time. *He'd be able to help.* Mikami genuinely believed that.

Suwa was becoming increasingly withdrawn, the cause more than simple fatigue. He had been overwhelmed by the scale, by the sheer number of reporters from Tokyo. He'd lost the ability to stand up to them. The shock had been devastating to his confidence, and to his ability to function as a press officer. Kuramae looked numb. He'd retreated back inside his shell, slipped back into his role as a pedestrian desk worker. Mikumo's focus was too narrow. Desperately concerned about Ochiai's wellbeing, she'd lost sight of anything else they needed to do. Each time Ochiai was made to visit the Investigative HQ, she marked a cross on her palm. *We can't let this go on. He'll die if this doesn't stop . . .*

Twenty to six. Having watched Ochiai and Suwa leave, Mikami left for the toilet. It was still pitch black outside. He felt a sudden and debilitating tiredness, stemming from his sense of impotence. His thoughts travelled to Minako. To Yoshio Amamiya. To Ayumi . . .

Have I done a single thing right . . .?

He felt his neck tense the moment he reached the corridor. A group was standing next to the half-lit doors of the lift, as though in ambush. Ten. Twenty figures.

The realization hit him as he walked closer.

Ushiyama, Utsuki, Sudou, Kamata, Horoiwa, Yanase, Kasai, Yamashina, Tejima, Kadoike, Takagi, Kakei, Kiso, Hayashiba, Tomino, Namie . . .

They were all looking in his direction. Akikawa was there, too, muted, leaning against a wall to one side.

'What the hell is going on here?'

Ushiyama was the first to mount an attack, making no attempt to keep his frustration at bay. *Can't you stop this? Just do something.* The others pitched in after him.

Mikami's only response was to sigh. He cut a path through them and kept walking. The disappointment spread through him. *Right. Joining in with the rest of them, huh?*

'It's too much, it really is,' Yamashina hissed.

Tejima's hands were balled into fists.

'We can't take it . . . them treating you like this. It's unacceptable.'

The words had come from Madoka Takagi. Mikami was bowled over. Her eyes were glistening. *Of course.* They weren't tourists. They weren't complaining about having been relegated into a supporting role. Mikami knew the sentiment well. Your first posting was special. It was the first time you stood on your own feet, after leaving home. It was where you learned your trade; you got to know the streets, the businesses. You survived, you ate, you slept, you suffered. You took your first steps into the real world. It was when you discovered who you really were. It was more home than home itself. Now it was being trampled on. It saddened them. It made them mad.

Mikami started to walk again, saying nothing. He had no words that could measure up to what they – his reporters – wanted to hear. But he was moved. If nothing else, he wanted Akikawa to know that. The man's eyes were on the floor. He looked dog-tired. He'd made up his mind and taken hold of the microphone, but it was suicide. He'd tried his best on the largest stage there was. He was their representative; he'd have felt pride, responsibility. Mikami didn't doubt that some part of it had also been to offer support.

Without stopping, Mikami tapped his hand on Akikawa's shoulder.

You did well. Now it's my turn . . .

71

The change came suddenly.

Ochiai got a second wind. It was 6.30 a.m. Returning to the conference room, he looked visibly different to when he'd left for the Investigative HQ. Some degrees brighter. He was still shaky on his feet as he climbed to the stage, but he made it without Suwa's assistance. When he sat, he held himself straight and surveyed the room. They'd given him something of use. Maybe more. There was nothing in his expression to suggest the girl was dead. She'd shown up, alive and well. The kidnapper had been arrested. Either would allow for the immediate termination of the coverage agreement. They could leave this abnormal space behind, the blackout curtains.

Mikami was standing to the side of the cameramen. He looked at his team. Suwa nodded in recognition. Kuramae and Mikumo both stepped closer. They seemed restless. They both wanted it to be over. Hope showed on their faces.

The people in the room, having also noticed Ochiai's transformation, had started to chatter. The atmosphere became one of tense anticipation, the reporters leaning forwards into their desks so as not to miss a word.

Lights indicated that the TV cameras were recording. The rest of the cameramen jostled, to the sound of shutters clicking. Goatee picked up the microphone. His expression didn't match that of the other reporters. He didn't look angry, but it was clear he wasn't happy to see Ochiai's sudden recovery.

'Shall we start with your homework? How many calls has the kidnapper made to the family? When? How long for? Were there any discernible sounds in the background?'

'I don't have that information yet.'

Ochiai was still smiling when he answered. Goatee's expression changed.

'Has something happened? Do you have the girl in custody? Have you arrested the kidnapper?'

Everyone held their breath.

'Oh, no. We haven't got that either yet.'

'Well, then, what is it?' Goatee said, losing patience.

Ochiai's smile remained unshaken.

'I have new information regarding the calls, something you've asked a number of times already. I can tell you where they were made. Both calls – the first and the second – originated inside Genbu City.'

The information was important, it went without saying. But the delivery was wrong. Ochiai had raised their hopes, set expectations, and, because of that, the reveal had come across as trifling. The room seemed for a moment to gasp for air.

What can we say to such an idiot?

Goatee thought he knew.

'Where in Genbu?'

'Sorry?'

'I believe you're able to narrow the signal to a three-kilometre radius. You still don't get it, do you? We need specifics, details.'

Ochiai managed only a croak.

'Back to the beginning!' Slick shouted from his place next to Goatee, sounding like a teacher ordering a child. With that, the room ignited, the shouts of ridicule all the louder because of the reporters' disappointment.

What are you, an errand boy? Try learning a thing or two. Waste of fucking space.

Ochiai was staring into thin air. He was expressionless. He

looked dead, every muscle in his face having gone limp. He'd no doubt gone crying to Arakida. Begged him for something that would gratify the press. He'd finally managed to extract the origin of the calls. On the way back, he'd imagined the press thanking him for his good work.

Then . . .

'Well? Don't drag your feet. Get going! This time bring us something worthy of a press conference.'

Ochiai remained seated. His motionless figure began to tip forwards . . . his forehead thumped into the desk. Still slumped, his elbows spread out until he was flat on the desk.

Forgive me. It looked like an apology.

'Call an ambulance!'

The shout had come from Mikumo. Goatee yelled back at twice the volume.

'It's not going to be that easy. Don't think this'll help you get away.'

Mikumo held up the markings on her palm. 'Twenty-nine. That's the number of round-trips he's had to make. He's been here for seven and a half hours; he hasn't slept.'

Goatee hardly spared her a glance. His eyes continued to drill into the man on the stage.

'Neither have we! Seven and a half hours straight. We've come all the way from Tokyo and not had a wink. We're packed in here like sardines; I wouldn't be surprised if we've all got DVT. Twenty-nine round trips? Great. At least the bastard got some exercise.'

Slick gave him a nudge from the side.

'Let them take him to the hospital, then the director or the chief will have to come out.'

'Yeah, and what if they send more dregs, like this one?' Goatee said, looking back at Ochiai.

'If you want to go to bed, go and talk to the director. Get on your hands and knees and beg him to take your place.'

On the stage, Suwa and Kuramae were running over to where

Ochiai sat. Mikumo was trailing behind with a kettle and a towel. They pulled his limp form upright. He'd snapped. Expended every last reserve of energy. A line of spit dribbled from the side of his mouth.

'Pull yourself together. You're already at the bottom of the ladder. Won't be much hope for you if you collapse under something like this.'

'That's enough,' Mikami said. The word seemed to come from deep inside.

Goatee turned around. His expression said he hadn't heard properly.

'You've done enough!' This time Mikami raised his voice. 'You're a lynch mob, nothing more. We're finished here.'

'I'm sorry?' Goatee was clambering towards him; he stretched out his arm and held his microphone in front of Mikami. 'Could you repeat that, please?'

'I'm not bringing anyone else in, knowing they're going to be hung out to dry. As of now, all announcements are suspended.'

Hands hit desks in their hundreds; everyone in the room got to their feet. The floor started to rumble. The air erupted in a storm of shouts. Mikami's team were staring open-eyed from the stage. Even Ochiai's half-open eyes were swimming in his direction. Goatee had the microphone in the air, waving it from side to side. *Leave this to me.*

The background roar finally subsided. Even then, there was a quiet muttering. The reporters were waiting to see what Mikami said next, still ready to launch into battle.

'A lynch mob, you say?' Goatee gave Mikami a testing look. 'You're press director here. Perhaps you're misreading what this is. We've been given this man, your chief of Second Division, who doesn't even know the kidnapped girl's name. Whoever's in charge has chosen to sacrifice a lackey while they run and hide. You tell me – isn't that the real lynch?'

Mikami shouted towards the stage, 'Get him to First-aid.'

Mikumo flinched in response.

'Hey, you, gargoyle. *So-called* press director. Are you even listening to me?'

Gargoyle. Mikami already knew the two men had taken to calling him that.

'Announcements are suspended, you say? Are you announcing your intention to forgo the coverage agreement?'

'We will convene another session from 8 a.m. If anything happens in the meantime, we'll send you paper bulletins.'

'Uh-huh, right, like your face isn't enough of a joke. How do you propose to do that when you don't even know what's happening yourself?'

Right! A wave of sound swelled towards him. *Enough of the bullshit. Bring us your director of Criminal Investigations.*

'You know, you police are pretty bad wherever we go. But I've never seen an office as messed up as this,' Goatee continued. His eyes locked with Mikami's. They were striking, handsome-looking. Mikami wondered if the glass-like clarity he saw there was what came from years of fighting for what you believed was right.

Mikami shouted towards the stage. 'Get him out of here!'

Suwa and Kuramae were lending their shoulders, helping Ochiai to his feet.

'Yes? And what do you propose to do next?'

'About what?'

'Who's going to take over here, if the doctor gives him a no-go?'

'I'll find a suitable replacement.'

'The director. Give us your word. Right here, right now.'

He's right! He's right! The agreement echoed around the room, as if it were coming through speakers. *The director! We want your word!*

Mikami ground his back teeth, saying nothing.

'Don't think you can stand there in silence. We're only asking for a *normal* press conference. Why can't you bring us the director? What is it that you're trying to hide?'

Ochiai came down from the stage, supported by the two men. They began to cross the packed floor. Mikami called Mikumo over, deciding it was dangerous to let her go through. The others were threading through the crowd, trying to find places to walk. Ochiai's shoes were hardly on the floor. Alone, he wouldn't have made a single step. It looked like Suwa and Kuramae were helping a wounded soldier navigate a minefield.

Stop them! A sharp voice rang out from somewhere towards the middle of the room. *We can't just let them go. We need to get his word on the director.*

Mikami cursed. One of the mines – it triggered another wave of explosions.

Don't let him out!

A group of excited reporters got to their feet. They blocked Ochiai's path. More pressed in from either side.

Get the promise first. We exchange him for the director.

The circle began to close around Ochiai. Suwa and Kuramae's faces were drawn tight. Mikami heard Mikumo shriek from behind.

'Lay a finger on him and I'm taking you in for obstruction.'

Mikami listened to his voice reverberate through the space. He'd shouted into the microphone, having wrenched it from Goatee. The room fell still. All 269 pairs of eyes were focused on him. He closed his eyes. *Eeee, eeee, eeee.* A powerful ringing vibrated in his eardrums, too loud to tell if it was a voice or empty noise. Someone had grabbed the microphone. Not Goatee. It was Slick – he'd pulled it right out of Mikami's hands.

'That's enough showing off, Gargoyle. Shock tactics like that only work on the local kids.'

Goatee was still staring. He took back the microphone. *Fighting the good fight.* His glass-clear eyes were burning with angry conviction.

'We've been patient with you so far. We took you at your word

537

when you said the kidnapping could be a teenager's hoax. We've been understanding about the circumstances, and we've permitted this nonsense around the identity of her family. But we've had enough.' His anger boiled suddenly over. 'You will not continue making fools of us. This conference is a sham. You are clearly abusing the provisions of our agreement. You are concealing the truth, even as you carry on the investigation with impunity. It's too much for us to overlook. We decide this now.'

He turned to face the rest of the room.

'First we report this nonsensical state of affairs to Tokyo. Then we get them to appoint someone more *appropriate*, someone from the Criminal Investigations Bureau, to lead the Investigative HQ. They take over all proceedings, including all matters pertaining to us, the press. Are there any objections?'

'Wait!' Mikami shouted. 'I guarantee you'll get proper announcements from this point forwards. We will give you everything we know. It's what you want.'

'Aren't we past that stage? Things are only like this now because you failed to do exactly that.'

'I understand. We have failed in our obligation to you. Give me some time so I can help correct that. I won't need long.'

'You'll get the director?'

'I'll get you the chief of First Division.'

It worked. The flames that had been raging through the room were gone in an instant. His words had reflected the intensity of the blaze. He'd used the final reserves of extinguisher foam, reserves he should never have touched.

'The next session will start at eight o'clock.'

'Stay by my side,' he said to Mikumo, still behind him as he started to walk. It felt like an attempt at breaking through enemy lines. At the halfway point, he put his hand on Ochiai's back. The foam was working, but the room was still smouldering, far from normal.

538

They made it to the corridor. To the doors of the lift. Even then, Mikami could still feel the piercing stares on his back.

'Thank you,' Ochiai groaned.

Mikami took his shoulder. It felt delicate, just like Akikawa's. The five of them stepped into the lift. Once the doors were closed, Mikami turned to Suwa.

'I'm going back to Station G.'

Suwa's head was hanging low. It was plain to everyone there. Mikami wouldn't be able to bring Matsuoka – the field commander of the investigation – back with him.

'I have to try. Maybe he won't be able to come here in person, but there's a chance I can send you some proper information.'

Suwa's head stayed where it was. Mikami was painfully aware of how he felt.

I'll get you the chief of First Division.

He couldn't withdraw the statement. Despite this, Matsuoka wouldn't come. Mikami wouldn't even be there to take responsibility. All that waited for Suwa, now he'd lost confidence in his ability as a press officer, was the harsh reality of standing defenceless before the press.

Even so . . .

'I have to try,' Mikami repeated. The words were to convince himself it was true.

'Yes, you should go.' It was Ochiai. 'I can . . . I can hold out a bit longer. I'll manage, somehow.'

Mikami took his shoulder again; he squeezed. There were no words. He didn't want to force Suwa into anything.

'Suwa.'

He didn't reply.

'Futawatari called earlier, asking if he could help. I can call him in.'

The lift chimed, pulled to a stop. The doors slid open. No one made to get out. Kuramae and Mikumo were both watching

Suwa. *We'll stand by you whatever you decide.* Their eyes conveyed the message.

The doors began to close. Suwa's finger pressed *open* the moment before they shut.

'That won't be necessary. I'll never make press director if the man in charge of personnel thinks I'm weak.'

72

Outside, the sun was shining.

On the way to his car, Mikami paused to take in the sense of open space. He soaked up the morning sun, taking deep breaths. He gave his arms and legs a full stretch.

He couldn't forget the look he'd seen on Suwa's face. Yet . . . he'd built up the courage to keep going. He'd kicked himself, forced himself back into the fight.

Mikami got into his car and checked the time: 7.22. *One circuit.* Telling himself that was okay, he drove slowly around the parking area. He was looking for Minako's compact car. The Undercover Unit was scheduled to meet at seven. She'd be inside if she'd decided to go through with it. He pressed hard on the accelerator and pulled out of the station grounds. He hadn't seen her car, but there were other places she could have parked. She'd be there. She'd be out – under the same, blazing sunlight.

Traffic was heavy on the prefectural highway.

Mikami had decided against speeding. He'd given up on the eight o'clock announcement. And he'd forced the next – scheduled for ten – from his head, too. Everything came down to the announcement planned for midday. That was the deadline for getting the ransom together. It was when everything would kick into gear. How close he got to the investigation. How much raw, real-time information he was able to scrape together and relay back to the conference room. That was what would determine their success or failure. It was clear now he was outdoors. He knew exactly what needed to be done.

In the conference room, every moment had felt critical. For more than eight hours through the night, Mikami had faced the press with the mindset of someone running a 100-metre sprint. The truth was, nothing had happened. Ochiai's twenty-nine round trips, the fervent support given by Suwa and the others, everything else – it had been nothing more than a warm-up. What mattered was yet to come. The press wouldn't bare their teeth, really kick into gear, until the case itself started to develop.

An unmarked police car drove by. The metallic-silver body blended with the rest of the traffic, the speed not too slow, not too fast.

Mikami put a cigarette in his mouth and lit it.

I'll get you the chief of First Division.

He'd made an impossible promise. But he'd known it was impossible even as he'd said it – he couldn't let himself become prisoner to the words themselves. At the same time, he realized that breaking the promise, made before all 269 of the assembled reporters, would compel them to make an appeal for NPA intervention.

The only way he could prevent that from happening was to supply them with information that had the same value as would bringing Matsuoka back with him.

A strategy was coming together.

Criminal Investigations was hiding something. If he had any leverage at all, it was that. *Arakida and the Investigative HQ. Matsuoka and the front line.* It was already apparent that they had different ideas on suppressing information. Matsuoka had given him Mesaki's name, even though he knew it would get to the press; Arakida still called him 'A'. And Mutsuko and Kasumi were still 'B' and 'C', even though their names had come out a long time ago. Matsuoka had refused to give Mikami the latter two, but that had been more out of his own personal consideration than out of any attempt to conceal their identity. Arakida was hiding *everything* so he could hide *something*. Matsuoka was only hiding what needed to be hidden. The distinction was significant.

It meant Matsuoka would release anything he didn't think confidential. He wasn't the kind of man to ignore a coverage agreement, and his response to Mikami in the Station G toilets had shown an empathy for his situation and point of view. It would be fine, as long as Mikami didn't insist on getting everything. It would be frustrating to skirt around some of the points, but it was nothing compared to the turmoil of the conference room. He would get all that he could from Matsuoka. That way, he could supply information that would have as much weight as if the man himself were present. Even if Matsuoka had been there in person, he would still refuse to say anything he didn't plan on revealing. He would have given the press Mesaki's name, but not Mutsuko or Kasumi's, however much they pressured him. As he'd said: *some things must never be spoken.*

Something hit Mikami, a feeling that was somewhere between doubt and anxiety.

Was that it?

The identity of the family. Was that all Criminal Investigations was hiding? It couldn't be. It wouldn't be something so minor. They had to be hiding something else, something fundamental to the kidnapping, perhaps even to the investigation itself. Something that had left Arakida no choice but to suppress the information, even if it meant making a wholesale enemy of the press; a secret with an explosive potential that was on par with the Koda memo.

The only fact he had was that Matsuoka, the lead commander of the investigation, had refused to give him Mutsuko and Kasumi's names. That was all.

Kasumi was understandable. That could be explained normally. She was a juvenile, one suspected of having orchestrated a hoax kidnapping. Matsuoka wasn't the kind of man to grant dispensation due to age, but it was hard to argue with him for holding her name back.

But what about Mutsuko?

The thought came to him for the first time. Why had Matsuoka refused to give him the name of Kasumi's mother? Was it because she was a woman? Because she was suffering? Because her daughter had been kidnapped, or betrayed her trust? Did considerations like that come into it?

It didn't feel right.

So . . . no.

What else could it have been? Perhaps he'd just decided to help. It was possible he hadn't intended to give out any of their names at first but that he'd seen the state Mikami was in and taken pity, decided to give him at least Masato's name.

No.

Some things must never be spoken.

He'd 'spoken' Masato's name. But he hadn't done the same for Mutsuko and Kasumi. His decency hadn't permitted it.

The clarity started to fade.

Had Matsuoka's words contained any hidden meaning? Or had they been empty? *If* they had meant something . . .

A mother, a daughter . . .

The combination brought only negative connotations. Another unmarked police car passed by. They had been mobilized across the prefecture. In a few hours, the pursuit would begin, tailing the ransom all the way to the handover point. A manhunt in broad daylight. There was a chance it would turn into that.

The billboard for the Aoi Café came sliding into view. It would be open for the morning trade. Would it be the starting point again? Mikami searched for Minako's face in the windows. Would she go there again? If so, would she sit on the same seat she had fourteen years ago?

Mikami experienced a jolt of fear, suddenly feeling as though he'd thrown his wife into a dark and bottomless whirlpool.

Something would happen. He knew it, even though the idea had no basis. But that was how terror took hold – *groundless fear.*

There's a phrase: 'It takes a heretic to catch a heretic.'

Matsuoka's words came ominously back to mind. Mikami never heard the phrase before. Was it something Matsuoka had thought up himself? Something to put words to an idea of his? If so, were they some kind of placeholder? Something that suggested what it was that needed to remain hidden?

The shadow of a bird crossed the front window.

Mikami pulled away as soon as the light turned green. He needed to stare into Matsuoka's eyes and check, and not just for the sake of Media Relations.

73

A wind was picking up.

A four-tonne truck was parked up ahead, bearing the logo of a soft-drink manufacturer. Three years ago, the logo on the van was that of a cigarette company. Before that, Mikami seemed to remember it had been one for a company making processed food. It was the prefecture's Mobile Command Centre, purchased the year following the Six Four kidnapping after a compensatory jump in their budget. In the thirteen years since, he'd never once heard of the computerized vehicle being deployed.

Mikami was in his car. *The parking area of a driving school, half a kilometre from Station G.* It had taken three trips around the city to find them. *A detective in the driving seat. An elbow poking from the passenger window.* There would be more inside, sitting in the glittering silver container that formed the back of the vehicle.

The engine was off, but the vehicle's design included an array of batteries fitted to the undercarriage, allowing air conditioning, communications devices and all digital components to function regardless.

Five past ten. The announcement would have started. More likely, the announcement scheduled for eight o'clock was still dragging on. He couldn't let it distract him. He would wait for Matsuoka. Any normal First Division Chief would set up base in the Investigative HQ and lead from there, but Mikami knew that wouldn't apply to a hunter like Matsuoka. He would take advantage of any tool that was available to him. If there was a command vehicle, he would be in it. Mikami's job now was to keep his eyes open, to keep watch.

He hadn't slept for twenty-eight hours. He didn't feel sleepy, but his experience from previous stake-outs told him that was a sign of danger. You just passed out. And when you did, you didn't wake again, not even if your mark prodded you in the head. Matsuoka would enter the command vehicle at ten thirty. Eleven at the latest. Mikami had to stay alert until then.

He lit a cigarette; keeping one eye on the vehicle, he opened his mobile. He called the retired officer, Mochizuki. No one answered. Maybe his phone was on drive mode. Mikami had missed his call while he'd been driving, his own phone also set to drive mode. Now he was parked and calling Mochizuki back, their situations reversed; perhaps he was out delivering some flowers.

Futawatari paid another visit.

Mikami was expecting the call to be something like that. It didn't stir up any emotions. It was something he had to get out of the way, but that was all. The issue of the commissioner's visit had been sorted. In its place was the kidnapping and the kidnapping alone, stretching as far as the eye could see.

Mikami stubbed his cigarette into the car's ashtray.

Futawatari called earlier, asking if he could help. I can call him in.

He hadn't meant to test Suwa. The situation had convinced him that help was needed. How would Futawatari have dealt with it? What would he have done to get through? Mochizuki's missed call had triggered the questions, but his thoughts in the lift had been different. *Someone to rescue Suwa and Ochiai.* Futawatari's name had been the first to come to mind.

He slapped himself on the cheeks. He'd jumped after seeing the numbers on the car's digital clock: 10.25. His watch read the same. It felt as if time had jumped forwards. *I've been passing out each time I blink.* The fear rose inside him. He leaned into the steering column and scanned the command vehicle.

Nothing out of the ordinary. It was parked in the same place.

Everything was normal. Mikami let out a breath and had just begun to settle back into his seat when . . .

Matsuoka.

A row of three four-door sedans pulled on to the road in front of the driving school. Mikami caught a glimpse of Matsuoka from the side. He was in the back of the first vehicle. The cars continued until they were in the shadow of the command vehicle; there was the screech of brakes.

Mikami was already out of his car, running towards them. Alerted by the sound, one of the detectives getting out of the third vehicle turned around. *Aizawa.* He brushed a hand towards the hem of his jacket, not recognizing who it was. For a split second, the holster carrying his gun came into view. *Was he going to draw?* Mikami held up his hands but refrained from coming to a full stop. Seeing it was Mikami, his old boss from Special Investigations, Aizawa called to the next detective emerging from the vehicle, his expression still tense. *Looks like we've got a complication . . .*

Still keeping his distance, Mikami circled around towards the front of the command vehicle. He could feel the glaring eyes before the others came into view. Seven, eight, nine . . . Nine detectives stood encircling Matsuoka, each with a concealed weapon around their hip or chest. Each was a big name. Among them were Ogata from Violent Crime Section One and Minegishi from Special Investigations. They were Matsuoka's best, with a long service of leadership – men in line to take charge of Criminal Investigations for the next generation. They stood there, intimidating, as they tried to gauge Mikami's purpose, but they were also the only ones to remember decorum and offer a silent nod of their heads.

Once again, Matsuoka showed no sign of surprise. Mikami felt a wave of nostalgia, as though they'd been reunited after a long trip, despite the fact that they had met only a day earlier, in the toilets of Station G. Matsuoka's eyes were not those of a heretic. There was no need for further scrutiny: they were the eyes of a man working on a case. They seemed compressed, half closed in concentration. When the time came, Mikami knew they would snap open, lifting, together with his thick eyebrows, to form the mask of a *Kongorikishi*, the muscular guardians that manned temple gates.

'What, you're stalking me now, Mikami?'

No doubt a calculated move, Matsuoka's casual remark immediately eased the tension among the detectives, bringing their guard down a notch. It had no effect on Mikami. He remained tightly wound.

'Let me come with you. In my role as press director.'

The nine detectives reacted simultaneously, looking astonished. With the cream of Criminal Investigations present, Mikami hadn't said anything that might sound as if he was bargaining for sympathy. There was the future to consider. He didn't care what they thought of him as an individual, but he couldn't undersell his office by kowtowing before these men, who were all detectives to their core. And he didn't have the time. Neither would Matsuoka. The commander would need to get inside and mobilize. It was all or nothing.

Matsuoka opened his mouth and spoke.

'I owe you my thanks. Nanao got in touch this morning to let me know.'

What?

'You didn't know? About Minako. She came in.'

'Right . . .'

She'd decided to do it.

'Yeah, sure. Get in.'

What?

'If you lose control of the press, we lose control of the front line. I want you to feed them until they fall asleep.'

The other detectives looked aghast, but it was Mikami who was truly lost for words. His follow-up proposal had already been on the tip of his tongue. *If not the command vehicle, at least a pursuit or an intercept car.*

'But, sir . . .'

Ogata had started to complain, but he held his tongue. Anyone who'd ever worked for Matsuoka would know why. It wasn't his rank as an officer or his title – whether as Chief Adviser or as First Division Chief – that had given Ogata pause. It was, instead, his trust in and reverence for Matsuoka's wishes that had prevented him from blurting out a poorly considered, emotive response. He would also know that the decision was no longer one he could reverse, not now Matsuoka had said it.

'Here's the condition. You wait at least twenty minutes before relaying anything you hear inside. We need to maintain a time lag between the investigation and the press,' Matsuoka said.

He hadn't given Mikami a condition. He'd given him permission to relay information directly, from the command vehicle to the conference room. Twenty minutes was well within the boundary of any administrative delay. During kidnappings in the past, there were many cases where the press had had to wait thirty minutes, even an hour, before they were brought up to speed.

'Yes, sir. That won't be a problem.'

'You concentrate on your job; we'll take care of ours.'

Make sure not to interfere with the investigation. He'd picked up on Mikami's rising adrenalin. But while it was true that the anticipation was building, Mikami's mind was not focused on the hunt. *The detective was stirring.* Matsuoka had doubtless interpreted it that way.

The steel bars rang out as the doors to the back of the vehicle's container came unlocked; they swung open. *The smell of his hands after pull-ups on the bar.* His nose registered the memory. Dully glowing orange ceiling lights. The area was cramped compared to how it had appeared from the outside, reminding Mikami of a submarine walkway he'd once seen in a film. Desks covered with screens and apparatus lined both sides. Seven stools were bolted to the floor in a zigzag pattern. Two men were already sitting inside, both wearing headphones. One was sitting before a phone attached to the desk; he was hairy, round, burly. The other was thin, pencil-faced, with a centre parting, and looked nothing like a detective. He was sitting in front of two computers, suggesting his role was something like Koichiro Hiyoshi's during the Six Four investigation.

The only people to get in were Matsuoka and the two team leaders, Ogata and Minegishi. Mikami, too, having secured his place. That made six but, despite there being seven stools, there was no room to move around. Elbows and knees knocked together as they took their seats.

'Closing up.'

Ogata pulled the handles on both doors, which were designed to be closed from the inside. They came together with a metallic thud. Both the view and any remaining light were shut out, compressing the air inside. Mikami immediately tensed, feeling his chest constrict. They had air-conditioning but no windows. The view from each side of the vehicle – front, back, left and right – was projected on to four different monitors sunk into the walls.

Minegishi picked up a radio microphone.

'Special Investigations, this is Mobile Command.'

'This is Special Investigations. Go ahead.'

'Confirm reception. Over.'

'Good: five bars. All tests okay. Over.'

'Copy. Commander and five more on board. Over.'

'Copy.'

'Mobile Command, over and out.'

The screens to the left were showing a rush of activity: a succession of car doors closing. The detectives outside were getting back into their cars. *Intercept 6. Intercept 7. Intercept 8.* Minegishi tested each of their radio responses. They were all part of the Intercept Unit; their role would be to conceal themselves in areas where there was a high likelihood of the kidnapper showing up, and move in if necessary. If the profiling was based around this being a copycat crime, the cars would have to be positioned near or at the areas designated by the kidnapper fourteen years earlier. They would be points, coming together to form a line. Also . . . right . . . around the area of yesterday's calls. Mikami took out his notebook, having come up with his first question. He was close enough for Matsuoka to feel his breath.

'Sir, do you know whereabouts in Genbu yesterday's calls were made?'

'The first was Tokiwamachi. The second was the area between Sumamachi and Nagimachi.'

'Can you give a general description of the areas?'

'They're west and east of Genbu's main station. Tokiwamachi is to the west; it's a downtown area based around an arcade-type shopping street. Bars, cinemas, that sort of thing. Sumamachi and Nagimachi are to the east, both red-light districts. Hostess bars, sex shops, love hotels, game centres. They've got it all.'

Matsuoka's answer was unguarded, detailed enough to dispel any suspicion that he was holding back. Mikami checked his watch: 10.38. He read through the notes he'd taken. *Tokiwamachi. Sumamachi. Nagimachi. The calls, both made from near the station.* Details. Exactly what he'd been waiting for. When he called it in, Ochiai would be euphoric. Suwa, the others, too – they would be able to stand tall before the other reporters. The embargo would hold until 10.58. Mikami stared at the second hand of the wall clock, willing time on. Twenty minutes felt different in a place like this. Like sitting on a bed of nails, it felt like a day, an eternity.

He could get more. If he didn't wait, he could report it all in one go at 10.58.

'The money – have they got the ransom of 20 million?'

He became aware of cold looks from Ogata and Minegishi.

'That's all done. We've taken the serial numbers and the notes have been marked.'

'Has the kidnapper been back in touch?'

'No.'

'And investigators – have you deployed people to the nine businesses from the Six Four investigation?'

'Naturally.'

And Minako? The thought came to him, but it wasn't the time to ask.

'And upstream, the Futago river?'

'Yes. We have officers near the Kotohira bridge, and the Ikkyu fishing lodge.'

That was as far as he got. The vehicle shuddered as the engine came to life.

'First we go to the house,' Matsuoka said.

Minegishi nodded in response. He got into a half-crouch and slid open a panel connecting the hold to the driver's side. *Take us out. Vicinity of Mesaki's home.*

The vehicle moved slowly forwards.

'This is Mobile Command, moving out.' Ogata used the radio to relay the information to the Investigative HQ.

'Copy.'

The speakers were silent again. Case information only. Nothing else was permitted.

They pulled out on to a main road. The four wall monitors projected the view on each side. Mikami knew the vehicle received yearly upgrades, that the computers and monitor system – which now enabled high-resolution recording and playback – had been added over time, and that the sensitivity of the directional microphones had also seen huge improvements. Using switches at the rear, they were able to cover the full 360-degree radius. Lying among the apparatus were nine mobile phones, all on a small, rimmed desk so they wouldn't fall. Each phone had a label: *S. Investigations, Station G, Home, Intercept, Pursuit, Outdoors, Locations, S. Ops, Kitou.* The numbers had been apportioned so the calls didn't come into a single phone. *Kitou* was the chief of Violent Crime, Section Two. He would be hiding in the car with Masato Mesaki and the ransom. Mikami had to wonder why they had included Special Operations. Most likely it was because the majority of work carried out during a kidnapping investigation was of a similar nature to theirs.

Matsuoka had moved Pencil-face to the side and was dividing his attention between two screens. One was a map of the Genbu city limits, the other a map of City D. They were scattered with blinking green and red lights, perhaps marking vehicles or officers in the field. The vast majority were in City D. The two cities were different in terms of size, but even then the distribution was surprising. Mesaki's home was in Genbu, and the kidnapper's calls had originated there, too, making it much more likely – under normal circumstances – to be the focus of an initial response than City D. The pattern suggested an emphasis on the Six Four elements of the case, but it felt like a gamble. Mikami wanted to find out the reason, but Matsuoka looked busy.

The vehicle shook. Perhaps because of bad suspension, the jolting was severe each time they crossed a bump or join in the road.

Minegishi was busy talking to the Home Unit on one of the mobiles; they were going through the details of the handover. The kidnapper would have Mesaki's mobile number from his daughter's phone. If the plan was to lead Mesaki and the money from point to point, as it had been with Six Four, it was likely he would call directly instead of using the businesses en route. Expecting this, they had attached a wireless microphone to his phone . . .

'Patching call to speakers,' Burly said to Minegishi. The voice of the man from the Home Unit echoed through the hold.

'Testing. Testing. Testing. Connection with target mobile. Repeat. Connection with target mobile.'

Loud and clear, Minegishi said, holding the mobile close to his mouth.

They had fitted a similar device to Mesaki's home phone. If a call came in, they would be able to monitor it in real time from the command vehicle. It was a different era. They no longer needed anyone on a radio to relay calls, as Mikami had done fourteen years earlier from the passenger seat of Pursuit 1.

He felt no regret. Just as he felt no need to compete with the present. Surrounded by real detectives, he'd have been lying to say he wasn't interested in their actions, their skills – but he still didn't feel like he was part of the hunt. His battle was with time. There were six minutes until the embargo lifted . . .

'Sir, we're almost there,' Ogata said. He was pointing at the corner of one of the monitors. His finger traversed away from the front monitor towards the one on the right. A normal-looking detached house on two floors, mortar and wood, behind a small-ish area for children to play in. The Mesaki family home.

'Okay, good,' Matsuoka said, studying the image. 'All we need to do is keep the house's relative position in mind. Take us on to the prefectural highway, towards City D.'

Ogata nodded, this time using a radio to relay the instructions to the driver.

The command vehicle was going to City D? Was the lead commander, the head of the army, really planning to leave Genbu? Genbu was where Mesaki's home was. It was also where the kidnapper's calls had originated – from the east and west sides of the main station. The east stood out, with its hostess bars, sex shops, love hotels, gaming centres. Wasn't that exactly the kind of place a kidnapper might use as a base of operations?

Something about that thought snagged. *Of course.* Lowlifes weren't the only kind of people who liked to hang out in the red-light districts. Out-of-control teenagers did, too, whatever their gender. What had happened to the idea of a hoax? Mikami's unexpected ticket into the investigation's central hub had, combined with the fact that no one had mentioned the possibility since, caused it to slip his mind completely.

But . . .

Mikami checked the clock. Two and a half minutes left. Matsuoka had leaned back from the screens and was watching the front monitor with a look that suggested the hunt was about to begin.

'Sir.'

'Uh-huh. What is it?'

'Have you begun the search for Kasumi Mesaki?'

Matsuoka looked unhappy with the question, which took Mikami by surprise. Had he offended him? *Right*. He'd used Kasumi's name, even though it was yet to be disclosed.

'Have you dismissed the possibility of this being a hoax?' Mikami asked, making sure not to repeat the offence.

'No, definitely not.'

'Are you searching the red-light district?'

'We're in the middle of a kidnapping; we can't do anything that might get us seen.'

Coming from Matsuoka, the answer sounded evasive. One of the hallmarks of modern policing, for Public Security and Criminal Investigations alike, was the ability to deploy large-scale investigations in the shadows.

'Do you know where she tended to go?'

'No.'

'Both calls originated in commercial districts, areas where lots of people go to hang out. Assuming this isn't a hoax, isn't there a strong possibility she's still in Genbu?'

'Mikami,' Ogata said, his eyes warning. Minegishi folded his arms, displeased.

Mikami nodded, but he couldn't stop the question.

'Why are we heading for City D?'

'Focus on your job,' Matsuoka said wearily. He jerked his chin up towards the clock on the wall.

The second hand was at the top of the dial: 10.58. Mikami was amazed. Was the timing coincidence, or had Matsuoka kept count of the twenty minutes, too?

'Excuse me.'

Mikami repositioned himself at the rear of the container,

stumbling each time the vehicle rocked. Burly's wide back was in the way. Mikami pulled out his mobile and opened it; he dialled Suwa's number, crouching forwards to hide some of the background noise.

The phone rang for a long time. When Suwa finally answered, the wave of sound was like a hammer on Mikami's eardrums. He was transported immediately back to the conference room. The volume was incredible, enough to make him physically recoil. Suwa was all but inaudible, his voice coming only in short bursts. He was making his way through the crowd, heading for the corridor. The line went dead even as Mikami pictured the image. He redialled straight away, but no one answered. He was left with nothing to do but wait for Suwa to call back once he'd found somewhere he could talk.

It was five minutes later when the mobile, gripped tight, started to vibrate.

'Sorry about that. I had to deal with something.'

Mikami didn't know what to say. Suwa had no doubt moved, but the background commotion could have been the worst he'd heard – if not for their last call.

'Anything wrong?'

He said the words then realized the phrase was Minako's. She had probably felt like he did now for a long time. The irritation that came from wanting to help, to take someone's place but be unable to do so. With no other way out, the emotion had become a stock question.

Suwa reported that Ochiai was still holding out. *The rest in Medical helped, I think; he's surprisingly resilient.* There was admiration in Suwa's voice as he spoke. At the same time, he said the situation was getting worse. The press had lost control when Matsuoka had failed to turn up at the eight o'clock announcement. They had taken the issue to the NPA, demanded that the Criminal Investigations Bureau send an executive in. Tokyo had refused outright. They'd taken the same position they had with the commissioner. There was no reason to expose themselves to the risk of another Dallas. Besides, they had no justification. Apart from its treatment of the press, Criminal Investigations had shown no deficiencies in its response to the kidnapping.

'. . . that really pushed them over the edge. They didn't like being snubbed like that. They've pushed Ochiai into fifty trips now, and the Investigative HQ still refuses to give him anything to help.'

Having listened to this point, Mikami opened his notebook. 'Listen. I'm inside the Mobile Command Centre. I can relay information to you as it comes in. Here's some for now. Take this down.'

Mikami relayed everything Matsuoka had given him. It was evident from Suwa's acknowledgements that he was already brightening. He was regaining his voice after a night of being beaten into submission. Mikami wanted to hear Kuramae and Mikumo's voices. He asked how they were.

'They're okay. Tougher than me, that's for sure,' Suwa said. 'There's no need to worry, we're getting used to things here,' he added, his voice rising an octave.

They both paused. *No one gets used to something like that.* Mikami looked at his scribbled-down notes. The information he'd given him wouldn't last long. He had to feed the press more, feed them until they were full, keep the information flowing until they couldn't take any more. It was the only way to put an end to the hell of the conference room.

'Suwa, listen . . .' *Take turns to get some sleep. Even if it's just fifteen minutes, half an hour.* Mikami was just getting ready to speak when he was interrupted.

'Incoming call. Mesaki's home phone.'

The voice had come from inside the hold. Mikami couldn't process what was happening.

'Patching it through, standby.'

One of Burly's hairy hands reached for a switch.

Mikami was now sitting bolt upright. Was it the kidnapper? Surely it was too early. It was 11.13. They had close to fifty minutes left until the deadline for getting together the ransom.

Ogata and Minegishi were on their feet behind Burly. Matsuoka was hidden in their shadow. A muffled sound emerged from the wall speakers. A phone, ringing. Once, twice . . . Pencil-face pulled his headphones half off and turned around.

'We've got a number. It's Kasumi Mesaki's mobile.'

The kidnapper. No one moved. No one breathed.

Three rings. Four. *Click.* Someone had picked up.

– H . . . hello? This is Mesaki. Hello . . .?

It was Masato Mesaki's voice. He sounded terrified.

– Hello? Can you hear me? H . . . hello?

– Do you have the money?

Mikami felt himself shiver. The kidnapper's voice, aliensounding from the helium, echoed crushingly through the hold.

– Yes . . . I've got it. It's all ready. Please, let me hear my daughter's voice. I'm begging you. Just for a moment . . .

– Leave now, bring the money and a phone. I want it at the Aoi Café in Aoi-machi, City D. Make sure you're there by 11.50.

The Aoi Café. The kidnapper really was planning to trace the Six Four route.

– Okay . . . 11.50. The Aoi Café. I think I know it. Right . . . yes . . . I think I've seen a billboard advertising it. Next to the main road . . . and a bookstore. I'm leaving right now. I'm bringing the money. If you could just let me—

Beep beep beep beep.

The line went dead.

Nobody moved. They were waiting. Matsuoka's eyes were locked shut. He looked like he was meditating.

'Sir, what is it?'

The voice leaked from the phone in Mikami's hand, hanging now by his side. It pulled him out of the reverie; he put the phone back to his ear.

'Sir, what is it? Has something happened?'

It's started.

Mikami came close to saying it. For a moment he thought it would be okay. Suwa just had to keep it to himself for twenty minutes . . .

But . . .

Get out. It would all be over if Matsuoka said the words.

Mikami made a note of the time: 11.16.

'I'll call back in exactly twenty minutes. Until then, try to get some sleep.'

74

'Pick it up.' Ogata issued the instruction through the panel leading to the front. The engine roared into life and the vehicle began to accelerate rapidly. They were on the verge of crossing into the city. Information was flying back and forth. Ogata was on the radio, Minegishi mostly on the mobiles. Both maintained constant communication with the Investigative HQ and the vehicles already mobilized.

'Get Forensics on to the background noise. ASAP.'

'Hold your position! Do not move in until we know the origin of the call. Repeat, standby.'

'Mesaki sounds like he's losing control. Tell him he needs to stop the car before he answers any more calls. We can't have him causing an accident.'

They were impressive, living up to their reputation as the future leaders of the department. They seemed able to read Matsuoka's thoughts, relaying his wishes with precise instructions, efficient and faultless as they dealt with the information coming in. More than anything, they were in tune with each other. They never repeated themselves, never got in the other's way, made sure always to seek confirmation before acting. It was like watching a two-headed dragon weave a dance through the hemmed-in container.

It was a different story outside the vehicle.

Evident in the communications between the Investigative HQ, Station G and the front-line vehicles, confusion and panic were rife. The officers had been caught off guard. Was that why the kidnapper had decided to bring the deadline forward? Or had something gone wrong with the plan?

'I want green lights, the whole way.'

It had been Matsuoka's first detailed instruction: fix the lights to make sure Mesaki's car makes it in time. They needed him to hurry. Mesaki had left his home at eleven fifteen, immediately after the kidnapper had ended the call. He'd had thirty-five minutes until the designated time. Getting to City D and Aoi-machi took forty minutes even without traffic; with traffic, the trip could last more than an hour. One of the screens inside the command vehicle was broadcasting information from Traffic Management. While there were no jams, the whole of the prefectural highway was flagged as having medium-to-heavy traffic. Matsuoka had given the order the moment Pencil-face had performed the calculation: Mesaki would be late by twelve or thirteen minutes. They already had people in place to manage the lights. Officers from Traffic were posted at every intersection en route, all in Tokyo Electric Power outfits. They would be notified by radio when Mesaki's car was approaching; then, taking care not to stand out, they would flip open the control box and fix the lights to green, returning them to normal once Mesaki was through. Like a game of Chinese whispers, the green lights would transmit down the line, preventing any major disruption of normal traffic.

'Mobile Command, this is Pursuit 1.'

'This is Mobile Command, go ahead.'

'We have a green at the Kuwabara intersection. Mesaki's through.'

'Copy.'

Kuwabara was three intersections behind the Mobile Command Centre. They'd passed it only two minutes earlier. The gap was closing. Around here, the road was a dual carriageway. Mesaki would be picking up speed. He would be on them in no time.

Mikami's notebook was permanently open. Whenever new information came in, he would take a note and mark the time. He would then add twenty minutes to the number and write the time the embargo lifted next to it. At 11.51, he could tell the press that Mesaki had passed the Kuwabara intersection. By that time, he would have probably already arrived at the Aoi Café. Still, as far as the press were concerned Mesaki was still at home. There were five minutes until the embargo lifted on the kidnapper's call. Mikami felt restless. He'd never thought twenty minutes could stretch out for so long.

They entered City D. The buildings were growing taller.

'We've got the area of the call.' Burly spoke up, after getting off the phone with DoCoMo. 'Yuasa Radio Tower. Genbu. Districts: Yuasa-cho and Asahimachi.'

'Genbu again,' Mikami muttered, taking the details down. The kidnapper was still in Genbu. What was the plan, having already sent Mesaki to City D? There was no way they could get to the Aoi Café ahead of him, not with Mesaki racing through green lights all the way. Besides, using the prefectural highway would mean passing twice through the N-system of automatic numberplate recognition. Maybe the kidnapper had no intention of going to City D and was instead planning to aim directly for another destination, somewhere already decided as the final handover point. A second possibility was that there was an accomplice, watching from somewhere near the Aoi Café.

It didn't feel right. It was sloppy, whether the kidnapper was working alone or as part of a group. They'd made two calls from Genbu City. Then, despite having a mobile that could be used anywhere, they'd made another call from inside the city limits. It didn't make sense. The calls would be traced to the general area. The circle would narrow.

What if the kidnapper didn't realize the danger? It was possible, if it was Kasumi. She hated her father and now she had him in a panic. She would be enjoying every minute of it. She would have no intention of taking the money – to her it wasn't even a hoax . . . just some practical joke.

No . . .

The kidnapper isn't female. That was what Mikami's intuition had told him the moment he'd heard the helium-altered voice. He hadn't been able to tell the gender outright, but it had been clear from the kidnapper's way of speaking, from the aggressive but not overstated tone, the mix of threat and restraint, that the speaker wasn't a seventeen-year-old girl. If it was a joke, an act she was putting on, she would have to be in it with an experienced, and male, accomplice.

'Let me see that.'

Mikami glanced at one of the screens over Matsuoka's shoulder. Brought up on the display was a map of the general area of the call, centred around Yuasa-cho and Asahimachi. At Matsuoka's request, Pencil-face zoomed in on the image. Yuasa-cho appeared mostly residential. The surprise was Asahimachi. It was located right next to Nagimachi, the area of the second call from the day before. Not part of the red-light district but crowded all the same. Lining the city road as it crossed the district were large out-of-town supermarkets, home-appliance stores, bowling alleys, outlet stores and a few of the large national chains selling business suits and shoes.

Out for a good time. The three areas seemed at first to shore up the idea of the kidnapping being a hoax. There were, of course, other explanations. The kidnapper was using the bustle to hide. Keeping near a train station to ensure an easy getaway should the need arise. Mikami couldn't decide. Was it a hoax? A genuine kidnapping? It was impossible to draw a conclusion either way.

'Sir, he's passing us now,' Ogata said. His finger was pointing towards one of the rear monitors. A white coupé, listing slightly towards the centre of the road. Fifty metres back. Still too far to make out the driver's face.

'Put us in the right-hand lane,' Minegishi instructed the driver over the radio.

A moment later, the vehicle drew smoothly towards the central division. The reason for the change became immediately clear. With the fast lane blocked, Mesaki had pulled left; he was overtaking on the inside. The driver's side was next to the command vehicle – they'd be able to see him close up.

All eyes turned to the monitors showing the left side of the vehicle. The moment they saw the white coupé pull up alongside them, it was gone.

But . . .

They'd had enough time to get a clear view of Mesaki's profile.

He'd been bent forwards, bunched over the steering column, his face all but pressed against the windscreen. *Forwards. Forwards.* His eyes had been glaring at something in the far distance. His teeth were bared, clenched tight, his gums bright red. He was a man on a warpath, a fire that was out of control. The expression had contrasted starkly with that of Yoshio Amamiya, who had looked as though his blood had frozen over.

Mikami shivered, feeling the tangible connection to the case. Mesaki was a fireball heading to a single destination. The Aoi Café.

'Sir . . .'

Matsuoka's eyes were still focused on the monitor. Pursuit 1 and Pursuit 2 were next to overtake the command vehicle. The camera picked up their fleeting eye contact.

'. . . is Minako at the Aoi Café?'

'No.'

'Where is she posted?'

'I can't tell you.'

'Mobile Command, this is Pursuit 1.'

'Why not?'

'This is Mobile Command, go ahead.'

'She's working with Special Operations.'

Mikami pulled back slightly. Minako, with Special Operations?

'We have a green at the Katayama-cho 3-chome intersection. Mesaki's through.'

'Copy.'

'What's she doing?'

'It's Special Ops. I can't tell you.'

'I'm her husband.'

'It doesn't matter.'

'Is it dangerous?'

'No, she'll be fine.'

Mikami regretted asking. Matsuoka had cooled since he'd said Kasumi's name. Although . . . maybe it wasn't just with him. The man's responses were increasingly terse, even with the others. And he hadn't issued any instructions since the lights. He was thinking in silence, looking almost lethargic, most of the time keeping his eyes closed. Was he sick? Mikami realized Matsuoka was starting to worry.

He jumped when he saw the time. 11.35. As it took a while to get past Burly, he should start towards the rear of the hold. He moved quickly, pushing forwards and past the man blocking the walkway. He opened his mobile; the moment the display switched to 11.36 he hit the button to dial Suwa's mobile. Probably already waiting, Suwa answered before the phone had a chance to ring.

The background was still noisy, but this time they were able to talk normally.

'The kidnapper made a third call to Mesaki's home,' Mikami said without pausing.

'Right! What time?'

'Twenty minutes ago. Wait . . . hang on. No. The call was at 11.13.'

Checking the numbers in his notebook, Mikami felt a rush of blood to his head. *Damn it. Idiot. Why didn't I use the time the call actually came in?*

'Sir? Hello . . .?'

'Sorry. I'll give you the details. Take this down.'

'Go ahead.'

Mikami related the details of the call. *Helium. Money and a phone. Aoi Café by 11.50.*

'But . . . 11.50? It's almost 11.50 now. It's already thirty-seven minutes past.'

'I know.'

'So Mesaki's already on his way?'

'That's right. He left the house at eleven fifteen.'

'Where is he now? Is he in City D?'

Mikami managed to catch himself. 'I can't say. I've got to wait twenty minutes.'

'Twenty minutes? I don't . . .'

'There has to be a time lag. I got in here on that condition.'

'Right, of course . . . okay. But you can tell me first, can't you?'

'Incoming call. Mesaki's mobile.' Burly spoke up again. 'The caller is . . . using Kasumi's mobile. Patching it through.'

'Sir?'

'I have to hang up. Just bear with me on this.'

The kidnapper's fourth call. The sound of the ringing resonated through the hold. Mesaki answered immediately.

— *This is Mesaki. What is it?*

His voice was close to a shriek.

— *Turn right at the Katayama-cho 3-chome intersection, join the ring road.*

Mikami couldn't believe it. They'd just passed the intersection at 3-chome. Which meant Mesaki's car had . . .

— *The 3-chome intersection? But I'm . . . I've already passed it!*

A pause followed.

— *Make a u-turn, right now.*

— *You want me to turn around? Okay, yes . . .*

Was the kidnapper hoping to throw them off course, moving

to an original script now the police were convinced it was a copy-cat crime? Or had something happened to force the kidnapper into making a quick revision of the plan? Whatever the case, Mesaki speeding through all the lights had been unexpected. The brief silence that followed Mesaki's answer had highlighted the kidnapper's surprise and disbelief.

'Urgent, urgent! Mobile Command, this is Pursuit 1. Mesaki has just made a u-turn. Continuing pursuit.'

'Pursuit 1, do not follow. Take the next two right turns, then turn left at the next intersection to join the ring road. Pursuit 2, left for three turns to follow.' Once he'd finished, Ogata turned to look at Matsuoka. 'Sir, what do you want us to do?'

'We follow Pursuit 1.'

'Affirmative.'

Ogata used the radio to relay this to the driver. To his side, Minegishi had the mobile labelled Kitou pressed to his ear. Burly was fixing various wires into the monitors, moving with a speed at odds with his size.

'Make sure Mesaki remains calm.'

'I can't.' The voice that came back was muffled. Kitou was speaking from under a blanket on the floor behind the front seats. 'He's still on the phone. I can't talk to him.'

'How fast is he going now?'

'Hold on. Eighty . . . no, closer to eighty-five.'

'Use your nightstick to give him a jab. Softly though, like he's a peach.'

— *Have you turned around?*

They were interrupted by the helium voice.

— *Yes! I just need to join the ring road, yes?*

— *That's right. Turn left at the intersection you passed: 3-chome.*

'Mesaki approaching now!' Pencil-face yelled.

The front-facing monitor. The white coupé was racing towards them in the opposite lane. Mesaki had his phone to his ear. He and the car flashed by. He was rocking violently backwards and forwards, like a kid having a tantrum behind the wheel of a broken pedal car.

'All Intercept Units in City D, this is Mobile Command. Intercept 1, hold position. Intercept 2, 3, 4 and 5, bring the back line forwards. Ogata! Mesaki's going to crash if he continues like this.'

'. . . cancel the green lights on the prefectural highway . . . cancel all green lights on the prefectural highway. Mesaki should be fine . . . he used to sell imported cars.'

'. . . we can't bring the line forwards. Three kilometres south . . . that's where we need the intercept cars. And Mesaki's doing eighty-five, with one hand!'

'This is Mobile Command. Copy. Okay, let's get him below seventy. Use two units to block his path – can you do that?'

Mikami was on edge. As if to suggest they couldn't work seated down, Ogata and Minegishi were both on their feet, backs pressed together. It was the best way of keeping balance. The command vehicle swung roughly to one side then the other, switching lanes before making a right. The road was bad, making the vertical jolting worse.

'Incoming call. DoCoMo. The origin of the call is . . . unchanged. Yuasa Radio Tower. Genbu. Districts: Yuasa-cho and Asahimachi.'

The kidnapper was still there. Perhaps moving, but still in the same general area.

'Can they narrow the area at all?' Mikami asked Pencil-face.

'Not possible. Not without more radio towers. Or the phone having GPS.'

'The phone having GPS?'

'Right. Some of the new models come with GPS antennas. KDDI put a few on sale last year. Fantastic phones, but they didn't catch on . . .'

Pencil-face looked for a moment like he'd forgotten everything else. He had long eyelashes, attractive eyes. Mikami sighed. It felt like he'd been treated as a guest. He *was* a guest, that much was true. But Matsuoka was showing no signs of hospitality, despite having invited him in. Instead of cushions, he'd been given a hard, mushroom-like stool. He'd had to bear witness to Ogata and Minegishi's impressive swordsmanship. It wasn't humiliation he felt, but it certainly wasn't comfortable. At the same time, he had to reflect on his luck, that he had managed to go with them in the command vehicle . . . To reflect on his luck . . .

The vehicle lurched into the air. Mikami caught a sharp breath. It took a moment to remember where he was. He'd almost gone under. No – he *had* gone under. The bump in the road had brought him back. *Amazing.* He was at the front line of the investigation, inside the lair of the true commander of Criminal Investigations, at the very top of the food chain. And yet the sandman had still come, unforgiving of even a momentary lapse. It had seized on his sense of good fortune and tried to lure him away by turning it to a sense of well-being, even elation.

He pinched the inside of his leg, twisting until the pain forced his mouth open.

'Incoming call. Forensics. Initial analysis of the calls to Mesaki's home has revealed a subtle reverberation. Potential matches are bathrooms, unfurnished studios, public toilets in government and/or commercial buildings built using reinforced concrete.'

Public toilets . . .

Mikami remembered the footsteps he'd heard the previous night. He saw again the map of the Asahimachi area. Large stores on a main road . . .

First he had to take down the new information. He opened his notebook, then stared in disbelief. *One of the details was missing.* He'd forgotten to record the time the kidnapper had instructed Mesaki to join the ring road. He'd been on the phone with Suwa. Then he remembered: Suwa had mentioned the time. *It's already thirty-seven minutes past.* The call had come in directly after that: 11.37. Mikami wrote down the time, then appended the details. The kidnapper's words. Making sure to get them right.

Holding the pen too tight, he tore the paper. *Damn idiot. What are you doing? Keep it together!*

'Mobile Command, this is Pursuit 1. Visual confirmation of Mesaki's car ahead. He's heading east on the ring road.'

'Copy. What's his speed?'

'Eighty-three, maybe eighty-four.'

'That's too fast. Pursuit 1 and Pursuit 2, get in front and slow him down to below seventy.'

'Pursuit 1, copy.'

'Pursuit 2, copy.'

'Mobile Command out.'

– Aaaaahhh . . . aaaaahhh.

Mesaki emitted a high-pitched moan. The kidnapper was still on the line. *– Please . . . please give Kasumi back . . .*

Heartbreaking was the only way to describe it. With guilty eyes, Burly lowered the volume a fraction.

– Where do you want me to go? Just tell me where. I need to see Kasumi. Please, I'm begging . . .

The question was a good one – where *was* the kidnapper trying to take him? Pencil-face was scrolling through the map on the screen. It was still too early to dismiss the Aoi Café. The ring road headed north, arrow-like, until it crossed the state road four kilometres on. From there, turning left at the Isogai intersection would lead south and back towards downtown and Aoi-machi. The route from there was the reverse of Six Four. Mesaki would pass Mahjong Atari first, then Four Seasons Fruits, before finally reaching Six Four's first stop, the Aoi Café.

But taking that route would be considerably longer than travelling straight down the prefectural highway. The switch had only taken Mesaki from one trunk line to another, so it couldn't have been designed to lose any cars in pursuit. And the kidnapper had gone so far as to make him do a u-turn . . . maybe he was thinking of the industrial area to the east. Or was he going to make Mesaki take a right off the state road, then a left off the prefectural highway, which would send him north and back on to the original route, the road from fourteen years ago that led to Neyuki, snaking into the mountains . . . to the Kotohira bridge . . . to the mercury lamps . . .?

Mikami had to shake his head. He felt like he'd reached his limit. It wasn't just the drowsiness now. The vehicle kept jerking him awake, and he was getting adrenalin rushes, periods of feeling low. Each came without warning. He remembered something and called out. *11.51!* The embargo was already up on Mesaki's crossing the Kuwabara intersection.

He fumbled, opening his phone. His hands froze. *Wait. Kuwabara . . .?* It seemed ridiculous. Mesaki had made a u-turn and was now racing down the ring road. Was Mikami to report that he was still heading towards Aoi-machi, down the prefectural highway? He'd be misleading them, as though he were taking part in some kind of sick prank. *I can't.* He would skip that particular report. He would call once the embargo was cleared about the kidnapper telling Mesaki to make the u-turn and join the ring road. There was no value in knowing he'd passed the Kuwabara intersection . . .

No . . . Wait . . .

He was wrong. Missing the point. It wasn't his job to assign value. That was for the people on the outside to determine. Wasn't that exactly what he'd learned?

The police weren't the entire world. They weren't at the centre of any universe. Outside, time was standing still. Mesaki had left the house . . . but he hadn't moved a metre since. Mikami needed to set him in motion. He was the only one who could.

He called Suwa. He fed him the information about the Kuwabara intersection, said he'd follow with more, and ended the call. 'It's a lot more like a normal conference now,' Suwa had said before he'd hung up. The feeling of achievement served as encouragement. *I'm more than just a spare part here.* With his eyes and ears, he would pay witness to everything that happened. And he would recreate it for the people on the outside.

75

'Mobile Command, this is Pursuit 1. Mesaki now at seventy-two. Approaching state road junction in 500 metres.'

The pursuit units had pulled back, having successfully lowered Mesaki's speed.

'Copy. Make sure you're positioned to follow, whether he goes left or right.'

— *Have you got to the state road?*

The helium voice. It set Mikami on edge; there was no way to stop it from ricocheting right through him.

— *I'm almost there. Should I go on? Do you want me to turn?*

The tension inside was palpable. Which would it be?

— *Go right.*

To the north, then. That meant the industrial area to the east was no longer viable. The kidnapper was planning to follow Six Four's original route.

'Incoming Call. DoCoMo. Caller still in vicinity of the Yuasa Radio Tower.'

Suggesting the kidnapper had an accomplice.

He would need one, if the handover point was to be near Ney-uki, as it had been during Six Four. There were no decent roads linking the area and Genbu. There were a few minor routes you could take through villages and the forest, but the kidnapper wouldn't make it in time even if he left now. Mesaki was going to join the state road and speed north; it wouldn't be possible to reach Neyuki before him.

'Do you know of any helipads near the Yuasa Radio Tower?' Mikami asked Pencil-face.

'No.' The man had regained his businesslike look and tone.

There had to be an accomplice at the handover point. But where? It was a difficult question. The kidnapper had designated the Aoi Café, but then skipped it, and the next two points of the Six Four route. It wasn't even clear if the kidnapper was still mimicking Six Four. Getting Mesaki to throw the suitcase off the Kotohira bridge. Collecting it at Dragon's Hollow. Was something else waiting for them, something no one had thought of yet, something even more inventive than the idea behind Six Four? It didn't feel real. It felt made up. Was that because some part of Mikami knew the kidnapping was a hoax after all?

'Mobile Command, this is Pursuit 1. Mesaki has turned right on to the state road. He's northbound.'

— I just made the turn . . . what next? Keep going forwards?

— Are you familiar with the area?

— Here? No . . . not at all.

— Keep going straight. I'll get back to you with more instructions.

— Where am I going?

— Just get a move on. You don't have much time.

— O–okay!

'Mobile Command, this is Pursuit 1. Mesaki is picking up speed again. Eighty. Eighty-five. Ninety . . .'

— I just want Kasumi back, okay? I'll do anything. I just want her back!

— If you want to see her again, you will do everything I tell—

Everyone listening in sat bolt upright. The voice had changed, flattening and twisting around *see her again*, almost fully reverting to normal by *everything I tell*. A man's voice. Mikami had been right.

The line went dead. The helium had worn off.

'Kitou! Now's your chance. Get Mesaki to calm down, and he needs to drive more slowly. Make sure to keep your head down.'

'Copy.'

'Get Forensics on to the voice analysis.'

'Copy.'

Mikami had both feet firmly on the floor, bracing himself against the vehicle's erratic movement. He'd have done so even without the shaking – that was the effect of the shock coursing through him. It hadn't been the man's natural voice. The helium had held, just, maintaining the thinnest shield.

Even then . . .

. . . it felt like he'd actually heard it . . . *the voice of the Six Four kidnapper*. The voice of a man in his thirties or forties, slightly hoarse, with no trace of an accent. The voice that none of the detectives had heard, all those years ago. The Six Four kidnapper, re-enacting his own crime. He'd never considered it a possibility before. He still didn't, even after hearing the voice. There was only a sense of other-worldliness. The sense of having heard a voice calling from a place where no one was supposed to exist. Of having heard *something* from *somebody*. It felt like the shapeless uncertainty that had been smouldering inside him had multiplied and taken on the clear sound of footsteps.

'Have requested voice analysis. Noise analysis just in for the longer call. No echo detected. Other background sounds unclear due to the high noise levels in Mesaki's car.'

'Mesaki. You need to stay in control. Drive a bit slower.'

Kitou's voice sounded through the speakers. The connection picked up Mesaki's shrieked response.

– *What the fuck am I supposed to be doing? Where is he taking me?*

'Mesaki . . . Mesaki! Stop the car for now. We should wait for the next call.'

'Incoming call. Mesaki's mobile.'

Another call. Multiple sets of eyes drilled into the speakers.

'We've got the number. Kasumi's mobile.'

The fifth call: 11.56.

– *Keep . . . going . . . straight.*

Mikami was stunned. The voice was scratchy and pinched, that of a man squeezing his windpipe as tightly as he could. He'd run out of helium. His hand was clamped around his throat. The image was graphic.

The greater surprise came next.

– Go . . . to . . . the . . . Cher— . . . Cherry Café . . . on the left, a kilometre past . . . the Ishida-cho intersection.

It was a shortcut to bring Mesaki back. With no warning, the kidnapper had designated the Cherry Café, the fourth stop of the Six Four route.

– A kilometre past the lights . . . okay! The Cherry . . . Café. I'll find it!

Would he stick to Six Four from there? The Cherry Café would take Mesaki out of City D and into Yasugi. From there it had been right at another intersection a kilometre on to reach the Ai'ai Hair Salon on the city road. Then a left, at the next set of lights, to join the prefectural highway heading north again. Furusato Foods . . . Ozato Grill . . . Miyasaka Folk Crafts. Then, finally, the Ikkyu fishing lodge.

– Floor it . . . if you . . . want . . . to see your daughter alive. Floor it!

– Ahhhhhh!

Mikami opened his phone to the sound of Mesaki's heart-rending screech. He hadn't lost sight of the time: 11.57. He spoke quickly, relaying the last chunk of information to Suwa. The kidnapper instructing Mesaki to join the ring road, to make a u-turn. Mesaki complying. Leaving the prefectural highway.

That was as far as he could go.

Someone was watching him.

It was Matsuoka. His eyes were still those of a man on a case. Otherwise, he was inscrutable. Had he wanted to check that Mikami was keeping his word? Or had the look been out of pity? Maybe he really was unwell. When he'd seen Matsuoka, his eyes closed, it had seemed a real possibility. Matsuoka was leaving Ogata and Minegishi to do all the work. They were good, there

576

was no doubt about that. Enough to make Mikami feel envious. But the command vehicle didn't have that energy of being engaged in a hunt. The men were following the investigation with impressive finesse, but, with Matsuoka subdued, the usual burning urgency to take down the target was missing.

Did he believe it was a hoax, after all? Mikami had to wonder how he would react if they got word that the girl had turned up dead.

An alarm started to ring on someone's watch. Midday. It happened just as the information spread among those in the back of the truck. Burly turned around, his mouth gaping wide. He was blinking in startled astonishment. Mikami felt the blood drain from his face, painfully aware of what he'd just imagined.

'That was Station G. Kasumi's in police custody. She's safe, in Genbu City.'

76

The command vehicle veered sharply to one side.

They had joined the state road. Unable to decide between surprise at the unexpected development or nodding at the confirmation of a suspicion, the atmosphere inside the container hovered between both. *Wait for more details.* Matsuoka's warning had also had an effect. For a while, their attention to the radio response became inattentive. Ogata and Minegishi moved sluggishly, as though their previous animation had been a mirage.

'Details coming in,' Pencil-face announced, holding up one side of his headphones. 'Kasumi Mesaki is . . . she was arrested. Shoplifting. Three cosmetic products. From Strike, one of the outlet stores in Asahimachi, Genbu. The store reported the theft to a *koban* in West Asahimachi. The duty officer brought her in. He only discovered who she was after sitting down with her for questioning. According to her statement, she lost her phone yesterday, sometime before dawn. She'd been sleeping outside, next to the shutters of a live music venue. She said it was gone when she woke up.'

Shoplifting. Arrested. A lost phone. Mikami let out a deep exhalation. The truth had revealed itself, like the inside of a crosssectioned watermelon. Not a hoax. Not a kidnapping. Just a plan to obtain the ransom, hatched in the wake of Kasumi's disappearance.

The 'kidnapper' had played off the fact that Kasumi hardly ever showed up at home. He had stolen her phone, made the calls demanding the ransom, convinced her parents that he'd abducted her. All the while, he'd been following Kasumi around. If she reported her lost property to a *koban* . . . If she went home . . . In either case, he'd have had to call off his plan. That was why he'd had to stick around the busy areas near the main station – because he'd been following her from one place to the next. Then, earlier this morning, his fears had come true, unexpectedly so. Kasumi had been stealing from an outlet store in Asahimachi. He'd seen her do it, realized the staff would probably pick up on what she was doing. That was why he'd tried to bring the schedule forwards. He'd rushed into the store toilets and, having checked that no one was coming or going, had sucked in some of the helium already concealed in his bag and made the call to Mesaki's home phone. Deciding it was all or nothing, he'd set his ransom plan in motion. As he'd feared, Kasumi had been caught shoplifting. She'd probably been escorted to a back office. Seeing this, the kidnapper had told Mesaki to take a shortcut. He'd sent Mesaki from the ring road to the state road, abandoning his intention to trace the whole Six Four route starting from the Aoi Café. Following the initial change in plan, he would have given the remaining instructions from his car in the store's parking area. That explained the disappearance of the echo. It had to be from the car, to ensure no one overheard his helium-altered voice. And there was another reason why he'd had to wait in the parking area . . .

He'd been keeping watch on the store entrance. If the store reported Kasumi's theft, the police would arrive. Trying to calm himself, he'd placed all his hopes on Kasumi's will to fight. She was a delinquent who hardly ever went home. She wouldn't just admit to having done it. She'd play dumb, lie, burst into tears. Even with the goods held out before her, she'd insist she planned to buy them, that she'd forgotten to go to the counter. They wouldn't learn her identity if she chose not to tell them. Her phone, with all her personal information, had been stolen. And she wasn't the type to walk around with a school ID card. The kidnapper had been staring at the store entrance, hoping, all the time he had been giving Mesaki instructions on the phone. Kasumi had, in fact, put up a struggle. She'd secured enough time for Mesaki to travel ten kilometres.

Eventually, however, a uniformed officer from a nearby *koban* had shown up at the store. Even then the kidnapper had refused to give up hope. The store had probably only reported it because Kasumi had refused point-blank to give them her name. And it was only a shoplifting; the police wouldn't waste much effort investigating it. Her identity would come out, it was only a matter of time, but – Mikami thought of the command vehicle's own embargo – there was always an administrative lag in information like that percolating out to the necessary places. The kidnapper had entrusted everything to that one hope. Hoping to end everything while the time lag was still in play, he'd decided to go through with the plan. That explained why he was urging Mesaki to hurry. The final handover point had to be close. But . . .

It was already over.

Fair enough, he hadn't kidnapped or killed anyone, but he'd caused far too much distress and frenzy.

'Mobile Command, this is Pursuit 1. Mesaki has passed the Ishida-cho intersection. Approaching Café Cherry in five hundred metres.'

Mikami flipped open his phone. He was about to press Suwa's speed dial when a voice stopped him. It was Matsuoka. He was glaring right at him.

'Who are you calling?'

'I need to call off the coverage agreement.'

'Remember the condition.'

'I don't think it applies any more . . .'

'Uh-huh, and is that something you decide?'

'The case is over.'

'Not yet.'

Maybe he meant the investigation. It was true, but it was Matsuoka who had told Mikami to do his job when he'd joined them in the command vehicle.

Mikami got to his feet.

'This is a matter of good faith. The coverage agreement was put in place to protect someone in potential jeopardy. I can't prolong it for the sake of the investigation.'

'I'd agree with you if Kasumi had turned up dead. But she's safe — waiting twenty minutes to tell that to the press won't change a thing. It's not going to make a corpse of her.'

Mikami couldn't believe what he was hearing. Had Matsuoka really just said that?

The screeching of brakes echoed through the hold. The sound had come through the wall-mounted speakers.

— I'm here. Cherry Café. That was the place? What should I do now? Do you want me inside . . .?

— Pull . . . out again.

— What?

— Pull out . . . unless you want your daughter to die.

— Ahhhhhh!

'What about the girl's parents?' Mikami pointed at one of the speakers. 'Are you telling me they need to wait twenty minutes, too?'

'It's too early to let them celebrate.'

'Sorry?'

'The girl who stole the cosmetic products only *said* her name was Kasumi Mesaki. That's all we know. We don't have confirmation it's actually her.'

'Does that really matter?'

'Mobile Command, this is Pursuit 1. Mesaki's picking up speed. He's going way too fast.'

Mikami looked at Ogata. He looked at Minegishi.

'What, are you two planning to stand by, too? What if he crashes? Weren't you worried about that happening just now?'

Neither would meet Mikami's gaze. At the same time, neither looked particularly guilty.

'I see. You were talking about him as *bait*, right? You didn't want to loose the *bait*. Not before you'd hooked the bastard kidnapper.'

— Wh— . . . where next?

— Doesn't matter . . . just hurry.

'You fucking idiots. You're still waiting for someone to take a good bite? The investigation's not going to come to a standstill if the *bait* twitches for a second. Just bring that helium-infused fucker in first. You don't have to worry about the girl being killed any more. What happened to the intercept car we left at the driving school? Dispatch it to the outlet store! The guy's in a car. He's got his hand on his throat. He's talking on a mobile. Swat him down and get him to spit out the location of his accomplice!'

— Please, just tell me! Where do you want me to go . . . ?

— Go straight . . . three . . . kilometres.

— Go straight?

— Ahead . . . there's a hairdresser's up ahead . . . the Ai'ai Hair Salon. Get there in ten minutes or . . . your daughter's dead.

— B— . . . but . . .

'Call Kitou right now. Tell him Kasumi's safe. Put a bloody end to the man's torture – stop wasting time!'

'Incoming call to Mesaki's phone. Routed to call waiting. The caller is . . .' Burly's voice grew louder. '. . . it's Mesaki's wife. Mutsuko. Her mobile. Patching it through now.'

Finally. Mikami made a fist in front of his chest. *Of course . . . of course.* Mutsuko was phoning to let Mesaki know. To tell him Kasumi was safe.

The phone was still ringing.

He wasn't switching calls. Why wasn't he switching calls?

Mikami breathed in sharply.

Of course he wasn't. He was still on the line with the kidnapper. He couldn't leave the call, not for a split second. It was obvious. The kidnapper had anticipated this. That was why he'd stayed on the phone – to prevent Mesaki from talking to his wife.

Mikami gritted his back teeth. His arm extended forwards, picked up one of the mobiles. *Kitou.* He accessed the call history and dialled the last number. He held the phone to his ear . . .

Someone grabbed his wrist. Matsuoka's face came up to fill his vision. His eyes were burning, stretched wide open, the eyebrows terrifying arched ridges.

Matsuoka had rendered him unable to move.

He had to say it. *Say it!*

'The investigation is a sham – this is heresy!'

'Do *not* interfere.'

'Mobile Command, this is Pursuit 1. Mesaki has taken a right. Repeat, a right at the Usami crossroads.'

An incredible force weighed down on Mikami's arm. He tried to fight but it was no good. *Hello? Hello? This is Kitou.* The voice grew distant as his arm was pressed down on to his leg. Ogata prised open his fingers. Minegishi reclaimed the phone. Mikami felt humiliated. Powerless. He collapsed on to his knees.

'Don't you understand?' The shout came from his heart. 'How long every moment feels when your daughter's missing? Every second, every single minute . . . You're desperate for her to come back. You need to see her face. To hold her in your arms . . . as soon as you possibly can. Don't you understand? How can you call yourselves detectives if you don't get that?'

The engine was the only sound.

The four monitors showed midwinter fields, reddish brown, a section of residential homes with striking cobalt roofs.

Matsuoka swung his head upwards. He stayed like that for a while before looking down again. His eyes briefly caught Mikami's. Then he turned away, plunging his hands into his pockets.

'This isn't an investigation into a faked kidnapping.'

What?

Matsuoka started to pull his hands out, then sunk them back into his pockets. Even deeper this time.

'It all started with information we got from you. Right here: this is the command hub of the Six Four investigation.'

Mikami felt as though someone had draped him in a large, soft sheet.

His world was spinning. He was stunned, but he didn't understand why.

The Six Four investigation . . .? Information from you . . .?

Something was vibrating on his shoes. His open phone was edging over his feet, faintly buzzing. Right. After he'd called Suwa, he'd tried to call . . .

Getting to his feet, he took up the phone, hearing the man's voice as he held it to his ear.

'Sorry you had to call so many times . . .'

It was Mochizuki.

'. . . is something going on?'

'Why?'

'Last night, I had a call from Matsuoka. He wanted to know if I'd had any silent calls recently. I was a little bewildered, so I just said I hadn't and ended the call. But, you know, something like that . . . it makes you think. A direct call from Chief Adviser Matsuoka. Do you have any idea what he might have been calling about?'

No.

None at all.

Mikami ended the call and collapsed on to one of the stools.

In that instant, the large, soft sheet seemed to slip away, crumpling at his feet before it vanished completely.

He'd woken up.

He could see something . . .

Information from you. That was it. When he'd visited Matsuoka's home, he'd talked about the silent calls with his wife. He'd found out afterwards that their family home had also received a silent call. As had Mizuki Murakushi. Concerned about Minako, Mizuki had spoken with Matsuoka's wife, Ikue, on the phone, and that was when they'd remembered that Mikumo's family home had had a silent call, too. All of the calls had been recent. And Minako had been obsessive about noting the dates, so they would have had a timeline. Matsuoka's family home. Mikami's home. Mikumo's family home. Mizuki's apartment. The calls had come in in that order. Mikami knew of more still. Mesaki had received a number of calls before the kidnapping. Mikami supposed the call left on Ryoji Meikawa's answer machine had been the same.

Everything seemed to fall into place. As he recited the names, they came together in a line. Like watching planets come into alignment.

Ma, Mi, Mu, Me, Me . . .

It was the 'M' row of the Japanese syllabary. Only the last of the syllables was missing – *Mo*.

Mikami raised his head. He looked at Minegishi.

'Your parents, your relatives, did they receive any silent calls?'

Minegishi's eyes conveyed the answer. *Yes.*

Mikami turned to Burly.

'And you? What's your family name?'

'Shi . . . Shiratori.'

Mikami couldn't help but chuckle. But the reaction was only surface deep. He forced it down and turned to Pencil-face.

'And yours?'

'Morita.'

'Did you receive any silent calls?'

'No.'

'Did Matsuoka call you to confirm that?'

'I can't . . .'

'Yes. I did,' Matsuoka answered. As though to stop the questions, to put an end to the torment.

Mikami saw a single, blackened finger.

Ahh——

585

It hadn't been Ayumi, after all . . .

He saw everything, the moment he accepted that one fact. He'd fought the truth for so long. The clarity brought with it an immeasurable feeling of loss. He held his hands to his face, balling them into fists. He pressed them hard into his forehead.

It was right there . . .

He saw it now . . .

> A, I, U, E, O.
> Ka, Ki, Ku, Ke, Ko.
> Sa, Shi, Su, Se, So.
> Ta, Chi, Tsu, Te, To.
> Na, Ni, Nu, Ne, No.
> Ha, Hi, Fu, He, Ho.
> Ma, Mi, Mu, Me . . .

It was beyond belief. Incredible. 580,000 households. 1.82 million people. And he'd done it all alone. One man, behind all the silent calls. He'd started with 'A', and it was only now, after all this time, that he'd finally reached 'M'.

When must he have started? Three, five years ago? Further back still? Every day and all day – morning, noon and night – his fingers had paged through the phone directory, drummed the buttons on his phone. Even after his index finger had swollen and blackened into a blister, even after the skin and nail had cracked, he'd been relentless in striking the buttons.

All to find the voice on the phone. All to find the voice of his daughter's kidnapper, which he'd heard on the phone fourteen years ago.

I'll recognize it if I hear it. Amamiya had made the declaration at the time of the kidnapping. He'd put his faith in the police investigation, but his hopes had been betrayed. He'd learned the truth, the disgrace of the cover-up. Eight years later, his wife had collapsed with a stroke. That would be when he'd started. As he'd nursed her, he'd started to make the calls. With nothing but his ears as a guide, he'd tried to seek out the kidnapper. *While Toshiko's still alive.* Maybe that had been his motivation. Voices changed over time, but he'd been confident he would recognize it. The voice of a man in his thirties or forties, slightly hoarse, with no trace of an accent. *No.* The voice of his tormentor, one he'd heard at home and at nine different businesses, the voice that had spoken into his ear and committed him to a lifetime of anguish.

It was staggering even to consider it. The phone directory issued in the sixty-third year of Showa. They were in the regions . . . no one at the time had thought it a risk to have their number listed. *Prefecture D, Central to East.* Astoundingly thick, the edition contained the numbers of everyone in City D and three cities more. It started with Aikawa, then moved on to Aizawa, Aoki, Aoyanagi, Aoyama . . . Lurking in the middle were the vast realms of popular names like Sato, Suzuki, Takahashi, Tanaka . . . And he wouldn't have got by making just one call per house-hold. That would have been the minority. If it was a female voice that answered, he would have kept calling until a man picked up. If the voice was male but too young or too old, he'd have had to assume they were living with someone the kidnapper's age and kept calling. There would have been numbers where no one answered, regardless of how many times he called. He'd per-sisted, despite all of this. Even after losing Toshiko, he'd refused to give up. Out of a thirst for vengeance. Out of his duty as a father. For the memory of his wife and child. He would have had any number of emotions driving him on. Then, finally, he'd found it – the voice from that day fourteen years ago.

– *There, I can see the billboard!*

Mesaki's voice trembled through the speakers.

– *The Ai'ai Hair Salon, right? That was the place?*

Forty-nine years old. The voice matched the age. He had no noticeable accent. He'd been screaming since the morning, so it

587

was impossible to know if his voice was usually hoarse. Even without the yelling, none of the detectives would have recognized it. None of them had heard the kidnapper's voice all those years ago. *I've got people doing their best to find out, as we speak.* Matsuoka's words from the night before. He'd been ticking through 'M'. He'd contacted any detectives whose family name fitted the bill, got them to check their families and relatives. He'd assigned others to call around people they knew whose family names started with the letter. The detectives were all in police accommodation: none would have their numbers listed publicly. The results would have come as a surprise, the silent calls never having cropped up in their conversation. By morning, they'd have had a towering stack of reports confirming silent calls. Another decent-sized pile for people who hadn't: *Mogi, Mochizuki, Mori, Morikawa, Morishita, Morita.* No one with family names starting with 'Mo', the last syllable of the 'M' row, had received a call. Even if they had, there would have been too few to highlight a correlation.

'Mobile Command, this is Pursuit 1. Mesaki is pulling up to his destination.'

'Copy. Is there space to park?'

'Yes, enough for one or two cars.'

Matsuoka was focusing on each word. His eyes were fierce. He'd sounded sure when he'd said they were part of the Six Four Investigation; that suggested he'd already worked through the other rows of the Japanese syllabary before stepping into the command vehicle. The 'M' calls were all recent, fresh in memory, more likely to be talked about. That was why the subject had come to his attention. But this was Matsuoka. He'd have no doubt considered it dangerous to focus only on 'M'. If the caller had been someone fixated on that letter, that row alone, that couldn't make Mesaki the Six Four kidnapper. So Matsuoka had set out to check the end of 'H', the previous row, and the beginning of 'Y', the row that followed. He would have unearthed a sizable list of names from 'H', names like Horita, Hori and Honda, and seen the same pattern as with the 'M' row. For 'Y', he'd have found nothing. He'd reached his conclusion. The run of silent calls had ended at names starting with 'Me'.

From his experience in past investigations, he would have already known that no one in Prefecture D had a family name starting with 'Re'. That there were only a handful of names starting with 'He' or 'Me'. Once you excluded those like Meikawa, names of people who had moved in from other areas, Mesaki was the only name left on the list.

– Okay, I'm here! I just stopped. What now? What do you want me to do? Should I go inside?

'This is Pursuit 1. Passing now.'

– What should I do? Tell me what you want me to do!

– Take . . . out the suitcase.

Mikami closed his eyes and focused on the voice.

It was Kazuki Koda.

He hadn't been able to tell from the sound. But he was sure of it. Stealing phones. Trailing someone around a red-light district. Amamiya wasn't capable of such things. And there'd been a letter from Koda in the letter rack in Amamiya's living room. Kakinuma had also told Mikami that Koda never failed to visit Shoko's grave on the anniversary of her death. Koda must have confessed everything to Amamiya. He'd relayed the contents of the memo and asked forgiveness for the duplicity of the force. He'd stayed in contact, even after his resignation.

Tell me if I can help. I want to help.

Koda was a man of his word, and profoundly honest. Mikami didn't doubt that he had continued his entreaty, regardless of how much time had passed.

'This is Pursuit 2. Passing now. Mesaki is taking out the suitcase.'

His sense of obligation would have come from more than just a sense of justice. Aside from the Amamiyas, no one else had had their lives turned upside down, or been forced to suffer, as much as Koda. His loathing of the kidnapper would have been greater than anyone's. Amamiya had known this. It was why he'd confided in him. And that was why Koda had escaped Kakinuma's surveillance and gone into hiding. Why he'd seen fit to abandon a job he'd only obtained after grovelling on his hands and knees, why he'd left behind a wife and child, the normal life he'd finally managed to secure himself, only to martyr himself to Six Four as part of Amamiya's final play. They had crossed the line together – chosen heresy. *It takes a heretic to catch a heretic.* They were forcing their torture back on to Mesaki. They'd thrown the life of his daughter into uncertainty and, in the process, torn his soul apart.

But . . .

How were they planning to end it?

What was Amamiya's final goal? What role had he assigned Koda to see through?

The cars they'd left at the driving school – Intercept 6, 7, 8 – had no doubt already fenced Koda in. Koda would know that, but still he stayed on the line.

– Where do you want the money?

– There's . . . an empty plot of land . . . at the back.

– An empty . . . yes, I see it! You want it there?

– Hurry.

The Mobile Command Centre turned right. They were heading directly for the Ai'ai Hair Salon. Ogata took up the mobile phone marked *Locations*. Burly connected a wire.

'Yoshikawa, report.'

'Yes, sir. Mesaki is pulling the suitcase behind him, rushing down a path to the side of the building.'

His voice was a whisper.

'Can you see what's beyond?'

'An empty plot of land. Old tyres, a fridge, a washing machine, more piles of junk. The hair salon is probably using it as a temporary dump. Mesaki just got there. He's looking around now, phone still to his ear . . .'

— *I'm here. The empty plot of land. What next?*

— *There's an . . . oil drum.*

— *An oil drum? Ahh, okay . . . I see it.*

— *Take the money . . . out from the suitcase . . . put it all inside.*

— *What? Inside the drum?*

— *You don't have time . . . for questions.*

— *Sorry! You'll give her back, if I put it in? You'll let Kasumi go?*

— *Do it.*

'I've moved around; I have a good view of Mesaki. The suitcase is open and . . . he's cramming the money into an oil drum.'

Minegishi was leaning over a map he'd called up on one of the screens. He suggested to Matsuoka they approach from the front, then slid open the panel to tell the driver.

'At the next corner, turn left at the Lawson. Right at the crossroads after that.'

'Is the road wide enough?'

'Should be fine.'

— *The money's all inside. I've put it all in.*

— *Look at your feet.*

— *What?*

— *There's . . . a round container.*

— *I can see it . . .*

— *Inside you'll find some petrol and some matches. Use them to set the drum on fire.*

Mikami had to catch his breath.

No . . . Ogata and Minegishi said together.

— *Set it . . . on fire? You want me to burn the money?*

— *Do it now.*

— *But . . . but . . . if I do that . . . if I burn the money, what about Kasumi? Are you really going to give her back to me?*

— *Do you want her to die?*

– Okay . . . I'll do it. Hold on, I'll do it now.

'Mesaki is pouring something in, from a plastic bottle. Wait . . . *Shit!* Sir, he's set the whole thing on fire. The oil drum is on fire.'

It looked like some kind of flare. Black smoke churned into the air, visible through the monitors in the command vehicle.

– It's done. I've set the money on fire. It's all burning. Just like you wanted. I've done everything you said. Now just give me my daughter back. Where is she? Please. Where is she?

– Under the container.

– Under the . . . ?

There were a series of clicks.

'The kidnapper has ended the call.'

'. . . Mesaki's holding up the container now. Peering underneath. He's got something . . . a piece of paper. Smallish. Notepad size. He's staring at it. Sir, he's on his knees! Mesaki has collapsed on to his knees. He's got his head on the ground, both hands stretched forwards, holding the sheet. He's . . . balling it up. He's wailing. Screaming. His daughter's name. "Kasumi, Kasumi!"'

A note to tell him his daughter was dead?

Was that the message Amamiya had left him?

Now you know the pain of losing a daughter. This moment will last for ever.

'Incoming call. Mesaki's phone. The caller is . . . Mutsuko, his wife. Patching it through.'

– Finally! Where are you? It's Kasumi. She's safe. Our daughter's safe!

– She . . . she's safe?

– Yes! There was no kidnapping. No one kidnapped her. No one touched her, she didn't know anything about it. I'm so glad I got through . . . everything's okay.

– She . . . She wasn't kidnapped?

– No. She's safe and well. She doesn't want to talk . . . but there's nothing to worry about. She's safe. Darling, isn't the news fantastic? Come back as soon as you can.

− . . .

− *Is something wrong? What is it? Darling?*

'Patching Yoshikawa through second speaker.'

'Mesaki's opening a sheet of paper, he's looking at it. It's the same one. He's giving it a funny look. He's stopped moving. He's not moving at all.'

The empty plot had come into sight from the command vehicle. The front-side monitor was showing a shot of the area. One of the stylists from inside the salon had come to stand outside the rear entrance. She'd hurried out, no doubt surprised at the commotion. One of the customers was peering dubiously through a back window, colouring foil in her hair. More people were venturing out from nearby shops and houses, having heard Mesaki's howls. They were converging on a single point − the oil drum, still heaving with black fumes, and Mesaki, now cross-legged on the ground next to it.

'Zoom in.'

'Affirmative.'

The camera drew closer to Mesaki. The image expanded until it took up the whole height of the monitor. The camera had a direct view of the man's face. His head was drooping forwards. His eyes were focused on a single point on the ground. There was something tranquil about the way he looked, despite his trip to hell and back. His temples were moving. Twitching? No. The movement was identical on both sides. His jaw betrayed a subtle motion.

'It's in his mouth!' Minegishi shouted. 'The bastard's eating the note.'

'No, wait. Look!' Ogata pointed.

The note was there in Mesaki's hands. He still had it. *Except . . .* Yoshikawa had said it was standard notepad size. The paper was too thin for that. It looked stretched out, a strip more than a sheet. He *was* eating it. He'd torn off half and put it in his mouth.

It was already too late. His jaw was moving sideways, and not up and down. He was using his back teeth to turn it to pulp.

'Yoshikawa, did you see him do it?'

'I . . . didn't see him tearing the paper. I saw him lift a hand to his face, but it looked like he was just rubbing his jaw.'

It made sense. He'd been careful to conceal the fact that he was putting the paper in his mouth. He'd come all this way with the police in tow, so he knew detectives would be watching. He knew they'd later ask him to give them the note. That was why he'd chosen to leave half of it. The half he was chewing on was the half he didn't want them to see. Most likely the part containing Amamiya's message . . .

Mesaki's expression became calm. His jaw and temples were motionless. In the next moment, his Adam's apple rose and fell. Mikami could almost hear the sound of the gulp.

'Damn it!'

Ogata drove his fist into the frame around the monitor. Minegishi punched the wall. The right-hand side of the monitor blurred a little, turning light brown. One of the onlookers had stepped in the way of the camera. Another figure, out of focus and faintly blue, emerged to fill the remaining space on the left. Mesaki's shape tapered, thinning out until it was completely invisible.

'That was it?' Minegishi said, palms stretched wide. 'Why leave it at that? He could have done so much more. He could have forced him to confess, threatened to kill Kasumi if he didn't.'

'Agreed. That was too easy,' Ogata breathed.

'All that intimidation, getting him to run, to burn the money – all he got from the bastard was that 20 million yen. There was that one time, in the car . . . But that's hardly anything. And Mesaki ate the fucking note. He should have gone straight for it, on the phone. That would have got a proper fucking response.'

Mikami's mouth was half open. His anger was rising; he felt that their comments were defiling something important.

Matsuoka cut in. 'What more could we hope for?' His gaze was divided equally between the two detectives. 'Yoshio Amamiya delivered us a suspect. What happens next is up to us. All he had was a voice on the phone. Whatever the message was, it wouldn't have been anything we could use in an arrest. Amamiya deserves an award – he gave Mesaki something that *wasn't* conclusive evidence and got him to swallow it. Don't ever forget this. *That was Mesaki's confession*. Now we know he's the kind of guy who panics, confesses, even without definitive evidence.'

Ogata and Minegishi were standing upright and motionless, concentrating like third-year recruits still bringing tea to the real detectives. Shiratori was nodding at one of the walls. Taking a deep breath, Morita pulled the zoom back on the camera. A huge number of onlookers had gathered around the empty plot.

Mesaki was out of view. All they could see was the line of smoke, tapered now, and white. The wind had dropped off, letting it reach up in what was almost a straight line. Why make him burn the money? It was unlikely that Amamiya wanted revenge for the money he'd lost. It was a second message – it had to be. One Shoko and Toshiko could see from the heavens. He had entrusted the trail of smoke to carry his voice.

It's done. I did everything I could.

'Moving to extraction,' Matsuoka said into the radio. 'Bring Mesaki in. Say it's to shield him from the press. I want him under guard and delivered to Central Station.'

Mikami nodded. Matsuoka had been right. The rest was up to them.

Sensing a parting of ways, Mikami flicked open his phone and pressed the button for Suwa's speed dial.

'Sir.'

'Kasumi Mesaki is in police custody – she's safe. Disband the coverage agreement, effective immediately.'

77

The glow of the phone box came into view, a point in the darkness.

Having asked his taxi to wait at the top of the hill, Mikami had started towards the riverside park. The path was a gradual downward incline. There was the faint sound of water. It wasn't yet 6 p.m., but as he walked his feet became increasingly shrouded in the dark. The park's mercury lamps were still off, making the bluish glow of the phone box the only artificial light in the area.

Mikami had left the Mobile Command Centre, returning to the Prefectural HQ by three o'clock. By that point, there were no longer any traces of the bizarre atmosphere that had prevailed on the fifth floor of the government building's west wing. The conference room had been deserted, the state of the room shocking. Empty of its inhabitants, it had looked to Mikami like Wall Street during the Great Depression, or the aftermath of a parade celebrating the return of an astronaut. The reporters had taken flight, scattering like birds the moment they learned of the agreement's termination. Knowing Kasumi was safe, half had returned to Tokyo. Those who had remained had either left for the empty plot of land behind the hair salon or Mesaki's house in Genbu.

The schedule of press announcements was pulled back to once every three hours. The colour had returned to Ochiai's face by the time the four o'clock announcement – which less than fifty reporters hurried back to – took place. With the coverage agreement no longer in effect, the police were under no obligation to supply the press with real-time case updates. While they were careful to give out as much information as possible, the fact that Masato Mesaki had been taken into custody at Central Station was, needless to say, not mentioned. The locations of his wife and daughter – Mutsuko and Kasumi – were also concealed. Matsuoka had met them in person and taken them into protective custody, transferred anonymously – together with Kasumi's younger sister – to a shelter in a neighbouring prefecture's Mutual Welfare Society. *Some things must never be spoken*. Mikami finally understood what Matsuoka had meant. When Masato Mesaki was arrested, Mutsuko would become the wife of a kidnapper and murderer. Kasumi, the daughter. He would do what he could to prevent their first names from coming out, for their sake. That was the decision Matsuoka had made.

You need to get some sleep. Go home and get some rest. We've been taking turns catching up. We've had plenty. Suwa and Mikumo had insisted. Kuramae had called the taxi even as they spoke. The idea to visit the park had come suddenly, Mikami giving the driver the new destination on the way home. Yoshio Amamiya's house was dark. His car was gone, too. Where was he now? Where had he been when Masato Mesaki was burning the money? Mikami pushed on the door of the phone box. It was old, but it opened easily and without a sound. The phone inside was light green, faded and in poor repair. The push buttons were blackened from use but, towards the centre, where the finger made most contact, they were polished to a dull and silvery shine. *Not surprising, after so much use*.

Mikami let out a deep sigh.

This is where Amamiya made his calls.

He would have used the phone to call Mikami's number, too. Sometime after eight o'clock, that day on 4 November. A female voice had answered. He'd called again at nine thirty. Again, the female voice. He'd made a third attempt, calling close to midnight – that was when he'd finally heard a male voice. He'd concentrated on the sound, then hung up, striking a line through the name *Moriyuki Mikami*. The name was that of Mikami's father, who had still been alive at the time the directory was issued. If Amamiya had used a later edition, or if Mikami had moved into police accommodation, he'd never have received the calls.

No doubt he'd started making the calls from his phone at home. Then he'd heard about the introduction of caller display. As often happened with people living by themselves, he'd only had a partial understanding of the service, and hadn't known about the option to withhold his number. That would have been when he'd started to use the phone box.

Perhaps there'd been other reasons, too.

The park was the nearest to his home. It had a children's play area. It went without question that he would have visited it with Shoko, when she was a child; with Toshiko, too; the three of them. Families with small children tended to avoid it after Six Four, partly because the location of Shoko's abduction was never determined. It was ironic that this very fact gave Amamiya a place where he could occupy a phone box for extended periods, day and night, without having to worry about people seeing him.

This is it, this is the place.

Mikami closed his eyes and listened. It was quiet. No sound reached inside the phone box. It had no doubt been different on the day of their call. That evening, the north of the prefecture had been deluged with an unseasonal torrent of rain. Many places had suffered landslides. Rivers had swollen, noisily tossing mud downstream. The noise hadn't been the buzz of a city. It hadn't been traffic. The phone box was in a riverside park, part of a flood plain. That was the truth behind the 'continuous' sound he'd heard.

Ayumi? I know it's you, Ayumi.

That was what he'd said to the caller.

Ayumi! Where are you? Come home. Everything will be fine, just come home right away!

Amamiya had known the reason for Mikami's tears in front of the Buddhist altar.

Are you better?

Amamiya's words on the phone last night.

Not everything is bad. There's good out there, too.

Where on earth was he now?

Mikami was starting to wonder if he'd been the one to set events into motion. His first visit to Amamiya had been seven days ago. But the silent call to Mesaki's home had been ten days ago; Amamiya would have already tracked down the kidnapper's voice by the time of Mikami's visit. He would have been debating whether or not to report it. Although . . . the fact that he hadn't reported it during the three-day gap, however short that seemed, already had to be a reflection of how deeply he mistrusted the force. Every detective he'd met had assured him they would catch his daughter's killer, but it hadn't happened, even after fourteen years. Single-handedly, he'd achieved something tens of thousands police officers taking the force as a whole – had failed to do. And why? *Because it wasn't their business.* Doubtless, that would have been his conclusion. The police had sought to cover up their own recording error. A seven-year-old girl had been kidnapped, met with a tragic end, and yet they had taken action to protect their own interests. They had systematically wiped all record of the third call's existence. It was no wonder he'd lost faith. Even if he did report Mesaki's details, who could say whether they would have trusted his ability to distinguish the voice after fourteen years? Even if they had, it would have meant a loss of face, to have the victim's father succeed where they had failed. They would have resented that; perhaps it would have dulled the edge of the investigation; maybe they would have told him he was wrong, after only a perfunctory investigation. Even so, Amamiya couldn't bring Mesaki in by himself. He could go and see him, try to pressure him, but telling Mesaki he thought his voice matched the kidnapper's wouldn't be enough to force him into a confession.

It would have been then that Mikami had turned up.

Amamiya would have recognized his voice. He'd heard so many on the phone, but Mikami's response would have left an impression. And the name on his card started with *Mi*. With the call still fresh in his mind, Amamiya would have drawn only one conclusion. *His daughter's run away. He's anxious for her safety.* Perhaps he'd seen an opportunity to forge a real, emotional connection, become convinced that the man before him was one of only a handful of officers capable of understanding his plight – the pain of a parent who'd lost a daughter. If Mikami had been there to talk of anything else, Amamiya might have confided in him that he'd tracked down the voice of the Six Four kidnapper.

But . . .

What had Mikami said instead? It hurt to think about it. He'd asked Amamiya to accept a visit from the commissioner. Made a blatant attempt to involve him in a PR exercise. He'd pressed him for an answer, suggesting it might help, that the coverage might even unearth new leads. Amamiya's suspicions would have been confirmed. *They haven't changed.* Fourteen years, and the force continued to display no regard for the victim; far from it – they were hoping to take advantage of his suffering and shore up their own defences.

I appreciate the offer, but it won't be necessary. There's no need for someone as important as that to come all this way.

That was how it had started. Amamiya's attitude had undergone a sudden transformation. Mikami was sure of it now.

He had decided he wanted to corner Mesaki himself. He reached out to Koda. Together, the two men, who had both suffered at the hands of the police, put their heads together and came up with a plan. They wanted revenge on Mesaki, but they also wanted to get back at the force. They decided to enact their plan on the day of the commissioner's visit, knowing that would deal the heaviest blow. In the end, the one variable they had no control over – Kasumi's absence from home – had forced them to move it forward a day. The timing had never been down to chance. In what looked like a twist of fate, a copycat kidnapping took place just a day before the commissioner's inspection into Six Four. It wasn't the fury of Criminal Investigations that had finally forced the cancellation, nor was it fate – it was Koda and Amamiya's unmerciful revenge. Mikami had pushed Amamiya when he'd been undecided. By notifying him of the commissioner's visit, he'd ended up giving him a date they could use. The haircut had been a token of that resolve.

The words on their call the previous night . . . they probably hadn't been for Mikami alone. *Not everything is bad. There's good out there, too.*

And yet . . .

Amamiya and Koda had crossed a line.

They had to shoulder the responsibility. Amamiya's share of the burden was particularly weighty. Heresy is heresy; there are no graduations. Whatever his reasons, he'd staged the kidnapping of a young girl. He'd subjected her mother, Mutsuko Mesaki, to the terrors of losing her daughter. All this despite having witnessed first hand the suffering of his wife, Toshiko, when they'd learned of their daughter's abduction; even though her feelings were indistinguishable from his own. Amamiya had abandoned morality. He had, in order to satisfy his personal desire for retribution, crushed underfoot a mother's innocent heart.

He was fully aware that that was what he'd done, more than anyone. That was why he hadn't come back. Was it possible he'd decided to . . .?

Mikami recognized the sound of a car horn.

It was coming from the top of the hill.

The taxi was independently owned, one the Prefectural HQ used constantly; it was unlikely that the driver suspected Mikami of lying or trying to dodge the fare. Then again, Mikami had had the look of a man who hadn't slept for thirty-six hours . . . he must have looked inescapably bleak – perhaps the driver was worried he might drown himself. Mikami could see him now, in the distance, already out of the car. He leaned out of the phone box and waved a hand in the air.

I won't be much longer.

He closed the door and opened his mobile. He was about to dial Matsuoka's number when the urge took him to lift the phone before him off the cradle. The crackling of the line sounded like it came from the past. Matsuoka's phone went straight to voicemail. Deciding it wouldn't be funny to leave a silent call from a phone box, Mikami left his name and a message, saying he'd try again. He hung up. Something told him Matsuoka would call back. There were things he wanted to say; questions he wanted to ask.

What had happened to Kazuki Koda?

He doubted Matsuoka would just let him go. *Theft. Open threats. Blackmail.* His actions were unmistakably criminal. And yet the whole time Mikami had been in the command vehicle, he hadn't heard Matsuoka mention his name once; nor had it been mentioned on the radio. Had the Intercept Units not been able to bring him in? Had they deliberately let him go? Koda had to have been in contact with Matsuoka. At the very least, Matsuoka would have received an anonymous tip-off before everything started. It was the only way some things could be explained.

Matsuoka hadn't seen Amamiya's blackened finger. Without anything to make the connection, how else could he have joined the dots between the 'M' calls and the kidnapping?

Still . . . there were more pressing issues. *Was* Mesaki the mastermind behind Six Four? That was the most important question.

Matsuoka had seemed convinced. But with no evidence beyond Amamiya's testimony, there was no case for prosecution, nothing that would stand up in court. Without a confession or some kind of real evidence, Mesaki's status would stay unchanged and he would just remain a man under 'police protection'.

Supposing he *was* the Six Four kidnapper, he'd done a good job of concealing it after leaving his house in the white coupé. He'd been genuinely concerned for his daughter's safety, so perhaps that had helped. But he'd slipped up at the end. His front had collapsed, for a brief moment, as he'd blurted out a response to Koda's instructions on the phone. It was after he'd been told to pull out from the Cherry Café, when he'd been driving north on the state road. It was what Ogata had been referring to when he'd said, *There was that one time, in the car . . .*

– *Please, just tell me! Where do you want me to go . . .?*

– *Go straight . . . three . . . kilometres.*

– *Go straight?*

– *Ahead . . . there's a hairdressers up ahead . . . the Ai'ai Hair Salon. Get there in ten minutes or . . . your daughter's dead.*

– *B— . . . but . . .*

Mikami had picked up on it, listening to the recording afterwards. Koda *had* caught Mesaki out. Even before he'd sent him on to the state road, Koda had asked if he was familiar with the area. He'd forced Mesaki to say, *Here? No . . . not at all.* As the Six Four kidnapper, Mesaki wouldn't have been able to admit knowledge of the route. Having forced the declaration, Koda had then told Mesaki to drive straight for three kilometres. Before he realized what he was doing – genuinely so – Mesaki had responded with a question. *Go straight?* He would have known the correct way to reach the salon was to take a right at the next intersection, one kilometre ahead. At that point, Koda hadn't even mentioned the name Ai'ai. He'd duped Mesaki into revealing his expectation that the next destination would be the Ai'ai Hair Salon.

For Mesaki, the kilometre leading to the intersection would have felt like half a lifetime. He'd been instructed to go straight, but also to go to the Ai'ai Hair Salon. Should he turn? Should he go straight? The choices had been equally terrifying. There was a

603

detective on the floor behind his seat. The call was being recorded. He didn't think the police suspected him of being the Six Four kidnapper, but they would realize he knew the salon's location if he made the turn. Meaning he had to go straight. But he couldn't do that. He had to think of what might happen if he didn't get to the salon as instructed. The kidnapper had told him his daughter would be dead if he wasn't there in ten minutes. *Are you sure you want me to go straight?* The words would have been on the tip of his tongue, but saying them would have been tantamount to making a confession. After exhausting every possible avenue in his mind, he chose to take the right. He chose his daughter's life.

But the real dilemma had been kept for the end. That was, it went without saying, the note on the paper.

Unexpectedly, there was still a pen-written message on the piece of paper Mesaki handed in to the police. Horizontal, on just one line.

Mikami shuddered.

A daughter. A child's coffin.

Having found and read the note from the bottom of the container, Mesaki had crumpled to the ground in tears. He'd begun to howl. *Kasumi is dead*. Mesaki had read this as the meaning of the two sentences. Then Mutsuko had called, telling him his daughter was alive and well. He read the message again. Noticed a detail. That it said 'child's coffin' and not just 'coffin'. It had dawned on him then. The note hadn't been referring to Kasumi: it had been referring to Shoko Amamiya.

Since the kidnapper's calls, since learning that the kidnapping was a carbon-copy of his own crime, Mesaki would have feared the possibility that the kidnapper was somehow related to the Amamiyas. At the same time, he would have assured himself that no amateur – relative or not – could track him down, not when the professionals had failed after fourteen years of investigation. *Coincidence, it's just coincidence*. He'd repeated the line like a mantra, attempting to drive his fears into submission.

But reading 'child's coffin', he had realized the truth. It had left him no room for doubt. The message was from someone in Shoko's immediate family. He'd realized this, yet he'd still handed the note to the police. What, then, had he chosen to eat?

Mikami had no idea. The paper had been torn above the message. The writing had been Western-style, horizontal, meaning Mesaki had chewed up the first half of the note. Specifically, he'd eaten two fifths of the sheet. The message they'd seen had filled the bottom half, the lower three fifths.

The first line would usually contain the addressee's name. It seemed plausible. *Masato Mesaki.* But no. Amamiya would have known the police would take possession of the note. He would have wanted something to spell out the fact that Mesaki was Shoko's murderer. Mesaki's voice was close to identical to the kidnapper's from fourteen years ago. That was all Amamiya knew for sure. Maybe that was exactly what he'd chosen to write. *Masato Mesaki. Slightly hoarse, no trace of an accent.*

It didn't constitute evidence of any kind. Yet Mesaki had put it in his mouth regardless. Because he was the Six Four kidnapper.

What would be the clever thing to do, knowing the police would ask for the note? Mesaki's mind had gone into overdrive. It would arouse suspicion to refuse. They would logically conclude that someone bore him a grudge, that he was trying to hide something from them. Yet he couldn't allow himself to give them the note as it was. The first line would create a connection between him and Shoko's murderer. And there was less than a year until the statute of limitations came into effect. Taking care not to be seen, he would put the top half in his mouth and leave the bottom as it was. That was his decision. To eat the part that would portray him as a suspect and leave the part that suggested he was a victim of a kidnapper who had murdered his child. He didn't imagine the phrase becoming a problem. *Child's coffin.* Offspring were always children in the eyes of their parents.

Carefully, he'd torn the paper in half. Carefully, he'd transferred one part to his mouth. Carefully, he'd begun to chew. At that point, he was no longer a father concerned for the well-being of his daughter. He'd become a savage, a man who – despite having a three-year-old daughter of his own – had collected a ransom after kidnapping and murdering a seven-year-old girl.

Why did you eat the paper?

What was written there?

Mesaki had protested at first, claiming he hadn't eaten anything. *It's on video. We can call a specialist to match the bite mark.* He was quick to drop the pretence. *Maybe I did eat a little bit, I wasn't myself. I hadn't eaten since yesterday. But this . . . this was all that was written down. Yes, I remember it clearly.* Mikami had been shaking with fury as he'd listened in to the report being made to Matsuoka. He had already changed his mind from earlier, understanding now why Ogata and Minegishi had become so worked up. Why *hadn't* Amamiya got Koda to push harder? They'd had plenty of time. All they'd needed to do was extract information on Six Four, drop by drop, back Mesaki slowly into a corner. They could have threatened to kill Kasumi if he didn't confess. Koda had been a detective. If not a full confession, he should have been able to extract something close enough.

And yet he hadn't. He hadn't made Mesaki confess.

The end result was exactly as Matsuoka had said. Amamiya had delivered them a suspect. Nothing more, nothing less. It wouldn't be hard for Mesaki to claim he didn't know about the Ai'ai Hair Salon. *The route came back to me, that's why I made the turn . . . I remembered having seen a billboard for it, a long time ago . . . I was panicking, I don't know what I was thinking . . .* All he had to do was say something like that and the interrogators would have nowhere to go.

Why had the plan been so oblique? The more Mikami thought about it, the more difficult it became to grasp. And the more he thought about it, the more it seemed to have been engineered that way. Amamiya had drawn the line at 'delivering a suspect' and then thrown the ball into their court. *It's up to you to make the arrest.*

Could what he'd done really be termed revenge?

The car horn sounded again. This time louder. *Coming.* The image came to him just as he was about to bring his hand up. The red baton. He saw Koda, in his guard's uniform, guiding cars into the Tokumatsu car park.

Because of Koda.

Koda was the only one who hadn't betrayed Amamiya's trust. He'd worked without sleep as a member of the Home Unit. He had never got over the cover-up. He'd stood up to the force, and lost his job for his efforts. Even then he'd stayed true to Amamiya. Now, with all that had happened, he'd given Amamiya proof of his word. *It'll mean becoming a criminal.* Koda had already been forced into the margins of society. It would have been only too easy to imagine the trials of having to serve time, then having to try to make a fresh start with his wife and child. Even then, Koda had agreed to help. He'd volunteered to become a kidnapper. That was when Amamiya had understood it, that there were still good men like Koda in the force.

Koda had endured the pain of putting the plan together. It had hurt — of that Mikami was sure. They were going to humiliate the force. Planning to expose the Six Four kidnapper, the very man the Prefectural HQ had failed to bring to justice for fourteen years. What would have happened if Koda had forced Mesaki to confess? Would Ogata and Minegishi have cheered in celebration? Koda would have ached to see the faces of his old colleagues. He knew he could deliver a physical blow to the Prefectural HQ, but the idea of humiliating them would have cut him up. No one had given him a second thought when he'd been forced to resign, yet he'd found a part of himself that couldn't hate them for it. His home ground was still exactly that, no matter how corrupt it was. Some part of you remains a detective, even after you leave the force. It was why Koda had never forgotten about Six Four, about Amamiya. Even after his resignation, he'd stayed a detective the whole time. He'd kept the vocation with him, as a last measure of pride.

That was why the plan had stopped short. Amamiya had made the decision, unable to bear Koda's anguish.

Mikami stepped out of the phone box.

The job's an easy one. Easiest in the world. How would Koda respond to something like that?

Cases test a person, time and time again. Mikami's feet were heavy as he stamped back through the dark.

78

The fare on the meter had shot up. The winter treads emitted a caustic sound on the road, but the taxi was like a dream compared to the command vehicle.

'Must've been cold out there?'

The driver had just struck up a conversation when Mikami's phone started to vibrate in his jacket pocket. It was Matsuoka. Mikami asked the driver to turn on the radio before he answered.

'Been making silent calls, Mikami?'

'I just happened across a phone box, so . . .'

'Is that a play or something?'

'I'm in a taxi.'

'What were you calling about?'

Mikami asked the driver to turn up the volume, then brought up a hand to cover his mouth. 'What's happening with Mesaki?'

'He's still in custody. We release him tomorrow.'

Mikami nodded. If Mesaki said he wanted to be out, they would have no choice but to comply.

'Did he say anything?'

'He told us to arrest the fucker that did this to him.'

Incredible.

'Well, maybe that's an option. You could use Amamiya's testimony to—'

'No, we're not doing that. We're going to get all we can on Mesaki. Cover all fourteen years. We're going to get enough circumstantial evidence to bury the man alive.'

Mikami made a deep nod.

'I remembered something you might be interested in, could be a motive for the kidnapping. It relates to the imported-car business.'

'Okay, go ahead.'

'This is going back eleven or twelve years . . .'

Seeing Ashida – Goggle Eyes – outside the assembly hall the previous day, Mikami had remembered him coming to ask about making an arrest on charges of fraud. A luxury import car-salesman had hanged himself. The man's wife had come to Ashida with the story. Her husband had been due to deliver a German car – valued at around 16 million yen – to a local Yakuza gang. Once payment was confirmed in full in the company account, he'd taken the car out at the pre-arranged time of 1 p.m. There he'd come across one of the Yakuza, a young man with a shaved head, waiting outside the building. The thug had said the *wakaga-shira* – the Number Two – was out, but that he had his personal stamp for the signature. The salesman had got him to press the stamp confirming delivery, then gone back to his office. At six that evening, he'd received a call from the *wakagashira*. *Where's my car?* The salesman had gone pale. *I delivered it to one of your people, a younger man.* The salesman had described the man's appearance, but was told they had no one of that description. He knew the *wakagashira* was lying, but he was Yakuza and the salesman didn't feel he could press the matter. The *wakagashira*'s name was Hagi-wara. The salesman saw then that the stamp said Ogiwara. In that moment, he was landed with a debt of 16 million yen. The crux was that the call had been made at 6 p.m. Five hours was enough to get the car to the Japan Sea or the Pacific. It would have been disassembled, or had its plates altered; it would be on a container vessel somewhere. When Mikami had told Goggle Eyes the only avenue was to go after the young man who'd used the stamp, he'd muttered something about it being difficult because the Yakuza used people from Kansai to take their deliveries.

'That could be useful, thanks. I'll get my people to check if anything like that happened before Six Four.'

'One more thing, about the phone calls . . .'

Mobile phones hadn't existed at the time of the Six Four kidnapping, but car phones were already in widespread use. It was possible that a dealer in luxury imported cars stocked models that hadn't yet been fitted.

'I don't understand the technical details, but say it was possible somehow to carry the phone, battery and the antenna; the kidnapper could have been near Dragon's Hollow when he called the fishing lodge.'

'Meaning he could have been working alone.'

'Exactly.'

'Okay, I've got people looking into the car phone. Was that all?'

'Does his sports store stock anything related to water sports?'

'Not much: no inflatables. Apparently, he has lots of stock for barbecues. Anything else?'

Mikami drew a long breath.

'Can I ask you a question?'

'Just one?'

'Hmm?'

'Look, I'm busy. If you've got more, just say it.'

'Fine . . . two questions.'

'Go on.'

'Koda and Amamiya. Are they still alive?'

Are they with you? If not, do you have an idea where they might be?

'Of course they are . . .'

The response was immediate. But . . .

'. . . why would anyone who staked their lives on something like this choose to die before seeing the result?'

Mikami was amazed.

'You're going to leave them alone?'

'Don't worry. They'll show up once we get Mesaki.'

'But . . .'

'They held the tip of a blade to our throats. It's only right we put an end to Six Four first. They'd be forced to live in dishonour if we did this back to front.'

A warrior's respect, perhaps. But was that all?

Mikami decided on his second question.

'The truth about today. How did you find out about it?'

He had to ask. How had Matsuoka been able to connect everything to Six Four without Amamiya's help and with only the 'M' calls to go on? He'd been in the command vehicle because he'd been able to predict what might happen. Unless Koda had tipped him off – in which case he would have had full knowledge of what was going to take place and been there as an observer. If that was true, he could even be implicated in conspiring with Amamiya and Koda from the start, running the entire thing to bring in the Six Four kidnapper.

'It was when I saw him, yesterday, at his house.'

The response was unexpected.

'Mesaki's house?'

Mikami thought he heard the man chuckle to himself. 'I let my eyes ask the question of everyone I meet. Are you the bastard behind Six Four?'

'But he . . .'

'No one admits to it. Mesaki, though . . . Well, he was more afraid of us detectives than he was of the kidnapper.'

Mikami was finally able to breathe out.

Testing everyone he met. That was how Matsuoka had spent the last fourteen years. His eyes had drilled mercilessly into those of a man whose daughter had been taken from him. There had been his age. The slightly hoarse voice. He'd been flustered, acting suspicious, even accounting for the effect of the kidnapping. His eyes had shied away from the detectives. He'd been targeted for revenge, a copycat crime . . . because he was the perpetrator of the original. Matsuoka would have constructed his hypothesis, and worked backwards from there. That would doubtless have been when he'd made the connection with the series of silent calls, the 'M' calls, already in the back of his mind.

The thought triggered a memory.

'There was a gap between the kidnapper's call and Mesaki reporting it in?'

'That's right. Twenty-five minutes.'

The kidnapper had abstained from using the stock phrase: *Don't tell the police*. Koda hadn't given Mesaki an excuse to hesitate. Despite this, there'd been a gap of twenty-five minutes. What would Mesaki have said when Mutsuko told him of the kidnapper's call? Whatever it was, there was no doubt his blood – that belonging to the father *and* to the monster – would have turned to ice. Mikami had to wonder, would Mesaki have reported it if the kidnapper *had* warned him against notifying the police?

'The man was probably terrified. Having the people he feared more than anything else milling around his house like that.'

And with Matsuoka there before him.

Are you the bastard behind Six Four?

Mesaki hadn't said anything, but he'd still given the game away.

Yes.

'Mikami, if you'd pass on my thanks to Minako.'

'Ah, of course. Was she able to help?'

'Very much so.'

'What did you have her doing?'

'As I said, Special Ops.'

'Right, of course . . .'

He thought he heard Matsuoka laugh again. 'Actually, it's fine. I'll tell you. She was right there, by your side.'

'She . . .?'

'I transferred everyone in the Undercover Unit who'd been in the Aoi Café during Six Four to the hair salon. They would all recognize Amamiya.'

'So, he . . .?'

'He was there. Right there in the middle of the onlookers. Watching Mesaki.'

Huh. Amamiya had been there, too.

'Minako spotted him first. She called in to let us know, just after you left for the headquarters in Pursuit 2.'

'Wow, I didn't . . . Where is he now?'

'I just wanted to check he was there. I don't see us needing him, not for a while yet, anyway.'

Matsuoka was talkative, considering his claim that he was busy. Was it the rush of having Six Four in his sights? Or was it the flip-side of the trepidation he would no doubt be experiencing? Mikami felt he had to ask. He needed to gauge the extent of Matsuoka's resolve. The matter was something closely related to Media Relations.

'Sir . . . you realize First Division won't be celebrated for this, even if you do finally get to put Six Four to rest?'

The message seemed to get through.

'You know?'

'Yes, I know what was in the Koda memo.'

'Okay, so you know.'

The Six Four investigation had become a double-edged sword. If Mesaki were to be arrested, make a full confession, the fact that he'd made three calls to Amamiya would almost certainly come out. The glorious press conference to mark the arrest would, at the same time, become ground zero for the explosive secret Criminal Investigations had kept hidden for fourteen years. After a considered pause, Mikami heard Matsuoka's low voice.

'Someone said something to me, a long time ago . . .'

Someone. For a detective, that was enough to know that Matsuoka was referring to Michio Osakabe, the erstwhile director of Criminal Investigations.

'. . . "Don't let it get you down. Use it, to get to the truth."'

Mikami nodded, understanding. There had been a time when

Matsuoka had agonized over the knowledge. Angry and disillusioned, having learned the hidden truth about Criminal Investigations, he'd gone to see the retired director in person. That was when Osakabe had told him. That the recording error was also a valuable resource, one they could leverage to arrest the kidnapper.

The Press Coverage Agreement had been disbanded the moment Shoko's corpse was found. Things had been different then. Fourteen years ago, the police had adhered strictly to the terms of the coverage agreement, supplying the press with comprehensive updates on the investigation's progress. Through the press, the information had become public knowledge. But none of the papers had mentioned a third call, the call the police had covered up. If a suspect mentioned it during their interrogation, it would show that they knew the truth – that they were the kidnapper.

Continue the investigation with that, and only that, in mind. You need to use every tool at your disposal to bring the kidnapper to justice, whatever it is, even if it's something capable of bringing the department to its knees.

Osakabe would have issued the reprimand.

Matsuoka would have agreed. He'd made the department's secret his own, drawn it in close. It would have been in that moment that he became the de facto director of Criminal Investigations.

Arakida hadn't been up to the task. He hadn't been seen or heard since the previous day – it was as though he wasn't even there. He'd gone into hiding. Matsuoka had told him the investigation was related to Six Four. He'd had visions of the bomb, concealed for eight generations of Criminal Investigations Directors, exploding during his term. He was due to move on within the year. His next post had already been decided. So he'd fled the enemy's jaws and assigned Matsuoka full jurisdiction over the investigation, throwing Ochiai out to handle the press. By keeping his hands clean, he'd tried to position himself outside the blast radius. Even beforehand, he'd been unable to shoulder the burden alone: that was why he'd passed the secret on to Matsuoka. The director's role had been beyond him from the start.

'That reminds me. Ogata and Minegishi are in shock, after that.'

'After what?'

'After you called them "fucking idiots". Hit them hard, the way you said that.'

'Ah. Tell them I'm sorry. The truth is, they were outstanding.'

'That they are.'

'The only problem . . . was that I found it a little hard to tell them apart.'

'Oh?'

'When I had my eyes closed, I couldn't tell which was Ogata and which was Minegishi.'

Matsuoka laughed out loud this time. Suppressing it, he said, 'Mikami, what would you say to working for me again?'

Mikami felt a sudden rush of heat. He sat upright in his seat.

'If the time should ever come, sir, it would be an honour.'

79

The lights were on when Mikami arrived home.

His eyes caught on something as he made his habitual scan for a takeaway bowl: white flowers blooming next to the wall, in the area that was too small to be called a front garden. Mikami didn't know much about flowers, but he was still surprised to see them bloom in December. The stems were slumped so the petals hung just above the earth. Only half open, they resembled the clenched hands of a child.

Minako looked no different to usual when she saw him in. *The calls weren't from Ayumi.* He found he couldn't broach the subject straight away.

Asking if she could make a bowl of ramen for him, he took a seat in the kitchen. The time was twenty past seven. The press conference would be under way. He felt as heavy as lead; not tired, but the front of his head felt taut.

'Those flowers outside, do you know what they're called?'

'Oh yes, they're in bloom,' Minako said from the counter.

'Do you know the name?'

'Christmas roses. I planted them not long before your father passed away. They haven't flowered for some years now . . . hardy little things.'

She seemed a little brighter than normal. Perhaps it was the effect of having been outside, of breathing the air, feeling the sun, of having been of help.

'So . . . you saw Amamiya?'

'Oh, err . . .'

Mikami grinned slyly. 'It's okay. Special Ops end once you're back home with your shoes off.'

'They do?'

'Sure. How did he look?'

Minako carried over his bowl of ramen, stayed where she was, then took a seat in front of him.

'Older, I suppose. Not in a bad way . . .'

Mikami fished at the ramen with his chopsticks.

'He was standing completely still, with this intense look. He was staring at the other man.'

'As though he hated him?'

'Yes, I suppose. But, then he . . .' Her eyes grew distant. '. . . then he stopped and looked up at the sky instead.'

'At the sky?'

'There was smoke, rising from the oil drum. He was watching that.'

Right. Smoke rising to the heavens.

'Our eyes met, just for a moment.'

Mikami's chopsticks hovered in mid-air. 'Really?'

'Yes. I was watching the smoke, too, I think; when I looked back down I saw he was looking straight at me. When our eyes met he gave me a little bow.'

'He bowed?'

'It looked that way, at least. I can't see how he would have recognized me, though. It was fourteen years ago, and he'd rushed straight out of the café. He wouldn't have seen me.'

'What happened next?'

'I bowed back, on auto-pilot. I told Chief Adviser Matsuoka later, I said I was sorry, but he said not to worry, that it was fine. He said it was exactly what he'd hoped to hear.'

Mikami breathed out. Everyone's eyes had been fixed on Mesaki. Only two people – Amamiya and Minako – had been watching the trail of smoke.

'Did you see the man when he set fire to the money?'

'The money? Was that what the smoke was?'

'Yeah, he burned the ransom money.'

'But, I don't . . . Why on earth would he do that?'

'The man you saw – he was Shoko's kidnapper.'

Minako gasped.

'Him? Really? But he was crying . . .'

'He was laughing.'

Mikami sunk his chopsticks into the ramen. Minako asked a new question each time he swallowed a mouthful. The conversation was getting difficult. He had to tell her how Amamiya had found out that Mesaki was the kidnapper – if he didn't, there was no point in having brought the subject up. He knew his courage to tell her wouldn't last the night.

It had to be now.

'Minako, I need you to listen to something.'

He left the remainder of the noodles and pushed the bowl to one side. He was close enough to touch her cheeks or hands if he reached out. He made sure he was close.

'Amamiya worked out he was the kidnapper by listening to his voice.'

That was how Mikami broached the subject. He was unhurried and methodical as he related the story, keeping nothing back. He went into particular detail when it came to the calls they'd had on 4 November. He wanted to make sure she knew why there had been three separate calls. Minako's hand stayed on her chest. She'd been silent – asked no questions, shed no tears, kept control of herself all the way to the end.

'Thank you,' she said.

Her voice was a whisper. Her expression had darkened, and it was clear that she was crestfallen, but it hadn't broken her poise. She was still sitting straight. It wasn't that she'd been prepared, or that she was trying to bear it, even that she was fighting the truth – none of that applied. None of the intensity with which she'd insisted the caller had been Ayumi came through in her reaction. Her eyes were on Mikami's chest. But they weren't desolate. They'd found serenity. That was how it looked to Mikami.

Because she was still supported, Mikami thought. By a faith that was too strong to come apart, even without the calls.

I just wonder . . . whether Ayumi just needs somebody else. Someone other than us.

Minako's words, muttered in the dark of their bedroom.

Someone has to be out there. Someone ready to accept Ayumi as she is, who won't try to change her one way or another. Someone who'll tell her she's perfect, who'll stand silently by her side and protect her. That's where she belongs. She'll be free to be herself, do what she wants.

He'd thought Minako had given up. He'd thought she'd become tired of waiting, of turning it over in her mind. But now he knew. She'd been listing the conditions for Ayumi's survival.

Ayumi had left with hardly any money. She couldn't talk to anyone. More than anything, she'd been terrified that people might see her, laugh at her. She wouldn't have survived without someone to extend a hand and rescue her. She wouldn't have survived without someone to be there by her side. Someone who would give her a place to stay, someone who would feed her and who wouldn't ask her name or try to find her parents, someone who wouldn't report her to the council or the police, someone who would sit patiently by and wait for her to emerge from her shell – that someone *needed* to exist for Ayumi to breathe, to listen to her heartbeat, to gaze out at the world. That was what Minako had decided.

So she had let go. *It's enough that she's alive. She doesn't have to be our daughter.* That was what Minako had told herself in the dark.

Not here, not with us. That's why she left.

Mikami's eyes began to close.

It felt like a wave lapping sand from his feet. Minako had never given up. Nor had she ever looked away from the truth. She'd looked death in the face and searched for the conditions necessary for their daughter's survival; and she'd come up with the idea of an inviolable 'someone' to meet those conditions. In her heart she'd built a world in which Ayumi *couldn't* die. Even though doing so had meant giving up her role as the girl's mother.

And what have I been doing?

Mikami had been hiding. He'd accepted the horrific reality thrust before him. He'd failed to nurture the unshakable faith of a parent, choosing instead to hold on to pragmatism, his experience as a detective.

The calls weren't from Ayumi.

He'd suspected it all along, but he'd pretended otherwise. Minako had been fighting to believe. She'd searched for reasons to differentiate the calls from the others, even as Mikami had looked the other way. Afraid of turning up the opposite result, he'd consigned them to the back of his mind. Earlier that day, when he'd finally had to accept the reality he'd feared all along, he'd done so with resignation. *It hadn't been Ayumi, after all . . .* He'd been forced into a corner. He'd started listing the conditions for her death.

He had, like Minako, focused on the conditions for her survival. He'd even considered the existence of that 'someone'. But he'd shut the idea from his thoughts, unwilling to believe a person so genuinely good-natured could exist, deciding only a criminal would take her in. Too painful to consider, he'd driven the world in which Ayumi was still alive out of his head. For his own peace of mind, he'd stopped thinking about survival and focused only on death.

He'd been getting prepared. Was that it? He'd given up the belief that his daughter was still alive.

His hand drifted to his left ear. What had happened to the dizziness? After so many attacks, where had they gone? Had they gone because he'd given up? Because he'd stopped trying to hide.

He'd accepted reality . . . had that ended the disconnect between his heart and his brain?

There was his appearance, too. He'd completely forgotten about it, even though it was inseparable from Ayumi herself. He'd felt nothing at Goatee and Slick's jeering, when they'd called him Gargoyle. All those reporters had burst into laughter. Even then, his feelings hadn't responded. He hadn't thought of Ayumi.

Had the bond been broken between them? Had he severed it himself?

Papa, Papa! Hey, Papa . . .!

Absurd. He hadn't given up on her. How could he do such a thing?

He wanted to see her again. From the bottom of his heart, he wanted to see her again. He hoped she was still alive. He needed her to be alive. He *knew* she was still alive. She would come home soon. She was just getting ready. Yes . . . she would be back, with the 'someone' by her side.

'Honey, you . . .'

Mikami's hands had come up to cover his face. His teeth were clenched tight. He was pressing down on his eyes, painfully hard, desperate to keep the tears at bay.

He felt a hand on his cheek.

He was supposed to have been the one to reach out. He was supposed to have touched her cheek, thumbed away the line of her tears, repeated those words from another age.

Are you okay?

'We'll get through this. She's doing fine, I'm sure of it.'

She was rubbing his wrists.

It's you. Minako was his 'somebody'. He'd already known it. He'd known it since the beginning. He'd pretended not to notice. Then, as he maintained the pretence, he'd actually stopped noticing. He'd been a fool. He'd been mistaken. He knew every sordid detail of his work, but what kind of a life was that if you didn't even notice your wife?

He would believe in it, too, the world Minako had created. The world in which that 'someone' existed. The world in which Ayumi was alive and well.

'You're exhausted. Why don't you lie down for a bit?'

Her hand came to rest on his forehead, as though checking for a temperature. He had the vague memory of his mother doing the same. He felt fiercely self-conscious. He rubbed his fingers over his eyes to extinguish the tears, then got to his feet.

'They'll need watering . . .'

'Sorry?'

'The rosemary.'

'The Christmas rose?'

'Right, those . . .'

'Now?'

'I mean . . . tomorrow, the day after. We should water them every day.'

'You think so? It is winter.'

'Yeah, we should. They're alive, after all.'

'Well, I suppose.'

'Why don't you buy a few more flowers – it'll liven the place up a little.'

'Listen to you!' Minako laughed, spurring him on.

'When work eases, we can go buy some from Mochizuki. You know him, right? Mochizuki?'

'Yes I think so – he retired, grows flowers now?'

'It's impressive. He's got these huge greenhouses, we could get some of those . . .' The name of the flowers refused to surface. 'Anyway, we should go and buy some. We can get some you like the look of.'

The conversation ending, Mikami looked at his watch. It was just after half past eight. The press conference would have finished by now.

'I have to make a call.'

'Is anything wrong?'

He looked her in the face. She was frowning, looking concerned.

Not yet, that's still to come, he thought. He looked her in the eyes.

'No, nothing's wrong. Never has been, not really,' he said.

He picked up the phone in the living room and dialled Media Relations. He felt clearer, almost cheerful.

'Media Relations.'

It was Suwa.

'Is the press director in?'

'Nice, sir. You're not still awake, are you?'

'How was the seven o'clock conference?'

'Terrible. The press were relentless, kept insisting we give them Mesaki's address.'

'That's not our remit. What about Ochiai? How's he doing?'

'He's full of beans. And we know why. It's Mikumo . . . Mikumo!'

Stop saying that! Mikumo sounded genuinely angry in the background. Mikami smiled. He left a few instructions then ended the call.

He pressed some more digits. Koichiro Hiyoshi's home number. When his mother picked up, Mikami asked if she would take the phone to the first floor, as she had the last time. From then on, time seemed to expand. Mikami grew wary of falling asleep.

Do a good deed, and it'll find its way back.

No, Dad. That's not why I'm . . .

Minako, tending to the flowers with a watering can. The clenched hands are open. Reds, yellows, blues. The area's in shadow; a dazzling ray of light shines on the flowers alone.

The phone's ringing . . .

Don't worry, I'll get it. It's fine, I'll get it . . .

Mikami started. He could hear a shuffling. Someone taking the phone into the room.

'It's Mikami. I'm just going to get straight to it, okay?'

'. . .'

'Hiyoshi, we got the kidnapper. Shoko's murderer.'

'...'

'It's big news, right? It won't be in the press for a while, but we've got the bastard. I saw his face. So did a guy just like you, called Morita. And this guy called Shiratori . . . you'd laugh to see the man's bulk after hearing that name. All of us had a good long look at the bastard's face.'

'...'

'Amamiya did, too. After fourteen years . . . he finally got to see the kidnapper's face. I think he's a lot calmer now. Grateful, too, to all the people who worked with him, all that time ago.'

'...'

'Hiyoshi, I hope you're listening to this. I guess you're tired. I am, too. Just hold on for another ten minutes. I'm going for a new record . . . thirty-nine hours without sleep. Thought I'd make a go of breaking the record I made at twenty-five.'

'...'

'Anyway, I'm going to put in a call every now and again. You've got the time, right? I have, too. My nights are free now I've been booted from detective work.'

80

The week hurtled by.

The press conferences were pulled back to twice a day. The majority of those still showing up were local, friendly faces, although any semblance of like-mindedness had all but faded away. Akikawa was back to his usual self. The others, too, had regained their aggressive edge and had taken to bulldozing their way into Media Relations after every announcement.

'You've got them in hiding, admit it. It's ridiculous . . . we've tried every trick in the book and we still can't track them down.'

'You can't blame us for your ineptitude.'

'Just give us a little more, on the girl's family. That was part of the coverage agreement. You have an obligation to let us in on the whole picture.'

'The agreement's no longer in effect. I can't hand out confidential case information.'

The Mesaki family were renting a house in a town in the north of the prefecture. Mesaki had brought someone in to run the sports business and had decided to sell their old house. No longer in police custody, his official status was now 'under observation'. After days of being questioned as the victim, he had revealed nothing that could be used against him. The only change was that the detectives had taken to calling him 'the honest man'; this was partly due to the first character in his name, meaning 'truth', but mostly due to the detectives' frustration with the way he always said exactly the right thing.

They'd held police 'line-ups' using recordings of his voice. Among those called in were the owners of the nine businesses where Amamiya had used the phone, together with people who had worked there; the detectives had also called in employees from Amamiya's pickle business, including Motoko Yoshida. The latter was now a patient in a closed psychiatric ward; the head warden had refused to let her leave and she hadn't been able to attend. A few of the remaining 'witnesses' had also failed to show, so that in the end only seven people listened to the recordings. Five agreed that the voice was similar; of these, three were convinced it was the same man. Out of the remaining two, one claimed not to remember, while the other said the voice wasn't the same. It was a result, but only a tiny part of the evidence they would need to bury Mesaki, as Matsuoka had said. They had nothing else from fourteen years ago that could help narrow the perpetrator down to Mesaki. It was going to take a while before 'the honest man' could be brought before a court of law.

'Would you prefer we let the tabloids and freelancers in, too?'

This time, the reporters had got hold of Suwa.

'You keep going on about the club, acting like it's an inalienable right. How about we hold another conference and give *all of you* the same information? *Ready, set, go!* You all go out and do your thing. If the tabloids beat you to it, you can think of it as motivation to improve on your reporting skills.'

'Right, hilarious. We've been helping you with information, too. You're making out like we're the bad guys, but this only started because of the way your organization likes to treat small fry like us. The police have always treated us as an agency for propaganda, refused to dole out any intelligence worthy of the name – my predecessors had to fight long and hard, waging their battles on the front lines and in government offices. The 'inalienable rights' that you're mocking? They're the result.'

'That's nothing *you* should be proud about. Maybe your predecessors did all that, but I'm talking about the here and now. You pester us for information, always more information, even as you sit in the Press Room with your feet up. That's not so hard to do.'

Suwa had matured. He no longer worried about upsetting the reporters. His tendencies towards calculation and brown-nosing were more subdued, and he'd developed a sharper edge.

The press had also undergone subtle changes. They were still worked up about having stumbled on to an important case, and that had made them more militant, caused them to talk big as they took their cues from Tokyo, yet they were showing signs of being able to rein themselves in when necessary. They still enjoyed laying siege, yet no longer rejoiced in breakdowns. They still exchanged blows, but they would shake hands afterwards. They'd even begun to exhibit a sense of altruism.

But . . .

. . . the true test of the relationship was still to come. Two days earlier, Mikami had gathered everyone in his department for a talk in a cramped basement meeting room. *This stays between us.* With the proviso in place, he had given them the truth about the investigation. He had talked about how it related to Six Four and told them everything about the cover-up Criminal Investigations had perpetrated.

Our relationship with the press dies the day they announce Mesaki's arrest. Those were his exact words. *What I want you to focus on is how we rebuild the relationship after that happens.*

Suwa had been thunderstruck. He'd navigated the problem of anonymous reporting and even put himself in the firing line when lobbying to get the Press Coverage Agreement signed. He'd grown in confidence and been ready to continue the fight – and his shock had been all the more apparent for it. Even so, Mikami didn't feel worried. That Suwa was still ready to battle on had been clear in the way he'd dealt with the press the day before, the way he continued to do so today. He would be the next press director. He'd woken up to his true talents.

Kuramae had listened with a pained look on his face; even

then, it wasn't until Mikami had explained about Amamiya and the silent calls that he'd looked genuinely crestfallen. Mikami had put a hand on his shoulder afterwards. *We don't know whether that was what happened with the message on Ryoji Meikawa's answerphone.* He wanted to believe it as much as Kuramae did. He wanted to believe the call had been someone from home.

Mikumo was the only one to give an opinion, her face blushing red.

'If I learned anything from this it's that our relationship with the reporters is always going to be like oil and water. If you stir hard enough we can move together, but only for a moment. I think . . . maybe the key is to engineer as many of those moments as possible.'

'How so?'

'We need to reach out to them, always . . . we can't give up, even if our relationship dies, even if they choose to disassociate themselves from us. We need to keep knocking, even when they don't answer. We can't give up . . .'

Directly afterwards, Mikumo had gone to the hospital, complaining of a sore throat. When she returned, Suwa had caught a glimpse of her medicine and saw it was to treat cystitis. She hadn't been able to use the toilet for the duration of that endless press conference. Mikami sympathized, felt worried even, but he still couldn't stop himself from chuckling at Kuramae's impromptu comment.

And all the time I thought Mikumo was like Ken Takakura, unable to lie . . .

He was sitting next to her now, both of them typing on computers. Media Relations had been given another computer following the Mesaki case. No doubt the time would come, as Akama had suggested, when they would get one for each member of staff.

'I'm going upstairs for a bit,' Mikami said, getting up.

Suwa was still busy with the reporters, but he managed to give Mikami a quick look.

First floor? Fourth floor?

Even further.

81

Wind gusted over the roof.

Mikami checked his watch. Two minutes after the arranged meeting time of two o'clock, and Futawatari was still to show.

Maybe he wasn't planning on coming. If so, that only backed up Mikami's theory.

Futawatari had been an instigator, too.

Now he'd had time to consider things properly, to run through the whole thing a number of times, Mikami had become convinced. Tokyo's plan to sequester the director's post. It had to have been Maejima, already in Tokyo on secondment, and therefore in a position to know, who had first sent word to Arakida. Mikami hadn't found anything to suggest Futawatari had been acting on instructions from Tsujiuchi or Akama – and yet he'd moved quickly into action. The natural conclusion was that Maejima, a contemporary and close friend of Futawatari, had told him about the development, as well as Arakida.

What, then, had a born-and-bred detective like Maejima expected Futawatari to do? The answer was obvious. Stop it from happening. Stop the commissioner's visit; make sure he didn't issue his proclamation from above.

If Mikami could establish the link, that would at least explain Futawatari's mysterious behaviour. He was the ace of Administrative Affairs, the secret overseer of personnel decisions with a modus operandi of working in the shadows, yet he'd jumped brazenly from detective to detective, spreading fear in his wake.

Like a serial arsonist, he'd ignited flames of hatred and directed them towards Administrative Affairs. He'd set off alarm bells. To incite an uprising.

Driven by his actions, Criminal Investigations had stepped up the intensity of its retaliation. They'd drawn closed the Iron Curtain and leaked details of misconduct to the press. They'd even made the misguided threat to set off a 'letter bomb' in Tokyo, a final notification of their intent. What, Mikami wondered, would they have had in waiting for the day of the commissioner's visit if the 'kidnapping' had never taken place?

Futawatari's machinations hadn't ended there. He'd set his sights on the press. Judging that a Criminal Investigations uprising would be insufficient to secure Prefecture D's status as Dallas, he'd opted for a double-pronged approach. Relations with the press had been falling apart. The troubles stemming from anonymous reporting had caused the press to threaten a boycott. Futawatari's goal had been to make powerless anyone trying to defuse the situation, thereby averting the boycott. Media Relations. He'd made Mikami – the press director – his target. Sure, they'd been pieces on the same board, but their repeated meetings had been no coincidence. Usually, it was a toss-up that they would meet once, twice a year. Futawatari had engineered each collision to pique Mikami's irritation. When Mikami's anger for the NPA was at its peak – having learned of their plans to take over – Futawatari had gone in for the kill, gunning straight at Mikami's sympathies as a detective.

Cool down. Nothing bad is going to come of this. If anything, it'll be a boost for efficiency.

You shouldn't take it so seriously. It's a symbol. It hardly matters who actually sits there. The detectives will do their job, regardless of the top. Isn't that right?

What else had he said?

You're a perfect example, Mikami.

A fine member of the Secretariat, in anyone's eyes.

Don't take it the wrong way. I meant it as a compliment.

Futawatari had wanted Mikami to dwell on his place in the organization. He'd known everyone would assume he was an agent for the NPA, and had used the misunderstanding to full effect. He'd been convinced that Mikami would side with Criminal Investigations, despite his posting in Administrative Affairs. He would have concluded that Mikami would forgo his duties as press director and take action to help his erstwhile department, letting the boycott go ahead and therefore completing Prefecture D's transformation into Dallas. He'd been single-minded in his efforts to push Mikami into taking action. It was no doubt how the man worked. Even so . . . had all those words – each one a burning-hot poker – been necessary for him to reach his goal? When he found out he'd lost, he hadn't accepted the defeat, masking his surprise at finding out Mikami had prevented the boycott with a single utterance: *I'll admit, there was some misjudgement on my part.*

All this time, Futawatari had been trying to save Criminal Investigations. He'd been trying to protect the Prefectural HQ. But Mikami felt no obligation to offer him praise or thanks. He'd fulfilled his duty as a member of Administrative Affairs. Nothing more, nothing less.

At least it ended well. That was what he'd said. After all the planning, all the strategizing, the kidnapping had robbed him of his endgame. Even so, when Mikami retraced it all back to the start, it was Maejima he saw, smiling and waving his hand. He felt no more anger. Everything had come together to cancel everything out; Mikami's emotional needle hung at zero.

But . . .

One mystery remained. One thing he still couldn't understand. The weapon in Futawatari's possession. Where could he have got wind of the Koda memo? It couldn't have been Maejima. The information was top secret, the knowledge restricted to Matsuoka and the last eight directors of Criminal Investigations.

Urushibara, Koda, Kakinuma, Hiyoshi . . . Mikami felt sure Futawatari wouldn't have succeeded in getting anything from the four members of the Home Unit. Who did that leave?

If he had to suggest a name . . .

Mikami looked up. The first thing he did was check his watch. Twenty-three minutes late. He looked back up. The man's slight frame seemed to cut through the wind as it approached.

'All done cleaning up?' Mikami called downwind, choosing to use the line he'd already prepared.

Futawatari stopped, leaving about three metres between them. He put a hand on the viewing pillar. No one came to see it, but the concrete cylinder was marked with the bearing and direction of every city and town in the prefecture.

'Not everything, not yet. People do like to leave a mess.' From his expression, it was clear his mind was already grappling with the next issue. 'What did you want to talk about?'

'No apologies for being late?'

'You'll know the reason why soon enough.'

'Uh-huh.'

Mikami moved closer and put a hand on the pillar. Futawatari was looking away from the wind.

If he had to suggest a name . . .

. . . it would be Michio Osakabe. With his own eyes, Mikami had seen Futawatari come and go from the director's house. He couldn't think of two men more diametrically opposed, but there was one point to connect them. Before too long Futawatari would assume his place as director of Criminal Investigations. They had met as one director to another, reaching beyond the constraints of time. They must have . . .

Mikami knew Futawatari wouldn't admit to anything, even if he asked. Besides, that wasn't why Mikami had called him to meet up.

'Have you started work on next spring's transfers?'

Futawatari showed no signs of a response. He became a brick

wall. It was no doubt a habit he'd developed over time. Erecting a barrier the moment anyone raised the subject.

'You know you made a right monkey of me with all this.'

'Hmm?'

Futawatari's eyes came up. Mikami stared right into them. Black and white, distributed evenly.

'You had me jumping all over the place.'

'I see.'

'I'd say you owe me one.'

'I don't ask for favours, and I'm in no one's debt.'

'There was that one time, when I lent you money for a train ticket.'

'I paid that back.'

'The day we went to see the Giants play in the Eastern League.'

'Definitely paid that back, the next day.'

'Anyway, are you getting ready for the spring?'

The corners of Futawatari's mouth came up, catching the meaning. 'Maybe you'd do better to focus on how many balls Matsui hits this season.'

Mikami grunted, laughing.

'All this time I'd had you pinned as an Ichiro fan . . .'

Ha! This time it was Futawatari who laughed. He went to say something but stopped before any words came out.

'I hear it gets cold in New York.'

Futawatari didn't answer.

The conversation had ended. They stood side by side but apart. Futawatari's eyes were narrowed, his jaw slightly raised. He might have been enjoying the breeze. He might have been thinking up solutions for whatever problem was next on his list.

The kind of people who made it to the top, the *survivors*, were those who kept their secrets close. The moment you let go of them, whether they were your own or someone else's, was the moment you lost. Standing next to Futawatari, Mikami couldn't help but think that was how it all worked.

But . . .

Futawatari was still standing there. He looked to be deep in thought, his hand still resting on the viewing pillar. Mikami glanced down to the man's feet. Spotless. His shoes weren't new, but the well-polished black leather reflected clearly the dull light of the overcast sky.

'Maybe you don't owe me anything. How about you let me owe you, for a change?'

The man's keen features came around, as though he'd been waiting to hear the words.

'I'm not going anywhere. Don't transfer me out of Media Relations.'

The Six Four investigation would continue, at least beyond the window for drawing up the plans for the next batch of transfers. The time would come, however, when Prefecture D would find itself cast fourteen years into the past, when it would make an enemy of the press. Mikami would be there to see it through. As press director, he would stand with Matsuoka at the announcement.

Futawatari was already walking away. He'd said nothing, and his expression had remained unchanged; all he'd done was flick his jacket collar up against the wind.

His insubstantial frame passed through the doorway. Mikami watched him go before he started to walk. Their shoes had been mirror images. No doubt the same was true of the weight of their convictions.

Mikami's hand came up to his forehead. He looked up at the sky.

Snowflakes, dancing.

The white brought to mind his discovery of the Christmas rose.

Read on for an exclusive Q & A with Hideo Yokoyama
by author David Peace.

Hideo Yokoyama – Man of Mystery
by David Peace

Hideo Yokoyama is one of Japan's most successful and acclaimed crime writers. *Six Four*, his last novel and first to be translated, has sold over one million copies and topped Japan's prestigious annual mystery polls. Set in 2002 in a regional police headquarters, *Six Four* follows Mikami, the reluctant head of police PR, whose own daughter is missing, but now finds himself caught between the conflicting demands of the bureaucrats, detectives and journalists of D Prefecture as the statute of limitations in a kidnapping-murder case run out and a new case unfolds. First published in 2012, the paperback is still front and centre in the bookshops of Tokyo. But although his novels are everywhere, Hideo Yokoyama remains something of a mystery. His public appearances and interviews are few and far between, and so I held out little hope of the following interview ever taking place. But at the end of a labyrinthine process, I found one of the most humble men you'll ever meet; a writer who even shuns the honorific *sensei*, obsessed not with titles but only words . . .

You used to work as a reporter on a regional newspaper in Gunma Prefecture; was there a particular moment when you were suddenly inspired to turn to fiction?

'Essentially, I started writing novels to say goodbye to the world of journalism. I had joined a local newspaper because I liked writing, however, after twelve years as a reporter, I realized that what I wanted to give people was not simply information or opinion, but stories that remain with us throughout our lives. However, I don't believe I had much talent for journalism anyway, and so I just hope I'm a better storyteller.'

Had you been interested in writing stories from an early age?

'As a child, I loved reading so much that one teacher called me 'the King of the Library'. And I was obsessed with the Sherlock Holmes stories, reading them at midnight, beneath a futon, by flashlight. But I was never satisfied with simply reading; I wrote sequels to *Treasure Island* and *Swallows and Amazons*, and even magically resurrected the dead boy and dead dog from *A Dog of Flanders* because I couldn't accept the ending of the story . . .'

But what made you write crime fiction?

'I've always believed in the power of stories, and then my experience as a journalist made me want to try to build a bridge between the two worlds of facts and fictions. Maybe because of this, my work has been compared to Seichō Matsumoto, the pioneer of what we call "social mysteries" in Japan. But though I had read a lot of Seichō's work when I was younger, I was never conscious of his influence when I began writing. Rather, the reason I choose to write "mystery novels" is purely because I love "mystery", but I define "mystery" as simply trying to recognize and understand the existence and mystery of lives other than my own.'

What do you feel fiction offers that non-fiction cannot?

'I like to read non-fiction books but, having abandoned the world of journalism, I always keep my eyes out for what is *not* written. If you read carefully between the lines, you'll find the hidden motive and position of the author, how certain elements or facts are ignored, forcing the reader to a desired conclusion. But if a book has one single unwritten line, even though every other word might be true, it cannot then be described as non-fiction.

'So I believe the purpose of fiction is hidden in the things not written about in non-fiction, the things I then *have* to write and can *only* write as fiction. But it is never easy for fiction to match the "power of facts". And ever since I made the decision to write fiction, I cannot escape a kind of inferiority complex that I quit being a reporter. So someday I want to write a novel that surpasses non-fiction; that might be my ultimate goal.'

Before the later success of your novels, you first became known for your very popular short stories; do you have a particular preference for either the short story or the novel?

'Japanese readers tend to prefer novels, but I am much more comfortable writing short stories; I am always hoping to write stories that have no superfluous flesh, that are dense and sharp. That is always my first instinct, no matter what my initial inspiration.'

But when you start to write, do you know from the beginning if a work will be a short story or a novel?

'Well, the times I have decided to write a novel are actually quite scarce, and only when I believed a multi-layered structure was essential to tell the story.'

Six Four *is a huge, multi-layered novel; what was your initial inspiration?*

'The first idea was, simply, the number 64. In Japan, each emperor's reign has a name and each year of the reign a number; for example, 2016 is *Heisei* 28, the 28th year of the *Heisei* Era, and

I was born in *Showa* 32, 1957. *Six Four* means *Showa* 64, the last year of the *Showa* Era. The *Showa* Emperor [*Hirohito*] died on January 7, 1989, and then the new *Heisei* reign began, meaning those first and last seven days of *Showa* 64 suddenly disappeared into some weird limbo. I felt this was somehow unfair; even though it had only lasted seven days, people had celebrated the New Year as *Showa* 64, and people had died and been born. So I got the idea to resurrect *Showa* 64. And then if a kidnapping-murder case had happened in those lost seven days, because the statute of limitations in Japan at that time was fifteen years, 2002 would be the last year before the statute of limitations expired and the case could be solved.'

You actually began writing Six Four *over ten years before it was finally published, putting it to one side for a while to write other books; why did it take such a long time to complete?*

'When I started writing *Six Four*, I was writing a lot of short stories for many different magazines. My writing style is to give a heavy burden to the main character in the beginning, and then to let the story go forward using the dilemma and desperation caused by this burden as its driving power. But when I started writing *Six Four*, because this was going to be my first novel, I gave the main character a load that was too heavy for him, both in his professional and private life. And it bounced back on me. I felt bound by four or five ropes, each rope carrying a heavy weight, and well, in those days, I did not have the strength to write while dragging those weights . . .

'I suffered a heart attack, then I had memory problems so I couldn't even remember the name of the main character. So it was a tough time. But what tormented me most was my own change of heart caused by the passing of the years. As the years of writing became two, three, four years, I noticed that there was a gap between the voice I had written in earlier years and my present sensibility. As six years, seven years passed, the gap became greater until it seemed that it was all written by someone else. So I started to rewrite the book again and again and again, but then my "gap detector" became even more sensitive, and I noticed the same gap appearing in the manuscript I had written only a couple of months before. I became terrified I might not complete the novel before I died . . .'

I heard you are such a perfectionist, you even re-wrote parts of Six Four *for the paperback publication . . .*

'The finished manuscript of *Six Four* still had traces of the different viewpoints, thoughts and emotions I had had while I was writing it, and they caused very slight distortions and inconsistencies in how characters acted, what they said, and how the story advanced. Eliminating all these discrepancies was tough work, like finding insects who are excellent mimics, and so it took a long time to replace and correct them.'

One of the great achievements of Six Four *is the incredible insight you give readers into the everyday workings and structure of the Japanese police force, their political machinations and rivalries, internal, local and national, and also their relationship with the press; were these particular issues you set out to highlight?*

'My goal was to set the benchmark for the Japanese police procedural novel; examining the relationship between the main character and the crime, his working environment, the friction between him and the organization for which he works, and from this the wider, more harmful elements in Japanese society. Because I believe writing about individuals is still writing about society. And so to then provide an informed discussion for anyone who wants to be a reporter, journalist, or policeman, or who wants to write police procedurals, or who simply believes they already know everything about the police and the press because of the growth of the internet.

'But for policemen and journalists – or any employee in any organization in any country – I sincerely hope this book also acts as a litmus test to see yourself: how *you* would behave and who *you* really are . . .

'When someone says something like "I am only really, truly myself in my private life", it sounds untrue. Your behavior as a member of an organization, or in any work you do, is your responsibility as an individual. Even if you would rather not see or recall what you did as a member of an organization, it was you and it is you. If you deny it was really you, it means your whole life is false, makes your life a lie. You have to accept yourself as a whole, accepting both your professional and private self.

'In that sense, *Six Four* contains all the themes of my work, describing the relationships between individuals and organizations far more carefully and minutely than I had ever done before. And writing about this relationship is not only my main theme or preoccupation, it has become my life's work.'

What are your daily writing routines and habits?

'My pace of writing is different each day; sometimes I am frozen in front of my computer from morning to night, sometimes I write through the night without any thought for food. However, my rule is to write more than 10 sheets of 400-squared Japanese manuscript paper a day [Six Four *would be approximately 1,500 of these pages in Japanese*], though I often throw away what I've written.'

And when you're not writing . . .

'My daily release is gardening, weeding, thinking about Herman Hesse in his garden, and occasionally I drive around town in my fifty-year-old-sedan. But I drive it so rarely, I feel like I am embarking on a big adventure rather than a leisurely drive.'

Finally, you live outside of Tokyo, in Gunma, and well away from 'the Literary Life'; how important is this relative isolation and distance for you and your writing?

'Isolation is an exaggeration, it's really just voluntary "canning" [*Japanese publishing jargon for isolating an author to meet a deadline, usually in a hotel room, as though they were "canned food"*]. But I never planned to live like this; one of the sub-themes of *Six Four* is that sometimes an accidental choice becomes your life, and the book is a reflection of that stage I had reached in my life. However, no matter the way we might have hoped things had gone, the taste of the fruits along the path we accidentally chose are always the most unpredictable and surprising. So I'd like to continue living my life this way . . .'

THRILLINGLY GOOD BOOKS
FROM CRIMINALLY
GOOD WRITERS

CRIME FILES BRINGS YOU THE LATEST RELEASES FROM
TOP CRIME AND THRILLER AUTHORS.

SIGN UP ONLINE FOR OUR MONTHLY NEWSLETTER AND BE THE FIRST
TO KNOW ABOUT OUR COMPETITIONS, NEW BOOKS AND MORE.